WATCHING TIME:
THE UNAUTHORIZED WATCHMEN CHRONOLOGY

By Rich Handley

Foreword by Brian Cronin
Essay by Duy Tano
Layout and Design by Paul C. Giachetti

HASSLEIN·BOOKS

New York

Author: Rich Handley
Foreword: Brian Cronin
Essay: Duy Tano
Layout and design: Paul C. Giachetti

ISBN-13: 978-0-692-78191-3
Library of Congress Cataloging-in-Publication Data
First Edition: September 2016

"*Quis custodiet ipsos custodes?*"

—*Satires*, by Decimus Iūnius Iuvenālis (Juvenal)

(Translated from the Latin:
"Who will guard the guards themselves?"
or "Who watches the watchmen?")

CONTENTS

"So many questions. Never mind. Answers soon."

—Walter "Rorschach" Kovacs

ACKNOWLEDGMENTS

Thermodynamic Miracles

"Do you comprehend the triumph which you have contributed, the secret glory that it affords? Do you understand my shame at so inadequate a reward?"

—Adrian "Ozymandias" Veidt

It takes an author to write a book, but it often takes a village to ensure that the author has the tools and resources necessary to make that book worth reading. I can't stress enough how vital the help of my particular village was during the writing of *this* book. My hearty and sincere thanks go out to the following individuals, without whom *Watching Time* would be a far lesser work.

• **Paul C. Giachetti**, my long-time friend and collaborator, whose amazing design skills have breathed life into my manuscript. Without visuals, a reference book is merely a bunch of words. Paul's visuals have enhanced tenfold every volume we've produced at Hasslein Books, and I cannot express how grateful I am for his friendship and partnership.

• **Brian Cronin** (comicbookresources.com), a noted comic book guru whose *thousands* of articles to date have fascinated fans—including yours truly—for years. Brian contributed this book's foreword, and I feel privileged and lucky to have him involved.

• **Duy Tano** (comicscube.com), the creator of the popular blog The Comics Cube, for penning an essay discussing why *Watchmen* is both dated and timeless. I'm ecstatic to have Duy aboard as well, as he and I have had many discussions in recent years about our mutual love of *Watchmen*.

• **Glenn Romanelli** (watchmencomicmovie.com), for creating the most important *Watchmen* fan site and forum on the Internet, for answering several questions I had while writing this book, and for giving the manuscript a test-read to make sure I didn't do anything stupid.

• **Prawit Sarathamwuthikul** (youtube.com/user/voeten) and **Alexandre Dias**, for filming playthrough videos of *Watchmen: The Mobile Game*, the one corner of *Watchmen* lore that eluded me as I wrote this chronology. I panicked while nearing the manuscript's completion, thinking I'd be unable to incorporate the mobile game's events, but these two came through when I'd exhausted all other options. Thanks also to **Jeff Ford** and **David Callipygous Smart** for aiding in my search.

• **Andrew Salmon** (tinyurl.com/andrewsalmon), an author and actor who worked as an extra on the *Watchmen* film and thrilled fans during its production by sharing on-set photos at comicrelated.com, under the pseudonym Cassandra Faust. Those photos provided me with a huge amount of valuable information, and Andrew also alerted me to his short story "Wounds," in Bobby Nash's *The Ruby Files, Volume One*, which contains some unexpected *Watchmen* cameos that I, of course, *had* to work into the timeline.

• **Robert Allen Rusk**, for his detailed *Watchmen: The End Is Nigh* game guide (tinyurl.com/ruskendisnigh), and YouTuber **RaSanBR**, for his complete *End Is Nigh* walkthrough videos (youtube.com/rasanbr), both of which saved me many hours I would otherwise have had to spend playing the game myself.

• **Christopher Beckett**, for his *Reading Watchmen* website (readingwatchmen.com), and **Doug Atkinson**, for *The Annotated Watchmen* (capnwacky.com/rj/watchmen.html), both of which proved invaluable as research.

Special gratitude goes to **Alan Moore**, **Dave Gibbons**, **John Higgins**, **Len Wein**, and **DC Comics** for giving us

Watchmen. The series' importance to the comic book world cannot be overstated. I also extend my appreciation to the many creative and talented individuals who brought us the role-playing books, the theatrical film, the video games, the *Before Watchmen* line, the *New Frontiersman* website and viral videos, and more, all of which expanded the world of *Watchmen* well beyond those twelve initial issues.

Thanks also to **Steve Almond, Joseph Dilworth, Hunter Goatley, Armando Saldaña, Frank Scaglioso, Ben Smith, Mike Sterling,** and **Lou Tambone** for their assistance big and small, and to **Steve Cafarelli** (monkeygripmusic.com), a close friend of 20 years, for designing and maintaining hassleinbooks.com for us. Like I said, it takes a village.

Finally, I dedicate this book to my wife **Jill** and our children, **Emily** and **Joshua**, who support everything I do—even when it means sequestering myself for large chunks of time to write a book discussing dysfunctional and impotent ex-crime-fighters, psychotic vigilantes, morally ambiguous geniuses, pointy-eared magicians, extradimensional alien squids, pirates, and giant blue penises. Those three are my thermodynamic miracle.

—Rich Handley

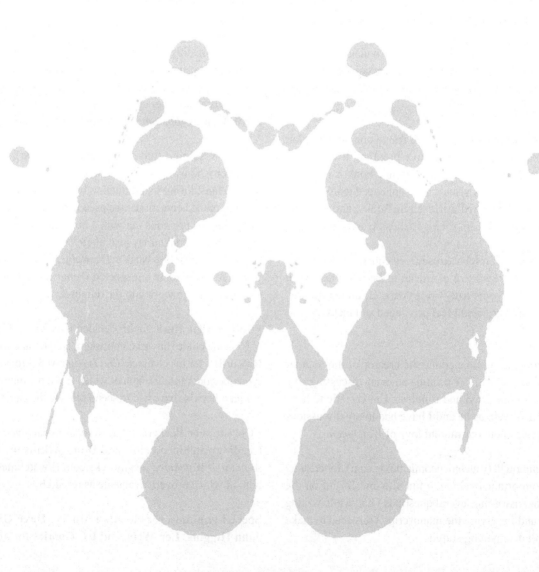

FOREWORD

How the Clock Was Crafted

By Brian Cronin

"Who makes the world? Perhaps the world is not made. Perhaps nothing is made. Perhaps it simply is, has been, will always be there. A clock without a craftsman."

—Jon "Dr. Manhattan" Osterman

In *Watchmen*, Doctor Manhattan often ponders the meaning of life and, in his case, the very creation of life itself. There is no "right" answer to Manhattan's questions of who made the world inside *Watchmen* the comic book, but we know who created that world outside the comic, and the story of how Alan Moore's, Dave Gibbons', and John Higgins' *Watchmen* came to be is a fine tale in and of itself.

In honor of the excellent and in-depth timeline by Rich Handley that you are about to read, I thought I'd present this story in timeline format.

Mid-1953
Fawcett Publications halted the production of their superhero line of comic books, primarily their "Marvel Family" of titles starring Captain Marvel and his supporting characters, like Captain Marvel Jr. and Mary Marvel. This was part of a settlement of a copyright-infringement lawsuit against them by National Comics Publications (DC Comics) over Captain Marvel allegedly infringing upon National's famed Superman character.

Late 1953
L. Miller & Son, Ltd., which had been licensing Fawcett's comic books for publication in England, had comic book creator Mick Anglo create a Captain Marvel knockoff to continue the stories. This character was Marvelman, with Young Marvelman taking over for Captain Marvel Jr. and Kid Marvelman taking over for Mary Marvel.

1963
L. Miller & Son, Ltd. went out of business and *Marvelman* comic books ceased publication. They had already turned to reprint-only status following a 1959 change to British law that allowed American comic books to be imported, leading to decreased sales for British-produced comic books.

Late 1967
The "Mighty Comics Group" was officially canceled. This was Archie Comics' attempt to get back into superheroes following DC's success in the genre in the late 1950s and then Marvel's even greater success in the 1960s. Archie Comics began as MLJ Magazines in 1939 (named after the initials of their three founders, Maurice Coyne, Louis Silberkleit, and John L. Goldwater) and soon had their own line of superheroes, including The Shield, a patriotic superhero who debuted a full year before Captain America.

Everyman teenager Archie Andrews was introduced as a back-up story in their superhero titles during the 1940s, before the entire company slowly became geared around Archie and his "gals and pals," to the point at which the company was eventually re-named after Archie. In 1959, Archie hired Joe Simon and Jack Kirby to restart their superhero line. That line was never particularly successful, even when Simon and Kirby were working there. Superman co-creator Jerry Siegel was their main writer during the mid-1960s. Characters like Fly, Jaguar, Private Strong, Comet, and The Hangman were now all in comic book limbo.

October 1976
Charlton Publications ceased production of new material for their Charlton Comics comic book line, which at this time was mostly marked by licensed comics (like *The Six Million Dollar Man*) and superhero characters created by Steve Ditko—namely, Captain Atom, The Question, and Blue Beetle (Ted Kord).

1981
DC Comics Managing Editor Dick Giordano met Alan Moore for the first time during a talent junket Giordano took to England. Giordano later recalled of Moore, "He was so brilliant, such a captivating speaker. He had so many interesting things to say."[1]

March 1982
Warrior #1 debuted, including Alan Moore's first regular comic book work, an updated version of Marvelman (which Moore and *Warrior* publisher Dez Skinn both felt was in the public domain).

December 1982
Dave Gibbons, a product of DC Comics' commitment to finding new talent in England, made his DC Comics art debut on a backup story in *Green Lantern Corps* #161 (DC editor Len Wein specifically made the call on hiring Gibbons).

Sometime After March 1982
Inspired by his success with *Marvelman*, Alan Moore came up with the idea of taking his approach on *Marvelman* and applying it to a larger comic book continuity. The L. Miller & Son, Ltd. *Marvelman* comics had their own self-contained universe, but it wasn't a broad one like the shared universes other comic book companies had achieved. Moore explained his plan to Jon B. Cooke:

> *So I'd just started thinking about using the MLJ characters - the Archie super-heroes - just because they weren't being published at the time, and for all I knew, they might've been up for grabs. The initial concept would've been the 1960s-'70s rather lame version of the Shield being found dead in the harbor, and then you'd probably have various other characters, including Jack Kirby's Private Strong, being drafted back in, and a murder mystery unfolding. I suppose*

> *I was just thinking, "That'd be a good way to start a comic book: have a famous super-hero found dead." As the mystery unraveled, we would be lead deeper and deeper into the real heart of this super-hero's world, and show a reality that was very different to the general public image of the super-hero.*[2]

November 1983
Another one of Len Wein's British hires, Alan Moore, made his DC Comics debut in *Saga of the Swamp Thing* #20 as that series' new writer. It did not take long before Moore (working with artists Stephen R. Bissette and John Totleben) made *Saga of the Swamp Thing* one of the most acclaimed comic books series of 1984.

Late 1983
After a brief, failed attempt to restart their comic book line, Charlton Publications sold their "Action Heroes" characters to DC Comics for reportedly $5,000 per character (Captain Atom, Blue Beetle, The Question, Peacemaker, Peter Cannon: Thunderbolt, Sarge Steel, Judomaster, and Nightshade were the primary acquisitions). Paul Levitz was the point man on the purchase, presumably acquiring them as a sort of gift to Dick Giordano, who had broken into the comic book industry working for Charlton Comics in the early 1960s, rising to becoming executive editor of the company in 1966.

Early 1984
Now working together at DC, Alan Moore and Dave Gibbons decided to propose a new series to DC Comics. Alan Moore revealed the genesis of the project to George Khoury:

> *I think that what started* Watchmen *was me and Dave Gibbons had done some work together on [the British comic book anthology - BC] 2000 A.D.; we'd done some very enjoyable little "Futhrer Shock"s together, and we liked working with each other and when we met up we got on well together. Since we both found ourselves working for DC, I think we came up with the idea of doing something for DC and we batted around a couple of different ideas - I know that at one point we were thinking of doing the* Challengers of the Unknown. *Another point Dave got as far as doing the rough pencil sketches for our version of* Martian Manhunter. *There may have been other ideas kicking*

[1] Eury, Michael; Giordano, Dick. Dick Giordano: Changing Comics, One Day at a Time. *TwoMorrows Publishing*, 2003.
[2] "Toasting Absent Heroes: Alan Moore discusses the Charlton-Watchmen Connection." Comic Book Artist (9). August 2000.

around, but eventually one of suggested - and I think that Dick Giordano had just acquired the Charlton characters - either Dick himself suggested it or Dave suggested it, or I suggested it - I can't remember whose idea it was - but the idea was, "Let's come up with a new treatment for the Charlton characters.[3]

Moore remembered his previous idea with the MLJ characters and decided to re-purpose it with the Charlton characters instead, with Peacemaker now taking the role of The Shield.

Mid-1984
Alan Moore sent in the proposal of "Who Killed Peacemaker?" to Dick Giordano, who loved the idea behind the story but did not think it was a good idea to use the Charlton characters. Giordano telephoned Moore in England to tell him:

Alan, we just bought the characters and you want to kill one of them off. Besides that, what you're doing is playing in somebody else's garden instead of your own. What you want to do with these characters is very exciting, but what you're going to end up with is something where nobody else can play in that garden. Why don't you create something that we can say belongs to Alan Moore, something that's brand new, a different setting. At first he was a little hesitant, because he wanted to do the Charlton characters.[4]

Gibbons had not even begun to design any of the Charlton characters for the series before Moore received the phone call to tell him to stop.

Later in 1984
Alan Moore **was** reluctant to use new characters at first, which he detailed to Khoury:

I'd hoped to have that kind of nostalgic background aura that using 1960s established characters would have given me. Once I stopped seeing that as a minus and started seeing it as a plus - the possibility of creating new characters - then it kind of flowed from there. That said, the ideas kind of evolved, but over the couple of months that me and Dave were putting the ideas together, you know, the characters came

into sharper focus - more extreme in a lot of cases, because we realized that if we weren't tied to the Charlton characters anymore, then we could make the characters more extreme. We could take them to their limits more than the Charlton characters had be taken to. Dr. Manhattan is a lot more interesting than Captain Atom.[5]

As mentioned, Captain Atom inspired Doctor Manhattan, while Blue Beetle inspired Nite Owl (specifically, the fact that Ted Kord was the second man to go by the name Blue Beetle, following the Golden Age Blue Beetle, Dan Garrett), Peter Cannon: Thunderbolt inspired Ozymandias, Peacemaker (with a little Nick Fury mixed in) inspired The Comedian, Nightshade inspired Silk Spectre, and The Question (mixed with Steve Ditko's independent creation, Mr. A) inspired Rorschach. The Nightshade/Silk Spectre connection was the loosest of them all, as Moore noted to Cooke:

I can't really say that Nightshade was a big inspiration. I never thought she was a particularly strong or interesting female character. The Silk Spectre was just a female character because I needed to have a heroine in there. Since we weren't doing the Charlton characters anymore, there was no reason why I should stick with Nightshade, I could take a different sort of super-heroine, something a bit like Phantom Lady, the Black Canary, generally my favorite sort of costumed heroines anyways. The Silk Spectre, in that she's the girl of the group, sort of was the equivalent of Nightshade, but really, there's not much connection beyond that.[6]

The remaining characters (The Minutemen, for example) appear to be original Moore-Gibbons creations, although it is possible that the MLJ heroes Hangman and Black Hood were inspirations for Hooded Justice.

1985
Once the approvals had been given for the project, Alan Moore and Dave Gibbons worked on it in England with limited oversight from Dick Giordano and the official editor on the project, Len Wein (Wein left his editing job at DC and moved from New York to California before the series was completed). Once the direct Charlton connection was

[3] Khoury, George. The Extraordinary Works of Alan Moore. *TwoMorrows Publishing, 2003.*

[4] Eury; Giordano, p. 124.

[5] Khoury, p 110.

[6] "Toasting Absent Heroes: Alan Moore discusses the Charlton-Watchmen Connection." Comic Book Artist (9). August 2000.

severed, Giordano trusted Moore's and Gibbons' instincts. Giordano recalled, "Who copyedits Alan Moore, for God's sake? This team had a vision and I got out of their way."[7] Once the issues started to come in, Giordano had no reason to question his decision. "After the fact, when I read all the issues, I realized that I was right in leaving them alone. There's nothing I would have changed."[8]

June 1986

Watchmen #1, by Alan Moore and Dave Gibbons (with colors by John Higgins) was released.

That was how the world of *Watchmen* originally came to be, but that world was expanded over the years with various new resources like role-playing games and the *Before Watchmen* prequel miniseries. That world has gotten so big that you will be amazed by how much detail Rich Handley found in it for his timeline. After all, someone has to keep track of the clock after the craftsman's job ended, and Rich is that guy.

Brian Cronin is the executive producer of the Comics Should Be Good *blog at Comic Book Resources (goodcomics.comicbookresources.com), as well as a Comic Book Resources staff writer, and is the founder of the urban legends website,* Legends Revealed *(legendsrevealed.com). He also covers the Yankees and Knicks at the* Replacement Level Yankees Weblog *(www.rlyw.net) and* KnickerBlogger *(knickerblogger.net), respectively. His work has appeared at I09, Gizmodo, the* Huffington Post, ESPN.com *and the* Los Angeles Times. *Brian lives in Astoria, Queens, with his wife, Meredith, and their cat, Hannah.*

---

[7] *Eury; Giordano, p. 124.*

[8] ibid

INTRODUCTION

I Watch the Watchmen

By Rich Handley

*"The country's disintegrating. What's happened to America?
What's happened to the American dream?"*

—Daniel "The Nite Owl" Dreiberg

Rich's Journal, July 10, 2016:

I feel that I should admit something right off the bat, and I don't want you to think any less of me when I do. Perhaps it would be best if I just ripped off that Band-Aid and worked through the pain. If I get this out in the open now, maybe we can move past it and you can enjoy this book unfettered by the spectre of an uncomfortable, unspoken truth. OK, here goes:

I've never been much into superhero stories.

That admission may seem surprising coming from a guy who has written a lengthy book about masked crime-fighters, but the truth is, while growing up I could never relate to characters who dressed up in Spandex costumes resembling humanized animals, adopted nicknames based on those animals, and then ran around the streets beating the tar out of similarly clad villains. It all struck me as a bit too much like what I'd expect Halloween to be if that holiday were combined with *Grand Theft Auto*… if *Grand Theft Auto* had existed when I was growing up, that is… which it didn't.

I'm sure you still get my point.

Sure, I enjoyed Christopher Reeve's *Superman* films, just like everyone else,[9] and I watched the *Super Friends* cartoons, as well as Adam West's *Batman*, Bill Bixby's *The Incredible Hulk*, Lynda Carter's *Wonder Woman*, and William Katt's *The Greatest American Hero*. And, yeah, I've adored Chris Nolan's

Batman trilogy, *Guardians of the Galaxy*, and nearly all of the *X-Men* movies—and *Deadpool* had me laughing to the point of abdominal pain. But beyond those and a few others (*The Incredibles* and *Unbreakable* chief among them[10]), the genre has historically not held much appeal for me.

I should point out that in the 1970s, we had only thirteen television channels from which to choose, a few of which showed static. So when I did watch superhero TV shows, it was often more the result of my not wanting to watch what was on the other channels, and less that I was truly into them. Lou Ferrigno smashing things and Lynda Carter doing… well, anything, really… were preferable to *The Love Boat*, *Hee Haw*, or *Leave It to Beaver* reruns any day of the week. With nothing else to choose, superheroes sufficed.

As I became a moody, withdrawn teenager, I delved deeply into science fiction franchises like *Star Trek*, *The Twilight Zone*, and *Planet of the Apes*, which greatly appealed to the part of my psyche that had a habit of watching news broadcasts and becoming embittered and depressed about the changes taking place in the United States in the 1980s. With crime rates skyrocketing, government corruption and civil-liberty incursions increasing, and the impending threat of nuclear destruction ever-present at the height of the Cold War, I found myself even less inclined to watch the superhero shows I saw as a child, which now seemed hopelessly naïve. *Trek*, *Apes*, and the *Zone*, on the other hand, offered powerful messages to

---

[9] Amusingly, my mother dropped me and my cousin off at a movie theater in 1977 so we could watch what she thought was a film called Superman, which she'd seen listed in a newspaper. (This was a year before Christopher Reeve's Superman hit theaters.) When we purchased our tickets, we discovered that the film was not quite what we'd (or she'd) expected. It was actually SuperVan, the latest in that peculiar genre of 1970s movies now known as "vansploitation," which tended to focus on hormonally driven college students who lived to show off their customized vans, often culminating in road competitions and a lot of sex and drugs. The titular vehicle was a solar-powered, laser-armed van with a mattress in the back for a different kind of riding, and the plot involved a wet T-shirt contest. We were nine years old at the time. The staff let us in to see it anyway. Come to think of it, that might explain a lot about me.

[10] Unbreakable's superhero and supervillain, of course, don't even wear comic-book costumes.

which I could far more easily relate. I (mistakenly) assumed that comics could not offer me that same relatability.

In college, my friend Tom pushed me to embrace superheroes. Tim Burton's first *Batman* film had just come out, and we'd gone to see it a few times because we'd both enjoyed it immensely (which surprised me, given how I generally felt about such characters). He was an avid collector of *Batman* comics and kept urging me to borrow them, claiming that they would alter my perception of masked crime-fighters.

I snobbily resisted, and continued to do so until a few years later, when I finally gave in and read the *Knightfall* saga, written by Chuck Dixon, Doug Moench, Alan Grant, and others. That intricately plotted, multi-title storyline is, of course, famous for introducing the steroid-enhanced, hyper-intelligent Bane, who did what no other member of Batman's rogues gallery had ever succeeded in doing: breaking the Caped Crusader's back and his spirit.[11] Bane deconstructed Batman, both on a figurative and literal level, exposing his vulnerabilities, and I found myself intrigued almost immediately.

I admit it: Tom was right. *Knightfall* was damn good storytelling, and after I finished reading it, I had to keep going. My eyes had been opened to the fact that not all superhero comics were corny slapstick, as I'd assumed them to be based on the TV shows from my childhood.

The *Knightfall* saga became my gateway drug to superheroes, and I kept reading Tom's other *Batman* titles. By the mid-1990s, he'd introduced me to Denny O'Neil's *Birth of the Demon*, Brian Augustyn's *Gotham By Gaslight*, Jim Starlin's heartbreaking "A Death in the Family" storyline, and Frank Miller's mesmerizing *Batman: Year One* and *The Dark Knight Returns*. (If you're noticing a pattern here—emphasizing the "dark" in "Dark Knight"—then you're keeping up just fine.) I needed more... but I didn't yet know that what I *really* needed was "more" with a second "o" in it.

Then Tom handed me Alan Moore's *Batman: The Killing Joke*.

I read that graphic novel twice in one sitting, each time having to catch my breath when I was done. Moore's chilling exploration of how a rational, ordinary individual could evolve into the twisted, psychotic, homicidal, maniacally laughing, and downright *scary* lunatic known as The Joker was like nothing I'd read before, not in all the dark, brooding *Batman* comics I'd just spent the previous few years devouring. His writing was beautiful, haunting, poetic, powerful and, above all else, literary. This wasn't a comic book I was looking at. It was literature—and it was some of the *best* literature I'd read in years.

If *Knightfall* had been my gateway drug to superhero comics, then *The Killing Joke* was my religious epiphany. There was a writing god out there of whom I'd been unaware, and he wrote stories like no other. His name was Alan Moore and, like Bane, he did the impossible: He made me *really* enjoy superheroes. Tom next gave me *Whatever Happened to the Man of Tomorrow?*, easily the best Superman tale I've encountered in any medium, and it brought me to tears.

A few years later, another friend, Joe, handed me his *Swamp Thing* collection after I shared with him the above memories. I was reluctant to read it, as I'd watched the *Swamp Thing* films and TV series and had found the character to be slightly ridiculous. But Joe mentioned that Alan Moore was among the writers on the comic (which, he assured me, was nothing like the filmed *Swamp Thing*), promising that I'd be blown away by the author's groundbreaking approach to Alec Holland's saga as multi-tiered, millennia-spanning mythology—much more than merely a murky tale of a muck-encrusted mockery of a man. Sighing (possibly due to the gratuitous overuse of alliteration in the previous sentence), I gave it a try.

Cue history: repeat. I admit it: Joe was right, too.

Alan Moore's *Swamp Thing* offered some of the most gripping storytelling I'd come across in the four-color medium, and the title character was no mere superhero—he was an elemental spirit tasked with protecting the entire planet, even from mankind. When I was done reading it, I didn't just give it a second read, as I had Moore's Joker story. No, I went out and tracked down every single *Swamp Thing* issue up to that point so that I could proudly feature the series in my own collection and re-read it as often as I liked—and I liked aplenty.

I didn't need to be hit over the head repeatedly to realize that I'd found a new favorite writer. *The Killing Joke* had dealt with mature subjects maturely, illustrating how comic books could truly terrify, while *Whatever Happened to the Man of*

---

[11] *And, in the process, setting the stage for Chris Nolan's* The Dark Knight Rises.

Tomorrow? had provided an emotional conclusion to the DC Comics pre-*Crisis on Infinite Earths* era, with Superman leaving crime-fighting behind to live an ordinary life as an automobile mechanic (something that should sound familiar to *Watchmen* fans). *Swamp Thing* upped the ante, regularly delving into examinations of societal problems that took me back to what had so enthralled me about *The Twilight Zone*, *Planet of the Apes*, and *Star Trek*.

I soon began hunting down Moore's other works as well, including *V for Vendetta*, *From Hell*, and even Marvel UK's weekly *Star Wars* magazine. (Yes, Moore wrote *Star Wars*, and it's just as weird and wonderful as you'd imagine.) It was somewhere in the midst of all this that I first picked up a graphic-novel collection of *Watchmen*, Moore's seminal twelve-issue miniseries, published from 1986 to 1987, that featured gorgeous artwork by Dave Gibbons and a vibrant, atypical color scheme from colorist John Higgins.

Set in an alternate version of 1985, *Watchmen* revolved around a group of dysfunctional, depressed ex-vigilantes living in a Nixon-controlled, borderline-fascist United States on the brink of nuclear war with the Soviet Union. I'd heard about this series many times during the decade since its debut, of course—it's almost impossible to run in geek circles and *not* hear about it—and knew that it was widely praised as having transformed the comic-book industry pretty much overnight.

Within only an issue or two, I understood why. *Watchmen* was a beautiful, unique, and wholly unexpected story, one that resonated with me personally since it examined the concept of costumed crime-fighters through a harshly critical lens, echoing the stance I'd held before reading *Knightfall*. Bradford W. Wright, in his book *Comic Book Nation: The Transformation of Youth Culture in America* (Johns Hopkins, 2001), characterized *Watchmen* as "Moore's obituary for the concept of heroes in general and superheroes in particular." His description couldn't have been more spot-on.

Wiped away were the long-held notions that crime-fighters always did the morally right things for the intellectually right reasons, that heroes and villains were rigidly defined constants, that good always prevailed over evil, and that happy endings were a foregone conclusion where the tights-and-mask crowd were concerned. In their place was a dystopian dissection of fascism, conservatism, liberalism, dogmatism, naïve idealism,

hypocrisy, and the slow, painful, deteriorating death of the American dream.

As if that weren't enough already, *Watchmen* contained a Batman analog (Dan Dreiberg), an amoral multiple-murderer prone to seeing everything as a joke (Eddie Blake), a crime-fighter who'd retired his costume to become an auto mechanic (Hollis Mason), and a powerful individual determined to save the planet from mankind (Adrian Veidt)—and it doesn't take much analysis to recognize the similarities between Rorschach and the unnamed antihero of *V for Vendetta*. *Watchmen* mixed and matched elements of almost every Alan Moore story I'd already enjoyed, creating a whole that was greater than the sum of its already impressive parts.

It was mind-bending—a wholesale deconstruction of the superhero genre and a harsh condemnation of mankind's violent nature—and it was glorious. To date, *Watchmen* remains my favorite work from Alan Moore. I've lost track of how often I've re-read it throughout the past twenty years, and I'm sure I'll do so again soon.

When rumblings arose in the mid-2000s of an impending *Watchmen* film (the latest in a string of such rumors, following the failures of several prior attempts to put Moore's most famous work in theaters), I decided to revisit the graphic novel yet again. I wanted to have it all fresh in my head when I eventually sat down to watch what would, no doubt, be an altered version of the story's events playing out on the big screen, so that I could compare and contrast from a position of knowledge, not one of hasty recollection.

While I was at it, I decided to look up whether or not anyone had used the *Watchmen* characters in any other media. In so doing, I learned about a trio of books that Mayfair Games had released, two in 1987 (*Who Watches the Watchmen?* and *Taking Out the Trash*) and a third in 1990 (*The Watchmen Sourcebook*), each of which incorporated the concepts and characters of *Watchmen* into the *DC Heroes Role Playing Game*. Set before the main events of Moore's saga, they served as DC's first *Watchmen* prequels.

The books looked intriguing, so I ordered all three online even though I wasn't an RPG player—and it turned out to be an excellent decision. Despite a number of frustrating continuity gaffes and contradictory dates (odd, given that

Moore himself co-wrote one of them), each volume was a data dump of valuable new information regarding the heroes' and villains' backstories, expanding *Watchmen*'s world into something even greater.

Players, assuming the roles of Rorschach, The Nite Owl, The Silk Spectre, Ozymandias, or The Comedian[12], thwarted an assassination attempt on Richard Nixon in one book and helped Captain Metropolis solve a spate of kidnappings in another, unaware that (*Spoiler alert!*) Metropolis himself had orchestrated the abductions in a misguided second effort to convince the heroes to form The Crimebusters.

Leafing through these books helped get me into the proper frame of mind to watch Zack Snyder's film. As Nite Owl might say, they were a hoot—and so was the movie. Say what you will about Snyder's rather divisive film, but I loved it and still do. Despite its changes to Moore's original work, I consider it one of the best adaptations of any story to the medium of film. Yes, it changed some things big and small, but it was beautifully shot and well acted, and it stayed remarkably close to the source material, proving wrong the oft-repeated claim that the graphic novel was entirely un-filmable.

In particular, the portrayals by Jeffrey Dean Morgan, Patrick Wilson, Billy Crudup, and Matt Frewer of, respectively, Eddie Blake, Dan Dreiberg, Jon Osterman, and Edgar Jacobi were spot-on—but the casting coup was Jackie Earle Haley, whose Rorschach leapt off the page with incredible fidelity. Everyone in the movie did a great job, as far as I'm concerned, but these five actors, in particular, captured their characters' nuances perfectly. Whenever they were on the screen, I felt that I was truly watching *Watchmen*. With all due respect to those who disliked it (including my friend Duy Tano—see his essay on page 311), I'll never quite understand the harsh criticism that the movie tends to receive in some circles.

To tie into the film's release, Warner Bros. commissioned four video games utilizing the on-screen depictions of the characters and the world they inhabit: *Watchmen: The Mobile Game*, a Java-based side-scroller for mobile phones; *Justice Is Coming*, an online role-playing game; *Minutemen Arcade*, an 8-bit arcade-game emulator; and *The End Is Nigh*,

a console and PC game for the Windows, PlayStation, and Xbox platforms. While each game added new content to the mythos, the first three were relatively unimportant (and two aren't even available anymore). Only *The End Is Nigh* made substantial additions, by showcasing Underboss and The Twilight Lady, supervillains mentioned merely in passing in Moore's story. If you haven't played *The End Is Nigh*, I recommend finding a copy. If you can get past the repetitive walking and fighting, there's a good story being told there.

In 2012, DC Comics announced its next major *Watchmen* undertaking: prequel comics spread out over multiple miniseries, under the umbrella title *Before Watchmen,* which spanned thirty-seven of a planned thirty-eight issues before the final issue, *Before Watchmen: Epilogue*, was canceled without explanation[13]. As divisive as the film was, the prequels were far more so, as the very idea of new stories not written by Alan Moore offended many fans who felt such a project was disrespectful to *Watchmen*'s creator.

I wasn't among them. Don't hate me, but I found *Before Watchmen* quite enjoyable, particularly *Minutemen, Silk Spectre*, and *Moloch*, which packed an emotional punch and more than a few laughs, as well as *Rorschach*, which was exquisitely drawn and exactly the sort of ass-kicking yarn one would expect the vigilante's story to entail. Some of the others (I'm looking at you, *Nite Owl* and *Comedian*) didn't always jibe with what Moore had laid down, and some of the character backgrounds in these new comics ignored those already created for the RPG books. (Alas, the otherwise excellent *Minutemen* is guilty on both counts.)

Hence, the genesis of the book you now hold.

In 2015, I sat down to re-read Moore's miniseries, the three Mayfair Games books, and *Before Watchmen*, and I began to notice some interesting trends. There were numerous instances in which the RPG books and *Before Watchmen* were wholly incompatible, most notably in the case of Rolf Müller and Hooded Justice. (Yes, I just mentioned them as being two separate individuals. Therein lies the biggest continuity quagmire of them all, as you'll discover while perusing the timeline.) But by and large, the two attempts at *Watchmen*

---

[12] *The books' editor astutely noted that Dr. Manhattan wouldn't make for a particularly playable role-playing game character, since his omnipotence, invulnerability, and simultaneous perception of all points within his lifetime effectively eliminated any sense of tension or danger, due to Jon knowing, from the outset of any adventure, how it would end. I find it amusing to picture the scenario: "OK, let's get started. Your mission begins with all of you in a room and—" "Captain Metropolis is the mastermind. Also, Moloch is secretly planning to start a riot." "What the—? Hey, nice job ruining the game for everyone else, jerk."*

[13] *I've always considered that a shame, as* Epilogue *would have rounded out* Watchmen *at an even fifty issues, including Moore's original miniseries. As it now stands, there are only forty-nine, which agitates my OCDish nature to no end. I've tried reaching out to author Len Wein to ask him about this lost issue, but, alas, have not received a response. Perhaps Mr. Wein will one day reveal what happened.*

prequels fit together surprisingly well (except when it came to characters' birthdates, when all hell tended to break loose).

What's more, in watching playthrough videos of the various video games, I discovered that their events mostly fit with both prequel lines as well. Contradictions inevitably arose—conflicting histories for Bill Brady, for instance, as well as differing accounts of the Woodward and Bernstein murders, the Police Riots, the passing of the Keene Act, Ursula Zandt's death, Dan Dreiberg's education, and Sally Jupiter's retirement—but an intricately interconnected tapestry of *Watchmen* history nonetheless emerged.

I began making mental notes about how everything did or didn't fit together, which quickly evolved into the makings of a book. Six months later, they'd grown into a manuscript of more than 350 pages, representing an exhaustive amount of research, reconciling, and contemplation. *Watching Time* presents a detailed timeline encapsulating every known event from all corners of the *Watchmen* franchise, including not only Moore's comics, *Before Watchmen*, and the film, RPG books, and video games, but also viral videos and websites, trading cards, promotional newspapers, reference books, and other ancillary sources—even unproduced film scripts.

When I began writing this book, I had no idea that DC Comics would soon make the controversial decision to transition *Watchmen*'s characters into its mainstream continuity via its *DC Universe Rebirth* concept (which I learned about a month before completing this book's manuscript, causing no small amount of panicking), or that director Zack Snyder would be working to bring the mythos to television, enabling us to watch *Watchmen* weekly[14]. I can only hope that future scribes, whether on screen or in print, will continue to hold a mirror up to society, exposing the deterioration that still plagues the United States—and the entire world—now, some thirty years after Alan Moore offered up what many consider his most influential work.

For my purposes (and yours), the timing couldn't have been better for such developments, because with major sea changes coming to the *Watchmen* franchise, now is a perfect time for veteran fans and new converts alike to revisit or discover all that has come before. If I've done my job properly, *Watching Time* will make that possible. I'll leave that to each of you to decide for yourself as you pull up a seat here at the Gunga Diner, order up some four-legged chicken, cold baked beans, and a cup of Nite Owl Dark Roast, and peruse the pages of this paperback primer.

Just understand one thing as we share this space: I'm not locked in here with you. *You're* locked in here with *me*.

Hrrm.

---

[14] *As this book goes to press, almost nothing is known about the impending TV show, but I hold out hope that it will involve The Minutemen. For my money, the best thing about Snyder's movie was the superb credits sequence, which made me yearn to see more of that earlier crime-fighting team in action. It's no surprise at all, then, that The Minutemen's story was my favorite aspect of* Before Watchmen.

ABBREVIATION KEY

Under the Hood

"What else have you got in there? Chocolate rations?
Boy Scout knife? Army-issue contraceptives?"

—Laurie "Silk Spectre" Juspeczyk

Watching Time draws from not only Alan Moore's *Watchmen* comics, the theatrical film, and the *Before Watchmen* prequel line, but a variety of other sources as well, some obscure. Everything plotted on the timeline has been carefully organized to present a cohesive, comprehensive chronology of all things *Watchmen*. To help readers keep track of it all, four-character codes indicate each entry's sources.

Canonicity is a hot topic among *Watchmen* fans. Some acknowledge only Moore's work, maintaining that only the creator should tell stories set in his world. Others disagree, noting that Moore himself has heavily mined other creators' characters for much of his work. Some accept the film adaptation and *Before Watchmen* in their own personal head canon, while others ignore those but fondly recall the fountain of information that the role-playing books added to the mythos. A recurring debate, therefore, has been what to deem canon or apocryphal. Do the RPG books count? How about the prequel comics? The video games? The officially licensed *Watchmen* condom[15]? And if one source contradicts another (which unfortunately does happen), which one takes precedence?

This book sidesteps that debate, adopting instead an all-inclusive approach. If an event occurs or is mentioned in a comic, the film, a video game, an RPG book, a behind-the-scenes guide, a viral video, etc., I considered it fair game for inclusion. The goal was not to adhere to any purist philosophy, but rather to examine how well everything gels. Contradictions were thus bound to occur. Potential workarounds are suggested when feasible, but sometimes there was just no way to make things fit. In such cases, a "CONFLICT:" tag alerts readers to the discrepancies. The one caveat: Alan Moore's miniseries is sacrosanct, so if a spinoff title contradicts anything *Watchmen*'s creator established, that secondary material is assumed to be in error.

Since all entries indicate their sources via the four-letter codes, readers are free to reject any aspects of the franchise that they prefer not to acknowledge. Don't like the film? No problem—just ignore any entries bearing its code. Prefer to ignore the events of *Before Watchmen*? That's OK, too—simply skip the correspondingly coded content. (Heck, if you're weird and accept everything *except* for Alan Moore's miniseries, the coding will still work for you… but I'm not sure anyone would take you seriously.) In this way, readers need not obsess about canonicity, and can simply enjoy the ride.

By way of examples, [ALAN] indicates that information contained in a particular entry is culled from Alan Moore's miniseries, while [BWMM] references *Before Watchmen: Minutemen*, [RPG3] signifies *The Watchmen Sourcebook*, and [CLIX] denotes trading cards packaged with the HeroClix *Watchmen* figures. The codes used are listed on the opposite page. For detailed information about each source, consult the list of works cited on page 315.

---

[15] *Yes, that actually exists—which is rather ironic, given that the story's protagonist is sexually impotent. The condom's packaging even boasts "We're society's only protection."*

CODE	SOURCE		CODE	SOURCE
ABSO	*Watchmen Absolute Edition*		**MIND**	*The Mindscape of Alan Moore*
ALAN	Alan Moore's *Watchmen* miniseries		**MOBL**	*Watchmen: The Mobile Game*
ARCD	*Minutemen Arcade*		**MOTN**	*Watchmen: The Complete Motion Comic*
ARTF	*Watchmen: The Art of the Film*		**MTRO**	*Metro* promotional newspaper cover wrap
BLCK	*Tales of the Black Freighter*		**NEWP**	*New Frontiersman* promotional newspaper
BWCC	*Before Watchmen—The Crimson Corsair*		**NEWW**	*New Frontiersman* website
BWCO	*Before Watchmen—Comedian*		**NIGH**	*Watchmen: The End Is Nigh, Parts 1 and 2*
BWDB	*Before Watchmen—Dollar Bill*		**PKIT**	*Watchmen* film British press kit
BWDM	*Before Watchmen—Dr. Manhattan*		**PORT**	*Watchmen Portraits*
BWMM	*Before Watchmen—Minutemen*		**REAL**	Real life
BWMO	*Before Watchmen—Moloch*		**RPG1**	*DC Heroes Role Playing Module #227: Who Watches the Watchmen?*
BWNO	*Before Watchmen—Nite Owl*			
BWOZ	*Before Watchmen—Ozymandias*		**RPG2**	*DC Heroes Role Playing Module #235: Taking Out the Trash—Curses and Tears*
BWRO	*Before Watchmen—Rorschach*			
BWSS	*Before Watchmen—Silk Spectre*		**RPG3**	*DC Heroes: The Watchmen Sourcebook*
CHEM	My Chemical Romance music video: "Desolation Row"		**RUBY**	"Wounds," short story published in *The Ruby Files Volume One*
CMEO	*Watchmen* cameos in comics, TV, and film:		**SCR1**	Unfilmed screenplay draft: Sam Hamm
	• Comic: *Astonishing X-Men* volume 3 issue #6		**SCR2**	Unfilmed screenplay draft: Charles McKeuen
	• Comic: *Hero Hotline* volume 1 issue #5		**SCR3**	Unfilmed screenplay draft: Gary Goldman
	• Comic: *Kingdom Come* volume 1 issue #2		**SCR4**	Unfilmed screenplay draft: David Hayter (2002)
	• Comic: *Marvels* volume 1 issue #4		**SCR5**	Unfilmed screenplay draft: David Hayter (2003)
	• Comic: *The Question* volume 1 issue #17		**SCR6**	Unfilmed screenplay draft: Alex Tse
	• TV: *Teen Titans Go!* episode #82, "Real Boy Adventures"		**SPOT**	*DC Spotlight #1*
			VRL1	Viral video: *NBS Nightly News with Ted Philips*
	• Film: *Man of Steel*		**VRL2**	Viral video: *The Keene Act and You*
	• Film: *Batman v Superman: Dawn of Justice Ultimate Edition*		**VRL3**	Viral video: *Who Watches the Watchmen? A Veidt Music Network (VMN) Special*
	• Film: *Justice League*		**VRL4**	Viral video: *World in Focus: 6 Minutes to Midnight*
CLIX	HeroClix figure pack-in cards			
DECK	*DC Comics Deck-Building Game—Crossover Pack 4: Watchmen*		**VRL5**	Viral video: *Local Radio Station Report on 1977 Riots*
DURS	*DC Universe: Rebirth Special* volume 1 issue #1		**VRL6**	Viral videos (group of ten): *Veidt Enterprises Advertising Contest*
FILM	*Watchmen* theatrical film			
HOOD	*Under the Hood* documentary and dust-jacket prop reproduction		**WAWA**	*Watching the Watchmen*
			WHOS	*Who's Who: The Definitive Directory of the DC Universe*
JUST	*Watchmen: Justice Is Coming*			
MATL	Mattel Club Black Freighter figure pack-in cards		**WTFC**	*Watchmen: The Film Companion*

In addition, a number of entries throughout the book are presented within a grey box. This shading denotes that those particular events occur in an alternate reality outside of the main *Watchmen* continuity (sometimes in the real world), in an effort to help readers more smoothly navigate the timeline.

Finally, a note about official timelines: Four attempts have been published to date, in *Watchmen: The Film Companion*, Mayfair Games' *Taking Out the Trash*, the video game *Watchmen: The End Is Nigh—The Complete Experience*, and the film's British press kit. It probably comes as little surprise to anyone familiar with licensed franchises that these brief chronologies contradict each other and Moore's miniseries on several points—especially the RPG version, which, while certainly fun to read, is riddled with inaccurate dating. As such, while all four timelines are discussed at length in notes accompanying the entries, none of them are treated as indisputable gospel.

I hope you enjoy the following attempt to make sense of the *Watchmen* mythos in all its various forms.

THE TIMELINE

"Time is simultaneous, an intricately structured jewel that humans insist on viewing one edge at a time, when the whole design is visible in every facet."

—Jon "Dr. Manhattan" Osterman

Part I:
A WORLD WITHOUT HEROES
(Prehistory to 1937)

—Circa 2,000,000 B.C.
The first light emitted by SN 1885A, a supernova in the Andromeda Galaxy, begins its two-million-year journey to Earth **[ALAN]**.

—Mid to Late 1800s
Hollis Wordsworth Mason, the future paternal grandfather of Hollis T. Mason, is born to a conservative Montana family **[ALAN]**.
> **NOTE:** *This placement is based on the younger Hollis being born in 1916.*

—1873
Moe Vernon, the future owner of Vernon's Auto Repairs, is born **[ALAN]**.

—August 20, 1885
German astronomer Ernst Hartwig detects SN 1885A, a two-million-year-old supernova in the Andromeda Galaxy **[REAL]**.

—1896
American businessman Henry John Heinz, the founder of H. J. Heinz Co., conceives of the slogan "58 Varieties" to describe his company's products **[ALAN]**.
> **NOTE:** *In the real world, Heinz coined the term "57 Varieties" in 1896, rather than Watchmen's "58." This subtly altered slogan (visible on a can of baked beans in Dan Dreiberg's home) provides an early indicator that the Watchmen universe is not quite the same world with which readers are familiar.*

Late 1800s or Early 1900s

The Esquire Hotel is built on Fifth Avenue in Manhattan. Standing thirty stories high, with more than nine hundred guest rooms, the hotel boasts three restaurants, a shopping arcade, and a highly reputable staff **[RPG2]**.

> **NOTE:** *The Esquire's age is unstated, but it is among New York City's oldest hotels, making this a logical placement, given the ages of the city's hotels in the real world.*

Between 1900 and 1910

Laurence Albert "Larry" Schexnayder, The Minutemen's future agent, is born **[ALAN]**.

> **NOTE:** *Schexnayder is said to be in his mid-thirties in 1939, setting his birth during this decade. His middle name appears in* The Watchmen Sourcebook.

1900s or 1910s

Linda Juspeczyk, future sister of Sally Juspeczyk, is born to a family in Skokie, Illinois. Her father is an insurance salesman **[RPG3]**.

> **NOTE:** *Linda's birth is undated, but she is an adult of marrying age when her younger sister Sally (the future Silk Spectre) is eleven years old in 1931, making this is a likely placement.*

William Dreiberg, future father of Daniel Dreiberg, is born **[BWNO]**.

1905

Rolf Müller is born **[RPG2]** to Henrik and Greta Müller **[RPG3]**.

> **CONFLICT:** *Alan Moore's miniseries strongly implies that Rolf Müller is Hooded Justice's true identity.* Taking Out the Trash *cements the connection, but claims that "Rolf Müller" is merely an alias. The Watchmen Sourcebook indicates that the Müllers hail from Kiel, Germany (*Taking Out the Trash *claims they are Austrian), and moves Rolf's birth year up to 1917, which contradicts* Taking Out the Trash's *1905 placement and makes little sense given his apparent physical age in* Watchmen.
>
> Before Watchmen: Minutemen *not only changes Hooded Justice's background, but also makes him a separate individual from Müller. That miniseries cites a birthdate of April 5, 1921, in a file containing Rolf's personal history (the handwriting used in the records is largely illegible—and in German—causing some online sources to incorrectly cite it as 1901). Neither date jibes with the character's physical appearance, however.* Taking Out the Trash's *dating of 1905 makes the most sense.*

After 1905

Right from childhood, Rolf Müller exhibits an almost inhuman strength and size. His parents' shortcomings shatter him psychologically, leaving him with a deep hatred that drives him throughout his life **[RPG2]**.

ABSO .... *Watchmen Absolute Edition*
ALAN ..... Alan Moore's *Watchmen* miniseries
ARCD .... *Minutemen Arcade*
ARTF ..... *Watchmen: The Art of the Film*
BLCK ..... *Tales of the Black Freighter*
BWCC ... *Before Watchmen—The Crimson Corsair*
BWCO ... *Before Watchmen—Comedian*
BWDB ... *Before Watchmen—Dollar Bill*
BWDM .. *Before Watchmen—Dr. Manhattan*
BWMM.. *Before Watchmen—Minutemen*
BWMO .. *Before Watchmen—Moloch*
BWNO ... *Before Watchmen—Nite Owl*

BWOZ.... *Before Watchmen—Ozymandias*
BWRO ... *Before Watchmen—Rorschach*
BWSS ... *Before Watchmen—Silk Spectre*
CHEM.... My Chemical Romance music video: "Desolation Row"
CMEO.... *Watchmen* cameos in comics, TV, and film:
 • Comic: *Astonishing X-Men* volume 3 issue #6
 • Comic: *Hero Hotline* volume 1 issue #5
 • Comic: *Kingdom Come* volume 1 issue #2
 • Comic: *Marvels* volume 1 issue #4
 • Comic: *The Question* volume 1 issue #17
 • TV: *Teen Titans Go!* episode #82, "Real Boy Adventures"
 • Film: *Man of Steel*

 • Film: *Batman v Superman: Dawn of Justice Ultimate Edition*
 • Film: *Justice League*
CLIX ...... HeroClix figure pack-in cards
DECK..... *DC Comics Deck-Building Game—Crossover Pack 4: Watchmen*
DURS .... *DC Universe: Rebirth Special* volume 1 issue #1
FILM ..... *Watchmen* theatrical film
HOOD .... *Under the Hood* documentary and dust-jacket prop reproduction
JUST ..... *Watchmen: Justice Is Coming*
MATL .... Mattel Club Black Freighter figure pack-in cards

—Early 20th Century

As a child, Friedrich Werner Veidt—the future father of Adrian "Ozymandias" Veidt—considers Alexander of Macedonia (Alexander the Great) a personal hero **[BWOZ]**.

—Circa 1910

A German child named Jacob is born **[BWMM]**.

> **NOTE:** Before Watchmen: Minutemen *seems to imply that Jacob, after being sexually abused by Rolf Müller, grows up to become Hooded Justice. Jacob's birthdate is not indicated, though he appears to be around ten years old in a photo taken in 1920.*

—March 22, 1910—Night

Byron Alfred Lewis, the future masked adventurer Mothman, is born **[RPG2]** to real-estate mogul Dr. Arthur Lewis and his wife Janet. The aristocratic millionaires reside in a mansion at 1142 Newcastle Lane, in New Haven, Connecticut **[RPG3]**.

> **NOTE:** *According to* Absolute Watchmen, *Alan Moore originally intended for Lewis to be born in 1915.*

—March 25, 1910

The *New Haven Register* publishes a birth announcement for Byron Lewis **[RPG3]**.

—August 11, 1912

Nelson Gardner, the future masked adventurer Captain Metropolis, is born **[RPG2, RPG3]** to New York residents Albert and Matilda Gardner **[RPG1, RPG3]**.

> **NOTE:** *According to* Absolute Watchmen, *Alan Moore originally intended for Gardner to be born in 1915.*

—In or After August 1912

Matilda and Albert Gardner nickname their young son "Nelly" **[RPG3]**.

> **NOTE:** *The term "nelly" denotes a foolish person and is also an offensive and derogative term for a homosexual man. "Nelly" is thus an ironic nickname for Gardner, a gay man who faces ridicule for his misguided attempts to form The Crimebusters.*

—January 9, 1913

Richard Milhous Nixon, future 37th President of the United States, is born to Francis A. Nixon and Hannah Milhous Nixon **[REAL]**.

MIND .... *The Mindscape of Alan Moore*
MOBL .... *Watchmen: The Mobile Game*
MOTN .... *Watchmen: The Complete Motion Comic*
MTRO .... *Metro promotional newspaper cover wrap*
NEWP .... *New Frontiersman promotional newspaper*
NEWW .... *New Frontiersman website*
NIGH ..... *Watchmen: The End Is Nigh, Parts 1 and 2*
PKIT ...... *Watchmen film British press kit*
PORT ..... *Watchmen Portraits*
REAL ..... Real life
RPG1 .... *DC Heroes Role Playing Module #227: Who Watches the Watchmen?*

RPG2 .... *DC Heroes Role Playing Module #235: Taking Out the Trash—Curses and Tears*
RPG3 .... *DC Heroes: The Watchmen Sourcebook*
RUBY .... *"Wounds," published in The Ruby Files Volume One*
SCR1 ..... Unfilmed screenplay draft: Sam Hamm
SCR2 ..... Unfilmed screenplay draft: Charles McKeuen
SCR3 ..... Unfilmed screenplay draft: Gary Goldman
SCR4 ..... Unfilmed screenplay draft: David Hayter (2002)
SCR5 ..... Unfilmed screenplay draft: David Hayter (2003)
SCR6 ..... Unfilmed screenplay draft: Alex Tse
SPOT ..... *DC Spotlight #1*
VRL1 ..... Viral video: *NBS Nightly News with Ted Philips*

VRL2 ...... Viral video: *The Keene Act and You*
VRL3 ..... Viral video: *Who Watches the Watchmen? A Veidt Music Network (VMN) Special*
VRL4 ..... Viral video: *World in Focus: 6 Minutes to Midnight*
VRL5 ..... Viral video: *Local Radio Station Report on 1977 Riots*
VRL6 ..... Viral videos (group of ten): *Veidt Enterprises Advertising Contest*
WAWA ... *Watching the Watchmen*
WHOS ... *Who's Who: The Definitive Directory of the DC Universe*
WTFC .... *Watchmen: The Film Companion*

Before 1914

The National Bank of New York **[ALAN]**, also known as the First National Bank of New York (FBNY) **[RPG3]** and National Bank Company **[BWDB]**, is founded **[RPG3]**.

> **NOTE:** *The bank has existed for more than a quarter-century as of 1939, indicating a founding date of before 1914.*

> **CONFLICT:** *In* Before Watchmen: Dollar Bill, *the bank is called National Bank Company, whereas* The Watchmen Sourcebook *calls it First National Bank of New York (FBNY). Since Alan Moore's miniseries uses the name National Bank of New York, that designation appears throughout this timeline.*

Circa 1910s

Liantha Mason, the sister of Hollis Mason, is born **[ALAN]**.

> **NOTE:** *It is unknown whether Liantha is older or younger than her brother, making a more specific placement impossible.*

1916

Hollis T. Mason, future masked adventurer The Nite Owl, is born to a Montana family. The boy is named after his paternal grandfather, Hollis Wordsworth Mason **[ALAN]**.

> **CONFLICT:** *Mason is said, in Alan Moore's miniseries, to have been born in 1916, despite being 46 years old in 1960, when he should be only 44 (a rare example of an internal inconsistency in Moore's story). Taking Out the Trash claims a birthdate of July 11, 1906, while timelines published in* The Film Companion *and in the film's British press kit cite a 1917 birth year. Each of these placements contradicts the comic.*

1916 to 1928

Hollis T. Mason lives on the Montana farm of his grandfather, Hollis Wordsworth Mason, along with his parents and his sister Liantha. The elder Mason, fiercely devoted to his family, the Bible, and the U.S. flag, impresses a strong moral code upon them all, teaching that people are morally healthier in country settings than in cities, which he sees as cesspools of dishonesty, greed, lust, and godlessness. Though some of that code sinks in, young Hollis re-thinks his granddad's appraisal upon witnessing his country neighbors' tendency toward drunkenness, domestic violence, and child abuse **[ALAN]**.

Before 1917

Gretchen Slovak, Ursula Zandt's future lover, is born in Austria **[BWMM]**.

> **NOTE:** *Gretchen's age is unstated, though she appears to be older than Ursula, born in 1917. Her surname, Slovak, is visible (though difficult to read) on a sign outside her office.*

—1917

William Benjamin "Bill" Brady, the future masked adventurer Dollar Bill, is born to a rural family **[RPG2]** under utterly normal circumstances **[BWDB]**.

> **NOTE:** *According to* Absolute Watchmen, *Alan Moore originally intended for Brady to be born in 1915.* Before Watchmen: Dollar Bill *reveals his middle name.*

> **CONFLICT:** Taking Out the Trash *provides a birthdate of November 6, 1917, and claims Brady is from Kansas.* Before Watchmen: Dollar Bill, *on the other hand, places his birth on July 4, 1917, and his home in Nebraska. Oddly,* The Watchmen Sourcebook *notes his being from Kansas, yet describes him as "an Omaha youngster," indicating Nebraska— thus making* Taking Out the Trash *and* Before Watchmen: Dollar Bill *simultaneously consistent and inconsistent.*

—May 29, 1917

John Fitzgerald Kennedy, future 35th President of the United States, is born to Joseph Patrick Kennedy, Sr., and Rose Elizabeth Fitzgerald-Kennedy **[REAL]**.

—September 4, 1917

Ursula Zandt, future masked adventurer The Silhouette, is born in Katzenbühl, Austria (located in the Alps), to a wealthy, aristocratic Jewish couple **[RPG2, RPG3]**. Her father, Dr. Gregor Zandt, is a kindly, successful physician **[RPG3]**.

> **NOTE:** *According to* Absolute Watchmen, *Alan Moore originally intended for Zandt to be born in 1914.*

—1918

Rolf Müller runs away from home at age thirteen to join the circus **[RPG2]**.

> **CONFLICT:** The Watchmen Sourcebook *cites Rolf running away from home on April 15, 1932, and claims he is fifteen years old at the time. That date does not jibe well with the character's apparent age in Alan Moore's miniseries, however, and contradicts* Taking Out the Trash's *background for young Rolf.*

—After 1918

Rolf Müller becomes famous as a circus strongman **[RPG2]**.

—In or Before 1919

Rolf Müller's family emigrates to the United States **[RPG2, RPG3]**.

> **CONFLICT:** *Ellis Island immigration records published in* The Watchmen Sourcebook *list the Müller family as arriving in the United States on June 14, 1919, whereas* Taking Out the Trash *has Rolf already living in America in 1918 and* Before Watchmen: Minutemen *depicts him as working at a German circus in 1920.*

MIND .... *The Mindscape of Alan Moore*	**RPG2** .... *DC Heroes Role Playing Module #235: Taking Out the Trash—Curses and Tears*	**VRL2**..... Viral video: *The Keene Act and You*
MOBL.... *Watchmen: The Mobile Game*		**VRL3**..... Viral video: *Who Watches the Watchmen? A Veidt Music Network (VMN) Special*
MOTN.... *Watchmen: The Complete Motion Comic*	**RPG3** .... *DC Heroes: The Watchmen Sourcebook*	
MTRO.... *Metro promotional newspaper cover wrap*	**RUBY** .... "Wounds," published in *The Ruby Files Volume One*	**VRL4**..... Viral video: *World in Focus: 6 Minutes to Midnight*
NEWP.... *New Frontiersman promotional newspaper*	**SCR1**..... Unfilmed screenplay draft: Sam Hamm	**VRL5**..... Viral video: *Local Radio Station Report on 1977 Riots*
NEWW.... *New Frontiersman website*	**SCR2**..... Unfilmed screenplay draft: Charles McKeuen	
NIGH ..... *Watchmen: The End Is Nigh, Parts 1 and 2*	**SCR3**..... Unfilmed screenplay draft: Gary Goldman	**VRL6**..... Viral videos (group of ten): *Veidt Enterprises Advertising Contest*
PKIT...... *Watchmen film British press kit*	**SCR4**..... Unfilmed screenplay draft: David Hayter (2002)	
PORT..... *Watchmen Portraits*	**SCR5**..... Unfilmed screenplay draft: David Hayter (2003)	**WAWA**... *Watching the Watchmen*
REAL..... Real life	**SCR6**..... Unfilmed screenplay draft: Alex Tse	**WHOS**.... *Who's Who: The Definitive Directory of the DC Universe*
RPG1 .... *DC Heroes Role Playing Module #227: Who Watches the Watchmen?*	**SPOT**..... *DC Spotlight #1*	
	VRL1..... Viral video: *NBS Nightly News with Ted Philips*	**WTFC** .... *Watchmen: The Film Companion*

—1910s or 1920s

As a child enrolled in the Straw Valley School System **[RPG3]**, Nelson Gardner spends time as a Boy Scout, internalizing many of that organization's values. A sickly child, he is often the butt of other children's jokes **[RPG2]**.

> **NOTE:** *The Boy Scouts of America have historically taken a strong stance against homosexuality among their membership. Nelson's involvement with that organization and embracing of its values is thus ironic, given his sexual orientation.*

When Byron Lewis is young, his father introduces him to high society, but the youth finds this lifestyle boring and pursues the intellectual arts instead **[RPG2]**. The two are not close as father and son, as Arthur Lewis spends little time with him, valuing money and power more than family **[RPG3]**.

Dr. Gregor Zandt plows through four-foot snow drifts in the middle of the night to treat the infant son of a neighbor in Katzenbühl, then gives her money to mend drafty holes in the walls of her home. On a separate occasion, Zandt lends another neighbor a horse and carriage to visit his pregnant wife in Vienna **[RPG3]**.

—In or Before 1920

Nelson Gardner develops severe bronchial asthma **[RPG3]**.

Rolf Müller begins molesting and murdering children as a serial killer dubbed The Friend of the Children **[BWMM]**.

> **CONFLICT:** *The depiction of Rolf Müller as a child-killer in* Before Watchmen: Minutemen *contradicts the character's background as established in* Taking Out the Trash *and* The Watchmen Sourcebook.

—1920

At Germany's Hauptzelt Zirkus circus, Rolf Müller abducts a young boy named Jacob and locks him in a cage **[BWMM]**.

> **CONFLICT:** Before Watchmen: Minutemen *implies that Jacob grows up to be Hooded Justice, contradicting other accounts in which Müller himself is Hooded Justice.*

—June 6, 1920

Edgar William Jacobi, the future supervillain Moloch the Mystic **[ALAN]**, is born to a Catholic couple **[BWMO]**. The child's large, pointed ears set him apart from others **[ALAN, RPG2]**, preventing even his parents from looking at or loving him **[BWMO]**.

> **NOTE:** *Alan Moore's miniseries establishes Moloch's birth year as 1920. The specific date appears in* Taking Out the Trash. *His parents' names are unknown.*
> *Moloch is a Canaanite god in* The Bible. *The name has been used figuratively in*

English literature, notably in John Milton's 1667 epic poem Paradise Lost, *to refer to a person or thing requiring a costly sacrifice—which Jacobi ultimately does in his later years, when Adrian Veidt gives him cancer and then shoots him as part of his plan to save the world from nuclear devastation.*

—August 3, 1920

Sally Juspeczyk, future masked adventurer The Silk Spectre, is born **[ALAN, RPG2]**.

> **NOTE:** *Alan Moore's miniseries establishes Sally's birth year as 1920. The specific date appears in* Taking Out the Trash. *According to* Absolute Watchmen, *Alan Moore originally intended for Sally to be born in 1926.*

> **CONFLICT:** *The* Watchmen *film, as well as timelines published in* The Film Companion *and in the movie's British press kit, all indicate a 1918 birth year. A police file in the press kit specifies October 29, 1918. David Hayter's unproduced 2002 screenplay changes Sally's first name to Dahlia.*

—September 14, 1920

Dr. Arthur G. Fabisher writes a letter to the Straw Valley School System, requesting that Nelson Gardner be excused from gym classes due to severe bronchial asthma, and warning that prolonged strenuous activity could trigger an attack **[RPG3]**.

—March 16, 1921

Melissa Murphy, a Straw Valley School System teacher, evaluates Nelson Gardner. In her report, she describes Nelson as the top student in his class, based on his reading-comprehension and mathematics scores, but notes that constant teasing from others, due to his sickly nature, impedes his ability to concentrate on his studies **[RPG3]**.

—Between March 16, 1921 and September 13, 1924

Nelson Gardner makes great progress in recovering from bronchial asthma **[RPG3]**.

—1923

A Caucasian male is born who will one day be murdered by The Brethren **[RPG2]**.

> **NOTE:** *This individual's name is not provided, merely his age.*

Phil Maddox joins the New York Police Department **[RPG3]**.

—Early 1920s

Bill Brady suffers typical childhood torments while in grade school **[BWDB]**.

MIND .... *The Mindscape of Alan Moore*
MOBL .... *Watchmen: The Mobile Game*
MOTN .... *Watchmen: The Complete Motion Comic*
MTRO .... *Metro promotional newspaper cover wrap*
NEWP .... *New Frontiersman promotional newspaper*
NEWW ... *New Frontiersman website*
NIGH ..... *Watchmen: The End Is Nigh, Parts 1 and 2*
PKIT ..... *Watchmen film British press kit*
PORT ..... *Watchmen Portraits*
REAL ..... Real life
RPG1 .... *DC Heroes Role Playing Module #227: Who Watches the Watchmen?*

RPG2 .... *DC Heroes Role Playing Module #235: Taking Out the Trash—Curses and Tears*
RPG3 .... *DC Heroes: The Watchmen Sourcebook*
RUBY .... "Wounds," published in *The Ruby Files Volume One*
SCR1 ..... Unfilmed screenplay draft: Sam Hamm
SCR2 ..... Unfilmed screenplay draft: Charles McKeuen
SCR3 ..... Unfilmed screenplay draft: Gary Goldman
SCR4 ..... Unfilmed screenplay draft: David Hayter (2002)
SCR5 ..... Unfilmed screenplay draft: David Hayter (2003)
SCR6 ..... Unfilmed screenplay draft: Alex Tse
SPOT ..... *DC Spotlight #1*
VRL1 ..... Viral video: *NBS Nightly News with Ted Philips*

VRL2 ..... Viral video: *The Keene Act and You*
VRL3 ..... Viral video: *Who Watches the Watchmen? A Veidt Music Network (VMN) Special*
VRL4 ..... Viral video: *World in Focus: 6 Minutes to Midnight*
VRL5 ..... Viral video: *Local Radio Station Report on 1977 Riots*
VRL6 ..... Viral videos (group of ten): *Veidt Enterprises Advertising Contest*
WAWA ... *Watching the Watchmen*
WHOS ... *Who's Who: The Definitive Directory of the DC Universe*
WTFC .... *Watchmen: The Film Companion*

Before January 1924

Connecticut millionaires Arthur and Janet Lewis hire Frank Madison as their family butler. Madison, a black man, forms a close bond with their son Byron, instilling in him a strong sensitivity against racial bigotry **[RPG3]**.

Early January 1924

Byron Lewis competes in a junior high school essay contest sponsored by Bryce University's English Department. His essay, titled "My Best Friend Frank" (about family butler Frank Madison), is chosen among the winners, for which he wins $100 and the collected works of Mark Twain **[RPG3]**.

January 5, 1924

The *New Haven Register* publishes an announcement about Byron Lewis's contest-winning essay **[RPG3]**.

May 13, 1924

Edward Morgan "Eddie" Blake, future masked adventurer The Comedian, is born **[ALAN, RPG2]**.

> **NOTE:** *Alan Moore's miniseries establishes Blake's birth year as 1924, as does a timeline packaged with* The End Is Nigh—The Complete Experience. *The specific date appears in* Taking Out the Trash. *According to* Absolute Watchmen, *Moore originally intended for Blake to be born in 1928.*
>
> *Blake's parents have not been identified in any medium. However, a prop replica of the crime-fighter's guns, released commercially as a tie-in to the* Watchmen *film, contained reproductions of his military dog tags, inscribed with the name Mrs. Kate Blake and an address, 3016 Woodrow St., Durham, N.C. Since dog tags traditionally list a soldier's next of kin, Kate is likely either his mother or sister, since there is no indication that Eddie ever marries. In addition,* Before Watchmen: Minutemen *briefly mentions Clarence Blake Jr., who could be his brother or another relative.*
>
> **CONFLICT:** *The* Watchmen *film claims a birth year of 1918, as do timelines published in* The Film Companion *and in the film's British press kit, while a police file in the press kit specifies April 19, 1918. Alan Moore's miniseries, however, is quite clear in establishing his age.*

September 13, 1924

Matilda Gardner requests permission from Dr. Arthur G. Fabisher for her son to take part in the Straw Valley School Board's annual steeple chase run. Despite his concern that cardiovascular activity might cause an asthma attack, the doctor gives approval since it would be good for Nelson's self-esteem **[RPG3]**.

September 14, 1924—12:00 PM or Earlier

Straw Valley's steeple chase run is held at Garden Green, raising more than $200 to benefit orphans at St. Albert's. More than five hundred people attend the event, including competitors from around the United States. Straw Valley JC student Marvin Bellows wins the race. Nelson Gardner also takes part, but suffers an asthmatic attack; Dr. Arthur Fabisher helps him get through this setback **[RPG3]**.

September 14, 1924—Shortly After 12:00 PM

Straw Valley Mayor Michael Dunhill awards Marvin Bellows a first-place medal at the start of a post-race carnival gala, which the St. Albert's orphans attend **[RPG3]**.

Between 1924 and January 1939

Eddie Blake experiences a number of traumatic childhood events that leave him prone to moments of uncontrollable rage **[BWMM]**.

1920s

The Treaty of Versailles, imposed on Germany and Austria-Hungary by the Allied Powers following World War I, financially ruins many Austrian families **[REAL]**. Ursula Zandt's family, however, retains their fortune and upper-class living standards. As a child, Ursula neither makes neighborhood friends nor attends a local school, though she is close with her Aunt Emma **[RPG3]**.

Sally Juspeczyk grows up in Skokie, Illinois. Her father (an insurance salesman) and mother care greatly for Sally and her sisters, Linda **[RPG3]** and Bella **[ALAN]**.

> **NOTE:** *Alan Moore's miniseries refers to Bella as Laurie Juspeczyk's maiden aunt, which would seem to indicate that she is Sally's unmarried sister. Although it's possible that Bella is Larry Schexnayder's sister, this seems doubtful since he leaves when Laurie is very young and she never sees him again, making it unlikely that Laurie would maintain a relationship with any of his relatives. As such, Bella is most likely another sister of Sally.*

In or Before 1925

Byron Lewis begins attending Van Buren Academy, where he excels as a student and maintains a spotless disciplinary record **[RPG3]**.

1925

Ursula Zandt breaks her leg while skiing. Her father, Dr. Gregor Zandt, sets the broken bone for her at a hospital in Katzenbühl, Austria **[RPG3]**.

MIND .... *The Mindscape of Alan Moore*
MOBL.... *Watchmen: The Mobile Game*
MOTN.... *Watchmen: The Complete Motion Comic*
MTRO.... *Metro* promotional newspaper cover wrap
NEWP.... *New Frontiersman* promotional newspaper
NEWW.... *New Frontiersman* website
NIGH ..... *Watchmen: The End Is Nigh, Parts 1 and 2*
PKIT...... *Watchmen* film British press kit
PORT..... *Watchmen Portraits*
REAL..... Real life
RPG1 .... *DC Heroes Role Playing Module #227: Who Watches the Watchmen?*

RPG2 .... *DC Heroes Role Playing Module #235: Taking Out the Trash—Curses and Tears*
RPG3 .... *DC Heroes: The Watchmen Sourcebook*
RUBY .... "Wounds," published in *The Ruby Files Volume One*
SCR1..... Unfilmed screenplay draft: Sam Hamm
SCR2..... Unfilmed screenplay draft: Charles McKeuen
SCR3..... Unfilmed screenplay draft: Gary Goldman
SCR4..... Unfilmed screenplay draft: David Hayter (2002)
SCR5..... Unfilmed screenplay draft: David Hayter (2003)
SCR6..... Unfilmed screenplay draft: Alex Tse
SPOT..... *DC Spotlight #1*
VRL1 ..... Viral video: *NBS Nightly News with Ted Philips*

VRL2..... Viral video: *The Keene Act and You*
VRL3..... Viral video: *Who Watches the Watchmen? A Veidt Music Network (VMN) Special*
VRL4..... Viral video: *World in Focus: 6 Minutes to Midnight*
VRL5..... Viral video: *Local Radio Station Report on 1977 Riots*
VRL6..... Viral videos (group of ten): *Veidt Enterprises Advertising Contest*
WAWA... *Watching the Watchmen*
WHOS ... *Who's Who: The Definitive Directory of the DC Universe*
WTFC .... *Watchmen: The Film Companion*

—May 16, 1925

Byron Lewis strikes a fellow Van Buren Academy student for using a racial epithet to describe a dark-skinned cafeteria worker. In light of his otherwise excellent record, Byron receives only two days of after-school discipline [**RPG3**].

> **NOTE:** *This date historically occurred on a Saturday, which could indicate that Van Buren Academy is a boarding school.*

—Mid-1920s to Early 1930s

Edgar Jacobi endures a great deal of bullying from other children due to his misshapen ears and unattractive face. He studies history, mathematics, and English at school, but learns about violence, cruelty, and brutality from his fellow students. More than anything, he longs for someone to care for him and accept him for who he is [**BWMO**].

—In or Before 1928

Moe Vernon amasses a large collection of risqué, tasteless novelty items at gag shops and during trips to Coney Island. These include a ballpoint pen featuring the image of a woman whose swimsuit vanishes when the pen is held upside down, salt and pepper shakers shaped like female breasts, plastic dog feces, and so forth. Vernon displays these gadgets to startle those visiting his office, which he finds amusing [**ALAN**].

The Owl Hotel opens in Manhattan, New York [**HOOD**].

—1928

When Hollis Mason is twelve years old, his father relocates their family from Montana to New York City. This sparks arguments with Hollis's grandfather, Hollis Wordsworth Mason, who had intended for his son to take over the family farm. The elder Mason condemns the decision to move east, predicting poverty and moral ruination [**ALAN**].

> **CONFLICT:** Under the Hood *contains a discrepancy regarding Mason's age when the family moves to New York. The text pages specify that he is twelve years old in 1928, but a "photograph" of Mason and his father at Vernon's Auto Repairs cites his age that same year as twenty-one. The latter does not jibe with a birth year of 1916, and must be a typographical error.*

Hollis Mason's father begins working at Vernon's Auto Repairs, located just off Seventh Avenue and owned by Moe Vernon. Also employed there is trusted senior mechanic Fred Motz. The elder Mason takes enthusiastic pride in his work, as he enjoys fixing cars and can provide for his family in a career of his choosing, dispelling his own father's dire predictions that he would be a failure in New York City [**ALAN**].

The Canada Malting Company begins constructing an enormous factory on the Hudson River shore, sparing no expense in building the largest factory of its kind **[BWMM]**.

—Before March 1928
Byron Lewis applies to Bryce University's School of Arts, located in New Haven, Connecticut **[RPG3]**.

—March 11, 1928
F. Stanley Dunn, the dean of Bryce University's School of Arts, writes a letter to Byron Lewis, welcoming him to the college for the 1928–1929 school year **[RPG3]**.

—Fall 1928
Byron Lewis begins studying at Bryce University's School of Arts **[RPG3]**.

—1928 to 1938
Hollis Mason grows increasingly repulsed by New York City's pimps, pornographers, protection artists, rapists, and shady landlords. The frequent suffering around him makes him feel ill, and he sometimes expresses a desire to return to Montana—not because he truly wishes to, but because it upsets his parents when he says it. Eventually, he comes to regret such statements **[ALAN]**.

Depressed by the gap between his grandfather's small-town teachings and the hellish world of city life, Hollis Mason finds refuge in reading pulp adventure fiction, such as *Doc Savage* and *The Shadow*, in which the line between right and wrong is always absolute. The brilliant, resourceful sleuths of these stories offer Hollis a glimpse of a perfect, moral world, inspiring in him a desire to become a police officer—and, later, a masked crime-fighter **[ALAN]**.

—Before 1929
Byron Lewis's family names a pet Buttons, which tries to eat any table scraps left unattended. Their butler, Frank Madison, often yells at the animal to stop **[RPG3]**.
> **NOTE:** *Buttons is presumably a dog or a cat, though this is unspecified.*

—In or Before 1929
German citizen Josef Osterman marries a Jewish woman named Inge, much to the displeasure of his friends and cousins **[BWDM]**.
> **NOTE:** *Inge, as drawn by artist Adam Hughes in* Before Watchmen: Dr. Manhattan, *strongly resembles model Riki "Riddle" Lecotey, a cast member on Syfy's* Heroes of Cosplay

MIND .... *The Mindscape of Alan Moore*
MOBL .... *Watchmen: The Mobile Game*
MOTN .... *Watchmen: The Complete Motion Comic*
MTRO .... *Metro* promotional newspaper cover wrap
NEWP .... *New Frontiersman* promotional newspaper
NEWW .. *New Frontiersman* website
NIGH ..... *Watchmen: The End Is Nigh, Parts 1 and 2*
PKIT ...... *Watchmen* film British press kit
PORT ..... *Watchmen Portraits*
REAL ..... Real life
RPG1 .... *DC Heroes Role Playing Module #227: Who Watches the Watchmen?*

RPG2 .... *DC Heroes Role Playing Module #235: Taking Out the Trash—Curses and Tears*
RPG3 .... *DC Heroes: The Watchmen Sourcebook*
RUBY .... "Wounds," published in *The Ruby Files Volume One*
SCR1 ..... Unfilmed screenplay draft: Sam Hamm
SCR2 ..... Unfilmed screenplay draft: Charles McKeuen
SCR3 ..... Unfilmed screenplay draft: Gary Goldman
SCR4 ..... Unfilmed screenplay draft: David Hayter (2002)
SCR5 ..... Unfilmed screenplay draft: David Hayter (2003)
SCR6 ..... Unfilmed screenplay draft: Alex Tse
SPOT ..... *DC Spotlight #1*
VRL1 ..... Viral video: *NBS Nightly News with Ted Philips*

VRL2 ..... Viral video: *The Keene Act and You*
VRL3 ..... Viral video: *Who Watches the Watchmen? A Veidt Music Network (VMN) Special*
VRL4 ..... Viral video: *World in Focus: 6 Minutes to Midnight*
VRL5 ..... Viral video: *Local Radio Station Report on 1977 Riots*
VRL6 ..... Viral videos (group of ten): *Veidt Enterprises Advertising Contest*
WAWA ... *Watching the Watchmen*
WHOS ... *Who's Who: The Definitive Directory of the DC Universe*
WTFC .... *Watchmen: The Film Companion*

reality show and a costumer who worked on the films X-Men: First Class *and* Captain America: Civil War. *Lecotey revealed to this book's author that Hughes is among her closest friends, and that the use of her likeness was intentional.*

●—1929

Jonathan "Jon" Osterman, the future superhuman Dr. Manhattan, is born **[ALAN, RPG2]** to Josef and Inge Osterman, a mixed-religion couple in Germany **[BWDM]**.

> **NOTE:** *Osterman's full first name, Jonathan, appears in* The Watchmen Sourcebook.

> **CONFLICT:** *Alan Moore's miniseries establishes Jon's birth year as 1929, as does a timeline packaged with* The End Is Nigh—The Complete Experience. *Taking Out the Trash specifies March 30, while* Before Watchmen: Doctor Manhattan, *oddly enough, cites both August 14 and May 5. Timelines published in* The Film Companion *and in the film's British press kit claim a birth year of 1930. A police file in the press kit specifies March 9, 1930.*

The stock-market crash kills The Canada Malting Company's desire for international trade, and the firm abandons its under-construction Hudson River factory **[BWMM]**.

●—In or Before March 1929

Byron Lewis begins maintaining a diary and dating a young woman named Linda, who uses opium and often calls him a dreamer **[RPG3]**.

●—March 17, 1929—Afternoon

Arthur Lewis tells his son Byron that the most important thing their family fortune has bought is respect, which translates to power. After riding the West Haven bus and seeing other passengers' loathing at his expensive clothing, however, Byron writes a diary entry condemning his father's values as a lie, and says he needs to get drunk **[RPG3]**.

●—March 17, 1929—11:00 PM

Linda comes by to visit Byron, and he samples her opium for the first time **[RPG3]**.

●—Before April 14, 1929

Nelson Gardner applies to Chesterfield College, in Chesterfield, Michigan **[RPG3]**.

●—April 14, 1929

Nelson Gardner receives a letter from Dr. Martin Frobe, Chesterfield College's dean of students, congratulating him on his acceptance for the fall semester **[RPG3]**.

—After April 14, 1929

Nelson Gardner contacts Maggie Meadows, in Chesterfield College's admissions office, to find out his dormitory assignment and financial arrangements **[RPG3]**.

> **NOTE:** *It is unknown whether Maggie Meadows is related to Hank Meadows, a Gila Flats scientist mentioned in Alan Moore's miniseries.*

—In or Before September 1929

Byron Lewis develops a drinking problem and, while drunk, makes unkind statements to family butler Frank Madison that he later regrets **[RPG3]**.

—Before September 7, 1929

Byron Lewis writes a letter to Frank Madison, expressing his desire to drop out of Bryce University, since the school only values him for his father's monetary contributions, and because people there place wealth above individuality and self-respect. Frank writes back, urging him to stay at school and endure it **[RPG3]**.

—September 7, 1929

Byron Lewis responds to Frank Madison's letter, agreeing to take his advice. Byron apologizes for having been unkind to Frank, says he has always been a father to him, and promises to decrease his alcoholic intake **[RPG3]**.

—Fall 1929

Nelson Gardner begins attending Chesterfield College **[RPG3]**.

—In or Before December 1929

The marriage between Henrik and Greta Müller becomes increasingly volatile, as she tends toward alcoholism and he frequently resorts to violence when they argue **[RPG3]**.

—December 11, 1929

Greta Müller files an incident report with the Macon County Sheriff's Office against her husband Henrik for domestic assault and battery, but presses no formal charges **[RPG3]**.

—1929 or 1930

Hollis Mason develops a crush on his math teacher, Miss Albertine, though she is engaged to his sarcastic English teacher, Mr. Richardson. At age thirteen or fourteen, he fantasizes about being a hero like those in his favorite pulp-fiction stories, saving the prettiest girl in school from bullies but refusing her reward of a kiss; or tracking down and killing gangsters who have kidnapped Albertine, causing her to leave Richardson and fall in love with him **[ALAN]**.

MIND .... *The Mindscape of Alan Moore*	**RPG2** .... *DC Heroes Role Playing Module #235: Taking Out the Trash—Curses and Tears*	**VRL2** ..... Viral video: *The Keene Act and You*
MOBL .... *Watchmen: The Mobile Game*		**VRL3** ..... Viral video: *Who Watches the Watchmen? A Veidt Music Network (VMN) Special*
MOTN .... *Watchmen: The Complete Motion Comic*	**RPG3** .... *DC Heroes: The Watchmen Sourcebook*	
MTRO .... *Metro* promotional newspaper cover wrap	**RUBY** .... "Wounds," published in *The Ruby Files Volume One*	**VRL4** ..... Viral video: *World in Focus: 6 Minutes to Midnight*
NEWP .... *New Frontiersman* promotional newspaper	**SCR1** ..... Unfilmed screenplay draft: Sam Hamm	**VRL5** ..... Viral video: *Local Radio Station Report on 1977 Riots*
NEWW .... *New Frontiersman* website	**SCR2** ..... Unfilmed screenplay draft: Charles McKeuen	
NIGH ..... *Watchmen: The End Is Nigh, Parts 1 and 2*	**SCR3** ..... Unfilmed screenplay draft: Gary Goldman	**VRL6** ..... Viral videos (group of ten): *Veidt Enterprises Advertising Contest*
PKIT ...... *Watchmen film British press kit*	**SCR4** ..... Unfilmed screenplay draft: David Hayter (2002)	
PORT ..... *Watchmen Portraits*	**SCR5** ..... Unfilmed screenplay draft: David Hayter (2003)	**WAWA** ... *Watching the Watchmen*
REAL ..... Real life	**SCR6** ..... Unfilmed screenplay draft: Alex Tse	**WHOS** ... *Who's Who: The Definitive Directory of the DC Universe*
RPG1 .... *DC Heroes Role Playing Module #227: Who Watches the Watchmen?*	**SPOT** ..... *DC Spotlight #1*	
	VRL1 ..... Viral video: *NBS Nightly News with Ted Philips*	**WTFC** .... *Watchmen: The Film Companion*

—1929 to 1939

The Canada Malting Company languishes during the Great Depression, its uncompleted Hudson River factory sitting abandoned for a decade **[BWMM]**.

—Late 1920s to Early 1930s

As a teenager, Hollis Mason enjoys occasional trips to Vernon's Auto Repairs with his father, and learns of owner Moe Vernon's passion for opera. Moe keeps a gramophone in his office, on which he plays scratchy old 78 RPM records of his favorite recordings at maximum volume. Among these is "The Ride of the Valkyries" **[ALAN]**, performed by the Vienna Philharmonic Orchestra, and conducted by Wilhelm Furtwängler **[BWMM]**. Although Hollis's dad lets him help out at the shop, he dislikes having his son exposed to the risqué novelty items that Moe keeps in his desk drawer **[ALAN]**.

> **NOTE:** "The Ride of the Valkyries" is the popular name for act 3 of Die Walküre (The Valkyrie), the second of four operas in Richard Wagner's Der Ring des Nibelungen (The Ring of the Nibelung) cycle. The music appears in the Watchmen film's soundtrack during Dr. Manhattan's battle scenes in Vietnam.

In college, Byron Lewis majors in philosophy **[RPG2]**, cultivates radical left-wing friendships **[ALAN]**, and adopts their bohemian lifestyle, attitudes, and idealism **[RPG2]**.

Blanche Zandt, the younger sister of Ursula Zandt, is born in Austria **[BWMM]**.

—1920s or 1930s

Future New York City news vendor Bernard is born to a family in Germany **[ALAN]**.

William Dreiberg secures his first job at age seventeen, making good money **[BWNO]**.

Frank Madison, the butler of Arthur, Janet, and Byron Lewis, marries a woman named Celia. The couple have a son, whom they name William **[RPG3]**.

—In or Before the 1930s

Clarence Blake Jr. graduates from Charlotte's Central High School **[BWMM]**.

> **NOTE:** It is unknown whether Clarence Blake is a relative of Eddie Blake.

—1930

John David Keene, future senator and proponent of the Keene Act, is born to a family in New York City's affluent Greenwich Village section **[NEWW]**.

> **CONFLICT:** Gary Goldman's unproduced 1992 screenplay changes the senator's name to Norman Keene.

ABSO .... *Watchmen Absolute Edition*
ALAN ..... Alan Moore's *Watchmen* miniseries
ARCD .... *Minutemen Arcade*
ARTF ..... *Watchmen: The Art of the Film*
BLCK ..... *Tales of the Black Freighter*
BWCC ... *Before Watchmen—The Crimson Corsair*
BWCO ... *Before Watchmen—Comedian*
BWDB ... *Before Watchmen—Dollar Bill*
BWDM .. *Before Watchmen—Dr. Manhattan*
BWMM .. *Before Watchmen—Minutemen*
BWMO .. *Before Watchmen—Moloch*
BWNO ... *Before Watchmen—Nite Owl*

BWOZ .... *Before Watchmen—Ozymandias*
BWRO ... *Before Watchmen—Rorschach*
BWSS ... *Before Watchmen—Silk Spectre*
CHEM .... My Chemical Romance music video: "Desolation Row"
CMEO .... *Watchmen* cameos in comics, TV, and film:
  • Comic: *Astonishing X-Men* volume 3 issue #6
  • Comic: *Hero Hotline* volume 1 issue #5
  • Comic: *Kingdom Come* volume 1 issue #2
  • Comic: *Marvels* volume 1 issue #4
  • Comic: *The Question* volume 1 issue #17
  • TV: *Teen Titans Go!* episode #82, "Real Boy Adventures"
  • Film: *Man of Steel*

  • Film: *Batman v Superman: Dawn of Justice Ultimate Edition*
  • Film: *Justice League*
CLIX ...... HeroClix figure pack-in cards
DECK ..... *DC Comics Deck-Building Game—Crossover Pack 4: Watchmen*
DURS ... *DC Universe: Rebirth Special* volume 1 issue #1
FILM ..... *Watchmen* theatrical film
HOOD .... *Under the Hood* documentary and dust-jacket prop reproduction
JUST ..... *Watchmen: Justice Is Coming*
MATL .... Mattel Club Black Freighter figure pack-in cards

In or Before January 1930
Martin Maxwell is named senior editor of *The Voice of the People*, a pro-communist newspaper. His staff includes associate editor Michael Kilmer, photo editor Laura Browning, and art director Ike Thompson **[RPG3]**.

January 4, 1930
Greta Müller files an incident report with the Macon County Sheriff's Office against her husband Henrik for domestic assault and battery, but presses no formal charges **[RPG3]**.

Between January 4 and January 11, 1930
The U.S. Internal Revenue Service (IRS) releases a report showing a major disparity between the poor and the wealthy in the United States **[RPG3]**.

January 11, 1930
The Voice of the People publishes an editorial citing the IRS report. The Stalinist newspaper condemns U.S. politicians for perpetuating a government that exists not to protect the average citizen, but to benefit the Rockefellers, Dreibergs, and other wealthy families who have earned fortunes by exploiting common laborers **[RPG3]**.

February 6, 1930
Greta Müller files another Macon County Sheriff's Office incident report against her husband Henrik for domestic assault and battery, but again presses no formal charges. Their son Rolf brutally beats Henrik in retaliation **[RPG3]**.

> **CONFLICT:** *Rolf is said to be thirteen years old in 1930 in* The Watchmen Sourcebook *when this occurs, but* Taking Out the Trash *cites a 1905 birth year, making him twenty-five at the time.*

Before 1931
Moe Vernon marries a woman named Beatrice **[ALAN]**.

1931
Beatrice Vernon begins a romantic affair with Fred Motz, a trusted mechanic working for her husband Moe at Vernon's Auto Repairs **[ALAN]**.

When Sally Juspeczyk is eleven years old, her sister Linda dies in a car accident shortly after marrying a Northwestern University medical student. Sally and her parents all suffer from depression as a result, their relationship permanently damaged **[RPG3]**.

MIND .... *The Mindscape of Alan Moore*
MOBL .... *Watchmen: The Mobile Game*
MOTN .... *Watchmen: The Complete Motion Comic*
MTRO .... *Metro* promotional newspaper cover wrap
NEWP .... *New Frontiersman* promotional newspaper
NEWW ... *New Frontiersman* website
NIGH ..... *Watchmen: The End Is Nigh, Parts 1 and 2*
PKIT ...... *Watchmen* film British press kit
PORT ..... *Watchmen Portraits*
REAL ..... Real life
RPG1 .... *DC Heroes Role Playing Module #227: Who Watches the Watchmen?*

RPG2 .... *DC Heroes Role Playing Module #235: Taking Out the Trash—Curses and Tears*
RPG3 .... *DC Heroes: The Watchmen Sourcebook*
RUBY .... "Wounds," published in *The Ruby Files Volume One*
SCR1 ..... Unfilmed screenplay draft: Sam Hamm
SCR2 ..... Unfilmed screenplay draft: Charles McKeuen
SCR3 ..... Unfilmed screenplay draft: Gary Goldman
SCR4 ..... Unfilmed screenplay draft: David Hayter (2002)
SCR5 ..... Unfilmed screenplay draft: David Hayter (2003)
SCR6 ..... Unfilmed screenplay draft: Alex Tse
SPOT ..... *DC Spotlight #1*
VRL1 ..... Viral video: *NBS Nightly News with Ted Philips*

VRL2 ..... Viral video: *The Keene Act and You*
VRL3 ..... Viral video: *Who Watches the Watchmen? A Veidt Music Network (VMN) Special*
VRL4 ..... Viral video: *World in Focus: 6 Minutes to Midnight*
VRL5 ..... Viral video: *Local Radio Station Report on 1977 Riots*
VRL6 ..... Viral videos (group of ten): *Veidt Enterprises Advertising Contest*
WAWA ... *Watching the Watchmen*
WHOS ... *Who's Who: The Definitive Directory of the DC Universe*
WTFC .... *Watchmen: The Film Companion*

—1932

At age fifteen, Ursula Zandt hears a police officer whistling at her good looks. Furious, she runs across the street and hits him, for which she is arrested **[RPG3]**.

—In or Before February 1932

Edgar Jacobi develops a crush on his classmate Marie **[BWMO]**.

—February 14, 1932

Edgar Jacobi's classmates exchange Valentine's Day cards. A student named Jimmy hands Edgar's card to Marie, but she rips it to shreds, then beats Edgar up in front of the other students, outraged that someone who looks like him would have the gall to give her a card **[BWMO]**.

—Fall 1932

Byron Lewis graduates from Bryce University **[RPG3]**.

—In or After 1932

Henrik Müller leaves his wife Greta to be with a young grocery lady named Mary, from Fulton County, Georgia. Henrik views Greta's alcoholism as godless, though he writes a letter before leaving, saying he still loves her and their son Rolf **[RPG3]**.

—Early to Mid-1930s

Bill Brady blossoms into a natural athlete while in high school, able to succeed at any sport. He earns scholarships to multiple colleges **[BWDB]**.

—1933

Janine "Janey" Slater, future girlfriend of Jon Osterman, is born **[WTFC]**.
  NOTE: *Slater's full first name appears in* Before Watchmen: Dr. Manhattan.

Beatrice Vernon withdraws all money from the joint bank account she shares with her husband Moe, then runs away to Tijuana, Mexico, with Fred Motz—who fails to show up for work as a result **[ALAN]**.

Shortly after his seventeenth birthday, Hollis Mason helps his father repair a busted-up Ford automobile at Vernon's Auto Repairs. In his office, Moe Vernon listens to Wagner operas while wearing foam-rubber breasts to amuse whoever delivers his morning mail. This has the desired effect, but a letter from Beatrice informs him of her decision to run away with Fred. Moe bursts open his office door and announces the affair. Despite the man's pain, the sight of him wearing fake bosoms and crying, with "The Ride of the Valkyries" playing in the background, makes everyone in the shop laugh **[ALAN]**.

An hour later, an employee apologizes for the mechanics' insensitivity. Moe accepts the apology, but sends everyone home early and commits suicide by breathing in the carbon monoxide fumes from a car's engine exhaust. Fred Motz later returns to New York City. Moe's brother takes over the business and re-hires Motz as his chief mechanic **[ALAN]**.

> **NOTE:** *It is unclear whether Motz and Beatrice end their relationship, causing him to leave Tijuana without her, or return to New York together following Moe's death.*

Nelson Gardner plays halfback for Chesterfield College's football team, the Gophers, as a late addition, but none of his fellow players pass him the ball during the entire season until the final game **[RPG3]**.

> **NOTE:** *Among Gardner's teammates are students named Tony Rotelli and Hal Mason. It is unknown whether Tony is related to Vittorio and Marie Rotelli, mentioned in* Justice Is Coming, *or whether Hal is a relative of Hollis Mason.*

The Edgar and Sons Pawn Shop opens in New York City **[MOBL]**.

> **NOTE:** *Presumably, there is no connection to Edgar Jacobi, whose only known child (in* Before Watchmen: Moloch*) is aborted during pregnancy.*

> **CONFLICT:** *In the* Watchmen *film, the store's sign indicates an establishment year of 1938 and cites the company's name as Edgar & Sons. It's possible that these are separate businesses.*

—Summer 1933

Rolf Müller joins the Sackson and Shanley circus's "Big Top Hello Mobile" troupe as Rolf the European Powerhouse. His colleagues never see the strongman in the company of young women, but shortly after Rolf's hiring, circus employee Daniel "Happy" Dahl witnesses him exiting a wardrobe tent looking shaken after having spent hours alone with fellow performer Frank Burrows. Dahl is unaware that the two men have had sex. Disgusted with himself, Müller grabs a red-hot poker and repeatedly burns his arms and thighs, then breaks down crying. Thereafter, Rolf wears a full body stocking to cover the scars **[RPG3]**.

—Before October 1933

Rolf Müller becomes a staunch anti-communist **[RPG2]** and joins the Ku Klux Klan. He, along with Frank Burrows and three other Klan members, are accused of murdering a black couple, Samuel and Eloise Horton, after they attend the circus in Atlanta, Georgia. The attackers break Samuel's neck and set Eloise on fire **[RPG3]**.

> **CONFLICT:** Taking Out the Trash *claims that Rolf joins the KKK in 1938. Perhaps he leaves and then rejoins the organization in the interim.*

MIND .... *The Mindscape of Alan Moore*	**RPG2** .... *DC Heroes Role Playing Module #235: Taking Out the Trash—Curses and Tears*	**VRL2** ..... Viral video: *The Keene Act and You*
MOBL .... *Watchmen: The Mobile Game*		**VRL3** ..... Viral video: *Who Watches the Watchmen? A Veidt Music Network (VMN) Special*
MOTN .... *Watchmen: The Complete Motion Comic*	**RPG3** .... *DC Heroes: The Watchmen Sourcebook*	
MTRO .... *Metro* promotional newspaper cover wrap	**RUBY** .... "Wounds," published in *The Ruby Files Volume One*	**VRL4** ..... Viral video: *World in Focus: 6 Minutes to Midnight*
NEWP .... *New Frontiersman* promotional newspaper	**SCR1** ..... Unfilmed screenplay draft: Sam Hamm	**VRL5** ..... Viral video: *Local Radio Station Report on 1977 Riots*
NEWW .... *New Frontiersman* website	**SCR2** ..... Unfilmed screenplay draft: Charles McKeuen	
NIGH ..... *Watchmen: The End Is Nigh, Parts 1 and 2*	**SCR3** ..... Unfilmed screenplay draft: Gary Goldman	**VRL6** ..... Viral videos (group of ten): *Veidt Enterprises Advertising Contest*
PKIT ...... *Watchmen* film British press kit	**SCR4** ..... Unfilmed screenplay draft: David Hayter (2002)	
PORT ..... *Watchmen Portraits*	**SCR5** ..... Unfilmed screenplay draft: David Hayter (2003)	**WAWA** ... *Watching the Watchmen*
REAL ..... Real life	**SCR6** ..... Unfilmed screenplay draft: Alex Tse	**WHOS** ... *Who's Who: The Definitive Directory of the DC Universe*
RPG1 .... *DC Heroes Role Playing Module #227: Who Watches the Watchmen?*	**SPOT** ..... *DC Spotlight #1*	
	VRL1 ..... Viral video: *NBS Nightly News with Ted Philips*	**WTFC** .... *Watchmen: The Film Companion*

In or Before October 1933

The *New York Gazette* begins publication **[RPG3]**. The newspaper's tag line: "We print the news" **[RPG2]**.

> **NOTE:** The Watchmen Sourcebook *features a* Gazette *article dated October 5, 1933, which is the earliest edition of the paper mentioned in* Watchmen *lore.*

October 3, 1933—Night

Rolf Müller, Frank Burrows, and three fellow Ku Klux Klan members are acquitted of murdering Samuel and Eloise Horton **[RPG3]**.

October 5, 1933

The *New York Gazette* covers the Horton murder acquittals, noting that the prosecutors, though suspicious of the jury having been highly biased in favor of the defendants, will not appeal the case **[RPG3]**.

In or After October 1933

Frank Burrows is outed as a homosexual **[RPG3]**.

November 10, 1933

The Chesterfield Gophers compete for the State College football title against fellow school Blakely. After successful plays by teammates Rich Fields, Tony Rotelli, Bill Burton, and Ed Jeremy, Nelson Gardner drops a well-thrown fourth-down touchdown pass from Burton, causing his team to lose the game and title during the final seconds. The dropped pass is Gardner's first and only action throughout the season **[RPG3]**.

November 11, 1933

The *Chesterfield Daily Reader* covers the Chesterfield Gophers' "crushing defeat," detailing Nelson Gardner's game-losing flub **[RPG3]**.

1933 and Beyond

Hollis Mason develops an emotional connection to "The Ride of the Valkyries," from Richard Wagner's *Der Ring des Nibelungen* (*The Ring of the Nibelung*) cycle, since it reminds him of the late Moe Vernon. Each time Mason hears this stirring refrain, he grows depressed and wonders about the lot of humanity and the unfairness of life **[ALAN]**.

Before March 22, 1934

Nelson Gardner graduates from college.

ABSO .... *Watchmen Absolute Edition*	**BWOZ**.... *Before Watchmen—Ozymandias*	• Film: *Batman v Superman: Dawn of Justice Ultimate Edition*
ALAN..... Alan Moore's *Watchmen* miniseries	**BWRO** ... *Before Watchmen—Rorschach*	• Film: *Justice League*
ARCD .... *Minutemen Arcade*	**BWSS** ... *Before Watchmen—Silk Spectre*	**CLIX** ...... HeroClix figure pack-in cards
ARTF ..... *Watchmen: The Art of the Film*	**CHEM**.... My Chemical Romance music video: "Desolation Row"	**DECK**..... *DC Comics Deck-Building Game—Crossover Pack 4: Watchmen*
BLCK..... *Tales of the Black Freighter*	**CMEO**.... *Watchmen* cameos in comics, TV, and film:	
BWCC .. *Before Watchmen—The Crimson Corsair*	• Comic: *Astonishing X-Men* volume 3 issue #6	**DURS** .... *DC Universe: Rebirth Special* volume 1 issue #1
BWCO .. *Before Watchmen—Comedian*	• Comic: *Hero Hotline* volume 1 issue #5	**FILM** ..... *Watchmen* theatrical film
BWDB .. *Before Watchmen—Dollar Bill*	• Comic: *Kingdom Come* volume 1 issue #2	**HOOD** .... *Under the Hood* documentary and dust-jacket prop reproduction
BWDM .. *Before Watchmen—Dr. Manhattan*	• Comic: *Marvels* volume 1 issue #4	
BWMM.. *Before Watchmen—Minutemen*	• Comic: *The Question* volume 1 issue #17	**JUST** ..... *Watchmen: Justice Is Coming*
BWMO .. *Before Watchmen—Moloch*	• TV: *Teen Titans Go!* episode #82, "Real Boy Adventures"	**MATL** .... Mattel Club Black Freighter figure pack-in cards
BWNO ... *Before Watchmen—Nite Owl*	• Film: *Man of Steel*	

March 22, 1934

After his college graduation, Nelson Gardner joins the U.S. Marine Corps to prove he is a man **[RPG2]**. He signs his enlistment papers at a recruiting center in Detroit, Michigan, in the presence of Sergeant Thomas Bascomb **[RPG3]**.

> **NOTE:** *In Alan Moore's miniseries, Gardner stays in shape thanks to a regimen of Canadian Air Force exercises. However, there is no evidence that he ever serves in that military organization.*

March 22, 1934 to December 22, 1937

During his three years as a Marine **[RPG2, RPG3]**, Nelson Gardner gains a strong knowledge of military technique and strategy **[ALAN]**.

December 6, 1934

Nelson Gardner receives orders from Major G. Holland to report to a Marine base in Annapolis, Maryland. From there, he ships out to join the Marine Postal Depot's service staff at Fort Whitman, in Farley, North Carolina, as the 415th infantry regiment's maintenance supervisor **[RPG3]**.

Mid-1930s

Police begin seeking an assassin known as The Italian Shadow, who eludes their pursuit for years **[FILM]**.

Arthur Lewis dies, leaving his son Byron in charge of his estate **[RPG2]**. A genius inventor, Byron creates and patents several aviation innovations, making him extremely wealthy **[BWMM]**, though this causes the Bohemian playboy much personal guilt **[RPG2]**. Thirsty for new challenges, Lewis travels the world seeking romantic adventure **[BWMM]**. He moves to New York City, where he witnesses misery and poverty on every corner. He spends much of his time at jazz clubs and poetry cafés in Lower Manhattan, volunteering twice weekly at a Harlem medical clinic **[RPG3]**.

Edgar Jacobi steals a quarter from his father's dresser to attend a carnival—his first criminal act, borne out of necessity since his parents give him very little. After watching Fantastico the Magician make a woman vanish, read minds, turn fire into live animals, and survive bullets and knives without injury, the teen pays to see the stage show four more times. He is instantly fascinated with magic, and by a magician's ability to be around pretty women and impress crowds, regardless of his appearance **[BWMO]**.

Jacobi later learns the art of magic from Fantastico, earning the respect of his peers. His classmate Marie, who beat him up in 1932 after he gave her a Valentine's Day card, pretends to find him attractive as a cruel trick to humiliate him once again. Upon overhearing her

MIND .... *The Mindscape of Alan Moore*	**RPG2** .... *DC Heroes Role Playing Module #235: Taking Out the Trash—Curses and Tears*	**VRL2** ..... Viral video: *The Keene Act and You*
MOBL.... *Watchmen: The Mobile Game*		**VRL3** ..... Viral video: *Who Watches the Watchmen? A Veidt Music Network (VMN) Special*
MOTN.... *Watchmen: The Complete Motion Comic*	**RPG3** .... *DC Heroes: The Watchmen Sourcebook*	
MTRO.... *Metro* promotional newspaper cover wrap	**RUBY** .... "Wounds," published in *The Ruby Files Volume One*	**VRL4** ..... Viral video: *World in Focus: 6 Minutes to Midnight*
NEWP .... *New Frontiersman* promotional newspaper	**SCR1**..... Unfilmed screenplay draft: Sam Hamm	**VRL5** ..... Viral video: *Local Radio Station Report on 1977 Riots*
NEWW... *New Frontiersman* website	**SCR2**..... Unfilmed screenplay draft: Charles McKeuen	
NIGH ..... *Watchmen: The End Is Nigh, Parts 1 and 2*	**SCR3**..... Unfilmed screenplay draft: Gary Goldman	**VRL6** ..... Viral videos (group of ten): *Veidt Enterprises Advertising Contest*
PKIT ...... *Watchmen* film British press kit	**SCR4**..... Unfilmed screenplay draft: David Hayter (2002)	
PORT..... *Watchmen Portraits*	**SCR5**..... Unfilmed screenplay draft: David Hayter (2003)	**WAWA**... *Watching the Watchmen*
REAL..... Real life	**SCR6**..... Unfilmed screenplay draft: Alex Tse	**WHOS** ... *Who's Who: The Definitive Directory of the DC Universe*
RPG1 .... *DC Heroes Role Playing Module #227: Who Watches the Watchmen?*	**SPOT**..... *DC Spotlight #1*	
	VRL1 ..... Viral video: *NBS Nightly News with Ted Philips*	**WTFC** .... *Watchmen: The Film Companion*

conspiring with her boyfriend David, Edgar vows revenge. To that end, he asks David to help with a magic trick involving a coffin-shaped vanishing cabinet, then kills him with a sword, sneaks the corpse into Marie's bed as she sleeps, hops a ride on a freight train, and begins working on the vaudeville circuit. Marie awakens next to her lover's bloody corpse, causing her great mental strife **[BWMO]**.

—Mid-1930s to Mid-1940s
Marie spends the next ten years in an asylum **[BWMO]**.

—Circa 1935
Bill Brady chooses a college from multiple scholarship offers **[RPG3, BWDB]**.
> **NOTE:** *This placement is conjectural, based on his birth in 1917.*
>
> **CONFLICT:** The Watchmen Sourcebook *cites Brady as attending Kansas State University, while* Before Watchmen: Dollar Bill *sees him choosing Ivy League research university Dartmouth College, in New Hampshire.*

—1935
When Ursula Zandt is eighteen years old, her father Gregor relocates their family to the United States to avoid atrocities being committed in Austria by Adolf Hitler's Nazi forces **[RPG3]**. The Zandts blend into upper-class Manhattan society. After her parents die, Ursula develops a wild streak **[RPG2]**. Underestimated due to her slender frame, she nonetheless exhibits a strong will and formidable fighting abilities **[BWMM]**.
> **CONFLICT:** Before Watchmen: Minutemen *depicts the Zandts as still living in Austria when Hitler's troops seize that country in March 1938. As a result, most of the family are killed in that account, during rioting at Linz.*

—Before January 7, 1935
Nelson Gardner completes officer's training, achieves the rank of lieutenant, and ships out for a ten-month stint in Guantanamo Bay, Cuba, where he receives instruction in field artillery. Gardner's Aunt Frieda suffers a bout of gall stones **[RPG3]**.

—January 7, 1935
Nelson Gardner writes a letter to his parents, Albert and Matilda Gardner, informing them of his promotion to lieutenant and his Guantanamo Bay assignment **[RPG3]**.
> **NOTE:** *In his letter, Nelson tells his parents to address any mail to the 3rd Division headquarters in Fairfax, Virginia, and that it will be forwarded to him. While this could be an entirely true statement, it could also be an indication—particularly in light of his Post Office maintenance duties—that Nelson is lying to his parents, and is not, in fact, in Guantanamo Bay for training.*

—Before Spring 1935

Sylvia Joanna Glick marries Peter Joseph Kovacs in Ohio **[ALAN]**.

> **NOTE:** The Watchmen Sourcebook *misspells her surname as Glicks.*

—Spring 1935

Sylvia and Peter Kovacs move from Ohio to New York City **[ALAN]**.

—Circa October 1935

Nelson Gardner completes a ten-month tour of duty with the U.S. Marines in Guantanamo Bay, then joins the 45th Battery as a junior staff officer **[RPG3]**.

—1930s (Estimated)

As the political scene in Germany deteriorates, a German citizen relocates his family, including his son, future news vendor Bernard, to the United States **[ALAN]**.

> **NOTE:** *Bernard's last name is never revealed in any* Watchmen *lore.*

—1936

At age sixteen, Sally Juspeczyk runs away from home and heads to New York, never returning to her parents in Skokie, Illinois **[RPG2, RPG3]**, though she does maintain contact with her sister Bella **[ALAN]**. Sally finds the experience liberating, but worries about ending up dead in an alley **[RPG2, RPG3]**

—1936 and Beyond

Bella Juspeczyk never marries **[ALAN]**.

—In or Before February 1936

Byron Lewis and his girlfriend Linda end their relationship **[RPG3]**.

—February 2, 1936

Byron Lewis writes a letter to Frank Madison, telling him about life in New York City and suggesting that what Harlem needs more than anything is a hero able to lift people out of their misery **[RPG3]**.

—1936 to 1939

Sally Juspeczyk survives life alone in New York City by taking jobs as a burlesque dancer and waitress **[ALAN]**. Despite several prostitution opportunities, she avoids having to sell her body **[RPG3]**.

MIND .... *The Mindscape of Alan Moore*
MOBL .... *Watchmen: The Mobile Game*
MOTN .... *Watchmen: The Complete Motion Comic*
MTRO .... *Metro* promotional newspaper cover wrap
NEWP .... *New Frontiersman* promotional newspaper
NEWW .... *New Frontiersman* website
NIGH ..... *Watchmen: The End Is Nigh, Parts 1 and 2*
PKIT ...... *Watchmen* film British press kit
PORT ..... *Watchmen Portraits*
REAL ..... Real life
RPG1 .... *DC Heroes Role Playing Module #227: Who Watches the Watchmen?*

RPG2 .... *DC Heroes Role Playing Module #235: Taking Out the Trash—Curses and Tears*
RPG3 .... *DC Heroes: The Watchmen Sourcebook*
RUBY .... "Wounds," published in *The Ruby Files Volume One*
SCR1 ..... Unfilmed screenplay draft: Sam Hamm
SCR2 ..... Unfilmed screenplay draft: Charles McKeuen
SCR3 ..... Unfilmed screenplay draft: Gary Goldman
SCR4 .... Unfilmed screenplay draft: David Hayter (2002)
SCR5 ..... Unfilmed screenplay draft: David Hayter (2003)
SCR6 .... Unfilmed screenplay draft: Alex Tse
SPOT ..... *DC Spotlight #1*
VRL1 ..... Viral video: *NBS Nightly News with Ted Philips*

VRL2 ..... Viral video: *The Keene Act and You*
VRL3 ..... Viral video: *Who Watches the Watchmen? A Veidt Music Network (VMN) Special*
VRL4 ..... Viral video: *World in Focus: 6 Minutes to Midnight*
VRL5 ..... Viral video: *Local Radio Station Report on 1977 Riots*
VRL6 ..... Viral videos (group of ten): *Veidt Enterprises Advertising Contest*
WAWA ... *Watching the Watchmen*
WHOS .... *Who's Who: The Definitive Directory of the DC Universe*
WTFC .... *Watchmen: The Film Companion*

Late 1930s
During college, Bill Brady excels at every sport but falters in his studies [BWDB].

In or Before 1937
Sally Juspeczyk begins dancing at New York City burlesque club Stage Left, just outside Times Square [RPG3].

In or Before October 1937
Bill Brady is named quarterback of his college's football team and quickly becomes its star player. Despite the many successes the team enjoys with Brady leading the charge, he remains humble and gracious throughout [RPG3].

1937
Wallace "Wally" Weaver, future colleague of Jon Osterman, is born [ALAN].
> **NOTE:** *Weaver's full first name appears in* Before Watchmen: Dr. Manhattan.

Peter and Sylvia Kovacs divorce amidst mutual accusations of adultery and mental cruelty. Following the divorce, the two have no further contact [ALAN].

Edgar Jacobi starts a career in nightclubs at age seventeen. As a stage magician, he fosters underworld contacts [ALAN] and develops an irrational attraction to demonic motifs and Dante décor [RPG1]. After considering several stage names, such as Mason, Mentallo, Morris, and Edgar the Entertaining, he chooses Moloch the Mystic due to its alliterative appeal, and because Moloch was an Ammonite god associated with the ritual sacrifice of children—which he deems appropriate since he began his criminal career by murdering a classmate [BWMO].
> **NOTE:** *Presumably, Jacobi's consideration of the stage name "Mason" is unconnected to Hollis Mason.*

Jacobi performs at Chicago's Palace Theatre, working alongside such vaudeville acts as clown Sacha Malden, singer La Reina del Vaudeville, Venus Gypsy, Joe & Jesse, and a stripper act called Striped. He performs three shows daily, but makes barely enough money to pay his assistant, so he utilizes stage-magic tricks to perpetrate bank heists. Great Britain's *Daily Mail* publishes an article about his crimes, titled "Mystery Man Robs International Bank." The police figure out his identity from the tuxedo he wears, but he enjoys crime enough that he makes it his full-time pursuit [BWMO].

October 31, 1937

Bill Brady's football team defeats the Michigan Wolverines. The game, held in Ann Arbor, ends with a score of 17 to 14 **[RPG3]**.

November 2, 1937

The *Michigan Sportsman* covers Bill Brady's October 31 win for his college football team, describing him as a "master of the comeback" with unique athletic abilities. The article attributes the victory not only to Brady's quarterback successes, but also to flubs by opposing players Todd Worrell, Tony Ross, Anton Edwards, and Carl Turrock **[RPG3]**.

Before December 22, 1937

The U.S. Marine Corps sends Nelson Gardner out on assignment to the Philippines **[RPG3]**.

December 22, 1937

Major G. Holland, at the Marines' Fort Whitman base in Farley, North Carolina, signs honorable discharge papers for Nelson Gardner. Since Gardner is on assignment in the Philippines, the papers await his return to the United States **[RPG3]**.

Late 1937 or Early 1938

Larry Schexnayder, an ex-Hollywood press agent **[RPG2]**, meets Sally Juspeczyk as she dances at Stage Left. Too naïve to perceive him as creepy for hanging out at clubs with younger women, she hires Larry as her agent. He gives her money and a home, which she finds attractive **[RPG3]**.

1937 to 1940

Sylvia Kovacs lives in a series of low-rent apartments, either alone or with a revolving door of male acquaintances **[ALAN]**.

Before 1938

Walter Zileski, future supervillain The Screaming Skull, attends the Massachusetts Institute of Technology (MIT). A bored graduate student, he develops several odd fetishes **[RPG3]**.

MIND .... *The Mindscape of Alan Moore*	**RPG2** .... *DC Heroes Role Playing Module #235: Taking Out the Trash—Curses and Tears*	**VRL2** .... Viral video: *The Keene Act and You*
MOBL .... *Watchmen: The Mobile Game*	**RPG3** .... *DC Heroes: The Watchmen Sourcebook*	**VRL3** ..... Viral video: *Who Watches the Watchmen? A Veidt Music Network (VMN) Special*
MOTN .... *Watchmen: The Complete Motion Comic*	**RUBY** .... "Wounds," published in *The Ruby Files Volume One*	**VRL4** ..... Viral video: *World in Focus: 6 Minutes to Midnight*
MTRO .... *Metro* promotional newspaper cover wrap	**SCR1** ..... Unfilmed screenplay draft: Sam Hamm	**VRL5** ..... Viral video: *Local Radio Station Report on 1977 Riots*
NEWP .... *New Frontiersman* promotional newspaper	**SCR2** ..... Unfilmed screenplay draft: Charles McKeuen	
NEWW ... *New Frontiersman* website	**SCR3** ..... Unfilmed screenplay draft: Gary Goldman	**VRL6** ..... Viral videos (group of ten): *Veidt Enterprises Advertising Contest*
NIGH ..... *Watchmen: The End Is Nigh, Parts 1 and 2*	**SCR4** .... Unfilmed screenplay draft: David Hayter (2002)	
PKIT ...... *Watchmen* film British press kit	**SCR5** .... Unfilmed screenplay draft: David Hayter (2003)	**WAWA** ... *Watching the Watchmen*
PORT ..... *Watchmen Portraits*	**SCR6** .... Unfilmed screenplay draft: Alex Tse	**WHOS** ... *Who's Who: The Definitive Directory of the DC Universe*
REAL ..... Real life	**SPOT** .... *DC Spotlight #1*	
RPG1 .... *DC Heroes Role Playing Module #227: Who Watches the Watchmen?*	**VRL1** ..... Viral video: *NBS Nightly News with Ted Philips*	**WTFC** .... *Watchmen: The Film Companion*

Part II:
RALLYING THE MINUTEMEN
(1938–1939)

—In or Before 1938

Friedrich Werner Veidt establishes a perfumery business in Germany, which proves quite successful **[BWOZ]**. He and his wife, Ingrid Renata Veidt, build a sizable fortune profiting from the Third Reich's activities in Europe **[WTFC]**.

> **NOTE:** *According to* The Film Companion, *actor Matthew Goode, in preparing to portray Ozymandias on film, conceived of the Veidts' Nazi connections as a motivation for Adrian to give away his entire fortune and start anew. No other* Watchmen-*related sources have acknowledged this concept, however.*

—1938

Hollis Mason graduates from the police academy at age twenty-two **[ALAN]**.

The Edgar & Sons Pawn Shop opens in New York City **[FILM]**.

> **NOTE:** *Presumably, there is no connection to Edgar Jacobi, whose only known child (in* Before Watchmen: Moloch*) is aborted during pregnancy.*

> **CONFLICT:** *In* Watchmen: The Mobile Game, *the store's sign indicates an establishment year of 1933 and gives the company's name as Edgar and Sons. It's possible that these are separate businesses.*

Rolf Müller joins the Shriner's Circus, permanently based in New York City. Sixteen days later, he debuts as Rolf the European Powerhouse, the persona he created for Sackson and Shanley **[RPG3]**.

Bill Brady, during the final game of the 1938 college football season and with recruiting scouts assessing his performance, runs quarterback against Texas Christian University's Horned Frogs. Late during the fourth quarter, Brady is tackled while catching a pass, badly

injuring his knee. Bill is benched, his football career ruined, and his college declines an invitation to play in the Rose Bowl. The talent scouts leave without speaking to him **[BWDB]**.

●—February 28, 1938
Nelson Gardner returns from his Philippines mission to find his U.S. Marines discharge papers awaiting him **[RPG3]**.

●—March 1, 1938
Nelson Gardner writes a letter telling his parents about his trip to the Philippines, and revealing that he'll be heading home in two weeks **[RPG3]**.

●—March 12, 1938
After Nazi forces seize control of Austria, Adolf Hitler marches into that country, stopping first in his hometown of Linz to deliver a speech to the masses **[REAL]**.

●—Shortly After March 12, 1938
Most of Ursula Zandt's family are killed during riots in Linz. Ursula and her sister Blanche survive, but suffer greatly at the hands of national socialists **[BWMM]**.

> **CONFLICT:** *In* The Watchmen Sourcebook, *the Zandts leave Austria in 1935, thereby avoiding Hitler's seizure of that nation by three years. Perhaps Blanche and Ursula return to their homeland in the interim for reasons unrevealed.*

Chemist Gretchen Slovak begins working at a large orphanage in Austria, which fills up after the Nazis invade Linz. Among the new arrivals are Ursula and Blanche Zandt. As Gretchen tends to Blanche's health, she and Ursula fall in love. While Gretchen takes care of the younger Zandt, Ursula reads to her sister from Robert Louis Stevenson's poetry collection, *A Child's Garden of Verses* **[BWMM]**.

> **NOTE:** *Taking Out the Trash and The Watchmen Sourcebook establish Ursula's birthdate as September 4, 1917, making her twenty years old at this time.*

The Nazi army assumes control of the orphanage, declaring certain areas off-limits. When children begin vanishing from their beds, Gretchen purchases forged travel papers so the three can escape to the United States, but Blanche disappears that same night. Ursula kills two guards outside the forbidden section, where she finds a hooded Nazi torturer cutting up Blanche's corpse. The two grapple until Gretchen shoots the man. The two lovers then flee the country, leaving the masked Nazi for dead **[BWMM]**.

> **NOTE:** *Blanche's murderer is Rolf Müller, though Ursula does not yet know this. According to* Taking Out the Trash *and* The Watchmen Sourcebook, *Rolf's family emigrate to the United States in 1918; apparently, he returns to Europe in the interim.*

—Circa March 15, 1938

Nelson Gardner returns home to Straw Valley, his military tour complete **[RPG3]**.

—In or After March 1938

Nelson Gardner moves to New York City, where he positions himself as an independent military consultant **[RPG3]**.

—June 1938

Action Comics issue #1 hits stores, featuring Superman's first appearance **[REAL]**, and sparking a brief love of superhero stories among children. Aware that others might mock him for reading a comic book, Hollis Mason asks a child to let him glance through the issue. He is particularly fascinated by Superman, whose story presents the same basic morality as pulp fiction without its inherent darkness, ambiguity, and repressed sexual urges. Mason is reminded of the fantasies of his early teen years, and reads the issue eight times before giving it back to the complaining youth **[ALAN]**.

> **NOTE:** *In the real world, of course, the superhero genre has been anything but brief—as of this book's writing, it is arguably experiencing its greatest success.*

—August 14, 1938

On his ninth birthday, Jon Osterman opens a present: an intricately designed clock, which his father Josef hopes will help him to understand that time—even a single second—has the power to change lives **[BWDM]**.

> **NOTE:** *The clock's design is the same as that of the glass dome Jon later constructs on Mars.*

> **CONFLICT:** Taking Out the Trash *cites his birthdate as March 30, 1929.*

August 14, 1938 (Alternate Realities)

In other quantum realities, Jon Osterman receives as his birthday gift a kitten, a teddy bear, a baseball and mitt, wooden soldiers, a toy castle, or construction blocks **[BWDM]**.

—Autumn 1938

Hollis Mason discreetly reads several more comics borrowed from "unsuspecting tykes," never telling anyone else about his interest in superheroes **[ALAN]**.

—Late 1938

Ingrid Renata Veidt tells her husband, Friedrich Werner Veidt, that she is pregnant. That day, Friedrich decides that they must move to the United States so their child can be

MIND .... *The Mindscape of Alan Moore*
MOBL .... *Watchmen: The Mobile Game*
MOTN .... *Watchmen: The Complete Motion Comic*
MTRO .... *Metro* promotional newspaper cover wrap
NEWP .... *New Frontiersman* promotional newspaper
NEWW .... *New Frontiersman* website
NIGH ..... *Watchmen: The End Is Nigh, Parts 1 and 2*
PKIT ...... *Watchmen* film British press kit
PORT ..... *Watchmen Portraits*
REAL ..... Real life
RPG1 .... *DC Heroes Role Playing Module #227: Who Watches the Watchmen?*

RPG2 .... *DC Heroes Role Playing Module #235: Taking Out the Trash—Curses and Tears*
RPG3 .... *DC Heroes: The Watchmen Sourcebook*
RUBY .... "Wounds," published in *The Ruby Files Volume One*
SCR1 ..... Unfilmed screenplay draft: Sam Hamm
SCR2 ..... Unfilmed screenplay draft: Charles McKeuen
SCR3 ..... Unfilmed screenplay draft: Gary Goldman
SCR4 ..... Unfilmed screenplay draft: David Hayter (2002)
SCR5 ..... Unfilmed screenplay draft: David Hayter (2003)
SCR6 ..... Unfilmed screenplay draft: Alex Tse
SPOT ..... *DC Spotlight #1*
VRL1 ..... Viral video: *NBS Nightly News with Ted Philips*

VRL2 ..... Viral video: *The Keene Act and You*
VRL3 ..... Viral video: *Who Watches the Watchmen? A Veidt Music Network (VMN) Special*
VRL4 ..... Viral video: *World in Focus: 6 Minutes to Midnight*
VRL5 ..... Viral video: *Local Radio Station Report on 1977 Riots*
VRL6 ..... Viral videos (group of ten): *Veidt Enterprises Advertising Contest*
WAWA ... *Watching the Watchmen*
WHOS ... *Who's Who: The Definitive Directory of the DC Universe*
WTFC .... *Watchmen: The Film Companion*

born in that country and someday become President. As Nazism sweeps across Europe, the couple book passage on one of the last freighters to safely leave Germany **[BWOZ]**.

—October 2, 1938
Bill Brady's college football team defeats a rival team from Notre Dame, thanks to strong plays by Brady, Howard Simpson, and Mike Stern, as well as a fumble by Notre Dame's quarterback, Red Owen. The game ends with a score of 24 to 21 **[RPG3]**.

—October 7, 1938
The Kansan covers Bill Brady's October 2 win, describing his performance during the game as a "miracle victory" **[RPG3]**.

—October 14, 1938
Three armed thugs rough up a man and his girlfriend in Queens **[RPG3]** after the couple enjoy a night at the theater. The criminals rob them of their valuables, beat up the man, and threaten to rape the woman, but a mysterious figure resembling a professional wrestler, clad in a black hood, cape, and neck noose, drops from above and beats the thugs so severely that all three are hospitalized **[ALAN]** at Our Lady of Mercy **[RPG3]**. One suffers a spinal injury, causing him to lose the use of both legs **[ALAN]**. A witness describes the vigilante as resembling the Grim Reaper **[RPG3]**.

—October 15, 1938
The *New York Gazette* runs a front-page story about the thwarted robbery. Hollis Mason reads the article and is stunned to find superheroes no longer confined to the world of comic books **[ALAN]**.

> **CONFLICT:** The Watchmen Sourcebook *cites the article's publication date as October 14, which contradicts Alan Moore's miniseries—and makes little sense, since the story would thus have been published before the actual robbery occurred.*

—Late October 1938
A week later, the noose-wearing crime-fighter stops a supermarket stickup by crashing in through the store's front window and attacking the robbers with such intensity that those not disabled drop their weapons and surrender. An article about this second incident, titled "Hooded Justice," includes an artist's impression of a cowl-clad vigilante. As the first masked adventurer outside of comic books, he comes to be known by that same nickname. After rereading this news item, Hollis Mason realizes that he must become the world's *second* superhero **[ALAN]**.

> **NOTE:** *According to* Amazing Heroes *issue #97 and* Absolute Watchmen, *Hooded Justice was originally called Brother Night. Moore's notes, reprinted in* Absolute Watchmen, *describe him as a "real weirdie" who may or may not have supernatural abilities, and*

who vanishes in 1951 without a trace.

Moore heavily implies that Hooded Justice's true identity is Rolf Müller. A character by that same name appears in Babylon 5 spinoff Crusade. There are few similarities between Crusade's Müller (a blackmailer and loan shark) and Hooded Justice (a crime-fighter), but by episode's end, Müller ends up with a permanent ring around his neck, similar to Hooded Justice's noose. Given that Babylon 5 creator J. Michael Straczynski would later write Before Watchmen titles Dr. Manhattan, Nite Owl, and Moloch, the Crusade character's naming may be an intentional Watchmen homage.

CONFLICT: Taking Out the Trash names the vigilante **The** Hooded Justice, but he is simply called Hooded Justice in Alan Moore's miniseries. Before Watchmen: Minutemen sees Rolf Müller vanishing from Nazi Germany in 1939, but this contradicts Moore's work, in which he is already fighting crime in the United States in October 1938. What's more, the miniseries reveals Müller and Hooded Justice to be separate individuals, conflicting not only with Moore's tale but also with Taking Out the Trash and The Watchmen Sourcebook, which specifically state them to be the same person.

—Late October 1938 to January 1939

For the first few months of his crime-fighting exploits, Hooded Justice remains a staple news item. Though he is technically a criminal and wanted by police, the cops let him be due to his dramatic success in battling the New York underworld **[RPG2]**.

During the three months following his vow to become a masked hero, Hollis Mason frequently doubts and ridicules this decision **[ALAN]**.

—In or Before December 1938

After reading about Hooded Justice at age eighteen **[HOOD]**, Sally Juspeczyk decides to become the first female masked adventurer, in the hope that the publicity will launch her modeling career. She makes no effort to hide her identity, but changes her surname to Jupiter to obscure her Polish heritage **[ALAN]**.

Sally chooses the moniker The Silk Spectre to sound mysterious, and as a play on "silk stalkings," to imply that she could slip out of an adversary's hands **[HOOD]**. Larry Schexnayder continues to represent Sally during her crime-fighting days **[ALAN]**. Intent on fostering her celebrity status, he recognizes that a female superhero could attract incredible media attention if properly handled, leading to lucrative merchandising and film contracts **[RPG2]**.

—December 1938

The Silk Spectre carries out her first crime-fighting "case"—a fake arrest involving an actor,

MIND .... The Mindscape of Alan Moore
MOBL.... Watchmen: The Mobile Game
MOTN.... Watchmen: The Complete Motion Comic
MTRO.... Metro promotional newspaper cover wrap
NEWP.... New Frontiersman promotional newspaper
NEWW... New Frontiersman website
NIGH ..... Watchmen: The End Is Nigh, Parts 1 and 2
PKIT...... Watchmen film British press kit
PORT..... Watchmen Portraits
REAL..... Real life
RPG1 ... DC Heroes Role Playing Module #227: Who Watches the Watchmen?

RPG2 .... DC Heroes Role Playing Module #235: Taking Out the Trash—Curses and Tears
RPG3 .... DC Heroes: The Watchmen Sourcebook
RUBY .... "Wounds," published in The Ruby Files Volume One
SCR1..... Unfilmed screenplay draft: Sam Hamm
SCR2..... Unfilmed screenplay draft: Charles McKeuen
SCR3..... Unfilmed screenplay draft: Gary Goldman
SCR4..... Unfilmed screenplay draft: David Hayter (2002)
SCR5..... Unfilmed screenplay draft: David Hayter (2003)
SCR6..... Unfilmed screenplay draft: Alex Tse
SPOT..... DC Spotlight #1
VRL1 ..... Viral video: NBS Nightly News with Ted Philips

VRL2 ..... Viral video: The Keene Act and You
VRL3 ..... Viral video: Who Watches the Watchmen? A Veidt Music Network (VMN) Special
VRL4 ..... Viral video: World in Focus: 6 Minutes to Midnight
VRL5 ..... Viral video: Local Radio Station Report on 1977 Riots
VRL6 ..... Viral videos (group of ten): Veidt Enterprises Advertising Contest
WAWA... Watching the Watchmen
WHOS.... Who's Who: The Definitive Directory of the DC Universe
WTFC .... Watchmen: The Film Companion

set up by Larry Schexnayder to attract press attention **[RPG3]**.

> **NOTE:** *According to* Absolute Watchmen, *Alan Moore originally intended for Sally to become The Silk Spectre in 1942, but changed it to shortly after Hooded Justice's arrival in 1938. The* Watchmen Sourcebook *specifies December 1938.*
>
> Absolute Watchmen *further notes that Moore had planned to depict her as a chemistry genius who used self-made scientific weapons until a preparation blew up, badly burning one hand. However, he ultimately dropped this aspect of her character. Per* Watching the Watchmen, *his original superhero name for Sally was The Silk.*

—Before December 21, 1938

Bill Brady's football team defeats Iowa during the Pioneer Bowl, thanks to plays made by Brady, Jim Bailey, Howard Simpson, Mike Stern, and Gary Luciano. Iowa nearly wins, due to strong plays by team members Everett, MacKenzie, and Todd Harris, but Brady throws four successive touchdowns, leading his team back to victory with a final score of 32 to 21 **[RPG3]**.

—December 21, 1938

The *Tulsa Times* covers Bill Brady's win in the Pioneer Bowl. In the article, Brady is humble about his successes, attributing them mostly to luck **[RPG3]**.

—December 1938 to Late 1939

Viewing masked adventuring as merely a social fad on which to cash in **[BWMM]**, Larry Schexnayder hires numerous actors and professional wrestlers to portray criminals so Sally Jupiter can foil their "crimes" before conveniently placed cameras, until she can learn how to take care of herself and fight crime for real **[RPG2]**. To prevent such fakery from being exposed, Larry bribes the local police chief to pretend the captures are legitimate, and to pose for reporters' photos. Despite this business arrangement, the cop and agent show each other little respect away from the cameras **[BWMM]**.

—1938 to 1954

Throughout his crime-fighting career, Hooded Justice never kills anyone, though he does leave some criminals maimed or crippled **[RPG2]**.

> **NOTE:** *Before Watchmen: Minutemen depicts Rolf Müller as a serial killer of children, while* The Watchmen Sourcebook *sees him killing a black couple while a member of the Ku Klux Klan. Since* Minutemen *also reveals Müller and Hooded Justice to be separate individuals, this does not constitute a continuity problem.*

—Late 1938 or 1939

After witnessing masked crime-fighters in action, Edgar Jacobi decides to match their motif by becoming a supervillain **[HOOD]**. Using his underworld contacts, Moloch positions himself as an ingenious, flamboyant criminal mastermind **[ALAN]**.

Jacobi hires goons to help him rob banks, hijack trucks, and carry out kidnappings. He invests his money in opium dens, at which he provides clients with heroin, cocaine, reefer, downers, uppers, and other drugs, then elicits information once they are stoned. Edgar creates bigger and better magic acts with which to perpetrate crimes, enjoying the company of women willing to please him sexually for a fix [BWMO]. From such dens of temptation, he soon controls a large portion of New York vice, including drugs, prostitution, and racketeering [RPG1]. He perpetrates his crimes under various aliases—not only as Moloch the Mystic, but also as Edgar William Vaughn, William Edgar Bright [ALAN], Satan of the Underworld [RPG1], and Arthur Gordon Scratch [RPG3].

After flipping a coin to decide whether to be good or evil, Walter Zileski begins a supervillain career as The Screaming Skull [RPG3].

> *NOTE: Zileski's coin-flipping is analogous to Batman villain Harvey "Two-Face" Dent, who often flips a two-headed silver dollar when making decisions.*

> *CONFLICT: Taking Out the Trash claims The Screaming Skull to be a Nazi saboteur, but no other sources indicate such a background—in fact, Under the Hood describes him as a nice guy who finds Christianity. The book's author may have confused the backgrounds of The Screaming Skull and Captain Axis.*

—In or Before 1939
Several businesses open in the Chinatown section of New York City, including Dragon's Lair (a chicken and steak restaurant) and a store called Lees [BWMM].

—1939
Superhero comic books continue to prosper for a time, featuring the exploits of such characters as Super-Man and Flash-Man [ALAN].

> *NOTE: In DC Comics lore, these characters are, of course, called Superman and The Flash. Given that news vendor Bernard mentions these comics in 1985, nearly fifty years after their publication, and that Superman is properly named in Hollis Mason's Under the Hood, it may be that Bernard is simply misremembering the names of characters who, in Watchmen continuity, would be considered obscure and long-forgotten by that point.*

Adrian Alexander Veidt, the future masked adventurer Ozymandias, is born to wealthy, upper-class German couple Friedrich Werner and Ingrid Renata Veidt [ALAN]. His middle name honors his father's childhood hero, Alexander of Macedonia [BWOZ].

> *NOTE: According to Absolute Watchmen, Alan Moore originally intended for Adrian to be born in Brooklyn to a working-class family.*

MIND .... *The Mindscape of Alan Moore*
MOBL.... *Watchmen: The Mobile Game*
MOTN.... *Watchmen: The Complete Motion Comic*
MTRO.... *Metro* promotional newspaper cover wrap
NEWP.... *New Frontiersman* promotional newspaper
NEWW... *New Frontiersman* website
NIGH ..... *Watchmen: The End Is Nigh, Parts 1 and 2*
PKIT...... *Watchmen* film British press kit
PORT..... *Watchmen Portraits*
REAL..... Real life
RPG1 .... *DC Heroes Role Playing Module #227: Who Watches the Watchmen?*

RPG2 .... *DC Heroes Role Playing Module #235: Taking Out the Trash—Curses and Tears*
RPG3 .... *DC Heroes: The Watchmen Sourcebook*
RUBY .... "Wounds," published in *The Ruby Files Volume One*
SCR1..... Unfilmed screenplay draft: Sam Hamm
SCR2..... Unfilmed screenplay draft: Charles McKeuen
SCR3..... Unfilmed screenplay draft: Gary Goldman
SCR4..... Unfilmed screenplay draft: David Hayter (2002)
SCR5..... Unfilmed screenplay draft: David Hayter (2003)
SCR6..... Unfilmed screenplay draft: Alex Tse
SPOT..... *DC Spotlight #1*
VRL1..... Viral video: *NBS Nightly News with Ted Philips*

VRL2..... Viral video: *The Keene Act and You*
VRL3..... Viral video: *Who Watches the Watchmen? A Veidt Music Network (VMN) Special*
VRL4..... Viral video: *World in Focus: 6 Minutes to Midnight*
VRL5..... Viral video: *Local Radio Station Report on 1977 Riots*
VRL6..... Viral videos (group of ten): *Veidt Enterprises Advertising Contest*
WAWA... *Watching the Watchmen*
WHOS ... *Who's Who: The Definitive Directory of the DC Universe*
WTFC .... *Watchmen: The Film Companion*

CONFLICT: *Alan Moore's miniseries establishes Veidt's birth as occurring in 1939.* Taking Out the Trash *changes it to October 7, 1933, while a timeline packaged with* The End Is Nigh—The Complete Experience *offers the year 1945. Timelines published in* The Film Companion *and in the film's British press kit cite 1950, with a police file in the press kit specifying September 6, 1950.*

The 1939 placement is appropriate, as Adrian is born in the same year in which all Minutemen except for Hooded Justice begin fighting crime, and in which superhero comic books enjoy their brief popularity in Watchmen *lore. Moreover, World War II—the era of the atomic bomb—began in 1939 in the real world, while DC's* Detective Comics *issue #27, featuring Batman's first appearance, hit stands that year as well.*

—In or Before January 1939

The Capitol Theater opens in New York City **[BWMM]**.

As a teen, Eddie Blake earns a criminal record with the State of New York Juvenile Correctional Services. Appended to his file is a photo of Eddie grinning, with a bruised eye. Blake is assigned a caseworker, who tells him he has moments of uncontrollable rage brought on by traumatic childhood events **[BWMM]**.

—January 1939

Dressing up in a mask and costume to protect one's neighborhood becomes a popular fad in the United States. Americans grow fascinated by this development as the media devotes a good deal of coverage to these individuals **[ALAN]**.
> **NOTE:** *This indicates that there may be many other masked crime-fighters than those spotlighted in Alan Moore's miniseries.*

Hollis Mason begins working for the New York City Police Department **[ALAN]**.
> **NOTE:** *Mason joins the police in 1939, before becoming The Nite Owl. Since his superhero days commence in January, he must become a cop within that same month.*

Friedrich Werner and Ingrid Renata Veidt emigrate from Germany and arrive in New York Harbor. Friedrich soon establishes a successful perfumery business **[BWOZ]**.

—Early January 1939

Four thugs perpetrate a triple homicide at a federal bank. Hooded Justice dispenses two of the criminals, Tony and Little Bob, before cornering the other two in a Battery Park factory. One, Monty, suggests they surrender to police rather than face the brute, but Hooded Justice finds them, battering both and tossing one out a window. The crook lands on a police car, shattering his body and the vehicle. Standing among the cops, Hollis Mason views Hooded Justice at the window and finds him terrifying. A nearby officer, traumatized at the sight, hands in his badge a few days later **[BWMM]**.

    NOTE: *Since* Taking Out the Trash *establishes that Hooded Justice kills no one throughout the course of his crime-fighting career, the thugs must survive the encounter.*

In preparation for becoming a masked crime-fighter, Hollis Mason frequently works out at the police gymnasium. A fellow cop invites him out for a beer a few times, but Mason repeatedly turns him down, preferring to work out before and after every shift. Given Mason's preference for going to bed by 9:00 PM, the other officer dubs him "The Nite Owl." Mason likes the moniker and adopts it as his superhero identity **[ALAN]**.

    NOTE: *Mason writes, in* Under the Hood, *that he became The Nite Owl during the early months of 1939. This can be narrowed down to early January, as he dons the costume three months after reading about Hooded Justice in October 1938, but begins fighting crime before Sally Jupiter, who is already doing so by January 12.*

    CONFLICT: Taking Out the Trash *claims that Mason makes his crime-fighting debut on March 11, 1939, but this contradicts evidence pointing to January.*

Hollis Mason creates a streamlined costume, opting for protective leather and steel mesh on his head and body, leaving his arms and legs free to fight **[ALAN, HOOD]**. Mason experiments with a cape like that of The Shadow, but finds it unwieldly. He builds a secret lair that he calls the Owl's Nest, then begins fighting crime as The Nite Owl. Mason's earliest adventures are unspectacular, but the media popularizes his exploits. His choice of mask nearly results in his death when a drunk criminal grabs it, obscuring his vision. Thereafter, he instead applies the mask via spirit gum **[ALAN]**.

    NOTE: *It is unclear whether or not the Owl's Nest is the same lair as the Owl Cave, introduced in* Before Watchmen: Nite Owl.

    CONFLICT: *Alan Moore's miniseries sets Nite Owl's debut in 1939. A timeline packaged with* The End Is Nigh—The Complete Experience *moves that debut back to 1938, contradicting the comic.*

Determined to be wherever crime is, Mason picks up overtime shifts in areas where he anticipates trouble, wearing his Nite Owl costume under his police uniform so he can change quickly in the event of a crime. When gunmen steal an armored car one night and speed through the city, endangering passersby, Mason makes a quick-change, heads them off by running through back alleys, and jumps into the vehicle. Startled, one gunman fires his machine gun, killing the driver and causing the car to flip. Nite Owl jumps free of the vehicle to protect a mother and child in its path **[BWMM]**.

The *New York Post* publishes exclusive photos of The Nite Owl, dubbing him "the city's newest hero" **[BWMM]**. The *New York Gazette* covers Mason's exploits as well, in an article titled "Mysterious Masked Man Cleans Up Wharf," while another newspaper's headline reads "Murderous Rampage Averted" **[FILM, ARTF]**.

> **CONFLICT:** *In the* Watchmen *film, the* Gazette *article is dated September 15, 1938—a month before Mason even decides to become a crime-fighter in the comics.*

—Before January 12, 1939

Larry Schexnayder licenses Sally Jupiter's image as The Silk Spectre for use in pinups, comic books, cigarette lighters, and other memorabilia **[HOOD]**. When Larry books an engagement at the Moritz, in Warsaw, Poland, a prince approaches Sally and calls her the most beautiful woman in Europe **[BWMM]**.

Sally Jupiter is photographed alongside Larry Schexnayder and six police officers, holding up an issue of the *New York Gazette* bearing the headline "Criminal World Goes Ga-Ga Over Silk Spectre" **[FILM]**. The article, written by Edwin Cooper, reports that arrest rates have risen since Sally's debut, while the crime rate has dropped **[ARTF]**.

On one occasion, Schexnayder works with Bergstein Jewelers, an uptown retailer facing hard times, to drum up mutual publicity for the store and Sally Jupiter. Larry hires an out-of-work actor to don a mask, call himself The Red Devil, and pretend to rob the jeweler. He then alerts the press so they'll be on hand when Silk Spectre thwarts the fake robbery and ties up the culprit **[BWMM]**.

Sally Jupiter arrests a thug named Claude Boke as he tries to rob a liquor store. Released on parole with a light fine, Boke gives up drinking, takes a job pumping gasoline, and grants an interview with the *Daily World*, saying he holds no grudge since he'd rather a sexy crime-fighting heroine bring him in than "two fat old cops" **[ALAN]**.

Larry Schexnayder shops around a Hollywood documentary about Sally Jupiter's crime-fighting career, titled *Silk Spectre: The Sally Jupiter Story*. Larry and Sally make a deal with Edmund "King" Taylor, of King Taylor Productions. Footage of Sally is shot, but studio involvement prevents the project from getting off the ground **[ALAN]**.

> **NOTE:** *Given the chronology of Hooded Justice's and Hollis Mason's crime-fighting, Sally must be a very new superhero when Larry makes this deal.*

—January 12, 1939

The *Daily World* runs an article about Sally Jupiter, titled "Villains Vie for Voluptuous Vigilante." The writer focuses on her good looks, citing her red hair, shapely curves, and revealing attire rather than on her (faked) crime-fighting accomplishments. The article

ABSO .... *Watchmen Absolute Edition*	**BWOZ**.... *Before Watchmen—Ozymandias*	• Film: *Batman v Superman: Dawn of Justice Ultimate Edition*
ALAN..... Alan Moore's *Watchmen* miniseries	**BWRO** ... *Before Watchmen—Rorschach*	• Film: *Justice League*
ARCD .... *Minutemen Arcade*	**BWSS** ... *Before Watchmen—Silk Spectre*	**CLIX** ...... HeroClix figure pack-in cards
ARTF ..... *Watchmen: The Art of the Film*	**CHEM**.... My Chemical Romance music video: "Desolation Row"	**DECK**..... DC Comics Deck-Building Game—Crossover Pack 4: Watchmen
BLCK..... *Tales of the Black Freighter*	**CMEO**.... *Watchmen* cameos in comics, TV, and film:	**DURS** .... *DC Universe: Rebirth Special* volume 1 issue #1
BWCC ... *Before Watchmen—The Crimson Corsair*	• Comic: *Astonishing X-Men* volume 3 issue #6	**FILM** ..... *Watchmen* theatrical film
BWCO ... *Before Watchmen—Comedian*	• Comic: *Hero Hotline* volume 1 issue #5	**HOOD** .... *Under the Hood* documentary and dust-jacket prop reproduction
BWDB .. *Before Watchmen—Dollar Bill*	• Comic: *Kingdom Come* volume 1 issue #2	**JUST** ..... *Watchmen: Justice Is Coming*
BWDM .. *Before Watchmen—Dr. Manhattan*	• Comic: *Marvels* volume 1 issue #4	**MATL** .... Mattel Club Black Freighter figure pack-in cards
BWMM.. *Before Watchmen—Minutemen*	• Comic: *The Question* volume 1 issue #17	
BWMO .. *Before Watchmen—Moloch*	• TV: *Teen Titans Go!* episode #82, "Real Boy Adventures"	
BWNO ... *Before Watchmen—Nite Owl*	• Film: *Man of Steel*	

quotes Larry Schexnayder as claiming that Sally is so attractive, thugs actually *try* to be arrested by her [ALAN].

—After January 12, 1939

King Taylor Productions, still tinkering with *Silk Spectre: The Sally Jupiter Story*, drops the documentary concept in favor of a Saturday-morning matinee approach, renaming the movie *Sally Jupiter: Law in Its Lingerie* [ALAN]. In one iteration of the script, Silk Spectre battles thugs named Ratso and Klinger, who work for a criminal called Mr. Weldon [RPG3]. Still, however, the film remains unmade [ALAN].

Underworld czar Jimmy Fantucci gives himself up to the police rather than shoot Silk Spectre. This becomes a standpoint moment in her crime-fighting career [ABSO].

—Before February 1939

To make his boring existence more interesting, and to compensate for his wealth by protecting others, Byron Lewis decides to become a crime-fighter [RPG2]. He creates a glider suit enabling him to fly, but testing it results in several accidents, some near-fatal. This causes him multiple injuries and constant pain [BWMM].

Nelson Gardner decides to become a masked crime-fighter called Captain Metropolis. He learns of The Canada Malting Company's uncompleted Hudson River factory, a massive building with the letters "CM" on one side, and decides to buy it as his personal headquarters. The Canadian government gladly sells him the factory for a very low sum, and Gardner spends months fortifying the building as his sanctum for the war on crime, hiring a personal servant to attend to his needs [BWMM].

After working several part-time jobs, Ursula Zandt gives up routine employment in order to become a crime-fighter [PORT] just for the sheer excitement of it, having followed stories of other superheroes already guarding the streets [RPG2].

—In or Before February 1939

Larry Schexnayder begins representing Hooded Justice as his agent [RPG3].

—February 1939

A month after Nite Owl's debut, Ursula Zandt begins fighting crime as The Silhouette [ALAN]. This pursuit demonstrates her individuality, while still commanding respect [RPG3], and she focuses her efforts on the tough neighborhoods bordering New York's Lower East Side and waterfront [PORT]. Ursula earns headlines by exposing a crooked publisher engaging in child pornography, beating up the entrepreneur and his two chief cameramen in the process [ALAN].

MIND .... *The Mindscape of Alan Moore*	**RPG2** .... *DC Heroes Role Playing Module #235: Taking Out the Trash—Curses and Tears*	**VRL2** ..... Viral video: *The Keene Act and You*
MOBL .... *Watchmen: The Mobile Game*		**VRL3** ..... Viral video: *Who Watches the Watchmen? A Veidt Music Network (VMN) Special*
MOTN .... *Watchmen: The Complete Motion Comic*	**RPG3** .... *DC Heroes: The Watchmen Sourcebook*	
MTRO .... *Metro* promotional newspaper cover wrap	**RUBY** .... "Wounds," published in *The Ruby Files Volume One*	**VRL4** ..... Viral video: *World in Focus: 6 Minutes to Midnight*
NEWP .... *New Frontiersman* promotional newspaper	**SCR1** ..... Unfilmed screenplay draft: Sam Hamm	**VRL5** ..... Viral video: *Local Radio Station Report on 1977 Riots*
NEWW .. *New Frontiersman* website	**SCR2** ..... Unfilmed screenplay draft: Charles McKeuen	
NIGH ..... *Watchmen: The End Is Nigh, Parts 1 and 2*	**SCR3** ..... Unfilmed screenplay draft: Gary Goldman	**VRL6** ..... Viral videos (group of ten): *Veidt Enterprises Advertising Contest*
PKIT ...... *Watchmen* film British press kit	**SCR4** ..... Unfilmed screenplay draft: David Hayter (2002)	
PORT .... *Watchmen Portraits*	**SCR5** ..... Unfilmed screenplay draft: David Hayter (2003)	**WAWA** ... *Watching the Watchmen*
REAL ..... Real life	**SCR6** ..... Unfilmed screenplay draft: Alex Tse	**WHOS** ... *Who's Who: The Definitive Directory of the DC Universe*
RPG1 .... *DC Heroes Role Playing Module #227: Who Watches the Watchmen?*	**SPOT** .... *DC Spotlight #1*	
	VRL1 ..... Viral video: *NBS Nightly News with Ted Philips*	**WTFC** .... *Watchmen: The Film Companion*

—February 14, 1939

On Valentine's Day, Hooded Justice barely avoids his secret homosexual lifestyle becoming public knowledge **[RPG3]**.

—In or After February 1939

The Gotham Opera House begins featuring several operas, including *Mefistofeles*, *Rigoletto*, *Die Fledermaus (The Bat)*, *Die Meistersinger von Nürnberg (The Master-Singers of Nuremberg)*, *Lucia di Lammermoor (The Bride of Lammermoor)*, and *Die Walküre (The Valkyrie)*. Hollis Mason thwarts the mugging of a wealthy couple outside the opera house. A photographer captures the scene on film as The Nite Owl punches the armed mugger in the face. The gun goes off, but no one is injured **[FILM]**.

> **NOTE:** *Gotham is Batman's home city in the DC Comics universe. Hanging on the opera house's wall are several posters for* Batman *comics, and among the operas listed is* Die Fledermaus (The Bat). *In essence, Mason prevents the murders of Batman's parents, Thomas and Martha Wayne—but only metaphorically, since Batman is a fictional character in* Watchmen *continuity.*

> **CONFLICT:** *A timeline published in* The Film Companion *sets the thwarted opera-house mugging in 1938, but Mason does not become The Nite Owl until 1939.*

In her efforts to stop child trafficking, Ursula Zandt chases a carpet-carrying man through Chinatown. The two fight in an alleyway, and he runs away after she slashes his chest with a knife, enabling her to rescue a young child rolled up in the rug **[BWMM]**.

At age fifteen, Eddie Blake decides to become a crime-fighter **[ALAN]**. After initially calling himself The Big Stick **[BWCO]**, he settles on the name The Comedian. Clad in a flimsy, yellow costume, he makes a name for himself by cleaning up New York City's waterfronts **[ALAN]**.

> **CONFLICT:** *A police file on Blake, in the* Watchmen *film's British press kit, changes his age at the start of his crime-fighting career to eighteen, which contradicts Alan Moore's miniseries.*

The Comedian gains citywide attention after thwarting a robbery of SoHo's Clef-Arpels jewelry store, and has several highly publicized clashes with the Garbino crime family **[RPG3]**. On one occasion, members of the press photograph Blake outside a bank, holding a would-be robber in a headlock maneuver with one hand and a bag of cash in the other. When apprehended, the thug is armed with a Colt M1921AC Thompson submachine gun **[FILM]**.

> **NOTE:** *The name Garbino is likely based on that of the real-world Gambino crime family.*

Though clever, Blake lusts for violence and holds humanity in disdain, viciously killing without pity or remorse **[MATL]**, and concluding that since life is violent, absurd, and full of suffering, he will participate in the "joke" by adopting amoral attitudes and willingly perpetrating brutality himself **[WHOS]**. A right-wing cynic, he recognizes society's flaws and parodies them by becoming a reflection of them—a gag that only he understands **[ALAN]**.

After beating every customer of The Bloody Ear senseless with a bat and trashing the bar in the process, Blake tells the bartender he should show some gratitude for helping to clean up the criminal element. Hitting the man with the bat, Blake helps himself to the cash register's contents and a bottle of alcohol, then leaves, laughing **[BWMM]**.

—Between February 1939 and 1946
Vogue magazine runs a feature story on The Silhouette, titled "Vigilance Chic" **[BWMM]**.

—February 1939 to 1949
To handle the pain caused during his glider testing, Byron Lewis initially uses aspirin pills and Absorbine Veterinary Linament, but eventually upgrades to morphine. Scared of his own creation, he suffers an ongoing fear that the suit will one day betray and kill him, and thus regularly drinks alcohol to take the edge off **[BWMM]**.

—In or Before April 1939
Bill Brady emerges as a hot prospect in professional football. Several teams make him lucrative offers to join their lineup **[RPG3]**, but he instead pursues a career outside the sports world **[ALAN, BWDB, BWMM]**.

—April 11, 1939
Executives at National Bank of New York hold a meeting, during which Thomas G. Younger announces the need for a new, contemporary promotions plan **[RPG3]**.
> *CONFLICT: In* Before Watchmen: Dollar Bill, *the bank is headed by Abie, Dewey, Cheatem, and Howe, while* The Watchmen Sourcebook *introduces Thomas Younger and Dick Loomis. This timeline assumes that all six men work at the bank, providing different functions, since corporate structures at large companies tend to be top-heavy with highly paid executives. Bill Brady's future meetings with each team, as depicted in the conflicting accounts of his hiring as Dollar Bill, can be reconciled by assuming that he undergoes multiple rounds of interviews.*

—April 14, 1939
Another National Bank of New York executive, Dick Loomis, writes a memo to Tom Younger, noting that costumed vigilantes earn a lot of publicity. He suggests that they hire an established hero, such as Hooded Justice or The Nite Owl, so they can advertise that all bank funds are protected by a "real-live superhero" **[RPG3]**.

MIND .... *The Mindscape of Alan Moore*
MOBL .... *Watchmen: The Mobile Game*
MOTN .... *Watchmen: The Complete Motion Comic*
MTRO .... *Metro* promotional newspaper cover wrap
NEWP .... *New Frontiersman* promotional newspaper
NEWW .... *New Frontiersman* website
NIGH .... *Watchmen: The End Is Nigh, Parts 1 and 2*
PKIT ...... *Watchmen* film British press kit
PORT ..... *Watchmen Portraits*
REAL ..... Real life
RPG1 .... *DC Heroes Role Playing Module #227: Who Watches the Watchmen?*

RPG2 .... *DC Heroes Role Playing Module #235: Taking Out the Trash—Curses and Tears*
RPG3 .... *DC Heroes: The Watchmen Sourcebook*
RUBY .... "Wounds," published in *The Ruby Files Volume One*
SCR1 ..... Unfilmed screenplay draft: Sam Hamm
SCR2 ..... Unfilmed screenplay draft: Charles McKeuen
SCR3 ..... Unfilmed screenplay draft: Gary Goldman
SCR4 ..... Unfilmed screenplay draft: David Hayter (2002)
SCR5 ..... Unfilmed screenplay draft: David Hayter (2003)
SCR6 ..... Unfilmed screenplay draft: Alex Tse
SPOT ..... *DC Spotlight #1*
VRL1 ..... Viral video: *NBS Nightly News with Ted Philips*

VRL2 ..... Viral video: *The Keene Act and You*
VRL3 ..... Viral video: *Who Watches the Watchmen? A Veidt Music Network (VMN) Special*
VRL4 ..... Viral video: *World in Focus: 6 Minutes to Midnight*
VRL5 ..... Viral video: *Local Radio Station Report on 1977 Riots*
VRL6 ..... Viral videos (group of ten): *Veidt Enterprises Advertising Contest*
WAWA ... *Watching the Watchmen*
WHOS ... *Who's Who: The Definitive Directory of the DC Universe*
WTFC ... *Watchmen: The Film Companion*

—April 16, 1939

Younger responds to Loomis, enthusiastic about the superhero idea but preferring to create their own in-house hero by hiring an athlete or wrestler, rather than dealing with anyone established. He asks Loomis to check with the New York Police Department to make sure no crackdown on vigilantism is imminent **[RPG3]**.

Byron Lewis makes his debut as the crime-fighter Mothman. Wearing wings and a black mask, he presents evidence to NYPD officials exposing a massive numbers racket run by Manhattan gangsters in and around Harlem. Based on this information, the police make three arrests **[RPG3]**.

> **NOTE:** *Oddly, Gary Goldman's unproduced 1992 screenplay names Mothman as a villain taken down by Dan Dreiberg and Rorschach.*

—April 17, 1939

The *New York Gazette* covers Mothman's arrival with an article titled "Oh No, Not Again!" **[RPG3]**.

—April 21, 1939

Dick Loomis compiles a list of possible names for National Bank of New York's patriotic superhero, including Finance Man, First National Man, Safety Man, Americaman, Mr. Americaman, Captain Americaman, and Red White and Blue Man. A coworker named Fred adds several "tough dramatic" names to the list, including Anti-Gangster Man, The Murderer, The Mutilator, The Butcher, The Pummeler, and The Crime Stomper **[RPG3]**.

—April 24, 1939

Nelson Gardner begins fighting crime as a gun-wielding, scarlet-costumed masked adventurer called Captain Metropolis. On his first night, he thwarts a gas station robbery in Hoboken, New Jersey. After capturing the perpetrator, he sticks around to speak with police and reporters, revealing that he is a former U.S. Marine lieutenant and promising to continue protecting the New York metropolitan area **[RPG3]**.

> **NOTE:** *Gardner's coverage area is quite large, as New York's metropolitan area comprises New York City, Long Island, New York's Hudson Valley, five cities in New Jersey, six cities in Connecticut, and five counties in northeastern Pennsylvania.*

—April 25, 1939

The *New York Gazette* covers Captain Metropolis's debut mission in an article titled "Jersey Gets Costumed Crusader of Its Own" **[RPG3]**.

—April 1939 to 1949

As Captain Metropolis, Nelson Gardner uses his knowledge of military technique and strategy to eradicate organized crime and vice in urban areas. Though decent and polite,

ABSO .... *Watchmen Absolute Edition*	**BWOZ** .... *Before Watchmen—Ozymandias*	• Film: *Batman v Superman: Dawn of Justice Ultimate Edition*
ALAN ..... Alan Moore's *Watchmen* miniseries	**BWRO** ... *Before Watchmen—Rorschach*	• Film: *Justice League*
ARCD .... *Minutemen Arcade*	**BWSS** ... *Before Watchmen—Silk Spectre*	**CLIX** ...... HeroClix figure pack-in cards
ARTF ..... *Watchmen: The Art of the Film*	**CHEM** .... My Chemical Romance music video: "Desolation Row"	**DECK** ..... *DC Comics Deck-Building Game—Crossover Pack 4: Watchmen*
BLCK ..... *Tales of the Black Freighter*	**CMEO** .... *Watchmen* cameos in comics, TV, and film:	**DURS** .... *DC Universe: Rebirth Special* volume 1 issue #1
BWCC ... *Before Watchmen—The Crimson Corsair*	• Comic: *Astonishing X-Men* volume 3 issue #6	**FILM** ..... *Watchmen* theatrical film
BWCO ... *Before Watchmen—Comedian*	• Comic: *Hero Hotline* volume 1 issue #5	**HOOD** .... *Under the Hood* documentary and dust-jacket prop reproduction
BWDB ... *Before Watchmen—Dollar Bill*	• Comic: *Kingdom Come* volume 1 issue #2	
BWDM .. *Before Watchmen—Dr. Manhattan*	• Comic: *Marvels* volume 1 issue #4	**JUST** ..... *Watchmen: Justice Is Coming*
BWMM . *Before Watchmen—Minutemen*	• Comic: *The Question* volume 1 issue #17	**MATL** .... Mattel Club Black Freighter figure pack-in cards
BWMO . *Before Watchmen—Moloch*	• TV: *Teen Titans Go!* episode #82, "Real Boy Adventures"	
BWNO ... *Before Watchmen—Nite Owl*	• Film: *Man of Steel*	

he holds old-fashioned values that include anti-black bigotry. Gardner has business cards created that identify him as a freelance consultant **[ALAN]**.

●—Between April 1939 and October 1939

With Hooded Justice, The Nite Owl, The Silhouette, Mothman, and The Comedian working in New York and surrounding areas, at least seven other masked vigilantes begin operating on or around the U.S. West Coast **[ALAN]**. New York becomes a haven for costumed crime-fighters, though the crime rate does not drop appreciably **[RPG2]**.

> **NOTE:** *The names and aliases of the other seven vigilantes are unknown.*

●—Before May 6, 1939

Designers working for the National Bank of New York conceive of a red, white, and blue costume for maximum appeal, including a billowing cape **[ALAN]**. Miss Fischer, in FBNY's records section, works with a public-relations team to create the outfit **[RPG3]**.

> **CONFLICT:** *In* Before Watchmen: Dollar Bill, *the costume already exists at the time of Bill Brady's job interview, whereas* The Watchmen Sourcebook *depicts the bank as creating the outfit after meeting with him.*

The bank decides that its in-house superhero should become an actual crime-fighter to boost bank publicity **[ALAN]**. Bank executive Dick Loomis reads coverage of Bill Brady's performance as a college football quarterback and is impressed, deeming him a possible candidate to be offered the job **[RPG3]**.

The *New York Daily Gazette*'s front-page headline reads "Rumors of War—Chamberlain Makes Bid for Peace" **[BWDB]**.

> **NOTE:** *Arthur Neville Chamberlain served as the United Kingdom's Prime Minister from 1937 to 1940. Despite his efforts to maintain peace with Germany, Britain declared war on that nation on September 3, 1939, after Adolf Hitler invaded Poland.*

Bill Brady graduates from college and moves into a small Manhattan apartment, but lacks the requisite skills listed in most classified ads. Noticing an auditions call for a Broadway revue at the Rialto Theatre, he prepares a song-and-dance routine. After the director scoffs at his performance, Brady spends several days drinking beer and feeling sorry for himself. He considers trying to make it in Hollywood, but lacks the train fare to get there. Finally, he notices an ad requiring only good looks **[BWDB]**.

A handsome, homophobic man in Manhattan passes up a date with a woman named Miss Sylvania for an interview at National Bank of New York. However, he angrily storms out upon learning that the job entails dressing up in costume as a superhero, worried that he might be mistaken for gay **[BWDB]**.

MIND .... *The Mindscape of Alan Moore*	**RPG2** .... *DC Heroes Role Playing Module #235: Taking Out the Trash—Curses and Tears*	**VRL2** ..... Viral video: *The Keene Act and You*
MOBL .... *Watchmen: The Mobile Game*		**VRL3** ..... Viral video: *Who Watches the Watchmen? A Veidt Music Network (VMN) Special*
MOTN .... *Watchmen: The Complete Motion Comic*	**RPG3** .... *DC Heroes: The Watchmen Sourcebook*	
MTRO .... *Metro* promotional newspaper cover wrap	**RUBY** .... "Wounds," published in *The Ruby Files Volume One*	**VRL4** ..... Viral video: *World in Focus: 6 Minutes to Midnight*
NEWP .... *New Frontiersman* promotional newspaper	**SCR1** ..... Unfilmed screenplay draft: Sam Hamm	**VRL5** ..... Viral video: *Local Radio Station Report on 1977 Riots*
NEWW ... *New Frontiersman* website	**SCR2** ..... Unfilmed screenplay draft: Charles McKeuen	
NIGH ..... *Watchmen: The End Is Nigh, Parts 1 and 2*	**SCR3** ..... Unfilmed screenplay draft: Gary Goldman	**VRL6** ..... Viral videos (group of ten): *Veidt Enterprises Advertising Contest*
PKIT ...... *Watchmen* film British press kit	**SCR4** ..... Unfilmed screenplay draft: David Hayter (2002)	
PORT ..... *Watchmen Portraits*	**SCR5** ..... Unfilmed screenplay draft: David Hayter (2003)	**WAWA** .. *Watching the Watchmen*
REAL ..... Real life	**SCR6** ..... Unfilmed screenplay draft: Alex Tse	**WHOS** ... *Who's Who: The Definitive Directory of the DC Universe*
RPG1 .... *DC Heroes Role Playing Module #227: Who Watches the Watchmen?*	**SPOT** ..... *DC Spotlight #1*	
	VRL1 ..... Viral video: *NBS Nightly News with Ted Philips*	**WTFC** .... *Watchmen: The Film Companion*

Bill Brady is the next to interview at the bank. Executives Able, Dewey, Cheatem, and Howe—short, cigar-puffing men who are physically identical aside from different bowtie designs—explain the in-house superhero concept. An assistant, Sheila, wheels out a mannequin displaying a red, white, and blue costume. Brady suggests removing the cape since it will restrict his movements, but the execs are adamant about keeping it **[BWDB]**.

> **NOTE:** *"Dewey, Cheatem, and Howe" is a gag name frequently applied to fictional law firms and accountancies, playing on the phrase "Do we cheat 'em? And how!" It's unclear how the additional name "Abie" fits into the joke—or whether the four executives are quadruplets, given their identical nature.*

> **CONFLICT:** *The* Under the Hood *documentary cites Brady as working for a major department store instead of a bank.*

May 6, 1939

Dick Loomis interviews Bill Brady as well. Having previously read about Brady's performance as a college football quarterback, Loomis considers him the right man to become the bank's superhero. Brady is hesitant to take the job until the banker explains that his duties will include fighting actual crimes, which the athlete finds appealing. Loomis recommends Brady to his boss, Tom Younger **[RPG3]**.

> **CONFLICT:** *In* Before Watchmen: Dollar Bill, *Brady is uneasy with the idea of fighting crime instead of working as an actor pretending to do so, but he embraces the opportunity in* The Watchmen Sourcebook *and accepts the gig for that very reason.*

Between May 6 and May 11, 1939

Based on Bill Brady's first name, Tom Younger finalizes a moniker for National Bank of New York's in-house hero: Dollar Bill **[RPG3]**. Bank representatives Abie, Howe, Cheatem, and Dewey show the proposed Dollar Bill costume to a test audience. The feedback on the soutfit is quite positive—especially regarding its red cape **[BWDB]**.

May 11, 1939

Tom Younger gives his approval for National Bank of New York to hire Bill Brady as Dollar Bill, instructing his staff to have Brady ready for training by May 23 **[RPG3]**.

May 23, 1939

National Bank of New York begins training Bill Brady to fulfill his duties as Dollar Bill **[RPG3]**.

Between May 23 and June 15, 1939

The National Bank of New York films promotional footage of Dollar Bill thwarting a mugging. The actor playing the thug is shown pinning the hero to the ground and aiming a .38-caliber gun at his head, but finding that his weapon is out of ammunition **[RPG3]**.

—Mid-1939

Nelson Gardner sees news coverage of Sally Jupiter and writes her a letter care of Larry Schexnayder, suggesting they meet to discuss the formation of a masked adventurer group who could pool resources and experience to combat crime. Signing the letter as Captain Metropolis, he lists Nelson Gardner as his representative. Though he is polite and reserved, whereas she swears, drinks, and wears skimpy clothing, she is the only vigilante with an agent listed in the telephone book. At Schexnayder's urging, Sally agrees to the team-up **[ALAN]**.

Gardner suggests calling the group The New Minute Men of America, then shortens it to The Minutemen. Schexnayder, who realizes an occasional gimmick will be needed to revitalize flagging public interest in superheroes **[ALAN]**, places ads in the *New York Gazette* and the *Daily News*, asking other "mystery men" to audition **[ALAN, BWMM]**. Gardner offers his headquarters—an abandoned malting company factory—as a base of operations. This new HQ is dubbed Freedom Tower **[BWMM]**.

—In or Before June 1939

Sylvia Kovacs begins dating Charlie **[ALAN]**, a short, freckled, dour-faced man with curly red hair and beady blue eyes, who often wears a pinstriped suit and a dirty brown overcoat. Sylvia and Charlie move into a third-floor apartment in a run-down tenement building. Their relationship is marked by mutual verbal abuse **[RUBY]**.

> **NOTE:** *Charlie will later become the father of Rorschach, who will share his physical appearance and mode of dress.*

—Circa June 1939

Sylvia Kovacs becomes pregnant with Charlie's child **[ALAN]**, though he denies the kid is his and sometimes threatens to leave her **[RUBY]**. Her friends urge her to abort the pregnancy, but she decides to have the baby anyway **[ALAN, RPG2]**.

> **NOTE:** Taking Out the Trash *establishes Rorschach's birthdate as March 21, 1940, indicating a conception sometime around June 1939.*

A magazine features Sally Jupiter in its "Women We Love" column for June, in an article titled "Sally Jupiter: Specter in Silk" **[BWMM]**.

—June 15, 1939

The National Bank of New York unveils Dollar Bill to the world as its in-house superhero. During the press event, the bank airs promotional footage of the masked crime-fighter stopping a mugger **[RPG3]**.

MIND .... *The Mindscape of Alan Moore*	**RPG2** .... *DC Heroes Role Playing Module #235: Taking Out the Trash—Curses and Tears*	**VRL2** ..... Viral video: *The Keene Act and You*
MOBL .... *Watchmen: The Mobile Game*	**RPG3** .... *DC Heroes: The Watchmen Sourcebook*	**VRL3** ..... Viral video: *Who Watches the Watchmen? A Veidt Music Network (VMN) Special*
MOTN .... *Watchmen: The Complete Motion Comic*	**RUBY** .... "Wounds," published in *The Ruby Files Volume One*	
MTRO .... *Metro promotional newspaper cover wrap*	**SCR1** ..... Unfilmed screenplay draft: Sam Hamm	**VRL4** ..... Viral video: *World in Focus: 6 Minutes to Midnight*
NEWP .... *New Frontiersman promotional newspaper*	**SCR2** ..... Unfilmed screenplay draft: Charles McKeuen	**VRL5** ..... Viral video: *Local Radio Station Report on 1977 Riots*
NEWW .... *New Frontiersman website*	**SCR3** ..... Unfilmed screenplay draft: Gary Goldman	
NIGH ..... *Watchmen: The End Is Nigh, Parts 1 and 2*	**SCR4** .... Unfilmed screenplay draft: David Hayter (2002)	**VRL6** ..... Viral videos (group of ten): *Veidt Enterprises Advertising Contest*
PKIT ...... *Watchmen film British press kit*	**SCR5** .... Unfilmed screenplay draft: David Hayter (2003)	
PORT ..... *Watchmen Portraits*	**SCR6** .... Unfilmed screenplay draft: Alex Tse	**WAWA** ... *Watching the Watchmen*
REAL ..... Real life	**SPOT** ..... *DC Spotlight #1*	**WHOS** ... *Who's Who: The Definitive Directory of the DC Universe*
RPG1 .... *DC Heroes Role Playing Module #227: Who Watches the Watchmen?*	**VRL1** ..... Viral video: *NBS Nightly News with Ted Philips*	**WTFC** ... *Watchmen: The Film Companion*

—After June 15, 1939

Within weeks, Dollar Bill's image adorns the front of every National Bank branch throughout New York State, gaining widespread recognition **[BWDB]**.

—June 16, 1939

The *New York Gazette* publishes an article announcing Dollar Bill's debut, noting "Now they're going commercial" **[RPG3]**.

—In or After June 1939

The National Bank of New York films a commercial to air in movie theaters, in which Dollar Bill thwarts two armed crooks, charms a bank teller with his good looks, and urges moviegoers to "Put your money where it's protected! National Bank… the bank with a hero in it!" Hollis Mason watches this commercial at a theater **[BWMM]**.

After being fully trained in security procedures and hand-to-hand combat, Bill Brady thwarts several actual attempts to rob National Bank of New York. The bank starts lending his talents to the local police force **[RPG2]**.

—September 1, 1939

World War II begins when Germany invades Poland. The conflict, also dubbed the Second World War, involves most of Earth's nations, including all sovereign states with sufficient expertise and ability to exert global influence **[REAL]**.

—After September 1, 1939

When Jon Osterman is ten years old, his father Josef tries to smuggle his Jewish wife and son out of Germany. Knowing that she'll never make it past the military, Inge urges Josef to get their son to safety, but he refuses to leave her behind. The couple head for the border with Jon hidden in the seat of their horse-drawn wagon. When Nazi troops halt the vehicle, Inge runs away to draw their attention from Jon's hiding place. A soldier named Sigmund shoots her. Josef kills the troops and runs to his wife's side, but she dies in his arms. Father and son escape Germany, relocating to New York **[BWDM]**.

Josef Osterman looks for work in New York and is hired by a watchmaker, who teaches him to be extremely delicate with his work. Determined to be the best at his new craft, Josef works day and night, hoping that by controlling this one bit of chaos, he might feel safe again and perhaps make peace with his wife's death. He soon earns the respect and admiration of his employer and the man's wife **[BWDM]**.

—Before September 11, 1939

Word of The Minutemen's fledgling formation begins to spread **[RPG3]**.

September 11, 1939

The National Bank of New York's Thomas Younger writes a letter to Larry Schexnayder, explains Bill Brady's dual status as a crime-fighter and a widely recognized media figure, and suggests him as a potential Minutemen member. Larry is enthusiastic about the prospect **[RPG3]**.

Before October 6, 1939

Impressed by accounts of The Comedian's campaign against the Garbino crime family in New York's waterfront, The Minutemen invite Eddie Blake to join their ranks **[CLIX]**.

October 6, 1939

The Comedian accepts the invitation, and Larry Schexnayder issues a press release announcing his membership in the crime-fighting team **[RPG3]**.

After October 6, 1939

The *New York Gazette* runs the announcement under the headline "Minutemen Adopt Kid Side-Kick," quoting Larry Schexnayder as anticipating no problems due to the newest member's young age **[RPG3]**.

Late October 1939

Clarence Blake Jr., a widely known business man from Charlotte, is named property manager of Alson Court Apartments. He and his family move into apartment 61B, on the first floor, and he places an ad in the *Daily News*, disguised as a news article, inviting anyone in the area to come view a model apartment **[BWMM]**.

> **NOTE:** *It is unknown whether or not Clarence Blake is a relative of Eddie Blake.*

The *Daily News*' front-page headline reads "War! Nazi Bombs Are Raining on Towns in Poland." Inside the newspaper is an advertisement inviting men of mystery, masked adventurers, and costumed crime-fighters to join a new team with Captain Metropolis and The Silk Spectre. Hollis Mason notices the ad that same day while helping Tino Musante, an immigrant youth from Italy, start his car **[BWMM]**.

> **NOTE:** *Mason notices the advertisement two weeks before auditioning, indicating a late October placement.*

Early November 1939

The National Bank of New York films a commercial in which Dollar Bill stops five armed gangsters from robbing one of its branches by tossing a large safe at them. In between takes, Abie, Dewey, Cheatem, and Howe show Brady a casting call for The Minutemen, asking that he audition for the crime-fighting team. He protests that he is just an actor, but they assure him it's all "flash and mirrors," with no real danger **[BWDB]**.

MIND .... *The Mindscape of Alan Moore*	**RPG2** ..... *DC Heroes Role Playing Module #235: Taking*	**VRL2** ..... Viral video: *The Keene Act and You*
MOBL .... *Watchmen: The Mobile Game*	*Out the Trash—Curses and Tears*	**VRL3** ..... Viral video: *Who Watches the Watchmen? A Veidt*
MOTN .... *Watchmen: The Complete Motion Comic*	**RPG3** .... *DC Heroes: The Watchmen Sourcebook*	*Music Network (VMN) Special*
MTRO .... *Metro* promotional newspaper cover wrap	**RUBY** .... "Wounds," published in *The Ruby Files Volume One*	**VRL4** ..... Viral video: *World in Focus: 6 Minutes to Midnight*
NEWP .... *New Frontiersman* promotional newspaper	**SCR1** ..... Unfilmed screenplay draft: Sam Hamm	**VRL5** ..... Viral video: *Local Radio Station Report on 1977*
NEWW .... *New Frontiersman* website	**SCR2** ..... Unfilmed screenplay draft: Charles McKeuen	*Riots*
NIGH ..... *Watchmen: The End Is Nigh, Parts 1 and 2*	**SCR3** ..... Unfilmed screenplay draft: Gary Goldman	**VRL6** ..... Viral videos (group of ten): *Veidt Enterprises*
PKIT ...... *Watchmen* film British press kit	**SCR4** ..... Unfilmed screenplay draft: David Hayter (2002)	*Advertising Contest*
PORT ..... *Watchmen Portraits*	**SCR5** ..... Unfilmed screenplay draft: David Hayter (2003)	**WAWA** .... *Watching the Watchmen*
REAL ..... Real life	**SCR6** ..... Unfilmed screenplay draft: Alex Tse	**WHOS** ... *Who's Who: The Definitive Directory of the DC*
RPG1 .... *DC Heroes Role Playing Module #227: Who*	**SPOT** ..... *DC Spotlight #1*	*Universe*
Watches the Watchmen?	**VRL1** ..... Viral video: *NBS Nightly News with Ted Philips*	**WTFC** .... *Watchmen: The Film Companion*

CONFLICT: In The Watchmen Sourcebook, Brady is excited by the idea of actually fighting crime, which convinces him to take the job.

—Mid-November 1939

Two weeks later, Nelson Gardner, Sally Jupiter, and Larry Schexnayder hold auditions for new Minutemen members. Hollis Mason is hired without having to audition, since the founders are well acquainted with his work. They initially dismiss Byron Lewis after he claims he can fly, but he eventually makes the cut **[BWMM]**. Bill Brady auditions as well. Some applicants recognize Brady as a celebrity, and an overweight Robin Hood impersonator promptly leaves, knowing he can't compete with Dollar Bill. Gardner and Jupiter recognize Brady from the movies and invite him to join immediately, knowing his presence would increase the group's public profile **[BWDB]**.

> **NOTE:** The auditions occur four weeks before The Minutemen's official formation, implying a mid-November setting.

Rejected would-be superheroes include The Frogman, a skinny, scuba gear-clad fellow who, according to his mother, is a good jumper; Liberty Lassy, a plump woman in a Statue of Liberty costume who can sing, dance, and cook "a mean brisket"; The Iron Lid, a large man encased in an iron suit who is anxious to "burn them all"; The Slut, who likes to take off her clothes and "do things"; and Hank, a slovenly, overweight fellow wearing a bucket on his head **[BWMM]**.

The National Bank of New York issues a public service announcement poster featuring Dollar Bill, urging children to stay off the streets in order to avoid being struck by cars **[RPG3]**.

—Late November or December 1939

The Minutemen add two other members to their lineup: Ursula "The Silhouette" Zandt **[ALAN]** and (the last to join) Hooded Justice, who refuses to reveal his true identity to most of the team **[RPG2]**. The crime-fighters also hire a maid, Frieda Jenkins, to clean their headquarters, launder their costumes, and keep their food pantry stocked **[RPG3]**.

Ursula Zandt and Sally Jupiter soon end up on bad terms **[ALAN]**. Recognizing Ursula's greater commitment to their craft, Sally feels cheap by comparison and dislikes her for being a better person—and for reminding Sally of things she'd prefer to forget. Ursula, in turn, looks down on Sally for running around in fishnet stockings and taking racy pictures instead of concentrating on crime-fighting **[BWMM]**, and goads her about being Polish, knowing it bothers Sally when she does so **[ALAN]**.

—December 14, 1939

Hooded Justice expresses approval of Adolf Hitler's Third Reich **[ALAN]** during an interview with *Newsworld*. In the article, the vigilante applauds the Führer for saving his nation from economic collapse, restoring dignity to his people, and "exterminating the undisciplined and perverse" from humanity **[RPG3]**. Ursula Zandt, a Jew, is highly offended by his comments, but Nelson Gardner sweeps the matter under the carpet to keep The Minutemen's reputation intact **[RPG2]**.

> **NOTE:** Under the Hood *indicates that the strongman offers such sentiments prior to Japan's 1941 attack on Pearl Harbor.* Taking Out the Trash *specifies 1940, but* The Watchmen Sourcebook *provides the actual quote, dated December 14, 1939.*

—December 16, 1939

The Minutemen officially launch as a crime-fighting team, with Larry Schexnayder managing their publicity **[RPG2]**. With the group's debut, Sally Jupiter ceases to fake arrests for publicity, thereafter fighting criminals for real **[RPG3]**.

> **NOTE:** *Alan Moore's miniseries sets the team's formation in fall 1939.* Taking Out the Trash *provides the specific date. According to* Absolute Watchmen, *Alan Moore originally intended for The Nite Owl to serve as acting president for most of the group's adventures. In the published comic, however, Captain Metropolis is the leader.*

> **CONFLICT:** The Watchmen Sourcebook *places the group's formation on August 16, contradicting Moore's story.* Taking Out the Trash's *December 16 setting, on the other hand, jibes with a fall launch.*
>
> *A preview of* Watchmen, *published in September 1985 in* DC Spotlight #1—*the characters' first appearance in any medium—claims the miniseries is set in a world in which superheroes do not appear until the 1960s. This, however, overlooks The Minutemen's existence.*

—Late December 1939

During the ensuing weeks, The Minutemen make the covers of every magazine on the racks except for *Good Housekeeping* **[BWDB]**. Some journalists dub the group "The Watchmen" **[ARTF]**.

> **NOTE:** *A timeline published in* The Film Companion *also calls the group The Watchmen.*

Nelson Gardner deems The Minutemen ready for battle and chooses their first mission to generate attention and promote patriotism: bringing down an Italian fifth-columnist cell rumored to be smuggling weapons into New York Harbor. Silk Spectre distracts a guard at the criminals' import-export warehouse as Nite Owl, Silhouette, and The Comedian scale a wall to enter from a skylight. However, the thugs are merely smuggling Chinese fireworks. Mothman drops a smoke grenade from the air as Metropolis, Dollar Bill, and Hooded Justice storm the building in a military tank, inadvertently igniting the stored fireworks. Gardner bullies the smugglers into keeping quiet and calls a press conference

MIND .... *The Mindscape of Alan Moore*
MOBL ..... *Watchmen: The Mobile Game*
MOTN .... *Watchmen: The Complete Motion Comic*
MTRO .... *Metro promotional newspaper cover wrap*
NEWP .... *New Frontiersman promotional newspaper*
NEWW .. *New Frontiersman website*
NIGH ..... *Watchmen: The End Is Nigh, Parts 1 and 2*
PKIT ...... *Watchmen film British press kit*
PORT ..... *Watchmen Portraits*
REAL ..... Real life
RPG1 ..... *DC Heroes Role Playing Module #227: Who Watches the Watchmen?*

RPG2 .... *DC Heroes Role Playing Module #235: Taking Out the Trash—Curses and Tears*
RPG3 .... *DC Heroes: The Watchmen Sourcebook*
RUBY .... "Wounds," published in *The Ruby Files Volume One*
SCR1 ..... Unfilmed screenplay draft: Sam Hamm
SCR2 ..... Unfilmed screenplay draft: Charles McKeuen
SCR3 ..... Unfilmed screenplay draft: Gary Goldman
SCR4 ..... Unfilmed screenplay draft: David Hayter (2002)
SCR5 ..... Unfilmed screenplay draft: David Hayter (2003)
SCR6 ..... Unfilmed screenplay draft: Alex Tse
SPOT ..... *DC Spotlight #1*
VRL1 ..... Viral video: *NBS Nightly News with Ted Philips*

VRL2 ..... Viral video: *The Keene Act and You*
VRL3 ..... Viral video: *Who Watches the Watchmen? A Veidt Music Network (VMN) Special*
VRL4 ..... Viral video: *World in Focus: 6 Minutes to Midnight*
VRL5 ..... Viral video: *Local Radio Station Report on 1977 Riots*
VRL6 ..... Viral videos (group of ten): *Veidt Enterprises Advertising Contest*
WAWA ... *Watching the Watchmen*
WHOS ... *Who's Who: The Definitive Directory of the DC Universe*
WTFC ... *Watchmen: The Film Companion*

to announce the takedown of a saboteur ring. No one catches the heroes in the lie, and The Minutemen make the front-page news [**BWMM, BWDB**].

The Minutemen lease a Manhattan brownstone from J.D. Dorchester, of Dorchester oil fame, to serve as their headquarters, for a monthly rate of $400. The building includes a conference room for regular and strategy meetings and social events, as well as quarters for Sally Jupiter and Hollis Mason, a trophy room, a basement gymnasium, and a communications room for contacting law-enforcement agencies worldwide [**RPG3**].

> **NOTE:** *This seems to be a separate location from The Minutemen's Freedom Tower headquarters.*

The Minutemen take on their second public mission when a gang of thieves robs a National Bank of New York branch, taking hostages. Though reluctant to risk being shot, Bill Brady notices a Dollar Bill statue outside the bank, which Hooded Justice lobs through the front window. Hooded Justice and Nite Owl charge the startled robbers, and Brady does the same a moment later, using wrestling moves to subdue a thief [**BWDB**].

Moloch the Mystic forces a scientist, Professor Tungren, to create a device called a solar mirror weapon. After killing Tungren with the device, Moloch uses it to perpetrate bigger heists, earning himself greater money and press [**BWMO**]. The mobster threatens to destroy the Empire State Building unless police provide him with a hand-rendered, illuminated copy of William Blake's "Marriage of Heaven and Hell," worth more than $16 million [**RPG3**]. He also robs a train filled with military weaponry, only to have his heist foiled by The Minutemen [**BWMO**]. The vigilantes defeat Moloch's plan and take the solar mirror weapon, displaying it in their headquarters' trophy room [**ALAN**].

> **NOTE:** *The Minutemen's first encounter with Moloch is undated in the* Watchmen *comic, but* The Watchmen Sourcebook *reveals the year to be 1939. Since this must occur after the team's first mission, that would place the encounter in late December. Before Watchmen: Moloch claims all Minutemen are present during this incident, but The Comedian is not visible among them.*

●—Winter 1939

Corrupt NYPD officer Peter Dacso is slain, his body burnt in a tenement fire set by the Shairp crime syndicate. Dacso's father, Alexei Dacso, meets with detective Richard "Rick" Ruby at the Gunga Diner, urging him to solve the murder. The P.I. accepts the case with reluctance, and his investigation brings him to the Keeler Mission, where he questions two survivors of the blaze: Sylvia Kovacs and her drunken boyfriend, Charlie. Ruby promises a nonexistent reward, and they put him on the trail of building owner Ed Shairp, the younger brother of syndicate boss Lou Shairp. Ruby solves the case, bringing down the Shairp crime family in the process [**RUBY**].

NOTE: *These events occur in the short story "Wounds," written by author and actor Andrew Salmon, who worked as an extra on the* Watchmen *film. Though not officially a* Watchmen *tie-in, the story, published in* The Ruby Files, Volume One, *offers a rare glimpse of Rorschach's parents before the events of Alan Moore's miniseries. Hollis Mason has a brief cameo as an off-screen police officer as well, sans dialogue.*

Presumably, the Shairp brothers are related to Rorschach's future landlord, Delores Shairp.

The Keeler Mission pays homage to social worker Edith Keeler, James T. Kirk's ill-fated love interest portrayed by Joan Collins in the classic Star Trek *episode "The City on the Edge of Forever." Edith's death is mentioned as having occurred a decade prior (she died in the episode, set in 1930), and the mission is decorated in rocketship images in honor of her forward-thinking view of the future.*

—Circa December 25, 1939

The Minutemen hold their first Christmas party, which turns out to be the group's last good time together before things begin to go bad **[ALAN]**.

—Between December 1939 and October 2, 1940

Bill Brady travels to Hollywood, hoping to leverage his newfound fame in The Minutemen to forge an acting career, but finds that he has become typecast due to his Dollar Bill commercials. Dejected, he returns to New York, accepts his role as a bank spokesperson and ribbon-cutter, and rents an upscale apartment **[BWDB]**.

NOTE: *This and the following events must occur between The Minutemen's founding in December 1939 and The Comedian's ouster on October 2, 1940.*

The earliest criminals thwarted by The Minutemen are gangs dressed up as pirates or ghosts, who find it funny to perpetrate heists while wearing costumes. The masks enable the thugs to quickly end up back on the streets, since no one can identify them out of a police lineup without having seen their faces **[FILM]**. Still, with Larry Schexnayder publicizing the team's exploits by arranging for newspaper and radio-show coverage, The Minutemen's popularity soars **[BWMM]**.

On one occasion, The *New York Gazette* reports the group's success in unearthing a hidden arsenal **[FILM]**. The crime-fighters also thwart a criminal called King Mob—then display, in a showcase, the ape mask he wears while committing crimes **[ALAN]**.

The Comedian gains renown for capturing an assassin known as The Italian Shadow, who for years has avoided police pursuit **[FILM]**. Blake also earns a reputation for stealing loot from the criminals he apprehends, however, as cops begin to notice that every crook he turns in is financially broke **[BWMM]**.

MIND .... *The Mindscape of Alan Moore*
MOBL .... *Watchmen: The Mobile Game*
MOTN .... *Watchmen: The Complete Motion Comic*
MTRO .... *Metro promotional newspaper cover wrap*
NEWP .... *New Frontiersman promotional newspaper*
NEWW .... *New Frontiersman website*
NIGH ..... *Watchmen: The End Is Nigh, Parts 1 and 2*
PKIT ...... *Watchmen film British press kit*
PORT ..... *Watchmen Portraits*
REAL ..... Real life
RPG1 .... *DC Heroes Role Playing Module #227: Who Watches the Watchmen?*

RPG2 .... *DC Heroes Role Playing Module #235: Taking Out the Trash—Curses and Tears*
RPG3 .... *DC Heroes: The Watchmen Sourcebook*
RUBY .... "Wounds," published in *The Ruby Files Volume One*
SCR1 ..... Unfilmed screenplay draft: Sam Hamm
SCR2 ..... Unfilmed screenplay draft: Charles McKeuen
SCR3 ..... Unfilmed screenplay draft: Gary Goldman
SCR4 ..... Unfilmed screenplay draft: David Hayter (2002)
SCR5 ..... Unfilmed screenplay draft: David Hayter (2003)
SCR6 ..... Unfilmed screenplay draft: Alex Tse
SPOT ..... *DC Spotlight #1*
VRL1 ..... Viral video: *NBS Nightly News with Ted Philips*

VRL2 ..... Viral video: *The Keene Act and You*
VRL3 ..... Viral video: *Who Watches the Watchmen? A Veidt Music Network (VMN) Special*
VRL4 ..... Viral video: *World in Focus: 6 Minutes to Midnight*
VRL5 ..... Viral video: *Local Radio Station Report on 1977 Riots*
VRL6 ..... Viral videos (group of ten): *Veidt Enterprises Advertising Contest*
WAWA ... *Watching the Watchmen*
WHOS ... *Who's Who: The Definitive Directory of the DC Universe*
WTFC .... *Watchmen: The Film Companion*

Eddie Blake makes no secret of his attraction to Sally Jupiter, despite being four years her junior, but she shows interest only in her close friend Hooded Justice, whom she calls "H.J." **[ALAN]**. Mason secretly loves Ursula Zandt, whom he considers an avenging angel for her efforts to thwart child pornographers **[BWMM]**.

The Minutemen cripple a crime ring plaguing the Metro Central Bank after the criminals wreak havoc on New York City for months. Mothman apprehends the suspects and helps their victims, urging New York's citizens not to lose hope. The *New York Gazette* covers the capture in a front-page story titled "'There Is Hope'—Mothman'" **[HOOD]**.
    CONFLICT: The crime ring's takedown is said to happen around September 20, 1939, but since Alan Moore's miniseries establishes The Minutemen's launch as occurring in December, that date must be ignored.

Eddie Blake expresses hope that the U.S. government will send The Minutemen to Europe to fight in World War II. Hooded Justice feels that they should remain non-political, while Byron Lewis fears the thought of fighting in a war **[ALAN]**.

Issue #1 of *Minutemen*, a new comic book about "America's greatest heroes," features adventures based on the exploits of the crime-fighting team **[RPG3]**.

Moloch earns a reputation for writing letters on parchment **[RPG1]**.

—Between December 1939 and May 13, 1946

Ursula Zandt remains aloof from her fellow Minutemen, becoming close only with Larry Schexnayder and, to some extent, Hollis Mason and Byron Lewis. She often tells them sabout her Aunt Emma in Katzenbühl, Austria, and comments that men tend to treat people like cars—if they could just know what was wrong, they could fix it **[RPG3]**.

—In or After 1939

The U.S. government abolishes laws banning vigilantism in order to accommodate the strategically useful talents of masked adventurers. Psychologists offer theories about why someone would choose to don a costume and fight crime, while others spread jokes, rumors, and innuendo about the superhero crowd's motives. For Hollis Mason, the answer is simple: because he enjoys it and feels better when doing so **[ALAN]**.

The U.S. Congress awards the Medal of Honor to members of The Minutemen for conspicuous gallantry and intrepidity involving risk of life above and beyond the call of duty **[ARTF, HOOD]**.
    NOTE: The Medal of Honor is dated March 27, 1936, but since that predates the group's existence by more than three years, this date must be ignored.

ABSO .... *Watchmen Absolute Edition*
ALAN ..... Alan Moore's *Watchmen* miniseries
ARCD .... *Minutemen Arcade*
ARTF ..... *Watchmen: The Art of the Film*
BLCK ..... *Tales of the Black Freighter*
BWCC ... *Before Watchmen—The Crimson Corsair*
BWCO ... *Before Watchmen—Comedian*
BWDB .. *Before Watchmen—Dollar Bill*
BWDM .. *Before Watchmen—Dr. Manhattan*
BWMM .. *Before Watchmen—Minutemen*
BWMO .. *Before Watchmen—Moloch*
BWNO ... *Before Watchmen—Nite Owl*

BWOZ .... *Before Watchmen—Ozymandias*
BWRO ... *Before Watchmen—Rorschach*
BWSS ... *Before Watchmen—Silk Spectre*
CHEM ... My Chemical Romance music video: "Desolation Row"
CMEO .... *Watchmen* cameos in comics, TV, and film:
  • Comic: *Astonishing X-Men* volume 3 issue #6
  • Comic: *Hero Hotline* volume 1 issue #5
  • Comic: *Kingdom Come* volume 1 issue #2
  • Comic: *Marvels* volume 1 issue #4
  • Comic: *The Question* volume 1 issue #17
  • TV: *Teen Titans Go!* episode #82, "Real Boy Adventures"
  • Film: *Man of Steel*

  • Film: *Batman v Superman: Dawn of Justice Ultimate Edition*
  • Film: *Justice League*
CLIX ...... HeroClix figure pack-in cards
DECK ..... *DC Comics Deck-Building Game—Crossover Pack 4: Watchmen*
DURS ... *DC Universe: Rebirth Special* volume 1 issue #1
FILM ..... *Watchmen* theatrical film
HOOD .... *Under the Hood* documentary and dust-jacket prop reproduction
JUST ..... *Watchmen: Justice Is Coming*
MATL .... Mattel Club Black Freighter figure pack-in cards

While working together in The Minutemen, Hollis Mason and Byron Lewis form a close bond. Hollis soon comes to consider Byron as his best friend **[BWMM]**.

—Between 1939 and 1947

The Silk Spectre makes two arrests of women involved in a string of thefts at funerals. After watching the women rob grieving families for a few weeks, Sally Jupiter attends several publicly announced funeral services and catches them in the act. A day later, she and The Minutemen are honored at a ceremony **[HOOD]**.

> **NOTE:** *The dating of this and the following events is unclear, though they must occur during the span of time in which Sally is still a member of The Minutemen.*

Silk Spectre takes down the Spring St. Bandits after working with an undercover reporter for two months to gather enough evidence to put the gang of thieves in jail for twenty years apiece. The thugs are arraigned before Magistrate F. Nelson and held on $10,000 bail, with $5,000 in recovered loot returned to the gang's victims **[HOOD]**.

While fighting a villain called The Fey Blade, Sally receives a scratch that becomes infected and swells up badly **[BWSS]**. She also defeats The Herald Square Gang **[ARTF]**. New York City Mayor Gordon Brunner and the New York City Council present her with a citation for outstanding service to the community, conspicuous gallantry, and going above and beyond the call of duty **[HOOD]**.

—1939 to 1950

Throughout The Minutemen's existence, Nelson Gardner suffers from the paranoid delusion that other members of the group are snickering behind his back. As a result, he spends much of his time desperate to earn their respect **[RPG2]**.

—Between 1939 and 1962

The Nite Owl fights a villain called The H(uman)-Bomb **[WAWA]**.

> **NOTE:** *This one-panel battle occurs in a pre-professional pen-and-pencil sketch that Dave Gibbons created at age fourteen. The artist suggested the name "Night Owl" to Alan Moore, who liked it but tweaked the spelling to the Americanized "Nite Owl."*

Hollis Mason builds a secret underground garage called the Owl Cave, accessible via a subway tunnel, in which he stores his costume, a selection of gadgets, and a rounded vehicle called the Owl Car. He develops rudimentary night-vision goggles (which fail to work properly) and adopts a signature phrase ("Hooty-hoot hoot!"), which fans—and some police officers—call out to him on the street. As Nite Owl, he vows to dispense "owl justice... because justice can find you in the shadows and the dark" **[BWNO]**.

> **NOTE:** *It is unclear whether or not the Owl Cave is the same lair as the Owl's Nest,*

MIND .... *The Mindscape of Alan Moore*
MOBL .... *Watchmen: The Mobile Game*
MOTN .... *Watchmen: The Complete Motion Comic*
MTRO .... *Metro* promotional newspaper cover wrap
NEWP .... *New Frontiersman* promotional newspaper
NEWW ... *New Frontiersman* website
NIGH .... *Watchmen: The End Is Nigh, Parts 1 and 2*
PKIT ...... *Watchmen* film British press kit
PORT ..... *Watchmen Portraits*
REAL ..... Real life
RPG1 .... *DC Heroes Role Playing Module #227: Who Watches the Watchmen?*

RPG2 .... *DC Heroes Role Playing Module #235: Taking Out the Trash—Curses and Tears*
RPG3 .... *DC Heroes: The Watchmen Sourcebook*
RUBY .... "Wounds," published in *The Ruby Files Volume One*
SCR1 ..... Unfilmed screenplay draft: Sam Hamm
SCR2 ..... Unfilmed screenplay draft: Charles McKeuen
SCR3 ..... Unfilmed screenplay draft: Gary Goldman
SCR4 ..... Unfilmed screenplay draft: David Hayter (2002)
SCR5 ..... Unfilmed screenplay draft: David Hayter (2003)
SCR6 ..... Unfilmed screenplay draft: Alex Tse
SPOT .... *DC Spotlight #1*
VRL1 ..... Viral video: *NBS Nightly News with Ted Philips*

VRL2 ..... Viral video: *The Keene Act and You*
VRL3 ..... Viral video: *Who Watches the Watchmen? A Veidt Music Network (VMN) Special*
VRL4 ..... Viral video: *World in Focus: 6 Minutes to Midnight*
VRL5 ..... Viral video: *Local Radio Station Report on 1977 Riots*
VRL6 ..... Viral videos (group of ten): *Veidt Enterprises Advertising Contest*
WAWA ... *Watching the Watchmen*
WHOS ... *Who's Who: The Definitive Directory of the DC Universe*
WTFC .... *Watchmen: The Film Companion*

introduced in Alan Moore's miniseries.

"Hooty-hoot hoot!" is likely an in-joke reference to "Zooty, zoot zoot!"—a catch-phrase used by comedians Rebo and Zooty, played by magician team Penn and Teller in Babylon 5 episode "Day of the Dead." Babylon 5 creator J. Michael Straczynski wrote Before Watchmen: Nite Owl, in which Mason's signature phrase is introduced.

Hollis Mason saves the life of an eight-year-old girl and her brother, despite being badly hurt in the process, and drags four policemen out of a burning building before it collapses **[BWMM]**. The press dubs him "The Light in the Darkness" **[BWNO]**.

> **NOTE:** This parallel's Batman's nickname "The Dark Knight."

●—1930s or 1940s

Josef Osterman expresses to his son Jon an admiration for the sky's precision **[ALAN]**. The watchmaker teaches his son how to repair watches, explaining that nothing is ever so badly broken that it can't be put back together with sufficient effort **[BWDM]**.

●—1930s and 1940s

Clandestine pornographic comic books, dubbed "Tijuana Bibles," flourish as an art form, featuring fictional characters like Chic Young's Blondie Boopadoop, as well as actor Mary Jane "Mae" West **[REAL]** and Minutemen crime-fighter Sally Jupiter. One such comic, portraying Sally's sexual exploits with a salesman from Acme Brush Co. **[ALAN]**, is titled *Silk Spectre and the Adventures of the Acme Brushman* **[FILM]**.

> **NOTE:** Tijuana Bibles were produced from the 1920s to the 1960s, peaking in popularity during the Great Depression. Sexually explicit in nature and typically eight pages in length, these satirical, palm-sized comics often perpetuated ethnic stereotypes and now command high prices among collectors. The Sally Jupiter comic is based on a real-world Tijuana Bible, The Adventures of a Fuller Brush Man.
>
> "Acme," a Greek word denoting the point at which something is the best or most successful (symbolizing masked adventurers before their decline), is also a common generic fictional company name, originating in Looney Tunes cartoons.

●—Late 1930s to 1950

Throughout his criminal career, The Screaming Skull is more interested in having fun playing the role of a typical comic-book supervillain than in reaping the rewards of his schemes. Though he steals more than $15 million worth of property, he clears only $2,000 or so in total, due to steep overhead and insurance costs **[RPG3]**.

Part III:
LIFE DURING WARTIME
(1940–1945)

—In or Before 1940

The Big Top Circus opens. The traveling circus performs three shows daily in cities along the U.S. East Coast **[BWMM]**.

—After the 1930s

The superhero comic-book genre fades away in a world populated by living crime-fighters, largely forgotten except among older readers who recall the fictional adventures of Superman and other heroes in the 1930s. In their place, pirate comics grow increasingly popular, including such titles as *Pirate* and *X-Ships* **[ALAN]**.

> *NOTE: X-Ships is likely an in-joke referencing Marvel Comics' X-Men, given the supplanting of the superhero genre by pirate lore.*

DC Comics publishes *The Curse of the Crimson Corsair*, a 28-chapter pirate comic written by Len Wein and John Higgins, illustrated by Higgins, and lettered by Sal Cipriano. The series, set in July 1771, comprises three storylines: "The Devil in the Deep," "The Evil That Men Do," and "Wide Were His Dragon Wings." In the series, sailor Gordon McClachlan mutinies against the cruel captain of British naval vessel *Pendragon*, but is knocked overboard during an attack by a Spanish frigate. Lying adrift for days, he is rescued by the *Flying Dutchman*—the ship of the damned—and learns that his act of mutiny has cursed him for eternity. McClachlan makes a deal with the undead pirate captain, the Crimson Corsair, for ownership of his own soul **[BWCC]**.

> *NOTE: The in-universe publication date of The Curse of the Crimson Corsair is unknown, though it likely occurs following the 1939 rise of the pirate comic genre.*
>
> *Wein, Higgins, and Cipriano are the real-world creative team on this back-up feature to 28 issues of Before Watchmen; previously, Wein and Higgins had served as the editor and colorist, respectively, of Alan Moore's miniseries.*
>
> *Just as* Tales of the Black Freighter *mirrors the plights of several* Watchmen

characters, Crimson Corsair *mirrors (whether intentionally or not) claims by some fans that those responsible for* Before Watchmen, *in crafting a prequel to the original comic, betrayed Moore's intentions, thereby cursing the series.*

January 1940
Sylvia Kovacs' boyfriend Charlie leaves her while she is pregnant with his son **[ALAN]**.

January 3, 1940
Byron Lewis records a diary entry expressing doubts about The Minutemen, which he has come to regard as an unimportant publicity stunt, and describes Hooded Justice as personifying the worst kind of hatred—the kind that needs to hide behind a mask. Eddie Blake scares him more, though, since his indiscretions are borne not of ignorance, like Hooded Justice's, but of high intelligence **[RPG3]**.

March 21, 1940
Sylvia Kovacs gives birth to Walter Joseph Kovacs, the future masked adventurer Rorschach **[RPG2]**. Many people, including Sylvia herself, deem him an unattractive child **[ALAN]**.

> **CONFLICT:** *Taking Out the Trash inexplicably switches Rorschach's first and middle names, calling him Joseph Walter Kovacs throughout the book.*
>
> *Alan Moore's miniseries sets Rorschach's birth in 1940, as does a timeline packaged with* The End Is Nigh—The Complete Experience. *Timelines published in* The Film Companion *and in the film's British press kit cite a birth year of 1942. A police file in the press kit specifies March 21, 1942, while Sam Hamm's unproduced 1988 screenplay claims a birth date of March 21, 1943.*

After March 21, 1940
With debts mounting, Sylvia Kovacs turns to prostitution to pay her bills. Shortly after Walter's birth, she is first arrested for soliciting **[ALAN]**.

May 26 to June 4, 1940
During World War II's Battle of Dunkirk, more than 330,000 Allied soldiers are evacuated after a Nazi advance on the French city is delayed **[REAL]**. Hans von Krupp, a top official under Adolf Hitler, falls out of favor with the Nazi Party for failing to act on intelligence that could have prevented the Allied Forces' escape **[RPG3]**.

After June 4, 1940
Hans von Krupp flees for his life and ends up in the United States. Though marked for death by the Third Reich, he remains fanatically loyal to Adolf Hitler. Allying with fifth-columnists in America, he takes on the role of a master saboteur known as Captain Axis, hoping to redeem himself in the eyes of the Führer **[RPG3]**.

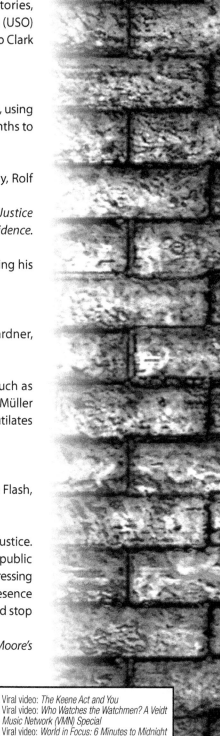

—June 1940 to 1945

As Captain Axis, Hans von Krupp becomes a famous saboteur, threatening factories, military installations, propagandistic war films, and United Service Organizations (USO) events. On one occasion, he tries to implant single-frame subliminal messages into Clark Gable movies that read "Germany Must Win!" **[RPG3]**.

—Mid-1940

Nelson Gardner has a meeting room constructed at The Minutemen's headquarters, using wood imported from Africa. He orders special chairs for the room, which take months to manufacture **[BWMM]**.

Hooded Justice breaks an arm while battling The Screaming Skull. Subsequently, Rolf Müller misses a month's performances at the Shriner's Circus **[RPG3]**.

> **NOTE:** *Given the revelation, in* Before Watchmen: Minutemen, *that Hooded Justice and Rolf Müller are separate individuals, this is apparently just an unusual coincidence.*

After interviewing Hooded Justice, the *New York Post* publishes an article describing his accent as "different, faintly Bavarian" **[RPG3]**.

—In or Before September 1940

Hooded Justice secretly enters into a homosexual relationship with Nelson Gardner, whom he calls "Nelly" **[ALAN]**.

The Big Top Circus arrives in New York City. The traveling circus features rides such as the Cyclone and the Tornado, carnival games like Cakewalk and Lucky 7, and Rolf Müller performing as "The Mighty Meuller." The strongman, a serial killer, abducts and mutilates children at each city in which the circus performs **[BWMM]**.

—September 1940

DC Comics' *All-Star Comics* issue #2 hits stands, featuring tales of The Spectre, The Flash, Johnny Thunder, The Sandman, and Red, White & Blue **[REAL, HOOD]**.

Larry Schexnayder discovers Nelson Gardner's secret relationship with Hooded Justice. Though Larry has no problem with the men being homosexuals, he decides the public would not react well to the news **[ALAN]**. The agent writes a note to Sally Jupiter, expressing concern about Hooded Justice's "problem," and suggests that she, when in the presence of photographers, snuggle up to the strongman so the press will infer romance and stop looking into his personal life **[RPG3]**.

> **CONFLICT:** *Larry's letter is dated February 16, 1939, which does not jibe with Alan Moore's miniseries and must thus be ignored.*

MIND .... *The Mindscape of Alan Moore*
MOBL .... *Watchmen: The Mobile Game*
MOTN .... *Watchmen: The Complete Motion Comic*
MTRO .... *Metro* promotional newspaper cover wrap
NEWP .... *New Frontiersman* promotional newspaper
NEWW .... *New Frontiersman* website
NIGH .... *Watchmen: The End Is Nigh, Parts 1 and 2*
PKIT ...... *Watchmen* film British press kit
PORT ..... *Watchmen Portraits*
REAL ..... Real life
RPG1 .... *DC Heroes Role Playing Module #227: Who Watches the Watchmen?*

RPG2 .... *DC Heroes Role Playing Module #235: Taking Out the Trash—Curses and Tears*
RPG3 .... *DC Heroes: The Watchmen Sourcebook*
RUBY .... "Wounds," published in *The Ruby Files Volume One*
SCR1 ..... Unfilmed screenplay draft: Sam Hamm
SCR2 ..... Unfilmed screenplay draft: Charles McKeuen
SCR3 ..... Unfilmed screenplay draft: Gary Goldman
SCR4 ..... Unfilmed screenplay draft: David Hayter (2002)
SCR5 ..... Unfilmed screenplay draft: David Hayter (2003)
SCR6 ..... Unfilmed screenplay draft: Alex Tse
SPOT ..... *DC Spotlight #1*
VRL1 ..... Viral video: *NBS Nightly News with Ted Philips*

VRL2 ..... Viral video: *The Keene Act and You*
VRL3 ..... Viral video: *Who Watches the Watchmen? A Veidt Music Network (VMN) Special*
VRL4 ..... Viral video: *World in Focus: 6 Minutes to Midnight*
VRL5 ..... Viral video: *Local Radio Station Report on 1977 Riots*
VRL6 ..... Viral videos (group of ten): *Veidt Enterprises Advertising Contest*
WAWA ... *Watching the Watchmen*
WHOS .... *Who's Who: The Definitive Directory of the DC Universe*
WTFC .... *Watchmen: The Film Companion*

—Late September 1940

At a Minutemen meeting, Larry Schexnayder reports that the team has achieved three newspaper headlines within the past week and scored record radio show ratings, and that a photographer will shoot publicity stills the following week. Nelson Gardner presents a patrol schedule to increase coverage area and efficiency. Ursula Zandt recommends focusing on child-trafficking rings, but Sally Jupiter and Schexnayder nix the idea, deeming molestation a sad topic, non-conducive to publicity. Byron Lewis suggests taking on Moloch, and Gardner agrees **[BWMM]**.

Following the meeting, Larry Schexnayder confronts Hooded Justice about his love affair with Nelson Gardner, suggesting he be seen in public with Sally Jupiter to prevent the press from noticing their lifestyle. The strongman says nothing, but hefts a saw and hammer in his hands menacingly. As Larry drives Sally home, she reluctantly agrees to be H.J.'s "beard." After they leave, Bill Brady and Eddie Blake are shocked to overhear Gardner and Hooded Justice engaging in sadomasochistic sex acts **[BWMM]**.

That night, Hollis Mason and Byron Lewis accompany Ursula Zandt as she works a case to locate a boy who went missing at the Big Top Circus. Mason flirts with Ursula as they investigate the grounds, but she rebuffs his advances, having no interest in men. They discover a bloody handprint and ropes, then track a putrid odor and the sound of crying to find a child's dead body hanging from the ceiling **[BWMM]**.

—September 1940 to June 1946

Ursula Zandt spends six years trying to identify the child-killer **[BWMM]**.

—After September 1940

Hollis Mason continues to help Ursula Zandt bring down child pornographers. The two become friends, meeting for coffee once a week at Deli Madison, with the agreement not to share their last names or details about their outside lives **[BWMM]**.

—Before October 2, 1940

Sally Jupiter begins posing as Hooded Justice's girlfriend, while also bolstering her own publicity. Sally adores the limelight and is often spotted holding his muscled arm in public, though Hooded Justice dislikes such "razzle dazzle" and prefers to be out on the streets. Hollis Mason notices that the strongman seems uninterested in her romantically, and that they never kiss **[ALAN]**.

—October 2, 1940

Scientists name the first artificial element "plutonium" **[REAL]**.

The Minutemen pose for a group portrait at their headquarters [ALAN], for a photographer called Weegee [FILM]. The team orders eight prints, one for each member (including Larry Schexnayder) [ALAN].

> **NOTE:** *Weegee was the pseudonym of Arthur Felliga, an Austria-born professional news photographer who documented many crimes, scandals, funerals, and fires that occurred in New York City during the 1930s and '40s. A June 2006* New York Times *article ("'Unknown Weegee,' on Photographer Who Made the Night Noir," by Holland Cotter) fittingly dubbed him the "night watchman of our American Babylon."*

After the meeting, Hollis Mason invites the others back to the Owl's Nest for a beer. Sally Jupiter remains behind to change in the trophy room, and Eddie Blake walks in on her undressing, presuming his interest in her to be mutual. When she refuses his advances, he becomes aggressive, forcing her to scratch his face in defense. Enraged, Blake beats her up and attempts to rape her, but Hooded Justice comes to her rescue, pummeling Blake badly. The hooded strongman is disturbed when Blake insinuates that he gets aroused by being rough with other men [ALAN].

> **CONFLICT:** Taking Out the Trash *dates Blake's attempted rape on June 25, 1940, but this contradicts Alan Moore's miniseries.*

—After October 2, 1940

Larry Schexnayder convinces Sally Jupiter not to press charges against Eddie Blake, for the good of The Minutemen [ALAN], though the team unanimously votes to expel him. When Blake pleads for forgiveness, Bill Brady sympathizes, partly blaming Sally's attire for the incident, but Hollis Mason is adamant, condemning Blake as a woman-beater and a crook. Eddie calls his ex-teammates hypocrites and perverts, flips Hooded Justice to the ground by his noose, and storms out, warning the strongman at gunpoint that he'll kill him someday [BWMM]. Blake's exit comes with a minimum of publicity [ALAN], other than Schexnayder issuing a press release announcing that The Comedian has resigned to fight crime in Washington, D.C. [RPG3].

Newspaper gossip writer Zelda Gotfried's "About the Town" column [RPG3] publishes a blurb about Sally Jupiter, calling her a "cheesecake crime-crusher." Gotfried claims that Sally and Hooded Justice are romantically involved, citing The Minutemen photo in which Sally is holding onto the hooded adventurer's arm [ALAN].

> **CONFLICT:** The Watchmen Sourcebook *dates the column's publication on January 3, 1940, but this must be ignored since the photograph would not yet exist.*

Nelson Gardner makes several derogatory statements regarding black and Hispanic Americans that others view as racially prejudiced and inflammatory [ALAN].

MIND .... *The Mindscape of Alan Moore*	**RPG2** .... *DC Heroes Role Playing Module #235: Taking Out the Trash—Curses and Tears*	**VRL2** .... Viral video: *The Keene Act and You*
MOBL.... *Watchmen: The Mobile Game*		**VRL3** .... Viral video: *Who Watches the Watchmen? A Veidt Music Network (VMN) Special*
MOTN.... *Watchmen: The Complete Motion Comic*	**RPG3** .... *DC Heroes: The Watchmen Sourcebook*	
MTRO.... *Metro* promotional newspaper cover wrap	**RUBY** .... "Wounds," published in *The Ruby Files Volume One*	**VRL4** .... Viral video: *World in Focus: 6 Minutes to Midnight*
NEWP... *New Frontiersman* promotional newspaper	**SCR1**..... Unfilmed screenplay draft: Sam Hamm	**VRL5** .... Viral video: *Local Radio Station Report on 1977 Riots*
NEWW.. *New Frontiersman* website	**SCR2**..... Unfilmed screenplay draft: Charles McKeuen	
NIGH .... *Watchmen: The End Is Nigh, Parts 1 and 2*	**SCR3**.... Unfilmed screenplay draft: Gary Goldman	**VRL6** .... Viral videos (group of ten): *Veidt Enterprises Advertising Contest*
PKIT...... *Watchmen* film British press kit	**SCR4**..... Unfilmed screenplay draft: David Hayter (2002)	
PORT..... *Watchmen Portraits*	**SCR5**..... Unfilmed screenplay draft: David Hayter (2003)	**WAWA**... *Watching the Watchmen*
REAL..... Real life	**SCR6**..... Unfilmed screenplay draft: Alex Tse	**WHOS** .... *Who's Who: The Definitive Directory of the DC Universe*
RPG1 .... *DC Heroes Role Playing Module #227: Who Watches the Watchmen?*	**SPOT**..... *DC Spotlight #1*	
	VRL1 ..... Viral video: *NBS Nightly News with Ted Philips*	**WTFC** .... *Watchmen: The Film Companion*

—October 3, 1940
Hollis Mason meets with Weegee at his photography studio on 21st Street to pick up the portraits of The Minutemen [**FILM**].

—Between October 1940 and 1941
Hooded Justice battles Moloch on several occasions, leading some to view the two as arch-enemies [**RPG3**].

—In or After 1940
Hollis Mason's parents both die, leaving him regretful that he never let them know they did right by him [**ALAN**].

—Between 1940 and 1951
Resentful of her financial problems, single-motherhood, and prostitution lifestyle, Sylvia Kovacs takes out her frustrations on her son Walter, frequently abusing him throughout the first decade of his life. Whenever Walter asks about his father, she lies that she threw him out due to his disapproval of President Harry S. Truman [**ALAN**]. Walter grows up thinking of her prostitution clients as his "uncles" [**BWRO**].

> ***NOTE:*** *Harry Truman, during World War II, ordered the bombing of Hiroshima and Nagasaki in the hope of ending the war—in essence, killing thousands of people in Japan to save millions worldwide. Thus, Truman's multiple mentions throughout Alan Moore's miniseries presage the nature of Adrian Veidt's plan to do the same on a larger scale to prevent World War III.*

Sylvia Kovacs tells young Walter that New York City is the greatest city on Earth. One New Year's Eve, she takes her son out on a fire escape and tells him he's lucky to live there—one of the few times she smiles at him. Her latest client calls her back to bed, and Walter waits outside in his pajamas despite the snow, causing his fingers to turn blue and his toes to blacken. The next morning, she brings him to a hospital emergency room to have his frostbite treated, angrily accusing him of ruining everything. She asks what made him this way, and he replies "You did" [**BWRO**].

—In or Before the 1940s
After corporate banker William Dreiberg impregnates a woman named Victoria, the two disagree about whether she should abort the pregnancy. The two get married despite not loving each other, and he routinely abuses her physically [**BWNO**]. William's brother Alan, meanwhile, marries a woman named Greta [**RPG3**].

> ***NOTE:*** *Rolf Müller's mother, according to* The Watchmen Sourcebook, *is also named Greta, and she ends up single after her husband Henrik abandons her. It is unclear whether the two Gretas—both of whom appear in the Sourcebook—are meant to be the same individual, implying Greta marries Alan Dreiberg after her first marriage ends. If that's*

the case, it would make Dan Dreiberg and Rolf Müller cousins, though neither would be aware of this since Rolf ran away from home years prior.

●—1940 (Most Likely)

Daniel M. "Dan" Dreiberg, future masked adventurer The Nite Owl, is born **[RPG3]** to William and Victoria Dreiberg **[BWNO]**. As the only child of wealthy parents, Dan is the sole heir to his father's fortune **[ALAN]**.

> **NOTE:** *Dan's middle initial appears in* The Watchmen Sourcebook.

> **CONFLICT:** *The question of Dan Dreiberg's birthdate is something of a nightmare. Before* Watchmen: Nite Owl *places Dan's birth in 1945, while timelines published in* The Film Companion *and the film's British press kit cite 1950, and a police file in the press kit specifies November 8, 1950.* Taking Out the Trash *offers a birth date of September 18, 1942, while* The Watchmen Sourcebook *cites September 18, 1940. Since Alan Moore's miniseries has him becoming The Nite Owl by the early 1960s and the* Sourcebook *has him graduating from Harvard in 1960, a birth year of 1950 is nonsensical; 1940 seems the most workable, though that would contradict his 1962 appearance as a teenager in* Before Watchmen: Nite Owl.

●—1940s

The Minutemen fight such American-born costumed villains as Mobster, who dresses like a 1920s Chicago gangster, and Spaceman, who commits crimes while clad in a pulp 1950s-style spacesuit **[WTFC]**. They eventually defeat Spaceman and display his ray-gun in their headquarters, alongside other confiscated weaponry **[ARTF]**.

●—1941

After being injured during a stabbing incident, Eddie Blake trades in his flimsy, yellow Comedian costume for leather armor **[ALAN]**.

> **NOTE:** *There is circumstantial evidence that Hollis Mason may have carried out the stabbing as retribution for Blake's attempted rape of Sally Jupiter. Not only does Mason harbor romantic feelings for Sally, but* Under the Hood *describes childhood fantasies of saving women from dangerous men. Moreover, since this occurs after Blake's ouster from The Minutemen, it seems unlikely that Mason would know the stabbing had even occurred unless he were there to witness it.*

During an interview, Hooded Justice describes Moloch as a "ringmaster"—a comment befitting a circus strongman **[RPG3]**.

> **NOTE:** *Given the revelation, in* Before Watchmen: Minutemen, *that Hooded Justice and circus strongman Rolf Müller are separate individuals, this is apparently just an unusual coincidence.*

MIND .... *The Mindscape of Alan Moore*	**RPG2** .... *DC Heroes Role Playing Module #235: Taking Out the Trash—Curses and Tears*	**VRL2** ..... Viral video: *The Keene Act and You*
MOBL .... *Watchmen: The Mobile Game*		**VRL3** ..... Viral video: *Who Watches the Watchmen? A Veidt Music Network (VMN) Special*
MOTN .... *Watchmen: The Complete Motion Comic*	**RPG3** .... *DC Heroes: The Watchmen Sourcebook*	
MTRO .... *Metro promotional newspaper cover wrap*	**RUBY** .... "Wounds," published in *The Ruby Files Volume One*	**VRL4** ..... Viral video: *World in Focus: 6 Minutes to Midnight*
NEWP .... *New Frontiersman promotional newspaper*	**SCR1** ..... Unfilmed screenplay draft: Sam Hamm	**VRL5** ..... Viral video: *Local Radio Station Report on 1977 Riots*
NEWW .... *New Frontiersman website*	**SCR2** ..... Unfilmed screenplay draft: Charles McKeuen	
NIGH ..... *Watchmen: The End Is Nigh, Parts 1 and 2*	**SCR3** ..... Unfilmed screenplay draft: Gary Goldman	**VRL6** ..... Viral videos (group of ten): *Veidt Enterprises Advertising Contest*
PKIT ...... *Watchmen film British press kit*	**SCR4** ..... Unfilmed screenplay draft: David Hayter (2002)	
PORT ..... *Watchmen Portraits*	**SCR5** ..... Unfilmed screenplay draft: David Hayter (2003)	**WAWA** ... *Watching the Watchmen*
REAL ..... Real life	**SCR6** ..... Unfilmed screenplay draft: Alex Tse	**WHOS** ... *Who's Who: The Definitive Directory of the DC Universe*
RPG1 .... *DC Heroes Role Playing Module #227: Who Watches the Watchmen?*	**SPOT** .... *DC Spotlight #1*	
	VRL1 ..... Viral video: *NBS Nightly News with Ted Philips*	**WTFC** .... *Watchmen: The Film Companion*

By age two, Adrian Veidt shows signs of being an extraordinary child, able to spell words like "genius" with his alphabet blocks **[BWOZ]**.

—February 1941

Pulp-fiction magazine *Detective Novel* publishes an issue containing complete novels by Frank Johnson and John L. Benton **[REAL, HOOD]**.

—December 7, 1941

Japan attacks a U.S. naval base at Pearl Harbor, a lagoon harbor on Oahu, Hawaii, causing the United States to declare war on Japan and enter World War II **[REAL]**.

—After December 7, 1941

The Comedian signs up to fight in World War II **[PKIT]**. The military trains Blake in counter-intelligence, advanced combat techniques, survival, sabotage, and more, then dispatches him and a U.S. Marine squad to Henderson Field, in Guadalcanal, Solomon Islands. Granted tangential authority over regional commanders and a uniform tailored to match his crime-fighting costume, Blake encounters hostile attitudes from several officers, including Captain Peterman, who calls him "a jackass in a shiny helmet." Painted on a wall is the phrase "Kilroy was here" **[BWMM]**.

During Blake's first command, he and his Marines are assigned to locate caves in which Japanese soldiers could be hiding. A sniper lures them into a minefield, killing six of his troops. Though deafened in the blast, Blake fires on the tree-line. He shoots the sniper, but the latter hits a Marine wearing a flamethrower, who lands on a mine, setting the field ablaze. Taking shrapnel in his side, The Comedian blacks out **[BWMM]**.

The next day, Blake awakens to find a scavenger and her son leaning over him. When he blacks out again, they alert the only surviving Marine, a Californian named Greg, and help him drag Blake to their cave, where she nurses him back to health. Greg and Blake swim to the beach in the dark, braving sharks and eels, and report in to Peterman, who orders an artillery barrage on the hills. Blake rushes to the cave to rescue his saviors, but arrives as a blast leaves the woman's scorched body stuck to her burnt skin. Peterman shoots her to end her misery, and Blake realizes that all enemies are dogs to be put down. That night, he sneaks into the captain's tent and slits his throat with a bayonet, then paints "Fuck Kilroy—Comedian was here" on the wall **[BWMM]**.

—December 1941

Around Christmas time, Sally Jupiter arranges a photo shoot for herself and Ursula Zandt, in order to send sexy photographs to U.S. troops overseas. Zandt has little use for the idea, and the two women end up insulting each other until Ursula leaves the set. Furious, Sally tells Larry Schexnayder that she wants The Silhouette gone **[BWMM]**.

—1942
John David Keene delivers his first public speech at age twelve while attending the prestigious Hunter College High School **[NEWW]**.

Artist Norman Rockwell paints a war-bonds poster of Sally Jupiter in her Silk Spectre costume. Rockwell poses her holding an American flag while standing atop an actor impersonating Adolf Hitler **[WTFC, PKIT, ARTF]**.

—January 1942
As Eddie Blake roughs up a Japanese explosives smuggler called Tojo, an FBI agent named Kaufax recruits him for U.S. government service **[BWMM]**. While performing covert duties in Manila, Philippines, he sustains a knife wound from an angry civilian, puncturing his right kidney. Dr. Edward Ross tends to his injury **[RPG3]**.

—January 6, 1942
Major G. Holland reactivates Nelson Gardner's military service, ordering him to report to North Carolina's Fort Bragg **[RPG3]**.

—January 1942 to April 1985
The Comedian serves as an operative for multiple branches, including the Office of Strategic Services (OSS), Army Intelligence, the Central Intelligence Agency (CIA), the Drug Enforcement Administration (DEA), and the U.S. Secret Service (USSS) **[RPG3]**.

—In or Before February 1942
Ursula Zandt and her girlfriend move into an apartment together in Manhattan **[RPG2]**.
> **NOTE:** *According to* Absolute Watchmen, *Alan Moore originally intended to depict Zandt as dating a much-older woman who worked as a sculptor.*

> **CONFLICT:** The Watchmen Sourcebook *identifies Zandt's lover as Dawn DeCarlo, while* Before Watchmen: Minutemen *names her Gretchen Slovak.* Minutemen *portrays her as a doctor, whereas the* Watchmen *film shows her wearing a nurse's outfit. The* New Frontiersman *website cites their address as Apartment 2371, Burns Street, but the* Sourcebook *offers an address of 771 Fifth Avenue, Apartment 32A.*

Byron Lewis attends a number of costumed meet-and-greets with Bill Brady for the National Bank of New York, in character as Mothman and Dollar Bill **[BWMM]**.

MIND .... *The Mindscape of Alan Moore*
MOBL .... *Watchmen: The Mobile Game*
MOTN .... *Watchmen: The Complete Motion Comic*
MTRO .... *Metro* promotional newspaper cover wrap
NEWP .... *New Frontiersman* promotional newspaper
NEWW .... *New Frontiersman* website
NIGH ..... *Watchmen: The End Is Nigh, Parts 1 and 2*
PKIT ...... *Watchmen* film British press kit
PORT ..... *Watchmen Portraits*
REAL ..... Real life
RPG1 .... *DC Heroes Role Playing Module #227: Who Watches the Watchmen?*

RPG2 .... *DC Heroes Role Playing Module #235: Taking Out the Trash—Curses and Tears*
RPG3 .... *DC Heroes: The Watchmen Sourcebook*
RUBY .... "Wounds," published in *The Ruby Files Volume One*
SCR1 ..... Unfilmed screenplay draft: Sam Hamm
SCR2 ..... Unfilmed screenplay draft: Charles McKeuen
SCR3 ..... Unfilmed screenplay draft: Gary Goldman
SCR4 ..... Unfilmed screenplay draft: David Hayter (2002)
SCR5 ..... Unfilmed screenplay draft: David Hayter (2003)
SCR6 ..... Unfilmed screenplay draft: Alex Tse
SPOT ..... *DC Spotlight #1*
VRL1 ..... Viral video: *NBS Nightly News with Ted Philips*

VRL2 ..... Viral video: *The Keene Act and You*
VRL3 ..... Viral video: *Who Watches the Watchmen? A Veidt Music Network (VMN) Special*
VRL4 ..... Viral video: *World in Focus: 6 Minutes to Midnight*
VRL5 ..... Viral video: *Local Radio Station Report on 1977 Riots*
VRL6 ..... Viral videos (group of ten): *Veidt Enterprises Advertising Contest*
WAWA ... *Watching the Watchmen*
WHOS ... *Who's Who: The Definitive Directory of the DC Universe*
WTFC .... *Watchmen: The Film Companion*

February 1942

Bill Brady is drafted into U.S. military service in the 3ʳᵈ Army **[RPG2]**, but the National Bank of New York arranges for his deferment **[BWMM]**. As a police officer, Hollis Mason is ineligible for drafting **[RPG2]**; though he tries to enlist, he is classified 4F—not acceptable for service in the Armed Forces—due to flat feet **[BWMM]**. Byron Lewis is classified as 4F as well **[BWMM]**. Hooded Justice avoids the draft entirely since his true identity is a complete mystery **[RPG2]**.

> **CONFLICT:** *In* The Watchmen Sourcebook, *Lewis is drafted into service and Brady does a tour of duty as well.*

Eddie Blake makes a name for himself as a war hero, with a camera crew capturing news footage of his exploits in the South Pacific **[ALAN]**. During the war, Blake fights alongside Major Montgomery Banner **[RPG2]**.

In or After February 1942

Hollis Mason and Ursula Zandt meet for coffee at Deli Madison and discuss World War II. Mason admits to feeling inadequate at not serving in the war, but she chalks that up to male pride, noting "The big fight is all around us, every day." He gives her the phone number of a police callbox that he checks hourly at ten past the hour, from 8:00 PM to 4:00 AM, in case she ever gets into trouble while fighting crime **[BWMM]**.

Later that day, the National Bank of New York opens a new branch. Unable to reach Byron Lewis, Bill Brady invites Hollis Mason to join him at a meet-and-greet for neighborhood children, where they perform superhero acrobatics and offer a pep talk about being good citizens. Afterwards, over beers, they discuss Nelson Gardner's relationship with Hooded Justice. Brady points out that The Bible calls homosexuality a mortal sin and worries that it could tarnish The Minutemen's image **[BWMM]**.

That night, Ursula Zandt spies on a gentlemen's club to photograph members' illicit activities. When she sees a little girl waiting to be molested, Ursula starts shooting the older men. Shot in the hip, she grabs the girl and runs out of the club, but a second bullet passes through her shoulder, fatally hitting the child in the chest and causing both to plummet down a staircase. Carrying the girl's body to a church, she calls Hollis Mason for help, then hallucinates Jesus saying he loves her—though it is actually Mason telling her this. He rushes Ursula to her girlfriend, a doctor, who tends to her wounds. The next day, Hollis buys fresh flowers for Zandt from a local woman, Mrs. Musante, but is embarrassed at his own obliviousness upon realizing Ursula is a lesbian **[BWMM]**.

March 1, 1942

After receiving a military draft notice, Byron Lewis registers as a conscientious objector.

Rather than using his family's congressional influence to secure a safe, comfortable posting, he writes a letter to the Secretary of Defense, refusing to take part in eradicating human life in what he sees as a repugnant war of the wealthy. To that end, he requests assignment to the Army Medical Corps as a field orderly, near the front line **[RPG3]**.

> **CONFLICT:** *In* Before Watchmen: Minutemen, *Lewis tries to enlist but is classified 4F (not acceptable for service in the Armed Forces).*

—After March 1, 1942

Byron Lewis is assigned as a medical aide at a Red Cross station in Europe **[RPG2]**.

—1942, After February

Hollis Mason, one of the few Minutemen remaining in the United States **[RPG2]**, battles Walter "The Screaming Skull" Zileski on several occasions, arresting the supervillain dozens of times **[ALAN, RPG3]**. Mason adds Zileski's weapon, an "electra-vibe," to the team's trophy room **[RPG3]**.

> **NOTE:** *Alan Moore's miniseries sets Mason's battles with The Screaming Skull in the 1940s. The specific year appears in* Taking Out the Trash.

The Minutemen foil several sabotage attempts by Hans von Krupp **[RPG3]**, a Nazi operative called Captain Axis who takes orders directly from the Third Reich **[RPG2]**. Mason floors Captain Axis with a powerful left hook **[ALAN]**.

> **CONFLICT:** *Gary Goldman's unproduced 1992 screenplay sets Mason's takedown of Captain Axis on August 5, 1944, contradicting* The Watchmen Sourcebook.

—Between February 1942 and December 1945

Bill Brady earns two Purple Hearts during his military service in World War II **[RPG3]**.

> **CONFLICT:** *In* Before Watchmen: Minutemen, *Brady avoids military service due to the National Bank of New York's efforts on his behalf to obtain a deferment.*

—November 1942

Pulp-fiction magazine *Black Mask* publishes an issue containing short stories by Robert Reeves, Dale Clark, and Norbert Davis **[REAL, HOOD]**.

—1942 to 1946

The Manhattan Project, a research and development venture during World War II, produces the United States' first nuclear weapons, with support from Canada and the United Kingdom. The project is overseen by Major General Leslie Groves of the U.S. Army Corps of Engineers, with physicist J. Robert Oppenheimer, the director of the Los Alamos National Laboratory, designing the bombs **[REAL]**.

MIND .... *The Mindscape of Alan Moore*	**RPG2** .... *DC Heroes Role Playing Module #235: Taking Out the Trash—Curses and Tears*	**VRL2**..... Viral video: *The Keene Act and You*
MOBL..... *Watchmen: The Mobile Game*		**VRL3**..... Viral video: *Who Watches the Watchmen? A Veidt Music Network (VMN) Special*
MOTN.... *Watchmen: The Complete Motion Comic*	**RPG3** .... *DC Heroes: The Watchmen Sourcebook*	
MTRO.... *Metro promotional newspaper cover wrap*	**RUBY** .... "Wounds," published in *The Ruby Files Volume One*	**VRL4**..... Viral video: *World in Focus: 6 Minutes to Midnight*
NEWP.... *New Frontiersman promotional newspaper*	**SCR1**..... Unfilmed screenplay draft: Sam Hamm	**VRL5**..... Viral video: *Local Radio Station Report on 1977 Riots*
NEWW... *New Frontiersman website*	**SCR2**..... Unfilmed screenplay draft: Charles McKeuen	
NIGH ..... *Watchmen: The End Is Nigh, Parts 1 and 2*	**SCR3**..... Unfilmed screenplay draft: Gary Goldman	**VRL6**..... Viral videos (group of ten): *Veidt Enterprises Advertising Contest*
PKIT...... *Watchmen film British press kit*	**SCR4**..... Unfilmed screenplay draft: David Hayter (2002)	
PORT..... *Watchmen Portraits*	**SCR5**..... Unfilmed screenplay draft: David Hayter (2003)	**WAWA**... *Watching the Watchmen*
REAL..... Real life	**SCR6**..... Unfilmed screenplay draft: Alex Tse	**WHOS** ... *Who's Who: The Definitive Directory of the DC Universe*
RPG1 .... *DC Heroes Role Playing Module #227: Who Watches the Watchmen?*	**SPOT**..... *DC Spotlight #1*	
	VRL1 ..... Viral video: *NBS Nightly News with Ted Philips*	**WTFC** .... *Watchmen: The Film Companion*

—1943

At age four and hungry for knowledge, Adrian Veidt reads all 24 volumes of his father's encyclopedia set. He discovers Sir Francis Bacon's philosophy that knowledge is power, and he agrees with the concept **[BWOZ]**.

—April 14 to August 2, 1943

While serving in the U.S. Navy, John F. Kennedy commands Motor Torpedo Boat *PT-109* in the South Pacific **[REAL]**. During this period, Kennedy forms a friendship with Eddie Blake, who becomes close with the entire Kennedy clan **[BWCO]**, despite his own hard-right political leanings **[ALAN]**.

—August 2, 1943

Motor Torpedo Boat *PT-109* collides with Japanese destroyer *Amagiri*, killing two of John Kennedy's crew **[REAL]**.

—November 1943

While performing covert duties in Bougainville, Papua New Guinea, Eddie Blake sustains a punctured eardrum due to a Japanese mortar burst, causing a permanent ten percent hearing loss. Dr. Edward Ross tends to Blake's injuries **[RPG3]**.

—Early 1940s

Sally Jupiter becomes one of the most popular wartime pinup girls **[WTFC]**.

Stellar Studios produces a World War II propaganda film titled *Okinawa Dawn*, portraying The Comedian as heroic, selfless, and merciful as he spares the life of a Japanese soldier whom he has defeated in armed combat **[RPG3]**.

Moloch perpetrates several heists, some successfully, others thwarted by the remaining Minutemen. He is incarcerated multiple times, but always manages to escape thanks to loyal thugs and money stashed in offshore accounts. Jacobi is sometimes drawn to the prison chapel, especially during Catholic mass, enjoying the ritual and the beauty of the Latin liturgy. Each time, however, he resists the pull of religion **[BWMO]**.

A shy and awkward child **[MATL]**, traumatized by his father's mistreatment of his mother **[BWNO]**, Dan Dreiberg grows up close with his Uncle Alan (his father's brother) and Aunt Greta **[RPG3]**.

—1944

Eddie Blake serves alongside a U.S. Marine whose future son, Greg, will date Laurie Jupiter **[BWSS]**.

—In or Before 1945

Jon Osterman snacks on a box of Karamal Korn while working to repair a watch. He inadvertently bites down on a small toy included in the box—a charm molded in the form of a blue-skinned man **[BWDM]**.

> **NOTE:** *The charm presages Osterman's transformation into Dr. Manhattan.*

Adrian Veidt hangs a poster on his bedroom wall, featuring a giant one-eyed, squid-like monster and the phrase "The Thing from Outer Space" **[BWOZ]**.

> **NOTE:** *This poster foreshadows Veidt's plan, during his adult years, to save the world by faking a deadly attack by an extra-dimensional, squid-like creature.*

—1945

While performing covert duties in Tokyo, Japan, Eddie Blake contracts syphilis. Dr. Edward Ross tends to Blake's condition **[RPG3]**.

The Minutemen engage in a pitched battle with Captain Axis on an Allied submarine located near the Arctic Circle. Hooded Justice tosses the supervillain into the ocean, and he never surfaces **[RPG3]**.

Adrian Veidt enters public school at age six. Although his parents are intellectually unremarkable and exhibit no genetic advantages, he proves exceptionally bright, scoring perfectly on early test papers **[ALAN]**—so high above the curve, in fact, that the principal accuses him of cheating. Adrian's father convinces her that the results were a fluke and will not be duplicated, then tells his son to maintain a low profile so no one will realize how smart he is or consider him a freak. Adrian does as he is told, but considers this unfair **[BWOZ]**.

—February 23, 1945

During World War II's Battle of Iwo Jima, The Comedian raises a U.S. flag atop Japan's Mount Suribachi **[WTFC]**.

> **NOTE:** *In the real world, the flag-planting, famously captured on film by Joe Rosenthal, was carried out by five U.S. Marines and a U.S. Navy hospital corpsman.*

—Before June 5, 1945

Eddie Blake bets a non-commissioned U.S. Army officer that he can kill seven Japanese prisoners-of-war with only eight bullets at a distance of fifty paces. Witnesses report the executions to military authorities **[RPG3]**.

MIND .... *The Mindscape of Alan Moore*
MOBL .... *Watchmen: The Mobile Game*
MOTN .... *Watchmen: The Complete Motion Comic*
MTRO .... *Metro* promotional newspaper cover wrap
NEWP .... *New Frontiersman* promotional newspaper
NEWW .... *New Frontiersman* website
NIGH ..... *Watchmen: The End Is Nigh, Parts 1 and 2*
PKIT ...... *Watchmen* film British press kit
PORT ..... *Watchmen Portraits*
REAL ..... Real life
RPG1 .... *DC Heroes Role Playing Module #227: Who Watches the Watchmen?*

RPG2 .... *DC Heroes Role Playing Module #235: Taking Out the Trash—Curses and Tears*
RPG3 .... *DC Heroes: The Watchmen Sourcebook*
RUBY .... "Wounds," published in *The Ruby Files Volume One*
SCR1 ..... Unfilmed screenplay draft: Sam Hamm
SCR2 ..... Unfilmed screenplay draft: Charles McKeuen
SCR3 ..... Unfilmed screenplay draft: Gary Goldman
SCR4 ..... Unfilmed screenplay draft: David Hayter (2002)
SCR5 ..... Unfilmed screenplay draft: David Hayter (2003)
SCR6 ..... Unfilmed screenplay draft: Alex Tse
SPOT ..... *DC Spotlight #1*
VRL1 ..... Viral video: *NBS Nightly News with Ted Philips*

VRL2 ..... Viral video: *The Keene Act and You*
VRL3 ..... Viral video: *Who Watches the Watchmen? A Veidt Music Network (VMN) Special*
VRL4 ..... Viral video: *World in Focus: 6 Minutes to Midnight*
VRL5 ..... Viral video: *Local Radio Station Report on 1977 Riots*
VRL6 ..... Viral videos (group of ten): *Veidt Enterprises Advertising Contest*
WAWA ... *Watching the Watchmen*
WHOS ... *Who's Who: The Definitive Directory of the DC Universe*
WTFC .... *Watchmen: The Film Companion*

June 5, 1945

Eddie Blake is court-martialed for killing the seven Japanese POWs. To keep his identity a secret, his trial is conducted by the Joint Chiefs of Staff [**RPG3**].

August 6, 1945

During the final stage of World War II, the U.S. military's B-29 Superfortress bomber *Enola Gay* drops a five-ton uranium-based atomic bomb, code-named "Little Boy," over Hiroshima, Japan. The detonation creates a blast equivalent to 15,000 tons of TNT and kills 80,000 people, with tens of thousands more dying from wounds and radiation poisoning [**REAL**].

> **CONFLICT:** *In the* Watchmen *film adaptation, the plane's name is changed to* Miss Jupiter, *while a timeline in the film's British press kit cites the bomber as a B-52 called* Sally Jupiter.

Before August 7, 1945

Josef Osterman learns about Albert Einstein's theories regarding time and special relativity, and wonders whether the world needs watchmakers if time is not a constant [**ALAN**].

August 7, 1945

In his family's Brooklyn home, sixteen-year-old Jon Osterman practices repairing his father's old pocket-watch, intending to follow in Josef's footsteps. The elder Osterman shows him the latest edition of the *New York Times*, bearing the headline "Atomic Bomb Dropped on Hiroshima," and deems atomic science the future. He tells Jon to become a physicist instead of a watchmaker, then drops the watch parts out a window [**ALAN**].

> **NOTE:** *The* Times' *actual headline on that date was "First Atomic Bomb Dropped on Japan; Missile Is Equal to 20,000 Tons of TNT; Truman Warns Foe of a 'Rain of Ruin.'"*

August 7, 1945 (Alternate Reality)

In another quantum reality, Jon Osterman asks his father Josef to bring him to a Brooklyn Dodgers baseball game. Josef's resultant good mood causes him to react less angrily when the Hiroshima bombing is announced, and he does not push his son to put aside watchmaking in favor of a career in physics—thus preventing Jon from eventually becoming Dr. Manhattan [**BWDM**].

August 9, 1945

The United States drops a plutonium implosion-type bomb, code-named "Fat Man," on the Japanese city of Nagasaki. Approximately 40,000 people die on this day, with the same amount dying during the coming months due to the effects of radiation [**REAL**].

Before August 22, 1945

King Taylor Productions again renames *Silk Spectre: The Sally Jupiter Story*, deeming the second

---

title, *Sally Jupiter: Law in Its Lingerie*, too long. The new name, conceived by an employee named Maurie, is *She-Devils in Silk*. This latest version retains plot elements from the movie's Saturday-morning matinee approach, and combines 1939 footage of Sally with new material shot using a younger actor, Cherry Dean, who resembles Sally from the back **[ALAN]**.

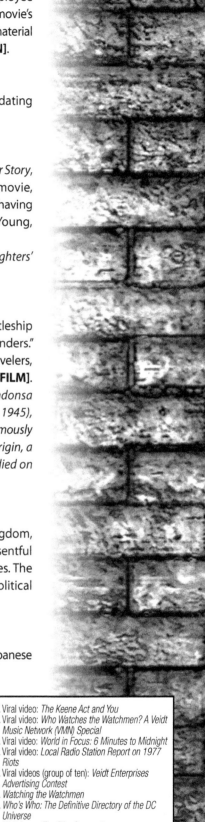

—August 22, 1945
Edmund "King" Taylor, of King Taylor Productions, writes a letter to Sally Jupiter updating her on the progress of her film, now retitled *She-Devils in Silk* **[ALAN]**.

—After August 22, 1945
King Taylor Productions releases the film originally titled *Silk Spectre: The Sally Jupiter Story*, under its fourth name (at least), *Silk Swingers of Suburbia*. The cheaply made B-movie, hack-directed by Edmund "King" Taylor, stars Cherry Dean in top billing (despite her having filled in for Sally), Rod Donovan (likely King himself under a pseudonym), Dana Young, Lola Booker, and Harry J. Peters **[ALAN]**.

> **NOTE:** *A poster for* Silk Swingers of Suburbia *hangs on the wall of the crime- fighters' headquarters in the* Watchmen *film.*

—September 2, 1945
World War II ends when Japan officially signs surrender documents aboard the battleship USS *Missouri* **[REAL]**. The *New York Gazette*'s front page reads "Victory! Japan Surrenders." As Americans celebrate in the streets, Ursula Zandt and her lover kiss among the revelers, unafraid of what others might think. The kiss is captured on film by a photographer **[FILM]**.

> **NOTE:** *The kiss mirrors a real-world exchange between U.S. sailor George Mendonsa and Austrian dental assistant Greta Zimmer Friedman on V-J Day (August 14, 1945), when Mendonsa spontaneously kissed Friedman in Times Square—a moment famously captured on film by photographer Alfred Eisenstaedt. Paying homage to that origin, a sailor walks by as Silhouette kisses her lover in the* Watchmen *film. Friedman died on September 8, 2016.*

—After September 2, 1945
The victorious great powers (the United States, the Soviet Union, the United Kingdom, France, and China) form the United Nations Security Council. The U.S.S.R. grows resentful when the United States takes credit for ending the war, despite huge Soviet losses. The Soviets and Americans emerge as rival superpowers, sparking a decades-long political and military tension known as the Cold War **[REAL]**.

—September 11, 1945
The Joint Chiefs of Staff, presiding over Eddie Blake's court-martial for killing seven Japanese prisoners-of-war, dismiss all charges, citing a lack of evidence **[RPG3]**.

MIND .... *The Mindscape of Alan Moore*
MOBL .... *Watchmen: The Mobile Game*
MOTN .... *Watchmen: The Complete Motion Comic*
MTRO .... *Metro promotional newspaper cover wrap*
NEWP .... *New Frontiersman promotional newspaper*
NEWW .... *New Frontiersman website*
NIGH ..... *Watchmen: The End Is Nigh, Parts 1 and 2*
PKIT ...... *Watchmen film British press kit*
PORT ..... *Watchmen Portraits*
REAL ..... *Real life*
RPG1 .... *DC Heroes Role Playing Module #227: Who Watches the Watchmen?*

RPG2 .... *DC Heroes Role Playing Module #235: Taking Out the Trash—Curses and Tears*
RPG3 .... *DC Heroes: The Watchmen Sourcebook*
RUBY .... *"Wounds," published in* The Ruby Files Volume One
SCR1 ..... *Unfilmed screenplay draft: Sam Hamm*
SCR2 ..... *Unfilmed screenplay draft: Charles McKeuen*
SCR3 ..... *Unfilmed screenplay draft: Gary Goldman*
SCR4 ..... *Unfilmed screenplay draft: David Hayter (2002)*
SCR5 ..... *Unfilmed screenplay draft: David Hayter (2003)*
SCR6 ..... *Unfilmed screenplay draft: Alex Tse*
SPOT ..... *DC Spotlight #1*
VRL1 ..... *Viral video: NBS Nightly News with Ted Philips*

VRL2 ..... *Viral video: The Keene Act and You*
VRL3 ..... *Viral video: Who Watches the Watchmen? A Veidt Music Network (VMN) Special*
VRL4 ..... *Viral video: World in Focus: 6 Minutes to Midnight*
VRL5 ..... *Viral video: Local Radio Station Report on 1977 Riots*
VRL6 ..... *Viral videos (group of ten): Veidt Enterprises Advertising Contest*
WAWA ... *Watching the Watchmen*
WHOS ... *Who's Who: The Definitive Directory of the DC Universe*
WTFC ... *Watchmen: The Film Companion*

—In or Before December 1945

Serial killer Geoffrey Dean systemically hunts down and murders several New York bowling alley pinsetters. Calling himself The Liquidator, he leaves an "L" scrawled in blood at the scene of each crime as his signature **[RPG3]**.

> **NOTE:** *It is unknown whether Geoffrey Dean is related to Taylor Dean, a fellow mass murderer whom Rorschach takes down in 1966, in* Before Watchmen: Nite Owl.

—December 1945

The National Bank of New York releases an advertising campaign reporting that Dollar Bill is returning home from service in World War II, and that gangsters should thus beware since the crime-fighter will again protect National Bank's investments **[RPG3]**.

—December 10, 1945

Dollar Bill disguises himself as a pinsetter to lure The Liquidator into a trap at Brooklyn's Hill Valley Bowl, in Bensonhurst. After the serial killer attacks him, The Silhouette and Mothman join the melee, forcing the killer to flee the scene. A high-speed chase ends at the George Washington Bridge, where The Liquidator strikes a stalled car while bound for New Jersey. A battle ensues, and Silhouette sends him plummeting off the bridge into icy waters. Mothman glides down, but fails to save him. The killer's body is not recovered from the river. Though presumed dead, he survives the fall **[RPG3]**.

—December 11, 1945

The *New York Gazette* reports on The Liquidator's apparent death, noting that police have not revealed whether they have determined his true identity **[RPG3]**.

—December 12, 1945—11:15 AM

The Liquidator seeks treatment at Saint Albion Hospital. Signing in using his actual name, Geoffrey Dean, he pretends to be homeless to prevent anyone from realizing who he is, and claims to have fallen into the river while drunk. The hospital treats him for a broken arm and exposure, then releases him **[RPG3]**.

—December 12, 1945 to May 31, 1946

Geoffrey Dean resumes his life of crime as The Liquidator **[RPG2, WTFC]**.

—1945 to 1949

Heeding his father's request to maintain a low profile so as to prevent others from realizing how smart he is, Adrian Veidt struggles to remain innocuous. He earns average grades, avoids participating in sports, forms no friendships, and finds himself victimized by bullies **[BWOZ]**.

Part IV:
A DEATH IN THE FAMILY
(1946–1955)

—Mid-1940s

Dan Dreiberg attends Tom's River Public Grade School, in New Jersey **[RPG3]**.

Hollis Mason's neighbor, Tino Musante, fathers a son, Tino Jr. **[BWMM]**.

—In or Before 1946

A superhero comic book called *Bluecoat and Scout* gains widespread popularity. In the series, the masked duo battle Japanese spies and other villains **[BWMM]**.

> **NOTE:** *In the* Watchmen *universe, superhero comic books fade away circa 1939, to be replaced by pirate comics.* Bluecoat and Scout's *popularity almost a decade later could be due to a temporary nostalgic fad, or to the anti-Japanese sentiment that pervaded the era.*

Gretchen Slovak begins dabbling in psychotherapy. She records hours of audiotaped notes discussing her thoughts about Ursula Zandt's cases, and about the individual members of The Minutemen. She deems Byron Lewis "a brilliant, gentle man," noting her concern that his frailties might consume him, and outlines her and Ursula's suspicion that Hooded Justice may be a serial killer of children **[BWMM]**.

Byron Lewis purchases a deserted machine shop containing a large sub-basement, which he transforms into a secret workplace. He and Hollis Mason often hang out there in their spare time as Byron tinkers with his flying suit and gadgets **[BWMM]**.

—Before January 3, 1946

Nelson Gardner returns home from his reactivated military service and resumes his secret relationship with Hooded Justice **[RPG3]**.

The *New York Gazette* re-publicizes Hooded Justice's past comments about Adolf Hitler, creating a public-relations nightmare for Larry Schexnayder, who knows the vigilante would be unwilling to issue a retraction at a press conference **[RPG3]**.

At Schexnayder's suggestion, Sally Jupiter takes a break from crime-fighting **[RPG3]**.

—January 3, 1946

Larry Schexnayder writes a letter to Sally Jupiter, reporting that Nelson Gardner and Hooded Jupiter are constantly fighting, with Gardner claiming the other doesn't love him anymore. Larry urges Sally to return from her break and help dispel the tension **[RPG3]**.

—March 29, 1946—Morning

The Minutemen catch their maid, Frieda Jenkins, stealing money from the group's petty-cash fund. Jenkins is fired, but the crime-fighters opt not to press charges, given her otherwise exemplary service **[RPG3]**.

—March 30, 1946

The *New York Gazette* interviews Larry Schexnayder regarding The Minutemen's decision to dismiss Frieda Jenkins from employment **[RPG3]**.

—April 11, 1946

The National Regaler advertises an upcoming issue in which Minutemen ex-maid Frieda Jenkins discusses Silk Spectre's attraction to Hooded Justice, Mothman's alcoholism, and what Dollar Bill *really* thinks of the National Bank of New York. The ad also promises "startling revelations" about The Silhouette's sexual orientation **[RPG3]**.

> **NOTE:** *The newspaper's name and motif spoof those of supermarket tabloid* The National Enquirer. *Jenkins does not expose the homosexual relationship between Hooded Justice and Nelson Gardner, but she may be unaware of that.*

—Between April 11 and May 13, 1946

New York Gazette investigative reporter Alfred Richter publishes a documented article backing up *The National Regaler*'s claims about The Silhouette's sexuality. *Chicago Tribune* reporter Michael Quinn writes a similar piece. Combined, the three articles create a major controversy for The Minutemen **[RPG3]**.

—In or Before May 1946

Byron Lewis begins eating hashish to alleviate chronic back and knee pain **[BWMM]**.

—May 4, 1946

The *New York Gazette*'s "Screen Reviews" column **[RPG3]** pans *Silk Swingers of Suburbia*, misspelling Sally Jupiter's name as "Sally Juniper" and calling the movie too awful even to be dignified with the term "pornography" **[ALAN]**.

—May 13, 1946

The National Regaler outs The Silhouette as living with another woman **[RPG3]**. Larry Schexnayder convinces The Minutemen to expel her from the group to avoid bad publicity. The vote is unanimous, despite Nelson Gardner and Hooded Justice also being gay **[ALAN, RPG2, RPG3]**, and Ursula does not bother to attend the meeting **[BWMM]**. Schexnayder issues a press release announcing Zandt's expulsion, saying the team will not seek a replacement. The *New York Gazette* publishes a brief article about the release **[RPG3]**, written by William Ball. The article, titled "Sex Scandal Ousts Silhouette from Minutemen," cites an unnamed source claiming that Zandt and The Silk Spectre were once lesbian lovers before their falling out **[PORT]**.

> **NOTE:** *Alan Moore's miniseries dates Zandt's ouster in 1946, as does a timeline packaged with* The End Is Nigh—The Complete Experience. *The specific date is provided in* Taking Out the Trash *and* The Watchmen Sourcebook.

That night, Hollis Mason meets Ursula Zandt on the roof of Deli Madison to inform her of The Minutemen's decision, which he claims was four to two against her. He suggests that he, Ursula, and Byron Lewis continue working together privately, and she agrees. She hands him an envelope containing photographs of several missing children, possibly the victims of the same killer, and asks that he look into their cases **[BWMM]**.

> **CONFLICT:** *Alan Moore's miniseries, as well as* Taking Out the Trash *and* The Watchmen Sourcebook, *establish the expulsion vote to be unanimous. It's likely that Mason, feeling guilty, tells Ursula otherwise for the sake of their friendship.*

—May 13, 1946 and Beyond

Although she dislikes Ursula Zandt personally, Sally Jupiter long regrets voting in favor of expulsion since Nelson Gardner and Hooded Justice are allowed to remain members despite being homosexuals **[ALAN, RPG2]**. Hollis Mason also harbors shame about the vote for the rest of his life **[RPG3]**.

—Late May 1946

Weeks after their rooftop meeting, Hollis Mason provides Ursula Zandt with information about the missing children, copied from police files. She and her girlfriend drop out of sight for an extended period of time to conduct an investigation at Marina Bay, in Quincy, Massachusetts **[BWMM]**.

MIND .... *The Mindscape of Alan Moore*
MOBL .... *Watchmen: The Mobile Game*
MOTN .... *Watchmen: The Complete Motion Comic*
MTRO .... *Metro promotional newspaper cover wrap*
NEWP .... *New Frontiersman promotional newspaper*
NEWW .... *New Frontiersman website*
NIGH ...... *Watchmen: The End Is Nigh, Parts 1 and 2*
PKIT ...... *Watchmen film British press kit*
PORT ..... *Watchmen Portraits*
REAL ..... Real life
RPG1 .... *DC Heroes Role Playing Module #227: Who Watches the Watchmen?*

RPG2 .... *DC Heroes Role Playing Module #235: Taking Out the Trash—Curses and Tears*
RPG3 ... *DC Heroes: The Watchmen Sourcebook*
RUBY .... "Wounds," published in *The Ruby Files Volume One*
SCR1 ..... Unfilmed screenplay draft: Sam Hamm
SCR2 ..... Unfilmed screenplay draft: Charles McKeuen
SCR3 ..... Unfilmed screenplay draft: Gary Goldman
SCR4 ..... Unfilmed screenplay draft: David Hayter (2002)
SCR5 ..... Unfilmed screenplay draft: David Hayter (2003)
SCR6 ..... Unfilmed screenplay draft: Alex Tse
SPOT ..... *DC Spotlight #1*
VRL1 ..... Viral video: *NBS Nightly News with Ted Philips*

VRL2 ..... Viral video: *The Keene Act and You*
VRL3 ..... Viral video: *Who Watches the Watchmen? A Veidt Music Network (VMN) Special*
VRL4 ..... Viral video: *World in Focus: 6 Minutes to Midnight*
VRL5 ..... Viral video: *Local Radio Station Report on 1977 Riots*
VRL6 ..... Viral videos (group of ten): *Veidt Enterprises Advertising Contest*
WAWA ... *Watching the Watchmen*
WHOS ... *Who's Who: The Definitive Directory of the DC Universe*
WTFC .... *Watchmen: The Film Companion*

May 31, 1946

Ursula Zandt takes down The Liquidator once again **[RPG2, WTFC]**. Following his arrest, police find a newspaper clipping of the *New York Gazette* report about The Silhouette's ouster from The Minutemen, her name circled in the article **[RPG3]**.

Before June 1946

Ursula Zandt finally identifies the child-killer she has sought since September 1940. Her suspect: German immigrant Rolf Müller, a strongman with the Big Top Circus, the show dates of which line up with each child's disappearance. Given the type of mask Müller wears during his performances, Zandt recognizes him as the Nazi torturer who murdered her sister Blanche in 1938—and believes that he may be Hooded Justice **[BWMM]**.

June 1946

The Comedian returns home from Europe. Considered a war hero, he is honored alongside U.S. soldiers and is featured on the cover of *Life* magazine **[BWMM]**.

Six weeks after Ursula Zandt's expulsion from The Minutemen **[ALAN]**, she calls Hollis Mason from the Marina Bay Motel, near Boston, asking that he meet her the following night to discuss their missing-child case **[BWMM]**. That same night, however, The Liquidator murders Zandt and her girlfriend **[BWMM, RPG3]** as revenge for their past encounters **[RPG2]**. He slays the two women in their home, then scrawls the phrase "Lesbian Whores" on one wall in their blood **[NEWW]**, and his usual signature, a blood-scrawled "L," on another. Blood covers the carpet, furniture, and walls **[RPG3]**.

> **NOTE:** The Watchmen Sourcebook *identifies Zandt's slain lover as Dawn DeCarlo, while* Before Watchmen: Minutemen *names her Gretchen Slovak.*

A neighbor in Apartment 2373, F.R. Williams, hears a commotion and calls the police. Attending officers R.F. Megson and R. Mayer discover the bodies **[NEWW]**, and investigator Detective Sergeant Phil Maddox finds a pornographic magazine of women under the bed. The bodies remain unidentified for an hour, until Patrolman Adam Green enters the crime scene and recognizes Zandt from news coverage **[RPG3]**.

> **NOTE:** *The* New Frontiersman *website lists the couple's address as Apartment 2371, Burns Street, whereas* The Watchmen Sourcebook *provides an address of 771 Fifth Avenue, Apartment 32A.*

The coroner, Dr. D. Moore, pronounces the cause of death to be gunshot wounds, dubbing Zandt's lover "Jane Doe" **[NEWW]**, though others present ascertain the woman's identity, given news reports of The Silhouette's lesbian scandal **[RPG3]**. No weapons are found at the scene **[NEWW]**. On the bed near their bodies is a newspaper bearing the headline "Sex Scandal Ousts Silhouette from Minutemen" **[FILM]**.

ABSO .... *Watchmen Absolute Edition*	**BWOZ**.... *Before Watchmen—Ozymandias*	• Film: *Batman v Superman: Dawn of Justice Ultimate Edition*
ALAN..... Alan Moore's *Watchmen* miniseries	**BWRO** ... *Before Watchmen—Rorschach*	• Film: *Justice League*
ARCD .... *Minutemen Arcade*	**BWSS** ... *Before Watchmen—Silk Spectre*	**CLIX** ......HeroClix figure pack-in cards
ARTF ..... *Watchmen: The Art of the Film*	**CHEM**.... My Chemical Romance music video: "Desolation Row"	**DECK**..... *DC Comics Deck-Building Game—Crossover Pack 4: Watchmen*
BLCK..... *Tales of the Black Freighter*	**CMEO** .... *Watchmen* cameos in comics, TV, and film:	**DURS** .... *DC Universe: Rebirth Special* volume 1 issue #1
BWCC .. *Before Watchmen—The Crimson Corsair*	• Comic: *Astonishing X-Men* volume 3 issue #6	**FILM** ..... *Watchmen* theatrical film
BWCO .. *Before Watchmen—Comedian*	• Comic: *Hero Hotline* volume 1 issue #5	**HOOD** .... *Under the Hood* documentary and dust-jacket prop reproduction
BWDB ... *Before Watchmen—Dollar Bill*	• Comic: *Kingdom Come* volume 1 issue #2	**JUST** ..... *Watchmen: Justice Is Coming*
BWDM .. *Before Watchmen—Dr. Manhattan*	• Comic: *Marvels* volume 1 issue #4	**MATL** .... Mattel Club Black Freighter figure pack-in cards
BWMM.. *Before Watchmen—Minutemen*	• Comic: *The Question* volume 1 issue #17	
BWMO .. *Before Watchmen—Moloch*	• TV: *Teen Titans Go!* episode #82, "Real Boy Adventures"	
BWNO ... *Before Watchmen—Nite Owl*	• Film: *Man of Steel*	

NOTE: *The coroner is presumably named after* Watchmen *creator Alan Moore.*

CONFLICT: *Moore's miniseries dates Zandt's death in 1946, with no month indicated. The* Watchmen Sourcebook *sets her ouster in May and* Taking Out the Trash *specifies May 13—but since Moore's story places her death six weeks after her departure from The Minutemen, that would indicate late June at the earliest.* Taking Out the Trash *has her death occurring only two weeks later instead of six; The* Watchmen Sourcebook *assumes a date of May 27, 1946; a police report published on the* New Frontiersman *website moves the murders to December 11, 1954; and timelines in* The Film Companion *and in the film's British press kit also cite 1954.*

While helping Byron Lewis repair his wings, Hollis Mason is stunned when a radio broadcast announces Ursula Zandt's murder **[BWMM]**. Bill Brady hears the radio coverage as well. Despite his religious-based condemnation of homosexuality, he raises a toast in her memory **[BWDB]**. Mason arranges for Zandt and her partner to be buried in adjoining, unmarked graves **[BWMM]**.

Nelson Gardner receives a tip that The Liquidator is hiding in Manhattan's Tenderloin redlight district, then summons The Minutemen so they can bring him down. Sally Jupiter beats the others to the killer's hideout and brutally murders him. When Gardner and Hooded Justice arrive, they find her waiting amidst a bloody mess. Sally tells them they never should have ousted Ursula Zandt since she was the best of them, then quits The Minutemen, leaving the men to clean up. Returning home, she informs Larry Schexnayder of her decision to leave the team **[BWMM]**.

> **NOTE:** *Although Sally quits The Minutemen, she does not officially retire from crimefighting until 1947, per Alan Moore's miniseries.*

Two days later, Byron Lewis and a weepy Hollis Mason visit the cemetery to pay their respects to Ursula Zandt and her girlfriend. After they leave, Sally visits their graves, apologizes for not standing up for Ursula during The Minutemen's vote to expel her, and tells her about The Liquidator's fate. Eddie Blake shows up at the grave site and opens up to Sally about his brutal experiences during World War II **[BWMM]**.

Byron Lewis and Hollis Mason arrange to meet at Ursula Zandt's home that evening to search for her child-killer evidence, but Byron gets drunk and fails to show up. Mason finds photos of dead children, a copy of Robert Louis Stevenson's poetry collection *A Child's Garden of Verses*, and Telefunken audio reels belonging to Gretchen Slovak, labeled with the names of individual Minutemen team members. He places these in a bag and brings them to Lewis's hideaway, unaware that Hooded Justice is in the apartment and has overheard their discussion **[BWMM]**.

MIND .... *The Mindscape of Alan Moore*	**RPG2** .... *DC Heroes Role Playing Module #235: Taking Out the Trash—Curses and Tears*	**VRL2** ..... Viral video: *The Keene Act and You*
MOBL .... *Watchmen: The Mobile Game*		**VRL3** ..... Viral video: *Who Watches the Watchmen? A Veidt Music Network (VMN) Special*
MOTN .... *Watchmen: The Complete Motion Comic*	**RPG3** .... *DC Heroes: The Watchmen Sourcebook*	
MTRO .... *Metro* promotional newspaper cover wrap	**RUBY** .... "Wounds," published in *The Ruby Files Volume One*	**VRL4** ..... Viral video: *World in Focus: 6 Minutes to Midnight*
NEWP .... *New Frontiersman* promotional newspaper	**SCR1** ..... Unfilmed screenplay draft: Sam Hamm	**VRL5** ..... Viral video: *Local Radio Station Report on 1977 Riots*
NEWW ... *New Frontiersman* website	**SCR2** ..... Unfilmed screenplay draft: Charles McKeuen	
NIGH ..... *Watchmen: The End Is Nigh, Parts 1 and 2*	**SCR3** ..... Unfilmed screenplay draft: Gary Goldman	**VRL6** ..... Viral videos (group of ten): *Veidt Enterprises Advertising Contest*
PKIT ...... *Watchmen* film British press kit	**SCR4** ..... Unfilmed screenplay draft: David Hayter (2002)	
PORT ..... *Watchmen Portraits*	**SCR5** ..... Unfilmed screenplay draft: David Hayter (2003)	**WAWA** .. *Watching the Watchmen*
REAL ..... Real life	**SCR6** ..... Unfilmed screenplay draft: Alex Tse	**WHOS** ... *Who's Who: The Definitive Directory of the DC Universe*
RPG1 .... *DC Heroes Role Playing Module #227: Who Watches the Watchmen?*	**SPOT** ..... *DC Spotlight #1*	
	VRL1 ..... Viral video: *NBS Nightly News with Ted Philips*	**WTFC** .... *Watchmen: The Film Companion*

Byron Lewis and Hollis Mason listen to Gretchen's tapes and learn about the death of Ursula's sister Blanche at the hands of a hooded butcher in 1938. That same night, Hooded Justice awakens screaming from a nightmare of childhood abuse. Nelson Gardner is stunned to see his lover sobbing **[BWMM]**.

—Before June 30, 1946
On the order of President Franklin D. Roosevelt, the War Relocation Authority (WRA) forcibly relocates nearly 120,000 Japanese-Americans to internment camps, following Japan's attack on Pearl Harbor; more than half of these individuals are U.S. citizens **[REAL]**. Among them are a boy who reads *Bluecoat and Scout* comic books, as well as his parents and grandfather. After the boy's mother dies in the camp, he, his father, and his granddad join a Japanese nationalist group out of a need for revenge **[BWMM]**.

> **NOTE:** *The family's internment is undated, but in the real world, those forced into relocation were freed when the WRA was disbanded on this date.*

—In or Before July 1946
Individuals named A. Sawyer and M. Cxxx pass away and are buried in a New York cemetery **[BWDB]**.

> **NOTE:** *These names are visible on gravestones at Bill Brady's funeral. "Cxxx" is actually one of the names, and is not a typographical error on this author's part.*

—Before July 23, 1946
Bill Brady grows increasingly self-assured during his time with The Minutemen. His success at crime-fighting restores the confidence and empowerment he once had as a high-school and college athlete **[BWDB]**.

—July 23, 1946
Three men rob National Bank of New York's Manhattan branch. Bill Brady intercedes, blocking their bullets with a statue of Dollar Bill. Two thugs run out the door, and he tries to follow **[BWDB]**. When his cape becomes entangled in the revolving door, the thieves shoot him at point-blank range. Unable to extricate himself, Brady dies instantly **[ALAN]**. Police apprehend the three thieves ten minutes after they leave the bank, holding them without bail at the New York Police Department's central city lockup **[RPG3]**.

> **NOTE:** *Alan Moore's miniseries dates Brady's death in 1946. The specific date is provided in* Taking Out the Trash *and* The Watchmen Sourcebook.

> **CONFLICT:** *Timelines published in* The Film Companion *and in the film's British press kit move his death to 1951, contradicting Moore's comic.*

—After July 23, 1946

The remaining Minutemen attend Dollar Bill's highly publicized funeral, along with Larry Schexnayder and bank executives Abie, Dewey, Cheatem, and Howe. Captain Metropolis delivers a stirring eulogy. Sally Jupiter comforts Byron Lewis, who is badly shaken by such a pointless loss. The crime-fighters notice a child wearing a Dollar Bill costume outside the cemetery, and are consoled that his memory lives on **[BWDB]**.

—July 24, 1946

The *New York Gazette* reports Dollar Bill's death, without mentioning his true identity **[RPG3]**.

—July 1946 and Beyond

In the wake of Bill Brady's murder, Byron Lewis grows increasingly depressed and starts drinking heavily **[ALAN]**.

—1946 to 1949

Scientist Elmo Greensback decides to become a superhero, then spends three years designing a flying costume and a weapon that he dubs an electro gun **[RPG3]**.

—In or Before 1947

Hollis Mason develops romantic feelings for Sally Jupiter, but never learns if she feels the same way since he lacks the courage to ask her out on a date **[HOOD]**.

The *New York Gazette* publishes several articles about Sally Jupiter's exploits, including "Grand Central Station Burglars Caught?" and "Silk Spectre Foils Greenwich Village Burglary Ring" **[FILM]**.

Larry Schexnayder writes a letter to Sally Jupiter informing her that Nelson Gardner believes Hooded Justice is cheating on him with other men, and is getting too rough during love-making. Larry expresses concern about the publicity backlash Sally could face—since she had posed as the strongman's girlfriend—if any of these men go to the police with convincing bruises. The agent suggests that he and Sally leave the crime-fighting game since it cannot last, and that they make their relationship more than business by moving in together out west **[ALAN]**.

> **NOTE:** *This letter bears a date of February 3, 1948, which must be discarded since that would be after Sally retires and marries Larry in 1947.*

A supervillain called The King of Skin begins committing crimes. The Minutemen have several encounters with him **[BWMM]**.

> **NOTE:** *The King of Skin's true identity and area of crime are unknown.*

Nelson Gardner purchases a boat for use in fighting crime **[BWMM]**.

MIND .... *The Mindscape of Alan Moore*
MOBL .... *Watchmen: The Mobile Game*
MOTN .... *Watchmen: The Complete Motion Comic*
MTRO .... *Metro* promotional newspaper cover wrap
NEWP .... *New Frontiersman* promotional newspaper
NEWW .... *New Frontiersman* website
NIGH ..... *Watchmen: The End Is Nigh, Parts 1 and 2*
PKIT ...... *Watchmen* film British press kit
PORT ..... *Watchmen Portraits*
REAL ..... Real life
RPG1 .... *DC Heroes Role Playing Module #227: Who Watches the Watchmen?*

RPG2 .... *DC Heroes Role Playing Module #235: Taking Out the Trash—Curses and Tears*
RPG3 .... *DC Heroes: The Watchmen Sourcebook*
RUBY .... "Wounds," published in *The Ruby Files Volume One*
SCR1 ..... Unfilmed screenplay draft: Sam Hamm
SCR2 ..... Unfilmed screenplay draft: Charles McKeuen
SCR3 ..... Unfilmed screenplay draft: Gary Goldman
SCR4 ..... Unfilmed screenplay draft: David Hayter (2002)
SCR5 ..... Unfilmed screenplay draft: David Hayter (2003)
SCR6 ..... Unfilmed screenplay draft: Alex Tse
SPOT ..... *DC Spotlight #1*
VRL1 ..... Viral video: *NBS Nightly News with Ted Philips*

VRL2 ..... Viral video: *The Keene Act and You*
VRL3 ..... Viral video: *Who Watches the Watchmen? A Veidt Music Network (VMN) Special*
VRL4 ..... Viral video: *World in Focus: 6 Minutes to Midnight*
VRL5 ..... Viral video: *Local Radio Station Report on 1977 Riots*
VRL6 ..... Viral videos (group of ten): *Veidt Enterprises Advertising Contest*
WAWA ... *Watching the Watchmen*
WHOS ... *Who's Who: The Definitive Directory of the DC Universe*
WTFC .... *Watchmen: The Film Companion*

—1947

As Moloch the Mystic, Edgar Jacobi becomes a major figure in the criminal underworld [**RPG2**].

Sally Jupiter officially retires from crime-fighting [**ALAN**], and the remaining Minutemen throw her a goodbye party [**FILM**].

> *CONFLICT: Alan Moore's miniseries sets Sally's retirement in 1947, as does a timeline packaged with* The End Is Nigh—The Complete Experience. *Timelines published in* The Film Companion *and in the film's British press kit move her retirement to 1953. In the* Watchmen *film, Sally is pregnant at her retirement party, contradicting Moore's series, in which Laurie is born a few years later. Moreover, Ursula Zandt and her girlfriend attend the party in the film, despite having died by this point in the comic, as does Eddie Blake, despite seven years having passed since his ouster.*

Hollis Mason and Byron Lewis work Ursula Zandt's last case, listening to hours of Gretchen Slovak's recorded notes for evidence of the child-killer's identity. Meanwhile, The Minutemen find the costumed-adventurer fad fading, with few supervillains left other than Moloch and The King of Skin. Without Larry Schexnayder coordinating their efforts, the team ceases to conduct regular meetings. For five weeks, Lewis and Mason have no contact whatsoever with Hooded Justice and Nelson Gardner [**BWMM**].

—In or Before June 1947

A Japanese father and son, who had joined a terrorist group after the boy's mother died in a U.S. internment camp, come to view the group's activities as wrong. When a dozen members—including the boy's grandfather—steal enriched uranium from Los Alamos to cause a meltdown in New York City as revenge for the Hiroshima and Nagasaki bombings, the two contact Nelson Gardner, clad as comic-book superheroes Bluecoat and Scout, to seek his help in foiling the plot. Gardner summons Byron Lewis and Hollis Mason to his headquarters, but Mason doesn't take the duo seriously, given the characters' fictional nature, until Bluecoat reveals the meltdown plans [**BWMM**].

That night at 10:00, the terrorists take hostages in the Statue of Liberty, announcing false demands to stall while the meltdown builds. The Minutemen rush to the monument with Bluecoat and Scout to prevent the disaster. Mothman drops a satchel from above filled with tracers, tear gas, and Chinese fireworks, while the others storm Liberty Island and run up the stairs to the torch. Bluecoat is shot and plummets to his death. Nite Owl shoots Scout's grandfather as the youth stops the meltdown, but the boy receives a fatal radiation dose in the process. It is The Minutemen's finest hour, but the government keeps the incident a secret to avoid public panic [**BWMM**].

NOTE: Sam Hamm's unproduced 1989 screenplay also features a terrorist attack on the Statue of Liberty, as do rewrites of that script by Charles McKeuen and Gary Goldman.

Byron Lewis pulls some strings to arrange for Hollis Mason and Scout to be treated at a private clinic. The child dies six days later, but Mason checks out fine thanks to the statue's metal structure having protected him from the radiation **[BWMM]**.

The Chicago Atomic Scientists, an international research team previously involved in the Manhattan Project **[REAL]**, learn about the barely averted Statue of Liberty attack and decide to alert the world about the dangers of atomic power **[BWMM]**. To that end, they add a symbol to the June 1947 cover of the *Bulletin of the Atomic Scientists*: the Doomsday Clock, the hands of which visualize the likelihood of possible global catastrophe, such as climate change or nuclear war **[REAL]**.

—June 1947 to 1949
Nelson Gardner grows depressed about the government cover-up of his Liberty Island victory, feeling useless as a warrior without a reward of glory **[BWMM]**, and the dwindling number of masked villains takes its toll on the superhero craze in general. Without opponents similarly fashioned, Hollis Mason begins to feel silly wearing his Nite Owl costume. Gradually, each of the remaining Minutemen loses his passion for costumed crime-fighting **[ALAN]**.

—Late 1947
Sally Jupiter marries Larry Schexnayder, and her former Minutemen teammates attend the wedding. Hollis Mason, who shows up in costume as The Nite Owl, deems the union a perfect pairing since they both love to see her get attention. During the reception, however, Sally has sex with another man in a bathroom **[BWMM]**.

The Minutemen hold out hope that Sally will someday return to the team, but this never happens. Recognizing that the age of the superhero will soon end, Larry Schexnayder officially steps down as the group's publicist **[ALAN]**. Having missed his chance to tell Sally how he feels about her, Hollis Mason never marries **[HOOD]**.

—1947 to 1955
Byron Lewis and Hollis Mason continue working Ursula Zandt's unresolved child-killer case, determined to identify the murderer and bring closure to her final investigation. Despite their canvasing and patrolling efforts, the killer eludes them, with another child or two turning up dead every year **[BWMM]**.

MIND .... *The Mindscape of Alan Moore*	**RPG2** .... *DC Heroes Role Playing Module #235: Taking Out the Trash—Curses and Tears*	**VRL2** ..... Viral video: *The Keene Act and You*
MOBL.... *Watchmen: The Mobile Game*		**VRL3** ..... Viral video: *Who Watches the Watchmen? A Veidt Music Network (VMN) Special*
MOTN.... *Watchmen: The Complete Motion Comic*	**RPG3** .... *DC Heroes: The Watchmen Sourcebook*	
MTRO.... *Metro* promotional newspaper cover wrap	**RUBY** .... "Wounds," published in *The Ruby Files Volume One*	**VRL4** ..... Viral video: *World in Focus: 6 Minutes to Midnight*
NEWP.... *New Frontiersman* promotional newspaper	**SCR1**..... Unfilmed screenplay draft: Sam Hamm	**VRL5** ..... Viral video: *Local Radio Station Report on 1977 Riots*
NEWW... *New Frontiersman* website	**SCR2**..... Unfilmed screenplay draft: Charles McKeuen	
NIGH ..... *Watchmen: The End Is Nigh, Parts 1 and 2*	**SCR3**..... Unfilmed screenplay draft: Gary Goldman	**VRL6** ..... Viral videos (group of ten): *Veidt Enterprises Advertising Contest*
PKIT...... *Watchmen* film British press kit	**SCR4**..... Unfilmed screenplay draft: David Hayter (2002)	
PORT..... *Watchmen Portraits*	**SCR5**..... Unfilmed screenplay draft: David Hayter (2003)	**WAWA**... *Watching the Watchmen*
REAL..... Real life	**SCR6**..... Unfilmed screenplay draft: Alex Tse	**WHOS** ... *Who's Who: The Definitive Directory of the DC Universe*
RPG1 .... *DC Heroes Role Playing Module #227: Who Watches the Watchmen?*	**SPOT**..... *DC Spotlight #1*	
	VRL1 ..... Viral video: *NBS Nightly News with Ted Philips*	**WTFC** .... *Watchmen: The Film Companion*

—1947 to 1967

Edgar Jacobi operates a vice-den for criminals to congregate and enjoy themselves with sexual and gambling diversions **[ALAN]**. His empire includes prostitution houses, fetish clubs, drug dens, and anything else that might prove the corruption of the "respectable" world. Despite his success, he loathes his ugliness and drowns his sorrows in business, booze, and the company of his own hookers. One of the women becomes pregnant with his child, but has an abortion. Upon overhearing her disgust at what the baby might have looked like, Moloch gives her $2,000 and puts her on a train out of town **[BWMO]**.

During his peak years, Moloch is hailed as "King of the Underworld." He develops numerous connections with street gangs and crime syndicates, becoming one of the planet's most dangerous active criminal geniuses, with a global mob of more than a hundred employees. A shrewd, clever manipulator, he executes complex plots to throw off his enemies, while perpetrating numerous Devil-themed crimes and operating front businesses such as The 666 Club and The Inferno. During this period, he battles The Comedian, who remains his arch-nemesis for decades **[ALAN]**.

—Late 1940s to Mid-1950s

John David Keene attends Yale University, where he spends seven years studying political science **[NEWW]**.

While growing up, Dan Dreiberg shows little interest in his father's banking career, despite the elder Dreiberg's hope that his son will follow in his footsteps. More fascinated with the concept of flying, Dan spends his time thinking about mythology, sword-and-sorcery stories, Pegasus, flying carpets, birds, airplanes, and the exploits of his crime-fighting idol, The Nite Owl **[ALAN]**.

—1948

Jon Osterman begins attending Princeton University to pursue an education in atomic science **[ALAN]**.

—May 15, 1948

Nelson Gardner insults a black cab driver for parking in front of a puddle outside Minutemen headquarters, causing him to splash mud on his costume. Angered by Gardner's racist comments, Byron Lewis punches him in the face, and police are called in to break up the fight. Throughout the melee, Hooded Justice stands nearby, laughing. A spokesman for The Minutemen tells the media that the "misunderstanding" between Captain Metropolis and Mothman has been patched up **[RPG3]**.

> **NOTE:** It's unclear who the spokesman is since Larry Schexnayder no longer represents the crime-fighters.

ABSO .... *Watchmen Absolute Edition*	**BWOZ**.... *Before Watchmen—Ozymandias*	• Film: *Batman v Superman: Dawn of Justice Ultimate*
ALAN..... Alan Moore's *Watchmen* miniseries	**BWRO** ... *Before Watchmen—Rorschach*	*Edition*
ARCD .... *Minutemen Arcade*	**BWSS** ... *Before Watchmen—Silk Spectre*	• Film: *Justice League*
ARTF ..... *Watchmen: The Art of the Film*	**CHEM** .... My Chemical Romance music video: "Desolation Row"	**CLIX** ...... HeroClix figure pack-in cards
BLCK..... *Tales of the Black Freighter*	**CMEO** .... *Watchmen* cameos in comics, TV, and film:	**DECK**..... *DC Comics Deck-Building Game—Crossover*
BWCC ... *Before Watchmen—The Crimson Corsair*	• Comic: *Astonishing X-Men* volume 3 issue #6	*Pack 4: Watchmen*
BWCO ... *Before Watchmen—Comedian*	• Comic: *Hero Hotline* volume 1 issue #5	**DURS** .... *DC Universe: Rebirth Special* volume 1 issue #1
BWDB ... *Before Watchmen—Dollar Bill*	• Comic: *Kingdom Come* volume 1 issue #2	**FILM** ..... *Watchmen* theatrical film
BWDM .. *Before Watchmen—Dr. Manhattan*	• Comic: *Marvels* volume 1 issue #4	**HOOD** .... *Under the Hood* documentary and dust-jacket
BWMM.. *Before Watchmen—Minutemen*	• Comic: *The Question* volume 1 issue #17	prop reproduction
BWMO .. *Before Watchmen—Moloch*	• TV: *Teen Titans Go!* episode #82, "Real Boy Adventures"	**JUST** ...... *Watchmen: Justice Is Coming*
BWNO ... *Before Watchmen—Nite Owl*	• Film: *Man of Steel*	**MATL** .... Mattel Club Black Freighter figure pack-in cards

—May 16, 1948

Free underground newspaper *The Harlem Teetotaler* publishes an article about the Mothman-Metropolis brawl. The writer questions who will protect the constitutional rights of minorities if even masked adventurers hold bigoted beliefs. The *New York Gazette* also covers the incident. Despite at least twenty-five people having overheard the conversation, the mainstream press fails to report Gardner's racial slurs **[RPG3]**.

—Between 1948 and April 18, 1955

While at Princeton, Jon Osterman attends a lecture given by Albert Einstein **[ALAN]**.

> **NOTE:** *No date is provided, but this must occur between Osterman's arrival at the university and Einstein's death.*

—1948 to 1959

Some of Jon Osterman's fellow students at Princeton view him as too stuffy, organized, and narrow to have fun or be spontaneous **[BWDM]**. Despite this, he forms friendships with several students from New Jersey **[ALAN]**.

—In or Before 1949

Dan Dreiberg reads Arthurian legends and deems Sir Galahad his favorite knight since he is brave and good, always does the right thing, and is strong enough to always defeat his enemies. Dan's father tells him such heroes no longer exist **[RPG3]**.

The Screaming Skull spends three months setting up a forty-member scheme to destroy The Minutemen's Manhattan headquarters building, but inadvertently blows up the wrong brownstone **[RPG3]**.

Adrian Veidt begins earning money by taking on a morning newspaper route **[BWOZ]**.

—1949

After three years spent preparing to be a superhero, scientist Elmo Greensback perfects his flying costume and a weapon he dubs an electro gun. Once finished, he calls in the only available person—his janitor, small-time hood Bob Krankk—to demonstrate his costume. Impressed, Krankk fatally shoots Greensback and steals the suit so he can become a supervillain **[RPG3]**.

With Ursula Zandt and Bill Brady dead, Sally Jupiter retired, and most of their enemies either in prison or focused on less glamorous activities, The Minutemen officially disband **[ALAN]**. The breakup is a quiet one, without scandal or drama **[BWMM]**. Byron Lewis retires from crime-fighting **[RPG2]**, falling further into alcoholism and drug abuse **[BWMM]**, while Hollis Mason, Nelson Gardner, and Hooded Justice continue their efforts individually

MIND .... *The Mindscape of Alan Moore*
MOBL .... *Watchmen: The Mobile Game*
MOTN .... *Watchmen: The Complete Motion Comic*
MTRO .... *Metro promotional newspaper cover wrap*
NEWP .... *New Frontiersman promotional newspaper*
NEWW .... *New Frontiersman website*
NIGH ..... *Watchmen: The End Is Nigh, Parts 1 and 2*
PKIT ...... *Watchmen film British press kit*
PORT ..... *Watchmen Portraits*
REAL ..... *Real life*
RPG1 .... *DC Heroes Role Playing Module #227: Who Watches the Watchmen?*

RPG2 .... *DC Heroes Role Playing Module #235: Taking Out the Trash—Curses and Tears*
RPG3 .... *DC Heroes: The Watchmen Sourcebook*
RUBY .... "Wounds," published in *The Ruby Files Volume One*
SCR1 ..... Unfilmed screenplay draft: Sam Hamm
SCR2 ..... Unfilmed screenplay draft: Charles McKeuen
SCR3 ..... Unfilmed screenplay draft: Gary Goldman
SCR4 ..... Unfilmed screenplay draft: David Hayter (2002)
SCR5 ..... Unfilmed screenplay draft: David Hayter (2003)
SCR6 ..... Unfilmed screenplay draft: Alex Tse
SPOT ..... *DC Spotlight #1*
VRL1 ..... Viral video: *NBS Nightly News with Ted Philips*

VRL2 ..... Viral video: *The Keene Act and You*
VRL3 ..... Viral video: *Who Watches the Watchmen? A Veidt Music Network (VMN) Special*
VRL4 ..... Viral video: *World in Focus: 6 Minutes to Midnight*
VRL5 ..... Viral video: *Local Radio Station Report on 1977 Riots*
VRL6 ..... Viral videos (group of ten): *Veidt Enterprises Advertising Contest*
WAWA ... *Watching the Watchmen*
WHOS .... *Who's Who: The Definitive Directory of the DC Universe*
WTFC .... *Watchmen: The Film Companion*

[RPG2]. Mason considers retiring as well, but his determination to solve Zandt's child-murder case keeps him in the game [BWMM].

> CONFLICT: *Alan Moore's miniseries sets the group's disbanding in 1949, as does a timeline packaged with* The End Is Nigh—The Complete Experience. *Timelines published in* The Film Companion *and in the film's British press kit cite 1954.*

At age nine, while attending Tom's River Public Grade School, Dan Dreiberg pens an essay titled "When I Grow Up," expressing his wish to be a knight like Sir Galahad and become friends with other knights; live in Washington, D.C., so the President can call on him when necessary; and fight wars and embark on quests in the interim. Another essay, "My Hobby," explores Dan's love of bird-watching, fascination with owls, and desire to be a scientist [RPG3].

When Adrian Veidt is ten years old, a schoolyard bully named Jerry beats him up and steals his lunch, aided by two other boys. His parents offer to intervene, but Adrian prefers to deal with it himself. He enrolls at a kung fu dojo, enduring months of daily beatings and lunch thefts while secretly training to defend himself. After graduating with honors in record time, he awaits the next attack and warns Jerry to walk away. When the bully ignores the warning, Adrian avoids every punch, shattering Jerry's kneecap with a single kick. The others run away in panic, and Jerry is permanently crippled. Adrian is expelled, until Friedrich buys the school a new library so he can stay enrolled. Upset that his father had to pay for his justified actions, Adrian stops hiding his talents [BWOZ].

—March 3, 1949

As Jon Osterman repairs a watch in the Princeton library, a fellow student tries to coerce him to join her on a group hike to a lake. Though attracted to her shapely figure, Jon declines, preferring to finish his watch repair [BWDM].

—August 16, 1949

The *New York Gazette* runs a front-page story about the supervillain Moloch, titled "Mystic's Reign of Terror Spreads" [HOOD].

—September 24, 1949

The *New York Gazette*'s headline reads "Russ Have A-Bomb" [FILM]. The article, written by William Ball, claims that Russia possesses a nearly completed atomic bomb, following reports of heightened security at a Soviet testing site at the Kazakhstan steppe [ARTF]. One of Sylvia Kovacs' prostitution clients reads the paper while awaiting his turn to have sex with her [FILM].

> NOTE: *In the real world, the* Los Angeles Times' *headline for this same date was "Truman Says Russ Have A-Bomb."*

ABSO .... *Watchmen Absolute Edition*
ALAN ..... Alan Moore's *Watchmen* miniseries
ARCD .... *Minutemen Arcade*
ARTF ..... *Watchmen: The Art of the Film*
BLCK ..... *Tales of the Black Freighter*
BWCC ... *Before Watchmen—The Crimson Corsair*
BWCO ... *Before Watchmen—Comedian*
BWDB ... *Before Watchmen—Dollar Bill*
BWDM .. *Before Watchmen—Dr. Manhattan*
BWMM .. *Before Watchmen—Minutemen*
BWMO .. *Before Watchmen—Moloch*
BWNO ... *Before Watchmen—Nite Owl*

BWOZ .... *Before Watchmen—Ozymandias*
BWRO ... *Before Watchmen—Rorschach*
BWSS ... *Before Watchmen—Silk Spectre*
CHEM .... My Chemical Romance music video: "Desolation Row"
CMEO .... *Watchmen* cameos in comics, TV, and film:
• Comic: *Astonishing X-Men* volume 3 issue #6
• Comic: *Hero Hotline* volume 1 issue #5
• Comic: *Kingdom Come* volume 1 issue #2
• Comic: *Marvels* volume 1 issue #4
• Comic: *The Question* volume 1 issue #17
• TV: *Teen Titans Go!* episode #82, "Real Boy Adventures"
• Film: *Man of Steel*

• Film: *Batman v Superman: Dawn of Justice Ultimate Edition*
• Film: *Justice League*
CLIX ...... HeroClix figure pack-in cards
DECK ..... *DC Comics Deck-Building Game—Crossover Pack 4: Watchmen*
DURS .... *DC Universe: Rebirth Special* volume 1 issue #1
FILM ..... *Watchmen* theatrical film
HOOD .... *Under the Hood* documentary and dust-jacket prop reproduction
JUST ..... *Watchmen: Justice Is Coming*
MATL .... Mattel Club Black Freighter figure pack-in cards

CONFLICT: *A version of this newspaper, produced as a prop for the* Watchmen *film, bears the date August 15, 1950.*

—In or After 1949

The Minutemen give up their lease of the J.D. Dorchester building housing their Manhattan headquarters **[RPG3]**. Nelson Gardner also abandons the Freedom Tower, his base at the abandoned Canada Malting Company factory, and moves back to New York City **[BWMM]**.

Following The Minutemen's breakup, a new villain emerges: Bob "Buzzbomb" Krankk, who uses a flying suit and electro gun that he stole from inventor Elmo Greensback after killing the man. The first time Krankk dons the costume, the former janitor mentally snaps, proclaiming himself invincible. Though a frequent foe of Hollis Mason, he never succeeds at any crime, yet he sees every encounter as a victory—even when sent to jail. Buzzbomb tries to steal the U.S. Constitution and actually manages to hold the document for several minutes until Nite Owl and local police beat him senseless, after which Krankk is sentenced to New York City's Rikers Island jail complex **[RPG3]**.

Some critics accuse the disbanded Minutemen of performing street theater while ignoring atrocities around the world **[WTFC]**.

—1949 to at Least 1986

Bob "Buzzbomb" Krankk serves time at Rikers Island, during which he claims to rule the world from his "island palace" **[RPG3]**.

—1940s or 1950s

William Dreiberg teaches his son Dan how to care for the pigeons living in a coop outside their home in Tom's River, New Jersey **[RPG3]**. But more often, he beats young Dan instead of showing him love **[BWNO]**.

—1940s and Beyond

From a young age, Walter Kovacs focuses on the immorality of society and comes to view the world around him as a disgusting plague **[MATL]**.

—Before 1950

Salvatore Rizzoli, the head of a prominent crime family, is succeeded by his son Anthony Rizzoli **[RPG3]**, also known as Anthony Vitoli **[RPG2]** and Underboss **[RPG3, NIGH]**. Shortly after Salvatore's death, the Rizzoli family becomes embroiled in a five-family gang war, from which they emerge victorious. Underboss incorporates two rival gangs into the Rizzoli hierarchy, greatly increasing his family's power **[RPG3]**.

MIND .... *The Mindscape of Alan Moore*
MOBL.... *Watchmen: The Mobile Game*
MOTN.... *Watchmen: The Complete Motion Comic*
MTRO.... *Metro* promotional newspaper cover wrap
NEWP.... *New Frontiersman* promotional newspaper
NEWW... *New Frontiersman* website
NIGH ..... *Watchmen: The End Is Nigh, Parts 1 and 2*
PKIT...... *Watchmen* film British press kit
PORT..... *Watchmen Portraits*
REAL..... Real life
RPG1 .... *DC Heroes Role Playing Module #227: Who Watches the Watchmen?*

RPG2 ..... *DC Heroes Role Playing Module #235: Taking Out the Trash—Curses and Tears*
RPG3 .... *DC Heroes: The Watchmen Sourcebook*
RUBY .... "Wounds," published in *The Ruby Files Volume One*
SCR1..... Unfilmed screenplay draft: Sam Hamm
SCR2..... Unfilmed screenplay draft: Charles McKeuen
SCR3..... Unfilmed screenplay draft: Gary Goldman
SCR4..... Unfilmed screenplay draft: David Hayter (2002)
SCR5..... Unfilmed screenplay draft: David Hayter (2003)
SCR6..... Unfilmed screenplay draft: Alex Tse
SPOT..... *DC Spotlight #1*
VRL1 ..... Viral video: *NBS Nightly News with Ted Philips*

VRL2 ..... Viral video: *The Keene Act and You*
VRL3 ..... Viral video: *Who Watches the Watchmen? A Veidt Music Network (VMN) Special*
VRL4 ..... Viral video: *World in Focus: 6 Minutes to Midnight*
VRL5 ..... Viral video: *Local Radio Station Report on 1977 Riots*
VRL6 ..... Viral videos (group of ten): *Veidt Enterprises Advertising Contest*
WAWA... *Watching the Watchmen*
WHOS ... *Who's Who: The Definitive Directory of the DC Universe*
WTFC .... *Watchmen: The Film Companion*

—Before 1950 to 1965

With Underboss in charge, the Rizzoli family's criminal empire dominates organized crime throughout New York City for more than fifteen years **[RPG3]**.

—In or Before the 1950s

The Gila Flats Test Base, a scientific research facility directed by Professor Milton Glass, is established in Arizona **[ALAN]**. Scientists at the base conduct experiments to subtract particles from an atomic pattern while leaving the governing electromagnetic pattern intact **[ABSO]**. Gila Flats' Weapons Testing Center separates gluons and gluinos by shattering their intrinsic fields, thereby creating a weapon providing instantaneous destruction on the scale of an atomic bomb, but without fallout and contamination. Since eliminating A-bombs would prove futile, Glass's team hopes to replace them with something more manageable and less likely to result in deadly accidents **[RPG3]**.

> **CONFLICT:** The Watchmen Sourcebook *erroneously places the base in White Lake, New Mexico.*

Dan Dreiberg idolizes The Nite Owl's crime-fighting exploits and fills his bedroom with pennants, magazines, news clippings, and other memorabilia of his hero **[BWNO]**.

Nelson Gardner begins a strict regimen of Canadian Air Force exercises **[ALAN]**.

> **NOTE:** *In Alan Moore's miniseries, Gardner stays in shape thanks to a regimen of Canadian Air Force exercises. However, there is no evidence that he actually serves in that military organization.*

—1950

Walter Kovacs walks in on his mother selling her body for money. Hearing Sylvia and her client (a married man) moaning, he thinks she is being hurt. The man leaves, creeped out by the child's presence, and pays her only five dollars for interrupted services. Sylvia beats her son, calling him an "ugly little bastard," and says she should have had an abortion. Walter suffers lifelong emotional scars from such abuse **[ALAN, WTFC]**.

> **NOTE:** *This event is undated in Alan Moore's miniseries. A timeline published in* The Film Companion *sets it in 1950.*

The Screaming Skull commits his last known criminal scheme **[RPG3]**.

—February 9, 1950

Senator Joseph McCarthy requests that the Federal Bureau of Investigation (FBI) sweep its files for possible subjects of interest, to aid House Un-American Activities Committee (HUAC) efforts to root out communist sympathizers **[RPG3]**.

> **NOTE:** *Although the real-world committee's hearings are sometimes conflated with*

McCarthy's anti-communist investigations, McCarthy served in the U.S. Senate, not the House of Representatives, and thus was not a member of HUAC. In Watchmen *continuity, he seems to have been directly involved in HUAC's activities.*

—Early 1950

Sally Jupiter has a one-time dalliance with Eddie Blake. Though he previously tried to rape Sally, her secret love for him prevents her from sustaining her anger. Their single encounter leaves her pregnant with Blake's child **[ALAN]**.

> **CONFLICT:** *Alan Moore's miniseries establishes their encounter as occurring in the summer, whereas* Taking Out the Trash *sets their affair in March 1950. Since the child, Laurie Jupiter, is born in December, a summer conception seems unlikely unless she is born prematurely.*

—June 25, 1950 to July 27, 1953

North and South Korea wage war against each other. During the conflict, a U.S.-led United Nations force fights for the South, while China and the Soviet Union help the North **[REAL]**. The Comedian fights in the so-called Korean War, alongside Major Montgomery Banner **[RPG2]**.

—Before August 15, 1950

The U.S. government dispatches those masked adventurers still active to Russia, to help prevent an atomic war between the United States and the Soviet Union **[ARTF]**.

New York City Mayor Vincent R. Impellitteri expresses concerns regarding The Minutemen's potential association with his predecessor, William O'Dwyer, who had resigned following a corruption scandal **[ARTF]**.

> **NOTE:** *In the real world, O'Dwyer did not retire until August 31.*

—August 15, 1950

The *New York Gazette* reports on the crime-fighters' trip to Russia, in an article by Jon Harris titled "Local Heroes Fight for Justice on Home Ground." A companion story, "Watchmen Not Worried By Reds," by Caroline Driscoll, quotes Silk Spectre as saying Russians are no different than Americans—both are scared people trying to protect themselves. The Comedian is quoted as disagreeing with this sentiment **[ARTF]**.

> **CONFLICT:** *This pair of articles, printed in a prop newspaper for the* Watchmen *film, has all members of The Minutemen taking part in the Russian mission. By this point in* Watchmen *history, however, Eddie Blake has long been estranged from the team, Sally Jupiter and Byron Lewis have retired, and Ursula Zandt and Bill Brady have been dead for years, with Hollis Mason, Nelson Gardner, and Hooded Justice each working solo.*

October 7, 1950

FBI Director J. Edgar Hoover writes a memo to Senator Joseph McCarthy, noting that his files indicate Mothman may be Byron Lewis, a "Negro rights" activist who was involved with a Stalinist newspaper at Bryce University, and who registered as a conscientious objector during World War II. If Lewis and Mothman are the same person, Hoover warns, there could be consequences **[RPG3]**.

December 2, 1950

Laurel Jane "Laurie" Jupiter, future masked adventurer The Silk Spectre, is born to Sally Jupiter. Larry Schexnayder helps Sally raise the baby, and Sally refuses to let Laurie's biological father, Eddie Blake, be part of her life **[ALAN]**. The couple let the press believe that Laurie is Larry's daughter **[RPG3]**.

> **NOTE:** *According to* Who Watches the Watchmen?, *Laurie is born with the last name Jupiter, then changes her surname to Juspeczyk after turning sixteen.*

> **CONFLICT:** *Both Alan Moore's miniseries and the* Watchmen *film set Laurie's birth in 1949, as do* Before Watchmen: Minutemen *and a timeline packaged with* The End Is Nigh—The Complete Experience, *but this is problematic since she turns 20 years old in 1970, necessitating a 1950 birth year.* Taking Out the Trash *gives her birthdate as December 2, 1950, which makes more sense, while timelines published in* The Film Companion *and in the film's British press kit both cite 1953; a police file in the press kit specifies June 22, 1953.* The Watchmen Sourcebook, *oddly enough, indicates two different dates: December 1 and December 2, 1949.*

A future criminal named Billy is born **[RPG1]**.

1950 to 1966

The United States operates without organizations of masked adventurers, though The Minutemen's exploits individually inspire the next generation of heroes. During this period, Nelson Gardner grows frustrated watching as specialized law enforcement stands still while crime continues to thrive **[ALAN]**.

In or Before 1951

An abusive ex-lover of Sylvia Kovacs comes back into her life. Her son Walter, after overhearing the man plotting to kill him and make it look like an accident, ties string at the top of a staircase, causing the man to fall to his death **[BWNO]**.

> **NOTE:** *It is possible (though not explicitly stated) that the abusive ex-lover may be Walter's biological father, Charlie. The man jokes about Sally having "a late-term—really late-term—abortion," which could be a callback to her friends' advice that she abort the baby after Charlie denied being the father. Moreover, her relationship with Charlie was*

one marked by frequent fighting. If this is, indeed, Charlie, then it is ironic that Walter grows up idolizing his absentee father, unaware that he unknowingly killed the man as his father was preparing to do the same to him.

—1951

Walter "The Screaming Skull" Zileski is captured and put on trial **[RPG3]**.

—June 15, 1951

The New York Police Department and the New York City Fire Department award plaques to former members of The Minutemen. Hollis Mason displays his on the wall of his apartment **[FILM, ARTF]**.

—June 1951 to November 1973

Leon Dorchester takes up residence in a building owned by his uncle, J.D. Dorchester, that previously contained The Minutemen's headquarters **[RPG3]**.

—July 1951

A pair of neighborhood teens bully ten-year-old Walter Kovacs outside a local store called Chen's. When they call his mother a whore and threaten to rape him, he angrily jams a cigarette into the eye of one thug, Richie, before biting a chunk out of the other's cheek. Richie is left partially blinded as a result **[ALAN]**.

> **NOTE:** *Walter is said to be ten years old at the time of this incident, but since he was born in 1940, he should be eleven by this point.*

—September 13, 1951

An investigation into Walter Kovacs' home life results in his removal from Sylvia's custody due to the frequent beatings he endures, and he is admitted to the Lillian Charlton Home for Problem Children, in New Jersey. A bright and likable but unusually quiet child (especially around women), he excels at his schoolwork, particularly in literature and religious education, and displays great skills in gymnastics and amateur boxing. Sylvia Kovacs never contacts him at the home **[ALAN]**.

> **NOTE:** *When Alan Moore proposed* Watchmen *to DC Comics, his original intention was to use superhero characters whom DC Comics had acquired from defunct publisher Charlton. The institution's name pays homage to this history.*

—Late 1951

Eleven-year-old Walter Kovacs writes an essay on the topic "My Parents," in which he describes an elaborate fantasy about the father he never knew having been an aide to President Harry S. Truman. In the essay, Walter claims his dad was killed during World War II while heroically fighting Nazis **[ALAN]**.

MIND .... *The Mindscape of Alan Moore*	**RPG2** .... *DC Heroes Role Playing Module #235: Taking Out the Trash—Curses and Tears*	**VRL2** ..... Viral video: *The Keene Act and You*
MOBL.... *Watchmen: The Mobile Game*		**VRL3** ..... Viral video: *Who Watches the Watchmen? A Veidt Music Network (VMN) Special*
MOTN.... *Watchmen: The Complete Motion Comic*	**RPG3** .... *DC Heroes: The Watchmen Sourcebook*	
MTRO.... *Metro* promotional newspaper cover wrap	**RUBY** .... "Wounds," published in *The Ruby Files Volume One*	**VRL4** ..... Viral video: *World in Focus: 6 Minutes to Midnight*
NEWP.... *New Frontiersman* promotional newspaper	**SCR1** ..... Unfilmed screenplay draft: Sam Hamm	**VRL5** ..... Viral video: *Local Radio Station Report on 1977 Riots*
NEWW... *New Frontiersman* website	**SCR2** ..... Unfilmed screenplay draft: Charles McKeuen	
NIGH ..... *Watchmen: The End Is Nigh, Parts 1 and 2*	**SCR3**..... Unfilmed screenplay draft: Gary Goldman	**VRL6** ..... Viral videos (group of ten): *Veidt Enterprises Advertising Contest*
PKIT...... *Watchmen* film British press kit	**SCR4**..... Unfilmed screenplay draft: David Hayter (2002)	
PORT.... *Watchmen Portraits*	**SCR5**..... Unfilmed screenplay draft: David Hayter (2003)	**WAWA**... *Watching the Watchmen*
REAL..... Real life	**SCR6**..... Unfilmed screenplay draft: Alex Tse	**WHOS** ... *Who's Who: The Definitive Directory of the DC Universe*
RPG1 .... *DC Heroes Role Playing Module #227: Who Watches the Watchmen?*	**SPOT**..... *DC Spotlight #1*	
	VRL1 ..... Viral video: *NBS Nightly News with Ted Philips*	**WTFC** .... *Watchmen: The Film Companion*

—1951 to 1971

Walter "The Screaming Skull" Zileski spends twenty years in jail **[RPG3]**.

—1952

Young Dan Dreiberg obtains a copy of *Silk Spectre and the Adventures of the Acme Brushman* **[FILM]**, a Tijuana Bible featuring Sally Jupiter's sexual exploits with a salesman from Acme Brush Co. **[ALAN]**.

—1953

Thirteen-year-old Walter Kovacs suffers a disturbing nightmare of his mother choking on food, and of a hideous beast resembling a man and woman intertwined (stemming from the memory of having walked in on his mother having sex when he was younger). He awakens from the dream with "dirty feelings" **[ALAN]**.

> **NOTE:** *A transcript of Walter's account of the dream to the staff at the Lillian Charlton Home for Problem Children, published in Alan Moore's miniseries and in* The Watchmen Sourcebook, *is dated "5/27/63," but that contradicts the rest of Rorschach's life, given that he would have been twenty-three in 1963, and that he left the children's home in 1956. The likely explanation is that he mistakenly wrote "63" instead of "53."*

E.C. Comics artist Joe Orlando poses for a photo **[ALAN]**.

While performing covert duties in Seoul, Korea, Eddie Blake contracts syphilis for a second time. This time, Dr. David Baines tends to Blake's condition **[RPG3]**.

At age fourteen, Adrian Veidt graduates from high school *cum laude* and begins attending Harvard University **[BWOZ]**.

—January 20, 1953

Dwight David "Ike" Eisenhower becomes the 34th President of the United States **[REAL]**.

—June 6, 1953

New York City resident Vittorio Rotelli, husband of Marie Rotelli, dies **[JUST]**.

> **NOTE:** *It is unknown whether the couple are related to Tony Rotelli, a college football teammate of Nelson Gardner, mentioned in* The Watchmen Sourcebook.

—After July 27, 1953

Major Montgomery Banner begins working for the U.S. Secret Service **[RPG2]**.

—August 4, 1953

The New York Fire Department names Sally Jupiter an honorary firefighter **[ARTF]**.

ABSO .... *Watchmen Absolute Edition*
ALAN..... Alan Moore's *Watchmen* miniseries
ARCD .... *Minutemen Arcade*
ARTF ..... *Watchmen: The Art of the Film*
BLCK..... *Tales of the Black Freighter*
BWCC ... *Before Watchmen—The Crimson Corsair*
BWCO ... *Before Watchmen—Comedian*
BWDB .. *Before Watchmen—Dollar Bill*
BWDM .. *Before Watchmen—Dr. Manhattan*
BWMM . *Before Watchmen—Minutemen*
BWMO ... *Before Watchmen—Moloch*
BWNO ... *Before Watchmen—Nite Owl*

BWOZ.... *Before Watchmen—Ozymandias*
BWRO ... *Before Watchmen—Rorschach*
BWSS ... *Before Watchmen—Silk Spectre*
CHEM.... My Chemical Romance music video: "Desolation Row"
CMEO.... *Watchmen* cameos in comics, TV, and film:
  • Comic: *Astonishing X-Men* volume 3 issue #6
  • Comic: *Hero Hotline* volume 1 issue #5
  • Comic: *Kingdom Come* volume 1 issue #2
  • Comic: *Marvels* volume 1 issue #4
  • Comic: *The Question* volume 1 issue #17
  • TV: *Teen Titans Go!* episode #82, "Real Boy Adventures"
  • Film: *Man of Steel*

  • Film: *Batman v Superman: Dawn of Justice Ultimate Edition*
  • Film: *Justice League*
CLIX ...... HeroClix figure pack-in cards
DECK..... *DC Comics Deck-Building Game—Crossover Pack 4: Watchmen*
DURS .... *DC Universe: Rebirth Special* volume 1 issue #1
FILM ..... *Watchmen* theatrical film
HOOD .... *Under the Hood* documentary and dust-jacket prop reproduction
JUST ..... *Watchmen: Justice Is Coming*
MATL .... Mattel Club Black Freighter figure pack-in cards

—August 23, 1953

New York City resident Marie Rotelli, widow of Vittorio Rotelli, dies **[JUST]**.

> **NOTE:** *It is unknown whether the couple are related to Tony Rotelli, a college football teammate of Nelson Gardner, mentioned in* The Watchmen Sourcebook.

—Early 1950s

While many look to the skies, fearing alien invaders or Soviet missiles, young Dan Dreiberg spends his summers in New England, owl-watching at night **[ALAN]**.

—Early to Mid-1950s

Without Larry Schexnayder as their publicist, the ex-Minutemen find newspaper coverage of their exploits decreasing in frequency and increasing in derision, and Hollis Mason comes to realize that masked adventuring had always been just a fad to fill newspapers. Jokes about hooded vigilantes become increasingly popular, with one suggesting that The Minutemen's name refers to their poor performance in the bedroom. Many sexual jokes focus on Sally Jupiter—which she seems to enjoy **[ALAN]**.

Many of The Minutemen's remaining enemies end their criminal careers, while others set aside costumes for a less extroverted, more profitable approach to crime. A new breed of villains arises who, despite having colorful names, operate in ordinary business suits. Their crimes are often deadlier and more horrible than those of their predecessors, but Hollis Mason finds the act of fighting them less fun—and more depressing. Mason grows dissatisfied with hearing beatniks, jazz musicians, poets, and rock musicians like Elvis Presley openly condemning American values, and finds himself losing interest in his secret profession **[ALAN]**.

A brief surge of anti-comic book sentiment has little lasting effect—and, in fact, boosts a publisher called E.C. To protect the reputations of the masked adventurers in its employ, the U.S. government (specifically, FBI Director J. Edgar Hoover) fully supports the comic book publishers **[ALAN]**.

With fear of communism rising in the United States, thousands of Americans—primarily government workers, union activists, entertainers, and educators—are accused of being communists or party sympathizers, many without evidence to support such claims. Those accused face aggressive investigations and questioning before government or private-industry committees, in a campaign spearheaded by Republican Senator Joseph McCarthy. As a result, many find their lives and careers destroyed **[REAL]**.

As superheroes fall out of favor and the political situation worldwide grows dire, The Comedian continues to earn headlines due to his government connections, and is groomed

MIND .... *The Mindscape of Alan Moore*	**RPG2** .... *DC Heroes Role Playing Module #235: Taking Out the Trash—Curses and Tears*	**VRL2** ..... Viral video: *The Keene Act and You*
MOBL .... *Watchmen: The Mobile Game*	**RPG3** .... *DC Heroes: The Watchmen Sourcebook*	**VRL3** ..... Viral video: *Who Watches the Watchmen? A Veidt Music Network (VMN) Special*
MOTN .... *Watchmen: The Complete Motion Comic*		
MTRO .... *Metro* promotional newspaper cover wrap	**RUBY** .... "Wounds," published in *The Ruby Files Volume One*	**VRL4** ..... Viral video: *World in Focus: 6 Minutes to Midnight*
NEWP .... *New Frontiersman* promotional newspaper	**SCR1** ..... Unfilmed screenplay draft: Sam Hamm	**VRL5** ..... Viral video: *Local Radio Station Report on 1977 Riots*
NEWW .... *New Frontiersman* website	**SCR2** ..... Unfilmed screenplay draft: Charles McKeuen	
NIGH ..... *Watchmen: The End Is Nigh, Parts 1 and 2*	**SCR3** ..... Unfilmed screenplay draft: Gary Goldman	**VRL6** ..... Viral videos (group of ten): *Veidt Enterprises Advertising Contest*
PKIT ...... *Watchmen film British press kit*	**SCR4** ..... Unfilmed screenplay draft: David Hayter (2002)	
PORT ..... *Watchmen Portraits*	**SCR5** ..... Unfilmed screenplay draft: David Hayter (2003)	**WAWA** ... *Watching the Watchmen*
REAL ..... Real life	**SCR6** ..... Unfilmed screenplay draft: Alex Tse	**WHOS** ... *Who's Who: The Definitive Directory of the DC Universe*
RPG1 .... *DC Heroes Role Playing Module #227: Who Watches the Watchmen?*	**SPOT** ..... *DC Spotlight #1*	
	VRL1 ..... Viral video: *NBS Nightly News with Ted Philips*	**WTFC** .... *Watchmen: The Film Companion*

as a patriotic symbol of the United States. At the height of the so-called "McCarthyism" era, his political motivations are never questioned **[ALAN]**.

The House Un-American Activities Committee (HUAC) begins issuing subpoenas to costumed superheroes **[RPG2]**, ordering them to reveal their identities in front of an FBI lawyer and swear an oath of loyalty. Each vigilante is placed in a room containing a two-way mirror, with Eddie Blake observing their responses on the other side, alongside FBI representatives **[BWMM]**. Given Nelson Gardner's military history and Hollis Mason's police career, each is cleared of suspicion. Unwilling to reveal his true identity, Hooded Justice refuses to testify **[ALAN]**.

> **CONFLICT:** *A timeline in the* Watchmen *film's British press kit sets the testimonies in 1950, while* Before Watchmen: Minutemen *chooses a setting of 1952. Taking Out the Trash and* The Watchmen Sourcebook *both place them in 1954.*

Dan Dreiberg enrolls as a student at Harvard University, earning undergraduate and dual graduate degrees **[RPG3]**.

Larry Schexnayder fails at being a loving stepfather to Laurie Jupiter. Frustrated at his wife's feelings for Eddie Blake, Larry takes it out on their love-child, often yelling at Laurie to the point of bullying **[ALAN]**.

—In or Before 1954

A member of the East German secret police—and a cousin of Rolf Müller—is arrested while trying to plant a listening device in the home of an American attaché. As a result, the U.S. government grows suspicious of Müller's loyalties **[RPG3]**.

—1954

Young Laurie Jupiter hears Sally Jupiter and Larry Schexnayder fighting. As her parents argue, she picks up a snow globe in the living room and stares at the tiny toy world inside it. Larry yells at her, startling her into dropping the globe, which shatters **[ALAN]**. Larry leaves angrily, and Sally tells Laurie that he won't be coming back. Laurie hugs her mother, assuring her they'll be okay **[BWSS]**.

> **CONFLICT:** *A timeline published in* The Film Companion *moves this event to 1966 and cites Laurie's age as thirteen, contradicting Alan Moore's miniseries, which establishes it as occurring in 1954.*

Future two-time hostage Jeffrey Iddings is born **[RPG1]**.

—February 1954

While performing covert duties in Pen Jomn, Eddie Blake sustains a fragmentation wound when mortar fragments shred his left deltoid. Dr. Hank Stevens tends to Blake's injuries [**RPG3**].

> ***NOTE:*** *There is no city called Pen Jomn in the real world, which could indicate that the name was misspelled in* The Watchmen Sourcebook, *or that this city exists only in the fictional* Watchmen *reality. There is a Penjom in Malaysia—a gold mine—but that was not founded until 1996.*

—April 16, 1954

When pressed to testify before The House Un-American Activities Committee, Hooded Justice opts to withdraw from society entirely [**ALAN**]. He makes a farewell speech to the press, then vanishes [**RPG3**], cutting all contact with Nelson Gardner [**BWMM**].

> ***NOTE:*** *The vigilante's vanishing is undated in Alan Moore's miniseries. The date appears in* The Watchmen Sourcebook.

—April 17, 1954

One day after Hooded Justice's disappearance, circus strongman Rolf Müller mysteriously vanishes as well [**RPG3**].

> ***NOTE:*** *Given the revelation, in* Before Watchmen: Minutemen, *that Hooded Justice and Rolf Müller are separate individuals, this is apparently just an unusual coincidence.*

—Before June 14, 1954

The U.S. Attorney General issues a subpoena to Byron Lewis, requiring him to testify before the House Un-American Activities Committee (HUAC), and noting that his testimony could be used in a court of law [**RPG3**].

> ***NOTE:*** *In the real world, the Attorney General in 1954 was Herbert Brownell, Jr. The signature on the letter is illegible, but the first name appears to be Jeff, indicating that a different official holds that position in* Watchmen *continuity.*

—June 14, 1954—3:00 PM

Byron Lewis testifies before HUAC [**RPG3**]. His left-wing college associations cause him to endure lengthy, ruthless investigations compared to those of other Minutemen members [**ALAN**].

—After June 14, 1954

Byron Lewis signs an oath of loyalty, as required by the U.S. government, but the ordeal saps his remaining will [**BWMM**]. For refusing to fight during World War II, he is labeled a communist sympathizer [**RPG2**]. Branded a societal outcast and emotionally scarred by his HUAC investigation, he fully succumbs to alcoholism and develops mental-health issues [**ALAN**].

MIND .... *The Mindscape of Alan Moore*
MOBL ... *Watchmen: The Mobile Game*
MOTN .... *Watchmen: The Complete Motion Comic*
MTRO .... *Metro* promotional newspaper cover wrap
NEWP .... *New Frontiersman* promotional newspaper
NEWW ... *New Frontiersman* website
NIGH ..... *Watchmen: The End Is Nigh, Parts 1 and 2*
PKIT ...... *Watchmen* film British press kit
PORT ..... *Watchmen Portraits*
REAL ..... Real life
RPG1 .... *DC Heroes Role Playing Module #227: Who Watches the Watchmen?*

RPG2 .... *DC Heroes Role Playing Module #235: Taking Out the Trash—Curses and Tears*
RPG3 .... *DC Heroes: The Watchmen Sourcebook*
RUBY .... "Wounds," published in *The Ruby Files Volume One*
SCR1 ..... Unfilmed screenplay draft: Sam Hamm
SCR2 ..... Unfilmed screenplay draft: Charles McKeuen
SCR3 ..... Unfilmed screenplay draft: Gary Goldman
SCR4 ..... Unfilmed screenplay draft: David Hayter (2002)
SCR5 ..... Unfilmed screenplay draft: David Hayter (2003)
SCR6 ..... Unfilmed screenplay draft: Alex Tse
SPOT ..... *DC Spotlight #1*
VRL1 ..... Viral video: *NBS Nightly News with Ted Philips*

VRL2 ..... Viral video: *The Keene Act and You*
VRL3 ..... Viral video: *Who Watches the Watchmen? A Veidt Music Network (VMN) Special*
VRL4 ..... Viral video: *World in Focus: 6 Minutes to Midnight*
VRL5 ..... Viral video: *Local Radio Station Report on 1977 Riots*
VRL6 ..... Viral videos (group of ten): *Veidt Enterprises Advertising Contest*
WAWA ... *Watching the Watchmen*
WHOS .... *Who's Who: The Definitive Directory of the DC Universe*
WTFC .... *Watchmen: The Film Companion*

—September 9, 1954

Sally Jupiter and Larry Schexnayder issue a press release denying any knowledge of Byron Lewis having anti-communist views. In the release, Sally claims that she was never as close to him as she was to other Minutemen members **[RPG3]**.

—September 11, 1954

Newsworld quotes The Comedian as describing Byron Lewis as "a flake" and a "nerdy little kid trying to hang out with big brother and his friends." Blake adds, however, that he doubts Lewis is "a goddamned Red" **[RPG3]**.

—Mid-1950s

A young woman named Carol-Anne, whose father works at the Gila Flats Test Base in Arizona, hangs up photos of up-and-coming singer Elvis Presley. Her dad deems the performer "pimp-eyed" **[ALAN]**.

William Dreiberg grows increasingly annoyed about his son Dan spending too much time dreaming and playing with action figures instead of finding a job and being productive. William frequently beats his wife Victoria, who tells her son to stay in his room whenever this occurs. During one fight, Dan overhears his parents arguing and learns that they only got married after she became pregnant with him **[BWNO]**.

Dan Dreiberg is sometimes bullied at school, and his father hits him each time for being weak. Dan endures the abuse, comforted that good men like The Nite Owl exist in the world. His mother covers his bruises with makeup, telling him to find a place deep within himself where no one can touch or hurt him **[BWNO]**.

After three bullies beat Dan up after school one day, he stops at an electronics store to watch TV footage of The Nite Owl subduing a gang of thugs, despite being injured and outnumbered. Inspired, he buys a Nite Owl mask at a toy store, puts it on, and confronts his bullies. They repeatedly knock him to the ground, but he keeps getting up to take another beating, knowing that they can't win as long as he refuses to give up **[BWNO]**.

—In or Before 1955

Tip Top Tailors opens in New York City **[BWMM]**.

The Big Top Circus begins performing in Boston **[BWMM]**.

A thug called Gangster commits a series of crimes. Hollis Mason brings him to justice, and a newspaper sports the front-page headline "Nite Owl Captures Gangster" **[BWNO]**.

—1955

Dan Dreiberg obtains a wall calendar bearing the image of Nite Owl **[BWNO]**.

—Early 1955

FBI Director J. Edgar Hoover approves a bureau-wide effort to find Hooded Justice **[BWMM]**, and The Comedian is assigned to track him down **[ALAN]**. Blake spies on Hollis Mason and Byron Lewis to determine if they know anything. He breaks into Byron's hideout, listens to Gretchen Slovak's tapes, learns of Ursula Zandt's suspicions that Rolf Müller is a child-killer, and heads to the Boston area to investigate police files about the women's murders **[BWMM]**. Concluding that Müller and Hooded Justice are the same man **[ALAN]**, he asks the FBI to obtain the circus strongman's file from the German government, which seemingly confirms his suspicions **[BWMM]**.

—April 16, 1955

Eddie Blake strangles Müller to death with a belt in his trailer at the Big Top Circus. Upon searching the trailer, however, he starts to doubt that the strongman, who looks around sixty years old, could be Hooded Justice. Blake finds a copy of Robert Louis Stevenson's poetry collection *A Child's Garden of Verses*, containing a photo of Müller as a young man with a boy named Jacob **[BWMM]**. He then shoots Müller's body and dumps it in a river **[ALAN]**. To cover up the murder, Blake tells his superiors that he failed to find his quarry **[ALAN, RPG2]**.

> **NOTE:** *Alan Moore's miniseries establishes the year of Rolf Müller's death as 1955. The specific date appears in* Taking Out the Trash.

> **CONFLICT:** *In Alan Moore's miniseries, Rolf Müller's corpse is found in a river with a bullet in his head, whereas Blake strangles him to death in* Before Watchmen: Minutemen. *This can be reconciled by assuming that Blake shoots the body and dumps it in the water to obscure the cause of death.*

—After April 16, 1955

Eddie Blake concocts a plan to disgrace Hooded Justice as revenge for their 1940 scuffle, using the child-killer case as a means of drawing the strongman out of hiding. Disguised as the noose-wearing vigilante, Blake kidnaps Hollis Mason's neighbor, Tino Musante Jr., and chains the boy to a table in a building near the circus—the same one in which Mason and Ursula Zandt found a dead boy hanging from the ceiling in 1940—so that Hollis will rescue Musante and track down Hooded Justice for him **[BWMM]**.

Tino Jr.'s grandmother asks Mason to find her grandson, and he spies on the circus that night. He follows Hooded Justice (The Comedian in disguise) into the nearby building, where Blake beats him unconscious and leaves. Mason awakens the next morning to

MIND .... *The Mindscape of Alan Moore*	**RPG2** .... *DC Heroes Role Playing Module #235: Taking Out the Trash—Curses and Tears*	**VRL2** ..... Viral video: *The Keene Act and You*
MOBL .... *Watchmen: The Mobile Game*		**VRL3** ..... Viral video: *Who Watches the Watchmen? A Veidt Music Network (VMN) Special*
MOTN .... *Watchmen: The Complete Motion Comic*	**RPG3** .... *DC Heroes: The Watchmen Sourcebook*	
MTRO .... *Metro* promotional newspaper cover wrap	**RUBY** ..... "Wounds," published in *The Ruby Files Volume One*	**VRL4** ..... Viral video: *World in Focus: 6 Minutes to Midnight*
NEWP .... *New Frontiersman* promotional newspaper	**SCR1** ..... Unfilmed screenplay draft: Sam Hamm	**VRL5** ..... Viral video: *Local Radio Station Report on 1977 Riots*
NEWW .... *New Frontiersman* website	**SCR2** ..... Unfilmed screenplay draft: Charles McKeuen	
NIGH ..... *Watchmen: The End Is Nigh, Parts 1 and 2*	**SCR3** ..... Unfilmed screenplay draft: Gary Goldman	**VRL6** ..... Viral videos (group of ten): *Veidt Enterprises Advertising Contest*
PKIT ...... *Watchmen* film British press kit	**SCR4** ..... Unfilmed screenplay draft: David Hayter (2002)	
PORT ..... *Watchmen Portraits*	**SCR5** ..... Unfilmed screenplay draft: David Hayter (2003)	**WAWA** ... *Watching the Watchmen*
REAL ..... Real life	**SCR6** ..... Unfilmed screenplay draft: Alex Tse	**WHOS** .... *Who's Who: The Definitive Directory of the DC Universe*
RPG1 .... *DC Heroes Role Playing Module #227: Who Watches the Watchmen?*	**SPOT** ..... *DC Spotlight #1*	
	VRL1 ..... Viral video: *NBS Nightly News with Ted Philips*	**WTFC** .... *Watchmen: The Film Companion*

find Tino Jr. chained to the table, unharmed. After returning the boy to his family, Mason searches day and night for any sign of Hooded Justice [**BWMM**].

Two weeks later, New York City's mayor awards The Nite Owl the key to the city for saving Tino Musante's life. In attendance are others whom the crime-fighter has helped during his career, along with actor Marilyn Monroe and athlete Joe DiMaggio. For the first time in years, Mason feels appreciated for all he has done [**BWMM**].

   NOTE: *Historically, New York City's mayor in 1955 was Robert F. Wagner, Jr.*

That night, Hollis Mason and Byron Lewis visit Nelson Gardner, seeking clues to Hooded Justice's whereabouts. They track him down to The Minutemen's abandoned Freedom Tower headquarters. Hooded Justice drops a wooden crate on them, badly injuring Lewis, and warns them to leave or die. Mason attacks and kills the strongman, unaware he is murdering the wrong person, then helps Byron leave on foot as Gardner arrives and cradles his ex-lover's corpse. After they leave, Nelson destroys the building, causing it to fall into the Hudson River [**BWMM**].

●—July 1955
A badly decomposed corpse washes up on Boston's coast with a bullet through the head. The body is tentatively identified as that of Rolf Müller [**ALAN**]. Eddie Blake's government connections prevent any serious investigation into the incident, and Hooded Justice's disappearance remains unsolved [**RPG2**].

●—1955 to 1956
Byron Lewis's mental health degenerates, to the point that he begins experiencing bouts of non-lucidity [**BWMM**].

Part V:
DAWN OF THE SUPERMAN
(1956–1960)

In or Before 1956

Sylvia Kovacs begins prostituting for a pimp named George Paterson **[ALAN]**.

Pioneer Publishing Inc. debuts a right-wing conspiracist newspaper called the *New Frontiersman*. Its slogan: "In your hearts, you know it's right" **[NEWP]**. Victor Godfrey is named the publication's editor **[RPG3]**.

> **NOTE:** *Victor Godfrey is very likely related to Hector Godfrey, the publication's editor from around 1977 (in a promotional* New Frontiersman *newspaper) until at least the 1980s (in Alan Moore's miniseries).*

The Gunga Diner, an Indian-cuisine fast-food chain **[ABSO]**, launches to great success. The company opens restaurants in many cities, including Boston **[BWOZ]** and Manhattan, near 40th Street and Seventh Avenue **[ALAN]**. The diner proves popular with New Yorkers, resulting in a great deal of garbage bearing its logo littering the streets **[ALAN]**. The Easy Travel Agency opens next to the New York City location **[NIGH]**.

> **NOTE:** *The restaurant chain exists at least as early as 1956, according to* Before Watchmen: Ozymandias.

Mid to Late 1950s

Several schools and colleges notice Adrian Veidt's abnormally developed talents, and he receives a scholarship to study in Europe **[ABSO]**.

1956

At age seventeen, Adrian Veidt takes post-graduate courses at Harvard University, majoring in the life of his namesake, Alexander of Macedonia. After reading every available volume on the subject, including *Alexander, Conquests of Alexander, Alexander the Great*, and *Empires of Alexander*, he realizes that he has only begun to scratch the surface **[BWOZ]**.

MIND .... *The Mindscape of Alan Moore*
MOBL .... *Watchmen: The Mobile Game*
MOTN .... *Watchmen: The Complete Motion Comic*
MTRO .... *Metro* promotional newspaper cover wrap
NEWP .... *New Frontiersman* promotional newspaper
NEWW .... *New Frontiersman* website
NIGH ..... *Watchmen: The End Is Nigh, Parts 1 and 2*
PKIT ...... *Watchmen* film British press kit
PORT ..... *Watchmen Portraits*
REAL ..... Real life
RPG1 .... *DC Heroes Role Playing Module #227: Who Watches the Watchmen?*

RPG2 .... *DC Heroes Role Playing Module #235: Taking Out the Trash—Curses and Tears*
RPG3 .... *DC Heroes: The Watchmen Sourcebook*
RUBY .... "Wounds," published in *The Ruby Files Volume One*
SCR1 ..... Unfilmed screenplay draft: Sam Hamm
SCR2 ..... Unfilmed screenplay draft: Charles McKeuen
SCR3 ..... Unfilmed screenplay draft: Gary Goldman
SCR4 .... Unfilmed screenplay draft: David Hayter (2002)
SCR5 ..... Unfilmed screenplay draft: David Hayter (2003)
SCR6 ..... Unfilmed screenplay draft: Alex Tse
SPOT .... *DC Spotlight #1*
VRL1 ..... Viral video: *NBS Nightly News with Ted Philips*

VRL2 ..... Viral video: *The Keene Act and You*
VRL3 ..... Viral video: *Who Watches the Watchmen? A Veidt Music Network (VMN) Special*
VRL4 ..... Viral video: *World in Focus: 6 Minutes to Midnight*
VRL5 ..... Viral video: *Local Radio Station Report on 1977 Riots*
VRL6 ..... Viral videos (group of ten): *Veidt Enterprises Advertising Contest*
WAWA ... *Watching the Watchmen*
WHOS .... *Who's Who: The Definitive Directory of the DC Universe*
WTFC .... *Watchmen: The Film Companion*

—Before February 11, 1956

In preparing an exposé on Hooded Justice's true identity, *New Frontiersman* editor Victor Godfrey interviews Sackson and Shanley employee Daniel "Happy" Dahl, who recalls a 1933 incident in which Rolf Müller repeatedly burned himself with a red-hot poker after spending hours alone with Frank Burrows, a gay man **[RPG3]**.

—February 11, 1956

The *New Frontiersman* publishes an article titled "Blacks, Whites, and Reds All Over." Victor Godfrey purports that Hooded Justice, long considered a U.S. patriot, was a highly placed communist spy—and possibly a homosexual—and lays out evidence that he was circus strongman Rolf Müller. Though condemning Müller for serving his "Red masters," Godfrey expresses continued support for the other Minutemen **[RPG3]**. The article theorizes that Müller went on the run for fear of being exposed as a communist, only to have his superiors execute him **[ALAN]**.

> *NOTE: The newspaper is dated "Monday, February 11th, 1956," which is historically inaccurate since that date fell on a Saturday.*

—March 11, 1956

Larry Schexnayder petitions the State of New York for a divorce from Sally Jupiter. Representing Larry is attorney Martin Baldridge, with Jason Hammacher representing Sally. The value of their marital assets is estimated at $1.2 million **[RPG3]**.

—May 11, 1956

Sally Jupiter and Larry Schexnayder divorce due to marital problems that include Sally's affair with Eddie Blake **[ALAN, RPG2]**, mental cruelty toward Larry on her part **[RPG3]**, and Larry's difficulty in reconciling his role as Sally's husband with his need, as her manager, to prey upon other men's attraction to her **[HOOD]**. Larry maintains no contact with his stepdaughter, Laurie Jupiter **[ALAN]**.

> *NOTE: Alan Moore's miniseries establishes the divorce as occurring in 1956. The specific date appears in* Taking Out the Trash.

> *CONFLICT: The Film Companion sets the divorce in the late 1960s.*

—Mid-1956

Sylvia Kovacs's pimp, George Paterson, forces her to ingest Drano cleaning fluid, then leaves her corpse in a South Bronx back alleyway. When her son Walter hears the news, his only comment is "Good" **[ALAN]**.

> *CONFLICT: A timeline in the* Watchmen *film's British press places Sylvia's death in 1954, contradicting Alan Moore's miniseries, which sets her murder in 1956.*

Upon turning sixteen, Walter Kovacs is deemed intelligent and stable enough to function in normal society, and is thus released from the Lillian Charlton Home for Problem Children. Taking up residence in the first of several small apartments, he secures a full-time job as a menial laborer in the women's apparel industry **[ALAN]**, at a company called Manhattan Fabrics **[RPG3]**.

> **CONFLICT:** Taking Out the Trash *indicates that Walter spends time in "a wide variety of detention homes," contradicting Alan Moore's miniseries, which has him living at the Charlton Home from 1951 to 1956, and then becoming independent.*

●—Before September 1956

Friedrich Werner Veidt and Ingrid Renata Veidt are killed in a traffic accident. Adrian Veidt, age seventeen, is their sole heir **[BWOZ]**. Though able to live an idol life of luxury, he yearns to experience as much as possible. With no living intellectual equals to turn to for advice, he explores how Alexander of Macedonia ruled most of the civilized world by age thirty-three, instituting his era's greatest seat of learning **[ALAN]**.

Adrian spends weeks studying a local museum's antiquities wing, staring silently at a large statue of his idol. Finally, after a voice in his head tells him, "Answers cannot be given. They must be learned" **[BWOZ]**, Veidt vows to measure his own successes against those of Alexander **[ALAN]**. To that end, he gives away his entire inheritance, donating much of it to worthy charities **[BWOZ]**, so that he can emulate the ruler by building an empire from nothing **[ALAN]**.

After traveling for weeks aboard a freighter, newly impoverished Adrian Veidt disembarks at a Black Sea coastal sea port, where he intimidates four thieves into backing down without a fight, merely by warning them away in Turkish **[BWOZ]**. He retraces his hero's steps through northern Turkey, Babylon, Kabul, and Samarkand; travels the Indus River; gathers martial wisdom in China and Tibet; and visits the leader's corpse in Alexandria. Finally, in Alexander's ruined Babylon ziggurats, Veidt ponders his idol's failure to rule the entire world and unite humanity in the long term **[ALAN]**. At each step of his journey, he pauses to improve his martial arts skills **[BWOZ]**.

Tibetan monks teach Veidt how to use his brain to one hundred percent capacity **[RPG1, RPG2]**. While in Tibet, he becomes romantically involved with a man who gives him a small ball of hashish, saying he'll know when to consume it. The night before returning to the United States, Adrian hears a voice whispering his name and wanders out into the desert **[BWOZ]**, where he consumes the drug and experiences a transformative vision of dead pharaohs **[ALAN]**. Returning to the Turkish port, he encounters the same thugs, who this time attack. He leaves their broken, bloodied bodies on the dock **[BWOZ]**.

> **NOTE:** *According to* Absolute Watchmen, *Alan Moore originally planned to have Veidt turn to crime-fighting following a vivid peyote experience under the supervision of South*

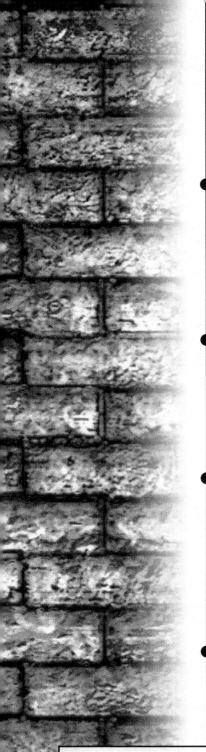

American witch-healers, known as brujos. The same year that DC published Watchmen, *Moore introduced the Brujería, a secret society of male witches, in his groundbreaking* Swamp Thing *storyline, "American Gothic."*

While Veidt is not explicitly stated to have been romantically involved with the male monk, the art is very suggestive of this. Had the monk character been female, there would be no question in readers' minds that the relationship was non-platonic. Therefore, intimacy is assumed on the part of this author.

September 1956
Weeks later, Adrian Veidt returns to New York City and eagerly begins his new life. He purchases a copy of *Financial News*, then spends a few weeks seated at a Gunga Diner booth, studying stocks to determine how best to invest his money. A beautiful woman, Miranda St. John, introduces herself at the restaurant after watching him throughout that time, and the two become lovers, eventually moving in together **[BWOZ]**.

> **NOTE:** *Veidt becomes Ozymandias in March 1958, eighteen months after returning to New York. This places his return in September 1956.*

Late 1956 to Early 1957
Adrian Veidt grows increasingly wealthy over a span of several months by focusing his investments on electric power stocks **[BWOZ]**. He adopts Alexander's free-booting style, embraces pacifism and vegetarianism, and studies science, art, religion, and a hundred philosophies, all in an effort to attain extraordinary capabilities **[ALAN]**. With an IQ of more than 240 **[PKIT]**, Veidt earns a reputation as "the world's smartest man" **[ALAN]**, a moniker bestowed upon him by several financial publications **[BWOZ]**.

Late 1950s
Despite daily exercise, Nelson Gardner begins to grow a paunch in middle age **[ALAN]**.

A boom in pirate-related merchandise occurs. As one of the few companies to anticipate this development, E.C. flourishes as its line of pirate comic books (such as *Piracy* and *Buccaneers*) dominates the marketplace **[ALAN]**.

While a student at Harvard University, Dan Dreiberg attends several lectures by Professor Joseph Westwood, an ornithological expert. The two form a bond **[RPG3]**.

1956 to Late 1960s
Sally Jupiter raises her daughter Laurie as a single mother. Throughout her childhood, Laurie assumes that her birth-father was Hooded Justice, whom she mistakenly believes to have been Sally's ex-boyfriend. She spends a great deal of time working out alone in a gymnasium, and thus grows accustomed to solitude **[ALAN]**.

As a child, Laurie often hears her Aunt Bella lament about being unable to part with unused belongings **[ALAN]**.

Sally buys Laurie a G.I. Joe action figure with a variety of spare uniforms **[ALAN]**.

—1957
While attending a charity function for retired police officers, Hollis Mason meets an officer who arrested fifteen-year-old Ursula Zandt in 1932 after she hit him for whistling at her good looks **[RPG3]**.

—1958
Jon Osterman graduates from Princeton University after a decade of study, with a Ph.D. degree in atomic science **[ALAN]**.

> **CONFLICT:** Taking Out the Trash *dates Osterman's graduation on March 14, 1959, contradicting Alan Moore's miniseries.*

—Before January 3, 1958
Frank Madison, Byron Lewis's family butler, dies **[RPG3]**.

—January 3, 1958
The *New Haven Register* announces funeral details for Frank Madison **[RPG3]**.

—January 5, 1958—3:00 PM
A funeral is held for Madison at Our Lady of Mercy, in Stamford, Connecticut **[RPG3]**.

—In or Before March 1958
Adrian Veidt orders an elaborate costume made from purple and yellow cloth for a Halloween party to be held later in the year **[BWOZ]**.

A drug dealer called Nico begins operating on New York's seedy South Side. Among his customers is a woman named Giselle **[BWOZ]**.

Several businesses open in New York City, including Portmeirion, Cispin's Food and Wine, and Heaven, the city's most exclusive supper club **[BWOZ]**.

Adrian Veidt creates a new type of knot, which he dubs the Gordian Knot **[BWOZ]**.

> **NOTE:** *The Gordian Knot, a legend associated with Alexander the Great, is often used as a metaphor for a problem that can be solved by thinking outside the box.*

MIND .... *The Mindscape of Alan Moore*
MOBL .... *Watchmen: The Mobile Game*
MOTN .... *Watchmen: The Complete Motion Comic*
MTRO .... *Metro* promotional newspaper cover wrap
NEWP .... *New Frontiersman* promotional newspaper
NEWW .... *New Frontiersman* website
NIGH ..... *Watchmen: The End Is Nigh, Parts 1 and 2*
PKIT ...... *Watchmen* film British press kit
PORT ..... *Watchmen Portraits*
REAL ..... Real life
RPG1 .... *DC Heroes Role Playing Module #227: Who Watches the Watchmen?*

RPG2 .... *DC Heroes Role Playing Module #235: Taking Out the Trash—Curses and Tears*
RPG3 .... *DC Heroes: The Watchmen Sourcebook*
RUBY .... "Wounds," published in *The Ruby Files Volume One*
SCR1 ..... Unfilmed screenplay draft: Sam Hamm
SCR2 ..... Unfilmed screenplay draft: Charles McKeuen
SCR3 ..... Unfilmed screenplay draft: Gary Goldman
SCR4 ..... Unfilmed screenplay draft: David Hayter (2002)
SCR5 ..... Unfilmed screenplay draft: David Hayter (2003)
SCR6 ..... Unfilmed screenplay draft: Alex Tse
SPOT ..... *DC Spotlight #1*
VRL1 ..... Viral video: *NBS Nightly News with Ted Philips*

VRL2 ..... Viral video: *The Keene Act and You*
VRL3 ..... Viral video: *Who Watches the Watchmen? A Veidt Music Network (VMN) Special*
VRL4 ..... Viral video: *World in Focus: 6 Minutes to Midnight*
VRL5 ..... Viral video: *Local Radio Station Report on 1977 Riots*
VRL6 ..... Viral videos (group of ten): *Veidt Enterprises Advertising Contest*
WAWA ... *Watching the Watchmen*
WHOS ... *Who's Who: The Definitive Directory of the DC Universe*
WTFC .... *Watchmen: The Film Companion*

—March 1958

Adrian Veidt, already a corporate mogul only eighteen months after returning from Tibet penniless, erects a Manhattan skyscraper to house his new business and penthouse apartment, including a trophy room filled with Alexandrian artifacts. This prevents him from spending much time with Miranda St. John. Bored one night, she goes out seeking excitement and ends up in a posh underground club owned by Moloch the Mystic. The gangster introduces her to heroin, and Veidt discovers her dead in bed from an overdose that same night. For the first time since his parents' deaths, he weeps **[BWOZ]**.

To avoid bad publicity for his young company, Veidt investigates Miranda's death himself. Combining his Halloween costume with ancient Greek artifacts, including Alexander's golden gauntlets and ricocheting headband, as well as several hidden weapons, he creates a crime-fighting costume for himself and decides his Gordian Knot shall be his calling card **[BWOZ]**.

—March 17, 1958

Inspired by The Minutemen's exploits, Adrian Veidt begins his crime-fighting career by tracking down the individual responsible for Miranda's death **[BWOZ]**.

—Late March 1958

Adrian Veidt spreads cash around New York City, seeking information about Miranda's drug supplier. Four days later, he receives an anonymous response directing him to a seedy South Side alleyway, where he confronts a drug dealer named Nico and renders him unconscious. When the pusher awakens, Veidt extracts the name of his supplier, then leaves him tied to a streetlamp in his signature Gordian Knot **[BWOZ]**.

The next night, Veidt visits an exclusive supper club called Heaven, orders a well-aired 1818 Château Lafite Rothschild, and surveys the room. He spots the manager handing an envelope to Hondo, a brutish mob enforcer, then trails the thug to a seemingly abandoned building in the warehouse district. Inside, young Asian women clad in underwear and facial masks process narcotics for their boss, Porcini **[BWOZ]**, a gangster who runs a major opium and heroin smuggling racket **[ALAN]**.

Warning the women to seek cover, Veidt takes out the mob within seconds, causes a gunman to fall into a pile of cocaine, and uses his ricocheting headband to drop a Klieg light onto Porcini. When police respond to the gunfire, Veidt introduces himself as Ozymandias, citing Percy Bysshe Shelley's same-named sonnet about Ramses II. The cops are less than thrilled by the arrival of yet another masked vigilante **[BWOZ]**.

—Mid-1958

Newspapers report Veidt's takedown of the drug racket, and he soon earns a reputation among criminals for his incredible intelligence and athletic prowess. This success leaves him optimistic that he can end injustice by demolishing crime syndicates, conquering evil by applying ancient teachings to modern society **[ALAN]**.

Veidt tracks down the mobile gambling dens of a high-roller called Wheeler-Dealer, captures a stolen-car czar known as Low Jack, thwarts an international counterfeiting ring run by Three Dollar Bill, and halts the operations of a hook-handed kingpin, The Ancient Mariner. Each morning over breakfast, he scours local newspapers for mentions of his exploits, maintaining scrapbooks of such articles that soon fill a bookcase. He makes a number of underworld contacts, including a man named Skeeter **[BWOZ]**.

The Nite Owl makes headlines by nabbing The King of Skin. Veidt reads about this and ponders about the decline in masked crime-fighters, vowing to learn what happened to The Minutemen so he can avoid a similar fate. For weeks, he scours microfiche and newspapers at the New York Public Library, then maps out Hooded Justice's final days in an effort to solve the mystery of his disappearance **[BWOZ]**.

—Before Fall 1958

Hank Meadows, a research scientist at Arizona's Gila Flats Test Base, spends a great deal of time with his wife at the Palisades Amusement Park, where he enjoys playing carnival games. A healthy individual, he doesn't smoke or drink and rarely goes near the base's heavy-radiation equipment **[BWDM]**.

> **NOTE:** It is unknown whether Hank Meadows is related to Maggie Meadows, mentioned in The Watchmen Sourcebook.
>
> The Gila Flats base is located in Arizona, whereas the Palisades Amusement Park is in New Jersey. As such, it seems odd that Hank and his wife would travel across the United States "all the time," as Janey Slater claims, to visit a local amusement park. There are amusement parks on the U.S. West Coast as well, after all.

—Fall 1958

Hank Meadows fails to notice an uncovered uranium container and unknowingly receives a fatal dose of radiation **[BWDM]**. He suddenly dies of a tumor **[ALAN]**, which Janey Slater finds perplexing, given his tendency toward clean living **[BWDM]**.

MIND	*The Mindscape of Alan Moore*
MOBL	*Watchmen: The Mobile Game*
MOTN	*Watchmen: The Complete Motion Comic*
MTRO	*Metro* promotional newspaper cover wrap
NEWP	*New Frontiersman* promotional newspaper
NEWW	*New Frontiersman* website
NIGH	*Watchmen: The End Is Nigh, Parts 1 and 2*
PKIT	*Watchmen* film British press kit
PORT	*Watchmen Portraits*
REAL	Real life
RPG1	*DC Heroes Role Playing Module #227: Who Watches the Watchmen?*
RPG2	*DC Heroes Role Playing Module #235: Taking Out the Trash—Curses and Tears*
RPG3	*DC Heroes: The Watchmen Sourcebook*
RUBY	"Wounds," published in *The Ruby Files Volume One*
SCR1	Unfilmed screenplay draft: Sam Hamm
SCR2	Unfilmed screenplay draft: Charles McKeuen
SCR3	Unfilmed screenplay draft: Gary Goldman
SCR4	Unfilmed screenplay draft: David Hayter (2002)
SCR5	Unfilmed screenplay draft: David Hayter (2003)
SCR6	Unfilmed screenplay draft: Alex Tse
SPOT	*DC Spotlight #1*
VRL1	Viral video: *NBS Nightly News with Ted Philips*
VRL2	Viral video: *The Keene Act and You*
VRL3	Viral video: *Who Watches the Watchmen? A Veidt Music Network (VMN) Special*
VRL4	Viral video: *World in Focus: 6 Minutes to Midnight*
VRL5	Viral video: *Local Radio Station Report on 1977 Riots*
VRL6	Viral videos (group of ten): *Veidt Enterprises Advertising Contest*
WAWA ...	*Watching the Watchmen*
WHOS	*Who's Who: The Definitive Directory of the DC Universe*
WTFC	*Watchmen: The Film Companion*

Fall 1958 (Alternate Reality)

In one possible timeline, Jon Osterman calls the Gila Flats Test Base on the advice of his professors, seeking information about the decay of certain atomic particles. As a result of this distraction, Hank Meadows notices the uncovered uranium container in time to avoid receiving fatal radiation exposure [**BWDM**].

—Before May 6, 1958

Jon Osterman submits his doctoral dissertation, "C Waves and Neutrino Theory," for consideration by Princeton University's faculty board [**RPG3**].

—May 6, 1958

Dr. Michael Florence, the chairman of Princeton University's Department of Physics, informs Jon Osterman that the college has accepted his doctoral dissertation [**RPG3**].

—June 7, 1958

Princeton University holds a graduation ceremony at its McDonlevy Hall, during which Jon Osterman is awarded a Doctorate of Philosophy in Physics degree [**RPG3**].

—1958 to 1968

Edgar Jacobi spends a decade developing a plan to elect a U.S. President connected to organized crime, in order to greatly increase his own influence and power [**RPG2**].

—Before February 2, 1959

Professor Milton Glass reads Jon Osterman's doctoral thesis from Princeton University, "C Waves and Neutrino Theory," and finds it brilliant [**ALAN**].

—February 2, 1959

Milton Glass invites Jon Osterman to visit Arizona's Gila Flats Test Base and view how scientists at that facility are working to separate gluons and gluinos by shattering their intrinsic fields, in order to create a weapon to replace atomic bombs [**RPG3**].

—In or Before May 1959

Milton Glass begins smoking Turkish cigarettes [**ALAN**].

—Before May 12, 1959

Milton Glass hires Jon Osterman to replace Hank Meadows at the Gila Flats Test Base [**ALAN**], in the facility's Weapons Testing Center [**RPG2**]. Jon's official job title is "project researcher" [**RPG3**].

Before May 12, 1959 (Alternate Reality)

In a quantum reality in which Hank Meadows does not die of fatal radiation exposure, Jon Osterman never replaces him at the Gila Flats Test Base **[BWDM]**.

May 12, 1959

Jon Osterman starts his first day of work at Gila Flats. Milton Glass introduces him to assistant Wally Weaver, who gives John a tour of the facility and shows him equipment used to conduct intrinsic field experiments, as well as a time-lock test vault designed to prevent radiation leakage when objects are separated from their intrinsic fields **[ALAN]**. Jon experiences déjà vu as his consciousness, connected with his future self, slides along the timestream **[BWDM]**.

Weaver and Osterman visit the Bestiary, an onsite cafeteria and bar. Wally introduces Jon to fellow physicist Janey Slater, who buys him a beer—the first time a woman has ever done that for him **[ALAN]**.

> **CONFLICT:** *The* Watchmen *film makes Wally a college friend of Jon Osterman, contradicting Alan Moore's miniseries, in which the two meet at Gila Flats.*

May 14, 1959

The Gila Flats Test Base issues Jon Osterman an official identification card, on which his first name is misspelled as "John" **[RPG3]**.

July 1959

Jon Osterman takes a vacation to New Jersey to visit friends from Princeton. Janey Slater travels with him to see her mother, who lives nearby. When her mom fails to answer the phone, they go to the Palisades Amusement Park, where a photographer snaps their picture, mistaking them for lovers **[ALAN, BWDM]**. Jon again experiences déjà vu as his consciousness, connected with his future self, slides along the timestream **[BWDM]**.

Jon wins Janey a stuffed animal while playing a carnival game called Big League Pitcher **[FILM]**. After enjoying a ride on the Tilt-A-Whirl, they head to the shooting gallery, where her watchband breaks and a fat man steps on it. Jon promises to fix the watch, and they head back to his hotel room to call her mother. There, the two make love for the first time **[ALAN]**.

> **NOTE:** *"Fat Man" was the codename for the atomic bomb detonated over Nagasaki, Japan, on August 9, 1945. The fat man stepping on a watch represents Osterman's background, symbolizing his transformation into an atomic superhuman.*

> **CONFLICT:** *In the* Watchmen *film, Wally Weaver and his girlfriend attend the amusement park with Jon and Janey. In Alan Moore's miniseries, the two are alone.*

July 1959 (Alternate Reality)

Jon Osterman buys Janey Slater a beer at a local tavern. As a result, the two never visit the Palisades Amusement Park, thereby altering their future fates **[BWDM]**.

August 1959

Scientists at the Gila Flats Test Base conduct fourteen experiments to remove the intrinsic fields from concrete blocks. All fourteen tests end with the concrete's disintegration **[ALAN]**.

Before August 20, 1959

Josef Osterman often tells his son Jon that if someone were to ask a centipede which foot went first, it would sit for hours, unable to move **[BWDM]**.

August 20, 1959—Morning

Jon Osterman fixes Janey Slater's watch and brings it with him to work **[ALAN]**.

> **NOTE:** Alan Moore's miniseries sets Osterman's transformation in August 1959. Before Watchmen: Doctor Manhattan provides the exact date.

> **CONFLICT:** Taking Out the Trash dates these events on September 11, 1959, contradicting the original comic.

August 20, 1959—Before 1:15 PM

After resetting the intrinsic field chamber, Jon Osterman accidentally leaves his lab coat, with Janey's watch in one pocket, inside the chamber **[ALAN]**. He heads out for lunch, then realizes he has forgotten the watch and returns to retrieve it. Wally Weaver praises his ability to put anything broken back together again. Neither is aware of Jon's future consciousness, Dr. Manhattan, observing these events **[BWDM]**.

August 20, 1959—Before 1:15 PM (Alternate Realities)

In various timelines, Jon Osterman either hurries into the chamber, saunters into it, stops to talk to Wally Weaver, or aches to return to Janey Slater. With each permutation, a new, unique quantum reality is created **[BWDM]**.

August 20, 1959—1:15 PM (All Realities)

To avoid changing his own history in any reality by inadvertently preventing Jon Osterman's transformation into a superhuman, Dr. Manhattan's consciousness expends a tiny amount of energy to reset the chamber's time clock. As a result, no matter when he enters, he will have only five seconds to exit, instead of the expected thirty. As infinite quantum possibilities collapse into a singular reality, every version of Jon Osterman in every universe becomes aware of the others' existence [**BWDM**].

August 20, 1959—1:15 PM

While Jon is still in the chamber, the door automatically locks as the generators warm up for an experiment to remove intrinsic fields from a fifteenth concrete block. Jon yells to be let out, but Milton Glass tells him there is no way to override the time-lock, and Janey runs away in tears, unable to watch her lover die. As the particle cannons fire, Jon's body is painfully reduced to its component atoms, and he screams in terror [**ALAN**].

August 20, 1959—1:15 PM (Alternate Reality)

Jon Osterman leaves the test chamber before the doors lock, and is not transformed into a superhuman. Unseen by Jon, his future consciousness, Dr. Manhattan, observes this alteration of his history, perplexed at how such a paradox could be possible [**BWDM**].

August 20, 1959—After 1:15 PM (Alternate Reality)

After leaving the test chamber, Jon Osterman notices that Janey's watch, despite having been repaired, has stopped ticking as of 1:15 [**BWDM**].

After August 20, 1959

Despite having a subtracted body, Jon Osterman's intelligence lives on at a subatomic level [**ABSO**], surviving as a purely electromagnetic pattern. Jon is presumed dead, but his incorporeal mind begins to build an approximation of its lost form. The military sends a telegram to his father, informing him of the accidental disintegration [**ALAN**]. Milton Glass pays respects to Josef Osterman, offering to handle his son's funeral arrangements. The watchmaker is devastated, refusing to accept Jon's death and demanding that the base find a way to put his pieces back together [**BWDM**].

After August 20, 1959 (Alternate Reality)

In a quantum reality in which Jon Osterman never becomes Dr. Manhattan, Josef Osterman dreams of government officials informing him that his son has died. The dream is disturbingly lifelike, staying with Josef for days [**BWDM**].

MIND .... *The Mindscape of Alan Moore*
MOBL .... *Watchmen: The Mobile Game*
MOTN .... *Watchmen: The Complete Motion Comic*
MTRO .... *Metro* promotional newspaper cover wrap
NEWP .... *New Frontiersman* promotional newspaper
NEWW .... *New Frontiersman* website
NIGH ..... *Watchmen: The End Is Nigh, Parts 1 and 2*
PKIT ...... *Watchmen* film British press kit
PORT ..... *Watchmen Portraits*
REAL ..... Real life
RPG1 .... *DC Heroes Role Playing Module #227: Who Watches the Watchmen?*

RPG2 .... *DC Heroes Role Playing Module #235: Taking Out the Trash—Curses and Tears*
RPG3 .... *DC Heroes: The Watchmen Sourcebook*
RUBY .... "Wounds," published in *The Ruby Files Volume One*
SCR1 ..... Unfilmed screenplay draft: Sam Hamm
SCR2 ..... Unfilmed screenplay draft: Charles McKeuen
SCR3 ..... Unfilmed screenplay draft: Gary Goldman
SCR4 ..... Unfilmed screenplay draft: David Hayter (2002)
SCR5 ..... Unfilmed screenplay draft: David Hayter (2003)
SCR6 ..... Unfilmed screenplay draft: Alex Tse
SPOT ..... *DC Spotlight #1*
VRL1 ..... Viral video: *NBS Nightly News with Ted Philips*

VRL2 ..... Viral video: *The Keene Act and You*
VRL3 ..... Viral video: *Who Watches the Watchmen? A Veidt Music Network (VMN) Special*
VRL4 ..... Viral video: *World in Focus: 6 Minutes to Midnight*
VRL5 ..... Viral video: *Local Radio Station Report on 1977 Riots*
VRL6 ..... Viral videos (group of ten): *Veidt Enterprises Advertising Contest*
WAWA ... *Watching the Watchmen*
WHOS ... *Who's Who: The Definitive Directory of the DC Universe*
WTFC .... *Watchmen: The Film Companion*

Between August 20, 1959 and May 14, 1961 (Alternate Reality)

In a quantum reality in which Jon Osterman never becomes Dr. Manhattan, Jon takes Janey Slater back to New Jersey's Palisades Amusement Park, discretely enlisting a worker's help in proposing marriage. As Jon plays the game the man operates, she reflects on Hank Meadows' sudden death, and how that tragedy enabled the couple to meet. Jon knocks down three milk bottles, winning her a stuffed blue bear. Hidden inside is a wedding ring, and she happily accepts his proposal **[BWDM]**.

Between August 20, 1959 and October 19, 1962 (Alternate Reality)

Jon Osterman tries unsuccessfully to fix Janey Sater's watch many times, but somehow never manages to do so. He hangs the watch on a nail in their home, with a tag labeled "The One That Got Away" **[BWDM]**.

—September 1959

A funeral is held for Jon Osterman, though there is no body to bury **[ALAN]**. Despite his having died on August 20, his gravestone lists a death date of August 30 **[BWDM]**.

—September 23, 1959

In New York City's port district, Adrian Veidt meets with an underworld contact, Skeeter, who tells him of rumors that the U.S. government is searching for Hooded Justice. Veidt finds dried blood on the docks, but before he can investigate, The Comedian fires at him. Adrian senses his presence, narrowly avoids injury, and lobs a stiletto into the gun barrel when Blake tries to shoot again, causing the weapon to explode. Adrian tackles him, but Blake gets the upper hand and tries to blind him with a cigar—which Veidt bites into, spitting the tip back in Blake's face **[BWOZ]**.

The two battle but are evenly matched, until Veidt lets his adversary win so he can observe the other's skills. The Comedian walks off, mocking Ozymandias's costume, abilities, and masculinity **[BWOZ]**. The encounter makes Veidt realize that criminals are not the only people capable of evil, and causes him to suspect (without hard evidence) that Blake may have killed Hooded Justice **[ALAN]**.

—In or After September 1959

Adrian Veidt abandons his search for Hooded Justice as more pressing concerns take precedence **[BWOZ]**.

Stepping back into the timestream after observing multiple realities, Dr. Manhattan's future consciousness realizes something is wrong with the universe—a static curtain now obscures his ability to experience the future, allowing silhouettes of death and destruction for which he is responsible, but no details. He visits Ozymandias at a point in time after their initial introduction, seeking advice from the world's smartest man **[BWDM]**.

—October 1959

A grieving Janey Slater places the amusement-park photo of her and Jon Osterman—the only picture anyone has of him—in a glass case at the Bestiary **[ALAN]**.

—November 1959

A ghastly image of Jon Osterman's floating nervous system appears in a bathroom mirror at the Gila Flats Test Base. The image terrifies two elderly employees discussing Fidel Castro's rise to power. During the coming weeks, Jon appears to several other workers as well, each time with more of his body reconstituted **[ALAN]**.

—November 9—11:30 PM

Dexter Redback, Gila Flats' night-shift janitor, is startled at the sight of an apparition in the north hall of Test Base Building 2A. He reports seeing the partially muscled skeletal body of a "blue man" punch the wall and utter an ear-piercing shriek before vanishing **[NEWW]**.

—November 10, 1959—1:00 AM

Captain T. Dixon and Second Lieutenant S. Chambers investigate Redback's claim. He reports a blue haze and electrical disturbances surrounding the figure **[NEWW]**.

—November 10, 1959—2:00 AM

Dixon and Chambers file an incident report, noting that Redback shows no signs of intoxication or narcotic influence **[NEWW]**.

—November 10, 1959—Daytime

Cooks at the Gila Flats facility are shocked when an image of Jon Osterman's circulatory system suddenly appears in the kitchen **[ALAN]**.

—November 14, 1959

Jon Osterman's partially muscled skeleton appears near the Gila Flats facility's perimeter fence, screaming for thirty seconds before vanishing **[ALAN]**.

—November 14, 1959—10:00 PM

While serving guard duty at Gila Flats' southeastern perimeter fence, M.P. Private James Sanderson summons M.P. officers Captain T. Dixon and First Lieutenant T. Phoenix, after

MIND .... *The Mindscape of Alan Moore*
MOBL.... *Watchmen: The Mobile Game*
MOTN.... *Watchmen: The Complete Motion Comic*
MTRO.... *Metro* promotional newspaper cover wrap
NEWP.... *New Frontiersman* promotional newspaper
NEWW... *New Frontiersman* website
NIGH ..... *Watchmen: The End Is Nigh, Parts 1 and 2*
PKIT ...... *Watchmen* film British press kit
PORT ..... *Watchmen Portraits*
REAL.....Real life
RPG1 .... *DC Heroes Role Playing Module #227: Who Watches the Watchmen?*

RPG2 .... *DC Heroes Role Playing Module #235: Taking Out the Trash—Curses and Tears*
RPG3 .... *DC Heroes: The Watchmen Sourcebook*
RUBY .... "Wounds," published in *The Ruby Files Volume One*
SCR1.....Unfilmed screenplay draft: Sam Hamm
SCR2.....Unfilmed screenplay draft: Charles McKeuen
SCR3.....Unfilmed screenplay draft: Gary Goldman
SCR4.....Unfilmed screenplay draft: David Hayter (2002)
SCR5.....Unfilmed screenplay draft: David Hayter (2003)
SCR6.....Unfilmed screenplay draft: Alex Tse
SPOT.....*DC Spotlight #1*
VRL1 .....Viral video: *NBS Nightly News with Ted Philips*

VRL2 .....Viral video: *The Keene Act and You*
VRL3 .....Viral video: *Who Watches the Watchmen? A Veidt Music Network (VMN) Special*
VRL4 .....Viral video: *World in Focus: 6 Minutes to Midnight*
VRL5 .....Viral video: *Local Radio Station Report on 1977 Riots*
VRL6 .....Viral videos (group of ten): *Veidt Enterprises Advertising Contest*
WAWA... *Watching the Watchmen*
WHOS... *Who's Who: The Definitive Directory of the DC Universe*
WTFC .... *Watchmen: The Film Companion*

being alerted to a strange figure suddenly appearing near the secondary fence. Sanderson describes the figure as a pair of eyes attached to a spinal column and ganglia. Dixon and Phoenix submit a report on Sanderson's claim, noting that he has no history of mental illness **[NEWW]**.

—November 22, 1959

Wally Weaver considers quitting the Gila Flats Test Base, convinced that recent ghostly sightings are due to a haunting. As Wally and Janey Slater dine in the Bestiary, energy fills the room, making everyone's hair stand on end and creating a shower of sparks. In a flash of ultraviolet light, Jon Osterman's full body appears floating in the room—naked, hairless, blue, and alive **[ALAN]**.

In reconstructing Jon Osterman's original form, this new entity achieves a mastery of all matter, able to reshape reality by manipulating its basic building blocks **[ALAN]**. He develops the ability to view quantum realities containing alternate permutations of his life's events, and to teleport himself anywhere in space and time—not by disassembling and re-assembling his component molecules, but by warping space-time around himself since it is less destructive to move the universe than his body **[BWDM]**.

—After November 22, 1959

Jon Osterman opts not to inform his father that he has returned to the living **[ALAN]**.

—November or December 1959

Osterman, now able to perceive past, present, and future events simultaneously, witnesses the assassination of U.S. President John F. Kennedy on December 22, 1963. He also experiences an argument that he and Janey Slater will have regarding his inaction in preventing that murder, followed by the couple's subsequent love-making **[ALAN]**.

—December 25, 1959

Janey Slater presents Jon Osterman with a gold ring on Christmas, hoping he still likes jewelry. When he describes its atomic structure, she admits to being scared at how everything has changed since he became god-like. He denies the existence of a god, but promises he'll always want her—knowing, even as he says it, that he is lying and will eventually leave her for a younger woman **[ALAN]**.

—Between December 1959 and February 1960

Jon Osterman ceases to feel heat or cold **[ALAN]**.

—1950s or 1960s
Walter Kovacs develops an appreciation for Senator Barry Goldwater, whom he considers a "true American" **[RPG2]**.

> **NOTE:** *Goldwater, an Arizona senator from 1953 to 1965 and from 1969 to 1987, ran for President in 1964 on the Republican ticket, losing to Lyndon B. Johnson.*

A beautiful woman (later known as The Twilight Lady) is used and abused by men only interested in her sexually. She endures the abuse and comes out a stronger person for it **[BWNO]**.

> **NOTE:** *The Watchmen Sourcebook lists her birth name as Leslie Chadwicke, while Before Watchmen: Nite Owl names her Elizabeth Lane. One or both could be an alias.*

—In or Before the 1960s
Eddie Blake apprehends an Italian drug dealer named Sal, attends his trial, and arranges for his deportation to the French island of Corsica. Blake keeps abreast of Sal's whereabouts, and thus learns of the criminal's relocation to Vietnam **[BWCO]**.

Hollis Mason, aware that he is getting older and putting on some extra weight, begins to doubt his ability to continue fighting crime **[BWDM]**.

—1960
Simon, a schoolmate of Laurie Jupiter, visits her home to invite Laurie outside to play baseball. Sally Jupiter, determined to protect her daughter from boys' attentions, scares him away by claiming she bullies and humiliates boys by pulling down their shorts. Dressed to play ball, Laurie sadly watches from her bedroom window as Simon runs away in fear **[BWSS]**.

—February 1960
The U.S. government prepares to announce Jon Osterman's existence to the world, intending to position him as an unstoppable weapon. Officials provide him with a black outfit and a helmet containing a logo symbolizing atomic power, designed by marketing experts. Deeming the helmet meaningless, Jon instead etches the image of a hydrogen atom directly on his forehead. The government nicknames him Dr. Manhattan, knowing the United States' enemies will associate it with the Manhattan Project, which produced the first U.S. nuclear weapon in 1942 **[ALAN]**. General Anthony Randolph is assigned as Dr. Manhattan's first "handler" **[FILM]**.

—Mid-February 1960
The National Regaler reports unconfirmed rumors of a "nuclear super-man" **[RPG3]**. Adrian Veidt also begins hearing buzz about a new superhuman force that could change the world's status quo **[BWOZ]**.

MIND .... *The Mindscape of Alan Moore*	**RPG2** .... *DC Heroes Role Playing Module #235: Taking Out the Trash—Curses and Tears*	**VRL2** ..... Viral video: *The Keene Act and You*
MOBL .... *Watchmen: The Mobile Game*		**VRL3** ..... Viral video: *Who Watches the Watchmen? A Veidt Music Network (VMN) Special*
MOTN .... *Watchmen: The Complete Motion Comic*	**RPG3** .... *DC Heroes: The Watchmen Sourcebook*	
MTRO .... *Metro* promotional newspaper cover wrap	**RUBY** .... "Wounds," published in *The Ruby Files Volume One*	**VRL4** ..... Viral video: *World in Focus: 6 Minutes to Midnight*
NEWP .... *New Frontiersman* promotional newspaper	**SCR1** ..... Unfilmed screenplay draft: Sam Hamm	**VRL5** ..... Viral video: *Local Radio Station Report on 1977 Riots*
NEWW ... *New Frontiersman* website	**SCR2** ..... Unfilmed screenplay draft: Charles McKeuen	
NIGH ..... *Watchmen: The End Is Nigh, Parts 1 and 2*	**SCR3** ..... Unfilmed screenplay draft: Gary Goldman	**VRL6** ..... Viral videos (group of ten): *Veidt Enterprises Advertising Contest*
PKIT ...... *Watchmen* film British press kit	**SCR4** ..... Unfilmed screenplay draft: David Hayter (2002)	
PORT ..... *Watchmen Portraits*	**SCR5** ..... Unfilmed screenplay draft: David Hayter (2003)	**WAWA** ... *Watching the Watchmen*
REAL ..... Real life	**SCR6** ..... Unfilmed screenplay draft: Alex Tse	**WHOS** ... *Who's Who: The Definitive Directory of the DC Universe*
RPG1 .... *DC Heroes Role Playing Module #227: Who Watches the Watchmen?*	**SPOT** ..... *DC Spotlight #1*	
	VRL1 ..... Viral video: *NBS Nightly News with Ted Philips*	**WTFC** .... *Watchmen: The Film Companion*

—In or Before March 1960

Veidt hires a personal assistant named Marla, whom he pays well. The two form a bond close enough that she is comfortable speaking sarcastically to him. Eventually, they become lovers **[BWOZ]**.

—Early March 1960

Top Eisenhower administration officials announce Dr. Manhattan's existence to the rest of mankind **[RPG3]**, releasing news reels of him dismantling weaponry and military tanks with his mind **[ALAN, RPG2]**. The announcement shocks nations around the world. A persistent *NBS Evening News* broadcaster **[FILM]** hounds Professor Milton Glass for comment, until the scientist tells him "God exists and he's American." The TV anchor misquotes him as saying "The superman exists and he's American" **[ALAN]**.

> **NOTE:** *Alan Moore's miniseries sets the announcement in March 1960.* Taking Out the Trash *specifies March 2,* The Watchmen Sourcebook *cites March 1, and the* NBS Nightly News *viral video uses the date March 11.*

> **CONFLICT:** *In the* Watchmen *film, Wally Weaver utters the quote, not Glass.*

The *New York Gazette* covers this development with a front-page article titled "Meet Dr. Manhattan: There Is a Superman, and He's American!" **[BWOZ]**. Quoted in the piece is Andrei Sokolov, the U.S.S.R.'s foreign minister, who dismisses the story as a hoax **[RPG3]**.

Adrian Veidt is outwardly unfazed when his assistant Marla shows him the article, but privately, he thanks God that this omnipotent entity is on the side of good. He instructs Marla to invest all liquid finance in fallout shelters and their renting and construction, so he can corner the market; to hire the world's three best architects, at least one of whom must be a cold weather construction expert; and to procure several square miles of Antarctica's most inaccessible and defensible land **[BWOZ]**.

—In or After March 1960

Unable to reach Jon Osterman for comment, a journalist interviews Nelson Gardner, who is unnerved at the news of Dr. Manhattan's existence, and Sally Jupiter, who remains skeptical. Janey Slater is delighted at the coverage Jon receives, though Jon himself remains nonplussed **[ALAN]**

For many, Dr. Manhattan's existence renders obsolete the concepts of "masked hero" and "costumed adventurer." Some initially express disbelief at the idea of an individual able to walk through walls, teleport instantly from one location to another, and completely re-arrange matter with a single thought, but disbelief turns to acceptance and even elation.

ABSO .... *Watchmen Absolute Edition*	**BWOZ**.... *Before Watchmen—Ozymandias*	• Film: *Batman v Superman: Dawn of Justice Ultimate Edition*	
ALAN..... Alan Moore's *Watchmen* miniseries	**BWRO** ... *Before Watchmen—Rorschach*		
ARCD .... *Minutemen Arcade*	**BWSS** ... *Before Watchmen—Silk Spectre*	• Film: *Justice League*	
ARTF ..... *Watchmen: The Art of the Film*	**CHEM** .... My Chemical Romance music video: "Desolation Row"	**CLIX** ...... HeroClix figure pack-in cards	
BLCK..... *Tales of the Black Freighter*	**CMEO** .... *Watchmen* cameos in comics, TV, and film:	**DECK**..... *DC Comics Deck-Building Game—Crossover Pack 4: Watchmen*	
BWCC ... *Before Watchmen—The Crimson Corsair*	• Comic: *Astonishing X-Men* volume 3 issue #6		
BWCO ... *Before Watchmen—Comedian*	• Comic: *Hero Hotline* volume 1 issue #5	**DURS** .... *DC Universe: Rebirth Special* volume 1 issue #1	
BWDB .. *Before Watchmen—Dollar Bill*	• Comic: *Kingdom Come* volume 1 issue #2	**FILM** ..... *Watchmen* theatrical film	
BWDM .. *Before Watchmen—Dr. Manhattan*	• Comic: *Marvels* volume 1 issue #4	**HOOD** .... *Under the Hood* documentary and dust-jacket prop reproduction	
BWMM.. *Before Watchmen—Minutemen*	• Comic: *The Question* volume 1 issue #17		
BWMO .. *Before Watchmen—Moloch*	• TV: *Teen Titans Go!* episode #82, "Real Boy Adventures"	**JUST**..... *Watchmen: Justice Is Coming*	
BWNO ... *Before Watchmen—Nite Owl*	• Film: *Man of Steel*	**MATL** .... Mattel Club Black Freighter figure pack-in cards	

For masked adventurers, it means being replaced **[ALAN]**. But because he is American, the United States' relationships with the Soviet Union and China degrade **[RPG2]**.

—March to June 1960

Three architects independently draw up plans for Adrian Veidt's Antarctic base **[BWOZ]**, which he calls Karnak after a huge monument once built by Ramses II, the Egyptian name for Ozymandias **[ALAN]**. Veidt deems each blueprint excellent and asks them to combine the best aspects into a single, focused design **[BWOZ]**.

—Between March 1960 and 1986

Imprisoned would-be supervillain Bob "Buzzbomb" Krankk often expresses a desire to face Dr. Manhattan—his self-imagined arch-nemesis—in man-to-man combat, despite having no history of having encountered the superhuman and no chance whatsoever of inflicting any damage on him **[RPG3]**.

—Before May 1960

Comic-book artist Joe Orlando draws a well-received run of "Sargasso Sea Stories" in E.C.'s *Piracy* comic series, adapting smoothly from a background drawing science-fiction and horror comics to being revered as the most respected artist in his burgeoning field. National Comics editor Julius Schwartz convinces Orlando to leave *Piracy* to illustrate a new title, *Tales of the Black Freighter* **[ALAN]**.

> **NOTE:** *Julius Schwartz was a prominent comic book editor and science fiction agent in the real world, while Joe Orlando was a well-respected writer, illustrator, cartoonist, editor, and publisher at DC Comics and* MAD Magazine. *Alan Moore reportedly intended, before his well-publicized falling-out with DC Comics, to work with Orlando on creating an actual* Tales of the Black Freighter *spinoff comic.*

—May 1960

National Comics publishes the first issue of *Tales of the Black Freighter* to much acclaim. Newcomer Max Shea writes the issue (which some see as sturdy but clichéd), naming the title vessel after a ship from Kurt Weill's *The Threepenny Opera*. The story, illustrated by Joe Orlando, involves three men who visit a dockside town in search of work and swap stories at a tavern. A nearby sea captain—who may be Satan—listens to their tales and offers passage aboard his ship, which turns out to be a vessel from Hell, sent out to take on board the souls of evil men for all eternity. Backup tale "Galapagos Jones," illustrated by another artist, is not as highly regarded **[ALAN]**.

—In or Before June 1960

Adrian Veidt obtains a trademark for his signature Gordian Knot. He also earns the nickname "Mr. O" **[BWOZ]**.

MIND .... *The Mindscape of Alan Moore*
MOBL .... *Watchmen: The Mobile Game*
MOTN .... *Watchmen: The Complete Motion Comic*
MTRO .... *Metro* promotional newspaper cover wrap
NEWP .... *New Frontiersman* promotional newspaper
NEWW ... *New Frontiersman* website
NIGH .... *Watchmen: The End Is Nigh, Parts 1 and 2*
PKIT ...... *Watchmen* film British press kit
PORT ..... *Watchmen Portraits*
REAL ..... Real life
RPG1 .... *DC Heroes Role Playing Module #227: Who Watches the Watchmen?*

RPG2 .... *DC Heroes Role Playing Module #235: Taking Out the Trash—Curses and Tears*
RPG3 .... *DC Heroes: The Watchmen Sourcebook*
RUBY .... "Wounds," published in *The Ruby Files Volume One*
SCR1 ..... Unfilmed screenplay draft: Sam Hamm
SCR2 ..... Unfilmed screenplay draft: Charles McKeuen
SCR3 ..... Unfilmed screenplay draft: Gary Goldman
SCR4 ..... Unfilmed screenplay draft: David Hayter (2002)
SCR5 ..... Unfilmed screenplay draft: David Hayter (2003)
SCR6 ..... Unfilmed screenplay draft: Alex Tse
SPOT ..... *DC Spotlight #1*
VRL1 ..... Viral video: *NBS Nightly News with Ted Philips*

VRL2 ..... Viral video: *The Keene Act and You*
VRL3 ..... Viral video: *Who Watches the Watchmen? A Veidt Music Network (VMN) Special*
VRL4 ..... Viral video: *World in Focus: 6 Minutes to Midnight*
VRL5 ..... Viral video: *Local Radio Station Report on 1977 Riots*
VRL6 ..... Viral videos (group of ten): *Veidt Enterprises Advertising Contest*
WAWA ... *Watching the Watchmen*
WHOS .... *Who's Who: The Definitive Directory of the DC Universe*
WTFC .... *Watchmen: The Film Companion*

The Red Cross and the Foundation for Relief for India plan a charity event to ease famine-related suffering in that nation. To help raise awareness, the organizations invite New York City's costumed crime-fighters to attend. Since Ozymandias's true identity remains a secret, they leave his invitation at police headquarters **[BWOZ]**.

—June 1960

Construction commences on Adrian Veidt's secret base in Antarctica, in what was previously a desolate wasteland. Veidt and his assistant Marla survey the project, then return to New York to conduct further business. Back in New York, Veidt manipulates the stock market by day, while fighting crime at night as Ozymandias **[BWOZ]**.

—June 3, 1960

Dan Dreiberg graduates from Harvard University with dual master's degrees in zoology and aeronautics **[ALAN]**. The commencement ceremony features speeches by Harvard President B.W. Thoreau ("Your New Responsibilities in the New Age"), Dean of Students Lucius Gallsworthy ("Who Would Have Dreamed?"), guest speaker Robert F. Kennedy ("The Bright Tomorrow"), and Dan himself as class valedictorian ("A Little Nostalgia"), with a closing prayer by Father George Berkeley **[RPG3]**.

> **NOTE:** *In the real world, Harvard's President in 1960 was Nathan Marsh Pusey. Dan's graduation from that school is mentioned in Alan Moore's miniseries. The* Watchmen Sourcebook *specifies his graduation date.*
>
> *Numerous sources have offered conflicting birth years for Dan. Even the earliest, 1940, would make him only twenty years old upon earning his master's degrees. Either way, Dan would seem to be a prodigy, befitting his status as* Watchmen's *Batman analog.*
>
> **CONFLICT:** *In* Before Watchmen: Nite Owl, *Dan has not yet graduated from college as of 1962.*

—June 11, 1960

The *New York Gazette* reports that the collection barrel of a Harlem mission for the underprivileged has received five suitcases containing more than a million dollars, each case bearing an anonymous clipped note indicating "For the needy" **[RPG3]**.

> **NOTE:** *The benefactor is unidentified, but is hinted at being Byron Lewis.*

—Mid-June 1960

Ozymandias topples a smuggling ring known as The Contraband, leaving them dangling outside police headquarters by a Gordian Knot. As he is about to leave, a police officer hands him an invitation that the Red Cross and the Foundation for Relief for India had left for him, inviting him to a charity function. Veidt initially declines, until learning that Dr. Manhattan will be among the attendees **[BWOZ]**.

●—June 17, 1960

A week later, Adrian Veidt attends the famine-relief event, held at Madison Square Garden. Others in attendance include Captain Metropolis, The Nite Owl, The Comedian, and Mothman. Veidt agrees to perform at the charity, but is annoyed when his acrobatics routine is paired with Eddie Blake's marksman demonstration. The Comedian hits every mark, and Veidt emerges unscathed, though tension remains between the two **[BWOZ]**.

After his routine, Veidt notices Byron Lewis having a panic attack that he might get himself killed during his performance. Adrian tells him that Mothman and his fellow Minutemen were his inspirations for taking up crime-fighting. His confidence bolstered, Lewis puts on an impressive flying routine, despite a few stumbles. Veidt watches from the backstage control room. Noticing a bank of television monitors, he decides to similarly equip his Antarctic citadel. Nelson Gardner asks him how to pronounce "Ozymandias," then mingles among the crowd. Veidt privately deems Gardner a Neanderthal, and the superhero crowd primitives **[BWOZ]**.

At the event, Hollis Mason finds Veidt to be "a nice young fellow," but considers Dr. Manhattan a bit distant, partly due to his own discomfort in the superhuman's physical presence. Manhattan finds that he has nothing in common with what he perceives as "friendly middle-aged men who like to dress up." The only attendee he finds interesting is Ozymandias **[ALAN, RPG2]**. Veidt is equally fascinated by him, though his arm hairs stand up and point toward Manhattan in the latter's presence **[ALAN, BWOZ]**.

> *NOTE: Alan Moore's miniseries establishes the charity event as occurring in June 1960. The specific date appears in* Taking Out the Trash.

> *CONFLICT: In* Before Watchmen: Minutemen, *Jon Osterman and Hollis Mason don't meet for the first time until the latter's retirement party in 1962, contradicting the original comic.*

Jon Osterman speaks to Indian President Rajendra Prasad about his country's severe famine. The superhuman offers to change the topsoil's nitrogen content to make India's land extremely fertile, but the politician cannot grasp the scale of the offer **[BWDM]**.

Mason peruses the room and sees Eddie Blake being obnoxious and smoking cigars, Byron Lewis acting drunk and incoherent, and Nelson Gardner showing some paunch. With the next generation of crime-fighters also in attendance, he doubts his own abilities and decides to quit the business. Eligible for police retirement, Mason considers what to do next with his life, then remembers that he was happiest while working with his father at Moe Vernon's garage **[ALAN]**. As he tells Jon Osterman of his plan, Janey Slater feels sick to her stomach and asks Jon to take her home **[BWOZ]**.

MIND .... *The Mindscape of Alan Moore*
MOBL.... *Watchmen: The Mobile Game*
MOTN.... *Watchmen: The Complete Motion Comic*
MTRO.... *Metro* promotional newspaper cover wrap
NEWP.... *New Frontiersman* promotional newspaper
NEWW.... *New Frontiersman* website
NIGH ..... *Watchmen: The End Is Nigh, Parts 1 and 2*
PKIT...... *Watchmen* film British press kit
PORT..... *Watchmen Portraits*
REAL..... Real life
RPG1 .... *DC Heroes Role Playing Module #227: Who Watches the Watchmen?*

RPG2 .... *DC Heroes Role Playing Module #235: Taking Out the Trash—Curses and Tears*
RPG3 .... *DC Heroes: The Watchmen Sourcebook*
RUBY .... "Wounds," published in *The Ruby Files Volume One*
SCR1..... Unfilmed screenplay draft: Sam Hamm
SCR2..... Unfilmed screenplay draft: Charles McKeuen
SCR3..... Unfilmed screenplay draft: Gary Goldman
SCR4..... Unfilmed screenplay draft: David Hayter (2002)
SCR5..... Unfilmed screenplay draft: David Hayter (2003)
SCR6..... Unfilmed screenplay draft: Alex Tse
SPOT..... *DC Spotlight #1*
VRL1 ..... Viral video: *NBS Nightly News with Ted Philips*

VRL2..... Viral video: *The Keene Act and You*
VRL3..... Viral video: *Who Watches the Watchmen? A Veidt Music Network (VMN) Special*
VRL4 ..... Viral video: *World in Focus: 6 Minutes to Midnight*
VRL5 ..... Viral video: *Local Radio Station Report on 1977 Riots*
VRL6 ..... Viral videos (group of ten): *Veidt Enterprises Advertising Contest*
WAWA... *Watching the Watchmen*
WHOS ... *Who's Who: The Definitive Directory of the DC Universe*
WTFC ... *Watchmen: The Film Companion*

●—Between June 1960 and 1967

Adrian Veidt introduces "The Veidt Method," a bodybuilding technique that he claims will turn customers into superhumans with "bodies beyond [their] wildest imagination." The four-tiered course combines meditation with physical and intellectual exercise. Advertisements for the physical-fitness and self-improvement program run on the back of the comic book *Tales of the Black Freighter* **[ALAN, NEWW]**.

> **NOTE:** *Veidt's bodybuilding advertisements are based on Charles Atlas's ads for his "dynamic tension" workout that ran for decades at the back of comics and boys' magazines, starting in the 1940s. The name also offers subtle foreshadowing that Adrian is the mastermind of the book's plot—it's all part of Veidt's method to save mankind.*

Joe Orlando remains on *Tales of the Black Freighter* for issues #2-9, while "Galapagos Jones" continues until issue #6. The comic greatly influences similar titles, with Max Shea's writing improving over time. Issue #3, "Between Breaths," is told from the viewpoint of a drowning man, culminating in dead sailors assuming control of the *Black Freighter*. Readers fully embrace the writing and artwork by issue #5, but Shea lets fame go to his head and resents Orlando's popularity, harassing him with impossibly detailed panel descriptions and frequent revision requests. Issue #7, "The Shanty of Edward Teach," is narrated in rhyme by Blackbeard **[ALAN]**.

> **NOTE:** *The Watchmen Sourcebook establishes the span of time during which the first thirty issues of* Tales of the Black Freighter *are published as seven years, which means a new issue must hit stores every three months or so.*

The friction between Shea and Orlando is well-publicized, and the latter steps down as of issue #9, to be replaced by unknown but skilled artist Walt Feinberg. Shea, possibly humbled by his fallout with Orlando, gets along well with Feinberg. Their run is as highly regarded as the Shea-Orlando years, featuring dark, sinister tales of metaphysical terror set against grim reality. These include "The Figurehead," an unflinching yarn about homosexuality, and "Marooned" (in issues #23-24) **[ALAN]**.

"Marooned" tells the story of a young mariner whose vessel is wrecked by the *Black Freighter* before its crew can warn their home port, Davidstown, of the Hellship's approach. The mariner, the sole survivor, becomes shipwrecked on a remote island, where he imagines conversing with the corpse of his friend, Bosun Ridley. Convinced that the evil pirate crew plan to attack Davidstown, the mariner has no choice but to use his shipmates' bloated bodies as an improvised raft so that he can either rescue or avenge his family **[ALAN, BLCK]**. Unlike other *Black Freighter* tales, "Marooned" is narrated almost entirely in captions **[ALAN]**.

> **NOTE:** *The storyline of "Marooned" presages Adrian Veidt's plan, for in order to save the world, Veidt must kill three million people—in essence, using their corpses as mankind's*

raft. The Black Freighter *tale's excerpts, peppered throughout* Watchmen, *mirror the miniseries' themes, character arcs, specific panels, and surrounding dialogue.*

CONFLICT: *The* Watchmen *film features an issue from the "Marooned" storyline, but the issue number, 307, contradicts the numbering indicated in Alan Moore's miniseries and in* The Watchmen Sourcebook.

Tales of the Black Freighter faces controversy as of issue #25, when Max Shea begins a series of tales about banned books in the freighter captain's library, which the pirate had plundered as they were headed to the Vatican for eternal suppression. When the concept is renounced as pornographic, DC Comics rejects four of the five planned storylines, and Shea quits the series—and the comics field—as of issue #31 **[ALAN]**.

The first thirty issues of *Tales of the Black Freighter* also feature the work of Michael Longfield, Tim Snowden, Xrat, Lisa Downing, Harvey Kurtzman, Alan Moore, Dave Gibbons, and other creators **[RPG3]**.
> **NOTE:** *Moore and Gibbons, of course, are* Watchmen's *original creators.*

—June 1960 and Beyond
Adrian Veidt keeps tabs on The Comedian's activities, disturbed by the immoral actions he commits in the name of fighting crime **[ALAN]**.

—In or Before August 1960
Dan Dreiberg's uncle Alan invites him to join the family banking business **[RPG3]**.

—August 16, 1960
Dan writes a letter to Alan, gratefully declining the job offer **[RPG3]**.

—In or After August 1960
Dan Dreiberg begins studying ornithology at the Bronx Zoo, in New York **[RPG3]**.
> **NOTE:** *Ornithology is a branch of zoology involving the study of birds.*

—September 9, 1960
Jon Osterman's initial Gila Flats Test Base identification card expires **[RPG3]**.

—Late 1960
Adrian Veidt hires three Asian servants to work for him at Karnak while the Antarctic citadel is still under construction **[BWOZ]**. He creates a vivarium (a glass-domed geodesic bubble housing a tropical paradise amidst the subzero conditions) in which to conduct research into teleportation and other sciences **[ALAN]**. His staff erects a wall of video

MIND	*The Mindscape of Alan Moore*	**RPG2**	*DC Heroes Role Playing Module #235: Taking Out the Trash—Curses and Tears*	**VRL2**	Viral video: *The Keene Act and You*
MOBL	*Watchmen: The Mobile Game*			**VRL3**	Viral video: *Who Watches the Watchmen? A Veidt Music Network (VMN) Special*
MOTN	*Watchmen: The Complete Motion Comic*	**RPG3**	*DC Heroes: The Watchmen Sourcebook*		
MTRO	*Metro* promotional newspaper cover wrap	**RUBY**	"Wounds," published in *The Ruby Files Volume One*	**VRL4**	Viral video: *World in Focus: 6 Minutes to Midnight*
NEWP	*New Frontiersman* promotional newspaper	**SCR1**	Unfilmed screenplay draft: Sam Hamm	**VRL5**	Viral video: *Local Radio Station Report on 1977 Riots*
NEWW	*New Frontiersman* website	**SCR2**	Unfilmed screenplay draft: Charles McKeuen		
NIGH	*Watchmen: The End Is Nigh, Parts 1 and 2*	**SCR3**	Unfilmed screenplay draft: Gary Goldman	**VRL6**	Viral videos (group of ten): *Veidt Enterprises Advertising Contest*
PKIT	*Watchmen* film British press kit	**SCR4**	Unfilmed screenplay draft: David Hayter (2002)		
PORT	*Watchmen Portraits*	**SCR5**	Unfilmed screenplay draft: David Hayter (2003)	**WAWA**	*Watching the Watchmen*
REAL	Real life	**SCR6**	Unfilmed screenplay draft: Alex Tse	**WHOS**	*Who's Who: The Definitive Directory of the DC Universe*
RPG1	*DC Heroes Role Playing Module #227: Who Watches the Watchmen?*	**SPOT**	*DC Spotlight #1*		
		VRL1	Viral video: *NBS Nightly News with Ted Philips*	**WTFC**	*Watchmen: The Film Companion*

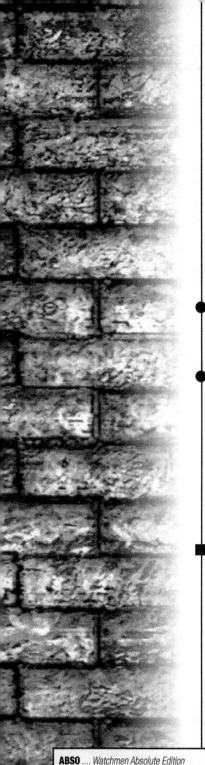

monitors tuned to every broadcast around the planet, so he can focus on the broadcasts randomly, combine the images with randomly selected print media articles, and thereby recognize societal patterns and trends not discernable through logical analysis [RPG3].

> **NOTE:** *Veidt's servants must be different individuals than the three Vietnamese refugees in Alan Moore's miniseries, who do not enter his employ until in or after 1971, following the Vietnam War's conclusion.*

Several months after the Red Cross charity event, construction is completed on the Karnak base. Soon thereafter, the three architects who designed it die in an airplane accident. Adrian Veidt and his assistant Marla fly to Antarctica to survey the completed retreat, which has state-of-the-art security preventing anyone from approaching undetected for miles in any direction. He tests his video monitors by calling up footage of Dr. Manhattan [BWOZ].

> **NOTE:** *The architects' deaths are likely orchestrated by Veidt to eliminate witnesses to his plan, though this is not explicitly stated.*

—Fall to Winter 1960

Adrian Veidt spends months fighting crime almost as an afterthought, lacking passion or joy for the task but compelled to do so since he possesses the requisite skills [BWOZ].

—November 1960

The press deems Dr. Manhattan a crime-fighter, so the Pentagon decides that he must fight crime, and he dispassionately complies. During a raid on Moloch's vice-den, the superhuman disrupts illegal activities by causing a criminal's head to explode. Although everyone in the room is horrified, Dr. Manhattan is unaffected by the morality of his own actions [ALAN].

> **CONFLICT:** *A timeline published in* The Film Companion *moves this event to 1964, contradicting Alan Moore's miniseries.*

Circa December 25, 1960 (Alternate Reality)

In a quantum reality in which Jon Osterman never becomes Dr. Manhattan, he and Janey Slater experience some rocky moments in their relationship during the Christmas season, but they move past these issues and continue planning their wedding [BWDM].

December 29, 1960

Adrian Veidt brings to justice a group of five criminals called The Flying Tigers, who commit crimes wearing orange, flexible cat costumes enabling them to glide on local updrafts for short distances. He leaves the gang dangling outside the local police headquarters, bound in his signature Gordian Knot **[BWOZ]**.

> **NOTE:** *In the real world, The Flying Tigers were a group of U.S. Army Air Corps, Navy, and Marine Corps pilots who defended China against Japanese military forces during World War II.*

1960 to 1975

With help from Jon Osterman, several sciences advance in leaps and bounds, including eugenics, quantum physics, and transport **[ALAN]**.

Between 1960 and 1963

Dr. Manhattan discovers how to synthesize sufficient lithium for manufacturers to mass-produce polyacetylene batteries, facilitating the introduction of electric automobiles **[ALAN]**. The use of electric cars alleviates the Arab oil crisis and helps to control the U.S. economy, curing inflation **[RPG2]**.

Between 1960 and 1985

Max Shea writes several well-received short stories, including "A Bucket of Blood and a Bottle of Rum," "Netherspace Slamdance," and "Angela Bradstreet's Dirty Face" **[RPG3]**. Several of Shea's stories feature the artwork of Indian surrealist painter Hira Manish, though the two do not meet in person while collaborating **[BWOZ]**.

Dr. Manhattan walks across the surface of Earth's sun **[FILM]**.

Part VI:
A NEW BREED OF CRIMEBUSTERS
(1961–1965)

—In or Before January 1961
Adrian Veidt supports John F. Kennedy's U.S. Presidential campaign, and the two become good friends **[BWOZ]**.

—1961
Eddie Blake begins working as a personal bodyguard for Findlay Setchfield South, an ex-Army major and a long-time political broker who, despite his cruel nature, has fooled many into considering him a humanitarian **[RPG2]**.

—January 20, 1961
John Fitzgerald Kennedy is inaugurated as the United States' 35th President **[REAL]**. As a wealthy campaign supporter, Adrian Veidt is invited to attend the event, where he meets JFK's wife, Jacqueline Kennedy. Veidt is troubled when he notices The Comedian congratulating Kennedy—Blake's close friend—on winning the Oval Office **[BWOZ]**.

—February 1961
Several weeks after Kennedy's inauguration, Adrian Veidt examines recorded footage of Dr. Manhattan. Upon viewing a recording of Manhattan reducing to atoms the head of Moloch the Mystic's henchman, Ozymandias realizes how little regard the superhuman has for human life **[BWOZ]**.

—March 11, 1961
Ford and General Motors both actively pursue electric cars, with prototypes expected within three months thanks to Dr. Manhattan's ability to synthesize mass amounts of lithium for battery use. *Science Today* reports that an electric charge should allow a vehicle to run for two hundred miles for as little as $2.00 **[RPG3]**.

MIND .... *The Mindscape of Alan Moore*
MOBL.... *Watchmen: The Mobile Game*
MOTN.... *Watchmen: The Complete Motion Comic*
MTRO.... *Metro* promotional newspaper cover wrap
NEWP.... *New Frontiersman* promotional newspaper
NEWW... *New Frontiersman* website
NIGH ... *Watchmen: The End Is Nigh, Parts 1 and 2*
PKIT...... *Watchmen* film British press kit
PORT..... *Watchmen Portraits*
REAL..... Real life
RPG1 .... *DC Heroes Role Playing Module #227: Who Watches the Watchmen?*

RPG2 .... *DC Heroes Role Playing Module #235: Taking Out the Trash—Curses and Tears*
RPG3 .... *DC Heroes: The Watchmen Sourcebook*
RUBY .... "Wounds," published in *The Ruby Files Volume One*
SCR1..... Unfilmed screenplay draft: Sam Hamm
SCR2..... Unfilmed screenplay draft: Charles McKeuen
SCR3..... Unfilmed screenplay draft: Gary Goldman
SCR4..... Unfilmed screenplay draft: David Hayter (2002)
SCR5..... Unfilmed screenplay draft: David Hayter (2003)
SCR6..... Unfilmed screenplay draft: Alex Tse
SPOT..... *DC Spotlight #1*
VRL1 ..... Viral video: *NBS Nightly News with Ted Philips*

VRL2..... Viral video: *The Keene Act and You*
VRL3 ..... Viral video: *Who Watches the Watchmen? A Veidt Music Network (VMN) Special*
VRL4 ..... Viral video: *World in Focus: 6 Minutes to Midnight*
VRL5 ..... Viral video: *Local Radio Station Report on 1977 Riots*
VRL6 ..... Viral videos (group of ten): *Veidt Enterprises Advertising Contest*
WAWA... *Watching the Watchmen*
WHOS... *Who's Who: The Definitive Directory of the DC Universe*
WTFC .... *Watchmen: The Film Companion*

—In or Before May 1961

William Water Schott, of Brooklyn, and his five member gang begin a reign of terror in the Bronx, carrying out acts of racketeering, theft, and murder. Schott, already wanted for a double homicide in Pennsylvania, calls himself The Bully **[RPG3]**.

May 1961 (Alternate Realities)

In a quantum reality in which Jon Osterman never becomes Dr. Manhattan, an issue of *Thrilling Space Mysteries* features the story "It Came from Dimension X," written by Max Shea, as well as *The Three Eternals*, a novel set in the 41st century. The cover depicts a naked, blue-skinned man and his sexy, yellow-clad, space-helmeted companion. In yet another quantum reality without Dr. Manhattan, the issue's cover depicts a nuclear explosion destroying the White House **[BWDM]**.

> **NOTE:** *The cover figures are, of course, Dr. Manhattan and The Silk Spectre. In the real world,* The Three Eternals, *written by Eando Binder (a pen-name of Earl Andrew Binder and his brother,* Captain Marvel *and* Superman *comic book scribe Otto Binder) was published in the December 1939 issue of* Thrilling Wonder Stories.

May 14, 1961—Before 3:00 PM (Alternate Realities)

In a quantum reality in which Jon Osterman never becomes Dr. Manhattan, he and Janey Slater prepare to wed in the Rose Ballroom. His father Josef helps him don his tuxedo, describing a dream he had of Jon's death. Jon reassures him that won't happen, then chats with a child reading *Thrilling Space Mysteries* in a hallway. The boy tells Jon that he wants to be a scientist like him, and to go to Mars to see "the blue people" like the man on the cover. Jon looks for Janey's dressing room, but finds two and is unsure which one contains his fiancée. In one permutation, he chooses the room on the left; in another, he checks the one on the right **[BWDM]**.

May 14, 1961—3:00 PM (Alternate Realities)

Jon Osterman and Janey Slater are married in multiple realities. In one permutation, Jon shares the first dance with Janey, with her father joining her for the last. In another, he shares the last dance with his wife, letting her father take the first **[BWDM]**.

After May 14, 1961 (Alternate Reality)

Jon and Janey Osterman move to Washington, D.C., where he teaches physics at Georgetown University [**BWDM**].

—Before May 22, 1961

Hollis Mason adopts a dog and names him Phantom [**RPG3**].

> **NOTE:** *Given Mason's love of pulp fiction heroes, it is safe to assume that the dog (as well as a cat he owns in 1985, also called Phantom) is named after Lee Falk's long-running comic strip adventurer The Phantom.*

—May 22, 1961

Hollis Mason and Phantom apprehend William Water "The Bully" Schott and his entire gang, then deliver them to the NYPD's Area Two Violent Crimes headquarters. Schott faces up to sixty years in prison for his crimes [**RPG3**].

—May 23, 1961

The *New York Gazette* reports on The Nite Owl's takedown of The Bully, quoting Mason as admitting that he's getting too old for crime-fighting and may soon give it up. When asked about Dr. Manhattan's effectiveness, he muses, "Who needs Sir Galahad when you've got God himself?" [**RPG3**].

—September 1961

At a press event, President John F. Kennedy shakes hands with Dr. Manhattan and asks what it's like to be a superhero. Manhattan tells Kennedy that he should know, which the leader finds amusing [**ALAN**]. The President adds that Manhattan's arrival assures U.S. soldiers that they will not need to become involved in situations like the Vietnam War [**BWDM**]. Wally Weaver and Janey Slater are both in attendance [**FILM**].

> **CONFLICT:** *Timelines published in* The Film Companion *and in the film's British press kit move this event to 1962, contradicting Alan Moore's miniseries.*

—September 1, 1961

Byron Lewis, inebriated and violent, is arrested during a civil-rights demonstration at a Greyhound bus terminal in Mobile, Alabama. The sit-in's organizers deny his involvement in the event [**RPG3**].

—September 4, 1961

The *New York Gazette* reports on Byron Lewis's Alabama arrest [**RPG3**].

MIND .... *The Mindscape of Alan Moore*
MOBL .... *Watchmen: The Mobile Game*
MOTN .... *Watchmen: The Complete Motion Comic*
MTRO .... *Metro promotional newspaper cover wrap*
NEWP .... *New Frontiersman promotional newspaper*
NEWW .... *New Frontiersman website*
NIGH ..... *Watchmen: The End Is Nigh, Parts 1 and 2*
PKIT ...... *Watchmen film British press kit*
PORT ..... *Watchmen Portraits*
REAL ..... *Real life*
RPG1 .... *DC Heroes Role Playing Module #227: Who Watches the Watchmen?*

RPG2 .... *DC Heroes Role Playing Module #235: Taking Out the Trash—Curses and Tears*
RPG3 .... *DC Heroes: The Watchmen Sourcebook*
RUBY .... *"Wounds," published in* The Ruby Files Volume One
SCR1 ..... *Unfilmed screenplay draft: Sam Hamm*
SCR2 ..... *Unfilmed screenplay draft: Charles McKeuen*
SCR3 ..... *Unfilmed screenplay draft: Gary Goldman*
SCR4 ..... *Unfilmed screenplay draft: David Hayter (2002)*
SCR5 ..... *Unfilmed screenplay draft: David Hayter (2003)*
SCR6 ..... *Unfilmed screenplay draft: Alex Tse*
SPOT ..... *DC Spotlight #1*
VRL1 ..... *Viral video: NBS Nightly News with Ted Philips*

VRL2 ..... *Viral video: The Keene Act and You*
VRL3 ..... *Viral video: Who Watches the Watchmen? A Veidt Music Network (VMN) Special*
VRL4 ... *Viral video: World in Focus: 6 Minutes to Midnight*
VRL5 ..... *Viral video: Local Radio Station Report on 1977 Riots*
VRL6 ..... *Viral videos (group of ten): Veidt Enterprises Advertising Contest*
WAWA ... *Watching the Watchmen*
WHOS ... *Who's Who: The Definitive Directory of the DC Universe*
WTFC .... *Watchmen: The Film Companion*

—In or Before 1962

A New York City grocery-store owner named Denise begins writing romance novels. She completes forty-two such manuscripts, none of which are published. While frequenting her shop, Hollis Mason grows fascinated by her literary prowess as she recounts to him the plots of twenty-seven of these books **[ALAN]**.

A company called Manhattan Fabrics creates a new type of textile for the women's apparel industry, which it markets as a Dr. Manhattan spinoff **[RPG3]**. The fabric consists of viscous fluids between two layers of heat- and pressure-sensitive latex, giving the effect of moving, ever-changing black and white shapes **[ALAN]**.

Hollis Mason obtains several comic books, including *Brigitte the Buccaneer*, *Tales of the Black Freighter* issue #10 (featuring "The Death Ship"), and *Minutemen* #1 **[BWMM]**.
   NOTE: *The first comic's title is alternately spelled as* Brigette the Buccaneer *in* Before Watchmen: Silk Spectre.

Sally and Laurie Jupiter move to a large home in Los Angeles, California, with a swimming pool and a great deal of land **[BWMM]**.

NYPD efforts fail to identify the base of operations of a car-theft ring. Unbeknownst to the police, the thugs operate out of Sparkys Garage **[BWNO]**.

Adrian Veidt meets Robert F. Kennedy, the United States' Attorney General **[BWOZ]**.

—1962

Newspapers dub scientist Wally Weaver "Dr. Manhattan's buddy" **[ALAN]**.
   NOTE: *Early DC comic books called Jimmy Olsen "Superman's pal."*

Sally Jupiter begins to worry that her daughter will turn out badly, just like she did, and thus pushes her to become a superheroine in order to instill in her a sense of honor and integrity **[RPG2]**. Laurie agrees to become the second Silk Spectre—not because she wants to, but to appease her mother. Sally begins instructing her daughter in the art of crime-fighting **[ALAN]**, and hires a trainer named Bruce to teach her acrobatics and martial arts **[RPG3]**. Although Laurie trains hard, her heart is not in it **[ALAN]**.
   NOTE: *David Hayter's unproduced 2002 screenplay changes Laurie's crime-fighting name to The Wraith, while his 2003 revision of that script calls her Slingshot.*

—February 16, 1962

Seven thousand people, many representing the Students for a Democratic Society (SDS), hold an anti-nuclear march on Washington, D.C., to protest Dr. Manhattan's existence. A news broadcast covers the march, as well as astronaut John Glenn's impending space mission aboard the *Friendship 7* **[BWNO]**.

> **NOTE:** *The SDS, a U.S.-based student activist movement, was most active in the mid-1960s before dissolving in 1969. The group held its first convention in 1962.*

—March 10, 1962

Wally Weaver attends a top-secret meeting at the White House with Senators George Malloy, Colin Newberry, and William Holmes, to offer testimony regarding "The Manhattan Phenomenon" **[NEWW]**.

> **NOTE:** *No such individuals served in the U.S. Senate in 1962 in the real world. Wally's surname is misspelled as "Weavers" on the envelope containing his testimony.*

—March 15, 1962

Wally Weaver next testifies in front of a U.S. Senate committee as a witness to the events involving Jon Osterman's transformation into Dr. Manhattan. Weaver's testimony is classified **[NEWW]**.

—Before May 1962

Hollis Mason begins composing an autobiography titled *Under the Hood*, covering the years before and during his stint as The Nite Owl. While writing the book, Mason seeks advice from his grocer, an unpublished novelist named Denise, who tells him to start with the saddest thing he can think of, so as to earn his audience's sympathies. Hollis thus pens a chapter explaining how "The Ride of the Valkyries," from act 3 of Richard Wagner's *Die Walküre* (*The Valkyrie*), reminds him of the tragic fate of his father's former employer, Moe Vernon **[ALAN]**. The writing of *Under the Hood* takes several months and helps Mason to purge the darker aspects of his former life **[BWMM]**.

> **NOTE:** *A timeline published in* The Film Companion *misidentifies the title of Mason's autobiography as* Dawn of the Superhero—*which is odd, since the book is correctly titled in the film itself.*

—In or Before May 1962

After completing all but the epilogue to *Under the Hood*, Hollis Mason sends a copy of the book's manuscript to Larry Schexnayder, seeking the agent's opinion **[BWMM]**.

The Stilton Hotel opens in New York **[BWMM]**.

> **NOTE:** *The hotel's name spoofs that of the real-world Hilton chain.*

Dan Dreiberg sets out to discover The Nite Owl's identity so he can become the crime-fighter's sidekick. He devises a number of plans for useful electronic equipment, including a flying vehicle and night-vision goggles **[BWNO]**.

MIND .... *The Mindscape of Alan Moore*
MOBL .... *Watchmen: The Mobile Game*
MOTN .... *Watchmen: The Complete Motion Comic*
MTRO .... *Metro* promotional newspaper cover wrap
NEWP .... *New Frontiersman* promotional newspaper
NEWW .. *New Frontiersman* website
NIGH ..... *Watchmen: The End Is Nigh, Parts 1 and 2*
PKIT ...... *Watchmen* film British press kit
PORT .... *Watchmen Portraits*
REAL ..... Real life
RPG1 .... *DC Heroes Role Playing Module #227: Who Watches the Watchmen?*

RPG2 .... *DC Heroes Role Playing Module #235: Taking Out the Trash—Curses and Tears*
RPG3 .... *DC Heroes: The Watchmen Sourcebook*
RUBY .... "Wounds," published in *The Ruby Files Volume One*
SCR1 ..... Unfilmed screenplay draft: Sam Hamm
SCR2 ..... Unfilmed screenplay draft: Charles McKeuen
SCR3 ..... Unfilmed screenplay draft: Gary Goldman
SCR4 ..... Unfilmed screenplay draft: David Hayter (2002)
SCR5 ..... Unfilmed screenplay draft: David Hayter (2003)
SCR6 ..... Unfilmed screenplay draft: Alex Tse
SPOT .... *DC Spotlight #1*
VRL1 ..... Viral video: *NBS Nightly News with Ted Philips*

VRL2 ..... Viral video: *The Keene Act and You*
VRL3 ..... Viral video: *Who Watches the Watchmen? A Veidt Music Network (VMN) Special*
VRL4 ..... Viral video: *World in Focus: 6 Minutes to Midnight*
VRL5 ..... Viral video: *Local Radio Station Report on 1977 Riots*
VRL6 ..... Viral videos (group of ten): *Veidt Enterprises Advertising Contest*
WAWA ... *Watching the Watchmen*
WHOS ... *Who's Who: The Definitive Directory of the DC Universe*
WTFC .... *Watchmen: The Film Companion*

Hollis Mason thwarts a car-theft ring at Sparkys Garage. Knocking the thugs senseless, he orders them to reassemble every stolen car and compile a list of vehicle identification numbers. Waving at his adoring fans, he then drives back to the Owl Cave, unaware that Dan Dreiberg has placed a microphone on the Owl Car so he can hear the sounds of the road and thereby determine the location of his secret lair **[BWNO]**.

Dan tracks the Owl Car to an abandoned building and follows tire tracks to a subway tunnel leading to the Owl Cave, containing the car, a gas pump, weapons, a typewriter, and more. After trying on the crime-fighter's mask, Dan types out a message requesting a meeting in Lincoln Park **[BWNO]**. He also writes a letter expressing admiration for Mason's crime-fighting efforts, indicates his plan to follow in Hollis's footsteps, and requests permission to use the Nite Owl name **[ALAN]**.

Hollis Mason finds the note and proceeds to the park, where he waits on a bench, a gun hidden beneath his coat, to see who approaches. Dan explains how he found Mason—and how to prevent others from doing the same—then asks to become his sidekick. Hollis promises to think about it **[BWNO]**.

Dan Dreiberg returns home to find his father beating his mother with a strap. Despite her plea not to be hit in front of their son, William continues, claiming it will make a man out of him. When the elder Dreiberg has a heart attack during the beating, Victoria heads outside to tell Dan, who counts to five before calling for an ambulance. William dies, and Dan, despite his father's abuse, harbors feelings of guilt for many years **[BWNO]**.
   NOTE: In David Hayter's unproduced 2003 screenplay, Dan's father is murdered by a mugger.

After reading a police report showing photos of Victoria Dreiberg's bruised body, Hollis Mason attends William's funeral and offers to take Dan on as his sidekick. During the funeral, Victoria spits in her late husband's face **[BWNO]**. Despite his disappointment in Dan's choices, the banker leaves his son a very large inheritance **[ALAN]**—enough to buy several small South American towns **[BWNO]**.

Dan Dreiberg uses his newfound wealth to create an array of crime-fighting technologies. Hollis Mason visits his home to view them, and the two form a close friendship **[ALAN]**. Hollis begins training Dan to fight, as well as how to recognize a crooked business from a legitimate one, and agrees not to call him a cute nickname like Owlie, Owl-Boy, or Owl-Kid. Dan shows him his plans for a proposed flying vehicle capable of vertical take-offs and landings. Hollis considers retiring and letting Dan assume the mantle of The Nite Owl, but decides to mull it over before making a decision **[BWNO]**.

—May 11, 1962

Italian-American woman Kitty Genovese orders a dress from Manhattan Fabrics **[RPG3]**. After she opts not to collect the garment, deeming it ugly, Walter Kovacs (employed at the factory) finds the textile's shape-changing quality and black-and-white motif beautiful. He takes the dress home, cuts the fabric into pieces, and uses heated implements to reseal the latex. With no immediate use for them, he places the pieces in a trunk and forgets about them **[ALAN]**.

> **NOTE:** *The 1964 murder of Catherine Susan "Kitty" Genovese in the real world inspires Walter Kovacs to become a crime-fighter in Alan Moore's miniseries. The comic sets her dress order in 1962; The Watchmen Sourcebook provides the exact date.*

—May 19, 1962

Film star Marilyn Monroe sings "Happy Birthday, Mr. President" to John F. Kennedy at a party held at Madison Square Garden to celebrate his 45th birthday **[REAL]**. Adrian Veidt attends the $1,000-a-plate dinner. Observing eye contact between the two, Veidt discerns that the President's relationship with Monroe is an intimate one. Following the performance, Kennedy introduces Adrian to the inebriated actor. Veidt notices Monroe exchanging similar glances with JFK's brother Robert as well **[BWOZ]**.

—Mid to Late May 1962

Dan Dreiberg decides to call his flying vehicle *Archimedes* **[BWNO]**.

> **CONFLICT:** *Alan Moore's miniseries establishes that Dan names the vehicle after watching the Disney animated film* The Sword in the Stone. *That film was released in theaters on Christmas 1963—more than a year beyond this point.*

Byron Lewis decides to check himself into a clinic in upstate New York for treatment. Before doing so, he purchases and refurbishes Vernon's Auto Repairs as a retirement gift for Hollis Mason. When he presents the garage to Mason, the latter cries, knowing his best friend is saying goodbye to him **[BWMM]**.

> **NOTE:** *According to Alan Moore's miniseries, Byron Lewis ends up committed in an asylum in Maine. This could indicate that his stay at the upstate New York clinic is a temporary one, predating his full-time institutionalization.*

Hollis Mason officially retires from crime-fighting **[ALAN, RPG2]**. Issuing a prepared statement to the press via FBI contacts **[BWNO]**, he also makes a public announcement on television, removing his mask and revealing his true identity **[BWOZ]**. When asked about future plans, Hollis says he intends to write a book and teach **[BWNO]**, and also announces the opening of his new garage, Mason's Auto Repair. After watching the TV broadcast, a man named Jerry brings his old Chevrolet to Mason's for service **[BWOZ]**.

> **NOTE:** *Alan Moore's miniseries sets Mason's retirement in May 1962, and a timeline*

MIND .... *The Mindscape of Alan Moore*
MOBL .... *Watchmen: The Mobile Game*
MOTN .... *Watchmen: The Complete Motion Comic*
MTRO .... *Metro promotional newspaper cover wrap*
NEWP .... *New Frontiersman promotional newspaper*
NEWW .... *New Frontiersman website*
NIGH ..... *Watchmen: The End Is Nigh, Parts 1 and 2*
PKIT ...... *Watchmen film British press kit*
PORT ..... *Watchmen Portraits*
REAL ..... Real life
RPG1 .... *DC Heroes Role Playing Module #227: Who Watches the Watchmen?*

RPG2 ..... *DC Heroes Role Playing Module #235: Taking Out the Trash—Curses and Tears*
RPG3 .... *DC Heroes: The Watchmen Sourcebook*
RUBY .... "Wounds," published in *The Ruby Files Volume One*
SCR1 ..... Unfilmed screenplay draft: Sam Hamm
SCR2 ..... Unfilmed screenplay draft: Charles McKeuen
SCR3 ..... Unfilmed screenplay draft: Gary Goldman
SCR4 ..... Unfilmed screenplay draft: David Hayter (2002)
SCR5 ..... Unfilmed screenplay draft: David Hayter (2003)
SCR6 ..... Unfilmed screenplay draft: Alex Tse
SPOT ..... *DC Spotlight #1*
VRL1 ..... Viral video: *NBS Nightly News with Ted Philips*

VRL2 ..... Viral video: *The Keene Act and You*
VRL3 ..... Viral video: *Who Watches the Watchmen? A Veidt Music Network (VMN) Special*
VRL4 ..... Viral video: *World in Focus: 6 Minutes to Midnight*
VRL5 ..... Viral video: *Local Radio Station Report on 1977 Riots*
VRL6 ..... Viral videos (group of ten): *Veidt Enterprises Advertising Contest*
WAWA ... *Watching the Watchmen*
WHOS ... *Who's Who: The Definitive Directory of the DC Universe*
WTFC .... *Watchmen: The Film Companion*

packaged with The End Is Nigh—The Complete Experience *reiterates that placement.* Taking Out the Trash *specifies May 16 (though another section of that same book moves his retirement to 1960), while* Before Watchmen: Nite Owl *cites May 12.*

CONFLICT: *A timeline in the* Watchmen *film's British press kit claims a 1964 retirement year, and a police file in the press kit moves the year up to 1967. Both placements contradict the original comic.*

Dan Dreiberg finds out about Mason's retirement while watching the news, then heads to the Owl Cave to ask his mentor about it. Mason admits that crime-fighting no longer has the same meaning for him, and says he's giving Dan everything—the cave, the car, the gadgets, and the Nite Owl name—provided that he finish his college education, train more, and build up his fighting weight **[BWNO]**.

> **CONFLICT:** *In* The Watchmen Sourcebook, *Dan has already finished college by this point, having graduated from Harvard on June 3, 1960. It could be that he is working toward another doctoral degree.*

Jon Osterman attends a civic banquet in Nite Owl's honor. Hollis Mason receives a statuette of himself, bearing the phrase "In Gratitude," which almost makes him regret retiring. When Osterman asks if his decision was age-based, Mason admits it was the other's arrival that prompted it, as he felt obsolete by comparison to a superhuman **[ALAN]**. Although Hollis considers Dr. Manhattan a "nice guy," he finds himself thinking "not human, not human" throughout their conversation **[BWMM]**.

> **NOTE:** *The phrase "In Gratitude" can be read as "ingratitude," representing the public's changing view of costumed heroes from the 1940s to the 1980s—especially since this same statue will eventually be the instrument of Mason's death in 1985.*

Hollis Mason moves to a new apartment, along with his dog Phantom **[BWMM]**, and officially opens Mason's Auto Repairs, specializing in obsolete vehicles. The *New York News* features a front-page article titled "Hero Retires," and he frames the clipping for his wall **[ALAN]**.

Four days after retiring, Hollis Mason begins writing *Under the Hood*'s epilogue, but he deems his first pass terrible for its forced attempt to wax philosophical. Larry Schexnayder calls him from the Stilton Hotel, asking him to come by so they can talk. The next morning, Hollis meets Larry to discuss *Under the Hood* over breakfast. Larry urges him not to publish the book, as it could damage other deals he has in the works, but Hollis refuses to back down, blaming The Minutemen's failure on the agent's greed and need for attention **[BWMM]**.

Dan Dreiberg buys a townhouse at Manhattan's 79th Street, located above a forgotten subway tunnel, then creates plans to turn the tunnel into a vast subterranean workshop, which he calls the Owl's Nest. The construction costs $3 million and is projected to be completed on February 7, 1963 **[RPG3]**.

> **NOTE:** *Hollis Mason gives Dan his existing Owl Cave in* Before Watchmen: Nite Owl, *but the two lairs do not appear to be the same location.*

Sally Jupiter tells Hollis Mason that her daughter Laurie wants to be a superheroine like her mother once she's old enough. This is only half-true, however, since Laurie is only giving in to Sally's wishes **[ALAN]**.

Hollis Mason finishes writing *Under the Hood*, in which he calls The Comedian a disgrace to crime-fighting and reveals that he choked and tried to rape Sally Jupiter, breaking several ribs. The book ponders Hooded Justice's identity, the psychology of masked adventurers, the changing world from the 1940s to the 1960s, the fall of The Minutemen **[ALAN]**, Nelson Gardner's secret homosexual lifestyle, and more. Mason recounts his personal memories of each team member **[BWMM]**, dubs Dr. Manhattan's arrival "the dawn of the superhero" **[FILM]**, and exposes Sally's murder of Geoffrey "The Liquidator" Dean **[BWMM]**.

Prior to *Under the Hood*'s publication, Hollis Mason sends copies of the manuscript to Sally Jupiter, Nelson Gardner, and Byron Lewis, seeking their feedback. Upon reading the manuscript, Gardner grows distraught and near-suicidal. A muscular friend of his, Norbert Veldon, visits Mason to demand that he not publish the book, then rips up the manuscript, warning that Hollis will hear from Nelson's lawyers. **[BWMM]**.

> **NOTE:** *It is unclear whether or not Veldon is Gardner's lover, though that seems to be the implication, given how strongly he feels about protecting Nelson.*

With *Under the Hood*'s publication imminent, Larry Schexnayder calls Sally Jupiter to express his frustration about what it will reveal. That same night, Nelson Gardner calls Sally in tears about his sexual orientation becoming public knowledge. Hollis Mason visits her and Laurie (now age twelve) in Los Angeles the next day. The three enjoy an afternoon at the pool, though Sally resents the book's revelations about her **[BWMM]**.

Mason awakens to the sound of a record playing in his apartment: Richard Wagner's "The Ride of the Valkyries," performed by the Vienna Philharmonic Orchestra and conducted by Wilhelm Furtwängler. He finds The Comedian sitting on a couch, petting Phantom. Blake tells Mason that his autobiography has upset many, including FBI Director J. Edgar Hoover. When Hollis counters that his book contains only the truth, Blake reveals that Hooded Justice was *not* Rolf Müller, and that Mason thus murdered an innocent man in 1955 **[BWMM]**.

Blake warns Mason to make *Under the Hood* a lighthearted remembrance rather than presenting the U.S. government in a negative light, or else his superiors will send him to execute not only Mason, but also Byron Lewis and Sally Jupiter. Hollis spends a week re-editing the manuscript to remove anything that might endanger his friends, though he keeps his comments about Blake's attack on Sally intact **[BWMM]**. The book does hint that Hooded Justice was Rolf Müller, but implicates Blake in the man's murder, omitting Mason's own role in his teammate's death **[ALAN, BWMM]**.

Under the Hood is released **[ALAN]**. Published by Chichester House **[RPG3]**, the autobiography—the only accounting of The Minutemen's careers **[BWMM]**—becomes a major bestseller **[HOOD]**. A hardcover version, published by Shenouda Publishing, features a dust-jacket portrait of Hollis Mason smoking a tobacco pipe, credited to Leah Hong and Clay Enos **[FILM]**.

> **NOTE:** *A scan of the book's dust jacket was featured on the* Watchmen *film's Director's Cut Blu-ray release. Leah Hong is a graphic designer who helped to create the movie, while Clay Enos photographed cast and crew members on set, which he later collected in the book* Watchmen Portraits.

> **CONFLICT:** *Alan Moore's miniseries establishes the book's publication in 1962, as does a timeline packaged with* The End Is Nigh—The Complete Experience. *A timeline in the* Watchmen *film's British press kit dates the book's writing in 1967, while the* Under the Hood *documentary sets its publication in 1975.*

Despite *Under the Hood*'s comments about The Comedian, Eddie Blake never brings a libel lawsuit against Hollis Mason—or kills him—once the book hits stores. Some readers dismiss the autobiography as melodramatic gossip-mongering **[NEWP]**, while others accept Mason's allegations as truth, given the lack of legal action **[ALAN]**.

●—May 27, 1962

A special presentation, *Dr. Manhattan: Man or Superman*, airs on television **[BWMM]**.

●—In or Before August 1962

Actor Marilyn Monroe obtains a prescription for Nembutal, a short-acting barbiturate, which she fills at Crolsins Pharmacy under the name "Janet Smith." Her address listed on the pill bottle is 1280 Surrey Square, in Los Angeles **[BWCO]**.

●—Before August 5, 1962

Eddie Blake visits the Kennedy family and plays football with John, Robert, and Ted Kennedy. After the game, Jacqueline Kennedy asks Blake to kill Marilyn Monroe, a "drug-addled peroxide whore" of whom her husband is fond, and whom Jackie deems a security threat since she is dating Chicago mobster Sam Giancana **[BWCO]**.

—August 5, 1962—Early Morning
Eddie Blake has sex with Marilyn Monroe in the bedroom of her home in Brentwood, California, then murders her and stages her death to make it appear to be a barbiturate overdose, kissing her naked buttocks on the way out **[BWCO]**.

—August 5, 1962
Monroe's death is ruled as a probable suicide **[REAL]**. Upon reading of her passing, Adrian Veidt consults his TV monitors for any clues to the true cause, suspecting that she may have been killed to tie up loose ends for the Kennedys **[BWOZ]**.

—August 28, 1962
Byron Lewis is committed to an asylum in Maine, following a mental breakdown and a long bout of alcoholism **[ALAN, RPG2, RPG3]**. Reporters photograph Lewis in his Mothman outfit, kicking and biting, as he is subdued by orderlies, placed into an ambulance, and transported away **[FILM, NEWW]**.

> **NOTE:** Alan Moore's miniseries establishes Byron's commitment to the Maine asylum. The Watchmen Sourcebook *provides the date of his incarceration. According to* Absolute Watchmen, *Moore originally intended for Lewis to die in 1962 of cirrhosis of the liver, rather than be committed to an institution.*

> **CONFLICT:** Timelines published in The Film Companion *and in the film's British press kit move this incident back to 1953, which does not jibe with Mothman's history in other sources. Byron is committed to Sunnycrest Asylum in* Taking Out the Trash, *whereas* The Watchmen Sourcebook *claims he is sent to the Holland Valley Alcohol Rehabilitation Centre.*

—September 5, 1962
The Holland Valley Alcohol Rehabilitation Centre files a patient evaluation on Byron Lewis, reporting no progress after his first week of treatment **[RPG3]**.

—September 11, 1962
Hollis Mason appears on *The Martha Edwards Show* to discuss *Under the Hood*. When asked about The Comedian's attempted rape of Sally Jupiter, Hollis expresses regret at having aired a good friend's dirty laundry. He describes Ursula Zandt as "real wild," saying she feared no one and would became angry if told not do something **[RPG3]**.

MIND .... *The Mindscape of Alan Moore*
MOBL .... *Watchmen: The Mobile Game*
MOTN .... *Watchmen: The Complete Motion Comic*
MTRO .... *Metro promotional newspaper cover wrap*
NEWP .... *New Frontiersman promotional newspaper*
NEWW ... *New Frontiersman website*
NIGH ..... *Watchmen: The End Is Nigh, Parts 1 and 2*
PKIT ...... *Watchmen film British press kit*
PORT ..... *Watchmen Portraits*
REAL ..... Real life
RPG1 .... *DC Heroes Role Playing Module #227: Who Watches the Watchmen?*

RPG2 .... *DC Heroes Role Playing Module #235: Taking Out the Trash—Curses and Tears*
RPG3 .... *DC Heroes: The Watchmen Sourcebook*
RUBY .... "Wounds," published in *The Ruby Files Volume One*
SCR1 ..... Unfilmed screenplay draft: Sam Hamm
SCR2 ..... Unfilmed screenplay draft: Charles McKeuen
SCR3 ..... Unfilmed screenplay draft: Gary Goldman
SCR4 ..... Unfilmed screenplay draft: David Hayter (2002)
SCR5 ..... Unfilmed screenplay draft: David Hayter (2003)
SCR6 ..... Unfilmed screenplay draft: Alex Tse
SPOT ..... *DC Spotlight #1*
VRL1 ..... Viral video: *NBS Nightly News with Ted Philips*

VRL2 ..... Viral video: *The Keene Act and You*
VRL3 ..... Viral video: *Who Watches the Watchmen? A Veidt Music Network (VMN) Special*
VRL4 ..... Viral video: *World in Focus: 6 Minutes to Midnight*
VRL5 ..... Viral video: *Local Radio Station Report on 1977 Riots*
VRL6 ..... Viral videos (group of ten): *Veidt Enterprises Advertising Contest*
WAWA ... *Watching the Watchmen*
WHOS ... *Who's Who: The Definitive Directory of the DC Universe*
WTFC .... *Watchmen: The Film Companion*

—Late 1962

While visiting Byron Lewis at the asylum, Hollis Mason asks if he has read *Under the Hood*, and if he's okay with what Hollis has written about him. Byron remains catatonic throughout the visit **[BWMM]**.

Sally Jupiter invites Nelson Gardner, Hollis Mason, and Byron Lewis to her home for a Minutemen reunion. Hollis and Nelson arrive, and as they reminisce with Sally, thirteen-year-old Laurie Jupiter finishes a workout. Mason asks if Laurie has yet read *Under the Hood*, but Sally prefers that her daughter not read such material. Byron shows up flanked by orderlies, who watch over him due to his fragile mental state. Laurie wonders if this is what she can look forward to as a crime-fighter **[ALAN]**.

> **NOTE:** *It would appear, given this reunion, that Mason's friends have forgiven him for the revelations in* Under the Hood.

—In or Before October 1962

President John F. Kennedy figures out that Ozymandias is his friend and campaign supporter, Adrian Veidt **[BWOZ]**.

—October 14, 1962

A U.S. U-2 spy plane captures photos of Soviet medium-range ballistic missile sites being constructed in Cuba, sparking a thirteen-day confrontation between the United States and the U.S.S.R. that nearly leads to full-scale nuclear war. The incident is later dubbed the Cuban Missile Crisis **[REAL]**.

—October 19, 1962

John F. Kennedy meets with the Joint Chiefs of Staff to discuss military options for responding to the Soviet missile deployment in Cuba **[REAL]**.

—October 21, 1962

President Kennedy institutes a blockade to impose a quarantine on Cuba, publicly urging the Soviet Union to withdraw its missiles from that country **[REAL]**.

—October 23, 1962

Soviet Premier Nikita Khrushchev responds to Kennedy's demand with a public address of his own, calling the American actions a threat to peace **[REAL]**.

—Between October 23 and October 28, 1962

The U.S. government sends two agents to Adrian Veidt's home to summon Ozymandias to Washington, D.C. Three hours later, Adrian Veidt circumvents White House security to enter the Oval Office. Kennedy says he is considering sending Dr. Manhattan to end the

Cuban Missile Crisis, but Veidt urges him to hold off, predicting that the Soviets will back down before war results, and offering to address the situation himself **[BWOZ]**.

Kennedy assigns Ozymandias to oversee U.S. aircraft carrier maneuvers in Cuba. *The Washington Post*'s front-page headline reads "Missiles in Cuba: Kennedy Confers With His Top Men." A subhead notes, "Jackie Gets New Outfit for Duration of Crisis; Nation Sleeps Better." Veidt advises the carriers' commander to open communications and talk rather than fight, and the crisis is averted **[BWDM]**. At Veidt's urging **[BWDM, BWOZ]**, the United States moves its Jupiter missiles out of Turkey, and the U.S.S.R. withdraws its missiles from Cuba **[REAL]**.

> **NOTE:** *A newspaper photo of Kennedy, Ozymandias, and the Joint Chiefs of Staff bears the caption "Dr. Manhattan gets laid a lot, but he always has blue balls." Presumably, the comic's creators assumed no one would notice. They were wrong.*

Between October 23 and October 28, 1962 (Alternate Reality)

In a quantum reality in which Jon Osterman never becomes Dr. Manhattan, Kennedy brings Eddie Blake in as an advisor during the Cuban Missile Crisis instead of Adrian Veidt, assigning him to oversee U.S. aircraft carriers stationed near the Russian fleet. The carriers' commander objects to Kennedy's orders to attack the Soviets, claiming the President lacks such authority, but Blake forces him to carry out the orders. The carriers open fire, causing the Russians to launch nuclear weapons, thereby destroying the White House and plunging the world into a full-scale nuclear war **[BWDM]**.

In or After 1962

A vandal spray-paints "Who Watches the Watchmen?" on the metal security gate protecting Hollis Mason's storefront **[ALAN]**.

> **NOTE:** *This phrase is a translation from "Quis custodiet ipsos custodes?"—a Latin question from Roman poet Juvenal's* Satires, *originally used in reference to marital fidelity. In modern usage, the phrase references the difficulty of controlling the actions of those in power.*

In or Before 1963

Eddie Blake forms a working relationship with G. Gordon Liddy, due to the latter's connections with the FBI **[BWCO]**.

> **NOTE:** *Retired lawyer G. Gordon Liddy, who served as the chief operative of the White House Plumbers unit during Richard Nixon's real-world presidency, directed the burglary of the Democratic National Committee headquarters in the Watergate office complex in Washington, D.C., that toppled Nixon's Presidency.*

MIND .... *The Mindscape of Alan Moore*
MOBL .... *Watchmen: The Mobile Game*
MOTN .... *Watchmen: The Complete Motion Comic*
MTRO .... *Metro promotional newspaper cover wrap*
NEWP .... *New Frontiersman promotional newspaper*
NEWW .... *New Frontiersman website*
NIGH ..... *Watchmen: The End Is Nigh, Parts 1 and 2*
PKIT ...... *Watchmen film British press kit*
PORT ..... *Watchmen Portraits*
REAL ..... Real life
RPG1 .... *DC Heroes Role Playing Module #227: Who Watches the Watchmen?*

RPG2 .... *DC Heroes Role Playing Module #235: Taking Out the Trash—Curses and Tears*
RPG3 .... *DC Heroes: The Watchmen Sourcebook*
RUBY .... "Wounds," published in *The Ruby Files Volume One*
SCR1 ..... Unfilmed screenplay draft: Sam Hamm
SCR2 ..... Unfilmed screenplay draft: Charles McKeuen
SCR3 ..... Unfilmed screenplay draft: Gary Goldman
SCR4 .... Unfilmed screenplay draft: David Hayter (2002)
SCR5 .... Unfilmed screenplay draft: David Hayter (2003)
SCR6 .... Unfilmed screenplay draft: Alex Tse
SPOT ..... *DC Spotlight #1*
VRL1 ..... Viral video: *NBS Nightly News with Ted Philips*

VRL2 ..... Viral video: *The Keene Act and You*
VRL3 ..... Viral video: *Who Watches the Watchmen? A Veidt Music Network (VMN) Special*
VRL4 ..... Viral video: *World in Focus: 6 Minutes to Midnight*
VRL5 ..... Viral video: *Local Radio Station Report on 1977 Riots*
VRL6 ..... Viral videos (group of ten): *Veidt Enterprises Advertising Contest*
WAWA ... *Watching the Watchmen*
WHOS ... *Who's Who: The Definitive Directory of the DC Universe*
WTFC .... *Watchmen: The Film Companion*

—February 7, 1963

Dan Dreiberg finishes constructing the Owl's Nest, his subterranean sanctuary spanning more than 10,000 square feet **[RPG3]**. The forgotten subway tunnel in which he builds it allows him to discreetly leave via a derelict warehouse located two blocks north, which he also owns **[ALAN]**. The workshop contains a VAX 880 computer database, networked with the databases of the NYPD, the FBI, and Interpol **[RPG3]**.

> *NOTE: In essence, Dreiberg builds* Watchmen's *analog to the Batcave, befitting his role as the story's surrogate Batman.*

—On or After February 7, 1963

Dreiberg stocks the Owl's Nest with multiple Nite Owl costumes **[RPG3]**, as well as numerous vehicles, including hover bikes, and an array of inventions, including night-vision goggles and a utility belt containing respirator masks, smoke bombs, a fingerprint kit, a pocket laser, and a console for the goggles **[ALAN]**.

—September 30, 1963

The Outer Limits airs an episode titled "The Architects of Fear" during its first season, written by Meyer Dolinsky and directed by Byron Haskin. The story involves a team of scientists who, convinced that the Cold War will lead to mankind's destruction, launch a nuclear attack to save the world by uniting mankind against a perceived common enemy **[REAL]**. Adrian Veidt misses the episode during its initial broadcast **[BWOZ]**.

—On or Before October 20, 1963

John F. Kennedy and Eddie Blake make a friendly wager on the outcome of a football game between the New York Giants and the Dallas Cowboys, with the loser buying the winner a steak dinner **[BWCO]**.

—October 20, 1963

The Giants defeat the Cowboys, 37 to 21, with Yelberton "Y.A." Tittle throwing a touchdown pass to Del Shofner **[REAL]**. Eddie Blake watches the game from a local bar. As the only person betting against the Giants, he is not pleased. During the third quarter, John Kennedy calls him at the pub to gloat **[BWCO]**.

—October 25, 1963

Eddie Blake flies from New York to Washington, D.C. As he steps off the plane, FBI Agent Luxem informs him that J. Edgar Hoover requires his assistance in bringing down Moloch the Mystic's drug empire, to show the American people that the Bureau takes seriously the threat of organized crime **[BWCO]**.

—October 25 to November 23, 1963

Eddie Blake works with the FBI to plan a takedown of Moloch's organization **[BWCO]**.

—October 26, 1963

Blake treats John Kennedy to a steak dinner at a restaurant called Dunston's **[BWCO]**.

—October 27, 1963

Kennedy and Blake get together to watch the Giants' next game, against the Cleveland Browns **[BWCO]**. The Giants win, 33 to 6 **[REAL]**.

—Before November 22, 1963

Jon Osterman orders a pair of earrings for Janey Slater, foreseeing that the mailman will deliver them to Wally Weaver's home by mistake **[ALAN]**.

The Comedian is assigned to guard Richard Nixon in Dallas, Texas, during John F. Kennedy's impending visit to that city **[ALAN]**.

—November 22, 1963—12:30 PM

John F. Kennedy's motorcade drives through Dealey Plaza, in Dallas, Texas **[REAL]**, with JFK and his wife Jackie traveling in an electric-powered limousine made possible by Dr. Manhattan's polyacetylene battery advancements **[ALAN]**. Kennedy is assassinated as the vehicle passes the Texas School Book Depository. The gunman is identified as Lee Harvey Oswald, though some report a second shooter firing from a grassy knoll **[REAL]**. That shooter—Eddie Blake—is never identified **[ALAN, FILM]**. Private citizen Abraham Zapruder captures the murder on a home-movie camera. With Kennedy dead, Lyndon B. Johnson assumes the Presidency **[REAL]**.

November 22, 1963—12:30 PM (Alternate Realities)

In one possible timeline, G. Gordon Liddy is the second shooter but is mistaken for Eddie Blake due to their strong physical resemblance **[BWCO]**. In a quantum reality in which Jon Osterman never becomes Dr. Manhattan, Blake is again the second gunman, while in yet another reality without the superhuman, a second gunman (neither Liddy nor Blake) is apprehended and Kennedy survives with only minor injuries **[BWDM]**.

—November 22, 1963—After 12:30 PM

Eddie Blake and Agent Luxem raid one of Moloch the Mystic's warehouses. Knowing the cameras are watching, Blake floors the gas pedal in Luxem's car, crashing the vehicle

MIND .... *The Mindscape of Alan Moore*
MOBL .... *Watchmen: The Mobile Game*
MOTN .... *Watchmen: The Complete Motion Comic*
MTRO .... *Metro promotional newspaper cover wrap*
NEWP .... *New Frontiersman promotional newspaper*
NEWW .... *New Frontiersman website*
NIGH .... *Watchmen: The End Is Nigh, Parts 1 and 2*
PKIT ...... *Watchmen film British press kit*
PORT ..... *Watchmen Portraits*
REAL ..... Real life
RPG1 .... *DC Heroes Role Playing Module #227: Who Watches the Watchmen?*

RPG2 .... *DC Heroes Role Playing Module #235: Taking Out the Trash—Curses and Tears*
RPG3 .... *DC Heroes: The Watchmen Sourcebook*
RUBY .... "Wounds," published in *The Ruby Files Volume One*
SCR1 ..... Unfilmed screenplay draft: Sam Hamm
SCR2 ..... Unfilmed screenplay draft: Charles McKeuen
SCR3 ..... Unfilmed screenplay draft: Gary Goldman
SCR4 ..... Unfilmed screenplay draft: David Hayter (2002)
SCR5 ..... Unfilmed screenplay draft: David Hayter (2003)
SCR6 ..... Unfilmed screenplay draft: Alex Tse
SPOT ..... *DC Spotlight #1*
VRL1 ..... Viral video: *NBS Nightly News with Ted Philips*

VRL2 ..... Viral video: *The Keene Act and You*
VRL3 ..... Viral video: *Who Watches the Watchmen? A Veidt Music Network (VMN) Special*
VRL4 ..... Viral video: *World in Focus: 6 Minutes to Midnight*
VRL5 ..... Viral video: *Local Radio Station Report on 1977 Riots*
VRL6 ..... Viral videos (group of ten): *Veidt Enterprises Advertising Contest*
WAWA ... *Watching the Watchmen*
WHOS ... *Who's Who: The Definitive Directory of the DC Universe*
WTFC ... *Watchmen: The Film Companion*

through a wall, then opens fire, taking out several armed thugs. He finds Edgar Jacobi sitting in his office, crying at the news of John Kennedy's shooting. Shaken, Blake finds a bottle of LV whiskey in Moloch's desk and takes a swig, then shares it with his nemesis, resting a hand on the weeping criminal's shoulder **[BWCO]**.

> **NOTE:** *Blake's reaction to Kennedy's death would appear to be feigned surprise, combined with the pain of having had to murder a close friend.*

—After November 22, 1963

Eddie Blake cuts ties with G. Gordon Liddy, claiming to hold a grudge over the latter's involvement in the JFK assassination. Liddy denies any involvement, saying there is no proof **[BWCO]**.

> **NOTE:** *Despite a seeming contradiction—Blake himself is JFK's murderer—it may simply be that Blake pretends to be upset to hide his own guilt in the matter, or that he holds Liddy personally responsible for making him carry out the assassination.*

Suspicious of a conspiracy, Adrian Veidt sequesters himself at Karnak to study all footage regarding Kennedy's assassination **[BWOZ]**. He learns that The Comedian was in Dallas at the time, guarding Richard Nixon—who had no reason to be there—and suspects the gunman may have been Eddie Blake **[ALAN]**. Others raise the same suspicion **[PKIT]**. Veidt finds no evidence of a conspiracy, however, and admits to himself that not even the world's smartest man can predict everything **[BWOZ]**.

President Lyndon B. Johnson meets with Dr. Manhattan, asking his help in dealing with enemies of the United States who will not be "spooked into submission" **[BWDM]**.

—November 23, 1963

A newspaper headline reads "President Shot—Fears Critical." Jon Osterman tells Janey Slater that he knew the assassination would occur but could not prevent it since, from his perspective, it was already happening. She accuses him of knowing how everything in the world works except for people, but he remains calm, having known this would happen since 1959, and that they would soon make love. Moments later, Wally Weaver arrives with a package that the mailman mistakenly delivered to his address. Inside are earrings Jon purchased for Janey. Though scared of what Jon is becoming, she has sex with him, as he'd always known she would **[ALAN]**.

> **CONFLICT:** *In the* Watchmen *film, these events happen on Christmas day, contradicting Alan Moore's miniseries.*

November 23, 1963 to April 1966

In the wake of John F. Kennedy's death, Adrian Veidt finds fighting crime a hollow pursuit, but continues to do so. Feeling helpless for failing to fix mankind's problems, he begins to despise himself as a sham **[ALAN]**.

On or After December 25, 1963

After watching Disney's *The Sword in the Stone*, Dan Dreiberg conceives of the Owlship, an advanced flying vehicle that he christens *Archimedes* (*Archie* for short), after Merlin's owl in that animated film **[ALAN]**. Construction of the vehicle is estimated to take approximately a year **[RPG3]**.

> **NOTE:** The Sword in the Stone, *Disney's final animated movie before Walt Disney's death, hit theaters on Christmas 1963. Assuming its release was the same in the* Watchmen *universe, that is the earliest date on which Dan could view the film.*

> **CONFLICT:** Before Watchmen: Nite Owl *has Dan naming the Owlship circa May 1962— more than a year prior to* The Sword in the Stone's *theatrical release.*

Dreiberg invents several new "owlsuits," including a variant containing compact electric generators, and also adds stun grenades to his arsenal of gadgets. The owlsuits afford him extraordinary strength and stamina, enabling him to lift extremely heavy items such as metal gates, while the grenades hold an electrical charge capable of causing temporary blindness and hearing loss **[NIGH]**.

> **NOTE:** *This information appears in the instruction manual for* The End Is Nigh, Parts 1 and 2.

Dreiberg also invents a reflective, razor-sharp, perfectly weighted metal boomerang, which he calls an owl-wing. The first time he uses it, however, it leaves a jagged scar on his leg **[SCR5]**.

> **NOTE:** *The owl-wing is analogous to Batman's batarang.*

1960s (Alternate Reality)

In a quantum reality in which Jon Osterman never becomes Dr. Manhattan, Jon and Janey host Milton Glass and Wally Weaver for dinner. They discuss the "Schrödinger's cat" thought experiment, in which a cat is placed inside a box containing a mechanism with a 50/50 chance of breaking a poison capsule. Until the lid is lifted, Wally explains, the cat is simultaneously dead and alive since an observer affects the observed—and the longer the box remains closed, the more quantum probabilities and pocket universe are created, before collapsing into a single reality once someone opens the lid **[BWDM]**.

MIND .... *The Mindscape of Alan Moore*	**RPG2** .... *DC Heroes Role Playing Module #235: Taking Out the Trash—Curses and Tears*	**VRL2** ..... Viral video: *The Keene Act and You*
MOBL.... *Watchmen: The Mobile Game*		**VRL3** ..... Viral video: *Who Watches the Watchmen? A Veidt Music Network (VMN) Special*
MOTN.... *Watchmen: The Complete Motion Comic*	**RPG3** .... *DC Heroes: The Watchmen Sourcebook*	
MTRO.... *Metro promotional newspaper cover wrap*	**RUBY** .... "Wounds," published in *The Ruby Files Volume One*	**VRL4** ..... Viral video: *World in Focus: 6 Minutes to Midnight*
NEWP... *New Frontiersman promotional newspaper*	**SCR1**..... Unfilmed screenplay draft: Sam Hamm	**VRL5** ..... Viral video: *Local Radio Station Report on 1977 Riots*
NEWW... *New Frontiersman website*	**SCR2**..... Unfilmed screenplay draft: Charles McKeuen	
NIGH .... *Watchmen: The End Is Nigh, Parts 1 and 2*	**SCR3**..... Unfilmed screenplay draft: Gary Goldman	**VRL6** ..... Viral videos (group of ten): *Veidt Enterprises Advertising Contest*
PKIT ...... *Watchmen film British press kit*	**SCR4**..... Unfilmed screenplay draft: David Hayter (2002)	
PORT ..... *Watchmen Portraits*	**SCR5**..... Unfilmed screenplay draft: David Hayter (2003)	**WAWA**... *Watching the Watchmen*
REAL..... Real life	**SCR6**..... Unfilmed screenplay draft: Alex Tse	**WHOS** .... *Who's Who: The Definitive Directory of the DC Universe*
RPG1 .... *DC Heroes Role Playing Module #227: Who Watches the Watchmen?*	**SPOT**..... *DC Spotlight #1*	
	VRL1 ..... Viral video: *NBS Nightly News with Ted Philips*	**WTFC** .... *Watchmen: The Film Companion*

NOTE: *Austrian physicist Erwin Schrödinger devised this thought experiment in 1935 to illustrate what he perceived as the inherent problem of applying the Copenhagen interpretation of quantum mechanics to everyday objects.*

Jon Osterman tries once more to fix Janey's watch, perplexed by its seeming violation of physical laws; although everything is in proper working order, the watch will not function. Janey jokes that time itself could be broken, then summons him to bed. Dr. Manhattan's consciousness, observing the exchange, realizes that Janey's quip may be right—in preventing his own transformation, he may have inadvertently damaged time. Seeing the couple's photo from the Palisades Amusement Park, he returns to Mars in 1985 **[BWDM]**.

—Early 1960s

Laurie Jupiter decides she wants to be a zookeeper or a veterinarian when she grows up. Sally dismisses the idea, determined that her daughter will fight crime **[BWSS]**.

Dr. Malcolm "Mal" Long, a psychiatrist, marries a woman named Gloria. The couple have at least one child **[ALAN]**.

> NOTE: *When the Longs marry is unspecified, but since their child (implied by Malcolm's mug having the word "Dad" printed on it) apparently does not live with them in 1985, he or she is likely an adult by that time. Given the couple's age, a 1960s setting is logical for their wedding. Sam Hamm's unproduced 1988 screenplay changes his wife's name to Sylvia—which is also the name of Rorschach's mother.*

Marion Lockley is elected to the U.S. House of Representatives as Illinois' senator **[RPG2]**.

> NOTE: *In the real world, Illinois had two senators during the 1960s: Paul Douglas, a Democrat, followed by Charles H. Percy, a Republican.*

Dr. Manhattan disintegrates several of Moloch the Mystic's top lieutenants and triggermen during a series of encounters, taking the supervillain down **[WTFC]**. Moloch breaks out of prison, then spends the rest of the decade tangling on and off with The Comedian and Ozymandias **[BWMO]**.

Adrian Veidt discusses with his assistant Marla the possibility of buying an island for his own private use, but makes no purchase at this time **[BWOZ]**.

—1960s to 1983

Former *Tales of the Black Freighter* scribe Max Shea graduates from comic books to writing novels and screenplays, several of which are deemed modern classics, including *The Hooded*

Basilisk and twice-filmed novel *Fogdancing*. According to the *Overstreet Guide*, his pirate comics fetch mint prices of almost a thousand dollars apiece **[ALAN]**.

—1964

Jon Osterman grows tired of unnecessary clothing and informs the Pentagon that he no longer intends to wear the entirety of his costume **[ALAN]**.

Moloch the Mystic kidnaps the governor of New Jersey **[WTFC]**.
   NOTE: *The outcome of this kidnapping is unknown.*

American novelist William S. Burroughs publishes *Nova Express*, a social commentary on how humans and machines control life. Burroughs writes the novel using the "fold-in" method of storytelling, a version of the Dadaist "cut-up" technique **[REAL]**.

Sally Jupiter catches her daughter Laurie playing spin-the-bottle with other teens in a friend's basement, with a boy waiting to kiss her in a closet. Laurie is humiliated when Sally removes her from the party, warning that all boys will leave her after getting what they want **[BWSS]**.

—In or Before February 1964

Sporting goods company Everaft begins selling boxing gloves **[BWCO]**.
   NOTE: *Cassius Clay wears a pair of Everaft gloves during a boxing match that Eddie Blake attends with Robert Kennedy. The name is based on real-world company Everlast, and may also play on the phrase "ever after."*

—Before February 25, 1964

U.S. Secretary of Defense Robert McNamara asks Eddie Blake to help the United States military win the Vietnam War, in the role of advisor **[BWCO]**.
   NOTE: *McNamara, who served as Secretary of Defense from 1961 to 1968 under Presidents John F. Kennedy and Lyndon B. Johnson, was a driving force in escalating U.S. involvement in the war.*

—February 25, 1964

Cassius Clay (later known as Muhammad Ali) becomes the world heavyweight boxing champion after defeating Sonny Liston during a six-round bout at the Miami Beach Convention Center **[REAL]**. Eddie Blake attends the event with Robert F. Kennedy, who tells Eddie that he will run for a seat in the U.S. Senate—and implies that the fight is fixed in Clay's favor **[BWCO]**.

—March 13, 1964—3:15 AM

As Catherine Susan "Kitty" Genovese fumbles with her keys to the high-rise apartment building in which she lives on 37th Street in Queens, four men emerge from nearby bushes and wrestle her to the ground **[RPG3]**. Winston Moseley brutally rapes, tortures, and murders her **[REAL]**. Nearly forty neighbors hear her screams, but none take action or call the police; some even watch the event take place **[ALAN, RPG3, BWNO]**.

> **NOTE:** The New York Times' *account of Genovese's murder, to which Alan Moore's miniseries adheres, has come under scrutiny in the years since the event. It is now known that there were far fewer witnesses than was reported at the time, and that the police were, in fact, called.*
>
> *Moseley died in prison on March 28, 2016, during the writing of this book.*

—March 14, 1964

The next day, Walter Kovacs reads about Kitty Genovese's death in the *New York Gazette* and becomes ashamed of humanity. That night, he retrieves the remains of her discarded dress fabric from his trunk and fashions a mask (his new "face") that will make it more bearable to look in a mirror **[ALAN]**.

—March 18, 1964

Walter Kovacs begins recording a daily journal containing notes about the cases he solves, observations about those whom he encounters, and his right-wing, conservative political leanings **[ALAN]**, as a "voucher to show the angels" when they come for him on Judgment Day. His first entry describes his "face" as being in black and white, "as all things should be" **[RPG3]**.

—March 20, 1964

Walter Kovacs becomes active as a vigilante called Rorschach **[RPG2]**. Wearing a pinstriped suit, a fedora, and a dirty brown overcoat **[ALAN]**, similar to the attire his father Charlie wore before abandoning his mother **[RUBY]**, Walter lives in squalor and sleeps only about four hours per night. He views his mask's black-and-white motif as a metaphor for life's ambiguity, believing that those he meets must read their own fates in the fabric's blots and judge themselves accordingly **[ABSO]**.

—March 20, 1964 to Summer 1975

Fighting crime at night and working in the garment industry by day, Walter Kovacs channels his misdirected aggression at his late mother. Though only five feet six inches in height and weighing 140 pounds, he is a formidable fighter in prime physical shape, capable of besting even much larger foes. Throughout this decade, Rorschach leaves criminals alive rather than killing them, causing no serious bodily harm when roughing up foes **[ALAN]**.

ABSO .... *Watchmen Absolute Edition*
ALAN ..... Alan Moore's *Watchmen* miniseries
ARCD .... *Minutemen Arcade*
ARTF ..... *Watchmen: The Art of the Film*
BLCK ..... *Tales of the Black Freighter*
BWCC ... *Before Watchmen—The Crimson Corsair*
BWCO ... *Before Watchmen—Comedian*
BWDB .. *Before Watchmen—Dollar Bill*
BWDM .. *Before Watchmen—Dr. Manhattan*
BWMM.. *Before Watchmen—Minutemen*
BWMO .. *Before Watchmen—Moloch*
BWNO ... *Before Watchmen—Nite Owl*

BWOZ.... *Before Watchmen—Ozymandias*
BWRO ... *Before Watchmen—Rorschach*
BWSS ... *Before Watchmen—Silk Spectre*
CHEM.... My Chemical Romance music video: "Desolation Row"
CMEO.... *Watchmen* cameos in comics, TV, and film:
• Comic: *Astonishing X-Men* volume 3 issue #6
• Comic: *Hero Hotline* volume 1 issue #5
• Comic: *Kingdom Come* volume 1 issue #2
• Comic: *Marvels* volume 1 issue #4
• Comic: *The Question* volume 1 issue #17
• TV: *Teen Titans Go!* episode #82, "Real Boy Adventures"
• Film: *Man of Steel*

• Film: *Batman v Superman: Dawn of Justice Ultimate Edition*
• Film: *Justice League*
CLIX ...... HeroClix figure pack-in cards
DECK..... *DC Comics Deck-Building Game—Crossover Pack 4: Watchmen*
DURS..... *DC Universe: Rebirth Special* volume 1 issue #1
FILM ..... *Watchmen* theatrical film
HOOD .... *Under the Hood* documentary and dust-jacket prop reproduction
JUST ..... *Watchmen: Justice Is Coming*
MATL ..... Mattel Club Black Freighter figure pack-in cards

March 20, 1964 to October 1985

Rorschach arrests more than fifty criminals who end up sentenced to the Sing Sing Correctional Facility, in Ossining, New York **[FILM]**.

April 3, 1964—Night

Rorschach apprehends four suspects in the Kitty Genovese murder, leaving them bound and gagged in front of the NYPD's Area Two Violent Crimes headquarters. He leaves a note pinned to one of them, reading, "With compliments—Rorschach" **[RPG3]**.

April 4, 1964

The *New York Gazette* covers the capture of the Kitty Genovese suspects, quoting Michael Martin, an Area Two Violent Crimes detective, as saying that while the police are grateful for the help, he finds "Rorsh-otch" to be "a dumb name" **[RPG3]**.

Spring 1964

New York City experiences a blackout **[BWOZ]**, culminating in the worst rioting in the city's history. After police warn citizens to stay indoors amidst widespread looting, Dan Dreiberg takes *Archimedes* out for its maiden voyage. As a gang of armed looters try to rape a lone woman, Dan hovers the Owlship, drops to the street, and pummels them all, saving her life. Once power is restored, he returns to *Archie* to find Rorschach waiting inside. Rorschach proposes a partnership, and the two begin working together **[BWNO]**.

> **NOTE:** *The riot is undated in Before* Watchmen: Nite Owl; Before Watchmen: Ozymandias *specifies spring 1964. In the real world, a major blackout occurred in November 1965, but not the year prior.*

Mid-1964

Rorschach fights a gang of six armed thugs who call him "Freak-Face," leaving them with a total of five broken ribs, three concussions, four dislocated limbs, and fourteen missing teeth **[BWOZ]**.

The Comedian travels to Vietnam, where U.S. Army officer Colonel Pitch greets him, glad to have a superhero on the team to boost troop morale. Assigned to eliminate Việt Cộng soldiers bombing the military base, Blake serves alongside Captain Holden, who believes full-fledged war would be bad for U.S. forces, and Pierce, who bemoans the U.S. government's refusal to give them adequate resources to defeat communism. Blake kills several enemy soldiers and decides that he will enjoy Vietnam **[BWCO]**.

> **NOTE:** *The Comedian's assignment to Vietnam is undated in Alan Moore's miniseries.* Before Watchmen: The Comedian *sets his tour of duty in 1964, though he is in the United States in 1966, per Moore's story,* Taking Out the Trash, *and* Before Watchmen:

Silk Spectre, *then serves alongside Dr. Manhattan in Vietnam in 1971. It may be that Blake is sent to the battlefield on several occasions throughout the conflict.*

With help from General Hnu, a Vietnamese military officer, The Comedian tracks down an old enemy—an Italian drug dealer named Sal. Blake forces Sal to help fund U.S. war efforts via the illegal drug trade, with the U.S. military flying narcotics to Corsica aboard Air America flights, to then be funneled to American drug users **[BWCO]**.

—August 2, 1964
The destroyer *USS Maddox* engages three North Vietnamese Navy torpedo boats in battle, in what will later be known as the Gulf of Tonkin incident **[REAL]**. When the U.S. government fails to respond militarily, Eddie Blake decides to take matters into his own hands **[BWCO]**.

—August 4, 1964
The National Security Agency reports a Second Gulf of Tonkin incident in which two U.S. destroyers, the USS *Maddox* and *Turner Joy*, are attacked in international waters. President Lyndon Johnson reveals the attack to the American people **[REAL]**. On Johnson's order, the U.S. military launches an air strike against North Vietnamese gunboats and support facilities. Eddie Blake takes part in the mission, painting a large yellow smiley face on his helmet **[BWCO]**.

> **NOTE:** *Former U.S. Secretary of Defense Robert McNamara admitted, in the 2003 documentary* The Fog of War, *that the August 4 attack was entirely fabricated by the NSA. Apparently, the attack actually occurs in the* Watchmen *universe.*

—Late Autumn 1964
Adrian Veidt, his business thriving, amasses more wealth than he could spend within one lifetime. Ever diversifying his empire, and following in his late father's footsteps, he instructs his laboratory scientists to create a new line of perfume. Early attempts are not quite right, and so Veidt suggests they add seven percent more lilac **[BWOZ]**.

—Between October and December 1964
Cuba's Fidel Castro meets with the Soviet Union's Leonid Brezhnev in Moscow. The two leaders watch as intercontinental ballistic missiles fly overhead **[FILM, WTFC]**.

> **NOTE:** *Brezhnev led the U.S.S.R. starting on October 14, 1964.*

> **CONFLICT:** *A timeline published in* The Film Companion *identifies the Soviet leader as Nikita Khrushchev, but the film's credits list him as Brezhnev.*

—November 3, 1964—Afternoon

President Lyndon B. Johnson and Vice President Hubert Humphrey are re-elected **[BWDM, FILM]**, defeating Barry Goldwater and William Miller by an unprecedented margin **[REAL]**. The *New York Gazette*'s front-page coverage of the election, written by Willis Rensie, bears the headline "LBJ Elected in Landslide" **[BWOZ]**.

> **CONFLICT:** *In* Taking Out the Trash, *set in 1968, the Republican nomination goes to the sitting Vice President; since Richard Nixon wins that election, per Alan Moore's miniseries, he must be that VP, which would make the winner of the 1964 election a Republican, and thus not Johnson (a Democrat, whose running mate was Humphrey). However, Johnson is the President in* Before Watchmen: Ozymandias, Before Watchmen: Doctor Manhattan, *and the* Watchmen *film.*

Veidt's laboratory staff brings him a sample of his new perfume line. Satisfied with its essence—which reminds him of his deceased mother—he instructs them to begin mass production immediately, with an eye toward having the product in stores by the holidays. He calls it Nostalgia **[BWOZ]**.

> **NOTE:** *This product's name appears throughout Alan Moore's miniseries, symbolizing the desire of several characters, including Hollis Mason, Dan Dreiberg, Sally Jupiter, Nelson Gardner, Janey Slater, Bernard, and others, to return to "better" or simpler days—despite those days having been just as fraught with conflict. It also presages Laurie's look back at her life's events in issue #9, thanks to Jon Osterman—and, in a way, to the nostalgia-riding release of the* Before Watchmen *prequel comics.*

—December 3, 1964

Dan Dreiberg finishes constructing the Owlcar, an all-purpose, all-terrain two-seater capable of traversing city streets and rugged country roads at speeds greater than 100 miles per hour. The car costs $55,000 to build and features a rear detention seat for housing criminals, a linkup with the Owl's Nest's computer, remote-control capability, machine guns discharging rubber bullets, and specially armored tires **[RPG3]**.

—Winter 1964

Veidt Enterprises introduces its Nostalgia perfume and aftershave line. The product's marketing tagline, "The times they are a'changing" **[ALAN]**, reminds consumers, who live under the constant threat of nuclear annihilation, of the classier, more carefree world of days past **[WTFC]**.

—In or After 1964

Adrian Veidt reads William Burroughs' novel *Nova Express*, the concepts of which align with his study of "futureology"—the circumvention of logical analysis in order to recognize societal patterns and trends, and thus predict future events **[RPG3]**.

MIND .... *The Mindscape of Alan Moore*
MOBL .... *Watchmen: The Mobile Game*
MOTN .... *Watchmen: The Complete Motion Comic*
MTRO .... *Metro* promotional newspaper cover wrap
NEWP .... *New Frontiersman* promotional newspaper
NEWW ... *New Frontiersman* website
NIGH .... *Watchmen: The End Is Nigh, Parts 1 and 2*
PKIT ...... *Watchmen* film British press kit
PORT ..... *Watchmen Portraits*
REAL ..... Real life
RPG1 .... *DC Heroes Role Playing Module #227: Who Watches the Watchmen?*

RPG2 .... *DC Heroes Role Playing Module #235: Taking Out the Trash—Curses and Tears*
RPG3 .... *DC Heroes: The Watchmen Sourcebook*
RUBY .... "Wounds," published in *The Ruby Files Volume One*
SCR1 ..... Unfilmed screenplay draft: Sam Hamm
SCR2 ..... Unfilmed screenplay draft: Charles McKeuen
SCR3 ..... Unfilmed screenplay draft: Gary Goldman
SCR4 ..... Unfilmed screenplay draft: David Hayter (2002)
SCR5 ..... Unfilmed screenplay draft: David Hayter (2003)
SCR6 ..... Unfilmed screenplay draft: Alex Tse
SPOT ..... *DC Spotlight #1*
VRL1 ..... Viral video: *NBS Nightly News with Ted Philips*

VRL2 ..... Viral video: *The Keene Act and You*
VRL3 ..... Viral video: *Who Watches the Watchmen? A Veidt Music Network (VMN) Special*
VRL4 ..... Viral video: *World in Focus: 6 Minutes to Midnight*
VRL5 ..... Viral video: *Local Radio Station Report on 1977 Riots*
VRL6 ..... Viral videos (group of ten): *Veidt Enterprises Advertising Contest*
WAWA ... *Watching the Watchmen*
WHOS ... *Who's Who: The Definitive Directory of the DC Universe*
WTFC .... *Watchmen: The Film Companion*

—Before 1965

Small-time hood Tom "Rocky" Ryan shows a great talent for burglary, earning the notice of larger street gangs despite his dwarf stature. Calling himself The Big Figure, the criminal genius quickly ascends the ranks of the organized-crime world **[RPG3]**.

> **NOTE:** *Sam Hamm's unproduced 1988 screenplay calls this character Little Bigger.*

—In or Before 1965

Several businesses open in Los Angeles, California, including Pay Day Loans, Liberty Menswear & Shoes, Ballpen, Mac Appliances, and Rick's Menswear **[BWCO]**, while Fogelsons Market opens in New York City **[BWNO]**.

Psychiatrist Malcolm Long begins using inkblot tests to help him diagnose patients **[RPG3]**.

—January 2, 1965

Dan Dreiberg finishes constructing the Owlship *Archimedes* (*Archie* for short), a hovering base of operations. The silent-running, remote-controlled vehicle costs $250,000 to build **[RPG3]** and is equipped with air-to-air missiles, floodlights, a flame-thrower, fog screens, electromagnetic systems, radiation shields, a public-address system, water cannons, screechers, a rear ramp, a starboard coffee machine, and an in-ship stereo. *Archimedes* can remain invisible to radar, thanks to concealed vents and turbines, along with a curved, corner-free surface. One closet contains auxiliary costumes for underwater work and other applications **[ALAN]**.

—January 20, 1965

The Republican Party's nominee becomes President of the United States, with Richard Nixon serving as his Vice President **[RPG2]**.

> **CONFLICT:** *In* Before Watchmen: Ozymandias, *as in the real world, Lyndon B. Johnson and Hubert Humphrey are re-elected in the 1964 election. Before Watchmen: Doctor Manhattan and the* Watchmen *film both depict Johnson's victory. However,* Taking Out the Trash, *set in 1968, sees the Republican nomination go to an unnamed sitting Vice President; since Richard Nixon wins the election (per Alan Moore's miniseries), he must be that VP, which would mean the President must be a Republican, and not Johnson, a Democrat.*

—Mid-1965

Dan Dreiberg attends a party to procure parts for a new invention. In attendance is a beautiful woman (later known as The Twilight Lady), accompanying the owner of a large manufacturing firm. She notices Dan's face, which sticks in her mind **[BWNO]**.

ABSO .... *Watchmen Absolute Edition*
ALAN ..... Alan Moore's *Watchmen* miniseries
ARCD .... *Minutemen Arcade*
ARTF ..... *Watchmen: The Art of the Film*
BLCK ..... *Tales of the Black Freighter*
BWCC .. *Before Watchmen—The Crimson Corsair*
BWCO ... *Before Watchmen—Comedian*
BWDB .. *Before Watchmen—Dollar Bill*
BWDM .. *Before Watchmen—Dr. Manhattan*
BWMM.. *Before Watchmen—Minutemen*
BWMO .. *Before Watchmen—Moloch*
BWNO ... *Before Watchmen—Nite Owl*

BWOZ.... *Before Watchmen—Ozymandias*
BWRO ... *Before Watchmen—Rorschach*
BWSS ... *Before Watchmen—Silk Spectre*
CHEM.... My Chemical Romance music video: "Desolation Row"
CMEO.... *Watchmen* cameos in comics, TV, and film:
• Comic: *Astonishing X-Men* volume 3 issue #6
• Comic: *Hero Hotline* volume 1 issue #5
• Comic: *Kingdom Come* volume 1 issue #2
• Comic: *Marvels* volume 1 issue #4
• Comic: *The Question* volume 1 issue #17
• TV: *Teen Titans Go!* episode #82, "Real Boy Adventures"
• Film: *Man of Steel*

• Film: *Batman v Superman: Dawn of Justice Ultimate Edition*
• Film: *Justice League*
CLIX ...... HeroClix figure pack-in cards
DECK..... *DC Comics Deck-Building Game—Crossover Pack 4: Watchmen*
DURS .... *DC Universe: Rebirth Special* volume 1 issue #1
FILM ..... *Watchmen* theatrical film
HOOD .... *Under the Hood* documentary and dust-jacket prop reproduction
JUST ..... *Watchmen: Justice Is Coming*
MATL .... Mattel Club Black Freighter figure pack-in cards

In or Before August 1965

As New York City street gang violence hits an all-time high, with gangs growing bolder and acting like they rule the streets **[MOBL]**, Rorschach and Nite Owl pool their efforts and make headway into battling the problem. Rorschach values Dan's friendship and deems them a good pair-up **[ALAN]**, though at times, he thinks he'd be better off by himself, and that Dan doesn't have what it takes **[BWDM]**. Dreiberg considers his partner tactically brilliant and rational, though quiet, grim, and unpredictable **[ALAN]**.

Anthony Rizzoli, also called Anthony Vitoli **[RPG2]** and Underboss **[RPG3, NIGH]**, emerges as a dangerous figure in the criminal underworld **[ALAN]**. Tom "Rocky" Ryan, a.k.a. The Big Figure, serves as a lieutenant in his syndicate **[RPG3]**.

Rorschach and Nite Owl apprehend Underboss at the height of his criminal empire. The mobster hides in a sewer, believing they won't be able to follow him aboard *Archimedes*, but the duo pursue him on hoverbikes instead. Underboss is shocked when a bike-riding Rorschach shoots out of a tunnel in a gas cloud, following a pack of frightened, scampering rats **[ALAN]**. The crime-fighters arrest the gangster, who is briefly jailed. The charges against him fail to stick, however, and he is set free **[RPG3]**.

During Underboss's incarceration, The Big Figure seizes control of his empire. The dwarf's gang quickly monopolizes narcotics, prostitution, and gambling sales throughout New York City. On one occasion, he wipes out an entire South Bronx police station **[RPG3]**. Nite Owl and Rorschach foil his plans several times **[ALAN, MOBL]**.

> **NOTE:** The Film Companion *notes that The Big Figure poses a powerful presence in the 1960s. Given that he is arrested and imprisoned in August 1965, his reign as boss is actually quite short (pun intentional).*

Washington Post reporters Robert Woodward and Carl Bernstein publish a series of articles about Underboss that finally lead to his conviction and imprisonment. The kingpin's underground hideout and other assets are auctioned off **[NIGH]**.

Early August 1965

Eddie Blake returns home from Vietnam aboard an American World Airlines (AWA) flight. As he steps onto U.S. soil, anti-war protestors greet him on the tarmac, which he finds disheartening. Among the hippies is a young woman resembling Laurie Jupiter, the daughter he has never known. As she hands him a flower, patriotic anti-protestors pummel her and other youths with tomatoes. Violence erupts between the two groups, and soldiers lead Blake to safety. Angry at himself for not taking action, he spends days mulling over what he should have done instead **[BWCO]**.

MIND .... *The Mindscape of Alan Moore*	**RPG2** .... *DC Heroes Role Playing Module #235: Taking Out the Trash—Curses and Tears*	**VRL2** ..... Viral video: *The Keene Act and You*
MOBL.... *Watchmen: The Mobile Game*		**VRL3** ..... Viral video: *Who Watches the Watchmen? A Veidt Music Network (VMN) Special*
MOTN.... *Watchmen: The Complete Motion Comic*	**RPG3** .... *DC Heroes: The Watchmen Sourcebook*	
MTRO.... *Metro* promotional newspaper cover wrap	**RUBY** .... "Wounds," published in *The Ruby Files Volume One*	**VRL4** ..... Viral video: *World in Focus: 6 Minutes to Midnight*
NEWP.... *New Frontiersman* promotional newspaper	**SCR1**..... Unfilmed screenplay draft: Sam Hamm	**VRL5** ..... Viral video: *Local Radio Station Report on 1977 Riots*
NEWW .... *New Frontiersman* website	**SCR2**..... Unfilmed screenplay draft: Charles McKeuen	
NIGH ..... *Watchmen: The End Is Nigh, Parts 1 and 2*	**SCR3**..... Unfilmed screenplay draft: Gary Goldman	**VRL6**..... Viral videos (group of ten): *Veidt Enterprises Advertising Contest*
PKIT...... *Watchmen* film British press kit	**SCR4**..... Unfilmed screenplay draft: David Hayter (2002)	
PORT..... *Watchmen Portraits*	**SCR5**..... Unfilmed screenplay draft: David Hayter (2003)	**WAWA** .... *Watching the Watchmen*
REAL..... Real life	**SCR6**..... Unfilmed screenplay draft: Alex Tse	**WHOS** ... *Who's Who: The Definitive Directory of the DC Universe*
RPG1 .... *DC Heroes Role Playing Module #227: Who Watches the Watchmen?*	**SPOT**..... *DC Spotlight #1*	
	VRL1 ..... Viral video: *NBS Nightly News with Ted Philips*	**WTFC** .... *Watchmen: The Film Companion*

—August 11, 1965

Lee Minikus, a white California Highway Patrol officer, pulls over African American motorist Marquette Frye for reckless driving. A roadside scuffle involving Frye's mother, Rena Price, causes community outrage, sparking what will later be dubbed the Watts riots **[REAL]**.

—August 12, 1965

The *Los Angeles Times'* front-page headline reads "1,000 Riot in L.A.—Police and Motorists Attacked" **[REAL, BWCO]**.

—Between August 12 and 17, 1965

After reading the *Times* article, Eddie Blake joins the fray, ignoring police orders to stand down. Shooting a sniper, he roughs up several protestors, inciting racial anger. After a rioter hits Blake with a brick, he shoots out store windows to cause widespread looting and thereby discredit the protestors in the eyes of the media. When LAPD Chief William H. Parker chastises The Comedian for escalating the situation and likens the rioters to monkeys, Blake flings dog feces at the officer and laughs hysterically **[BWCO]**.

—Mid to Late August 1965

Eddie Blake takes a vacation in Hawaii, where he has a fling with a beautiful woman at an establishment called Tiki Bar. Robert F. Kennedy calls to let him know there will be repercussions for his actions during the Watts riots, and that he must apologize to William Parker **[BWCO]**.

—August 22, 1965

Rorschach and Nite Owl bring down The Big Figure **[ALAN, RPG3]**, after the mobster lures the crime-fighters into a trap by sending out gang members to attack them. As Dan Dreiberg battles the lackeys, Rorschach tracks one to their hideout. Big Figure escapes in a missile-equipped aircraft, and the two partners pursue him aboard *Archimedes*. Dan brings the mobster's aircraft down using the Owlship's flame-throwers, then lands the vehicle to pursue Big Figure on foot. He finds the dwarf in a building rigged with TNT, then realizes they've been set up. As Dan disarms the bombs, Rorschach prevents Big Figure from escaping **[MOBL]**.

The vigilantes deliver Big Figure to the NYPD's Area Two Violent Crimes headquarters and provide cops with a ledger implicating him in two homicides, as well as a narcotics ring operating throughout New York City and parts of New Jersey **[RPG3]**. Big Figure is sentenced to the Sing Sing Correctional Facility, in Ossining, New York **[ALAN]**.

> **CONFLICT:** The Film Companion *moves Big Figure's arrest to 1970, contradicting Alan Moore's miniseries, which sets his capture in 1965. The Watchmen Sourcebook incorrectly places his incarceration at Rikers Island, not Sing Sing, and misspells the jail complex's name as "Riker's."*

—August 23, 1965—Afternoon

The *New York Gazette* covers The Big Figure's capture, quoting Nite Owl as saying he and Rorschach enjoy working together since the results speak for themselves **[RPG3]**.

—December 1965

Charlton Comics' *Blue Beetle* volume 3 issue #53 is published. The comic contains two stories, "The People Thieves" and "The Pyramids of Egypt" **[REAL, HOOD]**.

> **NOTE:** *Alan Moore based The Nite Owl on Blue Beetle. In the* Watchmen *universe, public interest in superhero comics dies out shortly after 1939, so the release of this issue a quarter-century later may indicate a brief resurgence.*

—December 25, 1965

Janey Slater cries on Christmas, but Jon Osterman turns her tear into a diamond **[WTFC]**.

—1965 to October 1985

The Big Figure spends twenty years at Sing Sing, with two largely built inmates **[ALAN]**, Michael "Mike" Stephens and Lawrence "Larry" Andrews, serving as his personal bodyguards. Larry keeps Big Figure's inmate uniforms clean, while Mike smuggles cigars into the prison for him **[CLIX]**. For two decades, the tiny kingpin looks forward to someday avenging himself on Rorschach and Nite Owl **[ALAN]**. Despite his imprisonment, The Big Figure's crime syndicate continues to operate. Among its members is a minor enforcer named Don "Big Daddy" Feroli **[RPG2]**.

> **NOTE:** *The surnames of Michael and Lawrence are revealed in HeroClix's* Watchmen *figure pack-in cards.*

> **CONFLICT:** *In the* Watchmen *film, Big Figure spends fifteen years in prison, not twenty, indicating an arrest in 1970, and contradicting Alan Moore's miniseries. Charles McKeuen's unproduced 1989 screenplay calls Lawrence "Fat Lawrence," while David Hayter's unproduced 2003 script draft and Alex Tse's 2006 version name him Billy and "Big Bill." In all three scripts, and in the final film, Michael is called Lloyd. Sam Hamm's 1988 screenplay, meanwhile, calls the dwarf Little Bigger.*

—In or After 1965

Dan Dreiberg creates a gas-powered grappling gun for Rorschach **[ALAN]**.

—Mid-1960s

The world's political balance changes drastically. The United States gains unquestioned military supremacy and economic leverage, enabling U.S. leaders to dictate the western world's economic policies. The American and Soviet governments each increase their stockpiles of nuclear weaponry, but the Russians back down in humiliation over several

MIND .... *The Mindscape of Alan Moore*
MOBL .... *Watchmen: The Mobile Game*
MOTN .... *Watchmen: The Complete Motion Comic*
MTRO .... *Metro* promotional newspaper cover wrap
NEWP .... *New Frontiersman* promotional newspaper
NEWW .... *New Frontiersman* website
NIGH ..... *Watchmen: The End Is Nigh, Parts 1 and 2*
PKIT ...... *Watchmen* film British press kit
PORT ..... *Watchmen Portraits*
REAL ..... Real life
RPG1 .... *DC Heroes Role Playing Module #227: Who Watches the Watchmen?*

RPG2 .... *DC Heroes Role Playing Module #235: Taking Out the Trash—Curses and Tears*
RPG3 .... *DC Heroes: The Watchmen Sourcebook*
RUBY .... "Wounds," published in *The Ruby Files Volume One*
SCR1 ..... Unfilmed screenplay draft: Sam Hamm
SCR2 ..... Unfilmed screenplay draft: Charles McKeuen
SCR3 ..... Unfilmed screenplay draft: Gary Goldman
SCR4 ..... Unfilmed screenplay draft: David Hayter (2002)
SCR5 ..... Unfilmed screenplay draft: David Hayter (2003)
SCR6 ..... Unfilmed screenplay draft: Alex Tse
SPOT ..... *DC Spotlight #1*
VRL1 ..... Viral video: *NBS Nightly News with Ted Philips*

VRL2 ..... Viral video: *The Keene Act and You*
VRL3 ..... Viral video: *Who Watches the Watchmen? A Veidt Music Network (VMN) Special*
VRL4 ..... Viral video: *World in Focus: 6 Minutes to Midnight*
VRL5 ..... Viral video: *Local Radio Station Report on 1977 Riots*
VRL6 ..... Viral videos (group of ten): *Veidt Enterprises Advertising Contest*
WAWA ... *Watching the Watchmen*
WHOS .... *Who's Who: The Definitive Directory of the DC Universe*
WTFC .... *Watchmen: The Film Companion*

issues, rather than risk a war they cannot win. Experts predict that in the event of a full-scale nuclear war, Dr. Manhattan could disarm or deflect sixty percent of all incoming Soviet warheads. Against such odds, many assume, Russia would not risk a global conflict. Jon Osterman is thus seen as a walking nuclear deterrent—a guarantee of lasting peace on Earth **[ALAN]**.

Edgar Jacobi becomes active again in the criminal underworld **[ALAN]**, conducting all business through a network of subordinates to avoid antagonizing masked adventurers **[RPG1]**. He develops connections with every major syndicate and street gang in New York City and grows his criminal empire around the entire world, including government officials both local and national **[RPG2]**.

Moloch makes his penthouse headquarters a protective fortress, tells only his most trusted employees the address, and is careful to remain free of incriminating evidence so his flunkies will take the fall in the event of his operations' exposure **[RPG1]**. Despite such precautions, the kingpin faces Dr. Manhattan during several conflicts, with the superhuman becoming his greatest nemesis since The Comedian **[ALAN]**.

> **NOTE:** It seems unlikely that Moloch would survive multiple encounters with Dr. Manhattan, given that not even Ozymandias could defeat the latter.

Moloch stops writing letters on parchment due to the high expense **[RPG1]**.

After busting numerous drug rings, Adrian Veidt is accused of being an establishment pawn **[ALAN]**.

In training her daughter to be the next Silk Spectre, Sally Jupiter begins ambushing her randomly, wearing a mask and a muscle suit. Though just a drill, Sally's attacks are intense, designed to hone Laurie's instincts. Laurie becomes an excellent fighter as a result, but grows to resent her mother for controlling her every move—and often sports bruises and cuts on her body **[BWSS]**.

—1965 and Beyond

With Dr. Manhattan working for the American government, the communist regimes of the world cease antagonizing the United States, fearful of his retaliation **[ALAN]**.

Part VII:
THE SMARTEST MAN ON THE CINDER
(1966)

In or Before 1966

Betsy Kensington, a schoolmate of Laurie Jupiter, searches her father's drawer for spare change and finds a Tijuana Bible featuring Silk Spectre's sexual exploits with an Acme Brush Co. salesman **[BWSS]**. The eight-page porn comic is titled *Silk Spectre and the Adventures of the Acme Brushman* **[FILM]**. Betsy recognizes the titular character as Sally Jupiter and decides to use this knowledge to humiliate Laurie **[BWSS]**.

Gang members scrawl graffiti tags on the walls of a San Francisco building, including "God Damn Mad Dog," "Tik Tok," "Pious Patrol," "Gila Monster," "Hot Mama," "Knight in Rusty Armor," "Sooper Seenius," "Skull Wise Kracker," "Likka Lika," "Homicidal Brainiac," "Acid Test," "Boggy Bob & Dirty Doug," "Wizards," "Sweet Charity," and more. One tagger warns others to "Respect the Raptor" **[BWSS]**.

In carrying out a variety of covert operations and military campaigns for the U.S. government, Eddie Blake becomes an expert at blackmail, torture, political assassinations, strategy, and tactics **[RPG1]**.

A crooner called The Chairman becomes immensely popular on the music charts, releasing such records as *Swing Low Swing High*, *Black & White & Swingin' All Over*, *In the Cards*, and *The Chairman's Greatest Hits*. Sally Jupiter becomes a fan of his music and buys several of his albums. Secretly, The Chairman is a criminal mastermind, protected by two beautiful bodyguards called The Shake Sisters **[BWSS]**.

> **NOTE:** *Though unnamed, The Chairman is drawn as Frank Sinatra, who earned the nickname "The Chairman of the Board" after forming Reprise Records in 1960.*

Gurustein, the proprietor of a San Francisco nightclub called Sand Doze, forms strong ties with several popular entertainers, including The Chairman. A drug manufacturer in

Gurustein's employ, Mr. Owsley, creates a new liquid pharmaceutical—Kesey Test 5 (KT-5 for short)—that overwhelms a person's rational thoughts. The drug can be blended into LSD, rendering a user susceptible to marketing, and The Chairman and Gurustein use it to brainwash fans to buy merchandise **[BWSS]**.

> **NOTE:** *KT-5 is a predecessor of KT-28, a street drug sold by the Knot-Tops in Alan Moore's miniseries. The drug's name is a reference to* One Flew Over the Cuckoo's Nest *author Ken Kesey, a prominent countercultural figure in the 1960s, who actually appears in* Before Watchmen: Silk Spectre.

Laurie Jupiter and a fellow high school student, Greg, develop a mutual attraction to each other, but Sally refuses to let Laurie date. Greg's father, a former U.S. Marine, tries to toughen Greg up by teaching him how to box, saying he'll have to join the military at age eighteen so the Marines can make a man out of him **[BWSS]**.

Several businesses open up in San Francisco, including The Blissful Boa (a seller of "psychedelic psupplies"), the Blue Unicorn Cafe, Bohemian Treasures, The Bootique, and Stellar Travels Car Rental **[BWSS]**.

> **NOTE:** *The spelling of "psupplies" is intentional, and not a typographic error on this author's part.*

A man named Hal Snyder borrows $12.50 from a friend. When he fails to pay it back, the lender scrawls graffiti on a San Francisco wall calling him a Nazi **[BWSS]**.

Laurie Jupiter adopts a pet bird, which she names Lamb **[BWSS]**.

Red D'eath and the Horseman play a gig with another band, Avalon, as their backup group **[BWSS]**.

> **NOTE:** *Red D'eath and the Horsemen are an earlier iteration of Pale Horse, a punk-rock band fronted by Red D'eath in 1985.*

The San Francisco Museum of Modern Art opens an exhibit on Jackson Pollock **[BWSS]**.

—1966

Laurie Jupiter watches television footage of a Vietnamese monk setting himself on fire **[WTFC]**.

> **NOTE:** *In the real world, Vietnamese Buddhist monk Thích Quảng Đức burned himself to death in Saigon on June 11, 1963.*

> **CONFLICT:** *Laurie is said to have watched this broadcast with her parents, contradicting Alan Moore's miniseries, which sets their divorce in 1956. At this point in the timeline, Larry Schexnayder is no longer in Sally's and Laurie's lives.*

—Early 1966

As Laurie Jupiter practices pole-vaulting one afternoon in high school, her friend Greg asks her out on a date, but she declines. Sally Jupiter drives her home, joking that if Laurie doesn't want Greg, she'll take him. Laurie is not amused. When Greg tells his parents about his crush on Laurie over dinner, they tell him about Sally's checkered past and his father shows him a copy of Sally's Tijuana Bible **[BWSS]**, *Silk Spectre and the Adventures of the Acme Brushman* **[FILM]**.

That night, Laurie tries on her mother's Silk Spectre costume, wishing her breasts were more shapely like Sally's. As she watches TV, Sally attacks her disguised as a home intruder, but their training turns into a fight when Laurie complains about not being able to enjoy her teen years, mocking Sally's sex-idol reputation. Maternal instincts replace Sally's anger, however, when she notices a cut on her daughter's face **[BWSS]**.

Sally calls Hollis Mason to discuss Laurie's rebelliousness, and he assures her that she's a great mother. Laurie, meanwhile, sneaks out to meet Greg. The two teens race around the high school track, and after she wins, they discuss their frustrations about their "hard-ass" parents. He takes off his shirt after splashing beer on it, and she notices bruises on his body. Showing him her own bruises, Laurie is delighted when Greg kisses one on her shoulder **[BWSS]**.

Laurie and Greg visit the 13 O'Clock Diner. A snobby schoolmate, Betsy Kensington, humiliates Laurie by calling her mother a whore. Furious, Laurie punches Betsy in the face, then returns home, packs a suitcase, and leaves, saying she's ashamed to be Sally's daughter. Greg meets her outside to make sure she's okay, tosses his father's Tijuana Bible into a sewer, and tells Laurie he loves her. The two run away from home, hitching a van ride to San Francisco **[BWSS]**. Laurie changes her surname to Juspeczyk, her mother's maiden name, to distance herself from Sally **[RPG1]**.

>   *NOTE: According to* Who Watches the Watchmen?, *Laurie is born with the surname Jupiter, then changes it to Juspeczyk after turning sixteen. Since she cuts ties with Sally after running away, this seems a logical placement for her name change.*

Laurie and Greg befriend the van's owners—Chappy, an artist, Gigi, a fashion designer, and their friend Eagle. Gigi and Chappy share their home with the two teens, introducing them to drug use and the hippie lifestyle, and they adopt a cat called Pigpen. Chappy sets up a silk-screening studio to make posters and T-shirts. Greg works with him to pay their share of the rent, while Laurie gets a job as a waitress at the Blue Unicorn Café. She writes a letter to Hollis Mason, asking him to assure her mother that she's fine, that she enjoys being free to think for herself, and that her life is a big adventure **[BWSS]**.

>   *NOTE: Eagle may simply be a fellow hitchhiker along for the ride, as he does not appear throughout the remainder of* Before Watchmen: Silk Spectre.

MIND .... *The Mindscape of Alan Moore*
MOBL .... *Watchmen: The Mobile Game*
MOTN .... *Watchmen: The Complete Motion Comic*
MTRO .... *Metro promotional newspaper cover wrap*
NEWP .... *New Frontiersman promotional newspaper*
NEWW .... *New Frontiersman website*
NIGH ..... *Watchmen: The End Is Nigh, Parts 1 and 2*
PKIT ...... *Watchmen film British press kit*
PORT ..... *Watchmen Portraits*
REAL ..... Real life
RPG1 .... *DC Heroes Role Playing Module #227: Who Watches the Watchmen?*

RPG2 .... *DC Heroes Role Playing Module #235: Taking Out the Trash—Curses and Tears*
RPG3 .... *DC Heroes: The Watchmen Sourcebook*
RUBY .... "Wounds," published in *The Ruby Files Volume One*
SCR1 ..... Unfilmed screenplay draft: Sam Hamm
SCR2 ..... Unfilmed screenplay draft: Charles McKeuen
SCR3 ..... Unfilmed screenplay draft: Gary Goldman
SCR4 ..... Unfilmed screenplay draft: David Hayter (2002)
SCR5 ..... Unfilmed screenplay draft: David Hayter (2003)
SCR6 ..... Unfilmed screenplay draft: Alex Tse
SPOT ..... *DC Spotlight #1*
VRL1 ..... Viral video: *NBS Nightly News with Ted Philips*

VRL2 ..... Viral video: *The Keene Act and You*
VRL3 ..... Viral video: *Who Watches the Watchmen? A Veidt Music Network (VMN) Special*
VRL4 ..... Viral video: *World in Focus: 6 Minutes to Midnight*
VRL5 ..... Viral video: *Local Radio Station Report on 1977 Riots*
VRL6 ..... Viral videos (group of ten): *Veidt Enterprises Advertising Contest*
WAWA ... *Watching the Watchmen*
WHOS .... *Who's Who: The Definitive Directory of the DC Universe*
WTFC .... *Watchmen: The Film Companion*

Laurie Juspeczyk and Greg amass art books about Pablo Picasso and Edvard Munch, Ken Kesey's novel *One Flew Over the Cuckoo's Nest*, and issues of several comic books, including *Tales of the Black Freighter* and *Brigitte the Buccaneer* **[BWSS]**.

While working at the café, Laurie overhears four thugs discussing plans to rough up an independent drug dealer the following Thursday night, as an example for others. She secretly starts fighting crime to protect the community, scoping out the site of the future attack—a building called The Mariposa. Gigi designs a slinky, yellow costume for Laurie, agreeing not to tell Greg or Chappy about her nocturnal pastime **[BWSS]**.

On Thursday night, Laurie sneaks out to The Mariposa and spots the thugs clad in gang garb, torturing a tied-up young man. She beats them up, frees their captive, and forces them to reveal their employer: Sand Doze owner Gurustein. Greg, meanwhile, attends a Dead Dogs gig and sells nineteen posters and twelve T-shirts. Chappy, Gigi, and their friends Fatima and Wilby go to the Sand Doze, where Gurustein gets them high on KT-5, giving them an overwhelming urge to buy consumer products **[BWSS]**.

The lead singer of rock group Red D'eath and the Horsemen gives amphetamines to two nubile, fourteen-year-old girls, making them open to his sexual advances **[BWSS]**.

The next morning, Laurie and Greg hang up fliers around town for a party hosted by Chappy and Gigi, asking "Can you pass the K-Test?" Outside the Haight Bank & Trust, Fatima leads a peaceful protest against corporate greed, while Greg and Laurie enjoy breakfast at the Blue Unicorn Café. Wilby enters, covered in smiley-face pins and craving inordinate amounts of coffee and brownies. He suddenly overdoses, and an ambulance transports him to a hospital **[BWSS]**.

At the Sand Doze, several entertainers enjoy alcohol and hookah pipes. The Chairman hits the nightclub stage, warning the assembled singers to stop influencing teenagers not to care about material things, as it's cutting into profits. His aide, Poindexter, displays slides showing a drop in sales of albums, singles, lunchboxes, and other products, and Owsley unveils his new drug, KT-5. Some entertainers dislike the idea of brainwashing fans to buy things, but Gurustein manipulates them into complying **[BWSS]**.

> **NOTE:** *Though not identified by name, the four musicians who protest the brainwashing drug are drawn to resemble The Beatles.*

When Fatima, Gigi, and Chappy arrive at the hospital, they seem obsessed with buying consumer goods, due to the effects of KT-5. Worried about her friends' state of mind, Laurie dons her crime-fighting outfit and investigates the Sand Doze. Two bodyguards,

The Shake Sisters, attack, but she gets the upper hand and forces them to reveal that Gurustein and The Chairman know of the drug's effects **[BWSS]**.

Laurie Juspeczyk returns home, where the party is in full-swing. Gurustein is emceeing the bash, with Red D'eath and the Horsemen performing. The punch is spiked with LSD, and Laurie experiences a heavy trip after drinking it, during which distorted visions of her pets talk to her; her mother has group sex with The Chairman, The Minutemen, and comedy team The Marx Brothers; and novelist Ken Kesey tells her to live like the world will soon end, whether tomorrow or in six months or in nineteen years **[BWSS]**.

> **NOTE:** The "nineteen years" reference foreshadows Adrian Veidt's 1985 murder of millions of New Yorkers in Alan Moore's miniseries. Laurie's hallucination also predicts her future involvement with Dr. Manhattan.

Hollis Mason receives Laurie's letter and calls Sally to let her know what her daughter has been up to. She hangs up and calls Eddie Blake to bring Laurie home. Hollis asks a neighborhood child to watch Phantom for him, then books a Pacific West flight to California **[BWSS]**.

Laurie awakens the morning after the party to find Greg overdosing on acid. Greg is hospitalized, and she tells him about her secret crime-fighting activities. Several others from the party have also been admitted for overdoses, and police take Chappy in for questioning. Laurie buys new boots for her costume at The Bootique, then bursts into the Sand Doze to find an orgy in progress. Pummeling Gurustein, she threatens to feed The Chairman his own testicles if more of her friends end up sick from KT-5 **[BWSS]**.

Eddie Blake arranges to have Greg brought to the hospital morgue, where he ties the youth up and gives him a choice: join the military and never see Laurie again, or be injected with a fatal combination of drugs. He makes Greg write a goodbye letter to Laurie, urging her to return home to her mother, then leaves it on her dresser as she sleeps, grabbing a smiley pin from her dresser to add to his costume. She finds the note in the morning and is devastated upon reading it **[BWSS]**.

> **NOTE:** This, presumably, is the same pin Blake dies wearing in 1985.

Hollis Mason arrives in San Francisco and elicits Laurie's address from Fatima and Wilby. The Chairman realizes Mason is a cop and sends The Shake Sisters to kill Gurustein, Owsley, and others at the Sand Doze in order to tie up loose ends. The two women try to kill Hollis as well, but he ties them up and awaits Laurie's return. Laurie heads to the nightclub and confronts The Chairman, who hits her with a pistol grip. Finally, she jams a boot heel into his neck and he runs out into the street, where he is run over by a bus carrying Ken Kesey and several hippies **[BWSS]**.

MIND .... *The Mindscape of Alan Moore*	**RPG2** .... *DC Heroes Role Playing Module #235: Taking Out the Trash—Curses and Tears*	**VRL2** ..... Viral video: *The Keene Act and You*
MOBL .... *Watchmen: The Mobile Game*		**VRL3** ..... Viral video: *Who Watches the Watchmen? A Veidt Music Network (VMN) Special*
MOTN .... *Watchmen: The Complete Motion Comic*	**RPG3** .... *DC Heroes: The Watchmen Sourcebook*	
MTRO .... *Metro* promotional newspaper cover wrap	**RUBY** .... "Wounds," published in *The Ruby Files Volume One*	**VRL4** ..... Viral video: *World in Focus: 6 Minutes to Midnight*
NEWP .... *New Frontiersman* promotional newspaper	**SCR1** ..... Unfilmed screenplay draft: Sam Hamm	**VRL5** ..... Viral video: *Local Radio Station Report on 1977 Riots*
NEWW .... *New Frontiersman* website	**SCR2** ..... Unfilmed screenplay draft: Charles McKeuen	
NIGH ..... *Watchmen: The End Is Nigh, Parts 1 and 2*	**SCR3** .... Unfilmed screenplay draft: Gary Goldman	**VRL6** ..... Viral videos (group of ten): *Veidt Enterprises Advertising Contest*
PKIT ...... *Watchmen* film British press kit	**SCR4** .... Unfilmed screenplay draft: David Hayter (2002)	
PORT .... *Watchmen Portraits*	**SCR5** ..... Unfilmed screenplay draft: David Hayter (2003)	**WAWA** ... *Watching the Watchmen*
REAL ..... Real life	**SCR6** .... Unfilmed screenplay draft: Alex Tse	**WHOS** ... *Who's Who: The Definitive Directory of the DC Universe*
RPG1 .... *DC Heroes Role Playing Module #227: Who Watches the Watchmen?*	**SPOT** ..... *DC Spotlight #1*	
	VRL1 ..... Viral video: *NBS Nightly News with Ted Philips*	**WTFC** .... *Watchmen: The Film Companion*

Laurie Juspeczyk bids farewell to her friends, one of whom gives her a skull ring as a going-away gift. Gigi makes her a new crime-fighting outfit, and Laurie adds the ring to it as a necklace. Laurie and Hollis return to San Francisco, where she tells her mother that she'll become the next Silk Spectre, but that she needs to do it her way **[BWSS]**.

> **NOTE:** *Laurie's proclamation that she needs to do things her way, after besting The Chairman, is a sly reference to Frank Sinatra's hit song "My Way."*

During the ensuing weeks, Laurie brings three different young men home just to annoy her mother, one of whom sports a goatee and a peace symbol tattoo. Eventually, the two relocate to New York, and she vows not to bother with men anymore **[BWSS]**.

—March 11, 1966—Afternoon
Laurie Juspeczyk makes her public debut as the second Silk Spectre, thwarting a jewelry-store heist in downtown Manhattan after noticing the theft in progress. Easily overpowering three armed thieves, she returns the stolen loot **[RPG3]**.

—March 12, 1966
The *New York Gazette* publishes an article about the second Silk Spectre, raising the question of whether or not she is related to her predecessor, Sally Jupiter **[RPG3]**.

—April 1966
France withdraws its military commitment to the North Atlantic Treaty Organization (NATO). The *New York Gazette* reports on this development, as well as on a recent heart-transplant operation, with the patient noted as being in stable condition, and the Russians calling Dr. Manhattan "an Imperialist weapon" **[ALAN]**.

> **NOTE:** *France's withdrawal occurred on June 21, 1966, in the real world, while the first heart transplant took place on January 23, 1964, when a chimpanzee heart was given to Boyd Rush, who died after ninety minutes; Christiaan Barnard performed the first successful heart transplant on Louis Washkansky on December 3, 1967. The newspaper reporting these events is dated April 1966, indicating that the histories of France, NATO, and heart transplants all unfold differently in* Watchmen *continuity.*

Frustrated that crime and immorality have thrived in the United States since The Minutemen's disbanding, Nelson Gardner decides to form a second masked adventurer team called The Crimebusters, to battle drugs, riots, promiscuity, black unrest, anti-war demonstrations, and other issues that concern him **[ALAN]**. To that end, he invites all active costumed heroes to attend a meeting at his home **[RPG1]**. He reaches Ozymandias by leaving a note for him with a local police department **[BWOZ]**.

> **NOTE:** *Nelson Gardner includes anti-war demonstrations, promiscuity, and black unrest on a list of "problems" he feels masked adventurers should be battling, reinforcing his*

racist, neo-fascist beliefs. The Watchmen *film adds other concerns to the list, including draft dodgers and illegal immigration.*

CONFLICT: *Oddly, the movie depicts Adrian Veidt, not Nelson Gardner, as the one who feels crime-fighters should be addressing these problems, despite such narrow-minded values being entirely contrary to Veidt's character.*

—April 5, 1966

Laurie Juspeczyk holds a press conference to reveal her true identity as the daughter of the original Silk Spectre, Sally Jupiter **[RPG3]**.

> **CONFLICT:** *A timeline in the* Watchmen *film's British press kit sets the second Silk Spectre's debut in 1970, while* Before Watchmen: Ozymandias *depicts Laurie going public in early 1965, contradicting both Alan Moore's miniseries and* Before Watchmen: Silk Spectre, *which place her debut in 1966.*

—April 6, 1966

The *New York Gazette* covers Laurie's announcement, claiming that while Sally Jupiter supports her daughter's choice to become a crime-fighter, Larry Schexnayder (believed to be Laurie's father) could not be reached for comment **[RPG3]**.

—Before April 14, 1966

Rorschach and Dan Dreiberg deliver a large file of evidence to detectives in the NYPD's Area Two Violent Crimes Unit, regarding the racketeering and conspiracy activities of Anthony Rizzoli **[RPG3]**, also known as Underboss **[RPG3, NIGH]**. The files link the mobster to illegal payments made to top city judges, lawmakers, employees, and law-enforcement officials **[RPG3]**.

—April 14, 1966—Morning

Detectives in the NYPD's Area Two Violent Crimes Unit apprehend Underboss on charges of conspiracy and racketeering **[RPG3]**.

> **CONFLICT:** *A police file on Rorschach in the* Watchmen *film's British press kit dates the mobster's takedown in 1967, which does not jibe with other sources.*

—April 14, 1966—Night

Laurie Juspeczyk, age sixteen, attends Nelson Gardner's Crimebusters meeting **[ALAN]**— one of her first public appearances in costume as the second Silk Spectre **[RPG2]**—which he hosts at his townhouse on New York City's East Side **[BWOZ]**. Sally Jupiter brings Laurie to the gathering in a limousine and waits for her outside until it ends. Though excited that her daughter is finally following in her footsteps **[ALAN]**, Sally is annoyed at Laurie's

MIND .... *The Mindscape of Alan Moore*	**RPG2** .... *DC Heroes Role Playing Module #235: Taking Out the Trash—Curses and Tears*	**VRL2** ..... Viral video: *The Keene Act and You*
MOBL .... *Watchmen: The Mobile Game*		**VRL3** ..... Viral video: *Who Watches the Watchmen? A Veidt Music Network (VMN) Special*
MOTN .... *Watchmen: The Complete Motion Comic*	**RPG3** .... *DC Heroes: The Watchmen Sourcebook*	
MTRO .... *Metro* promotional newspaper cover wrap	**RUBY** .... "Wounds," published in *The Ruby Files Volume One*	**VRL4** ..... Viral video: *World in Focus: 6 Minutes to Midnight*
NEWP .... *New Frontiersman* promotional newspaper	**SCR1** ..... Unfilmed screenplay draft: Sam Hamm	**VRL5** ..... Viral video: *Local Radio Station Report on 1977 Riots*
NEWW .... *New Frontiersman* website	**SCR2** .... Unfilmed screenplay draft: Charles McKeuen	
NIGH ..... *Watchmen: The End Is Nigh, Parts 1 and 2*	**SCR3** .... Unfilmed screenplay draft: Gary Goldman	**VRL6** ..... Viral videos (group of ten): *Veidt Enterprises Advertising Contest*
PKIT ...... *Watchmen* film British press kit	**SCR4** .... Unfilmed screenplay draft: David Hayter (2002)	
PORT ..... *Watchmen Portraits*	**SCR5** .... Unfilmed screenplay draft: David Hayter (2003)	**WAWA** ... *Watching the Watchmen*
REAL ..... Real life	**SCR6** .... Unfilmed screenplay draft: Alex Tse	**WHOS** ... *Who's Who: The Definitive Directory of the DC Universe*
RPG1 .... *DC Heroes Role Playing Module #227: Who Watches the Watchmen?*	**SPOT** ..... *DC Spotlight #1*	
	VRL1 ..... Viral video: *NBS Nightly News with Ted Philips*	**WTFC** .... *Watchmen: The Film Companion*

refusal to wear her Minutemen-era costume **[BWSS]**.

> **NOTE:** *Alan Moore's miniseries sets this meeting in April 1966. The specific date appears in* Taking Out the Trash.

> **CONFLICT:** *The* Watchmen *film moves the gathering to September 4, 1970, and a timeline published in* The Film Companion *also sets it in that year. In the movie, Veidt leads the meeting, not Gardner, who is absent. A timeline in the film's British press kit sees Veidt in charge, with Gardner merely an attendee, while Dan Dreiberg runs the show in David Hayter's unproduced 2003 screenplay, with no mention of Gardner at all.*
>
> *In the film, The Crimebusters are called The Watchmen.* Who's Who: The Definitive Directory of the DC Universe, Update '87 Vol. 4 *also identifies the group as The Watchmen, as do numerous prop newspaper articles created for the movie.* The Film Companion's *chronology calls them The New Watchmen, as do the card backs of several HeroClix* Watchmen *figures.*

Eddie Blake, Dan Dreiberg, Walter Kovacs, Jon Osterman, and Adrian Veidt also attend the Crimebusters meeting **[ALAN]**. Dan is intrigued by the concept, but Rorschach suspects a trap. Dan is flustered by Laurie's great beauty **[BWNO]**, but she sees him as a square—the kind of guy whom she could never date **[BWSS]**. Jon Osterman arrives accompanied by Janey Slater, who is visibly older than the non-aging Dr. Manhattan. The superhuman perceives the others as merely "people wearing disguises" **[ALAN]**. Dan snaps a photograph of the group for posterity **[FILM]**. During the meeting, Eddie Blake reads a news article announcing the launch of *Gemini 8* **[BWSS]**.

> **NOTE:** *In the real world, NASA launched* Gemini 8 *on March 16. This may indicate that the spacecraft's launch date is different in the* Watchmen *universe, or that The Comedian is simply reading a month-old newspaper.*

Nelson Gardner pairs off members so the team can learn about each other's ideas and goals, by placing names in a hat and pulling out two at a time. When he selects Dr. Manhattan's and Rorschach's IDs, Jon Osterman alters the latter's paper slip to display Laurie Juspeczyk's name instead so that he can spend time with her **[BWNO]**.

April 14, 1966—Night (Alternate Realities)

In that moment, Jon Osterman experiences other quantum realities in which he alternately becomes the partner of either Rorschach or Laurie Juspeczyk. In becoming his own quantum observer, he inadvertently splinters his quantum existence into infinite permutations based on every decision he makes **[BWDM]**.

—April 14, 1966—Night (continued)

The meeting goes awry when Eddie Blake calls the idea "bullshit," accuses Gardner of wanting to play "cowboys and Indians," mocks Adrian Veidt's reputed intelligence, and claims that none of them are equipped to understand what matters most: the inevitable threat of nuclear annihilation. Blake then leaves after setting fire to Gardner's display. Rorschach admires The Comedian's refusal to care whether or not people like him, and his ability to understand the true nature of the world, people, and society. The meeting opens Veidt's eyes to mankind's mortality and the possibility that Earth might actually die if things don't change. He vows to save humanity from itself **[ALAN]**.

Jon Osterman experiences his future romantic involvement with Laurie Juspeczyk. She admires his physique, but is put off by his blue skin. Janey Slater notices their mutual interest and demands that Jon leave with her, accusing him of "chasing jailbait." The others leave as well, to Gardner's dismay, with only Veidt remaining. Dan regrets the group's failure to form a fellowship of legendary beings like The Minutemen, or like King Arthur's Knights of the Round Table **[ALAN]**.

Outside, Blake calls Laurie over and lights a cigarette for her. Laurie finds him "cool," but Sally tells Blake to leave her daughter alone. Unaware that The Comedian tried to rape her mother—and that he's her father—Laurie is confused by Sally's fury and feels sorry for the man. Mother and daughter leave, then Sally pulls over, three blocks into the drive, and opens up to Laurie about the pain and fear she has silently suffered **[ALAN]**.

> **NOTE:** *This begs the question of why Sally would urge Laurie to join a crime-fighting team with Eddie Blake in the first place.*

Later that day, Dan Dreiberg rescues victims of a gas explosion, jetting them away from the flames aboard *Archimedes* **[RPG3]**.

—Between April 14, 1966 and June 6, 1966

Nelson Gardner broods about the failure of his Crimebusters concept, knowing that with evil on the rise, special forces will be required to combat subversion in the United States. Therefore, he sets out to find a way to manipulate the masked heroes into uniting against a common foe so that they will see value in working together as a team **[RPG1]**.

> **NOTE:** *This presages Adrian Veidt's plot to save mankind from nuclear war, possibly inspiring Veidt to use the same tactic on a larger scale.*

—After April 14, 1966

Despite the Crimebusters concept being a bust, its would-be members remain in contact and sometimes work together **[ALAN]**. The team is dubbed "The Watchmen" in the press,

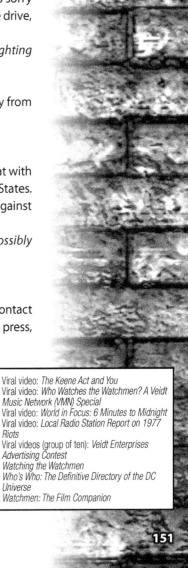

an allusion to a nickname formerly given to The Minutemen **[ARTF]**. Rorschach views his fellow masked adventurers, particularly Dan Dreiberg, as his friends **[ALAN]**.

Anthony "Underboss" Rizzoli faces trial for conspiracy and racketeering **[RPG3, NIGH]**.

—April 15, 1966

The *New York Gazette* covers Underboss's capture, noting that this time, unlike his 1965 arrest, the charges might stick. Detective Robert A. Mercer tells the reporter that the evidence is more than the NYPD has had in earlier attempts to put him away. The article quotes Nite Owl as saying that if he and Rorschach keep achieving such victories, he might continue to fight crime forever **[RPG3]**.

—Between April 1966 and June 6, 1966

Nelson Gardner begins investigating a flamboyant drug trafficker named Mole Varrows, but fails to find sufficient evidence to have him convicted. Meanwhile, the American Negro Alliance (ANA), a powerful civil-rights group, is formed. Viewing black unrest as a societal evil, the bigoted Gardner decides to bring the group down as well **[RPG1]**.

Matilda Gardner, Nelson Gardner's mother, moves into a nursing home in Long Island, New York. The facility's administrator is Carol Sinkfield **[RPG1]**.

> **NOTE:** *Since Gardner's father Albert (so named in* The Watchmen Sourcebook*) is not mentioned in* Who Watches the Watchmen?*, he may be deceased by this point.*

The Peace Front, a radical, law-breaking protest group bent on overthrowing the U.S. government, forms. Enthusiastic but inexperienced, they achieve little success. Their members comprise four white, middle-class hippie youths: Mary Ann Cooper, Dwight Finglass, Thomas Pawereski, and leader Alexander "Stickman" Gross **[RPG1]**.

Wally Weaver is assigned to the Fort Lee military base **[RPG1]**.

—In or After April 1966

Anthony "Underboss" Rizzoli is sentenced to prison **[ALAN]**.

—April 1966 to At Least 1968

Despite his imprisonment, Underboss continues to run his criminal empire **[RPG3]**.

—Mid to Late 1966

The Crimebusters meeting has a lasting effect on Adrian Veidt. With East-West distrust and hostilities escalating, he deems disarmament unlikely, even though both sides recognize the danger of mutual annihilation, since nuclear power is mandatory in an era

---

of diminishing natural resources and environmental ruin **[ALAN]**. He foresees that a third World War is certain to occur no later than 1990 **[ABSO]**.

Veidt examines the impact of Dr. Manhattan on the world and realizes that with Jon symbolizing the atomic age, and thus mankind's problems, masked adventurers will fall out of favor within a decade, bottoming out by the late 1970s. This leaves him ten years to build up sufficient fortune, power, and leverage to carry out a global plan to save humanity and still sustain himself beyond that point. To that end, he hires a public-relations firm and expands his personal empire **[ALAN]**.

—Between Mid-1966 and January 1976
Veidt Enterprises establishes the Veidt Building at 620 3rd Avenue, as well as a new headquarters at 1616 Avenue of the Americas **[NEWW]**. A branch of the company, Veidt Communications, produces television shows, including children's cartoons **[VRL1]**, while another branch, Veidt Energy, focuses on innovations in the energy field **[VRL4]**. Other major holdings include Veidt Cosmetics and Veidt Toys **[RPG3]**.

—Between Mid-1966 and 1985
Veidt launches several companies openly, purchasing others covertly by buying up shares using manufactured identities. Viewed as "a dream of free enterprise embodied in one perfect mind and body," he becomes a much-loved public figure, with the left wing respecting his moral, political, and pacifistic spiritual stances on issues. He occasionally speaks out against nuclear proliferation and the threat of war, his magnetic personality inspiring others to listen, and withdraws from his former life, having little to do with his crime-fighting colleagues **[ABSO]**.

—May 1966
A month after the failed Crimebusters meeting, Jon Osterman and Laurie Juspeczyk patrol the city together **[ALAN]**. They become romantically involved while surveying the rooftops of New York **[CLIX]**, and he leaves Janey Slater for her. When Jon informs Janey of his decision, she erupts in anger, calls him a pig for dating a teenager, and throws away the earrings he'd given her. She packs her bags to move out, but has trouble closing her suitcase **[ALAN]**.

> **CONFLICT:** Taking Out the Trash *establishes the relationship as ending on August 26, 1966, with Janey initiating the breakup, but this contradicts Alan Moore's miniseries. The* Watchmen *film claims that Jon and Janey date for eleven years, but in the comic, their relationship lasts from 1959 to 1966.*

MIND .... *The Mindscape of Alan Moore*
MOBL .... *Watchmen: The Mobile Game*
MOTN .... *Watchmen: The Complete Motion Comic*
MTRO .... *Metro promotional newspaper cover wrap*
NEWP .... *New Frontiersman promotional newspaper*
NEWW .... *New Frontiersman website*
NIGH ..... *Watchmen: The End Is Nigh, Parts 1 and 2*
PKIT ...... *Watchmen film British press kit*
PORT ..... *Watchmen Portraits*
REAL ..... Real life
RPG1 .... *DC Heroes Role Playing Module #227: Who Watches the Watchmen?*

RPG2 .... *DC Heroes Role Playing Module #235: Taking Out the Trash—Curses and Tears*
RPG3 .... *DC Heroes: The Watchmen Sourcebook*
RUBY .... "Wounds," published in *The Ruby Files Volume One*
SCR1 ..... Unfilmed screenplay draft: Sam Hamm
SCR2 ..... Unfilmed screenplay draft: Charles McKeuen
SCR3 ..... Unfilmed screenplay draft: Gary Goldman
SCR4 ..... Unfilmed screenplay draft: David Hayter (2002)
SCR5 ..... Unfilmed screenplay draft: David Hayter (2003)
SCR6 ..... Unfilmed screenplay draft: Alex Tse
SPOT ..... *DC Spotlight #1*
VRL1 ..... Viral video: *NBS Nightly News with Ted Philips*

VRL2 ..... Viral video: *The Keene Act and You*
VRL3 ..... Viral video: *Who Watches the Watchmen? A Veidt Music Network (VMN) Special*
VRL4 ..... Viral video: *World in Focus: 6 Minutes to Midnight*
VRL5 ..... Viral video: *Local Radio Station Report on 1977 Riots*
VRL6 ..... Viral videos (group of ten): *Veidt Enterprises Advertising Contest*
WAWA ... *Watching the Watchmen*
WHOS ... *Who's Who: The Definitive Directory of the DC Universe*
WTFC .... *Watchmen: The Film Companion*

—May 31, 1966 (Estimated)
Twelve-year-old Jeffrey Iddings is kidnapped by an extortion gang. His cruel abductors hold him hostage for almost two weeks **[RPG1]**.

—In or Before June 1966
Edgar Jacobi establishes a new hideout at 1023 Madison Avenue, a thirty-story glass and steel fortress with a penthouse lair, fallout shelter plates on its side, and a roof containing a sculpted garden, statues, fountains, and terraced paths. Nelson Gardner learns about this location while investigating the mobster, and discovers that the kingpin has given anonymous donations to radical protest groups so their increased activities will divert police attention away from his crimes. The donations are small and the effect on protests negligible, but Gardner sees this as an epic conspiracy among the forces of evil—and a catalyst to make the masked heroes join The Crimebusters **[RPG1]**.

Adrian Veidt befriends Ben Charles, the 34th Street precinct's chief of police. The two cooperate on a number of cases, though Veidt never tells Charles his identity **[RPG1]**.

Actor Cindy Radway becomes addicted to cocaine, using drug trafficker Mole Varrows as her supplier. She cleans up her act, stops using drugs, and tells him to get lost, which makes Mole angry. The Comedian meets Cindy at a state function; the two begin dating, though he never tells her his true name **[RPG1]**.

A police officer, Sergeant O'Malley, is assigned to the Town Hall police precinct. A switchboard operator, Kirk, is also assigned to the station **[RPG1]**.

Newton Ramsey, a U.S. Army private first-class and a chronic gambler, becomes heavily in debt to underworld figures, regularly losing his entire paycheck in shady poker games on the Lower East Side **[RPG1]**.

Sally Jupiter arranges for a photograph session on June 8 **[RPG1]**.

—June 4, 1966
Rorschach rescues Jeffrey Iddings from the extortion gang and returns the youth to his parents **[RPG1]**.

—June 5, 1966—Morning
Nelson Gardner identifies a person close to each masked adventurer he wants in The Crimebusters, then arranges for underworld figures to kidnap them, intending to frame subversive groups and Moloch the Mystic for the abductions. Gardner contacts members of the criminal world while wearing a red demon mask, distorts his voice via an electronic

scrambler, and calls himself "M" to make them think he is Moloch **[RPG1]**.

> **NOTE:** *Gardner's kidnappings and planning of same are undated. However, Rorschach rescues Jeffrey Iddings from his first kidnapping on June 4 and Gardner's abductions take place on June 6, so the planning of the latter (which must occur after Rorschach rescues Jeffrey the first time, or else Nelson would have no reason to link the boy to the vigilante) can only happen on June 5.*

To inspire the formation of The Crimebusters and simultaneously bring down Mole Varrows, Gardner hires the drug dealer to mastermind the kidnappings. In a series of phone calls, which Mole records, "M" instructs him to contract black kidnappers, posing as American Negro Alliance members, to capture Hollis Mason, Sally Jupiter, and his own mother, Matilda Gardner; and the Peace Front, a radical youth group, to abduct Wally Weaver, Ben Charles, Jeffrey Iddings, and Cindy Radway. He hires Milton Sabino, a small-time bagman, hood, and loan-shark, to help the kidnappers nab Wally Weaver from the Fort Lee military base. Throughout the plot, Sabino believes he is working for Moloch, not Captain Metropolis **[RPG1]**.

Nelson Gardner learns of Newton Ramsey's gambling debt through military connections. On Gardner's orders, Milton Sabino buys up Ramsey's debts, then extorts the soldier into acting as an inside man during Wally Weaver's abduction. Sabino threatens to break his kneecaps if he refuses, but promises to pay him if he does as he's told **[RPG1]**.

Mole Varrows contracts Lenard Harris, Billy Watts, and George Douglas Turner to carry out the American Negro Alliance kidnappings. He instructs them to join the Alliance, frequent its headquarters, wear the group's acronym on their black leather jackets, drop incriminating ANA pins at each abduction site, and avoid harming the victims. Mole then hires the Peace Front to abduct Charles, Weaver, and Iddings, agreeing to help the group destabilize the U.S. government in return. Varrows handles Cindy Radway's abduction himself, as revenge for her terminating their business dealings **[RPG1]**.

Nelson Gardner plants an incriminating letter in the American Negro Alliance's storefront headquarters files. The letter, signed by Mole Varrows, offers to pay the ANA three thousand dollars to kidnap Hollis Mason, Sally Jupiter, and Matilda Gardner. He also arranges for a stranger to be paid two thousand dollars to park a moving van in front of an abandoned Lower East Side drugstore and leave the scene on foot **[RPG1]**.

—June 5, 1966—Daytime

Dan Dreiberg finishes constructing an anti-cold suit that he dubs the Snow Owl, with a protective sheath allowing for unlimited operation in temperatures as low as -50 degrees Centigrade (-58 degrees Fahrenheit). The suit costs $10,000 to build, is colored white for quick retrieval, and can be worn over his standard uniform **[RPG3]**.

MIND .... *The Mindscape of Alan Moore*	**RPG2** .... *DC Heroes Role Playing Module #235: Taking Out the Trash—Curses and Tears*	**VRL2** ..... Viral video: *The Keene Act and You*
MOBL.... *Watchmen: The Mobile Game*		**VRL3** ..... Viral video: *Who Watches the Watchmen? A Veidt Music Network (VMN) Special*
MOTN.... *Watchmen: The Complete Motion Comic*	**RPG3** .... *DC Heroes: The Watchmen Sourcebook*	
MTRO.... *Metro promotional newspaper cover wrap*	**RUBY** .... "Wounds," published in *The Ruby Files Volume One*	**VRL4** ..... Viral video: *World in Focus: 6 Minutes to Midnight*
NEWP... *New Frontiersman promotional newspaper*	**SCR1**..... Unfilmed screenplay draft: Sam Hamm	**VRL5** ..... Viral video: *Local Radio Station Report on 1977 Riots*
NEWW... *New Frontiersman website*	**SCR2**.... Unfilmed screenplay draft: Charles McKeuen	
NIGH ..... *Watchmen: The End Is Nigh, Parts 1 and 2*	**SCR3**.... Unfilmed screenplay draft: Gary Goldman	**VRL6** ..... Viral videos (group of ten): *Veidt Enterprises Advertising Contest*
PKIT...... *Watchmen film British press kit*	**SCR4**.... Unfilmed screenplay draft: David Hayter (2002)	
PORT..... *Watchmen Portraits*	**SCR5**.... Unfilmed screenplay draft: David Hayter (2003)	**WAWA**... *Watching the Watchmen*
REAL..... Real life	**SCR6**.... Unfilmed screenplay draft: Alex Tse	**WHOS** ... *Who's Who: The Definitive Directory of the DC Universe*
RPG1 .... *DC Heroes Role Playing Module #227: Who Watches the Watchmen?*	**SPOT**..... *DC Spotlight #1*	
	VRL1 ..... Viral video: *NBS Nightly News with Ted Philips*	**WTFC** .... *Watchmen: The Film Companion*

—June 6, 1966—Morning

Several abductions occur on the same day, per Nelson Gardner's instructions. First, Harris, Watts, and Turner kidnap Hollis Mason from his West Side home. The capture requires considerable force, and Mason's dog Phantom bites one assailant **[RPG1]**.

> **CONFLICT:** *The dating of the abductions is inconsistent. All victims are said to vanish on the same morning, which would seem to be June 6, a Monday, since an anonymous caller (either Gardner or Varrows) alerts police to Mason's kidnapping on that date. But a police call sheet indicates that the disappearances are reported throughout a four-day period, while another page claims they all vanish on a Friday. June 6 seems the most logical date, despite these inconsistencies.*

Wally Weaver is forcibly abducted from the Fort Lee military base. Newton Ramsey, on guard duty at the base's Lab Compound, is assaulted during the kidnapping (per a pre-arranged plan) when a truck drives up near the end of his shift and its occupants attack him with a pipe. Knocked unconscious, he awakens in the infirmary **[RPG1]**.

Ben Charles vanishes while walking to the 34th Street precinct. Hearing a woman whimpering in an alley, the police chief stops to help her, but she puts a chloroformed handkerchief over his face and places him in a dented blue Oldsmobile, which drives off. When Charles fails to report for duty, midtown officers investigate but identify no witnesses or suspects, unaware that street rat Howie Jacobson saw it happen **[RPG1]**.

Two days after being rescued from previous kidnappers, Jeffrey Iddings is abducted for a second time. His parents witness him being taken by two men and a woman in a blue car, all of whom wear white masks adorned with a green peace sign **[RPG1]**.

Disguised as orderlies, Lenard Harris, Billy Watts, and George Douglas Turner abduct Matilda Gardner from her Long Island nursing home. One of them strikes the duty nurse in Section 3 before they flee **[RPG1]**.

—June 6, 1966—6:44 AM

In the Town Hall police precinct at 3600 N. Halstead, switchboard operator Kirk receives an anonymous call reporting Hollis Mason's abduction. Kirk logs the call for his watch commander, Sergeant O'Malley, noting little evidence and no suspects **[RPG1]**.

> **NOTE:** *The Town Hall police station is in Chicago, Illinois, located at 3600 N. Halsted St. (the book misspells the street name). The historic decommissioned station was replaced with a residential building, Town Hall Apartments, in August 2014. Why an Illinois police station would receive a phone call about New York City resident Hollis Mason is unknown.*
>
> *Kirk's badge number, SC 937-0176 CEC, is an in-joke referencing the Starfleet serial number of Star Trek's Captain James T. Kirk.*

—June 6, 1966—10:14 AM

Lenard Harris, Billy Watts, and George Douglas Turner abduct Sally Jupiter from her home, leaving signs of a forced entry and scuffle. Her grandfather clock is smashed during the skirmish, stopping at 10:14 **[RPG1]**.

—June 6, 1966—After 10:14 AM

Harris, Watts, and Turner deliver Hollis Mason, Sally Jupiter, and Matilda Gardner to Mole Varrows' apartment at 575 5th Avenue **[RPG1]**.

—June 6, 1966—10:37 PM

Lieutenant Colonel Howard Morgenstern, Fort Lee's commander, reports Wally Weaver's abduction and the assault and battery of Private First Class Newton Ramsey. Switchboard operator Kirk logs this on his call sheet, noting a lack of suspects. Morgenstern authorizes a two-day pass for Ramsey **[RPG1]**.

> **NOTE:** *Fort Lee is a U.S. Army base in Prince George County, Virginia. It is unknown why the Town Hall precinct, located in Chicago, would receive calls about crimes committed in Virginia.*

—June 7, 1966—9:32 AM

The midtown precinct requests an all-points bulletin on the disappearance of Chief of Police Ben Charles. Switchboard operator Kirk logs this on his call sheet **[RPG1]**.

—June 8, 1966—12:14 PM

After Sally Jupiter fails to show up at a scheduled photograph session, patrolling officers investigate and report a probable abduction. Switchboard operator Kirk logs this on his call sheet, noting that an investigation is pending **[RPG1]**.

—June 8, 1966—3:05 PM

Jeffrey Iddings' parents report their son's abduction and provide police with descriptions of the kidnappers. Switchboard operator Kirk logs this on his call sheet **[RPG1]**.

> **NOTE:** *Nelson Gardner's victims are all abducted on June 6. If Jeffrey's parents witness his kidnapping, it seems unthinkable that they would wait two days to report it—especially since he'd been rescued from* other *kidnappers only two days prior.*

—June 8, 1966—11:00 PM

Ralph Eastman, a doorman at the apartment building in which Cindy Radway lives, sees the actor enter her apartment right before his shift begins **[RPG1]**.

> **NOTE:** *Since Mole Varrows abducted Radway himself, instead of following Nelson Gardner's plan to have the Peace Front do it, this would account for her being taken on a different day than the other victims, and is thus not an inconsistency.*

MIND .... *The Mindscape of Alan Moore*
MOBL .... *Watchmen: The Mobile Game*
MOTN .... *Watchmen: The Complete Motion Comic*
MTRO .... *Metro promotional newspaper cover wrap*
NEWP .... *New Frontiersman promotional newspaper*
NEWW .... *New Frontiersman website*
NIGH ..... *Watchmen: The End Is Nigh, Parts 1 and 2*
PKIT ...... *Watchmen film British press kit*
PORT ..... *Watchmen Portraits*
REAL ..... Real life
RPG1 .... *DC Heroes Role Playing Module #227: Who Watches the Watchmen?*

RPG2 .... *DC Heroes Role Playing Module #235: Taking Out the Trash—Curses and Tears*
RPG3 .... *DC Heroes: The Watchmen Sourcebook*
RUBY .... "Wounds," published in *The Ruby Files Volume One*
SCR1 ..... Unfilmed screenplay draft: Sam Hamm
SCR2 ..... Unfilmed screenplay draft: Charles McKeuen
SCR3 ..... Unfilmed screenplay draft: Gary Goldman
SCR4 ..... Unfilmed screenplay draft: David Hayter (2002)
SCR5 ..... Unfilmed screenplay draft: David Hayter (2003)
SCR6 ..... Unfilmed screenplay draft: Alex Tse
SPOT ..... *DC Spotlight #1*
VRL1 ..... Viral video: *NBS Nightly News with Ted Philips*

VRL2 ..... Viral video: *The Keene Act and You*
VRL3 ..... Viral video: *Who Watches the Watchmen? A Veidt Music Network (VMN) Special*
VRL4 ..... Viral video: *World in Focus: 6 Minutes to Midnight*
VRL5 ..... Viral video: *Local Radio Station Report on 1977 Riots*
VRL6 ..... Viral videos (group of ten): *Veidt Enterprises Advertising Contest*
WAWA ... *Watching the Watchmen*
WHOS ... *Who's Who: The Definitive Directory of the DC Universe*
WTFC ... *Watchmen: The Film Companion*

—June 9, 1966—Before 10:47 AM

Mole Varrows, posing as actor Cindy Radway's producer, pays Ralph Eastman two thousand dollars to let him into her home. Ralph accepts the money, then Mole drugs Cindy and drags her outside, driving off with her in a Corvette decorated with a painted firebird image **[RPG1]**.

—June 9, 1966—10:47 AM

Ralph Eastman phones the police to report Cindy Radway's abduction, saying only that she is missing. Switchboard operator Kirk logs this on his call sheet **[RPG1]**.

—June 9, 1966—After 10:474 AM

After all seven kidnappings have taken place, Nelson Gardner shoots Mole Varrows, leaving evidence in the man's apartment pinning the murder on Edgar Jacobi: a letter telling Mole to deliver the hostages to someone called Stickman, and to have him deliver a speech against costumed heroes at a rally in Battery Park. Gardner moves the hostages to 666 Waterside Drive, a closed-down live-bait storefront in a seedy section of Manhattan **[RPG1]**.

—June 9, 1966—4:46 PM

Carol Sinkfield, the administrator of a Long Island nursing home, reports the abduction of Matilda Gardner from that facility. Switchboard operator Kirk logs this on his call sheet, describing the details of the kidnapping as "sketchy" **[RPG1]**.

> **NOTE:** *It seems odd that Chicago's Town Hall police precinct would receive a call about an abduction in New York—but it's odder still that it would take three days for the nursing home to report a resident's disappearance.*

—Before June 10, 1966

Edgar Jacobi arranges to have drug shipments brought into town on the following Sunday, knowing law enforcement will be busy with an anti-war protest that day. To ensure that the police will not notice his activities, he pays several militant youth organizations, including the Peace Front, to turn the peaceful event into a riot **[RPG1]**.

—June 10, 1966—Before 2:00 PM

Police fail to determine motives or find ransom notes for the seven abductions. Nelson Gardner sets in motion the next phase of his plan: contacting his stalled Crimebusters team to seek their help in finding the victims. Despite Wally Weaver being among the missing, Dr. Manhattan declines to help due to his busy work schedule. The others converge at Gardner's home and agree to combine their efforts **[RPG1]**.

The masked adventurers help Gardner investigate the abductions, starting with Hollis Mason's ransacked apartment. They determine that at least two assailants were involved, one of whom received a severe dog bite and wore a leather jacket. The heroes next visit the Fort Lee military base, where Howard Morgenstern brings them to speak with Newton Ramsey, who claims that two men in a truck attacked him with a pipe before taking Wally Weaver **[RPG1]**.

Looking into the disappearance of Ben Charles, the crime-fighters visit the L.A. Cafe Pool Hall and speak with Howie Jacobson. The street rat tells them that Charles was captured while helping an injured woman in an alleyway on his way to work. While investigating Sally Jupiter's home, they notice a pin bearing the acronym "ANA," indicating the American Negro Alliance. They then speak with Jeffrey Iddings' parents, who reveal that the attackers were two men and a woman in a blue car, wearing white hoods emblazoned with a green peace sign **[RPG1]**.

At Cindy Radway's apartment, the heroes intimidate doorman Ralph Eastman into revealing Mole Varrows' role in abducting her. This comes as a surprise to Nelson Gardner, who had not known of Mole's personal connection to Radway when hiring him, nor that Mole had done the indeed himself instead of contracting the Peace Front. The next search, at Matilda Gardner's nursing home, turns up little evidence **[RPG1]**.

Following their investigations, Gardner and his team meet aboard *Archimedes* to compare notes. A police contact receives a parchment letter written in red ink, warning that if any heroes are in New York on Sunday, the hostages will die in agony **[RPG1]**.

The crime-fighters spy on the storefront headquarters of the American Negro Alliance as Harris, Watts, and Turner arrive. The heroes enter and ask questions, with Gardner acting abusive and bigoted. The ANA's workers deny any wrongdoing, noting that the three men are recent members but do not fit the Alliance's dedication to peaceful change. When the heroes request blood samples, the thugs become violent but are subdued, and blood testing ties them to the scuffle at Mason's home. Gardner "finds" the planted letter from Mole Varrows in the ANA's files, framing the group for the abductions. The workers deny knowledge of this, but are arrested **[RPG1]**.

—June 10, 1966—2:00 PM
Newton Ramsey leaves the Fort Lee base and enters a taxi. Gardner's team discreetly follows the vehicle **[RPG1]**.

MIND .... *The Mindscape of Alan Moore*
MOBL.... *Watchmen: The Mobile Game*
MOTN... *Watchmen: The Complete Motion Comic*
MTRO.... *Metro* promotional newspaper cover wrap
NEWP.... *New Frontiersman* promotional newspaper
NEWW... *New Frontiersman* website
NIGH .... *Watchmen: The End Is Nigh, Parts 1 and 2*
PKIT...... *Watchmen* film British press kit
PORT..... *Watchmen Portraits*
REAL..... Real life
RPG1 .... *DC Heroes Role Playing Module #227: Who Watches the Watchmen?*

RPG2 .... *DC Heroes Role Playing Module #235: Taking Out the Trash—Curses and Tears*
RPG3 .... *DC Heroes: The Watchmen Sourcebook*
RUBY .... "Wounds," published in *The Ruby Files Volume One*
SCR1..... Unfilmed screenplay draft: Sam Hamm
SCR2..... Unfilmed screenplay draft: Charles McKeuen
SCR3..... Unfilmed screenplay draft: Gary Goldman
SCR4..... Unfilmed screenplay draft: David Hayter (2002)
SCR5..... Unfilmed screenplay draft: David Hayter (2003)
SCR6..... Unfilmed screenplay draft: Alex Tse
SPOT..... *DC Spotlight #1*
VRL1 ..... Viral video: *NBS Nightly News with Ted Philips*

VRL2..... Viral video: *The Keene Act and You*
VRL3..... Viral video: *Who Watches the Watchmen? A Veidt Music Network (VMN) Special*
VRL4 ..... Viral video: *World in Focus: 6 Minutes to Midnight*
VRL5 ..... Viral video: *Local Radio Station Report on 1977 Riots*
VRL6..... Viral videos (group of ten): *Veidt Enterprises Advertising Contest*
WAWA... *Watching the Watchmen*
WHOS ... *Who's Who: The Definitive Directory of the DC Universe*
WTFC .... *Watchmen: The Film Companion*

—June 10, 1966—After 2:00 PM

The cab brings Ramsey to an abandoned drugstore in the Lower East Side, where he climbs a fire escape into the building. A driver parks a moving van outside and leaves the scene. Inside the vehicle, the crime-fighters find a small, brass quartz clock, which lifts off and darts away, leaving a note that reads "Time flies when you're having fun." They question the driver but learn little, and a search turns up no clues **[RPG1]**.

Inside the building, Ramsey meets with Milton Sabino, who gives him a briefcase full of money, then tries to shoot him while he's counting it, intending to hide out at the Regis Hotel for three days before flying to Casablanca, Morocco. The crime-fighters thwart the murder, and Sabino admits he was hired by a man called "M," with a demonic mask and an electronically synthesized voice **[RPG1]**.

Gardner's team checks out Mole Varrows' blood-splattered Fifth Avenue apartment. They find the thug's bullet-ridden corpse in the kitchen, a recorded phone message of "M," and a photo of Alexander "Stickman" Gross. A letter from "M" indicates that Mole was supposed to deliver the hostages to Stickman and have him provide an anti-crime-fighter speech in Battery Park **[RPG1]**.

The crime-fighters travel aboard *Archimedes* to Battery Park, where a rally and concert are taking place to drum up support for a peaceful anti-war demonstration scheduled for the following Sunday. As a loud band plays, a rocket flare points to the park's large sundial, reminding the team that they are running out of time. They ask several hippies about Stickman and learn about his involvement with the Peace Front. The presenters express anti-war sentiments, infuriating Nelson Gardner, who sees this as communist. Finally, Stickman takes the stage and stirs up anger against "underwear heroes" **[RPG1]**.

Gardner's team interrogates Alexander Gross and learns that Moloch has hired the Peace Front to turn Sunday's peaceful protest into a violent rebellion so he can bring drugs into the city while police are dealing with the resultant riot. Moloch, he says, is holding the hostages at his new hideout at 1023 Madison Avenue. After his speech, Stickman heads home to his small apartment in Greenwich Village **[RPG1]**.

The crime-fighters visit Moloch's new lair and battle the mobster's goons while searching his penthouse, drug supplies room, pleasure palace, offices, private area, and suite. They interrogate Moloch's gang until the frightened thugs confess to abducting not only the heroes' friends and family, but also Amelia Earhart, Charles Lindbergh's baby, and other famous missing persons (none of which is true) **[RPG1]**.

Finally, the heroes locate Edgar Jacobi, barricaded behind steel blast doors, and question him about the kidnappings. He maintains his innocence, threating to call the police and his lawyers. During questioning, Gardner discreetly hides a parchment to incriminate Moloch, ordering his lieutenants to move the hostages to 666 Waterside Drive. The mobster denies any knowledge of this, calling it a frame-up. They arrest Moloch, but he is soon set free due to a lack of hard evidence **[RPG1]**.

The team rushes to 666 Waterside Drive, a closed-down bait shop, to find a young thug named Billy feeding pizza to the bound hostages. Upon seeing the crime-fighters, Billy holds a switchblade to Matilda Gardner until Nelson, speaking into his synthesizer as "M," orders the teen to drop the knife. The hostages are freed, and Gardner claims to have brought the device along after analyzing the message on Varrows' phone **[RPG1]**.

Nelson Gardner invites the masked adventurers to his home to celebrate, suggesting that they reform The Crimebusters, given how well they worked together to avert a "drugs-gangster-negro-radical-youth plot to disrupt the national fabric." The heroes suspect his involvement, but he denies it—until an analysis of the synthesized voices prove them to be identical. Gardner confesses, claiming it was necessary because mankind needs their protection, and that Vole's murder removed "human vermin" from the streets **[RPG1]**.

—June 12, 1966
An anti-war demonstration takes place **[RPG1]**.
> **NOTE:** *It is unclear whether Moloch's plan to bring in drugs during the protest, as well as the Peace Front's intended riot, still occur, given the crime-fighters' investigation.*

—Mid-June to Mid-July 1966
Several prostitutes in New York City are murdered, and many others end up missing. The NYPD show little interest in solving the crimes, however **[BWNO]**.

—In or Before July 1966
The Nite Owl and Rorschach establish a rooftop meeting place from which to coordinate their nightly crime-fighting efforts **[BWNO]**.

A rich, sexy, bored debutante becomes New York City vice queen The Twilight Lady because she views crime as a big game **[RPG3]**, and to take back the power she once lost from being sexually abused **[BWNO]**. Her initial schemes, focused on drawing attention to herself, tend not to hurt anyone, as she simply enjoys wearing dominatrix garb and committing crimes. However, she later upgrades to more traditional pursuits, including a small, upscale drug ring, becoming the first supervillain madam **[RPG3]**.

MIND .... *The Mindscape of Alan Moore*
MOBL .... *Watchmen: The Mobile Game*
MOTN .... *Watchmen: The Complete Motion Comic*
MTRO .... *Metro* promotional newspaper cover wrap
NEWP .... *New Frontiersman* promotional newspaper
NEWW .... *New Frontiersman* website
NIGH ..... *Watchmen: The End Is Nigh, Parts 1 and 2*
PKIT ...... *Watchmen* film British press kit
PORT ..... *Watchmen Portraits*
REAL ..... Real life
RPG1 .... *DC Heroes Role Playing Module #227: Who Watches the Watchmen?*

RPG2 .... *DC Heroes Role Playing Module #235: Taking Out the Trash—Curses and Tears*
RPG3 .... *DC Heroes: The Watchmen Sourcebook*
RUBY .... "Wounds," published in *The Ruby Files Volume One*
SCR1 ..... Unfilmed screenplay draft: Sam Hamm
SCR2 ..... Unfilmed screenplay draft: Charles McKeuen
SCR3 ..... Unfilmed screenplay draft: Gary Goldman
SCR4 ..... Unfilmed screenplay draft: David Hayter (2002)
SCR5 ..... Unfilmed screenplay draft: David Hayter (2003)
SCR6 ..... Unfilmed screenplay draft: Alex Tse
SPOT .... *DC Spotlight #1*
VRL1 ..... Viral video: *NBS Nightly News with Ted Philips*

VRL2 ..... Viral video: *The Keene Act and You*
VRL3 ..... Viral video: *Who Watches the Watchmen? A Veidt Music Network (VMN) Special*
VRL4 ..... Viral video: *World in Focus: 6 Minutes to Midnight*
VRL5 ..... Viral video: *Local Radio Station Report on 1977 Riots*
VRL6 ..... Viral videos (group of ten): *Veidt Enterprises Advertising Contest*
WAWA ... *Watching the Watchmen*
WHOS ... *Who's Who: The Definitive Directory of the DC Universe*
WTFC ... *Watchmen: The Film Companion*

NOTE: *The Twilight Lady's status as the first supervillain madam may indicate that others follow her lead.*

CONFLICT: The Watchmen Sourcebook *reveals The Twilight Lady's birth name to be Leslie Chadwicke, while* Before Watchmen: Nite Owl *provides the name Elizabeth Lane. One or both of these may be an alias.*

The Twilight Lady runs a stable of high-priced call girls and fetish operations, evading New York City's vice cops. Having been down "a hard road" in her past, she creates a safe environment for girls who make similar mistakes—even those working for other pimps or madams **[BWNO]**.

Reverend Taylor Dean begins hiring the services of a "full-service" prostitute twice weekly, under the pseudonym "Robert." After viewing news footage of Dean protesting a pornography shop, she tries to blackmail him into paying her a thousand dollars a week, so he strangles her to death and sets her apartment on fire. When her neighbors then evict other hookers living next door and establish a neighborhood watch to clean up the place, he realizes God has chosen him to deliver a message to mankind in a pillar of flesh and corruption, of fire and smoke—a bonfire of sin **[BWNO]**.

To that end, Dean begins killing those he perceives as sinners (young and old harlots, as well as young men), after using them all for his own sexual gratification. He then adds them to a macabre sculpture of corpses in the church's basement, forbidding others from entering that area to prevent them from undoing God's work. He realizes he's good at killing—and that he likes it—and believes God will send someone corrupted to take the blame for his crimes. In total, he kills twenty-seven victims **[BWNO]**.

NOTE: *It is unknown whether Taylor Dean is related to Geoffrey Dean (Ursula Zandt's killer, also called The Liquidator, according to* The Watchmen Sourcebook*).*

Walter Kovacs begins working at Reverend Dean's church by day, performing cleanup and other duties, and makes a habit of showing up early and staying late. As he works, Walter listens to news on the radio to numb himself to pain so that his hands will do what he needs them to do as Rorschach. Dean discovers that Walter is Rorschach and initially thinks the Devil has sent the vigilante to interfere with God's work, then decides that the Lord has sent him to complete that work **[BWNO]**.

Colombian pimp Carlos "Vincent" Onofrio starts up a prostitution ring on New York City's South Side. He recruits Polish, Czech, Russian, and South American immigrants as they arrive in the United States via boat or bus, then hooks the women on drugs and puts them to work as hookers on the docks, the lower track, and downtown streets. The girls initially

fetch six or seven hundred dollars per client, but once their ability to bring in such money fades, Onofrio sells them to unscrupulous buyers **[BWNO]**.

    NOTE: *The pimp is drawn to resemble similarly named actor Vincent D'Onofrio.*

Serial killer Taylor Dean buys several such women from Onofrio. One prostitute escapes and seeks help from The Twilight Lady, saying three women who came with her from the Ukraine have disappeared. The madam promises to look into it **[BWNO]**.

Hollis Mason vows to stop drinking before noon **[BWNO]**.

—July 14, 1966
Richard Benjamin Speck tortures and murders eight student nurses in their dormitory at South Chicago Community Hospital **[REAL]**.

—July 17, 1966
Richard Speck is arrested for his crimes while being treated at Cook County Hospital following a suicide attempt **[REAL]**.

—July 18, 1966—Night
Riots erupt in Hough, Ohio, an African-American community in Cleveland, after a sign is posted outside a bar called 79'ers, warning "No Water for Niggers" **[REAL]**.

Gemini 10, a manned NASA spaceflight, launches. The spacecraft docks with the Agena Target Vehicle (ATV) in low Earth orbit **[REAL]**.

Rorschach and The Nite Owl fight a pair of thugs in an alley. Dan Dreiberg chases one to a dilapidated building, in which The Twilight Lady is torturing a willing client. Naked aside from boots, gloves, and a mask, she subdues his quarry with a paddle. Dan is grateful but flustered, while Twilight Lady openly appreciates his costume. Rorschach catches the other hoodlum, then finds Dan in the S&M den. Reminded of his prostitute mother, Rorschach calls her a slut and a whore. When he tries to attack her, Dan has little choice but to hit his partner. Rorschach leaves in a huff, and Dan follows, carrying the unconscious thug. The dominatrix invites him to come see her again **[BWNO]**.

Rorschach returns to his filthy apartment, removes his mask, and eats cold baked beans from a can while watching television. A news anchor discusses Richard Speck's arrest, the Hough riots, and *Gemini 10*'s Agena Target Vehicle dock-up. A commercial for Playtex's Living Bra promises to lift and separate a woman's breasts "for a cleaner, more natural appearance." The image reminds Rorschach of his childhood, when he walked in on his

prostitute mother disrobing for a customer **[BWNO]**.

> **NOTE:** *Rorschach's appearance is remarkably similar to that of real-world mass murderer Speck.*

Dan Dreiberg visits Hollis Mason. Over beers, the two discuss The Twilight Lady, and Hollis warns Dan to avoid her. Being associated with the madam or any of her clients, Hollis explains, could taint the kid-friendly Nite Owl name **[BWNO]**.

—July 19, 1966—Night

The Nite Owl awaits Rorschach at their rooftop meeting place. When his partner fails to show, Dan heads out on his own. Rorschach, meanwhile, goes to church, where Taylor Dean delivers a sermon about how television, movies, and music are drowning out God's message. Dean holds up a sign warning "The End Is Nigh," urging his followers to "get louder" and spread the word to others **[BWNO]**.

Sally Rose, a prostitute, is murdered in her rented apartment at 327 Grant Street. Dan Dreiberg responds to the police call and notices that Rose's body is covered with bruises, which reminds him of his mother's abuse at the hands of his father. Rorschach arrives on the scene as well, likening the murder to the Kitty Genovese case, and informs Dan that other hookers have recently been killed as well. Out on the roof, the two friends clear the air and board *Archimedes*, their partnership renewed **[BWNO]**.

—Between July 19 and July 23, 1966

Determined to solve the prostitute murders, Dan pays a visit to The Twilight Lady, who offers to help him investigate **[BWNO]**.

—July 23, 1966—Early Morning

As the Hough riots continue, three white men kill Warren LaRiche, a black man, as he sits in his car on Euclid Avenue in Chicago. Meanwhile, the pretrial of mass-murderer Richard Speck begins **[REAL]**. Walter Kovacs listens to a news broadcast about both cases while performing his daytime church duties. Reverend Dean condemns the immorality and spiritual decay of society, commenting that if no one stops it, the world will end up a smoking cinder. Walter agrees **[BWNO]**.

—After July 23, 1966

The Twilight Lady brings Nite Owl to the mansion of Colombian prostitution ringleader Carlos Onofrio, under whose employ three Ukrainian women have gone missing. She kisses the vigilante and leaves, saying to let her know what he finds out. Dan roughs up Onofrio and three thugs, then strings up the gangster above a toilet, threatening to drown

him unless Onofrio tells him the missing hookers' whereabouts. Finally, the pimp provides the phone numbers of six men to whom he sold them **[BWNO]**.

Dan relays this information to The Twilight Lady at her home, and she disrobes to seduce him. The two make love—Dan's first time doing so. He panics when she recognizes his face, but she promises to keep his identity a secret. He tells her about the abuse his mother endured at his father's hands, and she comforts him **[BWNO]**.

> **NOTE:** *The Nite Owl's flirtatious relationship with The Twilight Lady mirrors that between DC Comics' Batman and Catwoman.*

Dan checks out the phone numbers. Most turn out to be dead ends, but one leads to a downtown pay phone. Using a molecular polymer extract, Dan separates the receiver's oil and fingerprint layers to identify any frequent users **[BWNO]**.

Hollis Mason, guilt-ridden over mistakes made in his past, types up a confession and gives it to Dan Dreiberg, trusting his judgment about whether he should face punishment for his crimes. Though horrified by his mentor's actions, Dan burns the pages without exposing him **[BWNO]**.

> **NOTE:** *Presumably, the typed confession pertains to Mason's murder of Hooded Justice, as depicted in* Before Watchmen: Minutemen.

Reverend Taylor Dean's church prepares to launch a television channel to carry God's word to millions of viewers. Dean makes arrangements with potential backers, asking Walter Kovacs to move some boxes from the basement to his office for him. Walter is shocked to find a pile of dead bodies in the basement. Realizing one victim is still alive, he dons his Rorschach costume and tries to help her. However, Dean enters the room, shoots him in the shoulder, shackles him to the top of the mass of corpses, and ignites his "bonfire of sin," intending for Walter to take the blame for his murders, while allowing Dean to build a bigger church from the ashes of this one **[BWNO]**.

Dan Dreiberg checks the phone booth fingerprints against employment databases and police records, which leads him to Reverend Dean. Dan and The Twilight Lady find the church in flames. Rorschach endures the fire to melt his handcuffs, while Dan and the madam rush in to find survivors. Dan frees his friend as The Twilight Lady confronts the reverend. Dean tries to shoot her, but Rorschach grabs Dean's "The End Is Nigh" sign and fatally impales the killer with it. Hearing police sirens, the three vacate the burning church, though Rorschach keeps the sign. A police investigation ties Dean to the corpses—about which the reverend's wife refuses to comment to the press **[BWNO]**.

Returning to the Owl Cave, Dan finds Hollis Mason drinking and depressed. He tells Hollis that he's the closest thing Dan has to a father, that he's a good man despite his past deeds, and that he doesn't want to ruin anyone's image of his mentor. Hollis says another copy of the confession lies in a safety-deposit box, for Dan to do with as he pleases once Hollis dies [BWNO].

Dan threatens to turn Rorschach in for Dean's murder. Rorschach accuses him of being soft around women, citing Dan's failure to stop his mother's abuse. Angry, Dan puts their partnership on hold for a few weeks, but opts not to call the police. He returns to The Twilight Lady's home to ask her on a date, but finds the place empty save for a framed photograph of her in costume, signed, "From one 'night bird' to another. Love from The Twilight Lady." He calls her, but she refuses to see him again, saying she can afford anything a woman might need—except to fall in love, which she has with him [BWNO]. Heartbroken, Dan keeps the picture for years to come [ALAN].

Rorschach begins going out unmasked by day, brandishing the "End Is Nigh" sign while disguised as a homeless prophet of doom [BWNO].

—In or After 1966
Dan Dreiberg nicknames Jon Osterman's teleportation abilities "the Manhattan transfer," though he never says this in the superhuman's presence [ALAN].
> **NOTE:** *The Manhattan Transfer was an American music group established in 1969 in New York City by Tim Hauser, Erin Dickins, Marty Nelson, and Pat Rosalia.*

Professor Milton Glass writes an article discussing science, war, capitalism, and other aspects of the human condition, as well as how Jon Osterman's transformation changed the world. The article, titled "Dr. Manhattan: Super-Powers and the Superpowers," notes that while conventional wisdom sees Osterman as "a man to end wars," he is actually "a man to end worlds." The U.S.S.R., Glass says, has held a grudge against the United States since World War II and will not permit itself to be threatened, no matter the cost—including destruction by Dr. Manhattan. Glass warns that the Soviets could choose mutually assured destruction over U.S. domination [ALAN].

Numerous other authors write books about Dr. Manhattan as well. Some speculate about how history might have unfolded differently had someone other than Jon Osterman been in Intrinsic Field Experiment #15, or whether the experiment could be recreated to give others the same powers [CLIX].

Janey Slater begins smoking three packs of cigarettes a day, hurting herself out of anger at Jon Osterman for leaving her [BWMO].

1966 to 1977

Laurie Juspeczyk serves as Silk Spectre for a decade, despite being uncomfortable with her costume's short skirt and navel-plunging neckline. Dan Dreiberg appreciates the garb's aesthetics, but keeps this fact to himself. The two become close friends, revealing their identities to each other. Laurie finds that she enjoys night patrols. She establishes nine routes across the rooftops of Washington, D.C., but considers route five the best since it takes her past the White House and the Lincoln Memorial **[ALAN]**. She often fights crime alongside Rorschach and The Nite Owl **[RPG3]**.

Late 1960s

Philip Hollier is elected mayor of New York City **[RPG2]**.
> **NOTE:** *John Lindsay was the city's mayor in the real world from 1966 to 1973.*

Ken Shade enters politics as a Cook County Circuit Court judge in Chicago. Heavy gambling debts make him a mob puppet, and Edgar Jacobi uses his criminal empire to push the crooked Shade up the political ladder, first to the Illinois state senate, and then to the U.S. House of Representatives. Shade unseats Senator Marion Lockley by such a wide margin that the Republican Party drafts him as a Presidential candidate **[RPG2]**.
> **NOTE:** *Charles H. Percy was the state's senator in the real world from 1967 to 1985.*

Findlay Setchfield South hires Eddie Blake to spy on his rivals and help him eliminate anyone who might stand in the way of South putting Richard Nixon in the White House **[RPG2]**.

Before 1967

A slum area of New York City near Brooklyn is christened New London **[RPG2]**.
> **NOTE:** *No such area of New York City exists in the real world, though there is a New London near Rome, New York, and others in Connecticut and other U.S. states.*

Late 1966 to 1967

Ozymandias spends months reading the works of mankind's greatest fantasists, in order to find inspiration for how to save the world. He speed-reads every science fiction novel ever published and watches every sci-fi film and TV show he can find. Uninspired, he starts over again and re-watches *The Outer Limits*. His inspiration arrives thanks to the episode "The Architects of Fear," about a team of scientists launching a nuclear attack in order to save the world by uniting mankind against a perceived common enemy. Veidt watches this episode repeatedly for days to determine why the plan failed, before deciding it's because the scientists didn't think on a large enough scale **[BWOZ]**.
> **NOTE:** *Despite the similarities between* Watchmen *and this* Outer Limits *episode, Alan Moore claims to have only learned of "The Architects of Fear" while writing issue #10*

MIND .... *The Mindscape of Alan Moore*
MOBL .... *Watchmen: The Mobile Game*
MOTN .... *Watchmen: The Complete Motion Comic*
MTRO .... *Metro* promotional newspaper cover wrap
NEWP .... *New Frontiersman* promotional newspaper
NEWW .... *New Frontiersman* website
NIGH ..... *Watchmen: The End Is Nigh, Parts 1 and 2*
PKIT ...... *Watchmen* film British press kit
PORT ..... *Watchmen Portraits*
REAL ..... Real life
RPG1 .... *DC Heroes Role Playing Module #227: Who Watches the Watchmen?*

RPG2 .... *DC Heroes Role Playing Module #235: Taking Out the Trash—Curses and Tears*
RPG3 .... *DC Heroes: The Watchmen Sourcebook*
RUBY .... "Wounds," published in *The Ruby Files Volume One*
SCR1 ..... Unfilmed screenplay draft: Sam Hamm
SCR2 ..... Unfilmed screenplay draft: Charles McKeuen
SCR3 ..... Unfilmed screenplay draft: Gary Goldman
SCR4 ..... Unfilmed screenplay draft: David Hayter (2002)
SCR5 ..... Unfilmed screenplay draft: David Hayter (2003)
SCR6 ..... Unfilmed screenplay draft: Alex Tse
SPOT ..... *DC Spotlight #1*
VRL1 ..... Viral video: *NBS Nightly News with Ted Philips*

VRL2 ..... Viral video: *The Keene Act and You*
VRL3 ..... Viral video: *Who Watches the Watchmen? A Veidt Music Network (VMN) Special*
VRL4 ..... Viral video: *World in Focus: 6 Minutes to Midnight*
VRL5 ..... Viral video: *Local Radio Station Report on 1977 Riots*
VRL6 ..... Viral videos (group of ten): *Veidt Enterprises Advertising Contest*
WAWA ... *Watching the Watchmen*
WHOS ... *Who's Who: The Definitive Directory of the DC Universe*
WTFC .... *Watchmen: The Film Companion*

of his miniseries. Editor Len Wein reportedly quit the series over this similarity, citing concerns about plagiarism. In later penning Before Watchmen: Ozymandias, *Wein made the connection more explicit.*

Veidt instructs his assistant, Marla, to retrofit one of his facilities as a bio-lab **[BWOZ]**. He learns about genetics technology, pays a great deal of money to create a hybrid lynx as a pet, which he names Bubastis **[ALAN]**, and begins experimenting in manipulating DNA to create a new life form. He soon realizes, however, that he must hire someone with more knowledge about such research, and asks Marla to shop for an island that he can purchase **[BWOZ]**.

NOTE: *In ancient Egypt, Bubastis was a city located along the River Nile.*

CONFLICT: Before Watchmen: Ozymandias *depicts Veidt as having created Bubastis, contradicting Alan Moore's miniseries, in which the billionaire pays someone else to do it for him.*

Part VIII:
ALL THE PRESIDENT'S MEN
(1967–1970)

—1967

Rorschach brings down a criminal known as Zebra, a tall thug with tattooed stripes covering his face and body. In prison, Zebra employs three hulking convicts—Tom, Dick, and Harry—to do his dirty work **[SCR3]**.

—Early 1967

Adrian Veidt sets into motion his plan to frighten mankind into seeking salvation, by creating a threat so terrible that nations will set aside their differences to fight it together. To ensure sufficient funding, he develops the basic patent for public spark hydrants, a curbside device capable of powering electric vehicles. Such hydrants are soon deployed throughout the world's major cities **[ALAN]**.

Ozymandias thwarts four thieves attempting to pilfer the British Museum's collection. Subduing them within seconds, he wonders if anyone can offer him a challenge anymore. Dr. Manhattan arrives a moment later, seeking his advice **[BWDM, BWOZ]**.

Manhattan teleports himself and Veidt to the latter's office, which leaves Adrian dizzy but fascinated by the process. Jon disables all recording devices with a thought, then describes his odyssey through multiple quantum realities, in which each new universe ended with Earth's nuclear destruction. Though he has collapsed them all into a single timeline, Jon says, he can no longer see his own future, as though a cataclysmic event has created a curtain of static. Fearing that any further action on his part might cause that very destruction, he asks Ozymandias to decide his next move for him **[BWDM]**.

Veidt suggests that they replace nuclear power with an unlimited energy source, by working together to synthesize and replicate the energy that the superhuman creates. This, he explains, would solve the world's energy crisis, eliminating poverty and the need

MIND .... *The Mindscape of Alan Moore*	**RPG2** .....*DC Heroes Role Playing Module #235: Taking Out the Trash—Curses and Tears*	**VRL2** .....Viral video: *The Keene Act and You*
MOBL.... *Watchmen: The Mobile Game*		**VRL3** .....Viral video: *Who Watches the Watchmen? A Veidt Music Network (VMN) Special*
MOTN.... *Watchmen: The Complete Motion Comic*	**RPG3** ....*DC Heroes: The Watchmen Sourcebook*	
MTRO.... *Metro* promotional newspaper cover wrap	**RUBY** ...."Wounds," published in *The Ruby Files Volume One*	**VRL4** .....Viral video: *World in Focus: 6 Minutes to Midnight*
NEWP.... *New Frontiersman* promotional newspaper	**SCR1**.....Unfilmed screenplay draft: Sam Hamm	**VRL5** .....Viral video: *Local Radio Station Report on 1977 Riots*
NEWW.... *New Frontiersman* website	**SCR2**.....Unfilmed screenplay draft: Charles McKeuen	
NIGH ..... *Watchmen: The End Is Nigh, Parts 1 and 2*	**SCR3**.....Unfilmed screenplay draft: Gary Goldman	**VRL6** .....Viral videos (group of ten): *Veidt Enterprises Advertising Contest*
PKIT ...... *Watchmen* film British press kit	**SCR4**.....Unfilmed screenplay draft: David Hayter (2002)	
PORT ..... *Watchmen Portraits*	**SCR5**.....Unfilmed screenplay draft: David Hayter (2003)	**WAWA**... *Watching the Watchmen*
REAL ..... Real life	**SCR6**.....Unfilmed screenplay draft: Alex Tse	**WHOS** ... *Who's Who: The Definitive Directory of the DC Universe*
RPG1 .... *DC Heroes Role Playing Module #227: Who Watches the Watchmen?*	**SPOT** .... *DC Spotlight #1*	
	VRL1 ..... Viral video: *NBS Nightly News with Ted Philips*	**WTFC** .... *Watchmen: The Film Companion*

for war. The static curtain could be due not to war, Adrian reasons, but to Jon's energies being used on a global scale in the future. Manhattan agrees, unaware that Veidt has an ulterior motive **[BWDM]**.

A former runaway and prostitute known as Mother forms a gang-cult called The Brethren as a "family" for New York City's homeless population, deep in the New London slums near Brooklyn. Its members wear leather jackets emblazoned with the gang's insignia, and many live in a large stronghold called Gehenna. The rat-infested building, located at 2312 Division Avenue, is badly damaged from fire, its windows all boarded over. Outside is a dumping ground for tons of trash and refuse **[RPG2]**.

> **NOTE:** *Mother's true name is never revealed.*
>
> *Gehenna, in the Hebrew Bible, is where followers of various Ba'als and Canaanite gods, including Moloch, sacrificed their children by fire. In Jewish Rabbinic literature, and in Christian and Islamic scriptures, it is a destination of the wicked.*

Deranged, narcotics-addicted, and possibly schizophrenic, Mother grows obsessed with the work of William Blake, endlessly rattling off passages from his *Proverbs of Hell*. Reading Blake's *Marriage of Heaven and Hell* sends Mother into a holy frenzy. She and her gang-cult "children" go on a spree of ritual killings and kidnappings, somehow avoiding the notice of police and masked crime-fighters. **[RPG2]**.

—January 30, 1967—11:15 AM
The U.S. Secret Service issues a communique to Agents Abner and Delacroix, ordering them to deny Jenny Slater any further access to Jon Osterman. Laurie Juspeczyk is added to Dr. Manhattan's list of cleared visitors **[RPG3]**.

—February 11, 1967
Adrian Veidt submits articles of incorporation to New York State for Dimensional Developments, Inc., registered to Veidt Industries. Adrian lists himself as CEO and principal owner, with Leroy Gibbons named as treasurer **[RPG3]**.

—March 6, 1967
Dan Dreiberg finishes construction on a lightweight underwater suit designed to mimic his standard Nite Owl costume, allowing for four hours of operation while submerged in liquid. The suit costs $13,000 to build, is colored green for quick retrieval, and contains enhanced infrared visual capabilities for viewing objects underwater from up to 75 feet away at a depth of a hundred feet **[RPG3]**.

—Mid-1967
Adrian Veidt procures a secluded tropical island far from normal shipping lanes. He asks

his assistant, Marla, to arrange for the island to be removed from all public records and maps, to have a number of buildings erected using local labor, and to pay those hired well enough to assure their silence about the project. Marla tells him the construction could take years to complete **[BWOZ]**.

> **NOTE:** *Veidt systematically kills off everyone else who helps him achieve his master plan, so it seems uncharacteristic of him to merely pay off those involved in building the very site where said plan is hatched. More likely, he plans to have them all killed after they complete their work.*

> **CONFLICT:** *In* Taking Out the Trash, *Veidt buys a Mosquito Coast island in October 1968, while* The Watchmen Sourcebook *has him purchasing Alguna Island from Ecuador on October 5, 1968, and* Before Watchmen: Ozymandias *depicts him acquiring another island in 1967. Each account is clearly meant to identify his island base from Alan Moore's miniseries, but Moore's comic dates the island's purchase in 1970. This can be reconciled by assuming that Veidt requires four separate islands for his plan.*

—In or After 1967

Claiming to be working toward solving the planet's energy problems, Adrian Veidt tasks his research-and-development team with synthesizing and replicating Dr. Manhattan's energies. He dubs these efforts the Manhattan Project **[BWOZ]**.

> **NOTE:** *The Manhattan Project, during World War II, produced the United States' first nuclear weapons, with support from Canada and Great Britain—and is the same project after which Dr. Manhattan himself is named.*

—1967 to 1970

The royalties earned from Adrian Veidt's public spark hydrants greatly increase his already vast fortune **[ALAN]**. Veidt spends a great deal of time at Karnak, studying Dr. Manhattan's quantum abilities and the world political spectrum **[BWOZ]**.

—1968

A subway map is printed that Rorschach will continue to use for the rest of his life, making frequent changes by hand **[ALAN]**.

Veidt Communications produces an animated television series called *The Adventures of Dr. Manhattan*, capitalizing on the superhuman's position as a role model **[VRL1]**.

Underboss's criminal empire achieves the height of its success, despite his being imprisoned in Chicago **[RPG3]**. He becomes one of the most feared mob leaders ever to operate on American soil, with crime syndicates throughout New York, Chicago, and Philadelphia **[RPG3, NIGH]**. The mobster's forces rival, in size, only those of Moloch the Mystic **[RPG3]**.

MIND .... *The Mindscape of Alan Moore*
MOBL .... *Watchmen: The Mobile Game*
MOTN .... *Watchmen: The Complete Motion Comic*
MTRO .... *Metro* promotional newspaper cover wrap
NEWP .... *New Frontiersman* promotional newspaper
NEWW .... *New Frontiersman* website
NIGH ..... *Watchmen: The End Is Nigh, Parts 1 and 2*
PKIT ...... *Watchmen* film British press kit
PORT .... *Watchmen Portraits*
REAL ..... Real life
RPG1 .... *DC Heroes Role Playing Module #227: Who Watches the Watchmen?*

RPG2 .... *DC Heroes Role Playing Module #235: Taking Out the Trash—Curses and Tears*
RPG3 .... *DC Heroes: The Watchmen Sourcebook*
RUBY .... "Wounds," published in *The Ruby Files Volume One*
SCR1 ..... Unfilmed screenplay draft: Sam Hamm
SCR2 ..... Unfilmed screenplay draft: Charles McKeuen
SCR3 ..... Unfilmed screenplay draft: Gary Goldman
SCR4 ..... Unfilmed screenplay draft: David Hayter (2002)
SCR5 ..... Unfilmed screenplay draft: David Hayter (2003)
SCR6 ..... Unfilmed screenplay draft: Alex Tse
SPOT ..... *DC Spotlight #1*
VRL1 ..... Viral video: *NBS Nightly News with Ted Philips*

VRL2 ..... Viral video: *The Keene Act and You*
VRL3 ..... Viral video: *Who Watches the Watchmen? A Veidt Music Network (VMN) Special*
VRL4 ..... Viral video: *World in Focus: 6 Minutes to Midnight*
VRL5 ..... Viral video: *Local Radio Station Report on 1977 Riots*
VRL6 ..... Viral videos (group of ten): *Veidt Enterprises Advertising Contest*
WAWA .... *Watching the Watchmen*
WHOS ... *Who's Who: The Definitive Directory of the DC Universe*
WTFC .... *Watchmen: The Film Companion*

Dr. Manhattan stops Russian troops from invading Prague, Czechoslovakia, by melting their military tanks. As the terrified soldiers exit the vehicles, angry Czech citizens barrage them with rocks **[SCR1, SCR2]**.

The Twilight Lady's pornography and prostitution empire evolves to include smut magazines and movies, studios, burlesque houses, and bordellos throughout New York City. She employs numerous dominatrices who, though capable of handling drunken patrons and admirers, typically leave any fighting up to the beefed-up bouncers guarding their employer's vice dens. Dan Dreiberg arrests The Twilight Lady while Rorschach is out of town working on a case involving someone named Schipono **[NIGH]**.

—1968 to 1970

The Twilight Lady spends two years in prison **[RPG3]**.

> **CONFLICT:** The Watchmen Sourcebook *claims that The Twilight Lady serves only two years in prison, then heads to France and vanishes, while* The End Is Nigh *depicts her as remaining behind bars until March 1977.*

—January 7, 1968—9:11 PM

The Brethren gang-cult seize and abduct a 45-year-old Caucasian male, stab him in the chest, drain all of his blood for a religious ritual, and dispose of his body **[RPG2]**.

> **NOTE:** *This individual's name is not revealed.*

—January 11, 1968

The New York Police Department's Special Investigations division finds the 45-year-old victim's corpse just off Houston Street, but are unable to identify him **[RPG2]**.

—January 28, 1968

The NYPD's Special Investigations division documents the 45-year-old victim's murder in its files on The Brethren **[RPG2]**.

—January to June 1968

Ben Richter, an investigative reporter with the *New York Gazette*, spends months working to expose The Brethren. In the course of his research, Richter pays local street youths to keep tabs on the gang-cult for him **[RPG2]**.

—March 14, 1968—9:30 PM

Members of The Brethren strangle Marianne Eliot and leave her body in an alley near Roehman Avenue **[RPG2]**.

—March 14, 1968—10:00 PM

The body of Marianne Eliot is discovered, with a pinned note stating, "The cut worm forgives the plow" **[RPG2]**.

> **NOTE:** *This phrase comes from William Blake's* Proverbs of Hell.

—Before March 16, 1968

As the Vietnam War continues, Eddie Blake is assigned to work with Charlie Company, 11th Battalion. The United States' director of central intelligence tells CIA advisor Raul Duke to afford The Comedian "a long rope." Blake does things his way, ignoring American economic and political considerations, much to the frustration of Duke and military officer William Benway. Blake befriends two young Vietnamese boys, whom he dubs "Hearts" and "Minds," and who call him "Mr. Eddie" **[BWCO]**.

> **NOTE:** *"Hearts and Minds" was a term used to describe the largely unsuccessful strategies employed by the U.S. and South Vietnamese governments to defeat the Việt Cộng by winning the popular support of the Vietnamese people.*
>
> *In 1968, the director of central intelligence was Richard M. Helms. In this story, Duke refers to the director as Bill. Helms replaced his predecessor, William F. Raborn, in real-world 1966, so it may be that Raborn retains his job in the* Watchmen *universe.*
>
> *Duke is apparently named after Raoul Duke, a fictional character from several stories, novels, and articles written by author Hunter S. Thompson, including the popular* Fear and Loathing in Las Vegas.
>
> **CONFLICT:** *Blake says he has been in Vietnam for several years, despite his having attended the Crimebusters meeting in Alan Moore's miniseries, carried out missions for Findlay Setchfield South in* Taking Out the Trash, *and traveled to San Francisco in* Before Watchmen: Silk Spectre, *all between 1966 and 1968. Given his status as an advisor, the likely explanation is that he can leave and return to Vietnam as needed.*

—March 16, 1968

The NYPD's Special Investigations division documents Marianne Eliot's murder in its files on The Brethren **[RPG2]**.

Robert F. Kennedy announces his intention to run for President of the United States **[REAL]**. Eddie Blake finds out about it from a fellow soldier, but when he tries to congratulate his friend, Kennedy is unavailable to take Blake's calls **[BWCO]**.

A member of Charlie Company, nicknamed Pizza-Face, is found murdered, while another soldier, Lucas, trips out on LSD. Blake decides that the war has become a joke and sets out to end it quickly by making the Việt Cộng terrified of the United States. He and his

squad drop acid, then torch and slaughter an entire VC-influenced village, leaving more than five hundred dead—including children, the elderly, and several raped and mutilated women. Realizing that none of the villagers were the enemy, a soldier known as Moose fatally shoots himself in the head **[BWCO]**.

Benway orders a soldier named Meadows to shoot Eddie Blake with tranquilizers. Blake awakens on a helicopter, where Duke and Benway urge him to stick to the military's game clock. As a joke, Blake grabs Benway and jumps out of the chopper. They survive freefall, though Benway breaks his leg on impact. Blake leads the injured officer through the jungle, killing several Việt Cộng along the way. Duke decides to cover up the operation and eliminate Benway. As Blake and Benway reach the helicopter, the CIA agent shoots Benway in the head, killing him **[BWCO]**.

—After March 16, 1968
Raul Duke writes a letter to the U.S. director of central intelligence, informing him of March 16's events. Duke calls Eddie Blake a maniac whose actions run counter to the U.S. rural-pacification program, blaming him for Charlie Company's atrocities. He recommends that Blake be removed from Vietnam, that the events be downplayed with the media in order to preserve public perception, and that Benway receive the highest posthumous honors. The U.S. Department of State approves these recommendations, and Blake is relieved of duty and sent back to the United States **[BWCO]**.

—Late March or Early April 1968
A member of The Brethren quits the gang-cult, no longer able to stomach its violent policies **[RPG2]**.

—Before April 7, 1968
Eddie Blake helps Findlay Setchfield South ensure Richard Nixon's Presidential election by putting pressure on Chicago mobster Joey Falcone and other criminals to divert their syndicate funds into South's campaign coffers. When Falcone refuses to pay, several other hoods do the same and the scam soon unravels **[RPG2]**.

—April 7, 1968
Eddie Blake ambushes Joey Falcone's car late at night, using a small explosive charge to stop the vehicle. Blake then shoots Falcone and his driver with a snub-nose .357 magnum, to make it appear to have been a typical gangland hit **[RPG2]**.

—April 12, 1968, Late Night

An entire 43-soldier platoon of U.S. Marines from the 6th Division's 42nd company are killed in Saigon during an incendiary strike from an American B-52 bomber **[RPG3]**.

—April 16, 1968

The *New York Gazette*, reporting on the friendly-fire mishap in Saigon, quotes General Walter Scott, commander of U.S. air operations in Vietnam, as blaming the incident on the pilot mistaking a "black light" near the platoon's bivouac for a blue signal flare marking a napalm target **[RPG3]**.

> **NOTE:** *It is unclear why these events are recounted in* The Watchmen Sourcebook's *section on The Comedian, as they seem unconnected to the crime-fighter's history, especially since he is not in Vietnam at this time. If the author intended to imply that the vigilante caused the mishap, that is not apparent.*

—May 15, 1968—10:14 PM

The Brethren kidnap a person near Wicker Park, stab the victim eleven times, decapitate the individual, and drain all blood from the body for use in a religious ritual **[RPG2]**.

—May 16, 1968

The decapitation victim's body is discovered but not identified. The NYPD's Special Investigations division adds this murder to its files on The Brethren **[RPG2]**.

—In or Before Early 1968

Eddie Blake carries out numerous blackmail and assassination missions for the CIA **[RPG2]**.

—Mid-1968

Rorschach and Dan Dreiberg spend weeks tracking a gang called The Rat Pack, who commit crimes while wearing rat masks. When the Rat Pack robs the First Bank & Trust, Eddie Blake tracks the gang to a bar called The Rat's Nest, where he beats them up and stabs one in the hand. Nite Owl and Rorschach crash through the front window to find The Comedian standing over the unconscious thugs. Blake mocks the duo, claiming Dan pretends to be something he's not beneath his suit **[BWCO]**.

> **CONFLICT:** *Dreiberg calls The Comedian "Blake," despite the latter's true identity being a secret from his fellow crime-fighters until 1985.*

The second floor of The Brethren's stronghold becomes so overrun with rats that the gang-cult's members thereafter ignore that level entirely **[RPG2]**.

MIND .... *The Mindscape of Alan Moore*
MOBL .... *Watchmen: The Mobile Game*
MOTN .... *Watchmen: The Complete Motion Comic*
MTRO .... *Metro* promotional newspaper cover wrap
NEWP .... *New Frontiersman* promotional newspaper
NEWW ... *New Frontiersman* website
NIGH ..... *Watchmen: The End Is Nigh, Parts 1 and 2*
PKIT ...... *Watchmen* film British press kit
PORT ..... *Watchmen Portraits*
REAL ..... Real life
RPG1 .... *DC Heroes Role Playing Module #227: Who Watches the Watchmen?*

RPG2 .... *DC Heroes Role Playing Module #235: Taking Out the Trash—Curses and Tears*
RPG3 .... *DC Heroes: The Watchmen Sourcebook*
RUBY .... "Wounds," published in *The Ruby Files Volume One*
SCR1 ..... Unfilmed screenplay draft: Sam Hamm
SCR2 ..... Unfilmed screenplay draft: Charles McKeuen
SCR3 ..... Unfilmed screenplay draft: Gary Goldman
SCR4 ..... Unfilmed screenplay draft: David Hayter (2002)
SCR5 ..... Unfilmed screenplay draft: David Hayter (2003)
SCR6 ..... Unfilmed screenplay draft: Alex Tse
SPOT ..... *DC Spotlight #1*
VRL1 ..... Viral video: *NBS Nightly News with Ted Philips*

VRL2 ..... Viral video: *The Keene Act and You*
VRL3 ..... Viral video: *Who Watches the Watchmen? A Veidt Music Network (VMN) Special*
VRL4 ..... Viral video: *World in Focus: 6 Minutes to Midnight*
VRL5 ..... Viral video: *Local Radio Station Report on 1977 Riots*
VRL6 ..... Viral videos (group of ten): *Veidt Enterprises Advertising Contest*
WAWA ... *Watching the Watchmen*
WHOS ... *Who's Who: The Definitive Directory of the DC Universe*
WTFC .... *Watchmen: The Film Companion*

In or Before June 1968

Due to riots and organized crime, the Republican National Convention is rescheduled from Miami Beach, Florida, to the McDaniel Convention Center, in Lower Manhattan, New York. Following this announcement, various threats and ominous warnings occur, which the police believe originate with The Brethren **[RPG2]**.

> **NOTE:** *In the real world, the convention was held at the Miami Beach Convention Center on August 5-8, 1968.*

Laurie Juspeczyk reads Hollis Mason's book *Under the Hood* and learns that Eddie Blake tried to rape her mother, Sally Jupiter, in October 1940 **[ALAN, RPG2]**.

> **NOTE:** *Alan Moore's miniseries establishes that Laurie reads the book, but not when.* Taking Out the Trash *indicates that she has already done so by June 1968.*

Edgar Jacobi recruits two bodyguards from the Far East, known as Sin and Temptation. The two martial arts experts wear leather pants and executioner's hoods **[RPG2]**.

Senator Ken Shade is accused by a fellow senator, Hunter, of being linked to organized crime, and of accepting campaign contributions from Underboss. Michael Barukis, a mob-paid special investigator appointed by the Justice Department, examines Hunter's evidence and clears Shade on all counts. Ike S. Lee, a contributing editor for *Probe* magazine, interviews the Presidential-hopeful, who denies the allegations, sharply criticizes the current President, and pushes for an upscaling of the United States' involvement in the Vietnam War, which he believes can be ended by 1969 **[RPG2]**.

Determined to have a U.S. President in his back pocket, Moloch calls in many old underworld debts, mobilizing his entire national organization to secure Ken Shade's nomination. This includes using wire taps to discover other candidates' campaign plans, as well as securing thousands of votes via extortion and blackmail, with the mob targeting anyone seen as a threat to Shade's election **[RPG2]**.

Findlay Setchfield South uses similar tactics to ensure Vice President Richard Nixon's nomination, hiring The Comedian to serve as his secret bodyguard, security advisor, and campaign consultant. Blake's illegal activities on his behalf prove instrumental in the campaign's success, for which he is paid a lot of money. Nixon comes out ahead in the primaries, with Shade in second and Mayor Philip Hollier of San Antonio, Texas, in third. A Republican Presidency—and a victory for Nixon—seems guaranteed **[RPG2]**.

> **NOTE:** *The VP is unnamed in* Taking Out the Trash *(perhaps to avoid political or legal ramification for DC Comics and Mayfair Games), but he must be Richard Nixon since, per Alan Moore's miniseries, that is who wins the election. In the real world, Nixon's opponents were Nelson Rockefeller, Ronald Reagan, George W. Romney, and Harold Stassen.*

To tip the scales in Shade's favor, Edgar Jacobi hires The Brethren to assassinate Richard Nixon. Moloch convinces Mother, the gang-cult's leader, that Nixon is an archangel sent down to destroy them, and that her "children" must eliminate the threat. Privately, he intends to betray Mother so Shade can expose The Brethren and take partial credit for capturing Nixon's killers **[RPG2]**.

Captain Charles Braddock of the New York Police Department puts Secret Service agent Montgomery Banner in charge of security at the Republican National Convention, and orders Banner to seek help from New York's costumed heroes. The major resents this, as the only crime-fighter he likes is The Comedian, alongside whom he fought during World War II and the Korean War **[RPG2]**.

Several masked adventurers work with Captain Arthur Bridwell of the NYPD's 14th Precinct to solve cases **[RPG2]**.

The Brethren purchase experimental army gas grenades on the black market. The canisters release a hallucinogenic compound designed to break the morale of enemy forces **[RPG2]**.

—June 2, 1968
Reporter Ben Richter meets a former member of The Brethren, who agrees to speak to him about the gang-cult's activities, using the alias "Iggy." The young man, who quit The Brethren two months prior, tells Richter about the group's leader, Mother, and about its stronghold, Gehenna, though not the building's precise location **[RPG2]**.

—Before June 3, 1968
While working to get Richard Nixon elected President, G. Gordon Liddy receives evidence from FBI contacts that Robert F. Kennedy's life is in danger. Liddy presents the evidence to Nixon and his campaign team at the Pied Piper Motel, and Nixon says to share the documents with Eddie Blake. Although Nixon and Kennedy have their differences, Nixon does not want to see his opponent killed, as it would galvanize the anti-war movement **[BWCO]**.

—June 3, 1968—Daytime
Eddie Blake flies to California to see Robert Kennedy, whose arrival is delayed due to the Democratic National Convention's hectic schedule. Liddy approaches Blake at a bar and tells him of an impending attempt on Kennedy's life, to be perpetrated by Sirhan Sirhan, a Palestinian nationalist brainwashed by the CIA to shoot the senator with a .22-caliber revolver, so as to give the impression of an amateur assassination. The FBI's director plans to let it happen, Liddy says, so he can discredit the CIA. Like Kennedy, Nixon wants to end the war—but by winning it, not by showing weakness before an enemy. Blake, who shares Nixon's view, agrees to fix the problem **[BWCO]**.

MIND .... *The Mindscape of Alan Moore*
MOBL .... *Watchmen: The Mobile Game*
MOTN .... *Watchmen: The Complete Motion Comic*
MTRO .... *Metro promotional newspaper cover wrap*
NEWP .... *New Frontiersman promotional newspaper*
NEWW .... *New Frontiersman website*
NIGH ..... *Watchmen: The End Is Nigh, Parts 1 and 2*
PKIT ...... *Watchmen film British press kit*
PORT ..... *Watchmen Portraits*
REAL ..... Real life
RPG1 .... *DC Heroes Role Playing Module #227: Who Watches the Watchmen?*

RPG2 .... *DC Heroes Role Playing Module #235: Taking Out the Trash—Curses and Tears*
RPG3 .... *DC Heroes: The Watchmen Sourcebook*
RUBY .... "Wounds," published in *The Ruby Files Volume One*
SCR1 ..... Unfilmed screenplay draft: Sam Hamm
SCR2 ..... Unfilmed screenplay draft: Charles McKeuen
SCR3 ..... Unfilmed screenplay draft: Gary Goldman
SCR4 ..... Unfilmed screenplay draft: David Hayter (2002)
SCR5 ..... Unfilmed screenplay draft: David Hayter (2003)
SCR6 ..... Unfilmed screenplay draft: Alex Tse
SPOT ..... *DC Spotlight #1*
VRL1 ..... Viral video: *NBS Nightly News with Ted Philips*

VRL2 ..... Viral video: *The Keene Act and You*
VRL3 ..... Viral video: *Who Watches the Watchmen? A Veidt Music Network (VMN) Special*
VRL4 ..... Viral video: *World in Focus: 6 Minutes to Midnight*
VRL5 ..... Viral video: *Local Radio Station Report on 1977 Riots*
VRL6 ..... Viral videos (group of ten): *Veidt Enterprises Advertising Contest*
WAWA ... *Watching the Watchmen*
WHOS ... *Who's Who: The Definitive Directory of the DC Universe*
WTFC ... *Watchmen: The Film Companion*

—June 3, 1968—Night

Robert Kennedy visits Eddie Blake's hotel room to discuss the massacre that his friend carried out in Vietnam in March 1968. Kennedy is upset by Blake's actions, and by the government's cover-up. To preserve U.S. integrity, he plans to expose the truth at a press conference after the primary votes have been tallied, but Blake offers to confess his crimes to the press himself, to prevent any backlash from hurting the senator **[BWCO]**.

—June 4, 1968

Robert F. Kennedy wins the Democratic nomination for the Presidency, defeating Minnesota Senator Eugene McCarthy **[REAL]**. Eddie Blake stands at his friend's side throughout the day's events **[BWCO]**.

—June 5, 1968—12:10 AM

Robert Kennedy delivers a speech in Los Angeles, to supporters in the Ambassador Hotel's Embassy Ballroom. During his speech, Kennedy pushes to halt racial and class divisions in American society, and to end the Vietnam War, the policies of which he describes as "unsuccessful" **[REAL, BWCO]**.

Eddie Blake stands at Kennedy's side during the speech, briefly speaks to a smiling man near the podium, and accompanies the senator through the hotel's kitchen to the nearby Colonial Room, where the press conference will be held. En route, Blake warns his friend of the CIA's plans to have him assassinated **[BWCO]**.

> **NOTE:** In the real world, Kennedy's escort through the kitchen was Karl Uecker, the Ambassador's assistant maître d'hôtel. Uecker may be the man to whom Blake speaks at the podium, as he was photographed smiling during Kennedy's speech.

—June 5, 1968—12:15 AM

Moments after Kennedy enters the ballroom, Sirhan Sirhan opens fire in full view of the press **[REAL]**. Eddie Blake pretends to guard his friend's life, but discreetly shoots him in order to save his own reputation, and for the good of the country **[BWCO]**.

—June 5, 1968—Early Morning

Blake leaves the hotel, discards his gun in a garbage truck, and drives away, slamming his head repeatedly into his car's steering wheel to dull the pain of having murdered another close friend and Kennedy. The impact bloodies his forehead and nose, causing a drop of blood to fall on a smiley-face pin adorning his lapel **[BWCO]**.

—June 6, 1968—1:44 AM

Robert F. Kennedy dies at Good Samaritan Hospital, 26 hours after the shooting, despite extensive neurosurgery to remove bullet and bone fragments from his brain **[REAL]**.

—June 10, 1968

New York City officials predict the numbers of homeless walking the streets will rise by eleven percent during the coming year, partly due to rising housing costs **[RPG2]**.

—June 11, 1968—Morning

The *New York Gazette* features a front-page article titled "Convention Set to Begin Tomorrow, Top GOP Officials Predict VP's Nomination," citing Richard Nixon as the nominee frontrunner for president, followed by Ken Shade and Philip Hollier. The paper publishes the first segment of a four-part special report on gang terror by investigative reporter Ben Richter, documenting the history of The Brethren **[RPG2]**.

Rorschach passes several transients on the street. He realizes how much New York City is changing and determines to find a new apartment the next day **[RPG2]**.

> **NOTE:** *Ironically, Rorschach spends much of his time posing as a transient during the years leading up to his death.*

—June 11, 1968—10:35 PM

On their nightly patrol of New York City, Dan Dreiberg and Rorschach leave *Archimedes* hovering above the city, descend into the subway on foot and head for the Bleecker Street station. Five members of The Brethren attempt to abduct an old man for a ritual sacrifice, but the crime-fighters save his life. Rorschach records a journal entry noting the weakness and sorrow on many people's faces, as well as the excessive, uncollected trash lying about in the tunnels **[RPG2]**.

—June 11, 1968—11:00 PM

Rorschach and Dreiberg wait for the police to arrive, and Captain Charles Braddock asks them to accompany him to NYPD headquarters **[RPG2]**.

—On or Before June 12, 1968

Senator Louis Conrad, a supporter and close friend of Mayor Philip Hollier, obtains tapes implicating Findlay Setchfield South and Eddie Blake in the murder of mobster Joey Falcone. The tapes come from Falcone's former rival, Tony Rossignoli. Conrad tries to force South into supporting Hollier as a Vice Presidential candidate, so that Conrad will be in a position to receive political favors. Although Hollier was initially South's first choice, the kingmaker changes his mind, unwilling to give in to blackmail **[RPG2]**.

—June 12, 1968—Morning

The *New York Gazette* publishes the second segment of Ben Richter's four-part special report on gang terror and The Brethren **[RPG2]**.

MIND .... *The Mindscape of Alan Moore*	**RPG2** .... *DC Heroes Role Playing Module #235: Taking Out the Trash—Curses and Tears*	**VRL2** ..... Viral video: *The Keene Act and You*
MOBL.... *Watchmen: The Mobile Game*		**VRL3** ..... Viral video: *Who Watches the Watchmen? A Veidt Music Network (VMN) Special*
MOTN.... *Watchmen: The Complete Motion Comic*	**RPG3** .... *DC Heroes: The Watchmen Sourcebook*	
MTRO.... *Metro* promotional newspaper cover wrap	**RUBY** .... "Wounds," published in *The Ruby Files Volume One*	**VRL4** ..... Viral video: *World in Focus: 6 Minutes to Midnight*
NEWP.... *New Frontiersman* promotional newspaper	**SCR1**..... Unfilmed screenplay draft: Sam Hamm	**VRL5** ..... Viral video: *Local Radio Station Report on 1977 Riots*
NEWW... *New Frontiersman* website	**SCR2**..... Unfilmed screenplay draft: Charles McKeuen	
NIGH ..... *Watchmen: The End Is Nigh, Parts 1 and 2*	**SCR3**..... Unfilmed screenplay draft: Gary Goldman	**VRL6** ..... Viral videos (group of ten): *Veidt Enterprises Advertising Contest*
PKIT...... *Watchmen* film British press kit	**SCR4**..... Unfilmed screenplay draft: David Hayter (2002)	
PORT..... *Watchmen Portraits*	**SCR5**..... Unfilmed screenplay draft: David Hayter (2003)	**WAWA**... *Watching the Watchmen*
REAL..... Real life	**SCR6**..... Unfilmed screenplay draft: Alex Tse	**WHOS** ... *Who's Who: The Definitive Directory of the DC Universe*
RPG1 .... *DC Heroes Role Playing Module #227: Who Watches the Watchmen?*	**SPOT**..... *DC Spotlight #1*	
	VRL1 ..... Viral video: *NBS Nightly News with Ted Philips*	**WTFC** .... *Watchmen: The Film Companion*

—June 12, 1968—12:35 AM

Two hours after saving the old man, Dan Dreiberg and Rorschach are escorted into a conference room in Lower Manhattan's 12th Precinct. Also present are The Comedian, Silk Spectre, Dr. Manhattan, and Ozymandias. Although Rorschach respects The Comedian, he has no interest in working with the others, and records a journal entry expressing as much **[RPG2]**.

> **NOTE:** *A timeline published in* Taking Out the Trash *breaks down the events of June 11 to 14, but the book's internal evidence negates much of that dating—such as this meeting, which is set on June 11, despite occurring two hours after the old man's 10:35 rescue, which places it on June 12.*

—June 12, 1968—12:35 to 12:55 AM

For twenty minutes, the crime-fighters await Braddock's arrival **[RPG2]**.

June 12, 1968—Circa 1:00 AM

New York City resident Ethel Clark is fatally stabbed by a mugger in an alley off of Eighth Avenue. Three seconds later, Robert Lincoln, of Gold Falls, New Jersey, dies when his car spins over an embankment into a river. Twenty seconds after that, Thomas Newcomb dies of kidney failure at a Cleveland hospital. Dr. Manhattan perceives all of these deaths but does not save them since he lacks the power to save every person who dies in the world, or the conscience to choose who will live or die **[RPG2]**.

> **CONFLICT:** *This seemingly contradicts how Dr. Manhattan's powers work. He repeatedly explains, in Alan Moore's miniseries, that he cannot choose to take action based on what he sees of the future, since all of his actions are pre-ordained. He does not predict the future—he experiences it in his present, so his actions have already occurred from his perspective.*

Charles Braddock enters the conference room with Montgomery Banner, who asks the heroes to handle security at the Republican National Convention. Dr. Manhattan declines, citing gluino experiments and the need to plan for when the President will ask him to invade Vietnam in three years. He departs, telling Laurie he will see her in seventy-six hours and thirty-seven minutes. The others accept the assignment **[RPG2]**.

—June 12, 1968—3:00 AM

After leaving the meeting with Banner, Eddie Blake confers with Findlay Setchfield South at the McDaniel Convention Center. South tells him about Senator Louis Conrad's blackmail attempt and says to obtain the tapes and coerce Conrad to stay out of South's way in the future, but not to kill him **[RPG2]**.

ABSO .... *Watchmen Absolute Edition*
ALAN ..... Alan Moore's *Watchmen* miniseries
ARCD .... *Minutemen Arcade*
ARTF ..... *Watchmen: The Art of the Film*
BLCK ..... *Tales of the Black Freighter*
BWCC ... *Before Watchmen—The Crimson Corsair*
BWCO .... *Before Watchmen—Comedian*
BWDB .. *Before Watchmen—Dollar Bill*
BWDM .. *Before Watchmen—Dr. Manhattan*
BWMM .. *Before Watchmen—Minutemen*
BWMO .. *Before Watchmen—Moloch*
BWNO ... *Before Watchmen—Nite Owl*

BWOZ .... *Before Watchmen—Ozymandias*
BWRO ... *Before Watchmen—Rorschach*
BWSS ... *Before Watchmen—Silk Spectre*
CHEM .... My Chemical Romance music video: "Desolation Row"
CMEO .... *Watchmen* cameos in comics, TV, and film:
 • Comic: *Astonishing X-Men* volume 3 issue #6
 • Comic: *Hero Hotline* volume 1 issue #5
 • Comic: *Kingdom Come* volume 1 issue #2
 • Comic: *Marvels* volume 1 issue #4
 • Comic: *The Question* volume 1 issue #17
 • TV: *Teen Titans Go!* episode #82, "Real Boy Adventures"
 • Film: *Man of Steel*

 • Film: *Batman v Superman: Dawn of Justice Ultimate Edition*
 • Film: *Justice League*
CLIX ...... HeroClix figure pack-in cards
DECK ..... *DC Comics Deck-Building Game—Crossover Pack 4: Watchmen*
DURS .... *DC Universe: Rebirth Special* volume 1 issue #1
FILM ..... *Watchmen* theatrical film
HOOD .... *Under the Hood* documentary and dust-jacket prop reproduction
JUST ..... *Watchmen: Justice Is Coming*
MATL .... Mattel Club Black Freighter figure pack-in cards

June 12, 1968—3:00 to 7:00 AM

Eddie Blake spends four hours calling numerous hotels in the area, before determining that Conrad is staying at the Esquire Hotel on Fifth Avenue **[RPG2]**.

June 12, 1968—Before 6:00 AM

The crime-fighters visit the NYPD's 14th Precinct to investigate The Brethren through a police contact, Captain Arthur Bridwell, who invites them to interrogate captured gang members. They learn little from the thugs, but Bridwell advises that they check out the Special Investigations division's files, stored in room 1417 at the NYPD headquarters. There, they find a file detailing the S.I.D.'s ongoing investigation of the gang **[RPG2]**.

June 12, 1968—Morning

The Republican National Convention commences at Manhattan's McDaniel Convention Center **[RPG2]**.

Reporter Ben Richter records a conversation with Iggy, a former Brethren member who claims something is "going down," and that a message drop will take place at midnight at Mex's Indy City, a seedy Manhattan rock club **[RPG2]**.

The crime-fighters question a snitch and junkie named Willy at The Sleep-r-y, a sleazy flop house in Lower Manhattan. Terrified of The Brethren, Willy reveals only that they're more than a gang—they're a religion. After finding a copy of Ben Richter's *New York Gazette* article on gang terror, the team visits the investigative reporter. Richter initially resists giving up sources, but eventually shares what he has learned from Iggy **[RPG2]**.

June 12, 1968—10:00 AM

When the heroes arrive at the McDaniel Convention Center to meet with Montgomery Banner, numerous hippie groups are protesting outside. Banner gives the team a tour of the facility, introduces them to Nixon, Shade, and Hollier, and puts Lieutenant Eddleson and seventy-five security guards under their command **[RPG2]**.

June 12, 1968—Daytime

Eddie Blake visits the Esquire Hotel and fights Louis Conrad's bodyguards. Inside the man's room, he finds a note from Conrad stating that in the event of his disappearance, four cassette tapes incriminating Findlay Setchfield South can be found at Philip Hollier's campaign office, in a file marked "Tango." Blake also finds a planning book listing a meeting with Tony Rossignoli, Joey Falcone's former rival **[RPG2]**.

MIND .... *The Mindscape of Alan Moore*
MOBL .... *Watchmen: The Mobile Game*
MOTN .... *Watchmen: The Complete Motion Comic*
MTRO .... *Metro* promotional newspaper cover wrap
NEWP .... *New Frontiersman* promotional newspaper
NEWW .... *New Frontiersman* website
NIGH ..... *Watchmen: The End Is Nigh, Parts 1 and 2*
PKIT ...... *Watchmen* film British press kit
PORT ..... *Watchmen Portraits*
REAL ..... Real life
RPG1 .... *DC Heroes Role Playing Module #227: Who Watches the Watchmen?*

RPG2 .... *DC Heroes Role Playing Module #235: Taking Out the Trash—Curses and Tears*
RPG3 .... *DC Heroes: The Watchmen Sourcebook*
RUBY .... "Wounds," published in *The Ruby Files Volume One*
SCR1 ..... Unfilmed screenplay draft: Sam Hamm
SCR2 ..... Unfilmed screenplay draft: Charles McKeuen
SCR3 ..... Unfilmed screenplay draft: Gary Goldman
SCR4 ..... Unfilmed screenplay draft: David Hayter (2002)
SCR5 ..... Unfilmed screenplay draft: David Hayter (2003)
SCR6 ..... Unfilmed screenplay draft: Alex Tse
SPOT ..... *DC Spotlight #1*
VRL1 ..... Viral video: *NBS Nightly News with Ted Philips*

VRL2 ..... Viral video: *The Keene Act and You*
VRL3 ..... Viral video: *Who Watches the Watchmen? A Veidt Music Network (VMN) Special*
VRL4 ..... Viral video: *World in Focus: 6 Minutes to Midnight*
VRL5 ..... Viral video: *Local Radio Station Report on 1977 Riots*
VRL6 ..... Viral videos (group of ten): *Veidt Enterprises Advertising Contest*
WAWA ... *Watching the Watchmen*
WHOS ... *Who's Who: The Definitive Directory of the DC Universe*
WTFC ... *Watchmen: The Film Companion*

June 12, 1968—Night

The crime-fighters patrol New London, seeking out random gang activity—Nite Owl aboard *Archimedes*, the others on the ground. Rorschach records a journal entry noting his belief that The Brethren will be out that night, per their usual pattern **[RPG2]**.

> **NOTE:** *Rorschach's journal entry is dated June 14, even though it is clearly June 12 at this point in the story.*

June 12, 1968—Between 9:30 and 10:00 PM

Four thugs hold up a liquor store on Yancy Street. The heroes fight them, but determine that they are not connected to The Brethren **[RPG2]**.

June 12, 1968—Between 10:30 and 11:00 PM

Four members of The Brethren attack a newspaper vendor, intending to kidnap the old man for use in a ritual killing. The masked heroes save the man's life and apprehend the gang members, but fail to discover the Gehenna stronghold's location **[RPG2]**.

June 12, 1968—Before 11:59 PM

Rorschach records a journal entry describing his feelings about The Brethren's territory, which he calls "a den of corruption deep in the land of shadows" **[RPG2]**.

June 13, 1968—12:00 AM

A runner working for Mother, leader of The Brethren, drops off a message at Mex's Indy City for members of the gang who don't live at Gehenna. Performing at the club is an acid-rock band called The Velour Overground. Scouting the loud club, the masked heroes witness the message exchange and chase the thugs outside, where they get ahold of one member's driver's license, which lists an address of 2103 Houston Street. The thugs escape, one making his way to the Houston Street safehouse, the other eluding the heroes while traveling to Gehenna by going miles out of his way **[RPG2]**.

> **NOTE:** *This event is said to occur at midnight on June 12, but midnight is actually 12:00 AM the next day.*
>
> *The band's name spoofs that of The Velvet Underground, a New York City-based group active from 1964 to 1973.*

June 13, 1968—Shortly Before 2:00 AM

Rorschach records a journal entry expressing excitement at finding The Brethren's safehouse, and noting "This could be fun" **[RPG2]**.

June 13, 1968—2:00 AM

The crime-fighters locate 2103 Houston Street and defeat five gang members within. On a wall is a photo of Richard Nixon with the word "Pig" scrawled on it, and the safehouse contains submachine guns and four New York National Guard uniforms. The message from Mother declares this to be "Judgement Day" **[RPG2]**.

—June 13, 1968—Early Morning
The *New York Gazette* publishes the third segment of Ben Richter's four-part special report on gang terror and The Brethren **[RPG2]**.

—June 13, 1968—Before 8:00 AM
Eddie Blake locates and destroys the incriminating cassette tapes in Louis Conrad's campaign office. To eliminate Conrad as a threat to Findlay Setchfield South, Blake sets out to find proof linking Conrad to Tony Rossignoli, and also plants the gun he used to kill Joey Falcone in order to frame Conrad for the murder **[RPG2]**.

—June 13, 1968—10:00 AM
Ken Shade makes a last-minute campaign speech in Central Park to more than a thousand peaceful spectators. Rorschach records a journal entry calling the senator dishonest and un-American. He, Dan Dreiberg, and Eddie Blake find a member of Shade's entourage familiar, though none immediately realize who he is: Don "Big Daddy" Feroli, a minor enforcer in The Big Figure's crime syndicate **[RPG2]**.

—June 13, 1968—9:00 PM
All lights in the convention center and surrounding area suddenly extinguish, in a blackout caused by time bombs set off in nearby relay stations. For security purposes, Lieutenant Eddleson locks each of the three candidates in his respective campaign room. The crime-fighters ascend to the roof to find a mob smashing windows and looting storefronts. Two blocks away, fifteen thugs armed with baseball bats try to tip a bus containing five passengers. The heroes take to the streets, battling rioters, some of whom admit they were informed of the blackout in advance **[RPG2]**.

> **NOTE:** *A timeline in* Taking Out the Trash *sets the blackout on June 16, but all internal evidence negates that placement.*

—June 13, 1968—9:02 PM
Police arrive on the scene, sirens wailing in all directions **[RPG2]**.

—June 13, 1968—9:15 PM
Seventy-five Brethren members surge forward and attack the convention center **[RPG2]**.

—June 13, 1968—After 9:15 PM
As security guards and crime-fighters attempt to restore normalcy, Nite Owl targets Brethren from the air via *Archimedes'* flame-throwers, sonic screechers, and water cannon. Fifteen

MIND .... *The Mindscape of Alan Moore*
MOBL.... *Watchmen: The Mobile Game*
MOTN.... *Watchmen: The Complete Motion Comic*
MTRO.... *Metro promotional newspaper cover wrap*
NEWP.... *New Frontiersman promotional newspaper*
NEWW... *New Frontiersman website*
NIGH ..... *Watchmen: The End Is Nigh, Parts 1 and 2*
PKIT...... *Watchmen film British press kit*
PORT..... *Watchmen Portraits*
REAL..... *Real life*
RPG1 .... *DC Heroes Role Playing Module #227: Who Watches the Watchmen?*

RPG2 .... *DC Heroes Role Playing Module #235: Taking Out the Trash—Curses and Tears*
RPG3 .... *DC Heroes: The Watchmen Sourcebook*
RUBY .... *"Wounds," published in The Ruby Files Volume One*
SCR1..... *Unfilmed screenplay draft: Sam Hamm*
SCR2..... *Unfilmed screenplay draft: Charles McKeuen*
SCR3..... *Unfilmed screenplay draft: Gary Goldman*
SCR4..... *Unfilmed screenplay draft: David Hayter (2002)*
SCR5..... *Unfilmed screenplay draft: David Hayter (2003)*
SCR6..... *Unfilmed screenplay draft: Alex Tse*
SPOT..... *DC Spotlight #1*
VRL1 ..... *Viral video: NBS Nightly News with Ted Philips*

VRL2..... *Viral video: The Keene Act and You*
VRL3 ..... *Viral video: Who Watches the Watchmen? A Veidt Music Network (VMN) Special*
VRL4 ..... *Viral video: World in Focus: 6 Minutes to Midnight*
VRL5 ..... *Viral video: Local Radio Station Report on 1977 Riots*
VRL6 ..... *Viral videos (group of ten): Veidt Enterprises Advertising Contest*
WAWA... *Watching the Watchmen*
WHOS ... *Who's Who: The Definitive Directory of the DC Universe*
WTFC .... *Watchmen: The Film Companion*

more cult members, disguised as National Guardsmen, attempt to enter the grounds, but the heroes spot Don Feroli in their truck, deduce that Ken Shade must be involved, and proceed to his campaign office **[RPG2]**.

The crime-fighters find Ken Shade bawling. Alongside him are Edgar Jacobi, bodyguards Sin and Temptation, and four other thugs. Moloch admits his role in the assassination attempt, and a brawl ends with the villains defeated and Moloch unconscious. In Jacobi's pocket, they find Gehenna's address: 2312 Division Avenue. At that stronghold, the heroes encounter several Brethren, are besieged by a huge pack of rats, rescue five kidnapping victims, and survive a gas attack that causes them to hallucinate a hostile crowd of diseased, rotted humans. Finally, they defeat The Brethren and apprehend Mother, who breaks down crying for her own mother **[RPG2]**.

Rorschach later records a journal entry maintaining that what his kind do is necessary because *someone* has to take out the trash **[RPG2]**.

—June 14, 1968—4:00 AM
After seven hours of rioting, the NYPD and the New York National Guard finally put an end to the violence. The riots result in eleven deaths and more than fourteen million dollars in damage **[RPG2]**.

—June 14, 1968—Morning
The *New York Gazette* publishes the final segment of Ben Richter's four-part special report on gang terror and The Brethren **[RPG2]**.

—June 14, 1968—7:30 AM
The masked adventurers convene at Montgomery Banner's police precinct office for a debriefing. On a nearby television, they watch as Richard Nixon receives the Republican Presidential nomination **[RPG2]**.
> **NOTE:** *In the real world, Nixon received the nomination on August 9, 1968.*

—June 15, 1968—6:12 AM (Estimated)
Dr. Manhattan and Laurie Juspeczyk see each other again, seventy-six hours and thirty-seven minutes after Dr. Manhattan's departure from the police station **[RPG2]**.

—June 16, 1968
The Republican National Convention concludes **[RPG2]**.

After June 1968

As punishment for his involvement in the Nixon assassination attempt, Senator Ken Shade is sentenced to thirty-five years in prison. Mother receives a thirty-year sentence, and The Brethren disband without her leadership **[RPG2]**.

September 1968

Edgar Jacobi's lawyers successfully argue his case, enabling him to get out of jail after only three months. Once back on the streets, he begins plotting revenge on those who put him behind bars **[RPG2]**.

October 1968

As part of an extremely complex corporate structure intended to obscure his plan to save mankind from nuclear war, Adrian Veidt uses his public spark hydrant royalties to form Pyramid Deliveries, a company that later funds the Institute for Extraspatial Studies—which, in turn, funds Dimensional Developments **[ALAN, RPG2]**. The company's Pyramid Transnational division operates out of Long Island City, N.Y. **[FILM]**.

> **NOTE:** *Alan Moore's miniseries establishes these events without dating them. The month and year of Pyramid Deliveries' formation appear in* Taking Out the Trash.

Adrian Veidt secretly purchases an island off the Mosquito Coast **[RPG2]**.

> **CONFLICT:** *In* Taking Out the Trash, *Veidt buys a Mosquito Coast island in October 1968, while* The Watchmen Sourcebook *has him purchasing Alguna Island from Ecuador on October 5, 1968, and* Before Watchmen: Ozymandias *depicts him acquiring another island in 1967. Each account is clearly meant to identify his island base from Alan Moore's miniseries, but that comic dates the island's purchase in 1970. It may be that Veidt requires four separate islands for his plan.*

October 5, 1968

Adrian Veidt, through purchase agent Worldwide Reality, buys Alguna Island from Ecuador. Simon Acquiare, Ecuador's minister of interior, signs the Certificate of Purchase **[RPG3]**.

> **NOTE:** *The island's naming is likely an in-joke, as "alguna" is Spanish for "any," making Veidt's secret base of operations "Any Island."*

November 5, 1968

Richard Nixon is elected to his first term of office as President of the United States, defeating Democrat nominee Hubert H. Humphrey. Nixon's Vice President is Gerald Ford, while Henry Kissinger is among his advisors **[REAL]**. Hollis Mason votes for Nixon, determined not to elect someone he views as a communist **[FILM]**.

MIND .... *The Mindscape of Alan Moore*
MOBL.... *Watchmen: The Mobile Game*
MOTN.... *Watchmen: The Complete Motion Comic*
MTRO.... *Metro* promotional newspaper cover wrap
NEWP.... *New Frontiersman* promotional newspaper
NEWW.. *New Frontiersman* website
NIGH ..... *Watchmen: The End Is Nigh, Parts 1 and 2*
PKIT...... *Watchmen* film British press kit
PORT..... *Watchmen Portraits*
REAL..... Real life
RPG1 .... *DC Heroes Role Playing Module #227: Who Watches the Watchmen?*

RPG2 .... *DC Heroes Role Playing Module #235: Taking Out the Trash—Curses and Tears*
RPG3 .... *DC Heroes: The Watchmen Sourcebook*
RUBY .... "Wounds," published in *The Ruby Files Volume One*
SCR1..... Unfilmed screenplay draft: Sam Hamm
SCR2..... Unfilmed screenplay draft: Charles McKeuen
SCR3..... Unfilmed screenplay draft: Gary Goldman
SCR4..... Unfilmed screenplay draft: David Hayter (2002)
SCR5..... Unfilmed screenplay draft: David Hayter (2003)
SCR6..... Unfilmed screenplay draft: Alex Tse
SPOT..... *DC Spotlight #1*
VRL1 ..... Viral video: *NBS Nightly News with Ted Philips*

VRL2 ..... Viral video: *The Keene Act and You*
VRL3 ..... Viral video: *Who Watches the Watchmen? A Veidt Music Network (VMN) Special*
VRL4 ..... Viral video: *World in Focus: 6 Minutes to Midnight*
VRL5 .... Viral video: *Local Radio Station Report on 1977 Riots*
VRL6 ..... Viral videos (group of ten): *Veidt Enterprises Advertising Contest*
WAWA... *Watching the Watchmen*
WHOS ... *Who's Who: The Definitive Directory of the DC Universe*
WTFC ... *Watchmen: The Film Companion*

—December 1968

While performing covert duties in Lik Dao, Eddie Blake sustains second-degree burns when a misfired flamethrower burns his chest and upper extremities. Dr. David Baines tends to Blake's injuries **[RPG3]**.

> **NOTE:** *There is no city called Lik Dao in the real world, which could indicate that the name was misspelled in* The Watchmen Sourcebook, *or that this city exists only in the fictional* Watchmen *reality.*

—Between 1968 and 1971

Adrian Veidt realizes that Dr. Manhattan must be eliminated as a threat in order for his plan to save mankind to succeed. Through Dimensional Developments, Veidt hires several former associates of Jon Osterman as his employees, including Wally Weaver, Janey Slater **[ALAN]**, and General Anthony Randolph **[FILM]**. Veidt slowly exposes them to radiation with the intention of giving them cancer, cultivating them as a future weapon to use against the superhuman **[ALAN]**.

> **CONFLICT:** *Taking Out the Trash dates Veidt's hiring of Jon's associates in July 1981, but this contradicts Alan Moore's miniseries, in which Wally dies in 1971.*

—Between 1968 and 1977

Abraham Lincoln's face on South Dakota's Mount Rushmore national monument is replaced with that of Richard Nixon **[VRL2]**.

—Between 1968 and 1985

To ensure that Dr. Manhattan will not foresee his plan to save the world, Adrian Veidt spends two billion dollars on tachyon research, hoping to block the superhuman's vision of the future **[FILM]**.

—In or Before 1969

Josef Osterman grows ill and is hospitalized. Since the watchmaker believes his son to be dead, Jon resists visiting him **[ALAN]**. When he eventually does so, the sight of a blue-skinned version of Jon makes his father recoil, and he leaves **[BWDM]**.

—1969

Josef Osterman passes away, after which Jon reveals his true identity to the public, no longer concerned with protecting his father's privacy **[ALAN]**.

Blair Roche is born to a blue-collar family, her father a bus driver **[ALAN]**.

A soldier named Joe Bird is dishonorably discharged from the U.S. military **[BWRO]**.

January 12, 1969

The *New York Gazette* publishes a front-page article about Dr. Manhattan, titled "He Is 'Awesome'" **[HOOD]**.

January 20, 1969

Richard Nixon is officially inaugurated into office as the 37th President of the United States **[REAL]**.

January 22, 1969

The Twilight Lady intercepts Richard Nixon's network feed as he delivers a state-of-the-union address. She replaces the feed in Seattle, Washington, with a video of herself in several erotic costumes, asking viewers which they prefer and making threats toward her rival criminals **[RPG3]**.

> **NOTE:** *In the real world, Richard Nixon gave his first state-of-the-union address in 1970. Lyndon B. Johnson delivered his last such address on January 14, 1969.*

> **CONFLICT:** *At this point, according to* The End Is Nigh, *The Twilight Lady should still be in prison. As such, she must arrange for this to happen from her cell.*

February 1969

While performing covert duties in Lik Dao, Eddie Blake contracts gonorrhea. Dr. Edward Ross tends to Blake's condition **[RPG3]**.

> **NOTE:** *There is no city called Lik Dao in the real world, which could indicate that the name was misspelled in* The Watchmen Sourcebook, *or that this city exists only in the fictional* Watchmen *reality.*

May 9, 1969

Dr. Manhattan's aides inform him that he is slated to be a guest on *The Martha Edwards Show*. He reacts in surprise, despite knowing his own future **[RPG3]**.

May 11, 1969

Dr. Manhattan appears on *The Martha Edwards Show*, where he discusses the nature of his powers, explaining that while he lives all points in his life simultaneously, he cannot alter the past or future. When asked if he knows the fate of his relationship with Laurie Juspeczyk, he surprises the audience (and Laurie) by replying that on October 19, 1985, at 6:35 PM, she will leave him for another man **[RPG3]**.

> **CONFLICT:** *During the interview, Dr. Manhattan recalls disassembling a rifle via telekinesis and displaying his powers to the world in 1958. However, Jon Osterman does not become a superhuman until 1959, and the government does not reveal his existence until 1960.*

MIND .... *The Mindscape of Alan Moore*	**RPG2** .... *DC Heroes Role Playing Module #235: Taking Out the Trash—Curses and Tears*	**VRL2** ..... Viral video: *The Keene Act and You*
MOBL.... *Watchmen: The Mobile Game*		**VRL3** ..... Viral video: *Who Watches the Watchmen? A Veidt Music Network (VMN) Special*
MOTN.... *Watchmen: The Complete Motion Comic*	**RPG3** .... *DC Heroes: The Watchmen Sourcebook*	
MTRO.... *Metro promotional newspaper cover wrap*	**RUBY** .... "Wounds," published in *The Ruby Files Volume One*	**VRL4** ..... Viral video: *World in Focus: 6 Minutes to Midnight*
NEWP ... *New Frontiersman promotional newspaper*	**SCR1**.....Unfilmed screenplay draft: Sam Hamm	**VRL5** ..... Viral video: *Local Radio Station Report on 1977 Riots*
NEWW... *New Frontiersman website*	**SCR2**.....Unfilmed screenplay draft: Charles McKeuen	
NIGH ..... *Watchmen: The End Is Nigh, Parts 1 and 2*	**SCR3**.....Unfilmed screenplay draft: Gary Goldman	**VRL6** ..... Viral videos (group of ten): *Veidt Enterprises Advertising Contest*
PKIT...... *Watchmen film British press kit*	**SCR4**.....Unfilmed screenplay draft: David Hayter (2002)	
PORT..... *Watchmen Portraits*	**SCR5**.....Unfilmed screenplay draft: David Hayter (2003)	**WAWA**... *Watching the Watchmen*
REAL.....Real life	**SCR6**.....Unfilmed screenplay draft: Alex Tse	**WHOS** ... *Who's Who: The Definitive Directory of the DC Universe*
RPG1 .... *DC Heroes Role Playing Module #227: Who Watches the Watchmen?*	**SPOT**.... *DC Spotlight #1*	
	VRL1 ..... Viral video: *NBS Nightly News with Ted Philips*	**WTFC** .... *Watchmen: The Film Companion*

What's more, although he correctly cites the date on which Laurie leaves him, their breakup occurs earlier than 6:35. Manhattan's memory is inexplicably faulty on these points. Perhaps it's due to the tachyons.

—May 12, 1969—11:46 AM

Dr. Manhattan performs gluino experiments **[RPG3]**.

—July 21, 1969

Neil A. Armstrong, an astronaut in NASA's *Apollo 11* mission, becomes the first human to step foot on Earth's moon. His fellow astronauts are Edwin "Buzz" Aldrin and Michael Collins **[REAL]**. Dr. Manhattan assists with the mission **[PKIT]**, arriving first to photograph the astronauts' landing **[FILM]**. Mission Control records several comments from Armstrong, including "That's one small step for Manhattan, one giant leap for mankind" **[VRL3]** and "Good luck, Mr. Gorsky" **[FILM]**.

> **NOTE:** *Armstrong's "Manhattan" comment subtly alters his real-world quote, "one small step for [a] man…" The Gorsky quote references a common urban legend that the astronaut, as a child, overheard his neighbor, Mrs. Gorsky, yelling to her husband, "Oral sex? Oral sex you want? You'll get oral sex when the kid next door walks on the moon!" According to Snopes.com, NASA transcripts prove Armstrong never said this.*

—Between 1969 and 1971

A plaque adorned with Richard Nixon's name is placed on Earth's moon **[ALAN]**.

> **NOTE:** *The date of this event is unknown. Since the first real-world spaceflight to land humans on the moon was Apollo 11, on July 20, 1969, the U.S. space program appears to have unfolded differently in the* Watchmen *universe. This makes sense, given the technological advancements enabled by Adrian Veidt and Dr. Manhattan.*

—Between 1969 and July 1977

Disgraced soldier Joe Bird pimps prostitutes and deals narcotics in New York City. During this period, he serves several stints in prison **[BWRO]**.

—Between the 1960s and 1985

Dan Dreiberg develops an interest in the music of such jazz and rhythm-and-blues performers as Billie Holiday, Nellie Lutcher, and Louis Jordan **[ALAN]**.

—Late 1960s to Early 1970s

Adrian Veidt exposes several plots by breakaway extremist factions within the Pentagon to release unpleasantly specific diseases upon the population of Africa. Outraged by Veidt's "unpatriotic" actions, *The New Frontiersman* denounces him as a "Puppet of Peking," referencing his youthful travels through the East **[ALAN]**.

ABSO .... *Watchmen Absolute Edition*
ALAN..... Alan Moore's *Watchmen* miniseries
ARCD .... *Minutemen Arcade*
ARTF..... *Watchmen: The Art of the Film*
BLCK..... *Tales of the Black Freighter*
BWCC ... *Before Watchmen—The Crimson Corsair*
BWCO ... *Before Watchmen—Comedian*
BWDB .. *Before Watchmen—Dollar Bill*
BWDM .. *Before Watchmen—Dr. Manhattan*
BWMM.. *Before Watchmen—Minutemen*
BWMO .. *Before Watchmen—Moloch*
BWNO ... *Before Watchmen—Nite Owl*

BWOZ.... *Before Watchmen—Ozymandias*
BWRO ... *Before Watchmen—Rorschach*
BWSS ... *Before Watchmen—Silk Spectre*
CHEM.... My Chemical Romance music video: "Desolation Row"
CMEO.... *Watchmen* cameos in comics, TV, and film:
• Comic: *Astonishing X-Men* volume 3 issue #6
• Comic: *Hero Hotline* volume 1 issue #5
• Comic: *Kingdom Come* volume 1 issue #2
• Comic: *Marvels* volume 1 issue #4
• Comic: *The Question* volume 1 issue #17
• TV: *Teen Titans Go!* episode #82, "Real Boy Adventures"
• Film: *Man of Steel*

• Film: *Batman v Superman: Dawn of Justice Ultimate Edition*
• Film: *Justice League*
CLIX ...... HeroClix figure pack-in cards
DECK..... *DC Comics Deck-Building Game—Crossover Pack 4: Watchmen*
DURS..... *DC Universe: Rebirth Special* volume 1 issue #1
FILM ..... *Watchmen* theatrical film
HOOD .... *Under the Hood* documentary and dust-jacket prop reproduction
JUST...... *Watchmen: Justice Is Coming*
MATL .... Mattel Club Black Freighter figure pack-in cards

U.S. police officers grow increasingly frustrated as costume-clad civilians are afforded glory, fame, and headlines for doing the same work as underappreciated and under-paid cops—and without facing the same watchdogging and rules as the police **[WTFC]**.

●—Long Before the 1980s

T.A. Crawford encounters an eagle owl in Norway. Another individual, Hudson, wounds a Magellanic eagle owl in Patagonia. Both writers document these incidents in published articles **[ALAN]**.

> **NOTE:** The publication dates of these articles are unknown, but they appear to have been written a long time before Dan Dreiberg reads them in 1983, given his description of them as "long-lost gems."

●—1970

The Gila Flats Test Base is shut down **[ALAN]**.

After serving two years in prison, The Twilight Lady is set free and moves to France, where she vanishes into obscurity **[RPG3]**.

> **CONFLICT:** The End Is Nigh, Part 2 *claims that The Twilight Lady serves nine years in prison, then resumes her pornography empire and eventually battles Rorschach and The Nite Owl, possibly dying in the process.*

On Laurie Juspeczyk's twentieth birthday, she and Jon Osterman move to a new apartment in Washington, D.C. **[ALAN]**. Although the superhuman's abilities enable him to carry out missions anywhere around the world, Laurie encourages the U.S. government to keep them on American soil **[CLIX]**.

> **CONFLICT:** *Laurie's birth year is a source of contradiction, as she is said to be born in 1949, yet turns twenty years old in 1970, when she should be turning twenty-one.*

Sally Jupiter attempts to visit Laurie Juspeczyk, but a government agent stops her from entering, saying she is not on the building's approved visitors list. Sally writes a letter to Laurie, warning that she's making a mistake in moving in with Dr. Manhattan, and urging her to contact Hollis Mason or Nelson Gardner to ask them about Jon's failed relationship with Janey Slater **[ALAN]**.

Adrian Veidt discreetly buys an island to conduct secret research with the long-term goal of saving mankind from nuclear war **[ALAN]**.

> **CONFLICT:** In Taking Out the Trash, *Veidt buys a Mosquito Coast island in October 1968, while* The Watchmen Sourcebook *has him purchasing Alguna Island from Ecuador on October 5, 1968, and* Before Watchmen: Ozymandias *depicts him acquiring another island in 1967. Each account is clearly meant to identify his island base from Alan Moore's*

miniseries, but that comic dates the island's purchase in 1970. It may be that Veidt requires four separate islands for his plan.

In recognition of meritorious service above and beyond the call of duty, Richard Nixon awards Eddie Blake a special pair of pistols emblazoned with his name, a smiley face, and the words "With Gratitude" on the grip. Blake displays them in a secret room in his apartment, along with his costume, newspaper clippings, and other items **[FILM]**.

NOTE: *A prop replica of the guns was released commercially as a tie-in to the* Watchmen *film.*

—February 1970

While performing covert duties in Lik Dao, Eddie Blake sustains a gunshot wound, requiring the removal of a .22-caliber bullet from his left thigh. Dr. Edward Ross tends to Blake's injuries **[RPG3]**.

> **NOTE:** *There is no city called Lik Dao in the real world, which could indicate that the name was misspelled in* The Watchmen Sourcebook, *or that this city exists only in the fictional* Watchmen *reality.*

—February 18, 1970

After a life of crime, Edgar Jacobi is finally imprisoned **[ALAN]**, on the same day that the "Chicago Seven" are acquitted. *The Boston Globe* runs a cover story on the mobster's capture, titled "The Comedian Gets the Last Laugh on Moloch" **[FILM]**. The warden taunts him that he'll never leave the prison alive **[BWMO]**.

> **NOTE:** *Alan Moore's miniseries sets Moloch's downfall in 1970. A news clipping in the* Watchmen *film establishes the actual date.*
>
> *Following anti-Vietnam War protests held at the time of the 1968 Democratic National Convention, the so-called "Chicago Seven" (Rennie Davis, David Dellinger, John Froines, Tom Hayden, Abbie Hoffman, Jerry Rubin, and Lee Weiner) were charged with conspiracy, inciting to riot, and other charges, but were found not guilty.*

—March 11, 1970—6:00 PM

NBS Nightly News airs a special report recalling ten years of Dr. Manhattan, co-anchored by Jim Sizemore and Ted Philips. Sizemore interviews passersby on the street, and the responses from both young and old are glowingly positive, with several using the pop-culture slogan "Better blue than red" **[VRL1]**, inspired by Manhattan's distinctive skin color and success in battling communists **[MTRO]**. Sizemore notes that the crime-fighter has been in recent talks with Richard Nixon, and ponders whether he could be the key to ending the Vietnam War **[VRL1]**.

May 4, 1970

The Ohio National Guard, in what will later be dubbed the Kent State Massacre, fires on a crowd of unarmed students at Kent State University protesting Richard Nixon's announcement of the Cambodian incursion during the Vietnam War. Four students die **[REAL]**, including a young woman placing a flower in a soldier's rifle barrel. Several protestors carry signs, including one bearing the slogan "Nixon Needs Fixin'" **[FILM]**.

> **NOTE:** *The slogan mocks an actual campaign phrase from that era, "The Country Needs Fixin'—Elect Nixon."*

May 22, 1970

President Richard Nixon, under advisement of the Secretary of Defense and the Offices of National Security, issues an Executive Order authorizing Operation Wrath of God, to strategically utilize Dr. Manhattan to ensure a swift, irrefutable victory in Vietnam. A badge is created for troops assigned to this operation, combining the motifs of The Comedian and Dr. Manhattan, including a blue-skinned smiley face emblazoned with a hydrogen atom symbol and the words "Comedy" and "Tragedy" **[NEWW]**. Among the pilots involved is Bill "The Kid" Dalgleish **[ARTF]**.

> **NOTE:** *Despite the order being issued in May 1970, Dr. Manhattan does not intervene in the war until almost a year later.*
>
> *The pilot is named after William Dalgliesh, a camera operator who worked on the* Watchmen *film.*

In or After 1970

The Twilight Lady returns to prison **[NIGH]**.

> **NOTE:** *This is conjectural, to reconcile a discrepancy.* The Watchmen Sourcebook *depicts the madam as serving prison time from 1968 to 1970 and then vanishing to France, whereas* The End Is Nigh *sees her still behind bars until 1977.*

Between 1970 and 1985

Veidt's teleportation experiments achieve only limited success, for without the guiding hand of Dr. Manhattan, anything living dies of shock upon transfer, or else materializes in an occupied space and explodes **[ALAN]**.

Although Adrian Veidt rarely brings Bubastis along on his travels (and when he does, it is typically to important fundraisers), his pet becomes quite well-known **[CLIX]**.

1970 to 1985

As the world changes, Dan Dreiberg loses some of his idealism and, in the process, his self-confidence **[ALAN]**.

Part IX:
WHO WATCHES THE WATCHMEN?
(1971–1976)

—January 4, 1971

President Richard Nixon asks Jon Osterman to intervene in the Vietnam War [**ALAN, RPG2**], then announces his plan to the American public. Watching the broadcast from Karnak, Adrian Veidt realizes there is no turning back now from the path toward war, and from the need to carry out his master plan [**BWOZ**].

>**CONFLICT:** *An article published on the* New Frontiersman *website—"Soviets Call Dr. M. 'Imperialist Weapon,'" by Allen Wynder—cites the U.S.S.R.'s complaints about Dr. Manhattan intervening in Vietnam, and quotes Soviet Foreign Minister Andrei Gromyko as condemning U.S. domination. However, that article (which also appears in the film) is dated June 19, 1970, which is half a year before Nixon asks Manhattan to do so in Alan Moore's miniseries, and four years after the "imperialist weapon" comment occurs in the comic.*

—January to March 1971

The U.S. Congress considers Richard Nixon's plan to send Dr. Manhattan to Vietnam [**BWOZ**].

—Early 1971

A U.S. military unit in Vietnam ends up missing in action while trying to locate an enemy landing area. The Comedian is assigned to find the unit, confirm intel of a helicopter gunship ferrying reinforcements for the Đặc Công (Vietnamese Special Forces), and dispose of all hostiles within the vicinity. Blake carries out his mission, killing many enemy soldiers (and noncombatants) in the process. Rescuing the U.S. troops, he scorches an entire village to punish them for covering for the Việt Cộng [**MOBL**].

—March 1971

Once Nixon secures approval from Congress [**BWOZ**], Jon Osterman travels to Saigon to intervene in the Vietnam War. There, he is reunited with The Comedian [**ALAN**], who

is surprised when Dr. Manhattan suddenly appears on the battlefield. Blake calls this development "the big blue man versus the big red menace." An officer named Charlie dispatches Osterman to deal with larger-scale strategic attacks while Blake infiltrates an enemy command center guarding a secret project **[MOBL]**.

During their time working together, The Comedian tries to rile up Dr. Manhattan by needling him about his dating a much younger woman **[MOBL]**. Jon finds the man's deliberate amorality interesting **[ALAN]**, and leaves the vigilante to battle soldiers on his own while Jon floats through the air, addressing more important matters. After blowing up a tank, Blake smiles for photographers despite frustration at his blue comrade's lack of ground assistance **[MOBL]**.

—March to May 1971

For two months, Jon Osterman uses his mental abilities to decimate the Việt Cộng forces, increasing his size to giant proportions and destroying enemy vehicles with a mere thought. Ultimately, many of the Việt Cộng soldiers surrender directly to him, their terror balanced by an almost religious reverence **[ALAN]**.

> **CONFLICT:** *In the* Watchmen *film, as well as in the movie's British press kit, the war only lasts for another week once Manhattan enters the conflict, contradicting Alan Moore's miniseries.*

During Operation Wrath of God, French photojournalist Alain Guillon captures images of Dr. Manhattan grown to enormous size and decimating Việt Cộng forces. Guillon is awed by the superhuman's power, yet terrified by his lack of emotional reaction to the mass destruction that he causes. The journalist also photographs The Comedian, whom he considers a monster. Guillon's photos are widely deemed among the defining images of the Vietnam War **[VRL4]**.

—April 16, 1971

Adrian Veidt submits articles of incorporation to New York State for Luxor Imports, Inc., registered to Dimensional Developments, Inc. Adrian names Leo Winston CEO, Dimensional Developments a principal owner, and Leroy Gibbons treasurer **[RPG3]**.

—May 1971

The U.S. government predicts that the Việt Cộng will surrender within a week **[ALAN]**.

—In or Before June 1971

The Comedian impregnates a young Vietnamese woman **[ALAN]** named Liao Lin **[SCR4, SCR5]**.

—June 1971

The war lasts a few weeks longer than expected, finally ending when Dr. Manhattan decimates the Việt Cộng's guerilla forces by molecularly restructuring the jungles in which they hide into noxious gases **[RPG3]**.

—Before June 29, 1971

A soldier named Tyson serves in the Vietnam War. A fellow soldier saves his life on several occasions, but ends up with his face badly burned, earning the nickname "Rawhead" **[BWRO]**.
> *NOTE: These events are undated, but must occur before the war ends.*

—June 29, 1971—Night

North Vietnam officially surrenders to the United States **[RPG3]**. Tôn Đức Thắng, President of the Democratic Republic of Vietnam, signs an Act of Military Surrender in the presence of Creighton Williams Abrams, head of the U.S. Military Assistance Command in Vietnam. The surrender is unconditional, with Vietnam agreeing to cease all hostilities, liberate all prisoners of war and civilian internees, and hand over all control and authority to Richard Nixon **[NEWW]**.
> *NOTE: Thắng was North Vietnam's second and final president in the real world, and the Socialist Republic of Vietnam's first president under Lê Duẩn.*

The Vietnam War ends with the United States victorious, and locals and troops celebrate Victory in Vietnam (V.V.N.) Night. The Comedian and Dr. Manhattan watch the revelry from inside the Saigon Officer's Club, discussing the war and their role in it. Blake considers the whole thing a joke. Richard Nixon arrives via helicopter to congratulate the troops, and to use the ceasefire and the presence of the press to secure his re-election **[ALAN]**.
> *NOTE: In the real world, without Dr. Manhattan's involvement, the Vietnam War ended on April 30, 1975.*

> *CONFLICT: Taking Out the Trash places Vietnam's surrender on February 1, 1971, while an Act of Military Surrender document created for the New Frontiersman website sets it on June 22, 1970. Both dates contradict Alan Moore's miniseries.*

As Eddie Blake awaits a helicopter ride back to the United States, Liao Lin confronts him **[SCR4, SCR5]**. Furious at his decision to abandon her, their unborn baby, and Vietnam, she slashes Blake's face with a bottle, for which he guns her down. Dr. Manhattan does nothing to stop him—which Blake points out when the superhuman condemns the murder **[ALAN]**. Dr. Edward Ross repairs Blake's facial lacerations, administering seventy-one stitches **[RPG3]**, but the resultant scar is permanent **[ALAN, FILM]**.
> *CONFLICT: The Watchmen Sourcebook sets Blake's injury in February 1971, contradicting Alan Moore's miniseries, in which V.V.N. Night takes place in June.*

MIND .... *The Mindscape of Alan Moore*
MOBL.... *Watchmen: The Mobile Game*
MOTN.... *Watchmen: The Complete Motion Comic*
MTRO.... *Metro* promotional newspaper cover wrap
NEWP.... *New Frontiersman* promotional newspaper
NEWW... *New Frontiersman* website
NIGH ..... *Watchmen: The End Is Nigh, Parts 1 and 2*
PKIT ...... *Watchmen* film British press kit
PORT ..... *Watchmen Portraits*
REAL ..... Real life
RPG1 .... *DC Heroes Role Playing Module #227: Who Watches the Watchmen?*

RPG2 .... *DC Heroes Role Playing Module #235: Taking Out the Trash—Curses and Tears*
RPG3 .... *DC Heroes: The Watchmen Sourcebook*
RUBY .... "Wounds," published in *The Ruby Files Volume One*
SCR1 ..... Unfilmed screenplay draft: Sam Hamm
SCR2 ..... Unfilmed screenplay draft: Charles McKeuen
SCR3 ..... Unfilmed screenplay draft: Gary Goldman
SCR4 ..... Unfilmed screenplay draft: David Hayter (2002)
SCR5 ..... Unfilmed screenplay draft: David Hayter (2003)
SCR6 ..... Unfilmed screenplay draft: Alex Tse
SPOT .... *DC Spotlight #1*
VRL1 ..... Viral video: *NBS Nightly News with Ted Philips*

VRL2 ..... Viral video: *The Keene Act and You*
VRL3 ..... Viral video: *Who Watches the Watchmen? A Veidt Music Network (VMN) Special*
VRL4 ..... Viral video: *World in Focus: 6 Minutes to Midnight*
VRL5 ..... Viral video: *Local Radio Station Report on 1977 Riots*
VRL6 ..... Viral videos (group of ten): *Veidt Enterprises Advertising Contest*
WAWA... *Watching the Watchmen*
WHOS .. *Who's Who: The Definitive Directory of the DC Universe*
WTFC .... *Watchmen: The Film Companion*

—After June 29, 1971

In the wake of the Vietnam War, the rest of the world grows terrified of the United States—and, specifically, of Dr. Manhattan **[BWOZ]**.

After June 29, 1971 (Alternate Reality)

In a quantum reality in which Jon Osterman never becomes Dr. Manhattan, The Comedian does not shoot Liao Lin. She delivers Blake's child, and he proudly holds the infant in his arms **[BWDM]**.

—June 30, 1971

The *New York Gazette* reports on North Vietnam's unconditional surrender **[RPG3]**.

—Between July 1971 and July 1977

After Rawhead's tour of duty in Vietnam ends, he decides to live up to the ugliness of his war-scarred face by becoming a criminal kingpin, operating out of a New York City nightclub called The Paradise Inferno. Joe Bird begins working for his organization as a drug pusher and pimp, as does Rawhead's Vietnam War buddy, Tyson **[BWRO]**.

—July 1, 1971

Eddie Blake is court-martialed for killing Liao Lin. To keep his identity a secret, members of the Joint Chiefs of Staff conduct the trial privately. He admits to the shooting, but claims it was in self-defense since she was attacking him **[RPG3]**.

Two days after V.V.N. Night, *Newsworld* quotes The Comedian as expressing relief at how the Vietnam War ended, since Americans' morale might have been damaged had the United States lost the war **[RPG3]**.

> *NOTE: The Watchmen Sourcebook dates the Newsworld article on February 4, 1971, contradicting Alan Moore's miniseries, which sets V.V.N. Night in June.*

—Mid-1971

Three years into his prison sentence, Ken Shade writes a book about his role in the failed assassination of Richard Nixon in 1968, titled *Sell Your Soul* **[RPG2]**.

—September 11, 1971

The Joint Chiefs of Staff, presiding over Eddie Blake's court-martial for killing an unarmed civilian in Saigon, dismiss all charges, citing a lack of evidence **[RPG3]**.

ABSO .... *Watchmen Absolute Edition*
ALAN..... Alan Moore's *Watchmen* miniseries
ARCD .... *Minutemen Arcade*
ARTF..... *Watchmen: The Art of the Film*
BLCK..... *Tales of the Black Freighter*
BWCC ... *Before Watchmen—The Crimson Corsair*
BWCO ... *Before Watchmen—Comedian*
BWDB .. *Before Watchmen—Dollar Bill*
BWDM .. *Before Watchmen—Dr. Manhattan*
BWMM.. *Before Watchmen—Minutemen*
BWMO .. *Before Watchmen—Moloch*
BWNO ... *Before Watchmen—Nite Owl*

BWOZ.... *Before Watchmen—Ozymandias*
BWRO ... *Before Watchmen—Rorschach*
BWSS ... *Before Watchmen—Silk Spectre*
CHEM.... My Chemical Romance music video: "Desolation Row"
CMEO.... *Watchmen* cameos in comics, TV, and film:
 • Comic: *Astonishing X-Men* volume 3 issue #6
 • Comic: *Hero Hotline* volume 1 issue #5
 • Comic: *Kingdom Come* volume 1 issue #2
 • Comic: *Marvels* volume 1 issue #4
 • Comic: *The Question* volume 1 issue #17
 • TV: *Teen Titans Go!* episode #82, "Real Boy Adventures"
 • Film: *Man of Steel*

 • Film: *Batman v Superman: Dawn of Justice Ultimate Edition*
 • Film: *Justice League*
CLIX ...... HeroClix figure pack-in cards
DECK..... *DC Comics Deck-Building Game—Crossover Pack 4: Watchmen*
DURS .... *DC Universe: Rebirth Special* volume 1 issue #1
FILM ..... *Watchmen* theatrical film
HOOD .... *Under the Hood* documentary and dust-jacket prop reproduction
JUST ..... *Watchmen: Justice Is Coming*
MATL .... Mattel Club Black Freighter figure pack-in cards

Before November 1971

Wally Weaver writes a book about how Dr. Manhattan has forever changed the geopolitical landscape by essentially making the idea of war obsolete **[HOOD]**.

November 1971

Wally Weaver dies of stomach cancer **[BWDM]** at age thirty-four. His death is sudden and painful **[ALAN]**.

> **CONFLICT:** *In the* Under the Hood *documentary, Weaver is alive and working alongside Dr. Manhattan in 1975. The* Watchmen *film sets his death on February 12, 1981, and a timeline published in* The Film Companion *reiterates the 1981 dating. These accounts contradict Alan Moore's miniseries, in which Wally dies in 1971.*

In or After 1971

Following the war, a purging takes place in Vietnam in which many die. Adrian Veidt hires three Vietnamese refugees to work as servants at his Karnak fortress in Antarctica. The men are grateful for his intervention, knowing they would likely have died otherwise, and remain happy and loyal employees. Veidt treats them more as friends than as workers, taking time to learn about their culture and language **[ALAN]**.

During a speech, Richard Nixon inadvertently refers to Dr. Manhattan as "God." This, combined with Manhattan's activities during the Vietnam War, results in growing hostility in the United States toward costumed crime-fighters. The radical left begins staging anti-hero demonstrations on college campuses, and ex-Beatle John Lennon and Yoko Ono record "The Forgotten Victims of Dr. Manhattan," an elegy for refugees of the Vietnam War. The song reaches number-one on national singles charts **[RPG2]**.

Walter "The Screaming Skull" Zileski finishes a twenty-year jail sentence, then moves to Queens, N.Y., gives up crime, and enters the insurance field **[RPG3]**. The former villain reforms and embraces Christianity, then marries and fathers two children **[ALAN]**.

In or Before 1972

Arms dealer Jimmy the Gimmick, who supplies weapons to thugs, government black-ops teams, and anyone else who will pay, establishes a lair at an abandoned amusement park waiting to be torn down in New York City's industrial dockland area. Morten's Moorage and Veidt Enterprises each build facilities in the dockland area, not far from that same amusement park **[NIGH]**.

A brand of beer called Bisons is introduced **[NIGH]**.

MIND .... *The Mindscape of Alan Moore*
MOBL .... *Watchmen: The Mobile Game*
MOTN .... *Watchmen: The Complete Motion Comic*
MTRO .... *Metro* promotional newspaper cover wrap
NEWP .... *New Frontiersman* promotional newspaper
NEWW ... *New Frontiersman* website
NIGH .... *Watchmen: The End Is Nigh, Parts 1 and 2*
PKIT ...... *Watchmen* film British press kit
PORT ..... *Watchmen Portraits*
REAL ..... Real life
RPG1 .... *DC Heroes Role Playing Module #227: Who Watches the Watchmen?*

RPG2 .... *DC Heroes Role Playing Module #235: Taking Out the Trash—Curses and Tears*
RPG3 .... *DC Heroes: The Watchmen Sourcebook*
RUBY .... "Wounds," published in *The Ruby Files Volume One*
SCR1 ..... Unfilmed screenplay draft: Sam Hamm
SCR2 ..... Unfilmed screenplay draft: Charles McKeuen
SCR3 ..... Unfilmed screenplay draft: Gary Goldman
SCR4 ..... Unfilmed screenplay draft: David Hayter (2002)
SCR5 ..... Unfilmed screenplay draft: David Hayter (2003)
SCR6 ..... Unfilmed screenplay draft: Alex Tse
SPOT ..... *DC Spotlight #1*
VRL1 ..... Viral video: *NBS Nightly News with Ted Philips*

VRL2 ..... Viral video: *The Keene Act and You*
VRL3 ..... Viral video: *Who Watches the Watchmen? A Veidt Music Network (VMN) Special*
VRL4 ..... Viral video: *World in Focus: 6 Minutes to Midnight*
VRL5 ..... Viral video: *Local Radio Station Report on 1977 Riots*
VRL6 ..... Viral videos (group of ten): *Veidt Enterprises Advertising Contest*
WAWA ... *Watching the Watchmen*
WHOS .... *Who's Who: The Definitive Directory of the DC Universe*
WTFC .... *Watchmen: The Film Companion*

1972

John David Keene, a Republican from New York, is elected that state's senator **[NEWW]**.

> **NOTE:** *In Gary Goldman's unproduced 1992 screenplay, Keene serves as Wisconsin's senator.*

Moloch arranges for the luxury liner *Queen Elizabeth II* to be hijacked **[WTFC]**.

> **NOTE:** *Alan Moore's miniseries establishes that Moloch spends the 1970s in prison. Presumably, he arranges the hijacking from his cell, via intermediaries.*

March 5, 1972

John Ehrlichman issues a check to Eddie Blake for fifty thousand dollars, drawn from a National Bank of New York account. The check's memo line reads "Creep Payment" **[RPG3]**.

> **NOTE:** *Richard Nixon's real-world re-election campaign was the Committee for the Re-Election of the President. Nixon's team used the acronym C.R.P., but others noted that it could also be abbreviated as C.R.E.E.P. Ehrlichman, Nixon's counsel, later played a key role in the Watergate scandal, for which he was sent to prison for conspiracy, perjury, and obstruction of justice.*

March 24, 1972

Francis Ford Coppola's crime-drama film *The Godfather* is commercially released in U.S. theaters. Based on Mario Puzo's best-selling novel, the movie stars Marlon Brando and Al Pacino as Vito and Michael Corleone, the leaders of a powerful New York crime family **[REAL]**. Brando bases his Oscar-winning performance on the persona of mob leader Anthony "Underboss" Rizzoli **[RPG3]**.

June 17, 1972

Five men are arrested for breaking and entering into the Democratic National Committee (DNC) headquarters at the Watergate office complex in Washington, D.C. The FBI finds a possible connection to Richard Nixon's campaign, the Committee for the Re-Election of the President **[REAL]**.

After June 17, 1972

Washington Post reporters Robert Woodward and Carl Bernstein investigate the Watergate scandal but are fired for their efforts. Their termination does not halt their efforts to expose the President's involvement, however. Rorschach dismisses the two journalists as paranoid conspiracy theorists **[NIGH]**.

> **NOTE:** *Rorschach's opinion of Woodward and Bernstein is rather ironic, given that he is an avid reader of the* New Frontiersman.

September 11, 1972

Dan Dreiberg finishes constructing a lightweight anti-radiation suit designed to mimic his standard Nite Owl costume, capable of withstanding intense radiation for up to five hours. The suit costs $30,000 to build and is colored orange for quick retrieval **[RPG3]**.

In or Before October 1972

A bar called Rumrunner opens in New York City. The establishment is frequented by ex-convicts and features performances by local bands **[ALAN, NIGH]**.

Construction begins on the Institute for Extraspatial Studies, in Manhattan **[NIGH]**.

A nihilistic youth gang, the Knot-Tops, forms in New York City, rapidly spreading from the docks throughout the entire area **[NIGH]**. Naming themselves after their samurai-like hairstyle **[WTFC]**, the Knot-Tops roam the streets vandalizing property, robbing people, selling illicit drugs, and otherwise causing trouble **[NIGH]**. The gang's hairdo and fashion sense permeate U.S. urban culture, even among non-members. The disaffected Knot-Tops reject authority figures, particularly costumed vigilantes, and often indulge in KT-28s ("katies"), 'luudes, and other street drugs **[WTFC]**. Armed with switchblades and Saturday-night specials, they become New York City's sole distributor of the highly addictive KT-28s **[CLIX]**.

> **NOTE:** *Knot-Tops appear in* The End Is Nigh, *set in October 1972, so the gang's formation must occur before that game's events. Gary Goldman's unproduced 1992 screenplay changes their name to "Topknots."*
>
> *KT-28 is a successor to KT-5, a street drug created circa 1966 by a drug maker called Mr. Owsley, in* Before Watchmen: Silk Spectre. *The "KT" in the drugs' names, according to that miniseries, is short for "Kesey Test," a reference to* One Flew Over the Cuckoo's Nest *author Ken Kesey, a prominent countercultural figure in the 1960s.*
>
> *Despite the different spellings, "'luudes" is likely short for "Quaalude," a brand name of sedative and hypnotic medication.*

October 1972

The bands Press Play on Tape, The Seawolves, Over Done, and DS Runners perform at New York City bar Rumrunner **[NIGH]**.

> **NOTE:** *These bands are identified on posters hanging on several walls.*

Before October 13, 1972

Washington Post reporters Robert Woodward and Carl Bernstein uncover evidence exposing Richard Nixon's involvement in a burglary of the Democratic National Committee

MIND .... *The Mindscape of Alan Moore*
MOBL .... *Watchmen: The Mobile Game*
MOTN .... *Watchmen: The Complete Motion Comic*
MTRO .... *Metro promotional newspaper cover wrap*
NEWP .... *New Frontiersman promotional newspaper*
NEWW .... *New Frontiersman website*
NIGH ..... *Watchmen: The End Is Nigh, Parts 1 and 2*
PKIT ...... *Watchmen film British press kit*
PORT ..... *Watchmen Portraits*
REAL ..... *Real life*
RPG1 .... *DC Heroes Role Playing Module #227: Who Watches the Watchmen?*

RPG2 .... *DC Heroes Role Playing Module #235: Taking Out the Trash—Curses and Tears*
RPG3 .... *DC Heroes: The Watchmen Sourcebook*
RUBY .... *"Wounds," published in* The Ruby Files Volume One
SCR1 ..... Unfilmed screenplay draft: Sam Hamm
SCR2 ..... Unfilmed screenplay draft: Charles McKeuen
SCR3 ..... Unfilmed screenplay draft: Gary Goldman
SCR4 ..... Unfilmed screenplay draft: David Hayter (2002)
SCR5 ..... Unfilmed screenplay draft: David Hayter (2003)
SCR6 ..... Unfilmed screenplay draft: Alex Tse
SPOT ..... *DC Spotlight #1*
VRL1 ..... Viral video: *NBS Nightly News with Ted Philips*

VRL2 ..... Viral video: *The Keene Act and You*
VRL3 ..... Viral video: *Who Watches the Watchmen? A Veidt Music Network (VMN) Special*
VRL4 ..... Viral video: *World in Focus: 6 Minutes to Midnight*
VRL5 ..... Viral video: *Local Radio Station Report on 1977 Riots*
VRL6 ..... Viral videos (group of ten): *Veidt Enterprises Advertising Contest*
WAWA .... *Watching the Watchmen*
WHOS ... *Who's Who: The Definitive Directory of the DC Universe*
WTFC .... *Watchmen: The Film Companion*

headquarters in Washington, D.C.'s Watergate office complex **[RPG2]**.

> **NOTE:** *In the real world, the two journalists provided much of the original news reporting on the Watergate burglary, culminating in Nixon's resignation.*

> **CONFLICT:** Taking Out the Trash *actually sets this in January 1973, but since they die in October 1972 in* The End Is Nigh, *that dating must be discarded.*

●—October 13, 1972

Eddie Blake abducts Mark Felt, associate director of the FBI, and brings him down to Underboss's former hideout in New York City's sewer. Blake tortures Felt to learn the locations of Bob Woodward and Carl Bernstein so he can prevent the reporters from exposing Richard Nixon's role in the Watergate scandal. He then hires Jimmy the Gimmick to help Underboss escape from Sing Sing Correctional Facility so he can murder the journalists and frame the kingpin for the crime **[NIGH]**.

> **NOTE:** *Mark Felt, using the name "Deep Throat," was an informant to Woodward and Bernstein during their Watergate investigation.*

●—October 19, 1972

The *New York Gazette* covers Mark Felt's disappearance in a front-page story, alongside another article titled "Nixon Leads McGovern By 10 Points, Re-election Almost Certain" **[NIGH]**.

> **NOTE:** *In the real world, George McGovern ran for President in 1972 as the Democratic nominee, losing to Nixon.*

When a cyclone threatens Sri Lanka, Dr. Manhattan teleports to that country to deal with the danger, accompanied by Silk Spectre **[NIGH]**.

Jimmy the Gimmick helps Underboss escape from Sing Sing by sabotaging the prison's power grid, causing a blackout that allows the inmates to riot. The arms dealer arranges for hardware to be delivered to Underboss's sewer hideout, playing into Eddie Blake's plan to frame him for the reporters' murders **[NIGH]**.

As Dan Dreiberg repairs *Archimedes* in his underground workshop, a police bulletin announces the riot at Sing Sing. He and Rorschach board *Archie* and head for the prison. The warden denies permission to land, but they enter the complex anyway, make their way to the backup generator, and leave a bloody trail of inmates as they investigate fires and explosions. The city restores power and guards return the prisoners to their cells, but Underboss has escaped. Rorschach and Dreiberg head for Rumrunner, a bar frequented by ex-convicts **[NIGH]**.

Dr. Manhattan and Sally Jupiter prevent an airplane carrying a Uruguayan rugby team from crashing in the Andes. Ozymandias, meanwhile, captures The King of Skin. Television reporter Jody Kramer interviews Veidt following the arrest **[NIGH]**.

October 19 (Late Night) to October 20 (Early Morning), 1972

Archimedes lands a few blocks from Rumrunner. Dreiberg and Rorschach make their way through a series of allies, battle hordes of biker thugs, and intimidate a bar patron into revealing Jimmy the Gimmick's involvement in Underboss's escape. They visit the industrial dockland area, fight several Knot-Tops, and find Jimmy in the amusement park. Cornering him atop The Rollercoaster, they learn that Underboss is back in his former hideout. Eddie Blake, unseen, cuts the ride's cable, causing the coaster—and Jimmy—to plummet off the tracks. Jimmy survives but is badly injured **[NIGH]**.

Dreiberg calls for an ambulance for Jimmy, then he and Rorschach take to the sewers to search for Underboss. Battling armored mercenaries throughout the sewer system, they find Mark Felt, the FBI's missing associate director, badly beaten and tied to a chair. Felt tells them that his captor plans to murder Robert Woodward and Carl Bernstein, but dies before he can identify the killer, Eddie Blake. Police confront the crime-fighters outside the sewer, and they realize they've been set up. With little choice, they fight the cops so they can stop the assassination and find Underboss **[NIGH]**.

October 20, 1972—3:00 AM

Eddie Blake assassinates Robert Woodward and Carl Bernstein at a construction site on 39th and Charlton, then hides their bodies in the trunk of Underboss's car **[NIGH]**.

> **NOTE:** *Charlton pays homage to Charlton Comics, on whose characters Alan Moore based his* Watchmen *heroes.*

> **CONFLICT:** *The* Watchmen *film and the* New Frontiersman *website both place the murders on November 5, 1973, contradicting Moore's comic, in which they are already dead before January 1973.*

October 20, 1972—After 3:00 AM

Dreiberg and Rorschach find a flamethrower-wielding Underboss at the construction site of the future Institute for Extraspatial Studies. The escapee discovers the corpses of Woodward and Bernstein inside the trunk of his car, but denies any involvement in their murders, saying he hasn't been back to his hideout. The heroes pursue him throughout the site, culminating in a standoff on the roof. Before Underboss can expose The Comedian's scheme, Blake shoots him from a nearby building, causing the mobster to plummet several stories to the ground. Underboss survives, but remains in a coma **[NIGH]**.

MIND .... *The Mindscape of Alan Moore*
MOBL .... *Watchmen: The Mobile Game*
MOTN .... *Watchmen: The Complete Motion Comic*
MTRO .... *Metro* promotional newspaper cover wrap
NEWP .... *New Frontiersman* promotional newspaper
NEWW .... *New Frontiersman* website
NIGH .... *Watchmen: The End Is Nigh, Parts 1 and 2*
PKIT .... *Watchmen* film British press kit
PORT .... *Watchmen Portraits*
REAL .... Real life
RPG1 .... *DC Heroes Role Playing Module #227: Who Watches the Watchmen?*

RPG2 .... *DC Heroes Role Playing Module #235: Taking Out the Trash—Curses and Tears*
RPG3 .... *DC Heroes: The Watchmen Sourcebook*
RUBY .... "Wounds," published in *The Ruby Files Volume One*
SCR1 .... Unfilmed screenplay draft: Sam Hamm
SCR2 .... Unfilmed screenplay draft: Charles McKeuen
SCR3 .... Unfilmed screenplay draft: Gary Goldman
SCR4 .... Unfilmed screenplay draft: David Hayter (2002)
SCR5 .... Unfilmed screenplay draft: David Hayter (2003)
SCR6 .... Unfilmed screenplay draft: Alex Tse
SPOT .... *DC Spotlight #1*
VRL1 .... Viral video: *NBS Nightly News with Ted Philips*

VRL2 .... Viral video: *The Keene Act and You*
VRL3 .... Viral video: *Who Watches the Watchmen? A Veidt Music Network (VMN) Special*
VRL4 .... Viral video: *World in Focus: 6 Minutes to Midnight*
VRL5 .... Viral video: *Local Radio Station Report on 1977 Riots*
VRL6 .... Viral videos (group of ten): *Veidt Enterprises Advertising Contest*
WAWA .... *Watching the Watchmen*
WHOS .... *Who's Who: The Definitive Directory of the DC Universe*
WTFC .... *Watchmen: The Film Companion*

October 21, 1972

Bob Woodward and Carl Bernstein miss a scheduled speaking engagement at Columbia University, at which they had planned to reveal information exposing Richard Nixon's involvement in the Watergate break-in **[NIGH]**.

> **NOTE:** *The deaths of Woodward and Bernstein in the* Watchmen *universe prevent Nixon from being disgraced, enabling him to remain in office for five terms.*

After October 21, 1972

Eddie Blake leaves the reporters' bullet-ridden corpses in the Key-Bridge underground garage in which they regularly met with informant "Deep Throat." Schoolgirl Rebecca Scorer finds their bodies and alerts police. An unidentified man is spotted fleeing the scene of the crime. Residents report having noticed the journalists there on a regular basis, leading some to speculate about the nature of their partnership. Their rumored research into a major scandal is never discovered **[NEWW]**.

Members of the underground press deem the double-murders suspicious, and the *Berkeley Barb* publishes an article suggesting a conspiracy **[ALAN]**. The *Wall Street Post*, in its coverage, quotes *Washington Times* editor Benjamin Bradlee as saying that their deaths have left the journalistic world "shaken to the core" **[NEWW]**.

November 7, 1972

Richard Nixon is re-elected for a second term of office as President of the United States. His Vice President remains Gerald Ford, while Henry Kissinger continues to serve among his advisors **[REAL]**. Hollis Mason again votes for him **[FILM]**.

November 8, 1972

The *New York Gazette*'s front-page headlines read "Nixon Wins in Landslide," "Underboss Still Comatose, Accused of Woodward/Bernstein Murders," and "Cuban Terrorists Linked to Death of FBI Official Felt." Rorschach buys the issue from news vendor Bernard, then records a journal entry pondering how long it will be before masked heroes will no longer be able to do what's right, and darkness wins **[NIGH]**.

In or After 1972

Underboss eventually awakens from his coma and is sentenced to New York City's Rikers Island jail complex **[RPG3]**.

1972 to 1976

During his first four years in the U.S. Senate, John David Keene makes little impact **[NEWW]**.

ABSO .... *Watchmen Absolute Edition*
ALAN ..... Alan Moore's *Watchmen* miniseries
ARCD .... *Minutemen Arcade*
ARTF ..... *Watchmen: The Art of the Film*
BLCK ..... *Tales of the Black Freighter*
BWCC ... *Before Watchmen—The Crimson Corsair*
BWCO ... *Before Watchmen—Comedian*
BWDB .. *Before Watchmen—Dollar Bill*
BWDM .. *Before Watchmen—Dr. Manhattan*
BWMM.. *Before Watchmen—Minutemen*
BWMO .. *Before Watchmen—Moloch*
BWNO ... *Before Watchmen—Nite Owl*

BWOZ.... *Before Watchmen—Ozymandias*
BWRO ... *Before Watchmen—Rorschach*
BWSS ... *Before Watchmen—Silk Spectre*
CHEM.... My Chemical Romance music video: "Desolation Row"
CMEO.... *Watchmen* cameos in comics, TV, and film:
 • Comic: *Astonishing X-Men* volume 3 issue #6
 • Comic: *Hero Hotline* volume 1 issue #5
 • Comic: *Kingdom Come* volume 1 issue #2
 • Comic: *Marvels* volume 1 issue #4
 • Comic: *The Question* volume 1 issue #17
 • TV: *Teen Titans Go!* episode #82, "Real Boy Adventures"
 • Film: *Man of Steel*

 • Film: *Batman v Superman: Dawn of Justice Ultimate Edition*
 • Film: *Justice League*
CLIX ...... HeroClix figure pack-in cards
DECK..... *DC Comics Deck-Building Game—Crossover Pack 4: Watchmen*
DURS .... *DC Universe: Rebirth Special* volume 1 issue #1
FILM ..... *Watchmen* theatrical film
HOOD .... *Under the Hood* documentary and dust-jacket prop reproduction
JUST..... *Watchmen: Justice Is Coming*
MATL .... Mattel Club Black Freighter figure pack-in cards

Before 1973

The *Journal of the American Ornithological Society* is founded **[JUST]**. The publication's offices are located in Chicago, Illinois **[RPG3]**.

1973

Dan Dreiberg begins writing occasional articles for ornithological journals **[ALAN]**, including "Crows and Ravens of the Upper Northeast Corridor," for the *Journal of the American Ornithological Society* **[JUST]**.

> **CONFLICT:** *In* Justice Is Coming, *Dan has already written for the publication as of 1973. The* Watchmen Sourcebook *includes a letter dated October 23, 1977 (four years later), in which he requests guidelines for submission, indicating he has not yet written for the journal by that time. It could be that a change in editorship has taken place in the interim, and that his letter is meant to introduce himself to the new management.*

Richard Nixon is photographed shaking hands with Eddie Blake **[WTFC]**.

> **NOTE:** *The image of the two shaking hands is based on a famous photograph of Nixon's meeting with singer Elvis Presley, taken on December 21, 1970.*

January 1973

Jon Osterman and Laurie Juspeczyk attend a banquet held in The Comedian's honor. Gerald Ford and G. Gordon Liddy also attend, resulting in much fanfare. Laurie becomes drunk on seven glasses of scotch and publicly confronts Blake about his having assaulted her mother in 1940. He comments that he only had to *force* Sally to have sex once, and Laurie throws a drink in his face, unaware that he is telling the truth. Jon takes Laurie home—her first time teleporting—which makes her vomit **[ALAN]**.

> **NOTE:** *Liddy, the chief operative of the White House Plumbers unit during Nixon's presidency, directed the burglary of the Democratic National Committee headquarters in Washington, D.C.'s Watergate office complex, and was convicted of conspiracy, burglary, and illegal wiretapping for his role in the scandal. With Bob Woodward and Carl Bernstein dead, Liddy is no longer disgraced in that scandal.*

March 14, 1973

Eddie Blake delivers a speech at a presidential fundraiser for Richard Nixon, noting that in this world, "being The Comedian is the only thing that makes sense." When asked if he ever lost to a villain, Blake claims that in 35 years of fighting crime, only one man has bested him—but Blake got the last laugh **[RPG3]**. Asked for comment regarding the deaths of reporters Woodward and Bernstein, Blake jokingly deflects the question, saying not to ask him where he was when John F. Kennedy died **[ALAN]**.

> **NOTE:** *Eddie Blake killed not only Kennedy, but also both reporters.*

MIND .... *The Mindscape of Alan Moore*
MOBL .... *Watchmen: The Mobile Game*
MOTN .... *Watchmen: The Complete Motion Comic*
MTRO .... *Metro* promotional newspaper cover wrap
NEWP .... *New Frontiersman* promotional newspaper
NEWW .. *New Frontiersman* website
NIGH .... *Watchmen: The End Is Nigh, Parts 1 and 2*
PKIT ...... *Watchmen* film British press kit
PORT ..... *Watchmen Portraits*
REAL ..... Real life
RPG1 .... *DC Heroes Role Playing Module #227: Who Watches the Watchmen?*

RPG2 .... *DC Heroes Role Playing Module #235: Taking Out the Trash—Curses and Tears*
RPG3 .... *DC Heroes: The Watchmen Sourcebook*
RUBY .... "Wounds," published in *The Ruby Files Volume One*
SCR1 ..... Unfilmed screenplay draft: Sam Hamm
SCR2 ..... Unfilmed screenplay draft: Charles McKeuen
SCR3 ..... Unfilmed screenplay draft: Gary Goldman
SCR4 ..... Unfilmed screenplay draft: David Hayter (2002)
SCR5 ..... Unfilmed screenplay draft: David Hayter (2003)
SCR6 ..... Unfilmed screenplay draft: Alex Tse
SPOT ..... *DC Spotlight #1*
VRL1 ..... Viral video: *NBS Nightly News with Ted Philips*

VRL2 ..... Viral video: *The Keene Act and You*
VRL3 ..... Viral video: *Who Watches the Watchmen? A Veidt Music Network (VMN) Special*
VRL4 ..... Viral video: *World in Focus: 6 Minutes to Midnight*
VRL5 ..... Viral video: *Local Radio Station Report on 1977 Riots*
VRL6 ..... Viral videos (group of ten): *Veidt Enterprises Advertising Contest*
WAWA ... *Watching the Watchmen*
WHOS ... *Who's Who: The Definitive Directory of the DC Universe*
WTFC .... *Watchmen: The Film Companion*

CONFLICT: *Blake's cryptic statement about getting the last laugh on the one person who bested him clearly refers to Hooded Justice. However, Before Watchmen: Minutemen retroactively renders his statement nonsensical, by revealing Hooded Justice and Rolf Müller to be separate individuals. In that story, The Comedian kills Müller, not Hooded Justice (whom Hollis Mason murders)—and Blake is well aware of that fact.*

April 1973 (Alternate Reality)

Namor McKenzie (a.k.a. The Sub-Mariner) leads an Atlantean invasion of New York City to rescue an extraterrestrial named Tamara Rahn, being held captive by the United Nations. The Nite Owl, The Silk Spectre, and Rorschach take part in the invasion, on the side of Namor, aboard *Archimedes* **[CMEO]**.

> **NOTE:** *The Owlship and its occupants have a rather uncharacteristic Marvel Universe cameo in* Marvels *issue #4, published in 1994. The scene in question recalls a prior story, published in 1973 in the pages of* Sub-Mariner *issue #60.*

May 23, 1973

A key to the city is awarded to New York City's masked crime-fighters **[ARTF]**.

> **CONFLICT:** *The Crimebusters, called The Watchmen in the film, appear to have functioned as an actual team in that version, unlike in Alan Moore's miniseries.*

Between December 6, 1973, and October 12, 1985

Eddie Blake is photographed shaking hands with Vice President Gerald Ford **[ALAN]**.

> **NOTE:** *In the real world, Ford assumed the Vice-Presidency on December 6, 1973. This placement presumes that Richard Nixon's first VP, Spiro T. Agnew, similarly resigned in the fictional universe, to be replaced by Ford.*

December 1973 to May 1986

The Dorchester building that once housed The Minutemen's headquarters remains vacant for thirteen years **[RPG3]**.

In or Before 1974

Rorschach begins leaving as his calling card a scrap of paper bearing an ink blot resembling an "R," attached to all criminals whom he leaves injured or dead for police to find **[FILM, WTFC]**.

Eddie Taylor, a student at Woodrow Wilson High School, in Springfield, earns a letterman's jacket for badminton, which he gives to his girlfriend, Stacy Sweet **[JUST]**.

NOTE: *The state containing Springfield is unidentified. This may be an in-joke reference to* The Simpsons, *in which the show's Springfield setting is purposely left unassociated with any particular state.*

A pimp named Exavier Micheals opens a nightclub and bar in New York City called The Strip Club. Micheals serves as the club's manager **[JUST]**.

A masked serial killer clad in enormous black wings begins preying on prostitutes in New York City. He kills each victim with a Bowie knife and leaves a black feather from *Corvus corax principalis* (the common raven) over her eyes. Rorschach investigates the multiple homicides **[JUST]**.

—1974

Rorschach roughs up two criminals and leaves their bloodied bodies tied to a fire hydrant for police to find, along with his ink blot calling card **[FILM, WTFC]**.

> **NOTE:** *This event is depicted but undated in the* Watchmen *film. The Film Companion establishes it as occurring in 1974.*

Ronin Press publishes *History of Underground Comics*, by Mark James Estren, in which the author discusses the origin of Tijuana Bibles **[RPG3]**.

Stacy Sweet graduates from Woodrow Wilson High School, in Springfield, then moves to Manhattan to become an actor. Stacy leaves her boyfriend, Eddie Taylor (though she keeps his letterman's jacket), and moves into a boarding house owned by landlady Mrs. Flint, sending her parents postcards describing her auditions and hope for the future. Desperate for money, she works at the Adult Theater, portraying Hordelia in an all-nude production of *Queen Lear*, "a tale of an aged doxy and three ungrateful strumpets." The theater also shows a mini-play titled *Roll Over & Screw U* **[JUST]**.

> **NOTE:** Queen Lear *is a spoof of William Shakespeare's* King Lear, *with Hordelia based on the titular monarch's daughter, Cordelia.*

—May 11, 1974

At a dinner honoring Richard Nixon, Eddie Blake raises a glass to toast Hooded Justice, whom he claims to miss the most from his days with The Minutemen **[RPG3]**.

> **NOTE:** *Blake's statement is ironic, given that he hated Hooded Justice and attempted to hunt down and kill him in 1955.*

August 9, 1974 (Alternate Reality)

In a quantum reality in which Jon Osterman never becomes Dr. Manhattan, Richard Nixon resigns in disgrace from the presidency during his second term in office due to his involvement in the Watergate scandal. Television journalist Walter Cronkite announces the resignation during a news broadcast **[REAL, BWDM]**.

October 3, 1974

Nelson Gardner is decapitated in a motor vehicle accident **[ALAN]** when the car he is driving spins off an embankment on the New Jersey Turnpike and catches fire. In his hand is a piece of paper charred beyond recognition. Despite the roads being wet and slippery, investigators estimate the vehicle's speed to have been seventy-five miles per hour. Police determine Captain Metropolis's true identity from the recovered body, but withhold this information to the press **[RPG3]**.

> **NOTE:** Alan Moore's miniseries sets Gardner's death in 1974. The specific date appears in Taking Out the Trash. It's unknown what the charred paper in Gardner's hand is, but the implication may be that it's a suicide note.
>
> **CONFLICT:** The Watchmen Sourcebook includes a New York Gazette article reporting his death on October 4, 1972. In Sam Hamm's unproduced 1988 screenplay, Gardner is still alive and fighting crime in 1976. Both contradict Moore's work.

September 5, 1974

Adrian Veidt submits articles of incorporation to New York State for Pyramid Deliveries, registered to Luxor Imports, Inc. Adrian names Howard Cart CEO, Luxor Imports the principal owner, and Leroy Gibbons treasurer **[RPG3]**.

Late 1974 or Early 1975

Stacy Sweet takes off during the night, still owing four weeks' rent to Mrs. Flint. Under the name Cherry Sweet, she begins working as a prostitute for a pimp, Exavier Micheals, as well as dancing at The Body House, a club on Bowery St. Eventually, Stacy falls victim to a masked serial killer who preys upon prostitutes **[JUST]**.

In or Before 1975

The film *The Funk Hole* opens in theaters. **[JUST]**.

Fast and safe zeppelins become economically viable, thanks to scientific innovation enabled by Dr. Manhattan **[ALAN]** and funded by Adrian Veidt **[BWOZ]**. The Gunga Diner chain uses such technology to advertise its business via an elephant-shaped airship floating above New York City **[ALAN]**.

> **NOTE:** Following the Hindenburg *disaster in 1937, hydrogen-fueled zeppelins fell into disuse, with the remaining airships deconstructed in 1940. The comic's use of zeppelins symbolizes the hydrogen atom emblazoning Dr. Manhattan's forehead.*

Roche Chemical is founded and becomes immensely successful **[ALAN]**.

Adrian Veidt develops an interest in electronic music (which he considers "superhero-ey"), and in avant-garde music in general, particularly dub music, a Jamaican hybrid of reggae and electronics. Among his favorite musicians are Pierre Henry, Terry Riley, and Andrew Lang, as well as Cage, Stockhausen, and Penderecki **[ALAN]**.

> **NOTE:** Veidt's musical tastes are rather eclectic. French composer Pierre Henry helped to pioneer electronic music; American musician Terry Riley pioneered the minimalist school of Western classical music; and Scottish writer Andrew Lang, best known for his novels and poetry, also published a volume of metrical experiments. Presumably, the others refer to American composer John Cage, German electronic music composer Karlheinz Stockhausen, and Polish conductor Krzysztof Penderecki.

Veidt Enterprises introduces an eight-bit arcade game called *Minutemen*. Set in 1942, the side-scrolling game enables players to "re-live the golden age of costumed fighters" on the streets and in the subways of Manhattan. Players can battle Moloch the Mystic's thugs in the role of either The Nite Owl or The Silk Spectre **[NEWW, ARCD]**.

> **NOTE:** The game contains a number of Watchmen *Easter eggs, including Charlton St. (Alan Moore based the Crimebusters after characters created by Charlton Comics), a poster advertising Rolf Müller's circus strongman act, and a theater featuring Moloch's stage-magic show.*
>
> *A parody video,* Watchmen—Dr. Manhattan Video Game Leaked, *was posted to liquidgeneration.com in 2009, and later to YouTube. Presented as footage from a vintage-style eight-bit scrolling video game, the video features Dr. Manhattan and the Jolly Green Giant dueling with giant penises.*

Dr. Manhattan is deemed the Eighth Wonder of the World, a national treasure, and the planet's greatest hope, though some view him as a freak of nature **[HOOD]**.

—October 27, In or Before 1975

A New York couple named Bernard and Rosa marry. The two share an admiration for masked adventurers. Although she wishes to leave Manhattan, they never move away.

MIND .... *The Mindscape of Alan Moore*
MOBL.... *Watchmen: The Mobile Game*
MOTN.... *Watchmen: The Complete Motion Comic*
MTRO.... *Metro* promotional newspaper cover wrap
NEWP.... *New Frontiersman* promotional newspaper
NEWW... *New Frontiersman* website
NIGH .... *Watchmen: The End Is Nigh, Parts 1 and 2*
PKIT ...... *Watchmen* film British press kit
PORT.... *Watchmen Portraits*
REAL..... Real life
RPG1 .... *DC Heroes Role Playing Module #227: Who Watches the Watchmen?*

RPG2 .... *DC Heroes Role Playing Module #235: Taking Out the Trash—Curses and Tears*
RPG3 .... *DC Heroes: The Watchmen Sourcebook*
RUBY .... "Wounds," published in *The Ruby Files Volume One*
SCR1..... Unfilmed screenplay draft: Sam Hamm
SCR2..... Unfilmed screenplay draft: Charles McKeuen
SCR3..... Unfilmed screenplay draft: Gary Goldman
SCR4..... Unfilmed screenplay draft: David Hayter (2002)
SCR5..... Unfilmed screenplay draft: David Hayter (2003)
SCR6..... Unfilmed screenplay draft: Alex Tse
SPOT..... *DC Spotlight #1*
VRL1 ..... Viral video: *NBS Nightly News with Ted Philips*

VRL2..... Viral video: *The Keene Act and You*
VRL3..... Viral video: *Who Watches the Watchmen? A Veidt Music Network (VMN) Special*
VRL4..... Viral video: *World in Focus: 6 Minutes to Midnight*
VRL5..... Viral video: *Local Radio Station Report on 1977 Riots*
VRL6..... Viral videos (group of ten): *Veidt Enterprises Advertising Contest*
WAWA... *Watching the Watchmen*
WHOS ... *Who's Who: The Definitive Directory of the DC Universe*
WTFC .... *Watchmen: The Film Companion*

After she passes away, her friends stop calling to check on Bernard, and he takes a job as a newsstand vendor to meet people [**ALAN**].

> **NOTE:** *These events are undated in Alan Moore's miniseries, though the* Under the Hood *documentary shows Bernard already working as a news vendor in 1975. Bernard's marriage to Rosa is said to occur on October 27, with no year indicated.*

●—After October 27, In or Before 1975

Bernard reads *Under the Hood* and finds the book fantastic. He is filled with pride that Hollis Mason, whom he considers a great man, is among his regular customers [**HOOD**].

●—1975

Andy Warhol produces a series of paintings of Dan Dreiberg as The Nite Owl, which he displays at an art gallery. Truman Capote attends the unveiling [**FILM, WTFC**].

> **NOTE:** *This event is depicted undated in the* Watchmen *film. The Film Companion and the movie's British press kit set the event in 1975.*

> **CONFLICT:** The Film Companion *misidentifies the paintings as being of Hollis Mason, not Dan Dreiberg. In the film, however, the image is clearly of Dan's costume.*

Shortly after its television debut, news program *The Culpeper Minute* profiles Hollis Mason regarding his book *Under the Hood.* Host Larry Culpeper meets with Mason at the Gunga Diner to discuss his crime-fighting days, his opinions of The Comedian and Dr. Manhattan, and more. Hollis admits to having romantic feelings for Sally Jupiter and holding out hope that they'll end up together. Culpeper also interviews Sally, who fondly recalls being a sex symbol but offers no comment on The Comedian's alleged rape attempt. Larry Schexnayder denies the attack happened, adding that his marriage to Sally was doomed from the start. When asked for comment about the rape incident, The Comedian threatens to stick a cigarette in Culpeper's eye [**HOOD**].

> **NOTE:** *Schexnayder's name is misspelled as Lawrence Shexnayder.*

During the broadcast, Culpeper asks several individuals for their opinions of masked adventurers. News vendor Bernard defends them, while local bar owner Joe calls crime-fighters dangerous, claiming they harass his customers and hurt his business. Psychiatrist Dr. Long deems vigilantes sociopathic, but adds that he hopes one day to psychoanalyze one. The Big Figure, from prison, mocks superheroes for wearing masks, while Edgar Jacobi says the existence of superheroes inspired the rise of supervillains in the first place, and that he worries that an adversary powerful enough to serve as a counterpoint to Dr. Manhattan might soon arrive [**HOOD**].

NOTE: *Since Edgar Jacobi spends the 1970s in prison, his interview with Larry Culpeper must be conducted from inside a correctional facility. Dr. Long's comment about psychoanalyzing a vigilante foreshadows his meetings with Rorschach in 1985.*

CONFLICT: *Dr. Long's first name is given as William, contradicting Alan Moore's miniseries, in which the psychiatrist is named Malcolm.*

Stacy Sweet's brother visits New York City to find his missing sister. He questions her landlady, Mrs. Flint, who says Stacy took off a few months prior. The brother pays Stacy's back rent, and Flint hands him a program to an all-nude Adult Theater production, *Queen Lear*, in which Stacy portrayed Hordelia. He finds the theater boarded up and notices a bum wearing the jacket of her ex-boyfriend, Eddie Taylor. The drunk no longer recalls how he obtained the coat **[JUST]**.

> **NOTE:** *Stacy's brother was not named in the now-defunct video game* Justice Is Coming, *since each player who assumed the role used his or her own character name.*

Police find Stacy's dead body in Central Park, her throat cut and a black feather over her eyes. Her brother identifies the body and informs their parents. In a pocket of Eddie's jacket, he finds a matchbook for a seedy hotel in the Red Light District, where he searches her room to find a number of food wrappers from the Gunga Diner. At the restaurant, he meets two of Stacy's fellow hookers, Trish and Wendee, who refer him to The Body House, a seedy nightclub at which his sister danced **[JUST]**.

At The Body House, Stacy's brother watches as Rorschach investigates a recent spate of prostitute deaths. Rorschach breaks the finger of a Knot-Top, who draws a well-dressed man whom he heard yelling at Stacy outside the club. An informant provides a possible lead, stockbroker J. Alex, who feigns knowledge of Stacy until the brother uses the same finger-bending tactic. Alex hands over the business card of Stacy's pimp, Exavier Micheals, but the brother finds Exavier dead—naked, his throat cut, with a black feather across his eyes—at his nightclub and bar, The Strip Club **[JUST]**.

Consulting a library for information about black-feathered birds, Stacy's brother finds an article about crows and ravens, written by Dan Dreiberg for the *Journal of the American Ornithological Society*. The brother visits Dreiberg, who identifies the feather as being from *Corvus corax principalis* (the common raven), and points him to a flock that frequents a corner of the city cemetery. There, near the graves of Vittorio and Marie Rotelli, the brother encounters Stacy's serial killer—a masked man with enormous black wings, armed with a Bowie knife—whom he kills, bringing his sister justice **[JUST]**.

In or Before January 1975

The Comedian begins leaving a bloody smiley-face pin on his victims' bodies, to serve as his calling card **[BWOZ]**.

January 20, 1975

President Richard Nixon's approval ratings soar, and his opponents on Capitol Hill and in the press become less vocal as a result **[NEWW]**. Leveraging the U.S. victory in Vietnam **[ALAN]**, as well as the country's prosperity brought on by the introduction of electric cars **[RPG2]**, Nixon announces plans to repeal Constitutional Amendment 22, enabling him to run for a third term in office. *The Washington Times* covers this announcement in a front-page story written by Alan Morgan **[NEWW]**.

> **NOTE:** *Amendment 22 was ratified in 1951, following President Franklin D. Roosevelt's fourth term in office.*
>
> *Alan Morgan is clearly named after* Watchmen *creator Alan Moore.*

Adrian Veidt watches a broadcast of Nixon's announcement on the monitors of his Karnak fortress. In that moment, Veidt decides to retire from crime-fighting and volunteer his true identity to the public **[BWOZ]**, so as to defuse accusations of secrecy and cover-up that could hurt him financially **[ABSO]**.

Richard Nixon's supporters adopt the name Campaign for the Re-election of the President (C.R.E.E.P.) **[ALAN]**, repurposing an acronym from his 1972 re-election campaign **[RPG3]**. The administration seeks donations from captains of industry, and C.R.E.E.P. builds an electoral war closet of hundreds of millions of dollars **[NEWW]**. Reminded of *The Man From U.N.C.L.E.*, Adrian Veidt finds the acronym ridiculous **[ALAN]**.

> **NOTE:** *In the real world, Nixon's campaign was called the Committee for the Re-Election of the President. Although Nixon's team used the acronym C.R.P., his adversaries took advantage of the fact that it could also be abbreviated as C.R.E.E.P.*

January 24, 1975

Disheartened by Nixon's unconstitutional motives, and by the realization that fighting individual evils does little good for the greater world, Adrian Veidt officially retires from crime-fighting, invites reporters to his office, and admits to having been Ozymandias **[ALAN, BWOZ]**. Journalist Doug Roth asks why he would give up his alter-ego, given the current social instability, and Adrian explains that Dr. Manhattan's actions in Vietnam have made masked adventurers superfluous **[BWOZ]**. A newspaper bears the headline "Ozymandias Quits: Smartest Man in the World Goes Public" **[ALAN]**.

> **CONFLICT:** *Alan Moore's miniseries sets Veidt's retirement in 1975. A timeline packaged with* The End Is Nigh—The Complete Experience *moves it to 1977.*

Between January 24 and March 7, 1975

While attending a banquet for Richard Nixon, Adrian Veidt witnesses a Presidential aide spilling a glass of water on Vice President Gerald Ford, who smiles and (misspeaking) assures the aide, "Oh, that's okay. Nobody's human." Amused, Veidt begins referring to Nixon's close subordinates as "humanoids" **[ALAN]**.

After January 24, 1975

Doug Roth calls Adrian Veidt to discuss his retirement in detail, and the former crime-fighter flies Roth to Karnak aboard his private jet to conduct a formal interview for *Nova Express*. The article, titled "After the Masquerade: Superstyle and the Art of Humanoid Watching," explores Veidt's background, philosophies, musical tastes, and politics, and features a photograph of him with Bubastis, courtesy of Triangle Inc. **[ALAN]**. During the interview, Adrian offers harsh words regarding his fellow crime-fighters, which further turns the American public against vigilantes **[RPG2]**.

Adrian Veidt sets up a company to sell posters, diet books, action figures, and other memorabilia, cashing in on his reputation as Ozymandias to further his media empire. Disgusted, Rorschach deems him a sellout and a prostitute **[ALAN]**.

Dr. Manhattan apprehends a criminal by making his handgun disintegrate, then bends a pole around him to hold him in place until police arrive. Elsewhere, Silk Spectre stops another lawbreaker, while The Comedian leaves a thug dead on the street, with three bullet holes in his body, along with Blake's bloody smiley-face calling card **[BWOZ]**.

March 7, 1975

Richard Nixon's administration passes a new amendment repealing Amendment 22, thereby allowing him to remain in office beyond a second term **[RPG2]**.

Between March 7, 1975 and July 1975

Adrian Veidt invites Jon Osterman and Laurie Juspeczyk to his Karnak retreat. As servants bring them Indonesian food, Jon perceives that their host is sad **[ALAN]**.

Between March 7, 1975 and November 2, 1976

The Republican Party nominates Richard M. Nixon for an unprecedented third term in office. Television journalist Walter Cronkite announces the nomination during a news broadcast **[BWDM]**.

July 1975

Nova Express magazine, Vol. XXII, publishes "After the Masquerade: Superstyle and the Art of Humanoid Watching," featuring Doug Roth's interview with Adrian Veidt **[RPG3]**.

MIND .... *The Mindscape of Alan Moore*
MOBL .... *Watchmen: The Mobile Game*
MOTN .... *Watchmen: The Complete Motion Comic*
MTRO .... *Metro* promotional newspaper cover wrap
NEWP .... *New Frontiersman* promotional newspaper
NEWW .. *New Frontiersman* website
NIGH ..... *Watchmen: The End Is Nigh, Parts 1 and 2*
PKIT ...... *Watchmen* film British press kit
PORT ..... *Watchmen Portraits*
REAL ..... Real life
RPG1 .... *DC Heroes Role Playing Module #227: Who Watches the Watchmen?*

RPG2 ... *DC Heroes Role Playing Module #235: Taking Out the Trash—Curses and Tears*
RPG3 .... *DC Heroes: The Watchmen Sourcebook*
RUBY .... "Wounds," published in *The Ruby Files Volume One*
SCR1 ..... Unfilmed screenplay draft: Sam Hamm
SCR2 ..... Unfilmed screenplay draft: Charles McKeuen
SCR3 ..... Unfilmed screenplay draft: Gary Goldman
SCR4 ..... Unfilmed screenplay draft: David Hayter (2002)
SCR5 ..... Unfilmed screenplay draft: David Hayter (2003)
SCR6 ..... Unfilmed screenplay draft: Alex Tse
SPOT ..... *DC Spotlight #1*
VRL1 ..... Viral video: *NBS Nightly News with Ted Philips*

VRL2 ..... Viral video: *The Keene Act and You*
VRL3 ..... Viral video: *Who Watches the Watchmen? A Veidt Music Network (VMN) Special*
VRL4 ..... Viral video: *World in Focus: 6 Minutes to Midnight*
VRL5 ..... Viral video: *Local Radio Station Report on 1977 Riots*
VRL6 ..... Viral videos (group of ten): *Veidt Enterprises Advertising Contest*
WAWA .. *Watching the Watchmen*
WHOS ... *Who's Who: The Definitive Directory of the DC Universe*
WTFC .... *Watchmen: The Film Companion*

—Summer 1975

Gerald Anthony Grice, a lowlife living in a disused Brooklyn dressmaking shop called Modern Modes, abducts six-year-old Blair Roche, mistaking her as being connected to the Roche Chemical fortune. After raping and torturing the little girl, he butchers her body and feeds her to his two German shepherds **[ALAN]**, Fred and Barney **[FILM]**.

> **CONFLICT:** *Sam Hamm's unproduced 1988 screenplay and Charles McKeuen's 1989 rewrite of that script both change the girl's surname to Franco, while Gary Goldman's 1992 rewrite gives her surname as Dupont.*

Days pass without ransom demands, and Rorschach, reminded of his own childhood, is troubled by the thought of young Blaire Roche being abused and frightened. He promises her parents that he will bring her home, then visits several underworld bars, injuring patrons to gain information. After putting fourteen people in the hospital, he learns Grice's name and address from the fifteenth **[ALAN]**.

Walter Kovacs visits Modern Modes, where he discovers Blair's underwear in a wood-burning stove and the German shepherds fighting over her bones. Horrified, he chops up Fred and Barney with a cleaver. As blood splatters on his chest, he closes his eyes, utters "Mother," and re-opens them, fully transformed and no longer considering himself Walter Kovacs—only Rorschach. When Grice returns home drunk that night, Rorschach throws the dogs' carcasses at the man through a window, cuffs him to the stove, gives him a hacksaw, douses the place with kerosene, and drops a cigarette. He then watches from outside for an hour as Grice burns to death, and feels reborn **[ALAN]**.

> **CONFLICT:** *In the* Watchmen *film, Rorschach kills Grice outright instead of leaving him to burn.*

No longer leading a dual life, Rorschach quits his garment-industry job and begins wearing his mask at all times—except when going out in public, when he hides his costume in a garbage dumpster or under his apartment's floor boards. The vigilante begins spending each night patrolling the streets and killing criminals instead of letting them live. By day, he goes out unmasked, disguised as a homeless prophet of doom carrying his "The End Is Nigh" sign **[ALAN]**, which enables him to roam the streets ignored or overlooked by others **[CLIX]**. At all times, his personal hygiene remains poor, causing others to comment on his putrid stench **[ALAN]**.

—Late 1975

"Who Watches the Watchmen?" becomes a rallying cry of anti-hero protestors, with the phrase spray-painted on walls and subway trains across the United States **[RPG2]**.

> **NOTE:** *This phrase is a translation from "Quis custodiet ipsos custodes?"—a Latin question from Roman poet Juvenal's Satires, originally used in reference to marital*

ABSO .... *Watchmen Absolute Edition*	**BWOZ**.... *Before Watchmen—Ozymandias*	• Film: *Batman v Superman: Dawn of Justice Ultimate Edition*
ALAN..... Alan Moore's *Watchmen* miniseries	**BWRO** ... *Before Watchmen—Rorschach*	• Film: *Justice League*
ARCD .... *Minutemen Arcade*	**BWSS** ... *Before Watchmen—Silk Spectre*	**CLIX** ...... HeroClix figure pack-in cards
ARTF..... *Watchmen: The Art of the Film*	**CHEM**.... My Chemical Romance music video: "Desolation Row"	**DECK**..... *DC Comics Deck-Building Game—Crossover Pack 4: Watchmen*
BLCK..... *Tales of the Black Freighter*	**CMEO**.... *Watchmen* cameos in comics, TV, and film:	**DURS**..... *DC Universe: Rebirth Special* volume 1 issue #1
BWCC .. *Before Watchmen—The Crimson Corsair*	• Comic: *Astonishing X-Men* volume 3 issue #6	**FILM** ..... *Watchmen* theatrical film
BWCO .. *Before Watchmen—Comedian*	• Comic: *Hero Hotline* volume 1 issue #5	**HOOD** .... *Under the Hood* documentary and dust-jacket prop reproduction
BWDB .. *Before Watchmen—Dollar Bill*	• Comic: *Kingdom Come* volume 1 issue #2	**JUST** ..... *Watchmen: Justice Is Coming*
BWDM .. *Before Watchmen—Dr. Manhattan*	• Comic: *Marvels* volume 1 issue #4	**MATL** .... Mattel Club Black Freighter figure pack-in cards
BWMM .. *Before Watchmen—Minutemen*	• Comic: *The Question* volume 1 issue #17	
BWMO .. *Before Watchmen—Moloch*	• TV: *Teen Titans Go!* episode #82, "Real Boy Adventures"	
BWNO ... *Before Watchmen—Nite Owl*	• Film: *Man of Steel*	

fidelity. In modern usage, the phrase references the difficulty of controlling the actions of those in power.

—1975 to October 1985

With his superhero days behind him, Adrian Veidt makes numerous televised appearances as a celebrity, gymnast, and athlete. He provides a series of stunning athletic performances, donates all proceeds to charity, and becomes a public heartthrob and sports-world sensation **[ABSO]**.

Every year on their anniversary, news vendor Bernard thinks about his late wife Rosa **[ALAN]**.

—Before 1976

Adrian Veidt forms a close friendship with one of his favorite American novelists, William S. Burroughs **[RPG3]**.

Punk-rock group Pale Horse forms. Among its members is musician Red D'eath **[RPG3]**.
> **NOTE:** *Adrian Veidt refers to the band in a January 1976 interview with* Probe *magazine, so the band must exist before that point. Pale Horse's name, symbolizing the fear of nuclear destruction, references Revelations 6:8 from The Bible: "I looked and there before me was a pale horse! Its rider was named Death, and Hell was following close behind him." The band's name (and that of Red D'eath) foreshadows Adrian Veidt's destruction of New York City in 1985.*

—In or Before 1976

Jacobs Motors introduces its Apache motor vehicle model, the fuel tank of which is vulnerable to dangerous flare-ups. The company's engineers devise a technological means of eliminating the problem, creating a plastic back-flow valve that would cost only $11.38. Another team works up a statistical survey of company liabilities in accidental death lawsuits **[RPG3]**.
> **NOTE:** *It is unclear why these events are recounted in* The Watchmen Sourcebook's *section on The Comedian, as they seem unconnected to his history.*

With the U.S. political scene changing, many anticipate an impending federal ban on costumed vigilantes **[RPG3]**.

—1976

Senator John David Keene allies with the New York Police Officer's Union, enabling him to become more prominent in U.S. politics **[NEWW]**.

Adrian Veidt, a regular at Studio 54 **[FILM, WTFC]**, earns a reputation as the "ultimate

MIND .... *The Mindscape of Alan Moore*
MOBL.... *Watchmen: The Mobile Game*
MOTN.... *Watchmen: The Complete Motion Comic*
MTRO.... *Metro promotional newspaper cover wrap*
NEWP.... *New Frontiersman promotional newspaper*
NEWW.. *New Frontiersman website*
NIGH ..... *Watchmen: The End Is Nigh, Parts 1 and 2*
PKIT ...... *Watchmen film British press kit*
PORT ..... *Watchmen Portraits*
REAL ..... *Real life*
RPG1 .... *DC Heroes Role Playing Module #227: Who Watches the Watchmen?*

RPG2 .... *DC Heroes Role Playing Module #235: Taking Out the Trash—Curses and Tears*
RPG3 .... *DC Heroes: The Watchmen Sourcebook*
RUBY .... *"Wounds," published in* The Ruby Files Volume One
SCR1..... *Unfilmed screenplay draft: Sam Hamm*
SCR2..... *Unfilmed screenplay draft: Charles McKeuen*
SCR3..... *Unfilmed screenplay draft: Gary Goldman*
SCR4..... *Unfilmed screenplay draft: David Hayter (2002)*
SCR5..... *Unfilmed screenplay draft: David Hayter (2003)*
SCR6..... *Unfilmed screenplay draft: Alex Tse*
SPOT ..... *DC Spotlight #1*
VRL1 ..... *Viral video: NBS Nightly News with Ted Philips*

VRL2 ..... *Viral video: The Keene Act and You*
VRL3 ..... *Viral video: Who Watches the Watchmen? A Veidt Music Network (VMN) Special*
VRL4 ..... *Viral video: World in Focus: 6 Minutes to Midnight*
VRL5 ..... *Viral video: Local Radio Station Report on 1977 Riots*
VRL6 ..... *Viral videos (group of ten): Veidt Enterprises Advertising Contest*
WAWA... *Watching the Watchmen*
WHOS ... *Who's Who: The Definitive Directory of the DC Universe*
WTFC .... *Watchmen: The Film Companion*

bachelor and international playboy." Veidt becomes romantically linked with singers Stevie Nicks, Sheena Easton, and Madonna; counts David Bowie and Mick Jagger among his best friends **[VRL3]**; and hangs out with the band Village People. On one occasion, portrait photographer Annie Leibovitz snaps his picture as he enters the club with Jagger and Bowie, during the latter's "Ziggy Stardust" days **[FILM]**.

> **NOTE:** *These events are depicted undated in the* Watchmen *film. The Film Companion places them in 1976.*
>
> *David Bowie is known to have been bisexual, and The Rolling Stones' Mick Jagger is rumored to be as well. Several Village People members are homosexual, and Studio 54 was operated by gay businessman Steve Rubell. Veidt's association with these celebrities reinforces Rorschach's suspicions, in Alan Moore's miniseries (confirmed in* Before Watchmen: Ozymandias*), that Adrian is gay (or, more accurately, bisexual, given his involvement with Nicks, Easton, Madonna, and—in* Before Watchmen—*Miranda St. John and his assistant Marla).*

Alan Greenfeldt, Jacobs Motors' vice president, issues an internal memo discussing two studies conducted by Jacobs employees to prevent fuel tank flare-ups and assess liability in the event of a lawsuit. The memo weighs the cost of a recall to fit all Apaches with an $11.38 back-flow valve against the potential cost of monetary judgments. No recall is ordered **[RPG3]**.

> **NOTE:** *It is unclear why these events are recounted in* The Watchmen Sourcebook's *section on The Comedian, as they seem unconnected to his history.*

—January 1976

Probe magazine interviews Adrian Veidt, who explains why he became Ozymandias, discusses Captain Metropolis's failed effort to launch The Crimebusters, explores his concept of "futureology," and notes that while it would be tragic if vigilantes were banned, the country could "afford to lose one or two." Asked if he'll miss wearing his costume, he says he'll be too busy building his businesses to save the world **[RPG3]**.

—January 11, 1976

Dan Dreiberg finishes constructing a battery-powered exoskeleton prototype capable of increasing a wearer's strength by a factor of sixteen or more. The suit costs $175,000 to build and can be worn over his standard uniform. The exoskeleton's bulk makes it difficult to control, however **[RPG3]**. The first time he uses it, in fact, he breaks his arm and decides never to do so again **[ALAN]**.

—Mid-1976

A masochistic, mentally ill individual, identity unknown, poses as a supervillain called Captain Carnage. For a span of several months, he begs costumed heroes to beat him up **[ALAN, RPG3]**. The asthmatic would-be criminal wears a hockey mask but is not very intimidating **[SCR1]**.

> **NOTE:** Carnage's activities are discussed but undated in Alan Moore's miniseries. The Watchmen Sourcebook specifies 1976.

Laurie Juspeczyk notices Captain Carnage exiting a jewelry shop one day and begins hitting him. Unaware that he enjoys the pummeling, she mistakes his aroused breathing for an asthma attack **[ALAN]**. He later devises an elaborate fake theft ring that lasts for months, during which he plants clues to his hideout at each crime scene, hoping to be apprehended and beaten. Laurie finds one such clue and tracks him down to a mirrored room in SoHo, featuring soft music and red flashing wall lights **[RPG3]**. The faux supervillain approaches Dan Dreiberg, begging to be punched in broad daylight. Having heard of Carnage's activities, Nite Owl tells him to get lost. When Carnage tries the same tactic with Rorschach, the vigilante drops him down an elevator shaft **[ALAN]**.

—In or Before July 1976

Nine members of the Radical Front are imprisoned **[SCR1, SCR2]**. Each sports a beard like that of Fidel Castro **[SCR3]**.

—July 1976

The Brain Trust, five corrupt scientists led by Dr. Cortex, take hostages inside the Statue of Liberty and threaten to destroy the monument unless the nine Radical Front prisoners are released. Network correspondent Cindy Chan and Channel 4 anchors Sheila Shea and Jim Bradley cover the standoff for the news. FBI Chief Ernest Bullard attempts to negotiate a release, but the statue is decimated when New York City's masked vigilantes, ignoring the orders of FBI and SWAT teams on the scene, accidentally trigger the bomb to detonate. This incident damages the reputation of masked adventurers in the eyes of the public and the government **[SCR1, SCR2, SCR3]**.

> **NOTE:** The Brain Trust and Bullard appear unnamed in Sam Hamm's unproduced 1989 screenplay, as well as in Charles McKeuen's rewrite of that script. Gary Goldman's version gives the criminals a moniker and Bullard a name.

> **CONFLICT:** Captain Metropolis is said to take part in this mission, despite having died in October 1974 in Alan Moore's miniseries.

—In or Before September 1976

Sally Jupiter begins meeting with a therapist to deal with her emotional issues stemming

from Eddie Blake's assault on her in 1940. When she admits that she feels as though she contributed to the attempted rape, the therapist suggests she may be experiencing misplaced guilt **[ALAN]**.

Probe magazine sends reporter Marth Braddock to Sally Jupiter's home in Burbank, California, to interview the "costumed cutie" **[RPG3]**.

●—September 1976

Probe magazine publishes a profile of Sally Jupiter, under the cover title "Silk Spectre: Hero or Just Another Sex Symbol?" **[RPG3]**. The interviewer's slanted questions focus on her sex life and those of her fellow superheroes. Sally admits to not having liked Ursula Zandt, but says The Minutemen were wrong to oust her for being a lesbian, since she wasn't the only homosexual on the team. (She refuses to reveal names, but cites two male members, now dead.) When asked about Hollis Mason's allegations that The Comedian tried to rape her, Sally says she holds no grudges and may have, on some level, wanted it to happen **[ALAN]**.

> **NOTE:** *This interview provides solid evidence that Nelson Gardner and Hooded Justice are a homosexual couple. When asked who else in The Minutemen was gay besides Ursula Zandt, Sally responds, "It was a couple of the guys, and they're both dead now." This establishes two male members of The Minutemen as being gay—and the only two dead by that point are Gardner and Hooded Justice. Moreover, in a letter from Larry Schexnayder to Sally Jupiter, Larry writes, "With Nelly and H.J. acting up it's a pretty sorry spectacle at the meetings these days." This indicates that Nelly (a nickname for Nelson) attends the meetings, and thus must be a team member, which can only point to Gardner. Artist Dave Gibbons has claimed that he and Moore did not intend for the two to be gay, but the text pages do not bear him out on this. It's important to remember that the above statements appear not in Gibbons' art panels, but on non-drawn text pages. Therefore, the artist's faulty memory is understandable.*

●—November 2, 1976

Richard Nixon is re-elected for a third term of office as President of the United States. His Vice President remains Gerald Ford, while Henry Kissinger continues to serve among his advisors **[ALAN]**. Hollis Mason once again votes for him **[FILM]**.

> **NOTE:** *This presumes Election Day in the United States occurs on the same day in Alan Moore's miniseries as in the real world.*

■— November 2, 1976 (Alternate Reality)

James Earl "Jimmy" Carter Jr. is elected as the United States' 39th President **[REAL]**.

ABSO .... *Watchmen Absolute Edition*	**BWOZ**.... *Before Watchmen—Ozymandias*	• Film: *Batman v Superman: Dawn of Justice Ultimate*
ALAN..... Alan Moore's *Watchmen* miniseries	**BWRO** ... *Before Watchmen—Rorschach*	*Edition*
ARCD .... *Minutemen Arcade*	**BWSS** .. *Before Watchmen—Silk Spectre*	• Film: *Justice League*
ARTF ..... *Watchmen: The Art of the Film*	**CHEM**.... My Chemical Romance music video: "Desolation Row"	**CLIX** ...... HeroClix figure pack-in cards
BLCK..... *Tales of the Black Freighter*	**CMEO** .... *Watchmen* cameos in comics, TV, and film:	**DECK**..... *DC Comics Deck-Building Game—Crossover*
BWCC ... *Before Watchmen—The Crimson Corsair*	• Comic: *Astonishing X-Men* volume 3 issue #6	*Pack 4: Watchmen*
BWCO ... *Before Watchmen—Comedian*	• Comic: *Hero Hotline* volume 1 issue #5	**DURS** ..... *DC Universe: Rebirth Special* volume 1 issue #1
BWDB ... *Before Watchmen—Dollar Bill*	• Comic: *Kingdom Come* volume 1 issue #2	**FILM** ..... *Watchmen* theatrical film
BWDM .. *Before Watchmen—Dr. Manhattan*	• Comic: *Marvels* volume 1 issue #4	**HOOD** .... *Under the Hood* documentary and dust-jacket
BWMM .. *Before Watchmen—Minutemen*	• Comic: *The Question* volume 1 issue #17	prop reproduction
BWMO .. *Before Watchmen—Moloch*	• TV: *Teen Titans Go!* episode #82, "Real Boy Adventures"	**JUST** ..... *Watchmen: Justice Is Coming*
BWNO ... *Before Watchmen—Nite Owl*	• Film: *Man of Steel*	**MATL** .... Mattel Club Black Freighter figure pack-in cards

Part X:
KEENE INTEREST
(1977–1984)

In or Before 1977

New York City's crime-fighters arrest supervillains Golden Boy, The Butcher, Electron, and Ogre. The Comedian takes down another criminal called Jack of Hearts, sending him to prison for white slavery **[SCR3]**.

While pursuing a dope dealer, Dan Dreiberg takes a moment to urinate. By the time he doffs and dons his costume, his quarry escapes. Afterward, Dan re-designs his outfit to make it easier to relieve himself in the future **[ALAN]**.

The following businesses open in New York City: Alfredo's Barber Shop, Burlesk, Discount Liquor, Freshsave Foods, J&K Television, M&G Variety Discount Store, Plantine's Liquidation Center, and Poseidon Laundromat **[FILM]**.
> **NOTE:** These companies are named on signage in the Watchmen film.

Rorschach begins making frequent visits to Bellevue Hospital's emergency room, sans costume, to steal medical supplies. Thanks to the hospital's overcrowded, understaffed conditions, no one notices his supply room raids. For a time, he types his journal entries instead of writing them by hand **[BWRO]**.

1977

Moloch the Mystic arranges for the New York Stock Exchange to be bombed **[WTFC]**.
> **NOTE:** Alan Moore's miniseries establishes that Moloch spends the 1970s in prison, so he must arrange the bombing from his cell, via intermediaries.

February 16, 1977

Television personality Dick Cavett interviews ex-Beatle John Lennon and his wife, Yoko Ono **[WTFC]**.

Francis Giancarlo, president of the New York Police Officers' Union, issues a letter to the city's mayor, warning that the union plans to strike in protest of costumed adventuring making police work increasingly dangerous **[NEWW]**.

—March 1977

The Twilight Lady is released from prison after nine years. Returning to her now-dilapidated Upper East Side mansion, she resumes the vice trade, paying off her police clients—including the chief, commissioner, and mayor—to protect her **[NIGH]**.

> **CONFLICT:** The Watchmen Sourcebook *claims The Twilight Lady serves only two years in prison, then heads to France and vanishes.*

—Spring 1977

The New York City Police Union enters into negotiations with the city council regarding their annual pay raise. The council denies the request on the grounds that masked adventurers have been doing the cops' job for them **[BWOZ]**.

—April 12, 1977

The *New York Gazette*'s front-page headline reads "City Council Denies Cops Raise!" Upon reading the article, Adrian Veidt deems the council's decision shortsighted **[BWOZ]**.

—June 1977

On her eighteenth birthday, an attractive woman named Violet Greene starts working for The Twilight Lady, performing sadomasochistic scenes in pornographic movies. Her parents receive a package in the mail, containing an excerpt from her first film, *Schoolgirls in Trouble*, in which the vice queen holds a riding crop to the girl as she stands shackled to window bars, begging not to be molested. Unaware that Violet took part in the film voluntarily and has not been abducted, her parents show the reel to Rorschach, who vows to find their daughter for them **[NIGH]**.

> **NOTE:** *Who sent Violet's parents the film footage is unknown.*

—Before July 1977

A New York City movie theater begins showing *Die Slowly* and *Demonoid* as a double-feature. The adult film *Babylon Blue* is released, starring Bridgette Money **[BWRO]**.

> **NOTE:** *The actor's name is based on real-world porn star Bridgette Monet, who starred in* Babylon Blue *in 1983.*

Street hustler Dwayne Carter earns Rorschach's notice for his activities selling fake gold chains and drugs **[BWRO]**.

Ronald James Randall begins killing women in New York City as a statement about society's growing decay. The killer, a cab driver, carves cryptic messages deeply into the skin of each corpse, causing the press to dub him The Bard **[BWRO]**.

—In or Before July 1977

Treasure Island, a Manhattan comic shop **[HOOD, FILM]**, opens near Dan Dreiberg's brownstone. The retailer sells maritime collectibles, including a poster of *Mutiny on the Bounty* **[ALAN]**.

> **NOTE:** *In the video game* The End Is Nigh, Part 2, *the shop is already in operation in July 1977.*

The Judo Master Karate Kung-Fu Academy opens in Times Square. The Paradise Inferno night club also opens in New York City **[BWRO]**.

Dan Dreiberg stores two hoverbikes near Manhattan's waterfront, in a building operated by Strigidae Industries **[NIGH]**.

> **NOTE:** *Presumably, Dan owns Strigidae Industries, given that the word "Strigidae" refers to a family of nearly 190 species of owls.*

Manhattan strip club The Honey Pit begins featuring female dancers called Pussy Cat, XXX, and the Titty Nipply Girls. In addition, an adult film called *Beautiful Bootys* is produced **[NIGH]**.

> **NOTE:** *The dancers are identified on posters hanging on the club's walls.*

Conrad, a chef, and Nancy, a waitress, obtain jobs at the Gunga Diner in New York City. Rorschach becomes a daily customer at the restaurant, sitting at the counter and ordering two chili dogs as his usual breakfast routine. Nancy is intrigued by her odd customer, despite his poor hygiene, while Conrad finds him off-putting **[BWRO]**.

New York City drug kingpin Rawhead buys a pet tiger **[BWRO]**.

An orderly named Dwayne begins working in Bellevue Hospital's emergency room **[BWRO]**.

—July 1, 1977

Rorschach records a journal entry recalling the childhood abuse his mother inflicted on him. He describes how, despite others' fear of him, he continues to prowl the streets, protecting the innocent **[BWRO]**.

MIND .... *The Mindscape of Alan Moore*
MOBL.... *Watchmen: The Mobile Game*
MOTN.... *Watchmen: The Complete Motion Comic*
MTRO.... *Metro* promotional newspaper cover wrap
NEWP.... *New Frontiersman* promotional newspaper
NEWW... *New Frontiersman* website
NIGH ..... *Watchmen: The End Is Nigh, Parts 1 and 2*
PKIT ...... *Watchmen* film British press kit
PORT..... *Watchmen Portraits*
REAL..... Real life
RPG1 .... *DC Heroes Role Playing Module #227: Who Watches the Watchmen?*

RPG2 .... *DC Heroes Role Playing Module #235: Taking Out the Trash—Curses and Tears*
RPG3 .... *DC Heroes: The Watchmen Sourcebook*
RUBY .... "Wounds," published in *The Ruby Files Volume One*
SCR1..... Unfilmed screenplay draft: Sam Hamm
SCR2..... Unfilmed screenplay draft: Charles McKeuen
SCR3..... Unfilmed screenplay draft: Gary Goldman
SCR4..... Unfilmed screenplay draft: David Hayter (2002)
SCR5..... Unfilmed screenplay draft: David Hayter (2003)
SCR6..... Unfilmed screenplay draft: Alex Tse
SPOT..... *DC Spotlight #1*
VRL1 ..... Viral video: *NBS Nightly News with Ted Philips*

VRL2 ..... Viral video: *The Keene Act and You*
VRL3 ..... Viral video: *Who Watches the Watchmen? A Veidt Music Network (VMN) Special*
VRL4 ..... Viral video: *World in Focus: 6 Minutes to Midnight*
VRL5 ..... Viral video: *Local Radio Station Report on 1977 Riots*
VRL6 ..... Viral videos (group of ten): *Veidt Enterprises Advertising Contest*
WAWA .... *Watching the Watchmen*
WHOS ... *Who's Who: The Definitive Directory of the DC Universe*
WTFC .... *Watchmen: The Film Companion*

Rorschach kicks in the door of a private porn theater booth, interrupting street hustler Dwayne Carter as the latter masturbates to an adult film. The vigilante breaks Carter's arm and demands information about his stash, coercing the pusher to reveal that the drugs are stored in a sewer tunnel. Rorschach heads out to find them **[BWRO]**.

—July 1 to 6, 1977

Rorschach spends several days wading through New York City's sewers without sleep, searching for Carter's drug supplier **[BWRO]**.

—July 6, 1977

Rorschach records a journal entry about his efforts in the sewer, describing himself as "a prospector in Hell, digging for the mother load" **[BWRO]**.

> **NOTE:** *The vigilante misspells the word "motherlode" in his journal entry.*

—July 6, 1977, Night

After days of searching, Rorschach tries to beat information out of two sewer-dwellers, but is quickly overpowered by their gang. Two others, Joe Bird and Big Cool, hold him while their burn-scarred boss, Rawhead, taunts him for being so easily defeated. Another thug, Lucky Pierre, tries to remove the vigilante's mask, but Rawhead says not to bother. The gang delivers a brutal beating instead, leaving him unconscious and bleeding in the muck. Rorschach later drags himself back to the surface, then breaks into a drugstore and downs prescription pain reliever **[BWRO]**.

The NYPD investigates the latest victim of serial killer The Bard, who is found lying face-down in a garbage dumpster with a message carved into her flesh: "I can't help myself but I don't need to / I can't see myself but neither can you" **[BWRO]**.

—July 7, 1977, Morning

Rorschach eats at the Gunga Diner, sans mask. The staff are shocked at his appearance, and he claims to have been mugged. A waitress, Nancy, cleans his bleeding face with a rag, but when she asks his name, he leaves without replying. Spotting two of Rawhead's cronies—one of his attackers and another called Tyson—selling drugs, he hotwires a truck, rams his attacker, leaves behind his ink-blot calling card, and tosses a Molotov cocktail, blowing up the pusher, the vehicle, and a few passersby. He later types up a journal entry in his apartment, admitting he underestimated the gang **[BWRO]**.

Tyson brings the ink-blot calling card to Rawhead, revealing that the vigilante is alive. Furious, Rawhead shoots Tyson in the head for failing him, feeds the corpse to his tiger, and orders other gang members to kill Rorschach **[BWRO]**.

Before July 8, 1977

The wife of Gunga Diner chef Conrad becomes pregnant. When she decides to get a job, Conrad refuses to let her do so, preferring to go on welfare **[BWRO]**.

July 8, 1977

Rorschach stumbles into the Gunga Diner for breakfast, even bloodier than the day prior. Conrad tells him to leave, but Nancy seats him at a back booth. After he vomits up blood and passes out, she has him transported to Bellevue Hospital **[BWRO]**.

July 8 to 10, 1977

The vigilante spends three days in Bellevue Hospital's emergency room **[BWRO]**.

July 10, 1977

After stealing medical supplies from Bellevue, Rorschach notices Nancy asking a nurse about his condition, but sneaks out without talking to her. He later records a journal entry noting that the rampant misery at the facility reminds him that he's at war, and that the city's growing garbage problem mirrors governmental corruption **[BWRO]**.

Rorschach finds Joe Bird punishing a prostitute at the Hotel Rio for failing to meet her quota. He roughs up the pimp, demanding Rawhead's whereabouts, then sticks glass in Bird's mouth and punches it. When others kick down the door, he lobs a gas grenade, steals a wad of money, and dives out a window. Gunfire dislodges the hotel's sign and fire escape, dropping the vigilante to the pavement, where he hails a taxi. The driver, Ronald James Randall—a serial killer called The Bard—recognizes him and praises his work, disgusted at the city's decay. Bird is hospitalized for his wounds **[BWRO]**.

> **NOTE:** *The Bard is drawn to resemble Travis Bickle, actor Robert De Niro's mentally ill title character from the 1976 film* Taxi Driver.

> **CONFLICT:** *The serial killer comments that outlawing vigilantes was a bad idea, but Alan Moore's miniseries sets the Keene Act's passing in August 1977, a month after this story takes place, so he should not yet know about that development.*

July 11, 1977

The Bard kills another victim, whose body is discovered lying naked in the street with a message carved into her corpse: "I'm not a monster / Innocent a child / Your future reflected / Growing up to [sic] soon" **[BWRO]**.

Rorschach visits the Gunga Diner to thank Nancy for her concern, offering to buy her dinner as a show of gratitude. She accepts, saying to pick her up at the restaurant after her shift ends **[BWRO]**.

MIND .... *The Mindscape of Alan Moore*	**RPG2** .... *DC Heroes Role Playing Module #235: Taking Out the Trash—Curses and Tears*	**VRL2** ..... Viral video: *The Keene Act and You*
MOBL .... *Watchmen: The Mobile Game*		**VRL3** ..... Viral video: *Who Watches the Watchmen? A Veidt Music Network (VMN) Special*
MOTN .... *Watchmen: The Complete Motion Comic*	**RPG3** .... *DC Heroes: The Watchmen Sourcebook*	
MTRO .... *Metro promotional newspaper cover wrap*	**RUBY** .... "Wounds," published in *The Ruby Files Volume One*	**VRL4** ..... Viral video: *World in Focus: 6 Minutes to Midnight*
NEWP .... *New Frontiersman promotional newspaper*	**SCR1** ..... Unfilmed screenplay draft: Sam Hamm	**VRL5** ..... Viral video: *Local Radio Station Report on 1977 Riots*
NEWW .... *New Frontiersman website*	**SCR2** ..... Unfilmed screenplay draft: Charles McKeuen	
NIGH ..... *Watchmen: The End Is Nigh, Parts 1 and 2*	**SCR3** .... Unfilmed screenplay draft: Gary Goldman	**VRL6** ..... Viral videos (group of ten): *Veidt Enterprises Advertising Contest*
PKIT ...... *Watchmen film British press kit*	**SCR4** ..... Unfilmed screenplay draft: David Hayter (2002)	
PORT ..... *Watchmen Portraits*	**SCR5** ..... Unfilmed screenplay draft: David Hayter (2003)	**WAWA** ... *Watching the Watchmen*
REAL ..... Real life	**SCR6** ..... Unfilmed screenplay draft: Alex Tse	**WHOS** ... *Who's Who: The Definitive Directory of the DC Universe*
RPG1 .... *DC Heroes Role Playing Module #227: Who Watches the Watchmen?*	**SPOT** .... *DC Spotlight #1*	
	VRL1 ..... Viral video: *NBS Nightly News with Ted Philips*	**WTFC** ... *Watchmen: The Film Companion*

—July 11, 1977—4:30 PM
News of The Bard's latest victim hits the news just as a thunderstorm begins **[BWRO]**.

—July 11, 1977—Night
Rorschach records a journal entry suggesting that The Bard must be confident about not being caught to have taken another victim so soon **[BWRO]**.

Rawhead orders his employees to find Rorschach before the vigilante picks them off individually. Lucky Pierre suggests using the fact that *he* knows *them* to their advantage, so Rawhead meets his hookers out on the street, sans bodyguards. Rorschach recognizes a trap and doesn't take the bait. Instead, he follows the gangster to his night club, The Paradise Inferno, where a pair of pimps threaten him for looking at their prostitutes. A moment later, New York City experiences a blackout, and he dons his mask to prepare for the inevitable chaos **[BWRO]**.

> **NOTE:** *A blackout in New York City took place in the real world on July 13-14, 1977, but Rorschach's journal entry establishes the date as July 11. Apparently, the power outage occurs two days earlier in* Watchmen *continuity.*

—July 11, 1977—Shortly Before 11:00 PM
Rorschach breaks into The Paradise Inferno, lets Rawhead's tiger loose, and fights gang members as they scramble to kill the animal. As he battles Lucky Pierre, Rawhead dances to disco music, dressed like John Travolta from *Saturday Night Fever*. The mobster ties Rorschach to a bed, removes his mask, and tries it on. Despite the stench, he jokes about being a superhero, then heads outside to have fun fighting looters—who promptly kill him with a bat. Lucky Pierre tortures Rorschach for his real name, but the tiger mauls the thug to death, enabling the crime-fighter to escape unnoticed. He then exits the club and retrieves his mask from Rawhead's corpse **[BWRO]**.

—July 11, 1977—11:00 PM
Nancy finishes her shift at the Gunga Diner, but when Rorschach fails to show up, Ronald James Randall (a regular customer) offers to walk her home to keep her safe during the blackout. Leading her into an alley, the serial killer pulls out a knife, slits her throat, and carves a message into her back: "Bright lies big city" **[BWRO]**.

—July 11, 1977—After 11:00 PM
Nancy survives and is found wandering naked and bleeding down the street. She identifies her attacker, having recognized Randall from the restaurant. Police arrest The Bard **[BWRO]**.

—After July 11, 1977

Power is restored to New York City, and the looting inhabitants return to their normal routine, resuming the façade of civility **[BWRO]**.

—Mid- or Late July 1977

The New York Police Officers' Union officially goes on strike **[NIGH]**. Union officials announce their demand that masked crime-fighting be abolished immediately **[VRL5]**.

> **CONFLICT:** *Alan Moore's miniseries sets the strike in 1977, but does not provide a specific starting date.* The Film Companion *cites late July, and* The End Is Nigh, Part 2 *specifies July 29.* The Watchmen Sourcebook *sees the strike already in progress on July 7, while* The New Frontiersman *website moves it back to March 2, 1977, and* Before Watchmen: Ozymandias *uses the date April 17.*

The strike lasts for three days **[ABSO]** and extends to other areas of the United States as well, resulting in widespread anarchy. Masked vigilantes step in to keep the peace, which only makes the situation worse since the strike is in protest of their actions. The press dubs the chaos the Police Riots. During the strike, Rorschach makes inflammatory anti-cop statements, for which many officers hold a grudge **[ALAN]**.

Radio journalist Greg Schwartz covers the situation, reporting that rioters have been rushed to hospitals after being attacked by Rorschach. Broadway is completely shut down, road blocks are erected along the Bowery, and several buildings are set ablaze on St. Ann's Avenue, Bergen Avenue, and Leonard Street **[VRL5]**. A large group of protestors are killed or injured when a man tosses a Molotov cocktail through the front window of J&K Television, causing the store to explode **[FILM]**.

Senator John David Keene represents the New York Police Officer's Union during the strike, demanding that the government "Give the American people uniforms over costumes." This sentiment is echoed by many right-wing citizens **[NEWW]**, though not the *New Frontiersman* staff, who staunchly defend the crime-fighters **[ALAN]**.

Adrian Veidt comes out of retirement to patrol the SoHo section of southern Manhattan. With looting and vandalism prevalent during the strike, he decides he'd be most effective in costume as Ozymandias. Veidt spots a teen spray-painting "Who Watches the Watchmen?" on a wall and orders him to stop. When the youth threatens him with the can, Adrian punctures it with a stiletto, spraying the boy's face with yellow paint. He finds looters emptying an appliance store and beats one badly, scaring the others into restocking the retailer's shelves **[BWOZ]**.

The *New York Gazette*'s front-page headline reads "Police Strike Enters Second Day." Rorschach records a journal entry noting that New York City seems feverish and on the verge of convulsions **[NIGH]**.

As Dan Dreiberg prepares *Archimedes* to help quell the riots, Rorschach shows him the footage of Violet Greene. Dan cleans up the film, recognizes Treasure Island's marquee in the background, and determines that the scene was shot at The Honey Pit, an adult-entertainment establishment. The two enter the strip club, battle bouncers and patrons while searching for clues, and find the room in which the film was made, which contains a movie camera but no sign of Violet **[NIGH]**.

Rorschach and Dreiberg seek out the film's director, whom Rorschach kills before they can question him. They find film reels in a closet, one of which contains the full version of *Schoolgirls in Trouble*, and discover that Violet's "captor" is The Twilight Lady. At the madam's residence, they fight gangs of Knot-Tops as the city erupts in fire and chaos around them. Making their way to a waterfront building owned by Strigidae Industries, Dan retrieves two hoverbikes from storage and they travel to The Twilight Lady's dilapidated mansion **[NIGH]**.

Inside, the crime-fighters battle thugs clad in sadomasochistic garb, then find Violet Greene engaged in S&M play with a U.S. senator. The vice queen says her whorehouse is protected by police, and that Violet is of legal age and employed voluntarily. Nite Owl suggests they leave since no abduction has occurred, but Rorschach refuses to compromise on morality, determined to return the girl to her parents. The madam flees the room and they pursue her throughout the huge house, battling numerous dominatrices and bondage-suited goons in her employ **[NIGH]**.

The two vigilantes confront The Twilight Lady atop her mansion, where she attacks them with an electrified cattle prod. Rorschach knocks her onto a glass roof, but when he tries to kill her, Dan intervenes, preferring to arrest her. Rorschach attacks his friend, accusing him of losing focus and tolerating child exploitation. The fight is brutal, seemingly ending their partnership **[NIGH]**.

> **NOTE:** *The outcome of* The End Is Nigh'*s storyline depends on who wins the fight during gameplay. If Rorschach gains the upper hand, he fires his grappling gun at the glass beneath The Twilight Lady, causing her to plummet several stories. Dan calls Rorschach a "fucking psycho" and tells him to leave, and Rorschach complies. If, on the other hand, Dan wins, he rescues The Twilight Lady but Rorschach falls through the roof instead, surviving the fall. In this scenario, the madam flirts with Nite Owl, but he angrily demands that she leave the city or else he will kill her himself.*

CONFLICT: The Watchmen Sourcebook *claims The Twilight Lady serves only two years in prison, then heads to France and vanishes.*

Still not on speaking terms with Rorschach **[NIGH]**, Dan Dreiberg teams up with The Comedian to quell a riot on Fire Island. Blake confuses the Owlship's flamethrower button for a cigarette lighter and nearly starts a fire in Dan's basement. When a rioter pelts Blake with a can as he rides *Archimedes'* exterior, he responds with riot gas and rubber bullets **[ALAN]**. The duo quell riots in the Bronx, where protestors cause $300,000 in damage. Nearby hospitals treat eleven eye and lung injuries caused by *Archie*'s tear-gas grenades **[RPG3]**.

As Rorschach works to hold the Lower East Side **[ALAN]**, Dan Dreiberg tries to find his friend and offer assistance. Laurie Juspeczyk questions this decision, condemning Rorschach's increasingly violent tactics, but Dan notes that recent years' events have had a heavy effect on his partner. She wishes Dan luck, then heads to Washington, D.C., with Jon Osterman. Dan battles rioters on the street, some of whom are merely innocent citizens scared of the chaos. He finds Rorschach, but his former partner accuses him of no longer being cut out for crime-fighting **[MOBL]**.

The Comedian contacts Nite Owl via radio, reporting that city officials need them to stop a mob from setting fires across town. Blake arranges to meet *Archimedes* at the top of the Teach Building, then battles his way through looters to the landing zone, including a protracted battle with one of the riot's leaders—a muscular giant of a man wearing a skintight purple outfit and arm-length fighting gloves. An old man witnesses the fight and accuses Blake of causing the chaos in the first place. Dan spots a helicopter setting the city ablaze and gives chase aboard the Owlship. The other aircraft fires missiles, but Dan brings the chopper down and retrieves The Comedian **[MOBL]**.

In D.C., Dr. Manhattan and Silk Spectre thwart an angry mob sporting signs proclaiming "Give Us Our Police Back," "Ban Vigilantes Now," and "Badges, Not Masks." As Laurie apprehends the riot's ring leaders, others call Jon "freak" and other derogatory names. The superhuman teleports the entire crowd to their homes, leaving the street empty save for the two crime-fighters. Two looters suffer heart attacks as a result **[ALAN]**.

—Mid-July 1977 to Mid-1980
Ronald James Randall spends three years in prison, awaiting trial **[BWRO]**.

—Late July or Early August 1977
The morning after the strike ends, the city council gives in to police union demands. Ironically, the rioting damages cost New York City more than the raise in police pay.

MIND .... *The Mindscape of Alan Moore*
MOBL .... *Watchmen: The Mobile Game*
MOTN .... *Watchmen: The Complete Motion Comic*
MTRO .... *Metro* promotional newspaper cover wrap
NEWP .... *New Frontiersman* promotional newspaper
NEWW .... *New Frontiersman* website
NIGH ..... *Watchmen: The End Is Nigh, Parts 1 and 2*
PKIT ...... *Watchmen* film British press kit
PORT ..... *Watchmen Portraits*
REAL ..... Real life
RPG1 .... *DC Heroes Role Playing Module #227: Who Watches the Watchmen?*

RPG2 .... *DC Heroes Role Playing Module #235: Taking Out the Trash—Curses and Tears*
RPG3 .... *DC Heroes: The Watchmen Sourcebook*
RUBY .... "Wounds," published in *The Ruby Files Volume One*
SCR1 ..... Unfilmed screenplay draft: Sam Hamm
SCR2 ..... Unfilmed screenplay draft: Charles McKeuen
SCR3 ..... Unfilmed screenplay draft: Gary Goldman
SCR4 ..... Unfilmed screenplay draft: David Hayter (2002)
SCR5 ..... Unfilmed screenplay draft: David Hayter (2003)
SCR6 ..... Unfilmed screenplay draft: Alex Tse
SPOT .... *DC Spotlight #1*
VRL1 ..... Viral video: *NBS Nightly News with Ted Philips*

VRL2 ..... Viral video: *The Keene Act and You*
VRL3 ..... Viral video: *Who Watches the Watchmen? A Veidt Music Network (VMN) Special*
VRL4 ..... Viral video: *World in Focus: 6 Minutes to Midnight*
VRL5 ..... Viral video: *Local Radio Station Report on 1977 Riots*
VRL6 ..... Viral videos (group of ten): *Veidt Enterprises Advertising Contest*
WAWA ... *Watching the Watchmen*
WHOS .... *Who's Who: The Definitive Directory of the DC Universe*
WTFC .... *Watchmen: The Film Companion*

Rumors abound that Ozymandias was spotted during the riots—which suits Adrian Veidt fine since he plans to release an Ozymandias action figure in stores the next day **[BWOZ]**.

Jon Osterman reads a newspaper article reporting that two rioters suffered heart attacks during the strike upon suddenly finding themselves teleported home. He is unfazed by the news since continued rioting would have caused increased fatalities **[ALAN]**.

—In or Before August 1977
Hector Godfrey is named the editor of the *New Frontiersman* **[NEWP]**.
> **NOTE:** *Godfrey is likely related to Victor Godfrey, who, according to* The Watchmen Sourcebook, *edited the conspiracy-theorist newspaper in 1956.*

—Before August 2, 1977
Senator John David Keene proposes an emergency bill known as the Keene Act, outlawing vigilantism in the United States. The *New York Post*'s front-page headline reads "Cops Say 'Let Them Do It.'" Public opinion turns against costumed adventurers, with many protestors spray-painting the phrase "Who Watches the Watchmen?" on building walls **[ALAN, FILM]**.
> **NOTE:** *The DC Comics Deck-Building Game's* Watchmen *Crossover Pack misspells the law's name as the Keane Act.*

> **CONFLICT:** *In Sam Hamm's unproduced 1988 screenplay, the police strike and the Keene Act result after the crime-fighters (collectively called The Watchmen, not The Crimebusters) inadvertently allow terrorists to topple the Statue of Liberty in 1976.*

Journalist Doug Roth brings a libel suit against the *New Frontiersman*. As part of its reparations to Roth, the newspaper agrees to provide the writer with a front-page space to contribute an op-ed piece opposing the editors' right-wing viewpoints **[NEWP]**.

—August 2, 1977
The *New Frontiersman* publishes a free Special Edition bearing the headline "Judgement Day!" The front page features three editorials discussing the Keene Act. "Wake Up America," by Hector Godfrey, warns that outlawing costumed heroes could lead to citizens losing voting rights and, ultimately, their freedom. Seymour Smith's "Punks Destroy England… Are We Next?" notes that as the U.S. government prevents patriots from dressing up in costumes to protect their country, the British punk-rock subculture are wearing leather S&M outfits in support of anarchy, and could influence American youths to embrace drug use and violence. Doug Roth's opposing op-ed piece, "Who Watches the Watchmen?", demands to know more about the mysterious vigilantes who have replaced due process. Roth urges readers to ignore the *New Frontiersman* and instead get their news from the more credible *Nova Express* **[NEWP]**.

August 3, 1977

The Keene Act (Title XIII of Public Law 95-111 and Title 18, Section 2726) **[VRL2, NEWW]**, passes the U.S. Congress, prohibiting the vigilante use of masks, capes, gadgets, experimental weapons, or dangerous unlicensed vehicles **[VRL2]**. The law deems the "improper investigation or prevention of any federal, state, or local criminal violation" by a person not duly licensed by the U.S. government a first-degree felony, and the failure by anyone making a citizen's arrest to disclose his or her name a second-degree felony **[RPG3]**. Opponents dub the law a "pseudo McCarthy witch-hunt"—a comparison that Keene, a staunch patriot and anti-communist, relishes **[NEWW]**.

> **CONFLICT:** Before Watchmen: Ozymandias *dates the Keene Act's passing on June 20, 1978. A timeline packaged with* The End Is Nigh—The Complete Experience *also cites 1978, while The* Watchmen *film moves the law's passing up to 1979. All of these dates contradict Alan Moore's miniseries, in which it occurs in August 1977. The* Watchmen Sourcebook *mentions Richard Nixon signing the bill into law in December 1977, which also contradicts the comic since Rorschach kills Harvey Furniss in protest of the new law that summer.*

The New York Post features the front-page headline "'Keene Act' Bans All Vigilantism" **[HOOD]**, while the *New York Gazette* announces "Keene Act Passed: Vigilantes Illegal" **[ALAN, BWOZ]**. Adrian Veidt buys a copy of the *Gazette* from news vendor Bernard, who comments that Ozymandias "got out while the getting was good" **[BWOZ]**.

Eddie Blake, Jon Osterman, and other crime-fighters are exempted from the Keene Act, provided that they work under U.S. supervision as "extranormal operatives." Blake accepts a position as a government hitman and mercenary, and Osterman also agrees to work for the government **[ALAN]**. Due to her relationship with Dr. Manhattan, Silk Spectre receives a government license to continue operating as a superheroine as well **[RPG3]**, though she opts not to **[ALAN]**.

> **NOTE:** *Alan Moore's miniseries implies that other vigilantes are exempted along with Eddie Blake and Jon Osterman, but offers no further details. The* Watchmen Sourcebook *reveals that Laurie Juspeczyk is among them.*

Most masked adventurers comply with the Keene Act, though others continue to operate outside the law, including Rorschach **[ALAN]**. Some go into hiding, which Senator Keene cites as proof that most vigilantes are merely criminals **[NEWW]**. Eddie Blake's first assignment is to make sure the others comply with the new law **[MOBL]**.

With vigilantism now illegal, some thugs take advantage of the situation by mounting a crime spree, so Dan Dreiberg carries out one final mission before hanging up the Nite Owl cowl. Taking *Archimedes* out for a last ride, he battles a helicopter and a blimp in the

MIND .... *The Mindscape of Alan Moore*	**RPG2** .... *DC Heroes Role Playing Module #235: Taking Out the Trash—Curses and Tears*	**VRL2** ..... Viral video: *The Keene Act and You*
MOBL.... *Watchmen: The Mobile Game*		**VRL3** ..... Viral video: *Who Watches the Watchmen? A Veidt Music Network (VMN) Special*
MOTN.... *Watchmen: The Complete Motion Comic*	**RPG3** .... *DC Heroes: The Watchmen Sourcebook*	**VRL4** ..... Viral video: *World in Focus: 6 Minutes to Midnight*
MTRO.... *Metro* promotional newspaper cover wrap	**RUBY** .... "Wounds," published in *The Ruby Files Volume One*	**VRL5** ..... Viral video: *Local Radio Station Report on 1977 Riots*
NEWP.... *New Frontiersman* promotional newspaper	**SCR1**..... Unfilmed screenplay draft: Sam Hamm	
NEWW... *New Frontiersman* website	**SCR2**..... Unfilmed screenplay draft: Charles McKeuen	**VRL6** ..... Viral videos (group of ten): *Veidt Enterprises Advertising Contest*
NIGH ..... *Watchmen: The End Is Nigh, Parts 1 and 2*	**SCR3**..... Unfilmed screenplay draft: Gary Goldman	
PKIT...... *Watchmen* film British press kit	**SCR4**..... Unfilmed screenplay draft: David Hayter (2002)	**WAWA** ... *Watching the Watchmen*
PORT.... *Watchmen Portraits*	**SCR5**..... Unfilmed screenplay draft: David Hayter (2003)	**WHOS** ... *Who's Who: The Definitive Directory of the DC Universe*
REAL..... Real life	**SCR6**..... Unfilmed screenplay draft: Alex Tse	
RPG1 .... *DC Heroes Role Playing Module #227: Who Watches the Watchmen?*	**SPOT**.... *DC Spotlight #1*	**WTFC** .... *Watchmen: The Film Companion*
	VRL1 ..... Viral video: *NBS Nightly News with Ted Philips*	

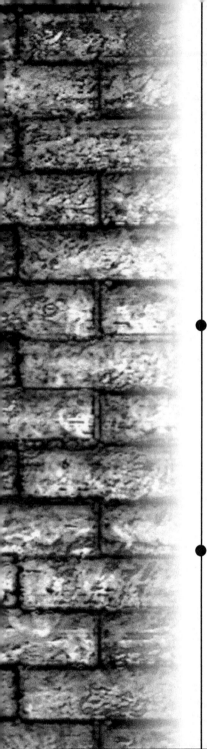

skies above New York City, then seeks out his colleagues to discuss the new law. Rorschach (whom he finds at Happy Harry's bar and grill) is angry at the situation, while The Comedian takes it in stride, Dr. Manhattan says his life will be unaffected, and Laurie views the law as a chance to grow up and lead a normal life **[MOBL]**.

Dan Dreiberg retires, keeping his alter-ego identity a secret from the masses. Laurie Juspeczyk also retires, having never enjoyed the superhero life in the first place **[ALAN]**. She holds a press conference in front of the historic Minutemen building to deny rumors that she will seek government exemption **[RPG3]**.

Rorschach harbors resentment at his friends' decision, which he sees as going soft and lacking staying power **[ALAN]**. He records a journal entry expressing his disgust at the Keene Act's passing. Having seen the city's black underbelly, he writes, he can never pretend it doesn't exist, no matter who tells him to look the other way. He spots a teenager spray-painting "Who Watches the Watchmen?" and beats him up **[NIGH]**.

—After August 3, 1977

The U.S. government, on behalf of the House Committee on Un-American Activities, releases a public-service film titled *The Keene Act and You*. The propaganda piece panders to patriotism, condemning The Minutemen and their successors for being prone to violence, perversion, and insanity. The film presents John Keene as an un-masked hero sympathetic to the masses, claims policemen are being undermined by "the costumed menace," and instructs anyone suspecting vigilante behavior in their vicinity to remain inside, lock all doors and windows, and notify police **[VRL2]**.

In the wake of the Keene Act's passing, newspapers stop reporting on The Comedian's exploits. Some journalists, unaware of the ex-crime-fighter's covert government duties, question whether he has retired—and, if so, why **[MOBL]**.

—August 5, 1977

Two days after the Keene Act's passing **[RPG3]**, Rorschach kills suspected multiple-rapist Harvey Charles Furniss in protest, leaving his corpse outside Manhattan's police headquarters, along with a paper note expressing his feelings toward compulsory retirement: "Never!" **[ALAN]**. For violating the Keene Act, Rorschach is placed on the FBI's "Ten Most Wanted" list **[FILM]**.

> **NOTE:** *Rorschach's murder of Furniss is undated in Alan Moore's miniseries, but is said to occur during the summer immediately following the act's passing. The Watchmen Sourcebook provides the exact date.*

ABSO .... *Watchmen Absolute Edition*	**BWOZ**.... *Before Watchmen—Ozymandias*	• Film: *Batman v Superman: Dawn of Justice Ultimate Edition*
ALAN..... Alan Moore's *Watchmen* miniseries	**BWRO** ... *Before Watchmen—Rorschach*	• Film: *Justice League*
ARCD .... *Minutemen Arcade*	**BWSS** ... *Before Watchmen—Silk Spectre*	**CLIX** ...... HeroClix figure pack-in cards
ARTF..... *Watchmen: The Art of the Film*	**CHEM**.... My Chemical Romance music video: "Desolation Row"	**DECK**..... *DC Comics Deck-Building Game—Crossover Pack 4: Watchmen*
BLCK..... *Tales of the Black Freighter*	**CMEO**.... *Watchmen* cameos in comics, TV, and film:	**DURS** .... *DC Universe: Rebirth Special* volume 1 issue #1
BWCC ... *Before Watchmen—The Crimson Corsair*	• Comic: *Astonishing X-Men* volume 3 issue #6	**FILM** ..... *Watchmen* theatrical film
BWCO ... *Before Watchmen—Comedian*	• Comic: *Hero Hotline* volume 1 issue #5	**HOOD** .... *Under the Hood* documentary and dust-jacket prop reproduction
BWDB .. *Before Watchmen—Dollar Bill*	• Comic: *Kingdom Come* volume 1 issue #2	**JUST** ..... *Watchmen: Justice Is Coming*
BWDM .. *Before Watchmen—Dr. Manhattan*	• Comic: *Marvels* volume 1 issue #4	**MATL** .... Mattel Club Black Freighter figure pack-in cards
BWMM .. *Before Watchmen—Minutemen*	• Comic: *The Question* volume 1 issue #17	
BWMO .. *Before Watchmen—Moloch*	• TV: *Teen Titans Go!* episode #82, "Real Boy Adventures"	
BWNO ... *Before Watchmen—Nite Owl*	• Film: *Man of Steel*	

Early August 1977

Adrian Veidt invites Jon Osterman to his Karnak lab on the pretense of discussing their efforts to replicate his teleportation abilities. Hidden video cameras record Osterman's every move, and Veidt is unnerved at the realization that Dr. Manhattan is aware of the cameras but simply doesn't care that they're there **[BWOZ]**.

August 29, 1977

A federal warrant is issued in New York City charging Rorschach with violations of federal homicide law (Title 18, Section 111) and the Keene Act (Title 18, Section 2726) **[NEWW]**.

September 10, 1977

A second federal warrant is issued in New York City charging Rorschach with violations of federal assault law (Title 18, Section 113), federal torture law (Title 18, Section 113C, S.Code 234DA), and federal malicious mischief law (Title 13, Section 1363) **[NEWW]**.

September 21, 1977

The Political Gazette publishes an article by writer Louise Easton titled "Senator Keene Acts," profiling John David Keene's rise to political power **[NEWW]**.

October 23, 1977

Dan Dreiberg writes a letter to Professor Joseph Westwood, editor of the *Journal of the American Ornithological Society*, expressing an interest in submitting articles for publication. As a writing sample, he includes an article titled "Blood from the Shoulder of Pallas" **[RPG3]**.

> ***CONFLICT:*** *In* Justice Is Coming, *Dan has already written for the publication as of 1973, though this might not necessarily constitute a contradiction—the 1977 letter could be due to a change in leadership, with Westwood replacing Dan's previous editor.*

Between 1977 and 1979

While serving his prison sentence, Edgar Jacobi finds religion **[WTFC]**. After pondering his past encounters with Dr. Manhattan, a being as powerful as God, he visits the prison's chapel and begs Christ's help and forgiveness **[BWMO]**, joins the Jesuit Fellowship, and sets aside his former criminal ways **[FILM]**.

> ***NOTE:*** *Alan Moore's miniseries states that Jacobi spends the 1970s in prison. The Film* Companion *establishes his finding religion during those years, but also has Moloch bombing the New York Stock Exchange in 1977 (presumably from his cell). Thus, his religious epiphany likely occurs between the bombing and his release.*
>
> *The Jesuits, also called the Society of Jesus, are a male-only congregation of the Catholic Church.*

MIND .... *The Mindscape of Alan Moore*
MOBL .... *Watchmen: The Mobile Game*
MOTN .... *Watchmen: The Complete Motion Comic*
MTRO .... *Metro* promotional newspaper cover wrap
NEWP .... *New Frontiersman* promotional newspaper
NEWW .... *New Frontiersman* website
NIGH ..... *Watchmen: The End Is Nigh, Parts 1 and 2*
PKIT ...... *Watchmen* film British press kit
PORT ..... *Watchmen Portraits*
REAL ..... Real life
RPG1 .... *DC Heroes Role Playing Module #227: Who Watches the Watchmen?*

RPG2 .... *DC Heroes Role Playing Module #235: Taking Out the Trash—Curses and Tears*
RPG3 .... *DC Heroes: The Watchmen Sourcebook*
RUBY .... "Wounds," published in *The Ruby Files Volume One*
SCR1 ..... Unfilmed screenplay draft: Sam Hamm
SCR2 ..... Unfilmed screenplay draft: Charles McKeuen
SCR3 ..... Unfilmed screenplay draft: Gary Goldman
SCR4 ..... Unfilmed screenplay draft: David Hayter (2002)
SCR5 ..... Unfilmed screenplay draft: David Hayter (2003)
SCR6 ..... Unfilmed screenplay draft: Alex Tse
SPOT ..... *DC Spotlight #1*
VRL1 ..... Viral video: *NBS Nightly News with Ted Philips*

VRL2 ..... Viral video: *The Keene Act and You*
VRL3 ..... Viral video: *Who Watches the Watchmen? A Veidt Music Network (VMN) Special*
VRL4 ..... Viral video: *World in Focus: 6 Minutes to Midnight*
VRL5 ..... Viral video: *Local Radio Station Report on 1977 Riots*
VRL6 ..... Viral videos (group of ten): *Veidt Enterprises Advertising Contest*
WAWA ... *Watching the Watchmen*
WHOS ... *Who's Who: The Definitive Directory of the DC Universe*
WTFC ... *Watchmen: The Film Companion*

—1977 to 1985

Eddie Blake spends several years engaged in so-called "diplomatic" work for the U.S. government, including knocking over Marxist republics in South America **[ALAN]**. Richard Nixon assigns him to keep tabs on his fellow former crime-fighters, to make sure they don't rock the boat following the passage of the Keene Act **[FILM]**.

Dan Dreiberg considers selling some of his crime-fighting equipment, but doesn't have the heart to part with it. From time to time, he returns to his subterranean workshop to tinker with his inventions **[ALAN]**.

—Late 1970s

Laurie Juspeczyk becomes a fan of Ohio-based rock band Devo **[ALAN]**.

—1978

Jacobs Motors issues a recall of its Apache cars after fuel tank flare-ups continue to occur, causing several injuries and fatalities, including the deaths of the twin children of a woman named Marla Givens. Givens and others bring a class-action lawsuit against Jacobs Motors that takes two years to proceed to trial **[RPG3]**.

> **NOTE:** *It is unclear why these events are recounted in* The Watchmen Sourcebook's *section on The Comedian, as they seem unconnected to his history. If the author intended to imply that the vigilante caused the kids' deaths, that is not apparent.*

—March 15, 1978

Alexander Haig, the White House's Chief of Staff, issues a memorandum on behalf of Richard Nixon to the directors of the CIA and the FBI, as well as the U.S. Secretary of Defense. The memo, titled "Special Talent Contingency," calls for a discussion of the extranormal operatives program to develop a contingency in case licensed superheroes become uncontrollable. Eddie Blake possesses critically sensitive information that could be detrimental to the Nixon administration, Haig notes, and a black-ops team could take him out if necessary; no plan exists, however, for what to do if Dr. Manhattan ceases to cooperate or turns his back on the United States **[NEWW]**.

March 16, 1978—2:00 PM

Richard Nixon convenes an off-the-record meeting to assess options for how to deal with Dr. Manhattan, with a view toward developing a long-term strategy **[NEWW]**.

—July 14, 1978

After aerial surveillance reveals widespread deployment of road-mobile SS-25 intercontinental ballistic missiles (ICBMs) within the U.S.S.R., the U.S. government asks Dr. Manhattan if he would be able to neutralize a Soviet strike, but the discussions prove inconclusive. The American intelligence community issues a top-secret document, "NIE 14-7-78, Soviet Aggression and Dr. Manhattan: The Case for Intervention in Afghanistan," outlining the Liddy Emergency Sub-Committee's proposal of a fast-track discussion of a "so-called Hiroshima strategy," by which Manhattan would use cataclysmic lethal force to shock and awe the Soviet regime. Laurie Juspeczyk's influence on Manhattan is noted to be an obstacle; an action requiring Presidential sanction is recommended, but later redacted via black marker **[NEWW]**.

—Before September 6, 1978

The Smithsonian Institute, in Washington, D.C., creates a "Law and Order" museum exhibit spotlighting costumed vigilantes, ranging from Hooded Justice to Dr. Manhattan. The exhibit contains a number of props, weapons, and memorabilia **[RPG3]**.

—September 6, 1978

Dr. Thomas M. Dewey, the Smithsonian Institute's special programs curator, writes a letter to Laurie Juspeczyk, asking her to donate her Silk Spectre costume for display in the "Law and Order" exhibit **[RPG3]**.

—September 27, 1978

Laurie Juspeczyk responds to Thomas Dewey, saying she would prefer to keep her costume, while recommending that he contact her mother, Sally Jupiter, who never throws anything away **[RPG3]**.

—Before October 28, 1978

After an individual named Loomis is extorted and murdered, two men are considered suspects: Franklin Smith and Daziel Amrand **[NEWW]**.

—October 28, 1978—6:45 AM

Three police officers from New York City's 67th Precinct respond to reports of a violent disturbance and shots fired at 1240 Telluride Avenue, and observe Rorschach leaving the building. After Rorschach injures Officer James Schwartz, Officers Mark Pallazo and Grevin Adell come to his assistance and also suffer injuries **[NEWW]**.

—October 28, 1978—7:05 AM

Support units arrive to assist the three officers, but Rorschach flees the location. Inside the building, the police find the dead bodies of Franklin Smith and Daziel Amrand, suspects in the Loomis murder-extortion case **[NEWW]**.

> **NOTE:** This Franklin Smith is a separate individual from the same-named New Frontiersman writer, who is still alive in 1985.

MIND .... The Mindscape of Alan Moore	**RPG2** .... DC Heroes Role Playing Module #235: Taking Out the Trash—Curses and Tears	**VRL2** ..... Viral video: The Keene Act and You
MOBL.... Watchmen: The Mobile Game		**VRL3** ..... Viral video: Who Watches the Watchmen? A Veidt Music Network (VMN) Special
MOTN.... Watchmen: The Complete Motion Comic	**RPG3** .... DC Heroes: The Watchmen Sourcebook	
MTRO .... Metro promotional newspaper cover wrap	**RUBY** .... "Wounds," published in The Ruby Files Volume One	**VRL4** ..... Viral video: World in Focus: 6 Minutes to Midnight
NEWP .... New Frontiersman promotional newspaper	**SCR1** ..... Unfilmed screenplay draft: Sam Hamm	**VRL5** ..... Viral video: Local Radio Station Report on 1977 Riots
NEWW... New Frontiersman website	**SCR2** ..... Unfilmed screenplay draft: Charles McKeuen	
NIGH ..... Watchmen: The End Is Nigh, Parts 1 and 2	**SCR3** ..... Unfilmed screenplay draft: Gary Goldman	**VRL6** ..... Viral videos (group of ten): Veidt Enterprises Advertising Contest
PKIT ...... Watchmen film British press kit	**SCR4** ..... Unfilmed screenplay draft: David Hayter (2002)	
PORT ..... Watchmen Portraits	**SCR5** ..... Unfilmed screenplay draft: David Hayter (2003)	**WAWA**... Watching the Watchmen
REAL ..... Real life	**SCR6** ..... Unfilmed screenplay draft: Alex Tse	**WHOS** ... Who's Who: The Definitive Directory of the DC Universe
RPG1 .... DC Heroes Role Playing Module #227: Who Watches the Watchmen?	**SPOT** ..... DC Spotlight #1	
	VRL1 ..... Viral video: NBS Nightly News with Ted Philips	**WTFC** .... Watchmen: The Film Companion

—October 28, 1978—11:45 AM

Sergeant Donald H. Malone, commanding officer of the 67th Precinct, files an internal NYPD report regarding Rorschach's suspected double-murder of Franklin Smith and Daziel Amrand **[NEWW]**.

—November 27, 1978

The FBI releases a wanted poster for Rorschach, citing murder in the first and second degrees, assault, aggravated assault, torture, breaking and entering, and violation of the Keene Act. Rorschach is said to be armed and dangerous, and a reward is offered of up to $10,000 for information leading to his arrest **[NEWW]**.

—Mid-December 1978

Iranian militants storm the United States' embassy in Tehran. Four days later, the U.S. government authorizes The Comedian to mount a rescue mission **[RPG3]**. Eddie Blake single-handedly rescues fifty-three American hostages and fatally shoots seventeen Iranian citizens—mostly armed militants **[RPG3]**. In ending the crisis and returning the captives home safely, Blake silences even his harshest critics **[ALAN, RPG2]**.

> **NOTE:** *The real-world standoff, during which the Muslim Student Followers of the Imams held more than sixty American diplomats and citizens captive for 444 days, lasted from November 4, 1979, to January 20, 1981.* Taking Out the Trash *and* The Watchmen Sourcebook *both set the crisis in December 1978—nearly a year earlier—while a timeline in the* Watchmen *film's British press kit moves the conflict to 1979, which is historically accurate but contradicts Alan Moore's miniseries.*

—December 21, 1978—Morning

The Comedian returns to U.S. soil after ending the Iranian hostage crisis, landing at Washington Dulles International Airport, in Virginia **[RPG3]**.

—December 22, 1978

The *New York Gazette* covers The Comedian's successful rescue of the U.S. hostages, noting that the operative merely laughed when asked to speak with reporters **[RPG3]**.

—1970s and 1980s

Sally Jupiter grows a bit bloated with age, though her popularity as an ex-superheroine continues in some fan circles **[ALAN]**.

—1979

The United States launches a retaliatory bombing of Beirut, Lebanon. Hector Godfrey, editor of the *New Frontiersman*, deems the action justified **[ALAN]**.

> **NOTE:** *What the United States is retaliating against is unstated. In the real world, this event did not occur.*

Dr. Manhattan forces Nicaragua's Sandinista National Liberation Front to sign a peace treaty with the United States. Manhattan is present as American Secretary of State G. Gordon Liddy and Sandinista leader Daniel Ortega sign the treaty **[SCR1, SCR2]**.

—February 1979

The Smithsonian Institute, in Washington, D.C., opens its "Law and Order" museum exhibit. Focused on masked adventurers from the 1930s to the 1970s, ranging from Hooded Justice to Dr. Manhattan, the exhibit includes numerous weapons, memorabilia, and props **[RPG3]**.

—August 14, 1979

Pursued by police officers, Rorschach runs into an ally. A cab driver recognizes him and offers a ride, calling the fugitive his hero in the war against sinners, politicians, and false prophets. Rorschach says the police fail to find him because they don't truly want to, but he knows they will eventually lock him up and then realize how much they need him. The vigilante later records a journal entry describing the conversation **[RPG3]**.

—End of the 1970s

While serving a decade in prison, Edgar Jacobi gets to know several fellow criminals, including Underboss, Jimmy the Gimmick, and The King of Skin **[ALAN, RPG2]**.

—Late 1970s or Early 1980s

Janey Slater quits smoking and her physician gives her a clean bill of health, though she suffers from a persistent cough that the doctor attributes to recurring bronchitis. When her health insurance company refuses to cover treatment, citing a pre-existing condition, Adrian Veidt tasks his medical contacts to find holistic, herbal treatments available only outside the United States. He pays for her treatment, designing a cigarette-based delivery system to make sure she'll use it every day. Unbeknownst to Janey, the cigarettes are designed to give her cancer **[BWMO]**.

—After the 1970s

Anthony "Underboss" Rizzoli dies at the Rikers Island jail complex while engaged in a knife fight over a cigarette lighter **[RPG3]**.

—Mid-1980

Ronald James Randall, the serial killer known as The Bard, faces trial after waiting for three years. Although his surviving victim, Nancy, testifies against him, the prosecution ineptly botches the case and the jury acquits. Nancy leaves town, scarred and scared, and Rorschach vows to bring Randall to justice **[BWRO]**.

MIND .... *The Mindscape of Alan Moore*	**RPG2** .... *DC Heroes Role Playing Module #235: Taking Out the Trash—Curses and Tears*	**VRL2** ..... Viral video: *The Keene Act and You*
MOBL .... *Watchmen: The Mobile Game*		**VRL3** ..... Viral video: *Who Watches the Watchmen? A Veidt Music Network (VMN) Special*
MOTN .... *Watchmen: The Complete Motion Comic*	**RPG3** .... *DC Heroes: The Watchmen Sourcebook*	
MTRO .... *Metro* promotional newspaper cover wrap	**RUBY** .... "Wounds," published in *The Ruby Files Volume One*	**VRL4** ..... Viral video: *World in Focus: 6 Minutes to Midnight*
NEWP .... *New Frontiersman* promotional newspaper	**SCR1** ..... Unfilmed screenplay draft: Sam Hamm	**VRL5** ..... Viral video: *Local Radio Station Report on 1977 Riots*
NEWW .... *New Frontiersman* website	**SCR2** ..... Unfilmed screenplay draft: Charles McKeuen	
NIGH ..... *Watchmen: The End Is Nigh, Parts 1 and 2*	**SCR3** ..... Unfilmed screenplay draft: Gary Goldman	**VRL6** ..... Viral videos (group of ten): *Veidt Enterprises Advertising Contest*
PKIT ...... *Watchmen* film British press kit	**SCR4** ..... Unfilmed screenplay draft: David Hayter (2002)	
PORT ..... *Watchmen Portraits*	**SCR5** ..... Unfilmed screenplay draft: David Hayter (2003)	**WAWA** ... *Watching the Watchmen*
REAL ..... Real life	**SCR6** ..... Unfilmed screenplay draft: Alex Tse	**WHOS** ... *Who's Who: The Definitive Directory of the DC Universe*
RPG1 .... *DC Heroes Role Playing Module #227: Who Watches the Watchmen?*	**SPOT** ..... *DC Spotlight #1*	
	VRL1 ..... Viral video: *NBS Nightly News with Ted Philips*	**WTFC** ... *Watchmen: The Film Companion*

—June 20, 1980

Sally Jupiter retires to the Nepenthe Gardens rest resort in California **[ALAN, RPG2]**.

> *NOTE: The date of Sally's move to the facility appears in* Taking Out the Trash. *When the resort debuts in issue #2 of Alan Moore's miniseries, only "Penthe Gardens" is visible on its sign. The full name appears in issue #12.* Penthe *is a Greek word meaning "to mourn," while* nepenthe, *in Greek mythology, is a medicine used to treat sorrow. Both terms describe Sally Jupiter's state of mind in the 1980s.*

—September 18, 1980

In Detroit, Michigan, a class-action lawsuit launches against Jacobs Motors, on behalf of the victims of fuel tank flare-ups in the company's Apache car. Lawyers for the plaintiffs produce a 1976 memo from Jacobs VP Alan Greenfeldt proving he knew of the problem before the vehicle's 1978 recall. At a press conference following the day's adjournment, Marla Givens, the mother of twins killed during a flare-up, calls for indictments against Greenfeldt and other executives, but State Attorney Dan Whiggins says U.S. law does not allow prosecutors to hold individuals responsible for a corporation's actions. The *New York Gazette* publishes an account of the proceedings **[RPG3]**.

> *NOTE: It is unclear why these events are recounted in* The Watchmen Sourcebook's *section on* The Comedian, *as they seem unconnected to his history.*

—November 4, 1980

Richard Nixon is re-elected for a fourth term of office as President of the United States. His Vice President remains Gerald Ford, while Henry Kissinger continues to serve among his advisors **[ALAN]**. Hollis Mason votes for Nixon yet again **[FILM]**.

> *NOTE: This presumes Election Day in the United States occurs on the same day in Alan Moore's miniseries as in the real world.*

November 4, 1980 (Alternate Reality)

Ronald Wilson Reagan is elected as the United States' 40th President **[REAL]**.

—1981

The Rockefeller Military Research Center is founded in New York **[ALAN]**.

Veidt Enterprises introduces the Nite Owl Dark Roast brand of "subversively good" specialty organic coffee **[FILM]**.

> *NOTE: This product appears in a* Watchmen *film scene set aboard* Archimedes, *following the tenement fire rescue. Photographer Clay Enos's Organic Coffee Cartel sold the coffee as a tie-in product in 2009, until the Massimo Zanetti Beverage Group brought a lawsuit*

ABSO .... *Watchmen Absolute Edition*	**BWOZ**.... *Before Watchmen—Ozymandias*	• Film: *Batman v Superman: Dawn of Justice Ultimate Edition*
ALAN ..... Alan Moore's *Watchmen* miniseries	**BWRO** ... *Before Watchmen—Rorschach*	• Film: *Justice League*
ARCD .... *Minutemen Arcade*	**BWSS** ... *Before Watchmen—Silk Spectre*	**CLIX** ...... HeroClix figure pack-in cards
ARTF ..... *Watchmen: The Art of the Film*	**CHEM** .... My Chemical Romance music video: "Desolation Row"	**DECK**..... *DC Comics Deck-Building Game—Crossover Pack 4: Watchmen*
BLCK..... *Tales of the Black Freighter*	**CMEO**.... *Watchmen* cameos in comics, TV, and film:	
BWCC ... *Before Watchmen—The Crimson Corsair*	• Comic: *Astonishing X-Men* volume 3 issue #6	**DURS** .... *DC Universe: Rebirth Special* volume 1 issue #1
BWCO ... *Before Watchmen—Comedian*	• Comic: *Hero Hotline* volume 1 issue #5	**FILM** ..... *Watchmen* theatrical film
BWDB .. *Before Watchmen—Dollar Bill*	• Comic: *Kingdom Come* volume 1 issue #2	**HOOD** .... *Under the Hood* documentary and dust-jacket prop reproduction
BWDM .. *Before Watchmen—Dr. Manhattan*	• Comic: *Marvels* volume 1 issue #4	
BWMM.. *Before Watchmen—Minutemen*	• Comic: *The Question* volume 1 issue #17	**JUST** ..... *Watchmen: Justice Is Coming*
BWMO .. *Before Watchmen—Moloch*	• TV: *Teen Titans Go!* episode #82, "Real Boy Adventures"	**MATL** .... Mattel Club Black Freighter figure pack-in cards
BWNO ... *Before Watchmen—Nite Owl*	• Film: *Man of Steel*	

against the cartel, as well as Warner Bros. and DC Comics, accusing the companies of stealing the design of its Chock full o'Nuts coffee can.

—March 1981

As Adrian Veidt's master plan grows closer to fruition, he realizes with regret that Marla, his faithful assistant of more than twenty years (and former lover), knows too much and must be eliminated. As she returns home from work one Friday, he arranges for her to stumble in front of an oncoming bus, which kills her instantly. Her funeral is small, attended only by Veidt, her parents, and a few close friends **[BWOZ]**.

—In or Before April 1981

Veidt hires a new personal assistant named Yvonne **[BWOZ]**.

—April 28, 1981

The *New York Gazette*'s headline reads "Scientists Move Doomsday Clock One Minute Closer to Midnight" **[BWOZ]**.

Veidt Enterprises' research-and-development team shows Adrian Veidt a prototype for the next generation of electric cars, offering twice the mileage at half the charge and passing every safety test. He orders the vehicles into immediate production, instructing the team to put all other projects on the back burner and focus on the Manhattan Project, his plan to duplicate Dr. Manhattan's teleportation abilities **[BWOZ]**.

—May 31, 1981

Jon Osterman is assigned to the Rockefeller Military Research Center's Special Talent Quarter. Laurie Juspeczyk moves to the base with him, tasked with keeping Jon happy and relaxed as he carries out projects for the government and military. Osterman deems the facility well-equipped for his work, but Laurie resents losing their privacy **[ALAN, RPG2]**. Among his team at the base are Major Adamson, William Charles Batts, Stephanie Boris, Dr. J.M. Candelaria, Colonel Brent Dabbs, and Susan White **[SCR1]**.

> **NOTE:** Alan Moore's miniseries sets the couple's relocation in 1981. The specific date appears in Taking Out the Trash.
>
> The base's logo incorporates the "S" from Superman's outfit, symbolizing Dr. Manhattan's status as Watchmen's only bona fide superhuman.

—Late October or Early November 1981

Dan Dreiberg embarks on a trip to Africa with Professor Joseph Westwood, his editor at the *Journal of the American Ornithological Society*. The two go out every morning to observe the local bird life **[RPG3]**.

MIND .... *The Mindscape of Alan Moore*
MOBL.... *Watchmen: The Mobile Game*
MOTN.... *Watchmen: The Complete Motion Comic*
MTRO.... *Metro* promotional newspaper cover wrap
NEWP.... *New Frontiersman* promotional newspaper
NEWW... *New Frontiersman* website
NIGH ..... *Watchmen: The End Is Nigh, Parts 1 and 2*
PKIT...... *Watchmen* film British press kit
PORT..... *Watchmen Portraits*
REAL..... Real life
RPG1 .... *DC Heroes Role Playing Module #227: Who Watches the Watchmen?*

RPG2 .... *DC Heroes Role Playing Module #235: Taking Out the Trash—Curses and Tears*
RPG3 .... *DC Heroes: The Watchmen Sourcebook*
RUBY .... "Wounds," published in *The Ruby Files Volume One*
SCR1..... Unfilmed screenplay draft: Sam Hamm
SCR2..... Unfilmed screenplay draft: Charles McKeuen
SCR3..... Unfilmed screenplay draft: Gary Goldman
SCR4..... Unfilmed screenplay draft: David Hayter (2002)
SCR5..... Unfilmed screenplay draft: David Hayter (2003)
SCR6..... Unfilmed screenplay draft: Alex Tse
SPOT..... *DC Spotlight #1*
VRL1 ..... Viral video: *NBS Nightly News with Ted Philips*

VRL2..... Viral video: *The Keene Act and You*
VRL3..... Viral video: *Who Watches the Watchmen? A Veidt Music Network (VMN) Special*
VRL4 ..... Viral video: *World in Focus: 6 Minutes to Midnight*
VRL5 ..... Viral video: *Local Radio Station Report on 1977 Riots*
VRL6 ..... Viral videos (group of ten): *Veidt Enterprises Advertising Contest*
WAWA... *Watching the Watchmen*
WHOS ... *Who's Who: The Definitive Directory of the DC Universe*
WTFC .... *Watchmen: The Film Companion*

—November 1981

Construction is completed on midtown Manhattan's Institute for Extraspatial Studies. At a ribbon-cutting ceremony, Adrian Veidt invites the world's greatest scientists to help him solve the universe's mysteries **[BWOZ]**. Veidt promotes the facility as searching for extra-dimensional energy sources, though it secretly plays an essential role in his plan to save humanity. The institute's chief physicist is Dr. Ed Corey **[ALAN]**.

—November 14, 1981

A couple of weeks after arriving in Africa, Dan Dreiberg sends a postcard to Hollis Mason describing his expedition. Dan admits that he misses being The Nite Owl and is having trouble accepting that he will never again wear the costume **[RPG3]**.

> **NOTE:** *Postcards are not mailed in envelopes, so anyone throughout the mail-delivery chain can read them. As such, it seems unthinkable that Dan would risk discussing his crime-fighting days on a postcard, thereby exposing his true identity.*

—Late November or Early December 1981

Dan Dreiberg returns home from his African jaunt a couple of weeks later **[RPG3]**.

—1982

Laetrile, a cancer medication made from apricot pits, is deemed phony and outlawed in the United States **[ALAN]**.

> **NOTE:** *Produced from amygdalin, a poisonous cyanogenic glycoside found in several fruits, Laetrile (the trade name for laevo-mandelonitrile-beta-glucuronoside) was banned in the United States in 1963 in the real world. In Alan Moore's miniseries, the drug's name is misspelled as "Laetril."*

Dominique Hirsch is born to a couple in New York City **[ALAN]**.

—Before July 1982

Adrian Veidt establishes the Veidt Foundation for Impoverished Inner City Children, registered charity #86744 **[NEWW]**.

—July 1982

Adrian Veidt, via J&L Auctioneers, auctions off an Ozymandias costume, including gauntlets, boots, greaves, tunic, mask, cape, and belt, for charity. The costume shows signs of wear but is in excellent condition; comes with a certificate of authenticity signed by Veidt; and is composed of fifty percent Kevlar, thirty percent Twaron, and 20 percent latex. He donates the winning bid to the Veidt Foundation for Impoverished Inner City Children **[NEWW]**.

July 11, 1982

Rorschach records a journal entry on the fifth anniversary of the 1977 blackout, describing how the loss of electricity and light exposed New Yorkers' true nature. He then tracks down and slays Ronald James Randall—a serial killer called The Bard—who tried to murder his friend Nancy that day but was acquitted in 1980 **[BWRO]**.

> *NOTE: A blackout in New York City took place in the real world on July 13-14, 1977, but Rorschach's journal entry establishes the date as July 11. Apparently, the power outage occurs two days earlier in* Watchmen *continuity.*

Before August 22, 1982

Adrian Veidt plays chess against 197 opponents during a simultaneous exhibition in New York, winning every single match, including one against Russian Grandmaster Garry Kasparov. In so doing, he shatters Cuban chess champion José Raúl Capablanca's 1922 record of 102 wins and one draw against 103 opponents **[NEWW]**.

August 22, 1982

Arnold Steinitz, president of the World Chess Association (WCA), writes a letter congratulating Adrian Veidt on his chess victories and inviting him to be a guest speaker at the organization's upcoming conference in October **[NEWW]**.

October 1982

The World Chess Association (WCA) holds its annual conference. Adrian Veidt is among the invited guest speakers **[NEWW]**.

In or Before 1983

Veidt Enterprises launches the Veidt Music Network (VMN). The television station broadcasts music videos and other programming, and its commercials feature footage of Neil Armstrong landing on Earth's moon, meeting Dr. Manhattan, and planting a flag bearing the VMN logo **[VRL3]**.

> *NOTE: Veidt creates an analog to MTV, possibly indicating that the latter (launched on August 1, 1981, in the real world) does not exist in* Watchmen *continuity.*

1983

Adrian Veidt begins recruiting creative individuals to help him design a massive, squid-like creature so he can fake an extradimensional alien invasion and trick mankind into uniting against it. Each person hired remains unaware of Veidt's true intentions, and is secretly transported to his isolated island facility for the duration of the project, with no contact allowed with the outside world. The team is misled into thinking they're creating a monster movie, and their disappearances spark a mystery in the press **[ALAN]**.

> *NOTE: In the* Watchmen *film, Veidt's plan does not involve an alien squid. Instead, he*

MIND .... *The Mindscape of Alan Moore*
MOBL.... *Watchmen: The Mobile Game*
MOTN.... *Watchmen: The Complete Motion Comic*
MTRO.... *Metro* promotional newspaper cover wrap
NEWP.... *New Frontiersman* promotional newspaper
NEWW... *New Frontiersman* website
NIGH .... *Watchmen: The End Is Nigh, Parts 1 and 2*
PKIT ...... *Watchmen* film British press kit
PORT..... *Watchmen Portraits*
REAL..... Real life
RPG1 .... *DC Heroes Role Playing Module #227: Who Watches the Watchmen?*

RPG2 .... *DC Heroes Role Playing Module #235: Taking Out the Trash—Curses and Tears*
RPG3 .... *DC Heroes: The Watchmen Sourcebook*
RUBY .... "Wounds," published in *The Ruby Files Volume One*
SCR1..... Unfilmed screenplay draft: Sam Hamm
SCR2..... Unfilmed screenplay draft: Charles McKeuen
SCR3..... Unfilmed screenplay draft: Gary Goldman
SCR4..... Unfilmed screenplay draft: David Hayter (2002)
SCR5..... Unfilmed screenplay draft: David Hayter (2003)
SCR6..... Unfilmed screenplay draft: Alex Tse
SPOT..... *DC Spotlight #1*
VRL1 ..... Viral video: *NBS Nightly News with Ted Philips*

VRL2..... Viral video: *The Keene Act and You*
VRL3..... Viral video: *Who Watches the Watchmen? A Veidt Music Network (VMN) Special*
VRL4 ..... Viral video: *World in Focus: 6 Minutes to Midnight*
VRL5 ..... Viral video: *Local Radio Station Report on 1977 Riots*
VRL6 ..... Viral videos (group of ten): *Veidt Enterprises Advertising Contest*
WAWA... *Watching the Watchmen*
WHOS ... *Who's Who: The Definitive Directory of the DC Universe*
WTFC .... *Watchmen: The Film Companion*

237

replicates Dr. Manhattan's power in order to frame the superhuman and make the world unite in peace against him.

CONFLICT: Taking Out the Trash *dates Veidt's hiring of this team in 1982, while* Before Watchmen: Ozymandias *sets their hiring in April 1981. Alan Moore's miniseries, however, specifies 1983.*

During a two-month span, four prominent creatives minds vanish without a trace: radical architect Norman Leith, Indian surrealist painter Hira Manish, respected science-fiction author James Trafford March, and avant-garde composer Linette Paley. Manish leaves behind a husband (whom she considers "a sexless oaf") and two spoiled sons. March owes massive debts to the Internal Revenue Service, which has frozen his earnings. Both Leith and Paley, meanwhile, are depressed and possibly suicidal. In addition, Dr. Whittaker Furnesse, a brilliant eugenics specialist, vanishes while walking his dog one evening, leaving behind a wife. Despite the different circumstances for each missing person, the *New Frontiersman*'s editors suspect a conspiracy, given the simultaneous disappearances of noted persons in multiple fields **[ALAN]**.

Veidt also hires author Max Shea as a screenwriter for the project **[ALAN]**. He meets the former *Tales of the Black Freighter* scribe at a Gunga Diner in Boston and invites him to help develop the "greatest science fiction film ever made." Adrian offers a huge payment, noting that those involved will be secluded to protect his use of a new technology **[BWOZ]**. The press cites Shea as the fifth missing creative person after he mysteriously vanishes from his Boston home **[ALAN]**.

After psychic and clairvoyant Robert Deschaines suffers a fatal stroke, Adrian Veidt secretly arranges for the man's head to be stolen while his body lies unattended on a mortuary slab, so that he can use the brain. Police investigate possible involvement by black-magic cultists, but no further evidence comes to light **[ALAN]**.

Veidt brings Shea to his private Pacific island a few days later, where he meets Hira Manish, who had illustrated several of the author's past stories. Also on the team is Professor Wickstein, who expresses concern over using an actual human brain to make the movie. Veidt mollifies the academic by lying that the brain comes from a cadaver **[BWOZ]**.

Manish begins illustrating Shea's script concepts as film storyboards, and the two become lovers. To create Veidt's "alien," Whittaker Furnesse and other geneticists clone material from the mystic's brain, which will act as a psychic resonator, amplifying a signal pulse and broadcasting it upon the creature's death. Furnesse's team codes a great deal of data into the signal, including Shea's descriptions of alien worlds, Manish's images, and Paley's compositions. Unaware of the life form's true nature, the scientists believe they are merely building a sophisticated film special effect **[ALAN]**.

Veidt Enterprises unveils new marketing for Nostalgia perfume and aftershave. The product's tagline is "Where is the essence that was so divine?" The Veidt Cosmetics & Toiletries division launches magazine and billboard advertising featuring a woman in erotic stockings. Androgynous models are chosen for the ads in order to afford a window into the gay community. The ads are successful due to the idyllic picture they paint of times past **[ALAN]**. Veidt Enterprises' television commercials for the perfume focus on lost love and the passage of time **[VRL6]**.

The Veidt Music Network (VMN) broadcasts *Who Watches the Watchmen?* The special, presented by Jenny Jones, offers a "caped-crusader countdown," during which Jones mocks The Comedian as being a "Where are they now?" candidate; calls Rorschach "violent, dangerous, and a little bit crazy"; deems The Nite Owl a "super geek"; and focuses on The Silk Spectre's good looks and Dr. Manhattan's lack of clothing. She concludes that only one man has the mind and body to fight crime and run a mega-corporation: Ozymandias. Following this program, two other hosts, Alan and J.J., interview A Flock of Seagulls and KISS, respectively **[VRL3]**.

> **NOTE:** *VMN is modeled after MTV, with Alan and J.J. named after Alan Hunter and John "J.J." Jackson, who were among the station's earliest video-jockeys.*
> *Adrian Veidt has not actively fought crime for eight years by this point.*

Dan Dreiberg immerses himself in academia. This, combined with the looming threat of war with the Soviet Union, brings on a sense of ennui and dulled passion. While visiting a sick acquaintance at a Maine hospital, he hears a hunting owl's cry and imagines that he can feel the fear of the bird's rodent prey. This awakens a long-submerged desire to experience thrills rather than merely record them. His fervor for bird study renewed, he discovers a new interest in revisiting dusty academic tomes on the subject, including works by T.A. Crawford and Hudson. Dan decides to share his experience with the *Journal of the American Ornithological Society*'s readership **[ALAN]**.

> **NOTE:** *The sick acquaintance is very likely Byron Lewis, who was committed to a mental hospital in Maine after having a nervous breakdown.*

—Fall 1983

The *Journal of the American Ornithological Society* publishes an article titled "Blood from the Shoulder of Pallas," in which Dan Dreiberg discusses his renewed passion for owls **[ALAN]**. Dan had first submitted the article in October 1977 **[RPG3]**.

> **NOTE:** *The title of Dan's article title is befitting of the* Watchmen *universe, for in Greek mythology, Pallas Athena was the goddess of war, wisdom, and justice.*

MIND .... *The Mindscape of Alan Moore*	**RPG2** .... *DC Heroes Role Playing Module #235: Taking Out the Trash—Curses and Tears*	**VRL2** ..... Viral video: *The Keene Act and You*
MOBL.... *Watchmen: The Mobile Game*		**VRL3** ..... Viral video: *Who Watches the Watchmen? A Veidt Music Network (VMN) Special*
MOTN.... *Watchmen: The Complete Motion Comic*	**RPG3** .... *DC Heroes: The Watchmen Sourcebook*	
MTRO.... *Metro* promotional newspaper cover wrap	**RUBY** .... "Wounds," published in *The Ruby Files Volume One*	**VRL4** ..... Viral video: *World in Focus: 6 Minutes to Midnight*
NEWP.... *New Frontiersman* promotional newspaper	**SCR1**..... Unfilmed screenplay draft: Sam Hamm	**VRL5** ..... Viral video: *Local Radio Station Report on 1977 Riots*
NEWW... *New Frontiersman* website	**SCR2**..... Unfilmed screenplay draft: Charles McKeuen	
NIGH ..... *Watchmen: The End Is Nigh, Parts 1 and 2*	**SCR3**..... Unfilmed screenplay draft: Gary Goldman	**VRL6** ..... Viral videos (group of ten): *Veidt Enterprises Advertising Contest*
PKIT...... *Watchmen* film British press kit	**SCR4**..... Unfilmed screenplay draft: David Hayter (2002)	
PORT..... *Watchmen Portraits*	**SCR5**..... Unfilmed screenplay draft: David Hayter (2003)	**WAWA**... *Watching the Watchmen*
REAL..... Real life	**SCR6**..... Unfilmed screenplay draft: Alex Tse	**WHOS** ... *Who's Who: The Definitive Directory of the DC Universe*
RPG1 .... *DC Heroes Role Playing Module #227: Who Watches the Watchmen?*	**SPOT**.... *DC Spotlight #1*	
	VRL1 ..... Viral video: *NBS Nightly News with Ted Philips*	**WTFC** .... *Watchmen: The Film Companion*

In or Before 1984

Richard Nixon runs for a fifth Presidential term, using the slogan "Stick With Dick in '84" **[ALAN]**.

1984

DC Comics' Flint Editions imprint publishes *Treasure Island Treasury of Comics,* which reprints the first thirty issues of *Tales of the Black Freighter* **[ALAN]**. The book presents seven years' worth of material from such creators as Max Shea, Michael Longfield, Tim Snowden, Xrat, Lisa Downing, Harvey Kurtzman, Alan Moore, Dave Gibbons **[RPG3]**, Joe Orlando, and Walt Feinberg **[ALAN]**.

> **NOTE:** *In the real world, cartoonist and comic book editor Harvey Kurtzman contributed to* MAD, Playboy, *and other publications. Moore and Gibbons, of course, are* Watchmen's *original creators.*

July 12, 1984

Adrian Veidt holds a benefit for African famine relief at New York's Yankee Stadium. Posters for the event urge citizens to "join in the fight against hunger" **[NEWW, FILM]**.

August 12, 1984

Ozymandias holds another charity benefit, this time for famine relief in southern India. Again, event posters encourage the public to "join in the fight against hunger" **[ARTF]**.

September 1984

Edgar Jacobi receives a sped-up parole for good behavior **[BWOZ]** following a decade of imprisonment **[ALAN]**, after Adrian Veidt speaks to the prison's officials and chaplain on his behalf. They agree that Jacobi is a changed man who deserves a chance to make amends for the crimes he committed as Moloch the Mystic. On his last day as an inmate, Edgar confesses his sins to a priest. Determined to face God without fear, he tells the clergyman his life's story, from birth up to his finding religion **[BWMO]**.

Adrian Veidt meets Jacobi at the prison exit, buys him a meal, and offers the ex-con a chance to do penance for his sins **[BWMO]** by accepting a temporary job at Veidt's research firm, Dimensional Developments **[ALAN]**. With an office and his own private entrance, Jacobi is tasked with proofreading the results of testing for a potential new energy source. Though the job is mundane, Jacobi is uniquely qualified due to the concentration skills he honed as Moloch. Edgar gratefully accepts the job **[BWMO]**, though Rorschach continues to distrust the former villain **[ALAN]**.

September 1984 to October 1985

Adrian Veidt exposes Edgar Jacobi's office to radiation during off-hours in order to induce cancerous tumors. Jacobi does his job dutifully, all the while growing sick and feeble—and unaware that the job is merely a ruse, the tasks he performs entirely meaningless **[BWMO]**.

Veidt doubles Jacobi's salary, praising his ability to notice infinitesimal errors in equations. He asks Edgar to deliver a package to Janey Slater—a box of herbal cigarettes of his design (secretly containing chemicals designed to give her cancer). Humbled at the trust that Adrian has shown him, the ex-supervillain cries in gratitude. After he leaves, Veidt prints up three more files of meaningless equations and has his assistant deliver them to Edgar's desk **[BWMO]**.

> **CONFLICT:** *Veidt calls his assistant Marla. However,* Before Watchmen: Ozymandias *depicts Marla as dying in 1981, to be replaced by another assistant, Yvonne. As such, this Marla must be a different individual—unless, of course, Veidt has figured out how to reanimate the dead. If anyone could do that, it would certainly be Ozymandias.*

October 14, 1984

Time magazine's cover features a photograph of Dr. Manhattan shaking hands with Adrian Veidt, under the headline "Supermen Unite for Peace." The issue includes an article calling the American poverty rate a "scandal" **[FILM, NEWW]**.

November 6, 1984

Richard Nixon is re-elected for a fifth term of office as President of the United States. His Vice President remains Gerald Ford, while Henry Kissinger continues to serve among his advisors **[ALAN]**. Once again, Hollis Mason votes for him **[FILM]**.

> **NOTE:** *This presumes Election Day in the United States occurs on the same day in Alan Moore's miniseries as in the real world.*

November 6, 1984 (Alternate Reality)

Ronald Wilson Reagan is re-elected President of the United States **[REAL]**.

Before 1985

Leo Winston, the president of Veidt Industries' marketing and development division, marries a woman named Josephine, with whom he fathers several children **[ALAN]**.

Part XI:
A TWIST OF VEIDT
(1985)

—In or Before 1985

Adrian Veidt exposes Jon Osterman's former teammates at Rockefeller Military Research Center's Special Talent Quarter—Major Adamson, William Charles Batts, Stephanie Boris, Dr. J.M. Candelaria, Colonel Brent Dabbs, and Susan White—to cancer-causing agents as part of his master plan to save the world **[SCR1]**. General Anthony Randolph, Dr. Manhattan's former "handler" at the base, is also diagnosed with cancer **[FILM]**.

Eddie Blake undertakes a mission for the CIA that angers Libya **[ALAN]**.

The constant threat of nuclear war results in a permanent malaise among Americans, many of whom begin to neglect their own environment. Buildings fall into disrepair, littered with graffiti, while new car sales drop. By 1985, the streets are filled with cars manufactured in the late 1960s or early 1970s **[WTFC]**.

Former villain Golden Boy develops Alzheimer's, while a quintet of criminals once called The Brain Trust die in prison **[SCR3]**.

A pair of films are released in theaters, titled *The Watchmen Return* and *Watchmen: The Final Hour*, detailing the exploits of New York City's masked vigilantes **[SCR3]**.

The following businesses open in New York City: Hanky-Head **[ALAN]**, Americana Appliances, Cohen's Jewelry, Copy Cottage, Criterion Apartments, Fantucci Electronics, Fast Food Market, French Quarters, Galaxy Arcade, the Kinky of Paris wig shop, Lucky Bar, Milton & Frye, Pioneer Copys, Show & Tell, Tattoo Studio **[FILM]**, Video Star, Love Nest, XXX, America Peep Show, and McAnn's Bar **[ARTF]**.

> **NOTE:** *These companies are named on signage in the* Watchmen *movie and in* The Art

of the Film. *Absolute Watchmen* references *underworld czar Jimmy Fantucci; whether or not the mobster is connected to Fantucci Electronics is unknown.*

Adrian Veidt obtains *The Great Pharaohs: Ramses II*, a book by Dr. Hans Dayal, as well as another titled *Egypt* and a copy of Hollis Mason's *Under the Hood* **[FILM]**.

Hollywood Twin Cinemas, a pornographic movie theater located in a seedy section of Manhattan, near the bar Rumrunner, begins showing X-rated films and featuring nude women on stage. Edgar Jacobi rents an apartment above the theater, at 806 West 43rd Street **[FILM]**. Adrian Veidt hides a listening device in Jacobi's apartment to monitor his employee's conversations **[ALAN]**.

Geodesic domes become a common architectural design **[ABSO]**.

Genetic manipulation results in a breed of chicken with four legs, which becomes a popular meal at restaurants **[ALAN, FILM]**.

Over the River and Through the Woods: The Pale Horse Story, by Howard Lauder, is published. Featuring essays and reminiscences by members of punk-rock group Pale Horse, the book covers the band's foundation and rise to power **[RPG3]**.

The Complete Max Shea reprints some of the author's notable works as a limited-edition book with a leather binding and gold endpapers. The reprinted stories, illustrated by Joe Orlando and other artists, include *Tales of the Black Freighter* issue #1-6, "A Bucket of Blood and a Bottle of Rum," "Netherspace Slamdance," "Angela Bradstreet's Dirty Face," and more **[RPG3]**.

Eddie Blake moves into a luxury Manhattan apartment on the Promethea Building's thirtieth floor. Maintaining little contact with his neighbors, including Dr. D. Gibbons **[MTRO]**, he drinks excessively and begins exhibiting aberrant behavior **[BWMO]**.
    NOTE: *Blake's neighbor is named after* Watchmen *co-creator Dave Gibbons.*

Painkilling medications called GoPain and Pain Away are introduced **[ALAN]**.

Angela Neuberg becomes the director of Veidt Cosmetics & Toiletries. She and Adrian Veidt forge a friendly working relationship, and he gets to know her husband Frank **[ALAN]**.

Veidt Enterprises introduces Veidt Hair Spray For Men **[NEWW, VRL4]**, Veidt Shampoo For Men, Veidt Conditioner For Men **[ARTF]**, and sneaker lines Veidt Sport **[VRL6]** and Veidt Victory **[NEWW, VRL4]**. The company produces television commercials promoting its products, with the hairspray ads announcing "Real men use Veidt" **[VRL6]**, the shampoo ads claiming "Hero is all in the look," and the footwear ads urging consumers to "Always be in your element" **[NEWW, VRL4]**. Adrian Veidt also signs a lucrative deal with a toy manufacturer to produce an Ozymandias action-figure line **[ALAN]**, and creates his own airline, Veidt Air **[NEWW]**.

Adrian Veidt tells Dan Dreiberg about Egyptian philosophies, noting that the ancient Egyptians regarded death as a voyage **[ALAN]**.

Hollis Mason and Dan Dreiberg begin a tradition of meeting at Mason's apartment every Saturday night to drink beer and reminisce about past adventures **[ALAN]**.

On separate occasions, Dr. Manhattan prevents a tidal wave from decimating Miami, contains an exploding nuclear reactor, and ends a mob riot by teleporting the rioters to the desert **[SCR3]**.

The *New York Gazette* publishes a front-page article titled "Afghanistan Strong Holds Discovered" **[ARTF]**.
> **NOTE:** *"Strongholds" is misspelled as two words.*

Dan Dreiberg obtains a 1985 calendar featuring images of owls **[ALAN]**.

—1985

World Book Encyclopedia, Vol. XIII, includes an entry on The Minutemen, claiming that the generally accepted history of the group—that it was founded by Captain Metropolis and the first Silk Spectre—has been disputed, with others claiming The Nite Owl, Hooded Justice, and Mothman were also among the team's creators **[RPG3]**.
> **NOTE:** *The* World Book *is in error, but this is not a continuity error. Rather, it denotes inaccurate in-universe reporting on the part of the encyclopedia's publisher.*

The Culpeper Minute reruns a 1975 episode profiling Hollis Mason and Sally Jupiter. Host Larry Culpeper discusses how opinions of masked heroes have changed during the decade since the show's initial broadcast, observing that masked heroes have become outdated and irrelevant in the post-Keene Act world **[HOOD]**.

The *New Frontiersman* publishes an editorial claiming that New York City is dying. Rorschach records a journal entry noting his disagreement with this sentiment, deeming the city—and the whole world—already dead, though no one knows or cares. It reminds him that the words "good" and "evil" once had meaning, and that crime-fighters' masks were symbols of justice, not disguises **[MOBL]**.

Rorschach records a series of journal entries recalling earlier days. He describes himself and Dan Dreiberg as having been "gutless" and soft on crime, condemns Adrian Veidt's decadence and cowardice, and praises The Comedian's refusal to retire following the Keene Act. He deems police in 1977 "spoiled children" who were jealous of masked crime-fighters, and says his kind had to adapt to survive the immorality around them. "The era of masks is ending," Rorschach writes, adding that he will never look for excuses to quit **[MOBL]**.

—March 31, 1985
Pyramid Deliveries reports an annual net income of $115.49 million **[ALAN]**.

—April 1985
Dan Dreiberg writes one final ornithological journal article, then stops penning such pieces, recognizing that most people find the study of birds boring **[ALAN]**.

While performing covert duties in El Salvador, Eddie Blake sustains a nine-millimeter gunshot wound to the right forearm. Dr. George Cook tends to Blake's injuries **[RPG3]**.

—In or Before July 1985
Adrian Veidt hires a former physician, license revoked, to work at Veidt Enterprises' free medical clinic. When Edgar Jacobi falls ill due to radiation poisoning, the doctor (on Veidt's orders) tells him it could be the flu or a virus and offers antibiotics and anti-nausea drugs. The doctor tells Veidt that the ex-villain is developing cancer as planned. Jacobi returns after excreting blood, and the physician reveals that he has stage-three prostate cancer, his prognosis not good. Veidt promises to pay all medical bills, and Edgar breaks down crying **[BWMO]**. Desperate to beat the disease, Jacobi begins taking Laetrile, a phony medication outlawed in the United States **[ALAN, BWMO]**.
> *NOTE: Both Alan Moore's miniseries and* Before Watchmen: Moloch *misspell the medicine's name as "Laetril."*

Eddie Blake is assigned to carry out a secret wetwork operation in Nicaragua for the U.S. government **[ALAN, BWOZ]**.
> *NOTE: The term "wetwork" is a euphemism for assassination, alluding to the spilling of a victim's blood.*

—July 1985
Adrian Veidt, wearing his Ozymandias costume, produces a televised Indian Famine Appeal charity performance at the New York Astrodome. The crowd and announcer are mesmerized as he warms up with a smooth, graceful gymnastic routine **[ALAN]**.

July 16, 1985

Eddie Blake returns to the United States via airship from his mission to Nicaragua. While cleaning his weapon, he glances out a window **[BWOZ]** and spots a freighter docking at an uncharted island. Suspecting Sandinista bases, he vows to investigate as soon as he can **[ALAN, RPG2]**.

> **NOTE:** *Alan Moore's miniseries establishes these events, but not when they occur. The specific date appears in* Taking Out the Trash.

After July 16, 1985

Days later, Eddie Blake returns to the island aboard a small dinghy **[BWOZ]**, reads Adrian Veidt's files, and learns that the world's smartest man has assembled a team of artists and scientists to fake an alien invasion and kill millions in order to save humanity. He discovers a list of those whom Veidt has used as pawns, including Janey Slater and Edgar Jacobi **[ALAN, RPG2]**, and also finds the "alien" creature in the island's largest warehouse **[BWOZ]**. Though appalled at Veidt's plans, Blake knows that exposing him would prevent mankind's salvation. He keeps the secret, but the thought of the brutal world he relishes being replaced by a Utopia breaks his spirit **[ALAN, RPG2]**.

July 23, 1985 (Estimated)

Eddie Blake drunkenly barges into the apartment of Edgar Jacobi, who sits terrified in bed as Blake rants about a terrible "joke" he recently uncovered, in which Jacobi and Janey Slater are unwitting pawns. Weeping at the foot of his former enemy's bed, Blake incoherently mentions an island and a list he discovered. Scared and confused, Edgar remains silent. Neither is aware that Veidt, who has bugged the room, overhears the exchange **[ALAN]**.

After July 23, 1985

Jacobi reports his encounter with Blake to Adrian Veidt **[BWMO]**, who decides to kill both men to protect his plan **[ALAN]**.

> **NOTE:** *Alan Moore's miniseries establishes these events, but not when they occur.* Taking Out the Trash *indicates that Blake, after finding the island, visits Jacobi "one week later." This placement seems odd, though, as it means Veidt waits three months to kill them.*

August 1985

Jon Osterman and Laurie Juspeczyk go for a walk in New York City. In Grand Central Station, they stop at a newsstand and buy a copy of *Time* magazine commemorating Hiroshima Week. On the cover is a damaged pocket-watch, stopped at the instant of the blast, which reminds Jon of his superhuman transformation. Dan Dreiberg also reads the issue and is disturbed by photos of children with their bodies burnt black **[ALAN]**.

MIND .... *The Mindscape of Alan Moore*
MOBL.... *Watchmen: The Mobile Game*
MOTN.... *Watchmen: The Complete Motion Comic*
MTRO.... *Metro* promotional newspaper cover wrap
NEWP.... *New Frontiersman* promotional newspaper
NEWW... *New Frontiersman* website
NIGH ..... *Watchmen: The End Is Nigh, Parts 1 and 2*
PKIT ...... *Watchmen* film British press kit
PORT..... *Watchmen Portraits*
REAL ..... Real life
RPG1 .... *DC Heroes Role Playing Module #227: Who Watches the Watchmen?*

RPG2 .... *DC Heroes Role Playing Module #235: Taking Out the Trash—Curses and Tears*
RPG3 .... *DC Heroes: The Watchmen Sourcebook*
RUBY .... "Wounds," published in *The Ruby Files Volume One*
SCR1 ..... Unfilmed screenplay draft: Sam Hamm
SCR2 ..... Unfilmed screenplay draft: Charles McKeuen
SCR3 ..... Unfilmed screenplay draft: Gary Goldman
SCR4 ..... Unfilmed screenplay draft: David Hayter (2002)
SCR5 ..... Unfilmed screenplay draft: David Hayter (2003)
SCR6 ..... Unfilmed screenplay draft: Alex Tse
SPOT ..... *DC Spotlight #1*
VRL1 ..... Viral video: *NBS Nightly News with Ted Philips*

VRL2 ..... Viral video: *The Keene Act and You*
VRL3 ..... Viral video: *Who Watches the Watchmen? A Veidt Music Network (VMN) Special*
VRL4 ..... Viral video: *World in Focus: 6 Minutes to Midnight*
VRL5 ..... Viral video: *Local Radio Station Report on 1977 Riots*
VRL6 ..... Viral videos (group of ten): *Veidt Enterprises Advertising Contest*
WAWA... *Watching the Watchmen*
WHOS ... *Who's Who: The Definitive Directory of the DC Universe*
WTFC .... *Watchmen: The Film Companion*

—August 26, 1985

The New Yorker magazine publishes a cover featuring an illustration of Dr. Manhattan shaking hands with Adrian Veidt **[NEWW]**.

—September 1985

Chris Duthrie, a spokesman for the New York Police Department, issues an official statement calling Rorschach "a violent masked murderer who believes himself to be above the law." Duthrie promises to bring the vigilante to justice **[MTRO]**.

—September 9, 1985

The Holland Valley Alcohol Rehabilitation Centre files a monthly patient evaluation on Byron Lewis, reporting no progress in his treatment **[RPG3]**.

—Before September 23, 1985

Punk-rock band My Chemical Romance plays a concert at a Manhattan club called Tower. As the group performs Bob Dylan's "Desolation Row," a fight breaks out near the ticket booth between members of several gangs, including Knot-Tops. Two police officers intervene, but are stomped and injured by gang members. Police reinforcements in riot gear disperse the crowd, then storm the concert, arresting and beating the band and many attendees **[CHEM]**.

> **NOTE:** *No year is specified (just the month and day), but this music video takes place in the world of* Watchmen, *suggesting a 1985 setting (in the real world, My Chemical Romance formed in 2001). This is reinforced by the "Four More Years" Richard Nixon campaign posters still hanging on the club's wall, and the fact the Pale Horse is still performing (see the next entry).*
>
> *The first chapter of Alan Moore's miniseries is titled "At Midnight All the Agents," which is a line from "Desolation Row."*

—September 23, 1985—7:00 PM

Punk-rock group Pale Horse performs at Manhattan's Tower club **[CHEM]**.

—In or Before October 1985

Adrian Veidt installs a private elevator at his penthouse office, accessible via the forward pulling of a particular book on his shelves **[BWOZ]**. He creates the Karnak Video Bank, in which tons of broadcast footage are archived for use by Veidt Enterprises **[VRL4]**.

The Economist and *Forbes* each publish cover stories about Adrian Veidt **[FILM]**.

Pale Horse, whose music in this era is similar to that of 1970s rock band Devo, schedules a series of concerts at New York City's Madison Square Garden. Laure Juspeczyk becomes a fan of the group **[ALAN]**.

> **NOTE:** *Laurie met Pale Horse's lead singer, Red D'eath, when he and his previous band (Red D'eath and the Horsemen) performed at a party in her home in 1966, according to* Before Watchmen: Silk Spectre.

Hollis Mason names his pet cat Phantom **[ALAN]**, just as he'd previously named his dog in the 1960s **[RPG1, BWMM]**.

> **NOTE:** *Given Mason's love of pulp-fiction heroes, it is safe to assume that both animals are named after Lee Falk's long-running comic strip adventurer.*

Former *Tales of the Black Freighter* artist Walt Feinberg begins drawing editorial cartoons for right-wing conspiracist newspaper *New Frontiersman*. Editor Hector Godfrey considers him lazy due to his frequent lateness in turning in work **[ALAN]**.

> **NOTE:** *David Hayter's unproduced 2002 and 2003 screenplay drafts change Feinberg's surname to Conheim, while Alex Tse's unproduced 2006 script calls him Dulmage.*

Sweet Chariot chewing sugar cubes become a popular confection. A candy known as MMeltdowns!! is also introduced, with a mushroom-cloud logo and the slogan, "With fruity fallout and a delicious molten center, they'll blow you all the way to China" **[ALAN]**, turning the threat of nuclear war into a dark joke **[WTFC]**. MMeltdowns!! are similar to American M&Ms or British Treets, with brightly colored atomic symbols on the wrapping **[ABSO]**.

Laurie Juspeczyk tries several times to quit smoking, but consistently fails **[ALAN]**.

Unknown individuals paint graffiti in an alley near Dan Dreiberg's apartment, including the sayings "Pale Horse," "K-Tops King," and "Castrate rapists" **[ALAN]**.

> **NOTE:** *Pale Horse is a punk-rock band mentioned several times in Alan Moore's miniseries and in* Before Watchmen: Silk Spectre. *"K-Tops" refers to the Knot-Top gang.*

New York City's Utopia Cinema begins showing classic science fiction films, including *This Island Earth*, *Things to Come*, and *The Day the Earth Stood Still* **[ALAN]**.

> **NOTE:** *In* This Island Earth *(1955), directed by Joseph M. Newman and Jack Arnold, aliens pretend to seek help from human scientists in saving their planet, Metaluna, but secretly plot to invade Earth.* Things to Come *(1936), directed by William Cameron Menzies and written by H. G. Wells, explores a society in which the threat of war accelerates technological progress.* The Day the Earth Stood Still *(1951), directed by Robert Wise, features an extraterrestrial named Klaatu trying to warn Earth about nuclear war but*

ending up hunted by U.S. government forces fearful of alien invaders. These films' themes, as well as the theater's name, all mirror Adrian Veidt's plan.

A New York City locksmith launches the Gordian Knot Lock Co., his van bearing the motto "They'll never undo *this* sucker!" His brother Milo opens the Promethean Cab Co., a taxi business with the slogan "Bringing light to the world." Among Promethean's drivers is a lesbian named Josephine (Joey for short), who lives with a magazine professional (and fan of Knot-Top fashion) named Aline. The two are very different, and Joey is frustrated that they've never had sex **[ALAN]**.

    NOTE: The Gordian Knot, a legend associated with Alexander the Great, is often used as a metaphor for a problem that can be solved by thinking outside the box. The company's name foreshadows Adrian Veidt's solution to the threat of nuclear war.

    In Greek mythology, Prometheus creates mankind and is its greatest benefactor, stealing fire from Mount Olympus and giving it to man. The image of Prometheus in Alan Moore's miniseries symbolizes both Dr. Manhattan (who leaves the galaxy to create human life elsewhere by story's end) and Ozymandias (who saves mankind from nuclear fire, becoming its greatest benefactor despite his horrific deeds).

Rorschach hears a joke in which a depressed man tells his doctor that life seems harsh and cruel, and that he feels alone. The doctor recommends that seeing the great clown Pagliacci might cheer him up. "But doctor," the man says, "I *am* Pagliacci" **[ALAN]**.

    NOTE: In the Italian opera Pagliacci, *by Ruggero Leoncavallo, a clown kills his unfaithful wife while performing onstage before an audience. The clown's nature mirrors that of Ozymandias—a benign public persona who commits a horrible crime.*

Enola Gay and the Little Boys perform at the Burlesk club in New York City. Located next door is an onstage peep show featuring live performers **[ALAN]**.

    NOTE: The Enola Gay, *a Boeing B-29 Superfortress bomber, was the first aircraft to drop an atomic weapon during the final stages of World War II, when it attacked Hiroshima, Japan. The warhead was code-named "Little Boy."*

Rorschach is accused of two counts of murder in the first degree, but evades capture. As Walter Kovacs, he rents an apartment in a bad part of town near the wharves. His landlady, Dolores Shairp—a prostitute, and a mother of five children by five different fathers—finds his lack of personal hygiene offensive, but is unaware that her tenant is a wanted fugitive **[ALAN]**.

Hollis Mason visits a supermarket to buy food for his cat Phantom, and runs into his former nemesis, The Screaming Skull. Despite their prior enmity, the reformed villain—who has since found God and built a family—exchanges contact information with Mason, who deems him a "nice guy" [ALAN].

Rorschach visits Happy Harry's bar and grill. His violent interrogation methods leave the pub's patrons—and owner Happy Harry—terrified [ALAN].

A rough-looking man named Steve moves to New York City. During his time in the Big Apple, he fails to learn about Rorschach's deadly reputation, leaving him unprepared for a future encounter with the vigilante [ALAN].

A Silk Spectre fan begins writing letters to Sally Jupiter at the Nepenthe Gardens rest resort. Laurie Juspeczyk finds it creepy when the man asks for her mother's old costume, but Sally is flattered to receive such attention, as it reminds her that men once found her desirable [ALAN]. The letter-writer sends her a copy of *Silk Spectre and the Adventures of the Acme Brushman* [FILM], a Tijuana Bible from the 1930s or '40s featuring Sally's pornographic exploits, which she saves. She hangs on her bedroom wall a painting of her younger self in costume, created by an artist named Varga [ALAN].

> **NOTE:** *The "Varga" poster references Joaquin Alberto Vargas, a Peruvian painter whose portraits of pin-up girls for* Esquire *magazine were prominent during World War II. Many American aircraft featured nose art inspired by his paintings.*

Hollis Mason displays an automobile maintenance manual and a copy of Philip Wylie's 1930 novel *Gladiator* on his bookshelf, alongside copies of his autobiography, *Under the Hood* [ALAN].

> **NOTE:** Gladiator *tells the story of a scientist who injects his pregnant wife with a serum designed to improve mankind, resulting in his son, Hugo Danner, being born with superhuman speed and strength, as well as bulletproof skin. The novel is widely considered an inspiration for the character of Superman.*

An automobile dealership adds a 1986 Buick model to its showroom [ALAN].

New York City news vendor Bernard allows a youth named Bernie to read a comic book called *Tales of the Black Freighter* without paying. The teen returns to reread the issue often, despite finding it difficult to comprehend, because his mother works many hours and his sister is rarely home. Bernie grows annoyed by the man's chattiness and constant ranting about the need to launch a nuclear attack on the Soviet Union, but keeps coming back anyway since the stand's spark hydrant keeps him warm. Despite their frequent interactions, the two Bernards never truly connect or even exchange names [ALAN].

Doctors diagnose Janey Slater with lung cancer, offering a prognosis of six months to live. Bitter and fatalistic, she begins smoking three packs of cigarettes a day **[NEWP]**.

U.S. President Richard Nixon undergoes two heart operations **[ALAN]**.

Adrian Veidt and Jon Osterman begin constructing a solution to the world's energy crisis, by means of a technology they call a **S**ub **Q**uantum **U**nified **I**ntrinsic field **D**evice (SQUID). Dr. Manhattan works on the SQUID system from the Rockefeller base, coordinating his efforts with Veidt at the latter's Karnak base in Antarctica **[FILM]**.

> **NOTE:** *The* Watchmen *film replaces the alien squid creature from Alan Moore's miniseries with a duplication of Dr. Manhattan's power as the mechanism of Veidt's plan to save mankind. The SQUID acronym is a subtle nod to the story's original climax.*

—October 1985

Dan Dreiberg's bird-themed calendar features an owl for October **[ALAN]**.

The *New York Gazette*'s front-page headline reads "New Skirmish on Afghan Border. Russkies Walk Out on Peace Powwow" **[SCR1]**.

—Before October 11, 1985

Professor Hal Eisner authors the controversial book *In the Shadow of Manhattan* **[VRL4]**.

French photojournalist Alain Guillon wins a Pulitzer Prize **[VRL4]**.

A toll-free number is set up for citizens to report possible vigilante behavior. The number, 1-555-NO-MASKS, is advertised in a logo featuring Rorschach's face inside a red circle and line **[VRL4]**.

—October 11, 1985—Daytime

Vietnam becomes the 51st state of the United States, earning the nickname "Viet Bronx." A 51st star is thus added to the U.S. flag **[ALAN]**.

> **CONFLICT:** *A timeline in the* Watchmen *film's British press kit moves this event back to 1977, contradicting Alan Moore's miniseries.*

The Soviet Union continues a recent series of military exercises by conducting a bomb test in the Bering Sea, 1,500 miles off the southern coast of Alaska. Richard Nixon issues a warning to the Soviets that the United States will maintain its strength to ensure peace. As a result, a watchdog group of scientists moves the Doomsday Clock to five minutes to midnight **[FILM]**.

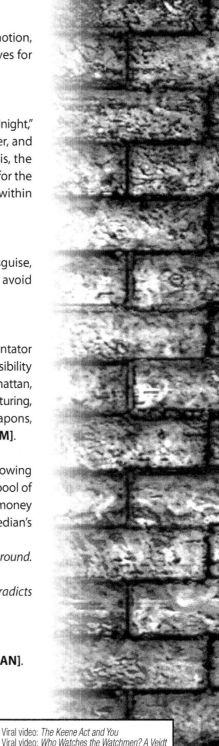

October 11, 1985—Night
During the final minutes before setting the last stage of his world-saving plot into motion, Adrian Veidt makes a recording outlining his life story. In it, he explains his motives for posterity, in case he fails to succeed in his mission [**BWOZ**].

October 11, 1985—10:30 PM
World in Focus, a late-night U.K. current-affairs show, airs the episode "6 Minutes to Midnight," in which French photojournalist Alain Guillon, U.S. professor and author Hal Eisner, and presenter Jeremy Miller discuss the Vietnam War, the emerging geopolitical crisis, the looming threat of nuclear war, and whether Dr. Manhattan's existence is to blame for the post-1959 political scene. Veidt Enterprises archives a recording of the program within its Karnak Video Bank [**VRL4**].

October 11, 1985—Before 11:30 PM
After sending his assistant Yvonne home for the evening, Adrian Veidt dons a disguise, drives to the apartment building of Eddie Blake, scales the building's exterior to avoid being seen, and makes his way from the roof to Blake's apartment [**BWOZ**].

October 11, 1985—11:30 PM
Inside the apartment, Eddie Blake watches a TV broadcast in which political commentator John McLaughlin and guest speakers Pat Buchanan and Eleanor Clift discuss the possibility of nuclear war. Buchanan sees no chance of that outcome since America has Dr. Manhattan, a walking nuclear deterrent, on its side. McLaughlin suggests the Soviets might be posturing, but Clift disagrees since the U.S.S.R. has stockpiled record amounts of nuclear weapons, and suggests that the nation might feel threatened by Manhattan's presence [**FILM**].

Veidt bursts down Blake's chain-locked door and beats the man to a pulp before throwing him through a large window. Blake falls thirty stories to his death, forming a large pool of blood on the sidewalk as the impact drives his head into his stomach. Adrian steals money from the apartment to mislead investigators away from his true motive. The Comedian's smiley-face button lands in the bloody puddle [**ALAN**].

> **NOTE:** *The time of Eddie Blake's death is established in the* Metro *newspaper wraparound.*

> **CONFLICT:** Taking Out the Trash *sets Blake's death on October 12, but this contradicts Alan Moore's miniseries.*

October 12, 1985—Morning
The New York Times announces Vietnam's status as the United States' 51st state [**ALAN**].

MIND .... *The Mindscape of Alan Moore*
MOBL .... *Watchmen: The Mobile Game*
MOTN .... *Watchmen: The Complete Motion Comic*
MTRO .... Metro *promotional newspaper cover wrap*
NEWP .... *New Frontiersman promotional newspaper*
NEWW .. *New Frontiersman website*
NIGH ..... *Watchmen: The End Is Nigh, Parts 1 and 2*
PKIT ...... *Watchmen film British press kit*
PORT ..... *Watchmen Portraits*
REAL ..... Real life
RPG1 .... *DC Heroes Role Playing Module #227: Who Watches the Watchmen?*

RPG2 .... *DC Heroes Role Playing Module #235: Taking Out the Trash—Curses and Tears*
RPG3 .... *DC Heroes: The Watchmen Sourcebook*
RUBY .... "Wounds," published in *The Ruby Files Volume One*
SCR1 ..... Unfilmed screenplay draft: Sam Hamm
SCR2 ..... Unfilmed screenplay draft: Charles McKeuen
SCR3 ..... Unfilmed screenplay draft: Gary Goldman
SCR4 ..... Unfilmed screenplay draft: David Hayter (2002)
SCR5 ..... Unfilmed screenplay draft: David Hayter (2003)
SCR6 ..... Unfilmed screenplay draft: Alex Tse
SPOT ..... *DC Spotlight #1*
VRL1 ..... Viral video: *NBS Nightly News with Ted Philips*

VRL2 ..... Viral video: *The Keene Act and You*
VRL3 ..... Viral video: *Who Watches the Watchmen? A Veidt Music Network (VMN) Special*
VRL4 ..... Viral video: *World in Focus: 6 Minutes to Midnight*
VRL5 ..... Viral video: *Local Radio Station Report on 1977 Riots*
VRL6 ..... Viral videos (group of ten): *Veidt Enterprises Advertising Contest*
WAWA.. *Watching the Watchmen*
WHOS .. *Who's Who: The Definitive Directory of the DC Universe*
WTFC .... *Watchmen: The Film Companion*

The U.S. government informs Jon Osterman and Laurie Juspeczyk of The Comedian's death. The CIA suspects that Libyans may be responsible **[ALAN]**.

Rorschach sees a dog carcass in an alley. Tire treads on the dog's body indicate that the animal has been run over by a vehicle. He walks past Eddie Blake's apartment sans mask as a local businessman hoses Blake's blood down a sewer drain. The vigilante tracks bloody footprints along the sidewalk **[ALAN]**.

Detectives Joe Bourquin and Steven Fine **[ALAN]**, from the NYPD's Area Two Violent Crimes division **[RPG3]**, investigate the crime scene. They suspect multiple perpetrators, given the murder's ferocity, but keep their findings low-profile to avoid drawing the interest of any masked adventurers **[ALAN]**.

> *NOTE: The detectives' concern about masked adventurers (plural) would seem to indicate that others continue to operate besides Rorschach. Nothing is known about these other vigilantes.*

> *CONFLICT: The Watchmen film changes Bourquin's surname to Gallagher, though a newspaper prop reporting Rorschach's capture retains the detective's original name. The Watchmen Sourcebook incorrectly cites his first name as James. In Sam Hamm's unproduced 1988 screenplay, as well as in Charles McKeuen's and Gary Goldman's rewrites of that script, the detectives are named Burns and Hyde.*

—October 12, 1985—Daytime
Russia, in protest of U.S. activities in Afghanistan **[ALAN]**, masses its troops on the country's border despite heated protests from Richard Nixon. In response, U.S. global military forces are placed on critical alert. At a meeting of the Senate Foreign Relations Committee, Secretary of State Henry Kissinger calls on the Kremlin to "stop lying" about the locations of Soviet troops **[MTRO]**.

—October 12, 1985—Night
Rorschach writes a journal entry mentioning the dog corpse. He condemns sex workers, murderers, politicians, lechers, communists, liberals, intellectuals, and smooth-talkers. Investigating Eddie Blake's murder, he pockets the bloody smiley-face pin, then scales the building to Blake's apartment. Hidden in a closet, he finds a compartment containing The Comedian's costume and weapons, a photo of The Minutemen **[ALAN, MIND]**, newspaper clippings of The Comedian's deeds, and photos of Sally Jupiter and Laurie Juspeczyk **[FILM]**. He realizes that Eddie Blake was The Comedian **[ALAN, MIND]**.

Following a weekly Saturday beer session with Hollis Mason, Dan Dreiberg heads home to find his front door knob busted. Inside, Rorschach eats cold Heinz baked beans from a can. His ex-partner tells him about The Comedian's death, and the two descend to Dan's long-unused Nite Owl workshop. Dan is skeptical about Rorschach's theory that someone is killing costumed heroes, and that Mason might be the culprit, given his autobiography's comments about The Comedian. After Rorschach leaves in a huff, Dan sits alone in his workshop, missing their friendship and glory days **[ALAN]**.

>**CONFLICT:** In the Watchmen film, the beans are from a fictional brand, Big Giant, presumably based on B&G Foods' Green Giant brand.

—October 13, 1985—Morning

A newspaper features the headline "Congress Approves Lunar Silos" **[ALAN]**.

>**NOTE:** This may indicate that international treaties prohibiting space-based nuclear weapons do not exist in the Watchmen universe, as they do in the real world.

The *Metro* free newspaper includes a wraparound featuring several articles syndicated from the *New Frontiersman*. Among them are "Public Enemy Number One," by Jed Ellis, discussing police efforts to bring Rorschach to justice; B. Thompson's "Who Watches the Watchmen?", which suggests that with crime soaring and the Cold War turning nuclear, the Keene Act may have been a step too far; "Police Seek Witness," by Jamie Hill, covering Eddie Blake's death; and Franklin Smith's "Doomsday Clock 5 to Midnight," pondering whether Dr. Manhattan is to blame for the world's nuclear crisis **[MTRO]**.

>**NOTE:** This Franklin Smith is a separate individual from the same-named criminal whom Rorschach murders in 1978.

>**CONFLICT:** The articles refer to The Crimebusters as The Watchmen, their name in the Watchmen film, and claim the group fought together for eight years, rather than disbanding after only a single meeting, as they do in Alan Moore's miniseries.

The *New York Gazette* reports Eddie Blake's death, citing police suspicions that the crime was committed by at least two hefty intruders armed with a lead pipe or a baseball bat **[RPG3]**.

—October 13, 1985—4:37 PM

After sleeping for most of the day, Rorschach awakens to the sound of his landlady, Dolores Shairp, complaining about the smell of his apartment **[ALAN]**.

—October 13, 1985—Night

The *New York Gazette*'s nighttime front-page headline reads "Nuclear Doomsday Clock Stands at Five to Twelve Warn Experts." A secondary headline notes "Geneva Talks: U.S. Refuses to Discuss Dr. Manhattan" **[ALAN]**.

MIND .... *The Mindscape of Alan Moore*
MOBL.... *Watchmen: The Mobile Game*
MOTN.... *Watchmen: The Complete Motion Comic*
MTRO.... *Metro* promotional newspaper cover wrap
NEWP.... *New Frontiersman* promotional newspaper
NEWW... *New Frontiersman* website
NIGH ..... *Watchmen: The End Is Nigh, Parts 1 and 2*
PKIT...... *Watchmen* film British press kit
PORT..... *Watchmen Portraits*
REAL..... Real life
RPG1 .... *DC Heroes Role Playing Module #227: Who Watches the Watchmen?*

RPG2 .... *DC Heroes Role Playing Module #235: Taking Out the Trash—Curses and Tears*
RPG3 ..... *DC Heroes: The Watchmen Sourcebook*
RUBY ..... "Wounds," published in *The Ruby Files Volume One*
SCR1..... Unfilmed screenplay draft: Sam Hamm
SCR2..... Unfilmed screenplay draft: Charles McKeuen
SCR3..... Unfilmed screenplay draft: Gary Goldman
SCR4..... Unfilmed screenplay draft: David Hayter (2002)
SCR5..... Unfilmed screenplay draft: David Hayter (2003)
SCR6..... Unfilmed screenplay draft: Alex Tse
SPOT..... *DC Spotlight #1*
VRL1 ..... Viral video: *NBS Nightly News with Ted Philips*

VRL2..... Viral video: *The Keene Act and You*
VRL3 ..... Viral video: *Who Watches the Watchmen? A Veidt Music Network (VMN) Special*
VRL4 ..... Viral video: *World in Focus: 6 Minutes to Midnight*
VRL5 ..... Viral video: *Local Radio Station Report on 1977 Riots*
VRL6 ..... Viral videos (group of ten): *Veidt Enterprises Advertising Contest*
WAWA... *Watching the Watchmen*
WHOS ... *Who's Who: The Definitive Directory of the DC Universe*
WTFC .... *Watchmen: The Film Companion*

Seated atop a building's chimney, Rorschach writes a journal entry about his suspicion that Dolores Shairp may be cheating on welfare. He notes his determination to uncover the truth about The Comedian's death, and his disgust at the reek of "fornication and bad consciences" pervading the city **[ALAN]**.

> *NOTE: Rorschach's complaint about bad smells is ironic, given the number of times that other characters comment on his putrid stench. Once again, the vigilante seems to be remarkably un-self-aware.*

Rorschach's investigation brings him to Happy Harry's bar and grill **[ALAN]**, where he roughs up several bar patrons, including criminals called Gideon (an arsonist), Johnny Gobs (a schoolyard drug pusher), and Nicky the Jap **[SCR1, SCR3]**. Another patron, Steve, mocks Rorschach's hygiene, unaware of the vigilante's deadly reputation. Rorschach breaks his fingers, one at a time, to induce others to talk. Frustrated that no one has the information he seeks, he leaves the bar and continues his journal entry, noting feelings of depression and his philosophy for dealing with disappointment: "Never despair. Never surrender" **[ALAN]**.

> *NOTE: Sam Hamm, after introducing Johnny Gobs in his unproduced 1988 screenplay, used the same name for a thug in his script for Tim Burton's first Batman film the following year.*

> *CONFLICT: Gary Goldman's 1992 rewrite of Hamm's script gives Steve's hygiene comment to a young punk named Harley, with Rorschach breaking the fingers of his companion, a criminal known as Jack of Hearts.*

Next, Rorschach visits Adrian Veidt to warn him that someone might be gunning for masked heroes. Veidt feigns surprise, suggesting that the Soviets could have been responsible, but Rorschach denies that possibility, since the existence of Jon Osterman would prevent any communist nations from antagonizing the United States **[ALAN]**.

—October 13, 1985—8:30 PM

Rorschach writes a journal entry deeming Adrian Veidt a pampered, decadent, shallow liberal—and possibly a homosexual—and condemning Dan Dreiberg as a flabby, whimpering failure. He considers the fates of several former vigilantes and wonders why so many of his kind fail to remain active and healthy **[ALAN]**.

As an army officer is about to have sex with a prostitute at a sleazy motel, Rorschach bursts into the room, breaks the man's arm, beats him unconscious with a blackjack, and slams the hooker into a wall, then steals the man's uniform and ID so he can gain access to the Rockefeller Military Research Center **[SCR6]**.

Entering the base's Special Talent Quarter, Rorschach warns Laurie Juspeczyk and Jon Osterman that someone might be plotting their murders. When he dismisses Blake's attempted rape of Sally Jupiter as a "moral lapse," however, Laurie grows angry and Jon teleports him out of the facility. Laurie calms her nerves by inviting Dan Dreiberg to dinner. Since Jon is on the verge of a scientific breakthrough—locating a gluino, thereby validating supersymmetrical theory—he declines to join them **[ALAN]**.

—October 13, 1985—9:30 PM

Dan Dreiberg and Laurie Juspeczyk meet for dinner at a restaurant called Rafael's. Laurie orders spaghetti Africaine, refusing to let Dan pick up the check since she plans to expense it to the military. The two reminisce about their days as crime-fighters. Laurie is glad to have her costumed days behind her, but Dan privately misses the adventure—and her costume **[ALAN]**.

—October 13, 1985—11:30 PM

Rorschach writes a journal entry claiming no one cares that The Comedian was murdered but him. With war imminent and millions of lives in the balance, he wonders why a single death bothers him so much, but vows that even in the face of Armageddon, evil must be punished without compromise **[ALAN]**.

—On or After October 13, 1985

An autopsy is performed on Eddie Blake, after which his body is released to the Pentagon **[MTRO]**.

—Before October 15, 1985

U.S. President Richard Nixon undergoes his third heart operation **[ALAN]**.

—October 15, 1985—Morning

The *New Frontiersman* publishes an article about Max Shea, titled "Missing Writer: Castro to Blame." *Nova Express* publishes an article titled "How Sick Is Dick?", discussing Richard Nixon's recent cardiac troubles **[ALAN, FILM]**.

—Before October 16, 1985

Utility company SAW Hydro & Power sends a letter to Edgar Jacobi letting him know that his account is overdue **[FILM]**.

—October 16, 1985—Morning

The *Palm Springs Gazette* publishes a front-page story titled "Soviets Escalate Nuclear Warhead Production," reporting that the Soviet Premier has reminded the United Nations

of the United States' "no first strike" promise **[FILM]**. The headline of the *New York Gazette*, meanwhile, reads "Soviets Will Not Tolerate U.S. Adventurism in Afghanistan" **[ALAN, FILM]**.

Jon Osterman, Adrian Veidt, and Dan Dreiberg attend Eddie Blake's funeral. Rorschach, sans garb, watches from outside the cemetery with his doomsday sign. He notices Edgar Jacobi placing flowers on his former enemy's grave. As Blake is laid to rest, Dreiberg tosses the smiley-face pin into the open grave **[ALAN]**.

    NOTE: *Dan Dreiberg has concealed his crime-fighting past ever since the Keene Act's passing. Attending a funeral with Dr. Manhattan and Ozymandias seems a risky action to take for someone determined not to let others know he was The Nite Owl.*

—October 16, 1985—2:00 PM

Unwilling to honor The Comedian, Laurie Juspeczyk visits Sally Jupiter at the Nepenthe Gardens rest resort, in California. Sally reminisces about the past and shows Laurie a Silk Spectre Tijuana Bible that she recently received. Laurie calls the comic degrading, but her mother reminds her that she "sleep[s] with an H-bomb" **[ALAN, FILM]**.

    NOTE: *The time is noted in the* Watchmen *film.*

—October 16, 1985—Night

Rorschach searches Edgar Jacobi's apartment and finds Laetrile pills, then ambushes the former criminal when he returns home, demanding to know why he was at the funeral. Edgar tells him about The Comedian's visit and admits that he is dying of cancer. Monitoring the conversation via his listening device, Adrian Veidt decides to frame Rorschach for murder to prevent the vigilante from exposing his plans **[ALAN]**.

After leaving Jacobi's apartment, Rorschach walks along 42nd Street, disgusted by the sexual imagery on every sign and billboard, and by the prostitutes selling their bodies. When he ignores a hooker's advances, she makes an obscene gesture at him. He sneaks into the cemetery to pay his last respects to The Comedian, then records a journal entry wondering if he, like Blake and The Minutemen, will die violently as well **[ALAN]**.

—Before October 19, 1985

The *New Frontiersman* hangs a poster near Hollis Mason's apartment, bearing the slogan "In Your Hearts, You Know It's Right." A vandal spray-paints the word "Wing" at the end of the slogan, mocking the newspaper's conservative politics **[FILM]**.

—On or Before October 19, 1985

Adrian Veidt arranges for Jon Osterman to be interviewed on television regarding their work to solve the world's energy crisis **[SCR6]**. Benny Anger, a journalist with the American Broadcasting Company (ABC), is chosen to conduct the interview **[ALAN]**.

ABSO .... *Watchmen Absolute Edition*	**BWOZ**.... *Before Watchmen—Ozymandias*	• Film: *Batman v Superman: Dawn of Justice Ultimate Edition*
ALAN..... Alan Moore's *Watchmen* miniseries	**BWRO** ... *Before Watchmen—Rorschach*	• Film: *Justice League*
ARCD .... *Minutemen Arcade*	**BWSS** ... *Before Watchmen—Silk Spectre*	**CLIX** ...... HeroClix figure pack-in cards
ARTF ..... *Watchmen: The Art of the Film*	**CHEM**.... My Chemical Romance music video: "Desolation Row"	**DECK**..... *DC Comics Deck-Building Game—Crossover Pack 4: Watchmen*
BLCK..... *Tales of the Black Freighter*	**CMEO** ... *Watchmen* cameos in comics, TV, and film:	
BWCC ... *Before Watchmen—The Crimson Corsair*	• Comic: *Astonishing X-Men* volume 3 issue #6	**DURS** ..... *DC Universe: Rebirth Special* volume 1 issue #1
BWCO ... *Before Watchmen—Comedian*	• Comic: *Hero Hotline* volume 1 issue #5	**FILM** ..... *Watchmen* theatrical film
BWDB ... *Before Watchmen—Dollar Bill*	• Comic: *Kingdom Come* volume 1 issue #2	**HOOD** ..... *Under the Hood* documentary and dust-jacket prop reproduction
BWDM .. *Before Watchmen—Dr. Manhattan*	• Comic: *Marvels* volume 1 issue #4	
BWMM.. *Before Watchmen—Minutemen*	• Comic: *The Question* volume 1 issue #17	**JUST** ..... *Watchmen: Justice Is Coming*
BWMO .. *Before Watchmen—Moloch*	• TV: *Teen Titans Go!* episode #82, "Real Boy Adventures"	**MATL** .... Mattel Club Black Freighter figure pack-in cards
BWNO ... *Before Watchmen—Nite Owl*	• Film: *Man of Steel*	

CONFLICT: *In the* Watchmen *film, Ted Koppel interviews Dr. Manhattan instead of Benny Anger, on a program called* Face to Face. *In Sam Hamm's unproduced 1988 screenplay, as well as in Gary Goldman's 1992 rewrite of that script, David Brinkley handles the interview. David Hayter's unproduced 2002 script draft names the interviewer Calvin Miller, and his program* Presswatch.

—October 19, 1985—Morning
The *National Examiner* reports the birth of a two-headed cat in Queens. News vendor Bernard sells this magazine alongside copies of *New Frontiersman*, *Tales of the Black Freighter*, *Knot Top*, *Music*, *Home Maker*, and *Bodyline* **[ALAN]**.

—October 19, 1985—Daytime
With the possibility of nuclear war increasing, New York City's Promethean Cab Co. is deemed a fallout shelter **[ALAN]**.

Rorschach, in doomsday prophet mode, buys a copy of the *New Frontiersman* from Bernard, promising that the world will end this day—but also reminding the news vendor to hold tomorrow's edition for him **[ALAN]**.

While having sex with Jon Osterman, Laurie Juspeczyk is startled to realize that he has duplicated himself twice to engage her in a foursome, with a fourth body continuing his research nearby **[ALAN]**. On a monitor is Adrian Veidt, with whom Jon is working to complete their **S**ub **Q**uantum **U**nified **I**ntrinsic field **D**evice (SQUID), which he teleports to Veidt's Karnak base in Antarctica **[FILM]**. Frustrated by Jon's inability to understand people anymore, and by his having put his work ahead of her needs, Laurie leaves in a huff, considering their relationship at an end **[ALAN]**.

Doug Roth interviews Janey Slater for *Nova Express* **[RPG3]** regarding her past romance with Jon Osterman, her bitterness at his having left her for Laurie Juspeczyk, and her recent cancer diagnosis. Janey claims that she and Jon were sexually disconnected. The interview comes to an abrupt end when her uncontrollable sobbing and cigarette-induced coughing leaves her unable to speak **[NEWP]**.
    CONFLICT: The Watchmen Sourcebook *includes an excerpt of the published article, dated October 15—four days before the interview occurs in Alan Moore's miniseries.*

—October 19, 1985—Shortly Before 6:15 PM
Laurie Juspeczyk hails a cab to Dan Dreiberg's brownstone, arriving as a locksmith from Gordian Knot Lock Co. fixes his busted door knob. She tells him she left Jon Osterman, then walks with Dan to Hollis Mason's apartment. En route, they are attacked by five Knot-Tops. The two fend off their would-be muggers, leaving them unconscious in an alley.

Filled with adrenaline, Laurie leaves to find a hotel for the night, while Dan continues on to visit Mason **[ALAN]**.

Dr. Manhattan prepares for a television interview with journalist Benny Anger, mentally summons a suit from a closet, and teleports himself to Studio 4 of the American Broadcasting Company (ABC), where his sudden arrival startles the staff **[ALAN]**. Director Kent Turner **[SCR1]** comments that there's no time for makeup to adjust his skin tone for the camera, so Jon darkens himself accordingly. Agent Forbes, an Army Intelligence officer, gives Manhattan a list of topics not to discuss **[ALAN]**.

> **NOTE:** The director is unnamed in Alan Moore's miniseries. Sam Hamm's unproduced 1988 screenplay names him Kent Turner.

> **CONFLICT:** Gary Goldman's unproduced screenplay replaces Forbes with Ernest Bullard and Adamson, agents from the Gestapo-like Civil Terrorism Unit (CTU). Goldman's script also mentions Comrade Justice, a superhuman Soviet counterpart to Dr. Manhattan—the existence of whom would entirely negate Alan Moore's miniseries, in which Jon Osterman is the world's only bona fide superhuman, thus giving the United States a major advantage.

Journalist Janet Black, speaking from the studio audience, notes that the Doomsday Clock stands at four minutes to midnight, and asks if Dr. Manhattan agrees that humanity is that close to nuclear annihilation. Jon cryptically replies that even without nuclear weapons, there will always be dangers in the world **[FILM]**.

Nova Express writer Doug Roth, also in the audience, asks about Wally Weaver, Edgar Jacobi, Janey Slater, and more than two dozen other associates of Dr. Manhattan all being diagnosed with cancer. Despite knowing his own future, Jon is shaken by news of Slater's illness. When Roth accuses him of giving them cancer, Forbes ends the interview, preventing Jon from responding to similar queries from *The Washington Post*'s Tina Price, *The Enquirer*'s Jim Weiss **[ALAN]**, and the *Los Angeles Times*' Rod Cage **[SCR2]**. When the press hammers him with more questions, Jon loses his temper and teleports everyone— and all cameras—away from the studio **[ALAN]**.

> **CONFLICT:** Taking Out the Trash *dates the beginning of Dr. Manhattan's cancer scandal on October 15, contradicting Alan Moore's miniseries.*

—October 19, 1985—Night

A late edition of *Nova Express* hits newsstands, containing Doug Roth's article linking Dr. Manhattan to the spate of cancers. Some who read the piece grow wary of Jon Osterman's powers—or conclude, given Janey Slater's claim of sexual incompatibility, that he must be a homosexual. In the wake of the TV interview, which airs continuously on the news, Jon returns to the Rockefeller Military Research Center to find a soldier hanging a radiation

---

warning outside his lab. He teleports himself to Mars, stopping first at the Gila Flats Test Base to retrieve a picture of himself and Janey **[ALAN]**.

—October 19 to 21, 1985
Rorschach goes two nights without any sleep, leaving him exhausted **[ALAN]**.

—On or After October 19, 1985
Adrian Veidt discreetly murders Doug Roth to prevent the journalist from uncovering his plans **[SCR6]**.

—October 20, 1985—Morning
The *New York Gazette*'s headline reads "Dr. Manhattan Leaves Earth." The *New Frontiersman* blames the Russians, opening with "Our Country's Protector Smeared by the Kremlin." Rorschach visits Bernard's newsstand, sans mask, and purchases both publications. Bernie returns to continue reading *Tales of the Black Freighter*, much to the annoyance of Bernard, who asks if he ever plans to buy the comic **[ALAN]**.

Laurie Juspeczyk returns to the military base to find U.S. Army personnel in hazmat suits removing the contents of Jon Osterman's lab. Agent Forbes informs her what has happened, then brings her to receive a cancer scan. When she reacts angrily, he tells her that her "meal ticket" is likely never coming back, that they are all in great trouble, and that it's her fault for causing him emotional stress **[ALAN]**.

Rorschach breaks Dan Dreiberg's new lock and helps himself to coffee and cereal while Dan sleeps. He awakens Dan to show him the *Gazette*'s headline about Dr. Manhattan's self-exile, wondering which of them will be the next to go **[ALAN]**.

—October 20, 1985—Night
The Soviet Union invades Afghanistan, and the United States takes a contrary position. The fighting escalates, leading many to conclude that a global nuclear war is imminent. Geneva talks to resolve the issue stall due to America's refusal to resume discussions unless the Soviets agree to exclude Dr. Manhattan from the agenda **[ALAN]**.

> **NOTE:** *In the real world, the Soviet occupation of Afghanistan lasted from 1979 to 1989, whereas in* Watchmen, *the invasion appears to have been delayed until 1985.*

> **CONFLICT:** Taking Out the Trash *dates the invasion on October 16, contradicting Alan Moore's miniseries.*

Chuck, a newspaper delivery man, drops off new issues at Bernard's newsstand. Nearby, Bernie reaches the end of *Tales of the Black Freighter*. Annoyed to see "Continued next

month" printed on the comic's last page, he refuses to pay for a story without an ending. Given the *New York Gazette*'s evening-edition headline, "Russians Invade Afghanistan," Bernard lets him have the comic for free **[ALAN]**.

Richard Nixon's advisors predict the Soviets will continue into Pakistan and Western Europe **[ALAN]**. Henry Kissinger says watchdog scientists have moved the Doomsday Clock to two minutes to midnight. A general recommends a first strike, reporting that Czechoslovakia, Poland, and East Germany have mobilized their forces but are letting Russia take the lead **[FILM]**. Projections predict the Eastern Bloc's destruction, though several Soviet warheads will still destroy Germany, the United Kingdom, and parts of the U.S. East Coast, including Boston, New York, Baltimore, and Washington, D.C. The U.S. Farm Belt will be mostly salvageable, with Mexico receiving the brunt of the fallout. Nixon ponders whether or not these constitute acceptable losses **[ALAN]**.

●—Before October 21, 1985

Hitman Roy Victor Chess begins renting apartment #3B at 52 Jackson Avenue in The Bronx **[FILM]**.

To throw Rorschach off the scent of the "mask killer," Adrian Veidt arranges for Pyramid Deliveries' freight coordinator to hire freight handlers to perform a series of illegal tasks. One handler, instructed to contract a hitman to carry out an assassination (on Veidt himself), hires Roy Chess for the job **[ALAN]**.

> **CONFLICT:** *In the* Watchmen *film, Roy Chess is an employee of Pyramid Transnational, which Rorschach learns while searching his apartment. Gary Goldman's unproduced 1992 screenplay renames him Harley.*

Adrian Veidt approves the creation of a Saturday-morning cartoon about his exploits as a masked crime-fighter, slated to air in fall 1986. He also authorizes *Ziggurat of Death* **[ALAN]**, the first adventure module of the *Ozymandias Role Playing Game* **[RPG2]**.

> **NOTE:** *A parody cartoon,* Saturday Morning Watchmen, *was posted to newgrounds. com in 2009, one day prior to the* Watchmen *film's release, and is currently available on YouTube. Created by Harry Partridge, the video satirizes how 1980s animators removed violence and other negative aspects from superhero cartoons to make them campy and kid-friendly. The cartoon's theme song depicts The Crimebusters (called The Watchmen) as happy, united, well-adjusted friends who sing, share pizza, and deliver positive messages for young viewers. Given the nature of 1980s television animation, Veidt's cartoon would likely be similar in tone.*

—October 21, 1985—Early Morning

Rorschach returns to Edgar Jacobi's apartment and ambushes the ex-villain in his kitchen, demanding to know who killed The Comedian and disgraced Dr. Manhattan, Jacobi's two greatest former enemies. Edgar maintains his innocence, even when Rorschach puts him in the refrigerator. Finally, Rorschach says to contact him if he remembers anything. Adrian Veidt monitors the conversation remotely **[ALAN]**.

—October 21, 1985—2:35 AM

Rorschach records a journal entry concluding that Edgar Jacobi is telling the truth, and is merely a pawn in someone else's plan. Exhausted, he returns to his filthy apartment and falls asleep without taking off his mask **[ALAN]**.

—October 21, 1985—Early Morning

Dr. Manhattan arrives on Mars twenty-seven hours after leaving the Gila Flats Test Base and relives key moments from throughout his life. After twelve seconds, he gazes at his photo of himself and Janey Slater, then drops it to the sand so he can view light emitted two million years earlier by supernova SN 1885A. He sits on Mars' pink sand and constructs a massive glass palace **[ALAN]**—a large-scale replica of a clock that his father gave him on his ninth birthday **[BWDM]**.

> **NOTE:** *The glass palace is a nod to Superman's Fortress of Solitude, while mirroring numerous aspects of Alan Moore's miniseries: Jon's former employer, Milton Glass; Eddie Blake crashing through a window to his death; Adrian Veidt's glass vivarium; Laurie's childhood snow globe; the destruction of New York City, in which the streets are showered with broken shards; and more.*

Dr. Manhattan attempts, for the first time, to extend his consciousness to before his transformation into a superhuman in 1959. In becoming his own quantum observer, he inadvertently changes history at Gila Flats so that the accident never occurred, thereby splintering his quantum reality into infinite permutations—an ability he did not previously know he possessed. After witnessing events from his life in these altered realities, Jon eventually returns to this same moment, realizing that to fix the fractured timelines he has caused, he must travel backward and forward through his own history, erasing all the divergent choices he made and thus restore the original reality—in essence, limiting his own powers for the sake of the world **[BWDM]**.

October 21, 1985—Early Morning (Alternate Reality)

In a quantum reality in which Jon Osterman never becomes Dr. Manhattan, Jon and Janey, now elderly, remain happily married **[BWDM]**.

MIND .... *The Mindscape of Alan Moore*
MOBL .... *Watchmen: The Mobile Game*
MOTN .... *Watchmen: The Complete Motion Comic*
MTRO .... *Metro* promotional newspaper cover wrap
NEWP .... *New Frontiersman* promotional newspaper
NEWW .... *New Frontiersman* website
NIGH .... *Watchmen: The End Is Nigh, Parts 1 and 2*
PKIT ...... *Watchmen* film British press kit
PORT ..... *Watchmen Portraits*
REAL ..... Real life
RPG1 .... *DC Heroes Role Playing Module #227: Who Watches the Watchmen?*

RPG2 .... *DC Heroes Role Playing Module #235: Taking Out the Trash—Curses and Tears*
RPG3 .... *DC Heroes: The Watchmen Sourcebook*
RUBY .... "Wounds," published in *The Ruby Files Volume One*
SCR1 ..... Unfilmed screenplay draft: Sam Hamm
SCR2 ..... Unfilmed screenplay draft: Charles McKeuen
SCR3 ..... Unfilmed screenplay draft: Gary Goldman
SCR4 ..... Unfilmed screenplay draft: David Hayter (2002)
SCR5 ..... Unfilmed screenplay draft: David Hayter (2003)
SCR6 ..... Unfilmed screenplay draft: Alex Tse
SPOT ..... *DC Spotlight #1*
VRL1 ..... Viral video: *NBS Nightly News with Ted Philips*

VRL2 ..... Viral video: *The Keene Act and You*
VRL3 ..... Viral video: *Who Watches the Watchmen? A Veidt Music Network (VMN) Special*
VRL4 ..... Viral video: *World in Focus: 6 Minutes to Midnight*
VRL5 ..... Viral video: *Local Radio Station Report on 1977 Riots*
VRL6 ..... Viral videos (group of ten): *Veidt Enterprises Advertising Contest*
WAWA ... *Watching the Watchmen*
WHOS ... *Who's Who: The Definitive Directory of the DC Universe*
WTFC .... *Watchmen: The Film Companion*

—October 21, 1985—Early Morning

Two hours later, Dr. Manhattan observes meteorites falling above the planet's Nodus Gordii mountain range and thinks about his father **[ALAN]**.

> **NOTE:** *Nodus Gordii, an actual mountain range on Mars, is named for the Latin translation of "Gordian Knot," a common image throughout Alan Moore's miniseries.*

—October 21, 1985—Morning

The *New York Gazette*'s front-page headline reads "Afghanistan Fighting Spreads." Another publication poses the question, "Afghanistan: Is Pakistan Next?" **[ALAN]**.

Two young children, Clare and Dominique Hirsch, are murdered by their father, who wishes to spare them the horror of a nuclear war with the Soviet Union. He kills them in front of his wife, then slices open his own jugular vein. Detectives Joe Bourquin and Steven Fine investigate the murder-suicide, assigning Officer Capaldi to bring the lone survivor to the hospital **[ALAN]**.

With Jon Osterman no longer working for the U.S. government, Laurie Juspeczyk is evicted from the Rockefeller base, her expense account suspended. Dan Dreiberg takes her out to lunch at the Gunga Diner, then invites her to stay at his apartment **[ALAN]**.

—October 21, 1985—11:00 AM

Rorschach awakens to shouting outside and notices teens spray-painting an abandoned building. On the way out of his apartment, he passes his landlady, Dolores Shairp, and her screaming children. Ignoring her complaints about his poor hygiene and late rent, he spots Dan Dreiberg and Laurie Juspeczyk leaving the diner. Rorschach records a journal entry wondering if the two are having an affair, and whether Laurie was involved in the downfalls of The Comedian and Dr. Manhattan **[ALAN]**.

—October 21, 1985, Midday

Adrian Veidt prepares to meet with a company that produces Ozymandias action figures, which hopes to expand the line with toys based on his enemies. Roy Chess confronts him in the lobby and fatally shoots his assistant. Adrian dodges the shooter's aim and beats him senseless. As police arrive on the scene, Veidt warns that the gunman has a poison capsule in his mouth. He pretends to try to stop Chess from biting down, but discreetly forces the would-be killer to swallow cyanide, killing him **[ALAN]**.

> **NOTE:** *Veidt's assistant is unnamed in Alan Moore's miniseries, though* Before Watchmen: Ozymandias *calls her Yvonne, a replacement for his longtime assistant, Marla. Gary Goldman's unproduced 1992 screenplay calls her Miss Wilcox, which could be Yvonne's last name.*

CONFLICT: *In the* Watchmen *film, Veidt is meeting with Lee Iacocca and other automobile captains of industry when Chess attacks, though Adrian's secretary does note that the toy company wants to meet with him as well. The secretary survives in the on-screen version (despite being shot in the leg and hand), while Iacocca dies. In Sam Hamm's unproduced 1988 screenplay, the assassin kills a television journalist named Justine James.*

—October 21, 1985—Night

The *New York Times* reports on the failed assassination of Adrian Veidt, with the front-page headline "Industrialist in Murder Bid." News vendor Bernard is shocked at the news, deeming Veidt a saint and a hero **[ALAN]**.

Rorschach checks his mail-drop (a public trash can near the Gunga Diner) and finds a note from Edgar Jacobi, indicating he has information to impart and asking that they meet at 11:30 that night. As the vigilante retrieves his hidden mask from a dumpster, he notices police in front of the Utopia Cinema restraining a teenager high on KT-28s, ranting about Richard Nixon and bombs. Rorschach records a journal entry about these events, wondering if everyone but him has gone mad **[ALAN]**.

—October 21, 1985—8:30 PM

Rorschach interrupts an attempted rape and mugging, taking great satisfaction from seeing fear in the attacker's eyes before he pummels the man **[ALAN]**.

—October 21, 1985—Night

Laurie Juspeczyk moves into Dan Dreiberg's apartment. Her beauty and mere presence unnerve him as he bids her goodnight **[ALAN]**.

Outside, rain pours down on Bernard's newsstand, but that doesn't deter young Bernie from continuing to read his comic book. Joey, a driver for the Promethean Cab Co., purchases a copy of *Hustler* and asks Bernard to display a poster for her, advertising an upcoming Pink Triangle benefit concert for a militant feminist group called Gay Women Against Rape (GWAR) **[ALAN]**.

> **NOTE:** *The cab company's name is a subtle reminder of Adrian Veidt's prevalent pyramid symbol, while the band's moniker foreshadows Joey's violence against Aline. The latter also ties in to* Watchmen's *repeated rape motif, with regard to Sally Jupiter, Kitty Genovese, Blair Roche, and Hooded Justice, as well as Rorschach being threatened with rape as a child and while in prison.*

While watching footage of Doug Roth's humiliation of Dr. Manhattan, Edgar Jacobi realizes that the cigarettes he has been delivering to Janey Slater have been hurting, not helping her. Adrian Veidt enters the room, explains his plan to prevent nuclear war, and gently asks

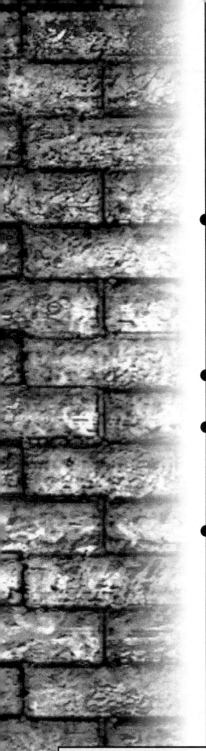

Edgar to accept his own death, adding that his sacrifice, like Christ's, will save humanity. Awed by the terrible but beautiful plot, the ex-magician calls it "the most amazing magic trick in history," then closes his eyes and awaits death **[BWMO]**. Veidt kills Edgar with a single bullet to the forehead, then leaves him for Rorschach and the police to discover. Veidt phones in an anonymous tip to Detectives Joe Bourquin and Steven Fine, claiming they can find Rorschach at Jacobi's apartment **[ALAN]**.

> **NOTE:** *In Alan Moore's miniseries, the broadcast airs on October 19, with Jacobi dying on October 21. Since* Before Watchmen: Moloch *shows Veidt killing Edgar after the latter watches the footage, it must not be the original broadcast.*

—October 21, 1985—11:30 PM

Rorschach finds Edgar Jacobi dead in his apartment. As he picks up a handgun to search for clues, police outside demand his surrender, and he realizes he's been set up. He fashions a makeshift weapon, sets a fire as a distraction, and injures police officers Willis, Shaw, and Greaves while trying to escape. Outnumbered, he is quickly subdued by cops, who rough him up and unmask him. Furious and foul-smelling, he demands that they give him back his face, which they ignore. The police discover Edgar Jacobi's corpse inside and assume Rorschach to be the killer **[ALAN]**.

—On or After October 21, 1985

Adrian Veidt hires a new assistant named Carol **[SCR5]**.

—Between October 21 and October 26, 1985

Police search Rorschach's apartment and find back issues of the *New Frontiersman*, but fail to notice his spare clothes, mask, gloves, hat, and shoes hidden beneath the floorboards. They confiscate the rough notes of his personal journal, but not the final draft, which lies hidden with his outfit **[ALAN]**.

—After October 21, 1985

Adrian Veidt begins killing off the Pyramid Deliveries freight handlers whom he'd hired to carry out his plan. The police deem these deaths accidents or overdoses, but one worker, who'd been paid to contract Roy Chess, grows suspicious after the freight coordinator who hired him falls under a subway train **[ALAN]**.

Adrian Veidt vetoes new action figures based on his former adversaries. Leo Winston, president of Veidt Industries' marketing and development division, suggests the product range still be expanded to increase marketplace profile, including figurines of Moloch, Rorschach, The Nite Owl, and Bubastis. Although the lynx was not part of Veidt's costumed-adventuring days, Winston says, she'll be featured in the upcoming Ozymandias cartoon as a feline sidekick. He offers a mockup leaflet showing the new figures, an Owlship model, and a replica of Rorschach's grappling gun [**ALAN**].

Adrian Veidt sends Leo Winston a handwritten note approving the Bubastis figure but not the others, for ethical reasons. He suggests instead releasing a costumed army of terrorists that would be incorporated into the cartoon as the primary villains, noting that the American public has never gone in much for superheroes [**ALAN**].

An investigation into Edgar Jacobi's murder reveals that he has left no estate [**ALAN**].

—October 22, 1985

Officer Shaw is admitted to a hospital for minor burns, while Greaves suffers a shattered sternum from being shot at point-blank range by Rorschach's grappling gun. Greaves is placed on the hospital's critical list [**ALAN**].

The *New York Gazette*'s front-page headline, "Rorschach Revealed," tops a pair of articles by M.J. Geisthardt and William Ball covering Rorschach's criminal history and capture, as well as the discovery of Edgar Jacobi's body [**FILM, ARTF**].

At his bail hearing, Walter Kovacs refuses to respond to anything but "Rorschach," then is jailed at the Sing Sing Correctional Facility, in Ossining, New York, to await trial for multiple murders, including those of Gerald Grice, Harvey Furniss, and Edgar Jacobi. In his pockets are a battery-powered flashlight, five Sweet Chariot chewing sugar cubes, a 1968 New York City subway map with red alterations, the withered remains of a red rose, loose change, his journal, a pencil, a broken bottle of Nostalgia cologne, and residue of ground black pepper [**ALAN**].

Dr. Malcolm "Mal" Long, from New York Psychiatric Hospital's West Branch, is assigned to evaluate Rorschach at Sing Sing [**RPG3**]. After reading Kovacs' file, the psychiatrist hopes to bolster his professional reputation by reforming the vigilante and writing a future article identifying a new syndrome. Long appends a note to the file, calling it a "complex case" and saying he looks forward to their first interview [**ALAN**].

> **NOTE:** *Long's case file on Rorschach, as shown in* Watchmen Portraits, *bears the name Dr. Terrance Roberts on its cover. This could constitute a name change for Long, but since he is called William Long in the* Under the Hood *documentary made to supplement the film, Roberts may simply be a colleague helping with the case.*

—October 23, 1985

Prior to his initial examination, Malcolm Long records a case history of Walter Kovacs [**RPG3**].

MIND .... *The Mindscape of Alan Moore*	**RPG2** .... *DC Heroes Role Playing Module #235: Taking Out the Trash—Curses and Tears*	**VRL2** ..... Viral video: *The Keene Act and You*
MOBL.... *Watchmen: The Mobile Game*		**VRL3** ..... Viral video: *Who Watches the Watchmen? A Veidt Music Network (VMN) Special*
MOTN.... *Watchmen: The Complete Motion Comic*	**RPG3** .... *DC Heroes: The Watchmen Sourcebook*	
MTRO.... *Metro* promotional newspaper cover wrap	**RUBY** .... "Wounds," published in *The Ruby Files Volume One*	**VRL4** ..... Viral video: *World in Focus: 6 Minutes to Midnight*
NEWP.... *New Frontiersman* promotional newspaper	**SCR1**..... Unfilmed screenplay draft: Sam Hamm	**VRL5** ..... Viral video: *Local Radio Station Report on 1977 Riots*
NEWW... *New Frontiersman* website	**SCR2**..... Unfilmed screenplay draft: Charles McKeuen	
NIGH ..... *Watchmen: The End Is Nigh, Parts 1 and 2*	**SCR3**..... Unfilmed screenplay draft: Gary Goldman	**VRL6** .....Viral videos (group of ten): *Veidt Enterprises Advertising Contest*
PKIT ...... *Watchmen* film British press kit	**SCR4**.... Unfilmed screenplay draft: David Hayter (2002)	
PORT..... *Watchmen Portraits*	**SCR5**..... Unfilmed screenplay draft: David Hayter (2003)	**WAWA**... *Watching the Watchmen*
REAL..... Real life	**SCR6**..... Unfilmed screenplay draft: Alex Tse	**WHOS** ... *Who's Who: The Definitive Directory of the DC Universe*
RPG1 .... *DC Heroes Role Playing Module #227: Who Watches the Watchmen?*	**SPOT**..... *DC Spotlight #1*	
	VRL1 ..... Viral video: *NBS Nightly News with Ted Philips*	**WTFC** .... *Watchmen: The Film Companion*

—October 25, 1985—Morning to Afternoon

A series of tenement fires erupt in New York City, allegedly started to remove sitting tenants **[ALAN]**.

With Dr. Manhattan no longer a deterrent to war, the Soviet Union moves the fighting in Afghanistan closer to the border of Pakistan, which asks the United States to intervene. Richard Nixon considers America's options and places the country's European military installations on full alert. At England's Greenham Common Base, several female peace demonstrators are arrested during scuffles with police officers **[ALAN]**.

After failing to open any new lines of investigation for two years, police call off their search for former *Tales of the Black Freighter* scribe Max Shea, who had mysteriously vanished from his Boston home in 1983 **[ALAN]**.

The Institute for Extraspatial Studies reports new possibilities for opening up new dimensions. Reporters speak to the agency's chief physicist, Dr. Ed Corey, who predicts early successes in the search for extra-dimensional energy sources **[ALAN]**.

—October 25, 1985—Afternoon

Malcolm Long has an initial meeting with Rorschach, whom he considers withdrawn and expressionless. Long is naïvely optimistic that he can reach Rorschach, oblivious to his dishonest responses to an ink-blot test. As guards return the vigilante to his cell, prisoners threaten to rape and kill him. He remains unfazed by their taunts **[ALAN]**.

> **CONFLICT:** The Watchmen Sourcebook *contains Long's notes about an October 23 meeting with Rorschach, contradicting Alan Moore's miniseries, in which the two first meet on October 25.*

—October 25, 1985—Afternoon to Night

Laurie Juspeczyk has her clothing and costume transferred from the Rockefeller base to Dan Dreiberg's apartment. She visits his underground lair, where she accidentally activates *Archimedes'* flamethrower, filling the cavern with fire. Dan rushes to her rescue and puts out the flames. As he performs a full systems check, the two reminisce about their days as masked heroes and their mutual loneliness **[ALAN]**.

—October 25, 1985—6:00 PM

Laurie and Dan watch the news together. Among the stories is footage of Rorschach's capture, including interviews with his landlady, Dolores Shairp (who calls him "a Nazi pervert" and lies that he propositioned her sexually), and *New Frontiersman* editor Hector Godfrey (who hails him as "a patriot and American") **[ALAN]**.

—October 25, 1985—After 6:00 PM

When Dan removes his glasses, Laurie sees him as handsome and kisses him. As they share an intimate evening, a repeat broadcast airs of Adrian Veidt's Indian Famine Appeal charity performance from July. While Veidt astounds audiences onscreen with his amazing physical prowess, Dan's performance with Laurie is less spectacular, as a lack of confidence causes temporary impotence **[ALAN]**.

—October 25, 1985—Night

Malcolm Long takes Rorschach's file home to study. His wife Gloria warns him not to become too wrapped up in the case, lest it ruin his cheerful disposition **[ALAN]**. The psychiatrist records notes about his patient, saying he's never met anyone so alienated and wondering how to help him **[RPG3]**.

—October 25, 1985—11:00 PM

Journalist Benny Anger wraps up a TV segment featuring Pale Horse member Red D'eath, after which *The Eleven O'Clock News* begins. Still unable to maintain an erection, Dan Dreiberg falls asleep on the couch **[ALAN]**.

—October 26, 1985—Early Morning

During the *Midnight Movie*, Laurie lays a blanket over Dan. Once the movie ends, she joins him on the couch to sleep **[ALAN]**.

—October 26, 1985—3:15 AM

Dan dreams of Laurie peeling off The Twilight Lady's costume and her own skin to reveal her Silk Spectre outfit underneath, while he removes his suit and skin to expose his Nite Owl garb. A nuclear blast burns them both alive, causing him to awaken in terror. Naked, he visits his workshop to take comfort in wearing his old outfit. Laurie follows him down, and he admits that the impending war and mask-killings have left him feeling powerless. To cure his midlife crisis, they suit up and board *Archimedes* **[ALAN]**.

—October 26, 1985—4:00 AM

Dan and Laurie spot a tenement fire at 5th Avenue and Grand Street **[FILM]**. He pilots the Owlship so she can rescue any trapped residents. Dousing the flames with water cannons, he drops off the residents on another rooftop, instructing them to head down to street level **[ALAN]**. Eleven people are saved, including Josephina Katz and her son Tim, whom the *New York Gazette* interviews in its coverage of the blaze **[RPG3]**.

> **CONFLICT:** Taking Out the Trash *and* The Watchmen Sourcebook *both date these events on October 22, contradicting Alan Moore's miniseries.*

MIND .... *The Mindscape of Alan Moore*
MOBL .... *Watchmen: The Mobile Game*
MOTN .... *Watchmen: The Complete Motion Comic*
MTRO .... *Metro promotional newspaper cover wrap*
NEWP .... *New Frontiersman promotional newspaper*
NEWW ... *New Frontiersman website*
NIGH ..... *Watchmen: The End Is Nigh, Parts 1 and 2*
PKIT ...... *Watchmen film British press kit*
PORT ..... *Watchmen Portraits*
REAL ..... *Real life*
RPG1 .... *DC Heroes Role Playing Module #227: Who Watches the Watchmen?*

RPG2 .... *DC Heroes Role Playing Module #235: Taking Out the Trash—Curses and Tears*
RPG3 .... *DC Heroes: The Watchmen Sourcebook*
RUBY .... *"Wounds," published in* The Ruby Files Volume One
SCR1 ..... Unfilmed screenplay draft: Sam Hamm
SCR2 ..... Unfilmed screenplay draft: Charles McKeuen
SCR3 ..... Unfilmed screenplay draft: Gary Goldman
SCR4 .... Unfilmed screenplay draft: David Hayter (2002)
SCR5 ..... Unfilmed screenplay draft: David Hayter (2003)
SCR6 ..... Unfilmed screenplay draft: Alex Tse
SPOT ..... *DC Spotlight #1*
VRL1 ..... Viral video: *NBS Nightly News with Ted Philips*

VRL2 ..... Viral video: *The Keene Act and You*
VRL3 ..... Viral video: *Who Watches the Watchmen? A Veidt Music Network (VMN) Special*
VRL4 ..... Viral video: *World in Focus: 6 Minutes to Midnight*
VRL5 ..... Viral video: *Local Radio Station Report on 1977 Riots*
VRL6 ..... Viral videos (group of ten): *Veidt Enterprises Advertising Contest*
WAWA ... *Watching the Watchmen*
WHOS .. *Who's Who: The Definitive Directory of the DC Universe*
WTFC .... *Watchmen: The Film Companion*

Re-invigorated and confident, Dan puts *Archimedes* on autopilot and makes love to Laurie while Billie Holiday's "You're My Thill" plays over *Archie's* in-ship stereo. Afterward, he decides to spring Rorschach from prison **[ALAN]**.

●—October 26, 1985—Daytime

Detective Steven Fine investigates the tenement fire. Witnesses describe an airship hovering between buildings, a goggle-wearing pilot, a female accomplice, and the provision of music and coffee. Fine determines to identity those who perpetrated the rescue **[ALAN]**.

Nova Express publishes an article titled "Spirit of '77," looking back at the passage of the Keene Act. In this article, Doug Roth compares costumed crime-fighters to Ku Klux Klan members. He reports that Rorschach's apartment, once searched, contained back issues of the *New Frontiersman*, illustrating the vigilante's fanatical tendencies and the newspaper's disreputable nature **[ALAN]**. The issue's cover features headshots of Dr. Manhattan, Rorschach, and Ozymandias **[NEWW]**.

> **NOTE:** *The title references "Spirit of '76," a patriotic sentiment often used to describe the desire for self-determination and individual liberty that was at the heart of the American Revolution.*

> **CONFLICT:** *The* New Frontiersman *website dates the issue on October 27, contradicting Alan Moore's miniseries.*

Malcolm Long meets with Rorschach, who dislikes the doctor's refusal to stop calling him Walter. Rorschach tells Long about the murder of Kitty Genovese that made him ashamed of humanity and inspired him to wear a mask. He accuses Long of caring not about his patient's well-being, but about getting his own name in medical journals. After guards return Rorschach to his cell, Long records notes indicating that the vigilante's misdirected aggression at his mother caused him to become a crime-fighter **[ALAN]**.

Later that day, as Rorschach waits in line for lunch at Sing Sing's canteen, an inmate named Otis tries to shank him, but Rorschach grabs a pan of hot cooking fat and douses the man with it, badly burning him. As guards drag Rorschach to solitary, he warns the prisoners that he's not locked up with them—*they're* locked up with *him*. Otis is taken to the hospital, and the deputy warden informs Long of the incident **[ALAN]**.

> **CONFLICT:** *Gary Goldman's unproduced 1992 screenplay replaces Otis with a trio of convicts called Tom, Dick, and Harry. In that version, Rorschach douses the latter two with oil when all three attack.*

October 26, 1985—Night

Malcolm Long's obsession with the Rorschach case takes its toll on his marriage that night when Gloria grows angry at him for choosing work over sex **[ALAN]**.

October 27, 1985

Rorschach tells Malcolm Long that he ceased to be Walter Kovacs when he decided to stop letting criminals live. He discusses his admiration for The Comedian and his philosophy of never compromising when fighting crime, noting that masked adventurers do what they do out of compulsion. Later that day, he receives death threats due to the hot-fat incident and is placed in solitary confinement for his own safety **[ALAN]**.

Long heads home, stopping at Bernard's newsstand. The news vendor shows off the latest issue of the *New York Gazette*, boasting that Rorschach was a regular customer. When he arrives home, his wife tells him she has invited their friends, Randy and Diana, over for dinner. He tries to sleep, but is unnerved by Rorschach's confessions **[ALAN]**.

After watching TV news footage of an airship saving tenement residents, Hollis Mason recognizes it as *Archimedes*. When Dan cancels their weekly beer session and admits he and Laurie carried out the rescue, Hollis calls Sally Jupiter to discuss old times and let her know what their successors have been up to. As they speak, an Acme Manicure specialist tends to Sally's feet **[ALAN]**.

> **NOTE:** *"Acme," a Greek word denoting the point at which something is the best or most successful (symbolizing masked adventurers before their decline), is also a common generic fictional company name, originating in* Looney Tunes *cartoons.*

The *New York Gazette* sports the headline "Reds Cross Pakistan Border" and also covers Rorschach's arrest. News vendor Bernard claims to have always suspected him **[ALAN]**.

In preparing to help Rorschach escape from prison, Dan Dreiberg buys the latest *Nova Express* to read its research into the Dr. Manhattan cancer scandal. He accesses his workshop computer and determines that cancer victims Janey Slater, Wally Weaver, and Edgar Jacobi were all employed by Dimensional Developments between 1967 and 1985. He and Laurie map out their jailbreak plans, opting not to tell Adrian Veidt since he might feel compelled to stop them **[ALAN]**.

October 28, 1985—Daytime

Russian troops fighting in Afghanistan spill over into Pakistan, which the Soviet government calls "accidental." Richard Nixon condemns the surge, and the *New York Gazette*'s front page reads "Nixon Promises Maximum Force," offering procedures for what to do in the event of a nuclear war **[ALAN]**.

MIND .... *The Mindscape of Alan Moore*
MOBL .... *Watchmen: The Mobile Game*
MOTN .... *Watchmen: The Complete Motion Comic*
MTRO .... *Metro* promotional newspaper cover wrap
NEWP .... *New Frontiersman* promotional newspaper
NEWW .... *New Frontiersman* website
NIGH .... *Watchmen: The End Is Nigh, Parts 1 and 2*
PKIT ...... *Watchmen* film British press kit
PORT .... *Watchmen Portraits*
REAL ..... Real life
RPG1 .... *DC Heroes Role Playing Module #227: Who Watches the Watchmen?*

RPG2 .... *DC Heroes Role Playing Module #235: Taking Out the Trash—Curses and Tears*
RPG3 .... *DC Heroes: The Watchmen Sourcebook*
RUBY .... "Wounds," published in *The Ruby Files Volume One*
SCR1 ..... Unfilmed screenplay draft: Sam Hamm
SCR2 ..... Unfilmed screenplay draft: Charles McKeuen
SCR3 ..... Unfilmed screenplay draft: Gary Goldman
SCR4 ..... Unfilmed screenplay draft: David Hayter (2002)
SCR5 ..... Unfilmed screenplay draft: David Hayter (2003)
SCR6 ..... Unfilmed screenplay draft: Alex Tse
SPOT ..... *DC Spotlight #1*
VRL1 ..... Viral video: *NBS Nightly News with Ted Philips*

VRL2 ..... Viral video: *The Keene Act and You*
VRL3 ..... Viral video: *Who Watches the Watchmen? A Veidt Music Network (VMN) Special*
VRL4 ..... Viral video: *World in Focus: 6 Minutes to Midnight*
VRL5 ..... Viral video: *Local Radio Station Report on 1977 Riots*
VRL6 ..... Viral videos (group of ten): *Veidt Enterprises Advertising Contest*
WAWA ..... *Watching the Watchmen*
WHOS .... *Who's Who: The Definitive Directory of the DC Universe*
WTFC .... *Watchmen: The Film Companion*

Malcolm Long meets once more with Rorschach, who recounts his murder of Gerald Grice in 1975 for the latter's torture, rape, and killing of young Blair Roche. This, he explains, fully transformed him from Walter Kovacs into Rorschach and made him stop leaving violent criminals alive **[ALAN]**.

Veidt Enterprises produces a television commercial promoting the Ozymandias line of action figures, in which a young child imagines that the superhero and his pet Bubastis stop a terrorist from attacking New York City. The commercial's director is D. Gibbons, and the tag line is "Ozymandias, protecting humanity from itself" **[VRL6]**.
> **NOTE:** *The director is named after* Watchmen *co-creator Dave Gibbons.*

—October 28, 1985—Night
Disturbed by Rorschach's recollections, Dr. Long records additional notes about his patient **[ALAN]**. His interest has become an obsession, he admits, and he has begun to see the world how Rorschach does—all in black **[RPG3]**. Long walks home along 40th Street, and a fellow black man calls him "nigger" for refusing to buy a Rolex watch. At dinner, he tells Randy and Diana details of the Blair Roche murder. After the uncomfortable couple cut the evening short, Gloria insults Mal's manhood and moves out. Sitting alone, the once-optimistic psychiatrist stares at an ink-blot test, seeing only a dead cat he once found, and realizing that everyone in the world is alone **[ALAN]**.

—October 29, 1985
The *New York Gazette*'s front-page story is titled "Tanks Mass in Eastern Europe." A secondary story is "California: Governor Reagan Urges Hard Line" **[ALAN]**.
> **NOTE:** *Ronald Reagan was the President of the United States in the real world from 1981 to 1989. With Richard Nixon retaining that job in* Watchmen *continuity, Reagan continues to serve as California's governor, just as he did from 1967 to 1975 in reality before turning his eye toward the Presidency.*

Malcolm Long resigns from Sing Sing Correctional Facility **[ALAN]**.

Rorschach's victim Otis slowly succumbs to his burns, and doctors predict that he could die within days **[ALAN]**. Tom "Rocky" Ryan (a.k.a. The Big Figure) **[RPG3]** and two henchmen **[ALAN]**, Michael "Mike" Stephens and Lawrence "Larry" Andrews **[CLIX]**, gain access to Rorschach's solitary-confinement cell by threatening to harm the wife and child of a prison guard named Mulhearney. Unfazed, Rorschach mocks Big Figure's size, and the dwarf promises to kill him during an impending riot **[ALAN]**.
> **CONFLICT:** *Big Figure and his henchmen undergo many changes in the six known unproduced* Watchmen *scripts. Sam Hamm's 1988 screenplay calls Big Figure "Little Bigger" and has him accompanied by three thugs: Carlos, Rafe, and T-Bone. Gary Goldman's*

1992 rewrite of that script replaces Big Figure with a tall, tattooed kingpin called Zebra, and his cronies with ex-supervillains The Butcher, Electron, and Ogre. Charles McKeuen's 1989 screenplay calls Lawrence "Fat Lawrence," while David Hayter's 2003 script draft and Alex Tse's 2006 version dub him Billy and "Big Bill." In all three scripts, as well as in Hayter's 2002 draft and the finalized film, Michael's name is changed to Lloyd. The surnames of Michael and Lawrence are revealed in HeroClix's Watchmen *figure pack-in cards.*

Dan Dreiberg hires the Gordian Knot Lock Co. to fix his front door knob for a second time **[ALAN]**.

Detective Steven Fine visits Dan Dreiberg at his home, hinting that he knows Dan's and Laurie's secret identities and that they saved the tenement residents. Fine opts not to arrest them, instead warning Dan that although no one would condemn them for rescuing fire victims, a return to crime-fighting would get them in trouble. After Fine leaves, Dan decides to spring Rorschach the next day **[ALAN]**.

> **NOTE:** *Despite Dan's decision, internal evidence in the comic indicates that the prison break actually occurs on October 31, two days later.*

At Adrian Veidt's island facility, his team puts finishing touches on his "alien" creature. Writer Max Shea looks forward to returning to the mainland after two years of working in total secrecy on what he and others believe to be a monster movie. After Hira Manish finishes a final sketch of the creature, the alien is refrigerated and transported to Veidt's Karnak lair in Antarctica **[ALAN]**.

●—October 30, 1985

To counter the *Nova Express* "Spirit of '77" anti-vigilante piece, the *New Frontiersman* publishes a front-page article appealing for clemency for costumed crime-fighters, titled "Honor Is Like the Hawk: Sometimes It Must Go Hooded." The story, by Hector Godfrey, calls Doug Roth a "coked-up commie coward"; features photos of Rorschach, Nite Owl, and The Comedian (which Godfrey deems appropriate for Halloween); and defends the Ku Klux Klan as having been formed by "decent people." Seymour Smith also runs a crank-file submission: a letter addressed to "the People of the Jewnited States of America." Additionally, the paper runs an article about Max Shea, titled "Missing Writer: Vanished Persons List Grows as Hunt Called Off," claiming the disappearances are part of a conspiracy with possible Cuban connections **[ALAN]**.

Otis dies of his burns, and Sing Sing officials fear a retaliatory riot **[ALAN]**.

As Laurie Juspeczyk and Dan Dreiberg prepare *Archimedes* for a trip to the prison, TV commentators discuss the imminent threat of nuclear war, which one reporter predicts

MIND .... *The Mindscape of Alan Moore*
MOBL .... *Watchmen: The Mobile Game*
MOTN .... *Watchmen: The Complete Motion Comic*
MTRO .... *Metro* promotional newspaper cover wrap
NEWP .... *New Frontiersman* promotional newspaper
NEWW .... *New Frontiersman* website
NIGH ..... *Watchmen: The End Is Nigh, Parts 1 and 2*
PKIT ...... *Watchmen* film British press kit
PORT ..... *Watchmen Portraits*
REAL ..... Real life
RPG1 .... *DC Heroes Role Playing Module #227: Who Watches the Watchmen?*

RPG2 .... *DC Heroes Role Playing Module #235: Taking Out the Trash—Curses and Tears*
RPG3 .... *DC Heroes: The Watchmen Sourcebook*
RUBY .... "Wounds," published in *The Ruby Files Volume One*
SCR1 ..... Unfilmed screenplay draft: Sam Hamm
SCR2 ..... Unfilmed screenplay draft: Charles McKeuen
SCR3 ..... Unfilmed screenplay draft: Gary Goldman
SCR4 ..... Unfilmed screenplay draft: David Hayter (2002)
SCR5 ..... Unfilmed screenplay draft: David Hayter (2003)
SCR6 ..... Unfilmed screenplay draft: Alex Tse
SPOT ..... *DC Spotlight #1*
VRL1 ..... Viral video: *NBS Nightly News with Ted Philips*

VRL2 ..... Viral video: *The Keene Act and You*
VRL3 ..... Viral video: *Who Watches the Watchmen? A Veidt Music Network (VMN) Special*
VRL4 ..... Viral video: *World in Focus: 6 Minutes to Midnight*
VRL5 ..... Viral video: *Local Radio Station Report on 1977 Riots*
VRL6 ..... Viral videos (group of ten): *Veidt Enterprises Advertising Contest*
WAWA ... *Watching the Watchmen*
WHOS ... *Who's Who: The Definitive Directory of the DC Universe*
WTFC ... *Watchmen: The Film Companion*

will erupt within ten days. The broadcast discusses the vigilante issue and quotes *Nova Express* writer Doug Roth as accusing the *New Frontiersman* article of grafting an acceptable face onto glorified Klan-style brutality **[ALAN]**.

—October 31, 1985

The prison riot begins. A newspaper covers the violence, reporting "Sing Sing Erupts: Captured Vigilante Sparks Riot: Five Dead" **[ALAN]**. The *New Frontiersman* runs a front-page story about Dr. Manhattan, with the headline "Does Super-Power Make U.S. a Superpower?" **[HOOD]**.

Two Knot-Tops, including one named Derf, stop by Bernard's newsstand to buy the latest *New York Gazette*, but it has yet to be delivered. Derf's buddy begs for some "katies" (KT-28s, a type of narcotics) so he can "get crazy." Also at the stand is cab driver Joey, who has ended her relationship with Aline and needs to look up apartments available for rent **[ALAN]**.

Under cover of the riot, The Big Figure heads to Rorschach's cell with Larry and Mike. As Larry prepares to cut through the door lock using an arc welder, the vigilante mocks his obesity, causing Larry to reach into the bars in anger, thus enabling Rorschach to tie them together with his shirt. With the lock now obscured, Big Figure tells Mike to kill Larry and open the cell. But as Mike does so, Rorschach breaks his toilet, flooding the floor with water and electrocuting him. Terrified, Big Figure runs away **[ALAN]**.

Archimedes arrives at Sing Sing in the midst of chaos. Dan Dreiberg activates the ship's screechers, assaulting the rioting convicts with a glass-shattering sound burst, then he and Laurie Juspeczyk make their way to the isolation ward as Rorschach corners The Big Figure in a bathroom. After killing the dwarf, Rorschach leaves with Dan and Laurie, who meet him unmasked for the first time. Their socially inept comrade fails to show gratitude for the rescue and angers Laurie in the process by insulting her costume and implying she might be the mask killer **[ALAN]**.

> **CONFLICT:** *In the* Watchmen *film, Rorschach stops at Long's office to retrieve his belongings. In Alan Moore's miniseries, however, he leaves without them.*

—October 31, 1985—11:00 PM

Knowing that the police will raid his apartment, Dan Dreiberg decides they need to hide, but stops to pick up a few items from his home and workshop **[ALAN]**.

—October 31, 1985—After 11:00 PM

Jon Osterman appears in Dan's living room, having come to bring Laurie to Mars since they will have an important discussion there in an hour. As Jon and Laurie vanish, Joe Bourquin

and Steven Fine bust down Dan's front door. By the time police find Dan's workshop, he and Rorschach are aboard *Archimedes* with Dan's Nite Owl gear **[ALAN]**.

Laurie falls to the Martian ground, unable to breathe until Jon generates an atmosphere. They debate whether he should save Earth, and she grows frustrated by his lack of compassion for life and incomprehensible perception of time. He flies his glass city across Mars, which he says gets along fine without life. Though unmoved by her pleas to prevent a war, Jon knows he will return to Earth amidst corpse-filled streets, but that some form of static—possibly due to mass warhead detonation—now obscures his view of the future **[ALAN]**.

To show how he perceives the world, Jon helps Laurie relive moments from her youth. Their discussion unlocks submerged memories, and she realizes that Eddie Blake is her birth-father. Horrified, she throws a snow-globe, which shatters the glass city, and Jon protects her by encasing her in a force-field. In that moment, he considers the statistical unlikelihood of Laurie's existence—conceived by her mother and a man she loved despite also hating—and changes his mind. Life, he realizes, is a thermodynamic miracle that must be protected. Therefore, he agrees to return with her to Earth **[ALAN]**.

After hearing a radio report about The Nite Owl breaking Rorschach out of prison, Derf's Knot-Top gang go to Hollis Mason's apartment to beat him up. Derf kills Hollis using the retirement statue he'd received in 1962. Hollis's final thoughts are of his glory days, when he single-handedly defeated an entire supervillain gang. As the thugs leave, trick-or-treaters arrive to find Hollis a bloody pulp **[ALAN]**.

> **NOTE:** *At Dan's apartment, Laurie changes the calendar page, saying it'll be November in an hour, thus establishing the time as 11:00 PM on Halloween. A short time later, the Knot-Tops kill Hollis; he mistakes them for trick-or-treaters, and actual trick-or-treaters soon arrive. However, it's unlikely that kids would be trick-or-treating so close to midnight.*

> **CONFLICT:** *Taking Out the Trash erroneously sets Mason's death in 1986, a year after the events of Alan Moore's miniseries.*

—October 31, 1985—Before 11:59 PM
The United States military moves to DEFCON 2 **[ALAN]**.

> **NOTE:** *The U.S. Armed Forces' DEFCON (**def**ense readiness **con**dition) scale prescribes five graduated levels of readiness for the military, ranging from DEFCON 5 (the least severe) to DEFCON 1 (the most severe), depending on the situation.*

—October 31, 1985—11:59 PM

In response to "Western alarmism," German tanks begin amassing. With DEFCON 1 imminent, *Air Force One* and *Air Force Two* bring Richard Nixon and Gerald Ford, respectively, to an Air Force Strategic Air Command base. Separate helicopters ferry them to Entrance Alpha of the underground complex, while the President's wife, Pat Nixon, is moved to a safe location. Henry Kissinger, G. Gordon Liddy, and others meet the two men at the complex and update Nixon on the political climate **[ALAN]**.

> **NOTE:** *Gerald Ford trips while exiting the aircraft, just as he did in the real world while visiting Austria in 1975.*

—Before November 1985

Pakistan denies that Soviet support is rising among generals with influence on the region's tribal leaders, but Soviet troops are spotted amassing in Kabul and the Khyber Pass. The Kremlin claims to have no influence on Afghanistan's government, while Soviet newspapers report that Richard Nixon's image among U.S. voters is worsening due to America's economic decline. At a Senate Foreign Relations Committee hearing, Secretary of State Henry Kissinger calls on the Kremlin to "stop lying" **[ARTF]**.

Nikita Khrushchev succumbs to a bout of alcoholism and drops out of the public eye, retreating to his private dacha in the southern Georgia woods of the Ukraine **[ARTF]**.

> **NOTE:** *In the real world, Khrushchev was removed from power in March 1964 and died on September 11, 1971. In the* Watchmen *universe, he is still alive in 1985—though not in power, since Mikhail Gorbachev leads the Soviet Union at this time in* Watchmen, *just as he did in reality.*

—In or Before November 1985

A writer submits an article to the *New Frontiersman*, claiming fluoride is turning people into homosexuals **[ALAN]**.

Adrian Veidt realizes that if mankind manages to avoid nuclear war, a new surge of social optimism will result, rendering outdated the concept behind advertisements for his Nostalgia perfume and aftershave. Therefore, he decides to create a new image for his company. To that end, he writes a letter to Angela Neuberg, director of Veidt Cosmetics & Toiletries, announcing his intention to replace the Nostalgia brand in summer 1986 with a new product line called Millennium **[ALAN]**.

> **NOTE:** *The product's name is misspelled as "Millenium" in Veidt's letter.*

—November 1985

Dan Dreiberg's bird-themed calendar features the image of a hawk taking a sparrow in flight **[ALAN]**.

November 1, 1985

The *New York Gazette* publishes a front-page article titled "Soviets Invade Afghanistan." Journalists William Ball and R.E. Klinghoffer report that the United Kingdom, despite its long-term friendship with Russia, has committed troops in solidarity with U.S. actions in the region, urging other European nations to do the same **[ARTF]**.

> **NOTE:** *The Soviet invasion occurs on October 20, per Alan Moore's miniseries, so it's unclear why the* Gazette *would choose such a headline twelve days later.*

November 1, 1985—4:30 AM

Adrian Veidt leaves his New York City home for his Karnak compound in Antarctica **[ALAN]**.

November 1, 1985—Daytime

The *New York Gazette's* front-page headline reads "Eastern Europe: Tanks Mass as Conflict Escalates" **[ALAN]**. The newspaper also reports Hollis Mason's death (in an article titled "Ex-Hero Killed in Brooklyn Break-in"), as well as Rorschach's escape (in "Nite Owl Breaks Rorschach Out of Riker's Island"), and publicly reveals Nite Owl's true identity as Daniel Dreiberg **[RPG3]**.

> **CONFLICT:** The Watchmen Sourcebook *places Rorschach's incarceration at Rikers Island (misspelling the jail complex's name as "Riker's"), contradicting Alan Moore's miniseries, in which he is sent to Sing Sing. Moreover, Hollis Mason lives in Manhattan, not in Brooklyn.*

Dan Dreiberg and Rorschach lay low aboard *Archimedes* for a few hours, then retrieve Rorschach's spare outfit and mask from his apartment, along with the final draft of his personal journal. Dolores Shairp finds them in the apartment and panics when Rorschach reminds her of her lies to the press about him molesting her. Upon seeing her scared children, he leaves without incident. They return to the Owlship, hidden on the Hudson River bed, where Dan performs computer searches that take most of the day, making Rorschach impatient **[ALAN]**.

Adrian Veidt flies to Karnak, where his servants and Bubastis greet him. Changing into his Ozymandias outfit, he instructs them to activate all TV monitors, timed to randomly change channels every hundred seconds so he can amass data about everything going on around the world. He deems war imminent after perusing broadcasts focused on violence and sexuality, and tells his staff to invest in munitions and major erotic video companies. Anticipating a future baby boom, he also says to negotiate controlling shares in baby food and maternity goods manufacturers **[ALAN]**.

> **NOTE:** *In David Hayter's unproduced 2002 and 2003 screenplay drafts, Veidt has a personal servant named Eric, who is described as "suspiciously beautiful," and whom Veidt kills with poisoned wine since Eric has been witness to his plans.*

—November 1, 1985—Night

Anxious to investigate the underworld for clues to the mask killer's identity, Rorschach snaps at Dan Dreiberg for wasting time with computers instead of doing something constructive. When he accuses his ex-partner of "lazing," Dan calls him a "goddamned lunatic" who uses and insults those who try to help him. Rorschach apologizes, acknowledging that Dan has always been a good friend **[ALAN]**.

News vendor Bernard warns his customers that war is inevitable. Seated nearby, Bernie continues to read *Tales of the Black Freighter*, ignoring the conversation. Two Jehovah's Witnesses try to offer him a copy of their magazine, *The Watchtower*, claiming God will soon end the world, but Bernard dismisses such sentiment as "baloney" **[ALAN]**.

> **NOTE:** *The magazine's mushroom-cloud cover image, warning Christians of the coming Apocalypse, also foreshadows the culmination of Veidt's plan.*

Rorschach and Dreiberg visit three bars to learn who hired Roy Chess. At the third, Happy Harry's, Rorschach hurts several patrons before the customers turn toward a man seated at the bar, and Rorschach crushes a glass in his hand. The man reveals that his boss at Pyramid Deliveries paid him to contract a killer, though he had no idea Adrian Veidt was the target until hearing about Chess's death on the news. When Dan notices a Knot-Top staring at him, the gang member hastily denies any role in Hollis Mason's murder—which is news to Dan. Stunned to learn of his friend's death, Dan beats the Knot-Top to a pulp. Rorschach calms him down and they depart **[ALAN]**.

> **NOTE:** *In the* Watchman *film, Dan learns about Mason's death while watching a Channel 3 news report from journalist Tiffany Burns.*

Max Shea, Hira Manish, Norman Leith, Linette Paley, James Trafford March, Whittaker Furnesse and their colleagues finish their work at Adrian Veidt's secret island base. After two years of seclusion, they board a ship that will return them to their homes. As their equipment is loaded on board, the team enjoys an evacuation party. Shea convinces Manish to have sex with him in the vessel's lower levels, but before they can make love, he discovers a bomb inside a storage crate, planted by Veidt to eliminate witnesses to his work. Moments later, the ship explodes, killing everyone aboard **[ALAN]**.

> **NOTE:** *Presumably, team member Professor Wickstein, from* Before Watchmen: Ozymandias, *is aboard the ship as well.*

Dan Dreiberg and Rorschach find Adrian Veidt's offices deserted. An appointment book refers to Karnak, while wall charts describe a rising global population, a nuclear hazard escalation index, and environmental decline. Dan access Veidt's computer, figures out his password ("Rameses II," the Egyptian name for Ozymandias), and discovers that Veidt owns Pyramid Deliveries—making him the mastermind behind recent events. Stunned, they collect Veidt's paperwork and head for Antarctica **[ALAN]**.

—November 1, 1985—Just Before Midnight

Rorschach records his final journal entry, admitting concern about going up against the world's smartest man. Aware that Adrian Veidt could kill them both, Rorschach exposes Veidt's recent actions and arranges for the journal to be delivered to those he trusts most: the *New Frontiersman*'s editors at Pyramid Publishing. He thanks them for their support, closing with this message: "For my own past, regret nothing. Have lived life, free from compromise, and step into the shadow now without complaint" **[ALAN]**.

—November 1 or 2, 1985

Detective Steven Fine is suspended from duty for failing to apprehend the three vigilantes **[ALAN]**.

—November 2, 1985—Daytime

The *New York Gazette* bears the simple front-page headline "WAR?" As patrons pick up this and other editions, news vendor Bernard muses about how recent events have left citizens vulnerable and unprotected, and wonders if society should have listened more to the masked adventurers against whom it turned **[ALAN]**.

A postman delivers Rorschach's journal to Seymour Smith at Pioneer Publishing. When Smith reads the first entry out loud, *New Frontiersman* editor Hector Godfrey deems it garbage and tells him to toss it on the crank file. Godfrey declares that war is coming, and that their publication must focus on truth and integrity, not drivel **[ALAN]**.

William J. Franklin, the U.S. director of central intelligence, issues a memorandum to all recipients of a document titled "NIE 14-7-78, Soviet Aggression and Dr. Manhattan: The Case for Intervention in Afghanistan," outlining the Liddy Emergency Sub-Committee's proposal of a fast-track discussion of a "so-called Hiroshima strategy," by which Jon Osterman would use cataclysmic lethal force to shock and awe the Soviet regime. Franklin cites an "overwhelming positive opinion" toward deploying Dr. Manhattan within Afghanistan's borders, noting that it remains unknown whether the superhuman could prevent more than 95 percent of Soviet ICBMs from reaching their targets if his intervention triggers a first strike **[NEWW]**.

> **CONFLICT:** *The memo is dated November 2, which makes little sense since the U.S. government is well aware that Dr. Manhattan has left for Mars.*

MIND .... *The Mindscape of Alan Moore*
MOBL .... *Watchmen: The Mobile Game*
MOTN .... *Watchmen: The Complete Motion Comic*
MTRO .... *Metro* promotional newspaper cover wrap
NEWP .... *New Frontiersman* promotional newspaper
NEWW .... *New Frontiersman* website
NIGH .... *Watchmen: The End Is Nigh, Parts 1 and 2*
PKIT ...... *Watchmen* film British press kit
PORT .... *Watchmen Portraits*
REAL ..... Real life
RPG1 .... *DC Heroes Role Playing Module #227: Who Watches the Watchmen?*

RPG2 ... *DC Heroes Role Playing Module #235: Taking Out the Trash—Curses and Tears*
RPG3 .... *DC Heroes: The Watchmen Sourcebook*
RUBY .... "Wounds," published in *The Ruby Files Volume One*
SCR1 ..... Unfilmed screenplay draft: Sam Hamm
SCR2 ..... Unfilmed screenplay draft: Charles McKeuen
SCR3 ..... Unfilmed screenplay draft: Gary Goldman
SCR4 ..... Unfilmed screenplay draft: David Hayter (2002)
SCR5 ..... Unfilmed screenplay draft: David Hayter (2003)
SCR6 ..... Unfilmed screenplay draft: Alex Tse
SPOT ..... *DC Spotlight #1*
VRL1 ..... Viral video: *NBS Nightly News with Ted Philips*

VRL2 ..... Viral video: *The Keene Act and You*
VRL3 ..... Viral video: *Who Watches the Watchmen? A Veidt Music Network (VMN) Special*
VRL4 ..... Viral video: *World in Focus: 6 Minutes to Midnight*
VRL5 ..... Viral video: *Local Radio Station Report on 1977 Riots*
VRL6 ..... Viral videos (group of ten): *Veidt Enterprises Advertising Contest*
WAWA ... *Watching the Watchmen*
WHOS ... *Who's Who: The Definitive Directory of the DC Universe*
WTFC .... *Watchmen: The Film Companion*

—November 2, 1985—Night

Rorschach and Dan Dreiberg arrive in Antarctica aboard *Archimedes*. For several hours, Dan pilots the Owlship along the coastline. Wet from submersion in the Hudson River, the vessel buckles as the water freezes. With no choice, he tries to set *Archie* down in the snow, but they crash near a cliff, twenty miles from Karnak. Dan dons a snow suit, and as they travel on hoverbikes, Ozymandias monitors their approach **[ALAN]**.

—November 2, 1985—8:00 PM

Pale Horse plays a sold-out concert at New York City's Madison Square Garden, with a band called Krystalnacht opening for them. Aline hopes to see the show, but puts her plans on hold to meet with Joey to discuss their future together **[ALAN]**.

> **NOTE:** *Pale Horse's name, referencing Revelations 6:8 from The Bible—"I looked and there before me was a pale horse! Its rider was named Death, and Hell was following close behind him."—symbolizes the fear of nuclear destruction. The opening band's name refers to Kristallnacht (The Night of Broken Glass), a coordinated Nazi attack on Jews on November 9, 1938. The bands' names, and the fact that one member of Pale Horse is called Red D'eath, foreshadow Adrian Veidt's plot, which will soon rain death down on New York City amid a shower of broken glass.*

—November 2, 1985—11:18 PM

While awaiting the arrival of Dan Dreiberg and Rorschach, Adrian Veidt records some random insights about the nature of multi-screen viewing, which he likens to the Dadaist "cut-up technique," popularized by William S. Burroughs, in which a literary work is broken into chunks and rearranged to create a new text **[ALAN]**.

> **NOTE:** *In essence, Ozymandias comments on the very storytelling technique that Alan Moore employed when writing* Watchmen.
>
> *Although Adrian says the time is 11:18, a nearby clock indicates that it is actually 11:14. It could be that Adrian purposely sets his clocks four minutes early, for reasons that only he, as the world's smartest man, knows.*

—November 2, 1985—11:20 PM

Joey and Aline talk near the Promethean Cab Co. When Aline urges her to read R.D. Laing's 1970 poetry book *Knots*, Joey rips it up and attacks her. Nearby, Gloria and Malcolm Long discuss the possibility of reconciliation, but she becomes angry when he decides to help Aline, ignoring her plea not to get involved in another person's problems, as he did with Rorschach **[ALAN]**.

—November 2, 1985—11:24 PM

Joe Bourquin and Steven Fine pull over to stop the fight. Joey's boss Milo runs over to the feuding couple as well **[ALAN]**.

—November 2, 1985—11:25 PM

Adrian Veidt launches the final step in his plan, and the squid-like creature teleports to the skies above the Institute for Extraspatial Studies. It explodes on contact, its death triggering mechanisms in its massive cloned brain. As a result, a psychic shockwave kills half the city, including Bernard, Bernie, Joey, Aline, Bourquin, Fine, Milo, and the Longs. The death toll is around three million. Those who survive are driven insane by a flood of grotesque sensations emanated by the creature's mind. A pregnant woman self-terminates her own fetus, convinced that it is eating her from the inside. Hector Godfrey and Seymour Smith both survive the tragedy **[ALAN]**.

> *CONFLICT: In the* Watchmen *film, the death toll is fifteen million, as Veidt targets other key cities as well, including Los Angeles, Moscow, Hong Kong, Tokyo, London, Paris, and Beijing. This is due to the movie changing the mechanism of Veidt's plan from an extradimensional squid to a recreation of Dr. Manhattan's powers, so that mankind will think the superhuman has turned against them.*

Stunned by what appears to be an attack by extradimensional aliens, governments around the world cease all hostilities to unite against a superior common foe. Richard Nixon and Soviet Premier Mikhail Gorbachev call for an immediate summit in Geneva, as well as the withdrawal of their troops from Afghanistan, effectively ending the threat of nuclear war **[ALAN]**.

—November 2, 1985—Between 11:25 and 11:59 PM

Adrian Veidt shares drinks with his servants in his vivarium in order to eliminate the only remaining witnesses to his plan. He poisons their drinks, and as they die, he tells them of his life and his fascination with Alexander the Great. After expressing gratitude for his friends' help and remorse for their necessary deaths, he opens the vivarium to the elements, causing their bodies to be buried in snow, so he can later claim they drunkenly opened the dome themselves **[ALAN]**.

A short while later, Rorschach and Dan Dreiberg—unaware of what has happened in New York—arrive at Karnak and search for Veidt. They try to take him by surprise as he dines, but he easily deflects every assault. Despite repeated attempts, they are unable to apprehend or hurt him. Eventually they stop trying, and Adrian outlines for them his entire plot to save mankind **[ALAN]**.

—November 2, 1985—11:59 PM

Dreiberg dismisses Veidt's alien-invasion concept as a ridiculous lie, but Adrian reveals that he carried out his plan thirty-five minutes prior so that they would be unable to prevent him from doing so **[ALAN]**.

MIND .... *The Mindscape of Alan Moore*
MOBL .... *Watchmen: The Mobile Game*
MOTN .... *Watchmen: The Complete Motion Comic*
MTRO .... *Metro promotional newspaper cover wrap*
NEWP .... *New Frontiersman promotional newspaper*
NEWW .... *New Frontiersman website*
NIGH .... *Watchmen: The End Is Nigh, Parts 1 and 2*
PKIT ...... *Watchmen film British press kit*
PORT ..... *Watchmen Portraits*
REAL ..... Real life
RPG1 .... *DC Heroes Role Playing Module #227: Who Watches the Watchmen?*

RPG2 .... *DC Heroes Role Playing Module #235: Taking Out the Trash—Curses and Tears*
RPG3 .... *DC Heroes: The Watchmen Sourcebook*
RUBY .... "Wounds," published in *The Ruby Files Volume One*
SCR1 ..... Unfilmed screenplay draft: Sam Hamm
SCR2 ..... Unfilmed screenplay draft: Charles McKeuen
SCR3 ..... Unfilmed screenplay draft: Gary Goldman
SCR4 ..... Unfilmed screenplay draft: David Hayter (2002)
SCR5 ..... Unfilmed screenplay draft: David Hayter (2003)
SCR6 ..... Unfilmed screenplay draft: Alex Tse
SPOT ..... *DC Spotlight #1*
VRL1 ..... Viral video: *NBS Nightly News with Ted Philips*

VRL2 ..... Viral video: *The Keene Act and You*
VRL3 ..... Viral video: *Who Watches the Watchmen? A Veidt Music Network (VMN) Special*
VRL4 ..... Viral video: *World in Focus: 6 Minutes to Midnight*
VRL5 ..... Viral video: *Local Radio Station Report on 1977 Riots*
VRL6 ..... Viral videos (group of ten): *Veidt Enterprises Advertising Contest*
WAWA ... *Watching the Watchmen*
WHOS .... *Who's Who: The Definitive Directory of the DC Universe*
WTFC .... *Watchmen: The Film Companion*

—November 3, 1985—12:00 AM

Dr. Manhattan and Laurie Juspeczyk return from Mars to find New York City a disaster area filled with bloody corpses, decimated buildings, and giant severed "alien" tentacles. Jon realizes the cause was not a nuclear detonation and detects the presence of tachyon particles. Tracing their source to Antarctica, he teleports with Laurie to Adrian Veidt's fortress to confront Ozymandias about what he has done **[ALAN]**.

> **NOTE:** *This event is said to occur at midnight on November 2, but midnight is actually 12:00 AM the next day, making it the 3rd. Ironically, the incorrect placement is stated by Dr. Manhattan, who should know better given his mastery of time. Odder still, he agrees to return to Earth with Laurie on the night of October 31, yet arrives at the start of November 3. Their whereabouts on November 1 and 2 is unaccounted for, since it only took Jon twenty-seven hours to travel from Earth to Mars.*

Ozymandias sacrifices Bubastis by having the lynx lure Dr. Manhattan into an intrinsic field subtractor. The machine reduces them both to their component molecules, recreating the accident that made Jon a superhuman. Laurie shoots Veidt, but he catches the bullet, pretends to be dead, and kicks her in the stomach. Reconstituted several stories high, Jon crashes through a wall—then stops when Veidt calls up news footage on his monitors of the New York disaster and the uniting of humanity. Adrian points out that exposing his plot would destroy any chance for world peace. Though horrified, Jon, Laurie, and Dan agree to remain silent, but Rorschach refuses to compromise, even in the face of Armageddon. He leaves the citadel, intent on exposing Veidt's crimes **[ALAN]**.

Veidt heads for his meditation chamber to contemplate his recent actions. Grateful to be alive, Laurie and Dan make love near his swimming pool. Dr. Manhattan follows Rorschach outside and vaporizes him, leaving a puddle of goo in the snow. Returning inside, he finds Dan and Laurie asleep, smiles at their happiness, then walks across the water, up and through a wall, and into Veidt's chamber. Adrian expresses regret for every death he's caused, but asks for Jon's understanding since it all worked out in the end. Jon tells him "Nothing ever ends," them leaves the galaxy for one less complicated, where he plans to create new life **[ALAN]**.

> **NOTE:** *In the* Watchmen *film, the conclusion plays out a bit differently. Dan follows Rorschach outside and witnesses his death at Manhattan's hands, after which Jon kisses Laurie goodbye before departing for another galaxy. Dan then attacks Adrian once more, who accepts every punch without putting up a fight.*
>
> *Sam Hamm's unproduced 1988 screenplay has a radically different ending, in which Veidt attempts to change time by killing Jon Osterman before he can become Dr. Manhattan in 1959. Manhattan vaporizes Veidt before he can do so, then realizes Adrian is right and alters his own history so that he survives the Gila Flats accident and never undergoes transformation. Moments later, Nite Owl, Silk Spectre, and Rorschach are*

pulled through time into another universe—the real world—where they are mistaken for fans dressed up as characters from Alan Moore's Watchmen *comics.*

Charles McKeuen's rewrite of that script uses the same rather bizarre ending as Hamm's version. Gary Goldman's rewrite has Manhattan snap Veidt's neck, while in David Hayter's 2002 and 2003 script drafts, as well as in Alex Tse's iteration, it is Dan Dreiberg who kills Veidt.

—November 3, 1985 and Beyond

For years to come, psychics around the world continue to experience unpleasant dreams as a result of the psionic assault from Adrian Veidt's creature **[ALAN]**.

—After November 3, 1985

Jon Osterman creates a new universe. On a world containing a large, looming moon, he extends a bit of energy to accelerate evolution by combining proteins and knitting DNA into a new form of life, hoping it will become something amazing **[BWDM]**.

—Between November 3, 1985, and December 25, 1986

Dan Dreiberg and Laurie Juspeczyk go into hiding under assumed names, Samuel M. and Sandra L. Hollis, dyeing their hair blonde to avoid recognition. Sally Jupiter assumes them to have perished during the New York City disaster **[ALAN]**. The couple relocate to 1200 W. Armory #2, in Philadelphia, obtaining driver's licenses under their new names. Dan's license lists his birthdate as September 18, 1940, with an issue date of May 14, 1983, while Sally's lists her birthdate as December 1, 1949, with an issue date of September 11, 1983 **[RPG3]**.

> **NOTE:** *The aliases' middle initials appear in* The Watchmen Sourcebook, *which contains illustrations of their fake licenses. Since the licenses have 1983 issue dates, Dan has likely forged them, as neither he nor Laurie could have possibly predicted a need for them two years before becoming fugitives and lovers.*

New York is cleaned up following the attack, with help from the Soviet Union and other countries. The Gunga Diner is replaced by a new restaurant, Burgers 'N' Borscht, while the Utopia Cinema becomes the New Utopia and starts showing Andrei Tarkovsky's *The Sacrifice* (a.k.a. *Nostalgia*). Bernard's news stand is replaced with an automated newspaper vending machine. With Milo dead, the Promethean Cab Co. comes under new management **[ALAN]**.

> **NOTE:** *Both titles attributed to* The Sacrifice, *made by Soviet and Italian filmmakers in 1983, symbolize the major themes of Alan Moore's miniseries. The restaurant's name represents the new alliance between Americans and Soviets.*

In a new spirit of world peace, posters proclaiming "One World," bearing the flags of both the United States and the Soviet Union, are placed on building walls. Members of the

MIND .... *The Mindscape of Alan Moore*
MOBL .... *Watchmen: The Mobile Game*
MOTN .... *Watchmen: The Complete Motion Comic*
MTRO .... *Metro promotional newspaper cover wrap*
NEWP .... *New Frontiersman promotional newspaper*
NEWW .... *New Frontiersman website*
NIGH .... *Watchmen: The End Is Nigh, Parts 1 and 2*
PKIT ...... *Watchmen film British press kit*
PORT ..... *Watchmen Portraits*
REAL ..... Real life
RPG1 .... *DC Heroes Role Playing Module #227: Who Watches the Watchmen?*

RPG2 .... *DC Heroes Role Playing Module #235: Taking Out the Trash—Curses and Tears*
RPG3 .... *DC Heroes: The Watchmen Sourcebook*
RUBY .... "Wounds," published in *The Ruby Files Volume One*
SCR1 ..... Unfilmed screenplay draft: Sam Hamm
SCR2 ..... Unfilmed screenplay draft: Charles McKeuen
SCR3 ..... Unfilmed screenplay draft: Gary Goldman
SCR4 .... Unfilmed screenplay draft: David Hayter (2002)
SCR5 .... Unfilmed screenplay draft: David Hayter (2003)
SCR6 .... Unfilmed screenplay draft: Alex Tse
SPOT ..... *DC Spotlight #1*
VRL1 ..... Viral video: *NBS Nightly News with Ted Philips*

VRL2 ..... Viral video: *The Keene Act and You*
VRL3 ..... Viral video: *Who Watches the Watchmen? A Veidt Music Network (VMN) Special*
VRL4 ..... Viral video: *World in Focus: 6 Minutes to Midnight*
VRL5 ..... Viral video: *Local Radio Station Report on 1977 Riots*
VRL6 ..... Viral videos (group of ten): *Veidt Enterprises Advertising Contest*
WAWA ... *Watching the Watchmen*
WHOS ... *Who's Who: The Definitive Directory of the DC Universe*
WTFC .... *Watchmen: The Film Companion*

press are discouraged from publishing negative articles about Russians, forcing the *New Frontiersman* to shift some of its reporting focus **[ALAN]**.

A newspaper features the front-page headline "NY Survivors Reveal Nightmare Under Hypnosis" **[ALAN]**.

—November 27, 1985

Veidt Industries holds a board meeting at 3:00 PM **[ALAN]**.
> **NOTE:** *This is noted in Adrian Veidt's appointment book.*

—November 28, 1985

Ted, an acquaintance of Adrian Veidt, has a birthday **[ALAN]**.
> **NOTE:** *This is also noted in Veidt's appointment book.*

—Before December 25, 1985

Angela Neuberg, director of Veidt Cosmetics & Toiletries, presents Adrian Veidt with dummy ad copy and artwork for a new product line called Millennium, for his perusal and comment prior to an expected summer 1986 launch **[ALAN]**.

Part XII:
AFTER MIDNIGHT
(1986 and Beyond)

—January 1, 1986
New Frontiersman editor Hector Godfrey decides to burn all crank-file submissions that he and Seymour Smith have never featured **[ALAN]**.

—1986
The Dorchester family donates the building containing The Minutemen's former headquarters to New York City for public viewing **[RPG3]**.

Who Watches the Watchmen, by Joel H. Keesman, examines costumed heroes past and present, both real and fictional, ranging from the Scarlet Pimpernel to Rorschach. The book includes a rogues gallery featuring entries on Moloch the Mystic, The Screaming Skull, Captain Axis, Buzzbomb, The Big Figure, Underboss, The Twilight Lady, and Captain Carnage **[RPG3]**.

—July 1986
After mud slides and an earthquake in Honduras leave thousands without food or water, a series of Quake Aid concerts raise money to purchase supplies and equipment to help the survivors **[RPG3]**.

—Summer 1986
Veidt Enterprises'Veidt Cosmetics & Toiletries division introduces its Millennium line. The new product's advertisements are controversial and modern, projecting a vision of a technological Utopia, as though new sensations and pleasures are just within a wearer's reach. The tagline: "This is the time, these are the feelings" **[ALAN]**.

—Fall 1986

A Saturday-morning cartoon debuts about Adrian Veidt's exploits as Ozymandias. The animated series features Bubastis as a feline sidekick—even though she played no part in his superhero adventures—and is heavily merchandised to children **[ALAN]**.

—October 4, 1986

An airplane carrying supplies and equipment purchased with funds from July's Quake Aid concerts crashes while en route to help earthquake survivors in Honduras. The crash kills two pilots and seventeen people on the ground, and the plane lands in the only operational fresh-water tank within seventy miles of a makeshift Red Cross landing strip, stranding thousands without drinking water **[RPG3]**.

> **NOTE:** *It is unclear why these events are recounted in* The Watchmen Sourcebook's *section on* The Comedian, *as they seem unconnected to the crime-fighter's history— particularly since this occurs a year after his death.*

—October 5, 1986

The *New York Gazette* reports on the crashed Quake Aid airplane. Red Cross volunteer Susan Daily says the situation will be dire if the mud slides continue **[RPG3]**.

—Before November 1, 1986

Veidt Enterprises hires a writer from Chicago to compose a second adventure module for the *Ozymandias Role Playing Game*. The manuscript contains information about Moloch and Rorschach, so Leo Winston, Veidt's marketing and development president, asks company lawyers to clear those bits from a legal standpoint. Research conducted by the marketing department indicates that few among the general public know that Edgar Jacobi was Moloch, while twenty-six percent doubt Moloch ever existed **[RPG2]**.

—November 1, 1986

Leo Winston drafts a letter to Adrian Veidt, informing him that the second *Ozymandias Role Playing Game* adventure module has been turned in **[RPG2]**.

—After November 1, 1986

After reading the module, Veidt responds to Winston, asking that the person in charge of the RPG revise it since he considers it too gloomy in its current form. He also suggests having the heroes bring perishable drugs to Algeria **[RPG2]**.

—December 25, 1986

Sally Jupiter relaxes at the Nepenthe Gardens resort on Christmas, watching an *Outer Limits* episode titled "The Architects of Fear." Dan Dreiberg and Laurie Juspeczyk visit to let her know that Laurie is alive, and she meets Dan for the first time. Laurie says she knows Eddie Blake was her father, but that she still loves Sally. After they leave, Sally hugs a photo of The Minutemen, kisses Blake's image, and cries. Outside, Dan and Laurie joke about becoming masked adventurers once more—but this time, Laurie wants a better costume and a gun **[ALAN]**.

> **NOTE:** *The year of this reunion is unspecified. Several online sources place it at Christmas 1985, but since Millennium (released in summer 1986) is already available for purchase, it must occur after that. A Christmas 1986 placement allows a year for Dan and Laurie to lay low, change their appearances and identities, and get married—which would be unrealistic within only a month's time.*
>
> *The plot of "The Architects of Fear" is remarkably similar to what Ozymandias does in* Watchmen. *Alan Moore claims to have only learned of the episode while writing issue #10, in which he acknowledged the story similarities.*

> **CONFLICT:** *In the* Watchmen *film, Laurie and Dan visit Sally immediately upon returning from Antarctica, without assuming new names and without any indication that they are wanted fugitives. In Gary Goldman's unproduced 1992 screenplay, Hollis Mason is still alive and now living with Sally in his apartment. In David Hayter's 2002 and 2003 script drafts, Dan and Laurie arrive with an infant daughter.*

—In or Before 1987

Donald DeWitt writes the book *Minutemen from A to Z*, detailing the team's lives before their days as crime-fighters. According to DeWitt, despite Ursula Zandt's claims of having had an Aunt Emma in Katzenbühl, surviving members of that Austrian town have no memory of such an individual **[RPG3]**.

—Before January 1, 1987

New Frontiersman reader Gill Burch, from Mill Bay, Kansas, sends a package to the newspaper, which ends up in the crank file alongside Rorschach's journal **[FILM]**.

> **NOTE:** *No such city exists in real-world Kansas, and the zip code on the envelope, 73942, is for Guymon, Oklahoma.*

—January 1, 1987

The *New York Gazette* publishes an article indicating that actor Robert Redford may run for President of the United States in 1988. The *New Frontiersman*'s Hector Godfrey refuses to give the announcement any coverage, dismissing the idea of a "cowboy actor" in the White House as ridiculous **[ALAN]**.

> **NOTE:** *Ronald Reagan, also a former "cowboy actor," served as President from 1981 to 1989 in the real world. The* Gazette's *headline says "RR," leading comic readers to initially assume this is a Reagan reference, but dialogue soon reveals those to be Redford's initials.*

January 1, 1987—11:59 AM

After buying lunch for himself and editor Hector Godfrey at Burgers 'N' Borscht, Seymour Smith returns to the *New Frontiersman*'s office. Hector has been forced to nix an anti-Russian column, so as replacement material, Seymour turns to his crank file, atop which sits the late Rorschach's journal **[ALAN]**.

> **NOTE:** *Apparently, Seymour failed to burn the submissions as instructed a year prior.*

1987

Applegate Press publishes *Run for the Shadows: The Story of Ursula Zandt*, a biography of the crime-fighter written by Martha McCormick **[RPG3]**.

New York City raises funds to renovate The Minutemen's former headquarters as a public museum, taking great pains to restore the building's exact condition when the crime-fighters left it behind in 1949 **[RPG3]**.

1987 (Alternate Reality)

Jon Osterman contributes an introduction and chronology of events for a *Watchmen*-themed role-playing game module. He discusses key moments in the life of Laurie Juspeczyk, comments on humans' inability to see time non-linearly, and notes that readers will skip over his introduction and read the pages following it, before coming back to read it later **[RPG2]**.

> **NOTE:** *Osterman's introduction, which appears in a pull-out section of* Taking Out the Trash, *contains a chronology of events from before and during Alan Moore's miniseries. Ironically, despite Jon's mastery of time, many of the dates listed on the chronology contradict those either inferred or directly stated in the comic.*
>
> *Given the metafictional nature of a* Watchmen *character contributing to a role-playing book about the* Watchmen *universe inside an actual role-playing book about the* Watchmen *universe, the question of how Dr. Manhattan could do this in 1987, despite having left Earth in 1985, becomes rather moot. It may be that he wrote the intro before departing, knowing that the book's writers would eventually need it.*

June 12, 1987—Afternoon (Alternate Realities)

President Ronald Reagan delivers a speech calling for Soviet leader Mikhail Gorbachev to open up the barrier that has divided East and West Berlin since 1961. Reagan makes an impassioned plea, saying, "Mr. Gorbachev, tear down this wall!" **[REAL]**. In a quantum reality in which Jon Osterman never becomes Dr. Manhattan and Reagan is not elected President, Richard Nixon considers a nuclear first strike against the Soviet Union, rather than risk the United States being "nuked into submission by the Reds" **[BWDM]**.

—1988 (Predicted)

Robert Redford possibly runs for President of the United States, per an article published in the *New York Gazette* **[ALAN]**.

June 1988 (Alternate Reality)

In a universe in which Alan Moore's *Watchmen* is a fictional tale, Vic "The Question" Sage buys a copy to read during an airplane flight. Fascinated by Rorschach, Sage considers asking his mentor, Dr. Aristotle "Tot" Rodor, to create a similar mask for his use. After falling asleep and dreaming about being Rorschach, The Question decides to be more like the fictional vigilante, asking himself "What would Rorschach do?" and adopting a more aggressive crime-fighting style. When this nearly gets him killed during a battle with criminals Butch and Sundance, he decides "Rorschach sucks" **[CMEO]**.

> **NOTE:** *The Question, a Charlton Comics character created by Steve Ditko and later acquired by DC Comics, was Alan Moore's basis for Rorschach. This story, titled "A Dream of Rorschach" and published in* The Question *issue #17, pays homage to the two characters' historical connection.*

In or Before 1989 (Alternate Reality)

In a reality populated by numerous superheroes, Dr. Manhattan poses for a photo with Nathaniel "Captain Atom" Adam for Harold "The Coordinator" Thompson, the owner of Hero Hotline. The photo is personalized with the phrase "$E=MC^2$! Your pals—Capt Atom & Dr. M!" **[CMEO]**.

> **NOTE:** *This cameo, in issue #5 of DC Comics' 1989 miniseries* Hero Hotline, *sees Dr. Manhattan hanging out in the mainstream DC Comics universe (predating DC's Rebirth by nearly thirty years) with Captain Atom, the Charlton Comics character on which Alan Moore based Jon Osterman. Since the story takes place in 1989, Jon Osterman apparently does not leave the galaxy in 1985, as he does in* Watchmen.

—1989

With restoration completed, New York City opens the doors of The Minutemen's former headquarters as a public museum and begins offering tours **[RPG3]**.

In or Before 1990 (Prevented Reality)

A third World War takes place on Earth **[ABSO]**.

> **NOTE:** *Adrian Veidt foresees that this will happen if he does not carry out his plan to bring about world peace. Given his status as the world's smartest man, it's safe to assume that he is successful in changing mankind's path to one less bleak.*

Mid-1990s (Prevented Reality)

Earth's rising global population, nuclear hazard escalation index, and environmental decline converge, creating a crisis for mankind **[ALAN]**.

> **NOTE:** *Presumably, Adrian Veidt prevents this from happening as well.*

—1998

Mother, the former cult leader of The Brethren, concludes her prison sentence for attempting to assassinate Richard Nixon in 1968 **[RPG2]**.

> **NOTE:** *This assumes that Mother has neither died nor been granted parole in the interim.*

—2003

Former Senator Ken Shade's thirty-five-year prison sentence for trying to assassinate Richard Nixon reaches its end as well **[RPG2]**.

> **NOTE:** *This assumes that Shade has neither died nor been granted parole in the interim.*

December 2004 (Alternate Reality)

When a firm called Benetech claims to have found a cure for mutants, a riot breaks out as mutated individuals vie for the vaccine. Rorschach takes part in the rioting **[CMEO]**.

> **NOTE:** *Rorschach has a non-speaking cameo in this story, published in Astonishing X-Men volume 3 issue #6, which adds the vigilante to the Marvel Comics universe—and apparently makes him either a mutant or someone who enjoys rioting.*

ABSO .... *Watchmen Absolute Edition*
ALAN ..... Alan Moore's *Watchmen* miniseries
ARCD .... *Minutemen Arcade*
ARTF ..... *Watchmen: The Art of the Film*
BLCK ..... *Tales of the Black Freighter*
BWCC .. *Before Watchmen—The Crimson Corsair*
BWCO .. *Before Watchmen—Comedian*
BWDB .. *Before Watchmen—Dollar Bill*
BWDM .. *Before Watchmen—Dr. Manhattan*
BWMM .. *Before Watchmen—Minutemen*
BWMO .. *Before Watchmen—Moloch*
BWNO ... *Before Watchmen—Nite Owl*

BWOZ .... *Before Watchmen—Ozymandias*
BWRO ... *Before Watchmen—Rorschach*
BWSS ... *Before Watchmen—Silk Spectre*
CHEM .... My Chemical Romance music video: "Desolation Row"
CMEO .... *Watchmen* cameos in comics, TV, and film:
 • Comic: *Astonishing X-Men* volume 3 issue #6
 • Comic: *Hero Hotline* volume 1 issue #5
 • Comic: *Kingdom Come* volume 1 issue #2
 • Comic: *Marvels* volume 1 issue #4
 • Comic: *The Question* volume 1 issue #17
 • TV: *Teen Titans Go!* episode #82, "Real Boy Adventures"
 • Film: *Man of Steel*

 • Film: *Batman v Superman: Dawn of Justice Ultimate Edition*
 • Film: *Justice League*
CLIX ...... HeroClix figure pack-in cards
DECK ..... *DC Comics Deck-Building Game—Crossover Pack 4: Watchmen*
DURS .... *DC Universe: Rebirth Special* volume 1 issue #1
FILM ..... *Watchmen* theatrical film
HOOD .... *Under the Hood* documentary and dust-jacket prop reproduction
JUST ..... *Watchmen: Justice Is Coming*
MATL .... Mattel Club Black Freighter figure pack-in cards

2011 (Alternate Reality)

Dr. Manhattan uses his abilities to alter a reality populated by multitudes of superheroes. As part of a larger plan only he knows, Manhattan rewrites that universe's history to remove crime-fighters' friendships and romantic relationships, makes them a decade younger and less experienced, and thereby weakens them as individuals **[DURS]**.

> **NOTE:** *This action on Dr. Manhattan's part, hinted at in 2016's* DC Universe Rebirth #1, *reverses the changes made to the DC mythos by the company's* New 52 *concept, launched in September 2011. In restoring the universe to its pre-New 52 status, DC has incorporated elements of* Watchmen *into its storylines. As of this book's writing, rumors abound that* Watchmen's *cast now exist in the mainstream DC universe, with Ozymandias as Superman's mentor, Mr. Oz; The Comedian as one of three individuals operating as The Joker; Rorschach as his Charlton Comics predecessor, The Question; and Nite Owl and Silk Spectre as a pair of new vigilantes protecting Gotham City. All stories published after* Rebirth #1, *however, are not covered in this book.*

In or Before 2013 (Alternate Reality)

A graffiti artist paints The Comedian's smiley-face logo on a wall in Metropolis **[CMEO]**.

> **NOTE:** *A painted image of the yellow smiley face is briefly visible during a scene in 2013's* Man of Steel.

February 2015 (Alternate Reality)

Dick "Robin" Grayson finds Victor "Cyborg" Stone feeling sad about no longer being a cybernetic person. Robin takes his friend on a "real boy adventure," during which many superheroes, including Nite Owl, sing about the advantages of being human. Cheered up, Cyborg tosses his robotic parts into a garbage chute **[CMEO]**.

> **NOTE:** *This rather absurd cameo occurs in "Real Boy Adventures," episode #82 of the* Teen Titans Go! *animated series.*

In or Before 2016 (Alternate Reality)

An unknown individual spray-paints "The End Is Nigh" on a billboard advertising Gotham Seaport's Union Local #234 **[CMEO]**.

> **NOTE:** *Rorschach's doomsday-sign phrase can be seen adorning a billboard in the Blu-ray release of* Batman v Superman: Dawn of Justice Ultimate Edition.

As Batman becomes increasingly violent, several journalists comment on his disturbing behavior. One writer claims Batman is acting as judge, jury, and executioner, accuses the Gotham City Police Department of being complicit, and poses the question, "If GCPD endorses vigilantes as our city's watchmen, who watches the watchmen?" **[CMEO]**.

> **NOTE:** *A snippet of this editorial piece also appears in the* Batman v Superman: Dawn of Justice Ultimate Edition *Blu-ray, as Clark Kent investigates the Dark Knight.*

2017 (Alternate Reality)

A line of *Tales of the Black Freighter* T-shirts is released. Barry "The Flash" Allen buys one, which he wears when meeting Bruce "Batman" Wayne for the first time **[CMEO]**.

> **NOTE:** *In the first trailer for 2017's* Justice League *film, released in July 2016, Ezra Miller's Barry Allen is sporting this shirt when Ben Affleck's Batman asks him to join his new superhero team.*

2020 (Alternate Reality)

Rorschach visits a bar for metahumans, where he interacts with Sherlock Holmes, The Shadow, and The Question, and also breaks the fingers of Brother Power the Geek. In this reality, Hollis Mason still writes *Under the Hood* **[CMEO]**.

> **NOTE:** *This cameo occurs in DC's* Kingdom Come, *a 1996 Elsewhere tale involving a conflict between traditional superheroes and irresponsible, amoral vigilantes. Like* Watchmen, *it takes place outside DC's mainstream mythos, with crime-fighters feeling betrayed and unappreciated by those whom they once protected. Unlike Rorschach's dream sequence in* The Question #17, Watchmen *is not a fictional tale in this series, with Rorschach and Mason part of in-universe continuity. Since the story takes place in the future, Rorschach must not die in 1985, as he does in* Watchmen.

Rorschach shares some similarities with Arthur Conan Doyle's fictional detective Sherlock Holmes; though brilliant at thwarting criminals, both are short on social skills and tidiness. The Shadow (Kent Allard), a pulp vigilante crime-fighter conceived by Walter B. Gibson, is among Hollis Mason's favorite heroes, while Brother Power the Geek is an obscure DC character created by Joe Simon. As for The Question (Vic Sage), Alan Moore based Rorschach on this mask-wearing Charlton Comics character.

—2021

William Water "The Bully" Schott finishes a sixty-year prison sentence after being convicted of racketeering, theft, and murder in 1961 **[RPG3]**.

> **NOTE:** *This assumes that Schott has neither died nor been granted parole in the interim.*

—2089

Adrian Veidt, the smartest man in the world, dies at age 150 **[ABSO]**.

> **NOTE:** *Alan Moore's original notes, reprinted in* Absolute Watchmen, *indicate that Veidt (born in 1939) lives to be 150 years old. Given his dual role as the ultimate villain and hero of the* Watchmen *saga, Ozymandias's death provides an appropriate conclusion to this chronology.*

MIND .... *The Mindscape of Alan Moore*
MOBL .... *Watchmen: The Mobile Game*
MOTN .... *Watchmen: The Complete Motion Comic*
MTRO .... *Metro* promotional newspaper cover wrap
NEWP .... *New Frontiersman* promotional newspaper
NEWW ... *New Frontiersman* website
NIGH ..... *Watchmen: The End Is Nigh, Parts 1 and 2*
PKIT ...... *Watchmen* film British press kit
PORT ..... *Watchmen Portraits*
REAL ..... Real life
RPG1 .... *DC Heroes Role Playing Module #227: Who Watches the Watchmen?*

RPG2 .... *DC Heroes Role Playing Module #235: Taking Out the Trash—Curses and Tears*
RPG3 .... *DC Heroes: The Watchmen Sourcebook*
RUBY .... "Wounds," published in *The Ruby Files Volume One*
SCR1 ..... Unfilmed screenplay draft: Sam Hamm
SCR2 ..... Unfilmed screenplay draft: Charles McKeuen
SCR3 ..... Unfilmed screenplay draft: Gary Goldman
SCR4 ..... Unfilmed screenplay draft: David Hayter (2002)
SCR5 ..... Unfilmed screenplay draft: David Hayter (2003)
SCR6 ..... Unfilmed screenplay draft: Alex Tse
SPOT ..... *DC Spotlight #1*
VRL1 ..... Viral video: *NBS Nightly News with Ted Philips*

VRL2 ..... Viral video: *The Keene Act and You*
VRL3 ..... Viral video: *Who Watches the Watchmen? A Veidt Music Network (VMN) Special*
VRL4 ..... Viral video: *World in Focus: 6 Minutes to Midnight*
VRL5 ..... Viral video: *Local Radio Station Report on 1977 Riots*
VRL6 ..... Viral videos (group of ten): *Veidt Enterprises Advertising Contest*
WAWA ... *Watching the Watchmen*
WHOS .... *Who's Who: The Definitive Directory of the DC Universe*
WTFC .... *Watchmen: The Film Companion*

THE CRIMELINE

A Mini-Chronology of Heroes and Villains

"The accumulated filth of all their sex and murder will foam up about their waists and all the whores and politicians will look up and shout 'Save us!'... and I'll look down and whisper 'No.'"

—**Walter "Rorschach" Kovacs**

At the very core of the *Watchmen* saga are heroes and villains. Sometimes, the line between the two blurs, and it's often the so-called heroes whose actions are the most villainous. Presented below is a brief mini-timeline highlighting the heroics and criminal activities of *Watchmen*'s many masked crime-fighters, vigilantes, supervillains, kingpins, and thugs. Birth and death dates are listed as well, in order to provide context. For more detailed information, including justifications for dating placeents, consult the corresponding dates in this book's main chronology.

- **Between 1900 and 1910**
  Laurence Albert "Larry" Schexnayder, The Minutemen's agent, is born.

- **1905**
  Rolf Müller, long rumored to be Hooded Justice, is born to Henrik and Greta Müller.

- **Circa 1910**
  A child named Jacob, possibly Hooded Justice's actual identity, is born.

- **March 22, 1910**
  Byron Alfred Lewis (Mothman) is born to Arthur and Janet Lewis.

- **August 11, 1912**
  Nelson "Nelly" Gardner (Captain Metropolis) is born to Albert and Matilda Gardner.

- **1916**
  Hollis T. Mason (the first Nite Owl) is born.

- **1917**
  William Benjamin "Bill" Brady (Dollar Bill) is born.

- **September 4, 1917**
  Ursula Zandt (The Silhouette) is born to Dr. Gregor Zandt and his wife.

- **In or Before 1920**
  Rolf Müller becomes a serial rapist and murderer called The Friend of the Children.

- **1920**
  Rolf Müller molests a youth name Jacob while working for the Hauptzelt Zirkus circus.

- **June 6, 1920**
  Edgar William Jacobi (Moloch the Mystic) is born.

- **August 3, 1920**
  Sally Juspeczyk (the first Silk Spectre) is born.

- **May 13, 1924**
  Edward Morgan "Eddie" Blake (The Comedian) is born.

- **1929**
  Jonathan "Jon" Osterman (Dr. Manhattan) is born to Josef and Inge Osterman.

- **February 6, 1930**
  Rolf Müller brutally beats his father Henrik in retaliation for the latter's abuse of Rolf's mother Greta.

- **Mid-1930s**
  Edgar Jacobi kills a classmate named David, then leaves his corpse in the bed of the boy's girlfriend Marie, as revenge for her trying to humiliate Edgar.

- **Before October 1933**
  Rolf Müller joins the Ku Klux Klan and, with Frank Burrows and three other members, murders a black couple, Samuel and Eloise Horton.

- **1937**
  Edgar Jacobi becomes a stage magician called Moloch the Mystic and begins using stage-magic tricks to perpetrate bank heists.

- **After March 12, 1938**
  Rolf Müller works as a torturer for Nazi forces in Austria. Among his victims is Ursula Zandt's sister Blanche.

- **October 14, 1938**
  Hooded Justice becomes the first masked crime-fighter. He makes his debut by beating up three armed thugs robbing a couple at a Queens theater.

- **Late October 1938**
  Hooded Justice stops a supermarket stickup, inspiring Hollis Mason to follow in his footsteps.

- **In or Before December 1938**
  Sally Juspeczyk reads about Hooded Justice's exploits and decides to do the same, in order to boost her modeling career. She calls herself The Silk Spectre.

- **December 1938 to Late 1939**
  Larry Schexnayder hires actors and professional wrestlers to pose as criminals so Silk Spectre can gain media attention by pretending to arrest them.

- **Late 1938 or 1939**
  Edgar Jacobi robs banks, hijacks trucks, and carries out kidnappings under aliases such as Moloch, Edgar William Vaughn, William Edgar Bright, Satan of the Underworld, and Arthur Gordon Scratch. He invests his money in opium dens.

  Walter Zileski becomes the supervillain The Screaming Skull after flipping a coin to decide whether to be good or evil.

- **1939**
  Adrian Alexander Veidt (Ozymandias) is born to Friedrich Werner and Ingrid Renata Veidt.

- **In or Before January 1939**
  As a teen, Eddie Blake earns a criminal record with the State of New York Juvenile Correctional Services.

- **Early January 1939**
  Hooded Justice thwarts four perpetrators of a triple homicide at a federal bank. He dispenses two, Tony and Little Bob, then tosses a third out a factory window.

  Hollis Mason becomes The Nite Owl. Early in his career, he stops gunmen from stealing an armored car and saves the lives of a mother and child in its path.

- **Before January 12, 1939**
  Larry Schexnayder conspires with Bergstein Jewelers to drum up publicity for Sally Jupiter by having her stop The Red Devil (an actor in costume) from robbing the store. Sally also arrests an actual criminal, Claude Boke, as he tries to rob a liquor store.

- **After January 12, 1939**
  Underworld czar Jimmy Fantucci surrenders to police rather than shoot Silk Spectre.

- **February 1939**
  Ursula Zandt becomes The Silhouette and exposes a crooked publisher trafficking in child pornography.

- **In or After February 1939**
  Hollis Mason stops the mugging of a wealthy couple outside The Gotham Opera House.

  Ursula Zandt rescues a child from traffickers in Chinatown.

Eddie Blake starts fighting crime, first as The Big Stick and then as The Comedian. He cleans up the waterfronts, thwarts a robbery of SoHo's Clef-Arpels jewelry store, and clashes with the Garbino mob. As much a thug as a hero, he beats the bartender and every customer at The Bloody Ear with a bat, then robs the bar's cash register.

- **April 16, 1939**
  Byron Lewis debuts as Mothman, exposing a massive numbers racket run by gangsters in and around Harlem.

- **April 21, 1939**
  The National Bank of New York, while coming up with names for an in-house superhero, considers calling him Finance Man, First National Man, Safety Man, Americaman, Mr. Americaman, Captain Americaman, Red White and Blue Man, Anti-Gangster Man, The Murderer, The Mutilator, The Butcher, The Pummeler, and The Crime Stomper.

- **April 24, 1939**
  Nelson Gardner, on his first night as Captain Metropolis, stops a gas station robbery in Hoboken, New Jersey.

- **Between April 1939 and October 1939**
  At least seven other masked vigilantes begin operating around the U.S. West Coast. New York becomes a haven for costumed adventurers.

- **May 11, 1939**
  The National Bank of New York hires Bill Brady as Dollar Bill, its in-house superhero.

- **Mid-1939**
  Nelson Gardner and Sally Jupiter partner to form a crime-fighting team called The New Minute Men of America, which they shorten to The Minutemen.

- **June 15, 1939**
  The National Bank of New York airs promotional footage of Dollar Bill apprehending a mugger.

- **In or After June 1939**
  Bill Brady stops several attempts to rob his bank, then begins working with local police.

- **Before October 6, 1939**
  The Minutemen invite The Comedian to join their ranks.

- **Mid-November 1939**
  Nelson Gardner, Sally Jupiter, and Larry Schexnayder hold auditions for The Minutemen and invite The Nite Owl, Mothman, and Dollar Bill to join the team. Rejected applicants include The Frogman, Liberty Lassy, The Iron Lid, The Slut, and Hank.

- **Late November or December 1939**
  The Minutemen add The Silhouette and Hooded Justice to their lineup.

- **December 16, 1939**
  The Minutemen officially launch as a crime-fighting team.

- **Late December 1939**
  The Minutemen try to take down Italian fifth-columnists rumored to be smuggling weapons into New York Harbor, who end up merely being Chinese fireworks smugglers. They also stop thieves from robbing a National Bank of New York branch.

  Moloch forces Professor Tungren to create a "solar mirror weapon," then kills the scientist, threatens to destroy the Empire State Building, and robs a train filled with military weaponry. The Minutemen foil Moloch's plans and confiscate the weapon.

- **Between December 1939 and October 2, 1940**
  The Minutemen defeat gangs dressed as pirates and ghosts, unearth a hidden arsenal, arrest King Mob, and cripple a crime ring plaguing the Metro Central Bank. The Comedian captures The Italian Shadow.

- **Between 1939 and 1947**
  The Silk Spectre arrests women robbing grieving families at funerals, works with a reporter to take down the Spring St. Bandits, battles The Fey Blade, and nabs The Herald Square Gang.

- **Between 1939 and 1962**
  The Nite Owl fights The H(uman)-Bomb. He also saves an eight-year-old girl, her brother, and four policemen from dying in a burning building.

- **Late 1930s to 1950**
  The Screaming Skull steals more than $15 million worth of property, but clears only $2,000 due to steep overhead and insurance costs.

- **March 21, 1940**
  Walter Joseph Kovacs (Rorschach) is born to single mother Sylvia Kovacs. His father, Charlie, is not part of his life.

- **June 1940 to 1945**
  Ex-Nazi officer Hans von Krupp, as the master saboteur Captain Axis, threatens factories, military installations, propagandistic war films, and USO events. He also tries to implant pro-Nazi subliminal messages into Clark Gable movies.

- **Mid-1940**
  Hooded Justice suffers a broken arm while fighting The Screaming Skull.

- **In or Before September 1940**
  Traveling with The Big Top Circus, Rolf Müller abducts and mutilates several children.

- **Late September 1940**
  Hollis Mason and Byron Lewis begin helping Ursula Zandt track down a serial killer and rapist of children. They know not that their quarry is Rolf Müller.

- **October 2, 1940**
  Eddie Blake tries to rape Sally Jupiter. Hooded Justice comes to her rescue, hurting Blake badly. The Comedian is expelled from The Minutemen.

- **Between October 1940 and 1941**
  Hooded Justice battles Moloch on several occasions.

- **1940 (Most Likely)**
  Daniel M. "Dan" Dreiberg (the second Nite Owl) is born to William and Victoria Dreiberg.

- **1940s**
  The Minutemen fight Mobster, who dresses like a 1920s Chicago gangster, and Spaceman, who commits crimes in a pulp 1950s-style spacesuit.

- **After December 7, 1941**
  The Comedian fights in World War II. During his first command, he murders an officer named Peterman for killing a Vietnamese woman and her son.

- **January 1942**
  An FBI agent named Kaufax recruits Eddie Blake for U.S. government service.

- **January 1942 to April 1985**
  The Comedian serves as an operative for multiple branches, including the OSS, Army Intelligence, the CIA, the DEA, and the U.S. Secret Service.

- **In or After February 1942**
  Ursula Zandt kills every member of a gentlemen's club after learning of its secret child-molestation ring.

- **1942, After February**
  Hollis Mason arrests The Screaming Skull dozens of times and confiscates his "electra-vibe" weapon. The Minutemen foil sabotage attempts by Captain Axis.

- **Early 1940s**
  Moloch perpetrates several heists, some successfully, others thwarted by the remaining Minutemen. He is incarcerated multiple times, but always escapes.

- **1945**
  The Minutemen fight Captain Axis on a submarine near the Arctic Circle. Hooded Justice tosses the villain into the ocean, and he never surfaces.

- **Before June 5, 1945**
  Eddie Blake kills seven Japanese prisoners-of-war to win a bet with an Army officer. He is court-martialed but cleared of all charges.

- **In or Before December 1945**
  Serial killer Geoffrey "The Liquidator" Dean stalks and murders several New York bowling alley pinsetters.

- **December 10, 1945**
  The Minutemen lure The Liquidator into a trap, and The Silhouette tosses him off the George Washington Bridge. He survives and continues killing.

- **March 29, 1946**
  The Minutemen fire their maid, Frieda Jenkins, for stealing money from petty cash. In retaliation, she outs Ursula Zandt to the press as a lesbian.

- **May 13, 1946**
  The Minutemen expel Ursula Zandt from their lineup to avoid bad publicity.

- **May 31, 1946**
  Ursula Zandt again arrests The Liquidator.

- **Before June 1946**
  Ursula Zandt finds evidence identifying Rolf Müller as serial killer The Friend of the Children—whom she believes may be Hooded Justice.

- **June 1946**
  The Liquidator murders Zandt and her girlfriend. Sally Jupiter tracks down and brutally murders him, then quits The Minutemen.

- **July 23, 1946**
  While trying to stop three men from robbing a National Bank of New York branch, Bill Brady is fatally shot after his cape becomes caught in a revolving door.

- **1946 to 1949**
  Scientist Elmo Greensback spends three years designing a flying costume and weaponry so he can become a superhero.

- **In or Before 1947**
  Sally Jupiter captures burglars at Grand Central Station and foils a Greenwich Village burglary ring. The Minutemen encounter The King of Skin on several occasions.

- **1947**
  Moloch becomes a major figure in the criminal underworld. Sally Jupiter retires from crime-fighting. The costumed-adventurer fad begins to fade.

- **In or Before June 1947**
  A father-and-son team pose as fictional comic-book superheroes Bluecoat and Scout to seek The Minutemen's

help in stopping Japanese terrorists from causing a nuclear meltdown in the Statue of Liberty. They succeed, but the two die in the process.

- **Late 1947**
  Larry Schexnayder steps down as The Minutemen's publicist.

- **1947 to 1955**
  Byron Lewis and Hollis Mason work Ursula Zandt's unresolved child-killer case, but Rolf Müller continues to murder children without being caught.

- **1947 to 1967**
  Moloch is dubbed "King of the Underworld." The Comedian becomes his arch-nemesis.

- **In or Before 1949**
  The Screaming Skull spends three months setting up a scheme to destroy The Minutemen's headquarters, but blows up the wrong brownstone.

- **1949**
  Elmo Greensback demonstrates his superhero gear for janitor Bob Krankk—who kills the scientist and steals his costume.

  The Minutemen disband. Byron Lewis retires from crime-fighting, while Hollis Mason, Nelson Gardner, and Hooded Justice continue their efforts individually.

  At age ten, Adrian Veidt commits his first crime-fighting act by permanently crippling a schoolyard bully named Jerry.

- **In or After 1949**
  As supervillain Buzzbomb, Bob Krankk becomes a frequent foe of Hollis Mason. None of his criminal endeavors succeed, but he nonetheless proclaims himself invincible. After trying to steal the U.S. Constitution, he is sentenced to Rikers Island.

- **Before 1950**
  Anthony Rizzoli (a.k.a Anthony Vitoli and Underboss) is named head of the Rizzoli crime family.

- **Before 1950 to 1965**
  With Underboss in charge, the Rizzoli family's criminal empire dominates organized crime throughout New York City.

- **1950**
  The Screaming Skull commits his last known criminal scheme.

- **Before August 15, 1950**
  The U.S. government dispatches masked adventurers to Russia to help prevent an atomic war between the United States and the Soviet Union.

- **December 2, 1950**
  Laurel Jane "Laurie" Jupiter (the second Silk Spectre, a.k.a. Laurie Juspeczyk) is born to Sally Jupiter. Her biological father, Eddie Blake, has no part in her life; stepfather Larry Schexnayder raises Laurie during her early years.

- **1950 to 1966**
  The United States operates without organizations of masked adventurers.

- **In or Before 1951**
  As a child, Walter Kovacks kills his mother's abusive ex-lover—who may be his father Charlie—after hearing the man plotting to murder young Walter.

- **1951**
  The Screaming Skull is captured and put on trial.

- **July 1951**
  Walter Kovacs jams a cigarette into the eyes of a local bully, Richie, and bites a chunk out of another boy's cheek after they threaten to rape him. He is thus sent to the Lillian Charlton Home for Problem Children.

- **1951 to 1971**
  Walter Zileski spends twenty years in jail.

- **Early to Mid-1950s**
  Many supervillains end their criminal careers, while others adopt a less extroverted, more profitable approach to crime. Superheroes fall out of public favor.

- **April 16, 1954**
  Pressed to testify before The House Un-American Activities Committee (HUAC), Hooded Justice vanishes. The government assigns Eddie Blake to find him.

- **In or Before 1955**
  Hollis Mason captures a criminal known as Gangster.

- **April 16, 1955**
  Eddie Blake murders child-killer Rolf Müller, mistaking him for Hooded Justice.

- **After April 16, 1955**
  Eddie Blake frames Hooded Justice for abducting a boy, making him appear to be Ursula Zandt's child-killer. As a result, Hollis Mason murders Hooded Justice.

- **Mid-1956**
  George Paterson, Sylvia Kovacs's pimp, kills her by forcing Sylvia to ingest Drano.

- **Before September 1956**
  Adrian Veidt, while studying in Tibet, is attacked by a gang of thugs and leaves their bodies in a broken, bloodied heap.

- **March 1958**
  To avenge the death of his lover, Miranda St. John, Adrian Veidt becomes Ozymandias and topples narcotics kingpin Porcini, on whose heroin Miranda had overdosed.

- **Mid-1958**
  Ozymandias defeats mobile gambling den operator Wheeler-Dealer, stolen-car czar Low Jack, international counterfeiting ring Three Dollar Bill, and hook-handed kingpin The Ancient Mariner. The Nite Owl nabs The King of Skin.

- **1958 to 1968**
  To increase his influence and power, Moloch schemes to elect a U.S. President connected to organized crime.

- **August 20, 1959**
  Jon Osterman dies during a scientific experiment. The physicist's body is reduced to atoms, but his consciousness survives and begins reconstructing his physical form.

- **September 23, 1959**
  While investigating Hooded Justice's disappearance, Adrian Veidt battles The Comedian.

- **November 22, 1959**
  Jon Osterman's body reconstitutes—naked, hairless, blue, and capable of mastering the building blocks of matter.

- **In or Before the 1960s**
  Eddie Blake apprehends Italian drug dealer Sal and has him deported to Corsica.

- **February 1960**
  The U.S. government dubs Jon Osterman "Dr. Manhattan," knowing that the country's enemies will associate the nickname with the Manhattan Project.

- **Mid-June 1960**
  Ozymandias topples smuggling ring The Contraband.

- **Late 1960**
  Adrian Veidt arranges for the architects who created his Karnak base to die in an airplane accident, so as to eliminate witnesses to his plan.

- **November 1960**
  During a raid on Moloch's vice-den, Dr. Manhattan causes a criminal's head to explode.

- **December 29, 1960**
  Adrian Veidt nabs The Flying Tigers, five flying criminals in cat costumes.

- **1961**
  Eddie Blake begins working as a personal bodyguard for Findlay Setchfield South.

- **In or Before May 1961**
  William Water Schott's gang perpetrates racketeering, theft, and murder in the Bronx. Already wanted for a double homicide in Pennsylvania, Schott calls himself The Bully.

- **May 22, 1961**
  Hollis Mason and his dog Phantom apprehend The Bully and his gang.

- **September 1, 1961**
  Byron Lewis is arrested during a civil-rights demonstration in Mobile, Alabama, for drunken disorderly behavior.

- **1962**
  Sally Jupiter pushes her daughter Laurie to become a superheroine and begins instructing her in the art of crime-fighting.

- **In or Before May 1962**
  Hollis Mason thwarts a car-theft ring at Sparkys Garage and orders the thieves to reassemble every stolen vehicle. He agrees to take Dan Dreiberg on as his sidekick.

- **Mid to Late May 1962**
  Hollis Mason retires from crime-fighting and gives Dan Dreiberg the Nite Owl identity and legacy.

- **August 5, 1962**
  At Jacqueline Kennedy's request, Eddie Blake murders Marilyn Monroe (after having sex with her) and stages her death to make it appear to be a barbiturate overdose.

- **August 28, 1962**
  Byron Lewis is committed to an asylum in Maine.

- **Between October 23 and October 28, 1962**
  Ozymandias assists John F. Kennedy in ending the Cuban Missile Crisis.

- **November 22, 1963**
  Eddie Blake assassinates John Kennedy by shooting him from a grassy knoll, letting Lee Harvey Oswald take the blame. Blake and FBI Agent Luxem raid one of Moloch the Mystic's warehouses.

- **November 23, 1963 to April 1966**
  Adrian Veidt grows to view crime-fighting as a hollow pursuit.

- **Early 1960s**
  Dr. Manhattan disintegrates several of Moloch's top lieutenants and trigger-men. Moloch breaks out of prison, then battles The Comedian and Ozymandias on several occasions.

- **1964**
  Moloch kidnaps the governor of New Jersey.

- **March 14, 1964**
  A day after reading about Kitty Genovese's murder, Walter Kovacs fashions a mask to make it more bearable to look in a mirror. A week later, he becomes Rorschach.

- **March 20, 1964 to October 1985**
  Rorschach arrests more than fifty criminals who end up sentenced to the Sing Sing Correctional Facility.

- **April 3, 1964**
  Rorschach apprehends four suspects in the Kitty Genovese murder, leaving them bound and gagged in front of NYPD headquarters.

- **Spring 1964**
  During a New York City blackout, Dan Dreiberg makes his crime-fighting debut to stop rioters. Rorschach boards the Owlship and proposes a partnership, to which Dan agrees.

- **Mid-1964**
  The Comedian travels to Vietnam to help end the war, then forces Italian drug dealer Sal to fund the war effort via the illegal drug trade.

- **Before 1965**
  Tom Ryan (a.k.a Rocky and The Big Figure) quickly ascends the ranks of the organized-crime world.

- **In or Before August 1965**
  Rorschach and Nite Owl tackle New York City's gang problem together.

  Big Figure seizes control of Underboss's syndicate while the latter is incarcerated. He specializes in narcotics, prostitution, and gambling sales, and wipes out an entire South Bronx police station.

- **Between August 12 and 17, 1965**
  During the Watts riots, Eddie Blake shoots out store windows to cause widespread looting and discredit protestors, then flings dog feces at LAPD Chief William H. Parker.

- **August 22, 1965**
  Rorschach and Nite Owl bring down The Big Figure, who is sentenced to Sing Sing.

- **Mid-1960s**
  Edgar Jacobi grows his criminal empire globally. Dr. Manhattan becomes Moloch's next arch-adversary, while Adrian Veidt busts several drug rings.

- **In or Before 1966**
  Eddie Blake carries out blackmail, torture, and political assassinations during covert operations and military campaigns for the U.S. government.

  The Chairman (who may be Frank Sinatra) becomes a criminal mastermind. Protected by bodyguards The Shake Sisters, and working alongside nightclub owner Gurustein and drug maker Owsley, he distributes a new drug to render teens susceptible to marketing.

  Singer Red D'eath gives amphetamines to two fourteen-year-old girls, then takes advantage of them sexually.

- **Early 1966**
  After several of Laurie Juspeczyk's friends overdose on the new drug, she beats up Gurustein and The Chairman, indirectly causing the latter's death.

- **March 11, 1966**
  Laurie Juspeczyk makes her public debut as the second Silk Spectre, thwarting a jewelry-store heist in Manhattan.

- **Before April 14, 1966**
  Rorschach and Dan Dreiberg deliver evidence to NYPD detectives regarding Underboss's racketeering and conspiracy activities.

- **April 14, 1966**
  Nelson Gardner tries to form a second masked adventurer team called The Crimebusters. He invites Dr. Manhattan, Ozymandias, Rorschach, The Comedian, The Silk Spectre, and The Nite Owl to take part, but the meeting is a bust and the team concept stalls. That same day, Nite Owl rescues gas explosion victims by taking them aboard *Archimedes*.

- **After April 14, 1966**
  Underboss is tried for conspiracy and racketeering.

- **Between April 1966 and June 6, 1966**
  Nelson Gardner begins investigating drug trafficker Mole Varrows, but fails to have him convicted. He vows to bring down The Peace Front, a radical protest group bent on overthrowing the government.

- **In or After April 1966**
  Underboss is sentenced to prison, but continues to run his criminal empire from his cell.

- **In or Before June 1966**
  Moloch gives anonymous donations to radical protest groups, including the Peace Front, so their increased activities will divert police attention from his crimes.

- **June 4, 1966**
  Rorschach rescues twelve-year-old Jeffrey Iddings from an extortion gang.

- **June 5, 1966**
  Nelson Gardner, hoping to revitalize his Crimebusters concept, arranges for six individuals (including Sally Jupiter, Hollis Mason, and his own mother) to be kidnapped, then frames Moloch, Mole Varrows, and the American Negro Alliance for the crimes.

- **Circa July 1966**
  The Twilight Lady (a.k.a. Leslie Chadwicke and Elizabeth Lane) launches a prostitution racket, then graduates to drug distribution. The Nite Owl helps her stop human-trafficker Carlos "Vincent" Onofrio.

  Reverend Taylor Dean murders a prostitute trying to blackmail him, then kills twenty-six more victims and burns their bodies in a bonfire of sin, intending to frame Rorschach for the deaths. Rorschach kills him instead.

- **1966 to 1977**
  Laurie Juspeczyk fights crime alongside Rorschach and Dan Dreiberg in New York City, and with Dr. Manhattan in Washington, D.C.

- **Late 1960s**
  Findlay Setchfield South recruits Eddie Blake to eliminate anyone standing in the way of Richard Nixon becoming President.

- **Late 1966 to 1967**
  Ozymandias begins concocting a plan to save mankind from itself by murdering millions of people and uniting humanity against a common foe.

- **1967**
  Rorschach brings down a criminal called Zebra. Imprisoned, Zebra hires three convicts (Tom, Dick, and Harry) as his lackeys.

- **Early 1967**
  Ozymandias thwarts four thieves attempting to pilfer the British Museum's collection.

  A former runaway and prostitute known as Mother forms a gang-cult, The Brethren, who go on a ritual killing and kidnapping spree.

- **1968**
  Underboss's criminal empire achieves the height of its success, despite his imprisonment in Chicago.

  Dr. Manhattan stops Russian troops from invading Prague by melting their military tanks.

  The Twilight Lady's pornography and prostitution empire evolves to include smut magazines and movies, studios, burlesque houses, and bordellos. Dan Dreiberg arrests her while Rorschach is working on the Schipono case.

- **1968 to 1970**
  The Twilight Lady spends two years in prison.

- **January 7, 1968**
  The Brethren abduct and stab a man, then drain his blood for a religious ritual.

- **March 14, 1968**
  The Brethren strangle Marianne Eliot and leave her body in an alley.

- **March 16, 1968**
  During the Vietnam War, Eddie Blake torches an entire Việt Cộng-influenced village, killing more than five hundred people, for which he is relieved of duty.

- **April 7, 1968**
  Eddie Blake shoots gangster Joey Falcone, making it appear to have been a typical gangland hit.

- **May 15, 1968**
  The Brethren kidnap, stab, and decapitate a person, then drain the body's blood for use in a religious ritual.

- **In or Before Early 1968**
  Eddie Blake carries out numerous blackmail and assassination missions for the CIA.

- **Mid-1968**
  Rorschach and Dan Dreiberg take down The Rat Pack.

- **In or Before June 1968**
  Edgar Jacobi hires martial arts experts Sin and Temptation as his bodyguards. He tries to secure Senator Ken Shade's Presidential nomination via extortion and blackmail, and hires The Brethren to assassinate Richard Nixon (which they fail to do).

- **June 5, 1968**
  Eddie Blake assassinates Robert Kennedy, letting Sirhan Sirhan take the blame.

- **June 11, 1968**
  Dan Dreiberg and Rorschach prevent The Brethren from abducting an old man for a ritual sacrifice.

- **June 13, 1968**
  The Brethren, working with Don "Big Daddy" Feroli, storm the Republican National Convention. Masked crime-fighters quell the riot, expose Ken Shade's and Moloch's involvement, and apprehend Mother. Moloch's lawyers get him freed from prison.

- **Between 1968 and 1971**
  To eliminate Dr. Manhattan as a threat to his plans, Adrian Veidt arranges for Wally Weaver, Janey Slater, Anthony Randolph, and others to develop cancer.

- **January 22, 1969**
  The Twilight Lady hacks into Richard Nixon's state-of-the-union address, replacing it with a video of herself in erotic costumes.

- **Between 1969 and July 1977**
  Joe Bird starts pimping prostitutes and dealing narcotics in New York City.

- **Late 1960s to Early 1970s**
  Adrian Veidt exposes breakaway extremist factions within the Pentagon planning to release diseases upon Africa's population.

- **1970**
  After two years in prison, The Twilight Lady is set free and vanishes to France.

- **February 18, 1970**
  Edgar Jacobi is finally sent away to prison.

- **In or After 1970**
  The Twilight Lady returns to prison.

- **Early 1971**
  The Comedian, assigned to find missing soldiers in Vietnam, scorches an entire village to punish them for helping the Việt Cộng.

- **March to May 1971**
  Jon Osterman works alongside The Comedian in Saigon to end the Vietnam War. Dr. Manhattan uses his mental abilities to decimate the Việt Cộng forces. He increases his size to giant proportions and destroys enemy vehicles with a mere thought.

- **June 1971**
  Dr. Manhattan decimates the Việt Cộng's guerilla forces by restructuring the jungles in which they hide into noxious gases. This action ends the Vietnam War.

- **June 29, 1971**
  Eddie Blake murders a Vietnamese woman, Liao Lin, who is pregnant with his child.

- **Between July 1971 and July 1977**
  A U.S. soldier, nicknamed Rawhead due to facial burns he received in Vitenam, becomes a prominent New York City gangster. Rawhead's war buddy Tyson and pimp Joe Bird join his organization.

- **July 1, 1971**
  Eddie Blake is court-martialed for killing Liao Lin, but claims it was in self-defense. All charges are dismissed on September 11.

- **In or After 1971**
  Walter Zileski (formerly The Screaming Skull) finishes a twenty-year jail sentence and gives up criminal pursuits.

- **In or Before 1972**
  Arms dealer Jimmy the Gimmick supplies weapons to thugs, black-ops teams, and others from his lair in an abandoned amusement park.

- **1972**
  Moloch arranges for the luxury liner *Queen Elizabeth II* to be hijacked.

- **June 17, 1972**
  Five employees of Richard Nixon's campaign team break into the Democratic National Committee headquarters at the Watergate complex in Washington, D.C., to peruse private files and plant listening devices. Nixon helps to cover up the men's crimes.

- **In or Before October 1972**
  A nihilistic youth gang, the Knot-Tops, forms. Its members vandalize property, commit robberies, sell drugs, and otherwise cause trouble.

- **October 13, 1972**
  Eddie Blake tortures the FBI's Mark Felt to learn the locations of Bob Woodward and Carl Bernstein before they can expose Nixon's Watergate involvement. He hires Jimmy the Gimmick to help Underboss escape from Sing Sing so he can frame the mobster for the journalists' murders.

- **October 19, 1972**
  Dr. Manhattan and Sally Jupiter prevent an airplane from crashing in the Andes. Ozymandias captures The King of Skin.

- **October 20, 1972**
  Eddie Blake assassinates Woodward and Bernstein.

- **October 20, 1972**
  Nite Owl and Rorschach locate Underboss, but The Comedian shoots him from a nearby building, causing the gangster to plummet several stories. After awakening from a coma, Underboss is sentenced to Rikers Island.

- **In or Before 1974**
  A masked, winged serial killer begins preying on New York City prostitutes. He kills each victim with a knife and leaves a black raven feather over her eyes. Rorschach investigates the multiple homicides.

- **1974**
  Rorschach roughs up two criminals and leaves their bloodied bodies tied to a fire hydrant for police to find, along with his ink blot calling card.

- **October 3, 1974**
  Nelson Gardner is decapitated in a motor vehicle accident.

- **Late 1974 or Early 1975**
  The feather-leaving serial killer murders prostitute Stacy Sweet.

- **1975**
  This same killer slays Stacy Sweet's pimp, Exavier Micheals. Stacy's brother tracks down and eliminates the masked murderer.

- **January 24, 1975**
  After Richard Nixon repeals Constitutional Amendment 22 so he can seek a third term in office, Adrian Veidt retires from crime-fighting and admits to being Ozymandias.

- **After January 24, 1975**
  Dr. Manhattan apprehends a criminal by making his handgun disintegrate, then bends a pole around him to hold him in place until police arrive. Silk Spectre stops another lawbreaker, while The Comedian leaves a third dead on the street.

- **Summer 1975**
  Gerald Anthony Grice rapes and tortures six-year-old Blair Roche, then feeds her corpse to his German shepherds, Fred and Barney. Rorschach burns Grice alive in a kerosene fire and thereafter ceases using the name Walter Kovacs.

- **Mid-1976**
  A mentally ill individual poses as a villain called Captain Carnage and begs costumed heroes, including Silk Spectre and Nite Owl, to beat him up. When he tries the same tactic with Rorschach, the vigilante drops him down an elevator shaft.

- **July 1976**
  The Brain Trust, led by Dr. Cortex, take hostages inside the Statue of Liberty and demand the release of nine Radical Front prisoners. Masked vigilantes try to stop them but inadvertently destroy the monument in the process.

- **In or Before 1977**
  New York City's crime-fighters arrest supervillains Golden Boy, The Butcher, Electron, and Ogre. The Comedian sends Jack of Hearts to prison for white slavery.

- **1977**
  Moloch arranges for the New York Stock Exchange to be bombed.

- **March 1977**
  The Twilight Lady, again released from prison, resumes her former vice trade.

- **June 1977**
  The Twilight Lady hires teenager Violet Greene to star in sadomasochistic porn films.

- **Before July 1977**
  Ronald James Randall begins killing women in New York City to protest societal decay. The press dubs him The Bard for his motif of carving phrases into his victims.

- **July 1, 1977**
  Rorschach breaks the arm of street hustler Dwayne Carter to learn the location of his drug supplier.

- **July 7, 1977**
  Rorschach kills two of Rawhead's enforcers by ramming one with a truck and blowing up the other (and some passersby) with a Molotov cocktail.

- **July 10, 1977**
  Rorschach badly injures Joe Bird to learn Rawhead's whereabouts.

- **July 11, 1977**
  As Rawhead's enforcer, Lucky Pierre, tortures Rorschach, Rawhead dons the vigilante's mask and heads out to have fun fighting looters—who kill the gangster with a bat. Rawhead's tiger eats Lucky Pierre.

  The Bard attacks Rorschach's friend Nancy, but she survives.

- **Mid- or Late July 1977**
  When the New York Police Officers' Union goes on strike, masked crime-fighters step in to stop the resultant looting. Nite Owl and The Comedian team up, as do Dr. Manhattan and Silk Spectre. Ozymandias comes out of retirement to lend assistance.

  Rorschach and Nite Owl bring down The Twilight Lady's vice empire, but their partnership ends after Dan stops his friend from killing her.

- **August 3, 1977**
  The Keene Act makes masked crime-fighting illegal. Eddie Blake and Jon Osterman are exempted from the law. Others retire, but Rorschach refuses to comply.

- **August 5, 1977**
  To protest the Keene Act, Rorschach kills suspected multiple-rapist Harvey Charles Furniss, leaving his corpse outside Manhattan's police headquarters.

- **Between 1977 and 1979**
  Edgar Jacobi finds religion in prison and renounces his criminal past.

- **1977 to 1985**
  Eddie Blake spends years engaged in "diplomatic" work for the U.S. government, including knocking over Marxist republics in South America.

- **Before October 28, 1978**
  Franklin Smith and Daziel Amrand are suspected of killing an individual named Loomis.

- **October 28, 1978**
  Rorschach murders Daziel Amrand and Franklin Smith. Police fail to capture the vigilante, who injures several officers.

- **November 27, 1978**
  The FBI releases a wanted poster for Rorschach, citing murder, assault, torture, breaking and entering, and violation of the Keene Act.

- **Mid-December 1978**
  After Iranian militants storm the U.S. embassy in Tehran, Eddie Blake rescues fifty-three American hostages and kills seventeen Iranians.

- **1979**
  Dr. Manhattan forces Daniel Ortega to sign a peace treaty between Nicaragua's Sandinista National Liberation Front and the United States.

- **August 14, 1979**
  Rorschach barely escapes capture by police officers, thanks to a cab driver who considers him a hero.

- **After the 1970s**
  Underboss dies at Rikers Island during a knife fight over a cigarette lighter.

- **Mid-1980**
  Ronald James Randall is acquitted of his crimes as The Bard, due to the prosecution botching the case. Rorschach vows to bring the serial killer to justice.

- **March 1981**
  Adrian Veidt murders his assistant Marla since she knows too much about his plans.

- **July 11, 1982**
  Rorschach tracks down and murders Ronald James Randall.

- **1983**
  Adrian Veidt recruits a team to design a squid-like creature so he can fake an alien invasion. Among them are Norman Leith, Hira Manish, James Trafford March, Max Shea, Linette Paley, Dr. Whittaker Furnesse, and Professor Wickstein.

- **September 1984**
  Edgar Jacobi is paroled for good behavior and begins working for Adrian Veidt, who gives him a chance to atone for his crimes as Moloch, but secretly exposes him to cancer-causing radiation.

- **In or Before 1985**
  Adrian Veidt also exposes Jon Osterman's former colleagues, Major Adamson, William Charles Batts, Stephanie Boris, Dr. J.M. Candelaria, Colonel Brent Dabbs, and Susan White, to carcinogenic agents.

  Eddie Blake undertakes a mission for the CIA that angers Libya.

  Former supervillain Golden Boy develops Alzheimer's. The Brain Trust die in prison.

  Dr. Manhattan prevents a tidal wave from decimating Miami, contains an exploding nuclear reactor, and ends a mob riot by teleporting the rioters to the desert.

- **April 1985**
  Eddie Blake performs covert duties in El Salvador.

- **In or Before July 1985**
  Eddie Blake carries out a U.S. government wetwork operation in Nicaragua.

- **After July 16, 1985**
  Eddie Blake finds Adrian Veidt's secret island and uncovers his plan to kill millions in order to unite the world behind a common foe.

- **In or Before October 1985**
  Rorschach is accused of two counts of murder in the first degree, but evades capture.

  Adrian Veidt and Jon Osterman construct a solution to the world's energy crisis, by means of a technology called a **S**ub **Q**uantum **U**nified **I**ntrinsic field **D**evice (SQUID).

- **October 11, 1985**
  Adrian Veidt murders Eddie Blake by tossing him out of his penthouse apartment window. Rorschach begins investigating what he believes to be a "mask killer."

- **October 13, 1985**
  Rorschach roughs up criminals called Gideon, Johnny Gobs, and Nicky the Jap to obtain information about the so-called mask killer.

- **October 16, 1985**
  Rorschach ambushes Edgar Jacobi after spotting him at The Comedian's funeral, but the former villain knows nothing useful. Adrian Veidt decides to frame Rorschach for Jacobi's murder to prevent the vigilante from exposing his plan.

- **October 19, 1985**
  Knot-Tops attempt to mug Laurie Juspeczyk and Dan Dreiberg, who leave them all injured or unconscious. Jon Osterman leaves Earth and relocates to Mars.

- **On or After October 19, 1985**
  Adrian Veidt murders Doug Roth to prevent the journalist from exposing his plan.

- **Before October 21, 1985**
  To prevent Rorschach from realizing he killed The Comedian, Adrian Veidt arranges for an assassination attempt on himself, hiring hitman Roy Chess to do the deed.

- **October 21, 1985**
  The father of Clare and Dominique Hirsch kills the two children, them himself, to spare them the horror of nuclear war.

  Roy Chess tries to shoot Adrian Veidt, who dodges his aim and forces him to swallow a cyanide pill, making it appear that Chess has committed suicide.

  Rorschach thwarts an attempted rape and mugging, then pummels the perpetrator.

  Adrian Veidt shoots Edgar Jacobi, summons Rorschach to the latter's apartment, and tips off the police, making it appear that the vigilante has murdered Moloch. Rorschach is apprehended and unmasked.

- **After October 21, 1985**
  Adrian Veidt kills a team of freight handlers whom he'd hired to carry out his plans. The police deem these deaths accidents or overdoses.

- **October 22, 1985**
  Rorschach is jailed at Sing Sing to await trial for the murders of Gerald Grice, Harvey Furniss, and Edgar Jacobi.

- **October 26, 1985**
  Laurie Juspeczyk and Dan Dreiberg don their costumes and rescue victims of a tenement fire. Dan decides they should also spring Rorschach from prison. At Sing Sing, an inmate named Otis tries to shank Rorschach, who douses him with hot cooking fat.

- **October 29, 1985**
  Fellow prisoner Tom Ryan (The Big Figure), accompanied by henchmen Michael Stephens and Lawrence Andrews, warns Rorschach that he'll soon be dead.

- **October 31, 1985**
  A prison riot erupts. The Big Figure tries to murder Rorschach, who dispatches Larry and Mike, then murders the dwarf as well. Silk Spectre and Nite Owl break Rorschach out, becoming wanted fugitives themselves. Several Knot-Tops hear about this and murder Hollis Mason, mistaking him for Rorschach's rescuer.

- **November 1, 1985**

  Adrian Veidt eliminates all witnesses to the creation of his squid creature by blowing up a boat containing Max Shea, Hira Manish, Norman Leith, Linette Paley, James Trafford March, Whittaker Furnesse, Professor Wickstein, and their colleagues.

  After some investigation, Rorschach and Nite Owl realize that Veidt is the mastermind behind recent events. The former partners set course for Karnak.

- **November 2, 1985**

  Adrian Veidt's "squid" kills millions in New York, causing the world's nations to cease hostilities and work together to defend Earth against this unknown enemy. Veidt poisons his servants to eliminate the only remaining witnesses to his actions. Rorschach and Dan Dreiberg confront Adrian, but are unable to hurt him.

- **November 3, 1985**

  Dr. Manhattan and Silk Spectre find New York a sea of gore and teleport to Karnak, but given the emerging world peace, they and Nite Owl agree to keep Ozymandias's secret. Rorschach refuses to compromise, so Manhattan vaporizes him, then departs this galaxy.

- **After November 3, 1985**

  Dan Dreiberg and Laurie Juspeczyk go into hiding under assumed names. Adrian Veidt spends the rest of his life feeling remorse for every death he has caused.

- **2011**

  For reasons only he knows, Dr. Manhattan alters a reality filled with superheroes, rewriting their history to remove their friendships and romantic relationships.

- **2089**

  Adrian Veidt dies at age 150.

REFLECTIONS

The Simultaneous Datedness and Timelessness of *Watchmen*

By Duy Tano

"Oh, how the ghost of you clings..."

—Nostalgia Perfume ad, Veidt Enterprises

Alan Moore's and Dave Gibbons' *Watchmen* is considered a comic-book classic, beloved by comics fans, taught in schools and universities, and constantly relevant since the time it was written. It's also seen by detractors as dated, since not too long after its release, the Cold War—an essential component of its backdrop—ended.

Truly, any adaptation of *Watchmen*, to be accurate, must be rooted in the era in which it's set and written, the mid-1980s. To translate the events of the book to a later time period would require too much of a change in the details that make up the story—and in *Watchmen*, the details make the story what it is. In spite (or maybe because) of this, however, *Watchmen* remains timeless, constantly relevant to our world today. As local Filipino writer Budjette Tan told me recently, "It's still the comic you throw at people who say comics are just for kids." It's true, and it wouldn't be the case if it didn't still speak to us today.

Watchmen would not translate to a modern-day telling of the tale without a major overhaul of the details, and—simply put—you can't do a major overhaul of the details of *Watchmen*. The miniseries paid so much attention to the minutiae that changing them would run the risk of making the whole thing unrecognizable except for the names of the characters and the sequence of events.

In his introduction, Rich talked about how much he liked the *Watchmen* movie, as he saw it as a faithful adaptation of the book. I didn't like it, *pretty much for the same exact reason*. So much of the greatness of *Watchmen* came in its essence, its willingness to buck convention, to try new things. In an industry in which everyone was trying to draw with the grandeur of Jack Kirby, *Watchmen* went in the exact opposite direction. For the strength of the film to simply be that it was "faithful" seemed, well, unfaithful, if not to its details, then to its spirit. But I also acknowledge that the film was in a tough spot in that regard. It was an adaptation, and for it to have remained true to the spirit of the book would have meant changing the details so much that it would have been unrecognizable. At the end of it, the film was recognizably *Watchmen*. Setting it in 2009 would have changed all that.

In his initial proposal for *Watchmen*, Moore lays out the concept like so[16]:

> *For one thing, I'd like the world that the Charlton characters exist in to be at once far more realistic in conception than any super-heroes' world has been before, and at the same time far different to our own world than the worlds presented as Earth One, Earth Two or Marvel Earth. To see what I'm trying to get at, you have to try and imagine what the presence of super-heroes would actually do to the world, both politically and psychologically.*

Moore goes on to outline the changes that the superheroic presence would mean for the world. In the work itself, the differences from our own world can be traced back to Dr. Manhattan's first appearance on November 22, 1959,

---

[16] *Moore, Alan and Gibbons, Dave.* Watchmen Absolute Edition. *DC Comics, 2005*

extrapolating from that point onward. While Moore worked on the political and socioeconomic ramifications—the more macro view, if you will—Gibbons conceptualized the more specific, minute details. In his sketches and lists, he writes, as examples, "geodesic domes," "less sexual restraint," "weather control," and "unusual fast foods." These are logical elements that one could conceptualize when working out the long-term effects of a super-powered being coming into existence. In 1986.

There is no mention of the internet as a medium for the masses. In 2016, surely, any such extrapolation of how the world would have changed due to a gigantic shift in the scheme of things would involve the internet, communication devices, and the digitization of our media. In the 1980s world of *Watchmen*, however, the primary media are very traditional. Despite the electric cars, the geodesic domes, and other advancements brought about by the coming of Manhattan, our characters still get their news from broadcast television, radio, and the printed newspaper.

One of the secondary characters is Bernie the news vendor, who must wait for shipments to come before he gets the news. Appointment viewing is still a thing—the last scene with Sally Jupiter shows this to be true. Rorschach writes and keeps multiple copies of his diary, with no electronic component (though this is easily justifiable with Rorschach, given his paranoia). And most tellingly of all, Ozymandias symbolically observes the world with his wide array of televisions. As impressive as that was when the comic was published in 1986, however, the average person with internet access and enough RAM today can simultaneously keep tabs on more than Veidt's television sets were able to.

There are more details that date *Watchmen* other than the lack of internet: the wires, the landlines, and Richard Nixon as President, to name a few. (Moore has admitted that using Nixon was a cheat, a kind of shorthand to emphasize that the President was meant to not be liked. Of course, as of this writing, the United States looks like it may soon elect a President that could take Nixon's place in the symbolism of these things.) But probably nothing dates *Watchmen* more than these two words: September 11.

Ozymandias's grand master plan, the thing that kicks off the events of *Watchmen*, is predicated on the idea that a big

enough threat and a large enough body count would get the world to come together in peace and unite against a common foe. The thing is, *that's already happened in our world*, and the nations of the world didn't exactly unite as one against their common foe. The attacks on the World Trade Center in 2001 divided the U.S. allies when it came to their course of action, and even divided the United States itself. Whatever camaraderie was felt didn't last long.

As a result, the ending of *Watchmen*—the open ending in which we, the readers, are invited to speculate whether or not the peace will last, with Seymour's hand hovering over Rorschach's journal—seems a foregone conclusion. It *won't* last. Rorschach's journal or not, it won't last. That fact colors *Watchmen* so much and even further roots it in its time period. Adrian Veidt absolutely, totally believes his plan will work. He is an idealist, Macchiavellan and twisted though he is, and we, the post-"War on Terror" crowd, can see his actions for what they are. We can see the intent, and we can still overlook the likely consequences. There's enough distance in terms of time. Set this story in the modern day, however, and that distance goes away.

None of this changes the relevance of *Watchmen* any more than Annie Lennox being the inspiration for Desire of the Endless changes the relevance of *Sandman*, or the numerous references to the bygone genre of Western movies changes the impact of *Preacher*. The themes remain universal, and likely always will. Whether it's coping with abuse, finding the thing you love doing to the point of dependence, or dealing with familial issues, it really doesn't matter that *Watchmen* remains a period piece. It resonates.

The big theme that overarched the entire book, of course, is that of mutually assured destruction, the idea that the world could go to war at any moment and humanity would destroy itself. Although 2016 has largely ignored the threat of another world war, something that always hung over the world of 1986, the advent of social media and a global connection has brought interpersonal tensions into the spotlight. When "Black Lives Matter" has to exist because racist policemen gun down African-Americans out of nowhere, when the usage of public bathrooms becomes a debate, and when the concept of equality for women gets shut down in the name of "ethics in gaming journalism" and "But *Ghostbusters* was really important to me," it's difficult not to see tension virtually anywhere and everywhere.

In 1986, there was the bomb. And now, there are still bombs. We're just waiting for which series of events could bring them out. The world always feels like it's on the brink of *something*, and *Watchmen* captures that paranoia, that fear, that tension so accurately. It did that in 1986. In 2016, the atmosphere it evokes is still accurate. Different sets of circumstances, same feeling.

Moore has always said that he sees science fiction as a way to talk about the present. Distancing the setting from the real world allows you to look at the latter from a different perspective. I don't think he wrote *Watchmen* believing that that line of thinking would still apply to the work 30 years later, but it does. Sadly, I do believe that the only way that *Watchmen* could stop being relevant to the casual reader, for it to stop being "the book that we throw at people who say comics are just for kids," and for its only merits to be as a how-to guide in storytelling, would be for the themes of the book to stop speaking to us as a society.

Maybe it would be worth it. Because while it would drop *Watchmen*'s stock in the world of comic books, it would mean the world had changed. And it would be a better world. A stronger world. A stronger, loving world to die in.

Duy Tano runs The Comics Cube (comicscube.com, facebook.com/comicscube), a website where he and his team write about whatever they want as long as it's about comics. He currently lives in his two-bedroom condo in the Philippines, surrounded by many comics, most of which he's sure he'll never read again, but can't bring himself to throw out, because, you know, he might! You can find him on Facebook at @comicscube or send him an email at comicscube@gmail.com.

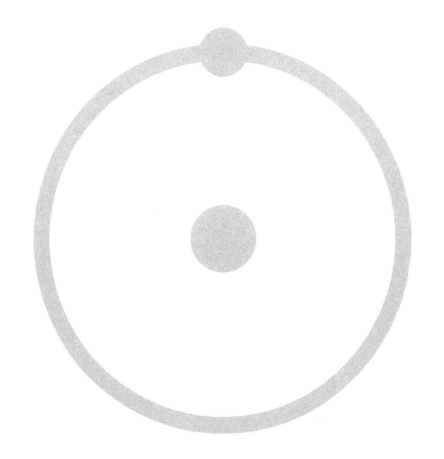

WORKS CITED

"Listen, I don't know from writing a book. I have all this stuff in my head that I want to get down, but what do I write about first? Where do I begin?"

—Hollis "The Nite Owl" Mason

The following works were extensively mined during the writing of *Watching Time: The Unauthorized Watchmen Chronology*. Covers for each title appear in the gallery that follows on page 320.

COMICS: *WATCHMEN*

Watchmen
Code: ALAN
Writer: Alan Moore
Artist: Dave Gibbons
- Issue 1: "At Midnight, All the Agents..."
- Issue 2: "Absent Friends"
- Issue 3: "The Judge of All the Earth"
- Issue 4: "Watchmaker"
- Issue 5: "Fearful Symmetry"
- Issue 6: "The Abyss Gazes Also"
- Issue 7: "A Brother to Dragons"
- Issue 8: "Old Ghosts"
- Issue 9: "The Darkness of Mere Being"
- Issue 10: "Two Riders Were Approaching..."
- Issue 11: "Look On My Works, Ye Mighty..."
- Issue 12: "A Stronger Loving World"

DC Comics, 1986–1987

Watchmen Absolute Edition
Code: ABSO
Writer: Alan Moore
Artist: Dave Gibbons
DC Comics, 2005

Watchmen: The Complete Motion Comic
Code: MOTN
Writer: Alan Moore
Artist: Dave Gibbons
DVD, Cruel & Unusual Films and Warner Home Video, 2008

COMICS: *BEFORE WATCHMEN*

Before Watchmen: Minutemen
Code: BWMM
Writer and Artist: Darwyn Cooke
- Issue 1: "The Minute of Truth, Chapter One: Eight Minutes"
- Issue 2: "The Minute of Truth, Chapter Two: Golden Years"
- Issue 3: "The Minute of Truth, Chapter Three: Child's Play"
- Issue 4: "The Minute of Truth, Chapter Four: War Stories"
- Issue 5: "The Minute of Truth, Chapter Five: The Demon Core"
- Issue 6: "The Minute of Truth, Chapter Six: The Last Minute"

DC Comics, 2012–2013

Before Watchmen: Silk Spectre
Code: BWSS
Writers: Darwyn Cooke and Amanda Conner
Artist: Amanda Conner
- Issue 1: "Mean Goodbye"
- Issue 2: "Getting into the World"
- Issue 3: "No Illusion"
- Issue 4: "The End of the Rainbow"

DC Comics, 2012

Before Watchmen: Comedian
Code: BWCO
Writer: Brian Azzarello
Artist: J.G. Jones
- Issue 1: "Smile"
- Issue 2: "I Get Around"
- Issue 3: "Play With Fire"
- Issue 4: "Conquistador"
- Issue 5: "Kicks"
- Issue 6: "Eighties"

DC Comics, 2012–2013

Before Watchmen: Nite Owl
Code: BWNO
Writer: J. Michael Straczynski
Artists: Andy Kubert, Joe Kubert, and Bill Sienkiewicz
- Issue 1: "No Such Thing as a Free Lunch"
- Issue 2: "Some Things Are Just Inevitable"
- Issue 3: "Thanks for Coming"
- Issue 4: "From One Nite Owl to Another"

DC Comics, 2012–2013

Before Watchmen: Ozymandias
Code: BWOZ
Writer: Len Wein
Artist: Jae Lee
- Issue 1: "I Met a Traveler...!"
- Issue 2: "The Hand That Mocked Them...!"
- Issue 3: "The Heart That Fed...!"
- Issue 4: "Shattered Visage...!"
- Issue 5: "These Lifeless Things...!"
- Issue 6: "Nothing Beside Remains"

DC Comics, 2012–2013

Before Watchmen: Rorschach
Code: BWRO
Writer: Brian Azzarello
Artist: Lee Bermejo
- Issue 1: "Damntown, Part One"
- Issue 2: "Damntown, Part Two"
- Issue 3: "Damntown, Part Three"
- Issue 4: "Damntown, Part Four"

DC Comics, 2012–2013

Before Watchmen: Dr. Manhattan
Code: BWDM
Writer: J. Michael Straczynski
Artist: Adam Hughes
- Issue 1: "What's in the Box?"
- Issue 2: "One-Fifteen P.M."
- Issue 3: "Ego Sum"
- Issue 4: "Changes in Perspective"

DC Comics, 2012–2013

Before Watchmen: Moloch
Code: BWMO
Writer: J. Michael Straczynski
Artist: Eduardo Risso
- Issue 1: "Forgive Me, Father, for I Have Sinned"
- Issue 2: "The Eleven-Thirty Absolution"

DC Comics, 2013

Before Watchmen: Dollar Bill
Code: BWDB
Writer: Len Wein
Artist: Steve Rude
- Issue 1: "I Want to Be in Pictures"

DC Comics, 2013

Before Watchmen: The Crimson Corsair
(Inside title: "The Curse of the Crimson Corsair")
Code: BWCC
Writers: Len Wein and John Higgins
Artist: John Higgins
- "The Devil in the Deep, Part One" (*Minutemen* #1)
- "The Devil in the Deep, Part Two" (*Silk Spectre* #1)
- "The Devil in the Deep, Part Three" (*Comedian* #1)
- "The Devil in the Deep, Part Four" (*Nite Owl* #1)
- "The Devil in the Deep, Part Five" (*Ozymandias* #1)
- "The Devil in the Deep, Part Six" (*Minutemen* #2)
- "The Devil in the Deep, Part Seven" (*Silk Spectre* #2)
- "The Devil in the Deep, Part Eight" (*Comedian* #2)
- "The Devil in the Deep, Part Nine" (*Nite Owl* #2)
- "The Devil in the Deep, Part Ten" (*Ozymandias* #2)
- "The Evil That Men Do, Part One" (*Rorschach* #1)
- "The Evil That Men Do, Part Two" (*Dr. Manhattan* #1)
- "The Evil That Men Do, Part Three" (*Minutemen* #3)
- "The Evil That Men Do, Part Four" (*Silk Spectre* #3)
- "The Evil That Men Do, Part Five" (*Comedian* #3)
- "The Evil That Men Do, Part Six" (*Nite Owl* #3)
- "The Evil That Men Do, Part Seven" (*Ozymandias* #3)
- "The Evil That Men Do, Part Eight" (*Rorschach* #2)
- "Wide Were His Dragon Wings, Part One" (*Dr. Manhattan* #2)
- "Wide Were His Dragon Wings, Part Two" (*Minutemen* #4)
- "Wide Were His Dragon Wings, Part Three" (*Silk Spectre* #4)
- "Wide Were His Dragon Wings, Part Four" (*Moloch* #1)
- "Wide Were His Dragon Wings, Part Five" (*Ozymandias* #4)
- "Wide Were His Dragon Wings, Part Six" (*Comedian* #4)
- "Wide Were His Dragon Wings, Part Seven" (*Minutemen* #5)
- "Wide Were His Dragon Wings, Part Eight" (*Rorschach* #3)
- "Wide Were His Dragon Wings, Part Nine" (*Dr. Manhattan* #3)
- "Wide Were His Dragon Wings, Conclusion" (*Moloch* #2)

DC Comics, 2012–2013

Before Watchmen: Epilogue
Code: Not applicable
Writers: Len Wein and others
Artists: John Higgins and others
DC Comics, unpublished
Comic book one-shot—solicited in 2013 but canceled for reasons unknown.

COMICS: OTHER (DC Comics Titles)

DC Spotlight #1
Code: SPOT
Writers and Artists: N/A
DC Comics, 1985

Who's Who: The Definitive Directory of the DC Universe (*Update '87 Vol. 4*)
Code: WHOS
Writers and Artists: Various
DC Comics, 1987

Who's Who: The Definitive Directory of the DC Universe (*Update '87 Vol. 5*)
Code: WHOS
Writers and Artists: Various
DC Comics, 1987

The Question volume 1 issue #17 ("A Dream of Rorschach")
Code: CMEO
Writer: Dennis O'Neil
Artists: Denys Cowan and Rick Magyar
DC Comics, 1988

Hero Hotline volume 1 issue #5 ("Lo, the Firebug")
Code: CMEO
Writer: Bob Rozakis
Artists: Stephen DeStefano and Karl Kesel
DC Comics, 1989

Kingdom Come volume 1 issue #2 ("Truth and Justice")
Code: CMEO
Writers: Mark Waid and Alex Ross
Artist: Alex Ross
DC Comics, 1996

DC Universe: Rebirth Special volume 1 issue #1 ("Lost")
Code: DURS
Writer: Geoff Johns
Artist: Ethan Van Sciver and Gary Frank
DC Comics, 2016

COMICS: OTHER (Non-DC Titles)

Marvels volume 1 issue #4 ("A Time of Marvels")
Code: CMEO
Writer: Kurt Busiek
Artist: Alex Ross
Marvel Comics, 1994

Astonishing X-Men volume 3 issue #6 ("Gifted, Part 6")
Code: CMEO
Writer: Joss Whedon
Artist: John Cassaday
Marvel Comics, 2004

SHORT FICTION

"Wounds"
Code: RUBY
Author: Andrew Salmon
Airship 27, 2012
Published in *The Ruby Files Volume One*, by Bobby Nash

GAMES

DC Heroes Role Playing Module #227: Who Watches the Watchmen?
Code: RPG1
Author: Dan Greenberg
Artist: Dave Gibbons
Mayfair Games, 1987

DC Heroes Role Playing Module #235: Taking Out the Trash—Curses and Tears
Original Title: *The Harlot's Curse*
Code: RPG2
Author: Ray Winninger (with Alan Moore)
Artist: Dave Gibbons
Mayfair Games, 1987

DC Heroes: The Watchmen Sourcebook
Code: RPG3
Author: Ray Winninger
Artist: DC Staff
Mayfair Games, 1990

Watchmen: The Mobile Game
Code: MOBL
  • Chapter 0: "Whatever Happened to the Good Ol' Days?"
  • Chapter 1: "Changing of the Guard"
  • Chapter 2: "To Protect and Serve?"
  • Chapter 3: "Red Versus Blue"
  • Chapter 4: "The Beginning of the End?"
Glu Mobile, 2008
JAVA-based video game for mobile phones.

Watchmen: Justice Is Coming
Code: JUST
   • Mission 1: "Stepping into the Shadow"
   • Mission 2: "We Are Compelled"
Warner Bros. and Interactive Entertainment, 2009
Massively multiplayer online role-playing game (MMORPG) for iPhone and iPod Touch; removed from Internet due to software bugs.

Watchmen: The End Is Nigh—The Complete Experience
Code: NIGH
Designer: Uffe Friis Lichtenberg
Director: Soren Lund
   • *The End Is Nigh*: Chapters I to VI
   • *The End Is Nigh, Part 2*: Chapters I to V
Deadline Games, 2009
Video game for Microsoft Windows, PlayStation Network, and Xbox Live Arcade platforms; packaged with foldable timeline and in-universe instruction booklet.

Minutemen Arcade
Code: ARCD
LittleLoud, 2009
Eight-bit video game presented online as a tie-in to the *Watchmen* film.

DC Comics Deck-Building Game—Crossover Pack 4: Watchmen
Code: DECK
Cryptozoic Entertainment, 2015
Supplement for use with DC's playable card game.

FILM AND VIDEOS

Watchmen theatrical film
Code: FILM
Writers: David Hayter and Alex Tse
Director: Zack Snyder
Legendary Pictures, DC Comics, and Warner Bros., 2009

Under the Hood
Code: HOOD
Writer: Hans Rodionoff
Director: Eric Matthies
Legendary Pictures, DC Comics, and Warner Bros., 2009

Tales of the Black Freighter
Code: BLCK
Writers: Zack Snyder and Alex Tse
Directors: Daniel DelPurgatorio and Mike Smith
Legendary Pictures, DC Comics, and Warner Bros., 2009

NBS Nightly News with Ted Philips
Code: VRL1
Writer and Director: Unknown
Viral video, posted at thenewfrontiersman.net, 2009

The Keene Act and You
Code: VRL2
Writer and Director: Unknown
Viral video, posted at thenewfrontiersman.net, 2009

Who Watches the Watchmen? A Veidt Music Network (VMN) Special
Code: VRL3
Writer and Director: Unknown
Viral video, posted at thenewfrontiersman.net, 2009

World in Focus: 6 Minutes to Midnight
Code: VRL4
Writer and Director: Unknown
Viral video, posted at thenewfrontiersman.net, 2009

Local Radio Station Report on 1977 Riots
Code: VRL5
Writer and Director: Unknown
Viral video, posted at thenewfrontiersman.net, 2009

Veidt Enterprises Advertising Contest
Code: VRL6
Writer and Director: Unknown
Two sample spots and eight contest-winners
Spearheaded by Zak Snyder, winners posted at joblo.com, 2008

The Mindscape of Alan Moore
Code: MIND
Writers and Directors: Dez Vylenz and Moritz Winkler
Shadowsnake Films, 2003

"Desolation Row" (*Watchmen* tie-in music video)
Code: CHEM
Song Lyrics: Bob Dylan
Band: My Chemical Romance
Director: Zack Synder
Reprise/Warner Bros., 2009

Teen Titans Go! (episode #82, "Real Boy Adventures")
Code: CMEO
Writer: Ben Joseph
Director: Peter Rida Michail
Cartoon Network and DC Entertainment, 2015

UNFILMED SCREENPLAY DRAFTS

Watchmen
Code: SCR1
Writer: Sam Hamm
Dated: September 9, 1988

Watchmen
Code: SCR2
Writer: Charles McKeuen (rewrite of Sam Hamm)
Dated: May 1, 1989

Watchmen
Code: SCR3
Writer: Gary Goldman (rewrite of Sam Hamm)
Dated: August 12, 1992

Watchmen
Code: SCR4
Writer David Hayter
Dated: August 2, 2002

Watchmen
Code: SCR5
Writer: David Hayter
Dated: September 26, 2003

Watchmen
Code: SCR6
Writer: Alex Tse
Dated: 2006

NON-FICTION BOOKS

Watching the Watchmen
Code: WAWA
Author: Dave Gibbons
Titan Books, 2008

Watchmen: The Art of the Film
Code: ARTF
Author: Peter Aperlo
Titan Books, 2009

Watchmen Portraits
Code: PORT
Author: Clay Enos
Titan Books, 2009

Watchmen: The Film Companion
Code: WTFC
Author: Peter Aperlo
Titan Books, 2009

MISCELLANEOUS

Watchmen Film British Press Kit
Code: PKIT
DC Comics and Warner Bros., 2009

HeroClix Figure Pack-in Cards
Code: CLIX
NECA/WizKids, 2011

Club Black Freighter Figure Pack-in Cards
Code: MATL
Mattel, 2012–2013

Metro
Code: MTRO
Picture Production Co., March 6, 2009
Newspaper articles published in promotional cover wrap.

New Frontiersman
Code: NEWP
Picture Production Co., 2012
Promotional newspaper published to coincide with *Before Watchmen*.

New Frontiersman
Code: NEWW
Picture Production Co., 2009–2013
Viral website containing numerous in-universe articles, photos, and videos.

ADDITIONAL RESOURCES

The following titles do not have corresponding codes in this timeline, but should still prove interesting to *Watchmen* fans:

Watchmen Portfolio
Artist: Dave Gibbons
DC Comics, 1988

Minutes to Midnight: Twelve Essays on Watchmen
Editor: Richard Bensam
Sequart, 2011

Watchmen and Philosophy: A Rorschach Test
Editors: Mark D. White and William Irwin
Wiley, 2009

Watchmen as Literature: A Critical Study of the Graphic Novel
Author: Sara J. Van Ness
McFarland, 2010

Considering Watchmen: Poetics, Property, Politics, Comics Culture
Author: Andrew Hoberek
Rutgers University Press, 2014

COVER GALLERY

"Its atomic structure is a perfect grid, like a checker board."

—Jon "Dr. Manhattan" Osterman

If you're looking to expand your *Watchmen* collection, the following gallery should facilitate the hunt. For more information about individual titles, consult the list of works cited on page 315.

COMICS: WATCHMEN

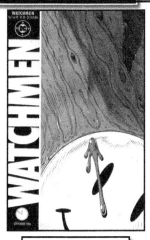

WATCHMEN #1

WATCHMEN #1
(DC COMICS ESSENTIALS)

WATCHMEN #1
(MILLENNIUM EDITION)

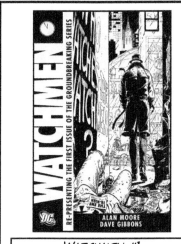

WATCHMEN #1
(WONDERCON 2009 EXCLUSIVE)

WATCHMEN #2

WATCHMEN #3

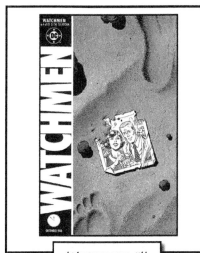

WATCHMEN #4

WATCHMEN #5

WATCHMEN #6

WATCHMEN #7

WATCHMEN #8

WATCHMEN #9

WATCHMEN #10

WATCHMEN #11

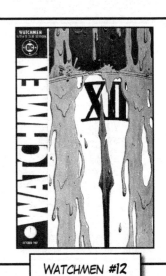

WATCHMEN #12

COMICS: WATCHMEN-RELATED

DC SPOTLIGHT #1
(WATCHMEN PREVIEW)

WHO'S WHO UPDATE '87
VOL. 4

WHO'S WHO UPDATE '87
VOL. 5

WATCHMEN (GRAPHITTI
DESIGNS HARDCOVER)

WATCHMEN
(ABSOLUTE EDITION)

WATCHMEN
GRAPHIC NOVEL

WATCHMEN
GRAPHIC NOVEL

WATCHMEN
GRAPHIC NOVEL

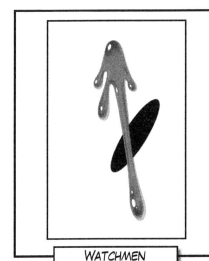

WATCHMEN
GRAPHIC NOVEL

WATCHMEN
GRAPHIC NOVEL

WATCHMEN
(DELUXE EDITION)

WATCHMEN
(INTERNATIONAL EDITION)

WATCHMEN NOIR
(HARDCOVER)

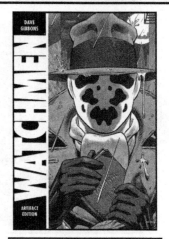

WATCHMEN
(ARTIFACT EDITION)

WATCHMEN
(ARTIFACT EDITION)

WATCHMEN
(ARTIFACT EDITION)

WATCHMEN
(ARTIFACT EDITION)

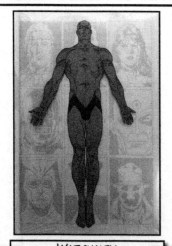

WATCHMEN
(DELUXE EDITION-SPANISH)

WATCHMEN (URBAN
COMICS EDITION-FRENCH)

WATCHMEN (INTEGRAL
EDITION-FRENCH)

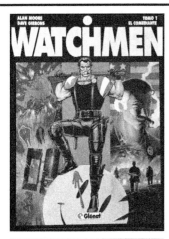

WATCHMEN TOMO 1
(FRENCH)

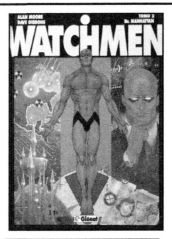

WATCHMEN TOMO 2
(FRENCH)

WATCHMEN TOMO 3
(FRENCH)

WATCHMEN VOLUME 1
(FRENCH)

WATCHMEN VOLUME 2
(FRENCH)

WATCHMEN VOLUME 3
(FRENCH)

WATCHMEN VOLUME 4
(FRENCH)

WATCHMEN VOLUME 5
(FRENCH)

WATCHMEN VOLUME 6
(FRENCH)

WATCHMEN
(COLLECTOR'S EDITION)

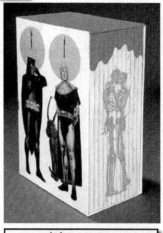

WATCHMEN
(COLLECTOR'S EDITION)

WATCHMEN 20 ANNI DOPO
(ITALIAN)

COMICS: BEFORE WATCHMEN

WATCHMEN (NORMA
EDITORIAL EDITION-SPANISH)

MINUTEMEN #1

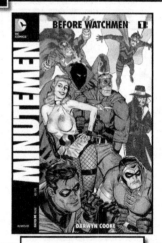

MINUTEMEN #1

MINUTEMEN #1

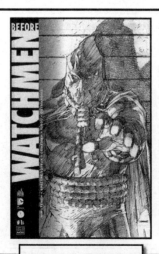

MINUTEMEN #1

MINUTEMEN #2

MINUTEMEN #2

MINUTEMEN #3

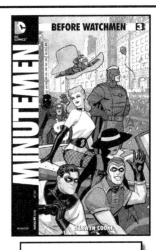

MINUTEMEN #3

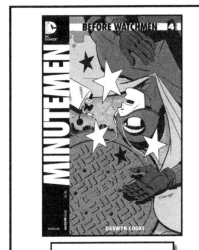

MINUTEMEN #4

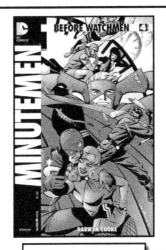

MINUTEMEN #4

MINUTEMEN #5

MINUTEMEN #5

MINUTEMEN #6

MINUTEMEN #6

NITE OWL #1

NITE OWL #1

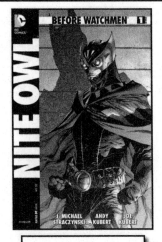

NITE OWL #1

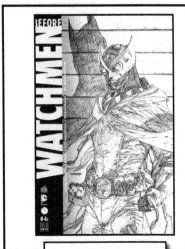

NITE OWL #1

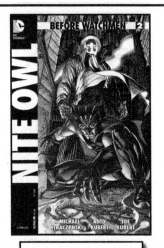

NITE OWL #2

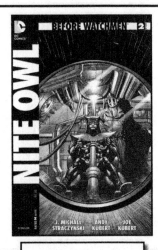

NITE OWL #2

NITE OWL #3

NITE OWL #3

NITE OWL #4

NITE OWL #4

NITE OWL #4

OZYMANDIAS #1

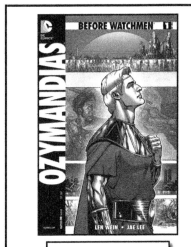

OZYMANDIAS #1

OZYMANDIAS #1

OZYMANDIAS #1

OZYMANDIAS #2

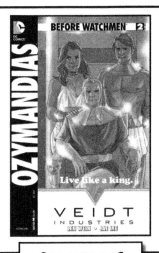

OZYMANDIAS #2

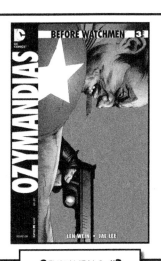

OZYMANDIAS #3

329

OZYMANDIAS #3

OZYMANDIAS #4

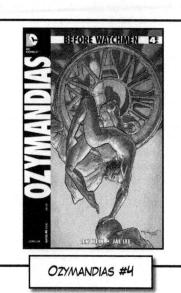

OZYMANDIAS #4

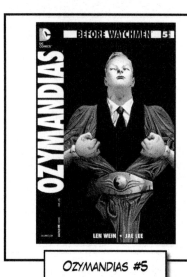

OZYMANDIAS #5

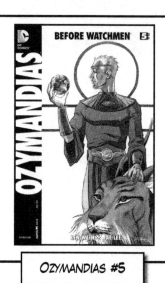

OZYMANDIAS #5

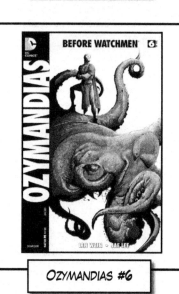

OZYMANDIAS #6

OZYMANDIAS #6

RORSCHACH #1

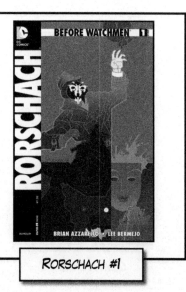

RORSCHACH #1

RORSCHACH #1

RORSCHACH #1

RORSCHACH #2

RORSCHACH #2

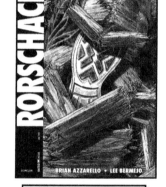

RORSCHACH #3

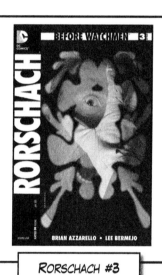

RORSCHACH #3

RORSCHACH #4

RORSCHACH #4

RORSCHACH #4

SILK SPECTRE #1

SILK SPECTRE #1

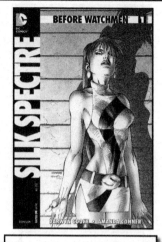

SILK SPECTRE #1

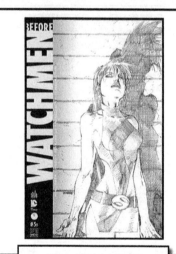

SILK SPECTRE #1

SILK SPECTRE #2

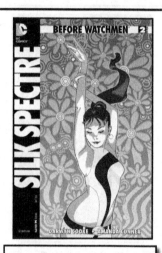

SILK SPECTRE #2

SILK SPECTRE #3

SILK SPECTRE #3

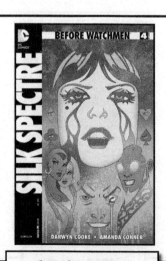

SILK SPECTRE #4

SILK SPECTRE #4

MOLOCH #1

MOLOCH #1

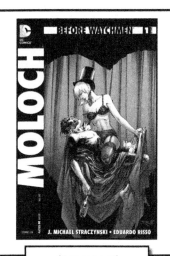

MOLOCH #1

MOLOCH #2

MOLOCH #2

DOLLAR BILL #1

DOLLAR BILL #1

DOLLAR BILL #1

COMEDIAN #1

COMEDIAN #1

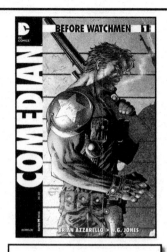

COMEDIAN #1

COMEDIAN #1

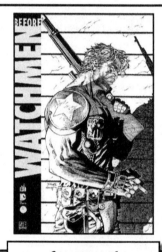

COMEDIAN #1

COMEDIAN #2

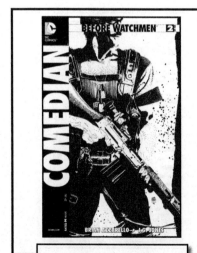

COMEDIAN #2

COMEDIAN #2

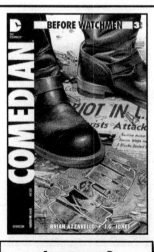

COMEDIAN #3

COMEDIAN #3

COMEDIAN #4

COMEDIAN #4

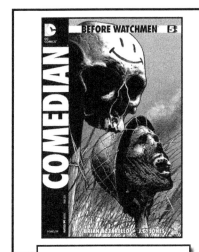

COMEDIAN #5

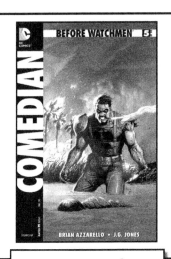

COMEDIAN #5

COMEDIAN #6

COMEDIAN #6

COMEDIAN #6

BEFORE WATCHMEN
SAMPLER

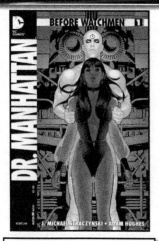

DR. MANHATTAN #1

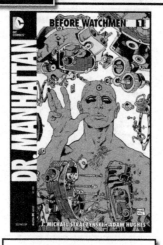

DR. MANHATTAN #1

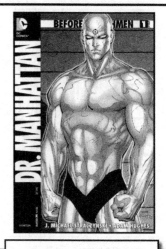

DR. MANHATTAN #1

DR. MANHATTAN #1

DR. MANHATTAN #2

DR. MANHATTAN #2

DR. MANHATTAN #3

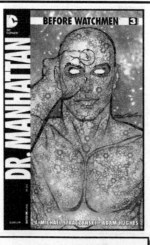

DR. MANHATTAN #3

DR. MANHATTAN #4

DR. MANHATTAN #4

MINUTEMEN

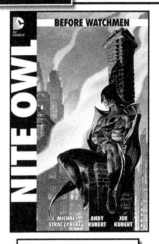

NITE OWL

OZYMANDIAS

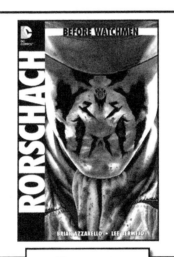

RORSCHACH

COMEDIAN

SILK SPECTRE

DR. MANHATTAN

THE CRIMSON CORSAIR

COMEDIAN/RORSCHACH
DELUXE EDITION

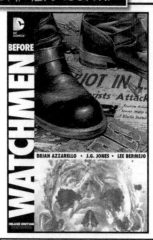

COMEDIAN/RORSCHACH
DELUXE EDITION

DR. MANHATTAN/NITE OWL
DELUXE EDITION

DR. MANHATTAN/NITE OWL
DELUXE EDITION

MINUTEMEN/SILK SPECTRE
DELUXE EDITION

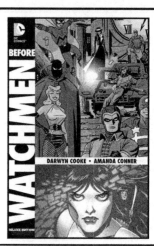

MINUTEMEN/SILK SPECTRE
DELUXE EDITION

OZYMANDIAS/CRIMSON
CORSAIR DELUXE EDITION

OZYMANDIAS/CRIMSON
CORSAIR DELUXE EDITION

MINUTEMEN HARDCOVER
(FRENCH)

COMEDIAN HARDCOVER
(FRENCH)

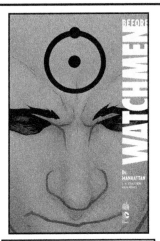

DR. MANHATTAN
HARDCOVER (FRENCH)

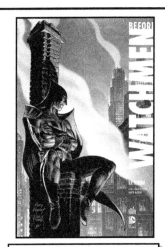

NITE OWL HARDCOVER
(FRENCH)

OZYMANDIAS HARDCOVER
(FRENCH)

RORSCHACH HARDCOVER
(FRENCH)

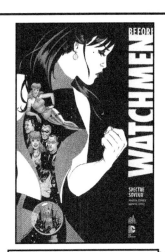

SILK SPECTRE HARDCOVER
(FRENCH)

COMPANION HARDCOVER
(FRENCH)

BEFORE WATCHMEN
ABSOLUTE (ITALIAN)

THE QUESTION #17

HERO HOTLINE #5

KINGDOM COME #2

MARVELS #4

ASTONISHING X-MEN #6

DC REBIRTH SPECIAL #1

ROLE-PLAYING GAMES

DC HEROES: WHO
WATCHES THE WATCHMEN?

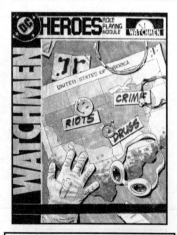

DC HEROES: WHO WATCHES
THE WATCHMEN? (UNUSED)

DC HEROES: WHO WATCHES
THE WATCHMEN? (UNUSED)

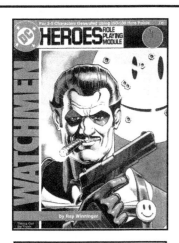

DC HEROES:
TAKING OUT THE TRASH

DC HEROES: THE
WATCHMEN SOURCEBOOK

WATCHMEN:
THE MOBILE GAME

WATCHMEN:
JUSTICE IS COMING

MINUTEMEN ARCADE

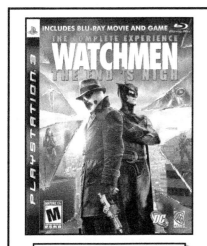

WATCHMEN: THE END IS
NIGH (PLAYSTATION)

WATCHMEN: THE END IS
NIGH (PLAYSTATION)

WATCHMEN: THE END IS
NIGH (XBOX)

DC COMICS
DECK-BUILDING GAME

WATCHMEN
HEROCLIX BOX SET

AFTER WATCHMEN

PUBLICATIONS

WATCHING
THE WATCHMEN

WATCHING
THE WATCHMEN

MINUTES TO MIDNIGHT:
TWELVE ESSAYS ON WATCHMEN

WATCHMEN: THE ART OF THE FILM

WATCHMEN PORTRAITS

WATCHMEN: THE FILM COMPANION

CONSIDERING WATCHMEN

WATCHMEN AND
PHILOSOPHY

WATCHMEN AND
PHILOSOPHY

THE RUBY FILES
VOLUME ONE ("WOUNDS")

WATCHMEN AS
LITERATURE

WATCHMEN PORTFOLIOS

WATCHING TIME: THE
WATCHMEN CHRONOLOGY

WATCHMEN
FILM PRESS KIT (BRITISH)

CRITICS CHOICE MAGAZINE
FOCUS ON WATCHMEN

TALES OF THE BLACK FREIGHTER
#307 (PROP REPLICA)

UNDER THE HOOD: AN
AUTOBIOGRAPHY (PROP REPLICA)

METRO (PROMOTIONAL
NEWSPAPER)

NEW FRONTIERSMAN
(PROMOTIONAL NEWSPAPER)

DVDS

WATCHMEN:
WIDESCREEN EDITION

WATCHMEN:
DIRECTOR'S CUT

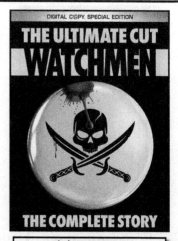

WATCHMEN:
THE ULTIMATE CUT

WATCHMEN: THE
COMPLETE MOTION COMIC

TALES OF THE BLACK
FREIGHTER

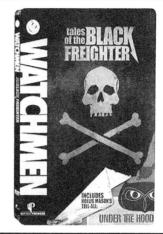

TALES OF THE BLACK FREIGHTER:
STEELBOOK EDITION

WATCHMEN DOUBLE
MOVIE COLLECTION

DVD DOUBLE FEATURE

3 MOVIE PACK ACTION
COLLECTION

5 MOVIE COLLECTION

TEEN TITANS GO!
SEASON TWO

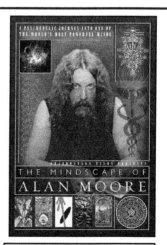

THE MINDSCAPE
OF ALAN MOORE

WATCHMEN:
DIRECTOR'S CUT

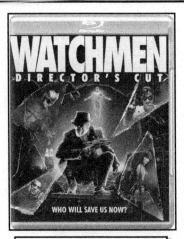

WATCHMEN:
DIRECTOR'S CUT

WATCHMEN: DIRECTOR'S CUT
(AMAZON EXCLUSIVE)

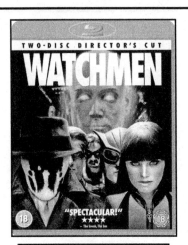

WATCHMEN: TWO-DISC
DIRECTOR'S CUT

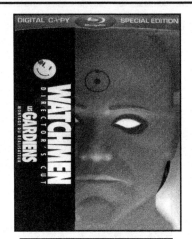

WATCHMEN: DIRECTOR'S
CUT LIMITED EDITION

WATCHMEN: DIRECTOR'S
CUT LIMITED EDITION

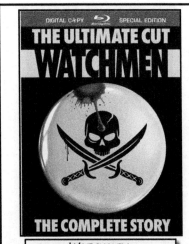

WATCHMEN:
THE ULTIMATE CUT

WATCHMEN: DIRECTOR'S
CUT LIMITED EDITION

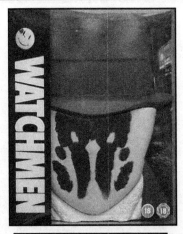

WATCHMEN: DIRECTOR'S
CUT LIMITED EDITION

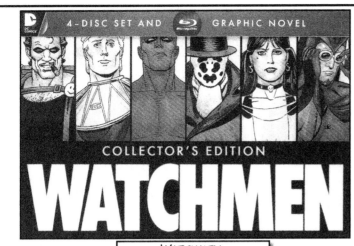

WATCHMEN:
COLLECTOR'S EDITION

WATCHMEN: 2-DISC
SPECIAL EDITION

WATCHMEN:
STEELBOOK EDITION

WATCHMEN: 100TH ANNIVERSARY
EDITION (SPANISH)

WATCHMEN:
COLLECTOR'S EDITION

TALES OF THE BLACK
FREIGHTER

MOTION COMIC/TALES
OF THE BLACK FREIGHTER

2 MOVIES COLLECTION

2 MOVIE PACK
ACTION COLLECTION

BLU-RAY DOUBLE FEATURE

BLU-RAY TRIPLE FEATURE

4 FILM FAVORITES:
COMICS COLLECTION

SOUNDTRACK

HEROES GENRE PACK

KAPOW! BOX 1

WATCHMEN: MUSIC FROM
THE MOTION PICTURE

ABOUT THE AUTHOR

"I don't mind being the smartest man in the world.
I just wish it wasn't this one."

—Adrian "Ozymandias" Veidt

Rich Handley, a cofounder of Hasslein Books, is the author or co-author of *Timeline of the Planet of the Apes: The Definitive Chronology*, *Lexicon of the Planet of the Apes: The Comprehensive Encyclopedia*, *Back in Time: The Back to the Future Chronology*, *A Matter of Time: The Back to the Future Lexicon*, and the novel *Conspiracy of the Planet of the Apes*.

Rich co-edited and contributed to *Planet of the Apes: Tales From the Forbidden Zone*, a short fiction anthology to be published in 2017 by Titan Books, as well as five Sequart essay anthologies to date—*The Sacred Scrolls: Comics on the Planet of the Apes*; *Bright Eyes, Ape City: Examining the Planet of the Apes Mythos*; *A Long Time Ago: Exploring the Star Wars Cinematic Universe*; *A Galaxy Far, Far Away: Exploring Star Wars Comics;* and *A More Civilized Age: Exploring the Star Wars Expanded Universe*. In addition, he has penned essays for IDWs five *Star Trek* comic strip reprint hardcovers, Sequart's *New Life and New Civilizations: Exploring Star Trek Comics* and *The Cyberpunk Nexus: Exploring the Blade Runner Universe*, and ATB Publishing's *Outside In Boldly Goes*.

Rich has also contributed to numerous magazines and websites, including StarTrek.com, StarWars.com, *Star Trek Communicator*, *Star Trek Magazine*, *Cinefantastique*, *Cinescape*, *Movie Magic*, *Dungeon/Polyhedron*, and various Lucasfilm *Star Wars* licensees. By day, he is the managing editor of *RFID Journal* and *IOT Journal* magazines.

ABOUT HASSLEIN BOOKS

Hasslein Books (hassleinbooks.com) is a New York-based independent publisher of reference guides by geeks, for geeks. The company is named after Doctor Otto Hasslein, a physicist and time travel expert portrayed by actor Eric Braeden in *Escape from the Planet of the Apes*.

In addition to *Watching Time*, the company's lineup of unauthorized genre-based reference books includes *Timeline of the Planet of the Apes*, *Lexicon of the Planet of the Apes*, *The Back to the Future Lexicon*, *The Back to the Future Chronology*, *Total Immersion: The Comprehensive Unauthorized Red Dwarf Encyclopedia*, *Lost in Time and Space: An Unofficial Guide to the Uncharted Journeys of Doctor Who*, and *Who Beyond 50: Celebrating Five Decades of Doctor Who*, with future volumes slated to feature *G.I. Joe*, *Alien vs. Predator*, *Fringe*, *Red Sonja*, James Bond, and more. Hasslein has also published the humor book *Messing With Telemarketers*.

To stay informed regarding the company's projects, follow Hasslein Books on Facebook (facebook.com/hassleinbooks) and Twitter (twitter.com/hassleinbooks), and at the Hasslein Blog (hassleinbooks.blogspot.com).

CPSIA information can be obtained
at www.ICGtesting.com
Printed in the USA
LVOW02s1455050117
519876LV00001B/41/P